NOT TAKEN

Not Taken by Terry Ulick

Paperback Edition

ISBN: 979-8-9892425-4-2

Copyright 2024, Library of Congress by Terry Ulick

Creator:
The Creator of this property asserts a moral right to identify as Terry Ulick and to identify as the Creator, Identity and Owner of this property regardless of law in any domain, having the moral right to oppose all use of Creator's identity, identities, writings, names, texts, scrolls, works and ideas.

Disclaimer:
This is a work of fiction, drawn entirely from the imagination of the Creator. Characters, dialogue, events, locations, and situations are all fabrications and entirely fictional. Characters and identities are not drawn upon or intended to represent any persons or identities living or dead nor any commercial names, identities or images. Any resemblance to actual identities or business identities is unintentional and entirely coincidental. Any song lyrics are used as in public conversation and to the benefit of the song writer and not intended to infringe on any copyright for use as original material.

Book designed, written and presented by Terry Ulick.

Photographs and Images Created by Terry Ulick, Copyright 2024, Terry Ulick.

Published by:

Wherever Books LLC
A Division of Renegade Company LLC
Littleton, CO 80127
www.whereverbooks.com

TRIGGER WARNING
EXTREME SEXUAL CONTENT

**THIS BOOK DOES NOT HOLD BACK ON
SEX, VIOLENCE, LANGUAGE OR DISTURBING EVENTS.**

If you are sensitive to obscene
language, graphic descriptions of
explicit sex acts, use of language
describing bodies that is anatomical
and degrading, obscene dialogue
between despicable and disgusting
characters, please do not read any
further. This book will upset you
and you will be offended.

If you are suffering from any form
of physical, mental, verbal, or sexual
abuse, or suffer PTSD from such abuse
or other types of violence or harm, please,
shut this book. It will trigger you throughout.

If you have religious beliefs based on the
teachings in the Bible, either one or both
Testaments, this book contains concepts and
references to religion, clergy, and Christian
teachings that will upset and offend you.
This is not a book about the Bible or of
religious teachings or existing or real
organized religions.

Terry Ulick
Author

INTRODUCTION

At this very moment, when reading this, a young girl is being taken, trafficked, and she will be sold to be used for sex or sold to be a possession of a wealthy or powerful man.

When I say young, I mean a child under the age of 18. Many are taken when young as 5.

Are you okay with that?

If you are, you may, or could be, a trafficker of human beings for sale as merchandise.

If not, you, your child, or someone you know has a child that could be trafficked. Trafficking of children is growing and is now more profitable than drugs sales. It happens everywhere in the world, and to every economic class. Children can be grabbed off the street, from an event, or meet with a person they think is another young girl or boy they met on social media. If taken, they are shipped outside of the country within a day and will not likely ever be found.

The message of this book is the only way to stop trafficking is to stop the traffickers.

This book is about two women who don't allow it to happen. I think they are true heroes. Knowing the only way to stop trafficking is to stop traffickers, they take it upon themselves to do what our government doesn't. Stop them. Dead.

Hold on. This is the most brutal story of sex and violence you'll ever read. It is impossible to write about sex traffickers and not be explicit in how they talk, what they do, and how sex is a commodity and young girls are merchandise. It's a world where terror is the language, enslaving and owning humans is the measure of success, and killing a child means nothing.

There is no way to tell this story without showing the depravity and horror of the world of trafficking.

Welcome to the nightmare that takes place where you live, and all over the world.

Terry Ulick

CHEAT SHEET
This book picks up where Aurora, the first book in the Not Taken Series, left off. If you haven't read Aurora, please read on.

This is a stand-alone book. All the events and characters from *Aurora* will be featured, and they will talk about events from *Aurora* that will fill in the blanks.

And be warned! I don't mean blanks in their weapons. They use the real thing. To set the stage, the following is a short synopsis of *Aurora*, and this book begins where it ended.

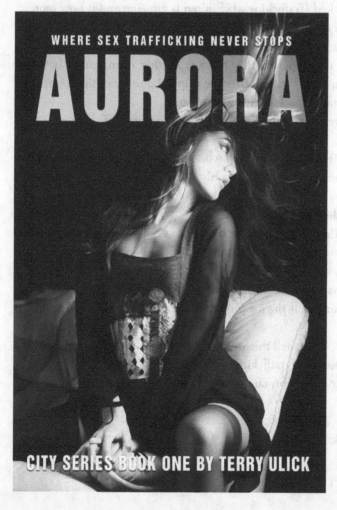

WHERE SEX TRAFFICKING NEVER STOPS

AURORA

CITY SERIES BOOK ONE BY TERRY ULICK

Not Taken

Synopsis:
AURORA

Cindy and her daughter Angie lived in a mobile home park in Aurora, a place where the worst of people live. Surrounded by drug dealers, pimps, and lost souls, they are there to hide from immigration. Cindy was born in the Ukraine, and when raped by her father when twelve, she was impregnated by him. Both her father and mother had learned to thrive in the Communist-controlled country before the collapse of the USSR by selling drugs, selling women for sex, and trafficking young women to USSR officials. Cindy's mother, Eliana, learned Angie and her brother were both raped by her husband. She went along with drug sales and trafficking, but not touching her children. She killed her husband in front of the two thinking they needed to know how life worked. Selling all their drugs and taking the large amount of money they had made, she bought their way out of the country by bribing – or shooting — anyone in her way.

Making it to the US, Eliana feared retaliation and decided it was safest to leave her children in America and return to the Ukraine. She bought a mobile home in Aurora, a place where people went to evade the law. Cindy gave birth to Angie when she was thirteen after Eliana returned to the Ukraine – and trafficking. Determined to make as much money as possible, Eliana became the most successful sex trafficker in Europe. To keep her children safe, she ceased all contact with Cindy or her newly born granddaughter, Angie.

The story begins with Angie, approaching her sixteenth birthday, getting up at dawn to avoid the men living in the trailer park who solicited her for sex since she could walk. Not having a working refrigerator, each morning at dawn Angie went shopping for food, and would look at the bulletin board there for ways to make money. Although too young to work as not of age, she longed to move out of Aurora, and make enough money for Cindy to become a citizen. Cindy, hiding from Ukrainian traffickers and drug dealers operating the US and seeking revenge on her mother, chose not to become a citizen. Keeping Angie out of school, she couldn't work a conventional job and offered herself as an escort, operating on her own, selling sex to lonely, respectable men, from the Ukraine and Russia.

For her sixteenth birthday, Cindy gave Angie two special gifts. A simple yet expensive black dress, and a flier she found seeking young girls to become "*the next big thing*" in modeling. Cindy and Angie look alike, both classic beauties, and she thought Angie could find a way to make money without needing to be discovered as a young girl not attending school. The invitation sought girls from their early teens through eighteen.

Going to an audition, Angie meets Jamie, who runs the modeling business, and Vlad, the photographer. After a photo session with Vlad, Angie is stunningly attractive and invited to come back for a full photo shoot. Excited, she returned with Cindy, who is even more stunning, and the photo shoot changes to include them both. What they didn't know was the photo audition was a front for sex trafficking. Jamie and Vlad were traffickers looking for very young girls. Immediately after the photo shoot, Jamie and Vlad ask them to stay and talk about their career opportunities. Having refreshments as they talked, they are drugged, put on a plane, and taken to Russia where they are put up for auction as a "*mother-daughter team*," and bought by an billionaire Arabian sheik.

Returning from Russia, Jamie confronts Vlad for murdering young girls meant for rich clients for his sexual perversion, and horrified at what he has done, kills him.

Replacing Vlad with a former glamour photographer, Mike, who answered her ad on the dark web, he presented a portfolio of sexual images of young girls, and she decides he is a good replacement for Vlad. What Jamie didn't know was that Mike was a CIA agent working undercover to find the heads of trafficking organizations. His sister had been "taken" when still in college while in Morocco. Trying to track her down, a CIA operative admired his methods and recruited him. As a CIA agent busting traffickers, he hoped to find her using agency resources.

Learning about Cindy and Angie when stepping in to replace Vlad, he decided to rescue them. Tolerating such activities, the agency was focused on taking down the traffickers – not rescuing girls taken. In the process, Mike and Jamie find themselves attracted to each other, and we learn that Jamie was trafficked since a child and is working as a trafficker to get to Brian, the Russian trafficker she was sold too, and even if it meant dying, kill him.

Cindy and Angie were at Brian's home, waiting to be collected by the sheik. Fulfilling his duty as a CIA agent Mike busts Jamie but recommends to his supervisor that she would provide valuable insider information in exchange for not being prosecuted. Jamie, determined to kill Brian, takes the deal and works with the agency as an undercover operative working with Mike.

Returning to Russia to kill Brian, finding Cindy and Angie at Brian's home, they learn Cindy offered Brian's bodyguard, who had previously worked for her mother, Eliana, a deal. The bodyguard knows Cindy's mother is a powerful trafficker, and to stay in her good graces, he kills Brian.

Although free, Cindy was not okay that some man, a sheik, "*bought*" them. Cindy and Angie pretend Brian is still alive, that they are captives, and dressed in burkas and hijabs, they wait for him. Once he arrives; alone with his "*merchandise*," Cindy shoots him in the head while he kneels before her, giving her oral sex as Angie watches.

The bodyguard knew Jamie, and she and Mike were welcomed by Cindy and Angie, learning how they also wanted to stop Brian. Cindy and Angie, in making a deal with the bodyguard, called Eliana and explained how he helped, and what happened to them both. Before they leave Eliana visits them, glad they are both safe – and that they turned to her for help.

Heading back to the US on a CIA private jet, Cindy looked at her bank balance on Mike's cell phone as she didn't think she'd enough money to pay utility bills. She discovers that her mother had wired $50 million into her bank account. Asking Mike if he thought she'd have enough in the bank to move out of Aurora and buy a home, he explains if she can't pay basic bills, it would be hard to buy a house.

Showing him her account balance, she doesn't act surprised as she knew her mother had made a fortune from selling young women. Jamie explains she can move anywhere and live a lush life, not having to be an escort anymore.

Cindy explained she just wanted a safe place to live – but planned to use her millions to take down traffickers and bring girls home. Knowing the money was made from selling girls, she explained she wanted to use it to save them. Explaining she and Angie wanted to go after traffickers the same way they took down Brian and the sheik, on their own and

outside the law, she asks Mike and Jamie to join their renegade anti-trafficking team.

The book ends with Cindy telling Mike she wants, "Lots of guns and hollow core bullets just like the one she shot the sheik with."

She had watched his head explode from the shot, and she wanted no less for any traffickers.

Mike, looking at Jamie, knows they both know they are in love and they join Cindy and Angie in a new life going after the sickness in the world that had hurt them all. Trafficking.

Characters featured in Aurora:

Cindy. Daughter of a powerful Ukrainian trafficker, working as an escort.

Angie. Cindy's sixteen-year-old daughter who is trafficked at a model audition.

Jamie. Sex trafficker who finds and exports girls showing up for fake model auditions.

Mike. Former glamour photographer who turned CIA operative to find his trafficked sister.

James. Heads CIA sex trafficking operations, and Mike's friend and supervisor.

Brian. Russian sex trafficker who is killed while Cindy is captive.

Charles. CIA psychiatrist who is supportive of Mike's need to find his sister.

Eliana. Cindy's mother who is a feared, powerful sex trafficker living in the Ukraine.

PART ONE
The Desert

CHAPTER 1

"Jamie? Are you fuckin' crazy? She's only goin' to be five this month!"

"If you want to stay fixed, what the fuck you bitching about? Yeah, so what? She's four goin' on five."

Brenda was shaking. Jonze was holding a bag of smack in one hand, a 45 in the other. He made the choice clear and the decision was hers. Either way, he'd leave with Jamie. The decision was simple in his mind. Take the bag, or have his gun stuck in her mouth to end her nightmare.

"Why you doing this to me? I'm the best ass you have working this shithole."

Looking at Brenda, he knew from fucking her when she first showed up she'd been hot ass one time. But that was before she got pregnant. Before getting hooked on smack when she used to eat enough. Now, she was worthless to him. Every time he went to collect money from her she looked emaciated, and even the most pathetic of truckers had started turning her away for a ten-dollar blowjob. Some thought she had AIDS, others knew there were better looking girls working the stop who'd blow them for the same ten.

The winds in the high desert were always brutal, and he was being pelted with sand and small debris. Feeling the temperature, the radio weather had said the Mojave would be hitting 120. He knew it was already that hot, or worse. Jonze was tired of standing outside of her camper and wanted to get back in his Land Cruiser. Even with its black tinted windows, it would be near as hot inside it as it was outside in the middle of nowhere.

He stood thinking how she could possibly think she was still worth fucking, let alone the best ass he had in his stable.

"Not with taking care of that little bitch, you're not. You're spending more time with mommy shit than blowing truckers, that's why. You choose. Either way, she's gone…"

Standing looking at her, he couldn't feel sorry for her. She had a big mouth and she was about to use it, and not for a blowjob.

"Ah, fuck, Brenda. I can't have you blow one of those fuckers to take you to the ER and tell them I took your brat. Fuck… I was going to let you blast off with this bag, but you're too far gone… Too fuckin' far gone. I'm fuckin' hot standing here. Ah, fuck… Why'd you go have that brat?"

Putting the bag of heroin in his pocket, he lifted his 45 and before she could stop him, he put it in her mouth as she opened it to answer him and fired.

"No need to answer that one, you dumb fuckin' cunt."

Walking over her body hanging out of the door of her camper, he went to the playpen that filled half of it and took the crying girl who had been watching her mother, crying nonstop. Wearing only underpants she fought to hold onto the playpen slats, he pulled her away from it and carried her by the waist to put her in the back of his Land Cruiser. It had a gate behind the rear seat to keep anything from flying when he had to stop quickly, and it would do as her new playpen.

Taking a knapsack he kept there along with a collection of junk he'd accumulated, he closed the hatch, then turned the truck on so the air conditioner would keep the girl cool enough to not die from heat. Looking at her as he was about to close the hatch, she knew something was wrong. She stared at him, blank, no expression, not even crying. Saying he was taking her for a ride, he shut the hatch then walked back to the camper.

Pulling Brenda fully inside the camper, he turned everything off and looked around for anything that may connect him to her. Finding nothing he need worry about, he opened a battered ice chest laying in the pool of blood where her head had been blown off. Pissed, it held just water, now hot. He had wanted a cold drink before doing what he needed to do next. Taking the 45, it was one he had taken from a trucker at the rest stop on the Interstate after getting a blowjob from Brenda but refused to pay. Climbing into the trucker's cab to settle matters, he felt energized from beating him unconscious. Looking at the half-toothed trucker, he shook his head at how low people could sink, then took all his money, and the 45, as payment.

Opening his knapsack, he rummaged for a bottle of solvent and latex gloves he had taken from an urgent care visit. Taking the gun, after putting on the gloves he spent time wiping it clean, then wiped it again. He stood thinking of how best to make it where it had been her holding the gun. He pulled her right hand up and put the gun in it, made sure her fingers were all over it first, then on the grip and trigger.

Pulling her hand up far as he could, using her hand under his, he fired one round to hit behind where she had been standing. He wanted

it to look like she blew the first shot by aiming at her head, and not wanting to miss again, put it in her mouth which worked that time. That would make sense, and her hand would have powder burns. That would be plenty as the sheriff could care less about the addicts and hookers who were the main population of the Mojave. Most going there were interested in getting high on a choice of fucked-up drugs, then doing sick shit to the hookers.

Checking everything over, he was confident things looked good enough for anyone to call it suicide. He was tired of the things he had to do to stay alive. He was disposable to a man with a bigger gun, and he knew one day it would be him making a choice to die — or, to die. For now, it was just another day and another dead bitch. There was no need to burn the trailer, but he did take the heroin after putting some of it in one of her pill bottles, then put the bottle in her pocket.

Taking a grocery bag and filling it with the girl's clothes and some toys, with one final look, he walked away leaving the camper door open. Anyone investigating would see the playpen and he knew they'd probably look for the girl. With the door of the playpen and the camper both left open, they would search in a small radius around the camper for her, sure she had scurried away to find someone to give her food and died of exposure. It didn't matter one way or another. The desert took care of small creatures, even humans. Birds of prey and other animals even ate bones. There were dozens of reasons she wouldn't be found, and she wouldn't be missed as Brenda had no family or friends. Just a drug addiction, an ass, and mouth.

Getting in the Land Cruiser with the bag of clothes and toys, it was cold enough inside. Sitting there, he didn't hear anything from the girl in the back, so decided to ask her what she was doing.

"Jamie, what the fuck you doin' back there?"

"Waiting."

"Waiting for what?"

"I'm hungry. Waiting to eat."

Pulling away, he headed for the Interstate and looked at the dust cloud made by his tires in the rear-view mirror. Getting out of the Mojave, he was planning to stop at a drive-through in Barstow to get her food. He was hungry too. Rummaging in the knapsack, finding some trail mix and a bottle of water, he stopped the truck, got out and opened the hatch.

"Going to be a while before I can get us some food. I'm hungry too, okay? This shit will have to do until then."

Opening the bag, he put it between her legs, saying not to spill it, and she nodded at him. Closing the hatch, driving at the posted speed, once in Barstow he stopped for food at a McDonalds for both of them.

Driving to the next rest stop, he took her from the cargo hold, telling her she'd be riding up front with him. Eating her kid's meal, looking at the toy but not opening it or playing with it, he'd bought the meal with a chocolate shake, and she sipped at it as they left the rest stop.

"You sure don't talk much. That shit will have to hold you over for a while. After we get out of this desert we can stop and get more to eat. Now, listen. When we do, I don't want any shit from you, okay? No crying or trying to talk to people. Understand?"

Sipping her shake, she nodded as she looked at him.

"You my daddy?"

Thinking how fucked up hookers' kids were, he looked at her and nodded.

"Yeah. For now, I'm your daddy."

Driving into the sunset, then the night, after a stop for gas and another meal, he was glad to reach Los Angeles. It was always busy, even late at night, not like the desert, and he fit right in.

Looking over at Jamie, he was glad he'd taken good care of her on the way. Henry, whose strip club he was headed to, would only pay if Jamie was unmarked, undrugged, and didn't understand what had happened to her mother. Seeing the tacky neon sign near the airport saying, "Girls Girls Girls," he pulled in the lot behind the cinderblock box that held losers putting dollar bills in the pussies of drugged out strippers, and the place was always full. Standing at the back service door was Bill, a large brute who was Henry's bodyguard and the one who'd kick the shit out of guys crossing the line or failing to say yes and pay for a lap-dance.

Rolling down his window, leaning out he told Bill, "Fragile goods." Bill leaned in and seeing Jamie, nodded, then went in the back door. Waiting, only a few minutes passed, Henry came out, got in the back seat and told Jamie to join him in the back.

Jonze did business, but he didn't do children. He didn't want to listen or watch what Henry was about to do to Jamie. Rolling his window up he told Henry he'd be right outside talking to Bill so he'd have some

privacy. Henry said he appreciated that. Jonze knew he would.

Getting out of the car, he went and stood with Bill. Looking over at the car, Bill shaking his head, he was muscle, but he also knew Henry was a sick fucker. They both knew what was being done. Both knew they were okay letting it happen. For them, it was only about money and pussy they'd get.

For Jonze, it was ten grand. More than he'd make in a month from pimping whores at the truck stops. All he had to do to get it was kill a woman who had just headed down a bad road, and take her child to be used by perverts. He was thinking how fucked up that was. Lives. One gone, the other a fucking hell waiting. And, he'd have ten grand.

Starting out a teen street hustler, Henry found him and said he needed a guy for truck stops, then provided an endless line of burned-out strippers for him to pimp. They were too far-gone on smack to work the club, but soon he was learning that wasn't all it was. Henry knew out in the desert some would be fucked up enough to have kids. They'd have no one to turn to, and after the thrill of being a mother, the thrill of a fix would take over and they'd give up their kid. Henry wanted a supply of unwanted children for himself, and clients. It also kept Jonze alive. He knew too much about how Henry trafficked children to do anything other than what he was told.

Bill was different. He didn't pimp, and he didn't care about anything people did. Not the strippers, the hookers, the patrons, and not what Henry did. He was there for free pussy. He was paid well and kept it all as he didn't have to pay for ass.

Staring at the Land Cruiser starting to shake and hearing thumping, both knew how low they had sunk to standing by while a little girl was being fucked by a perverted, sick man. Each managed to fool themselves it was just the way the world worked. They were right about that. If it wasn't them standing there, it would be some other losers, and the sick shit would still go down.

Bill heard his name called from the slightly rolled down back seat window of the Land Cruiser. He went over to see what Henry wanted him to do. Jonze watched as Bill went and got Henry's long Cadillac from the back of the lot and pulled it next to the side of the Land Cruiser. Opening doors, he carried an unconscious Jamie from one door to the other, then closed them both. Jonze knew Henry had given Jamie

an injection to keep her quiet.

Getting out, Henry told Bill to watch his car, then told Jonze to follow him inside.

Unlocking his small office in the back of the club, Henry opened a safe and took a banded bunch of twenties, marked $10k, handing it to Jonze. Putting it in his pocket, Jonze had nothing to add. Henry was a man in his 40s, a short beard, wore glasses and looked like everybody and nobody. He was much like any man living in the suburbs, yet showed little reaction to most anything said or asked when talking to him. He wore Dockers and a polo shirt, smoking a Camel most times he saw him.

Getting up to leave, Jonze saw Henry make a motion with his hand indicating to sit, and not to leave yet.

"That's good merchandise out there. I have new buyers who want as much as I can provide. Listen, I think it's time you stop fucking around with the whores out there. I want you to supply me with more Jamies. You do it right, you get rich and get any pussy out there in the club. Do it wrong? Get in trouble? You get dead. Fuck the desert shit. Work the suburbs, here. The valley. Bakersfield. Understand?"

He did. It was that or end up like Brenda. He knew the rules of the sick world he was in. He'd be happy to be out of the Mojave, and Henry knew he like the seriously experienced pussy like the strippers had, not the cum-filled cunts of the hookers. Nodding, he said sure, he'd clear out his place in the Mojave and be back in a few days. Getting only a nod from Henry, he walked out the back door thinking at least he wouldn't have to put up with the heat and hot wind — or the burned-out whores anymore.

late teens, she'd get curious and want to know about life outside of the private world they lived in. Her job was to make sure they understood they were lucky, and well taken care of when so many weren't. She asked how much Jamie had read.

"Some of it. It said that he was in trouble for making movies, like the ones we make with me in them. Oh, and that he made a lot of money from them. That's the part that I don't understand. Since I'm in them, shouldn't I make a lot of money too?"

That's when Erma asked what she had to complain about. She lived in mansions and flew in private jets and what was the big deal? Jamie had read more than she shared, primarily it was illegal to do the things they did, and Jakob was doing something wrong.

"Erma, I don't know why he'd run out like he did and miss his blowjob and all unless he was in bad trouble. I'm worried I could be in trouble too if he is."

Thinking Jamie had reached a time where she'd either got sold off or become a recruiter, her instincts told her that she'd be good at bringing other girls in. She was the right age to start learning how, and she had reached a point where she thought of sex the same as eating or grocery shopping. It was a matter of fact for her until getting online and reading it was illegal and girls were being groomed and used. Erma also thought Jamie had a sensibility that would work as a recruiter. She was already asking why she wasn't getting money after reading about sex trafficking online. Sold off, she'd go for a decent price, but 18 was older than desired for most clients. As a recruiter, she could bring in endless income.

"Jamie, I'm actually glad you got online and learned a bit about the world. You've lived a special life, one most people don't know about. From when you were little, you were fawned over by rich and powerful people and wanted for nothing. And all the people you know? They love your body, just like mine. They have sex all the time, but they especially like fucking you. Since you were little. That's why they're rich. They know what great sex is and they're very smart. You've fucked hundreds of men, and they all treated you nice and gave you gifts and took you places. You've always told me you like fucking and sucking them off, right?"

Jamie couldn't argue that she didn't. She'd always liked attention and

being pampered. All the girls and grownup women she knew fucked all the time as well, but she was told she was the best, and everyone's favorite. That wasn't what she was thinking about. She didn't know that the men paid money, or it was a business.

"Sure, who doesn't? Not as much when I was little. It mostly hurt. I like it now that I have orgasms. But, if a man pays money to fuck me, or makes a movie of me doing him, shouldn't I get paid? I didn't know they paid to do things with them. Who gets the money?"

Thinking she was right about Jamie having a business sense, there was no need to hold back on how things worked. If she didn't get Jamie righted, she'd be on a plane to the middle east or Russia. If she wanted to be part of things, it was the right time to find out.

"Well, all of us here… we work for a man in Russia. He arranges for men to fuck you, and they pay him. Then he pays me, and I pay for all the things you have and need. Remember, you were an orphan, and we took you in and took good care of you. Most orphans aren't so lucky. When you're young, money isn't what you need. You need to get good at doing men every way possible, and you have. Now, at your age, you're a grownup, and you can start making money for yourself. One way is with that sweet ass of yours. But you know… men, the rich ones? They pay for pussy that's young. At your age now… 18, that's too old for them. They'll pay to fuck you, but not very much. They like young girls. The younger the better. Do you understand?"

Thinking about it, she started nodding.

"Well, I used to get all kinds of questions about how old I was, and told I was a little sweetie to be with. Lately, nobody talks about me being young, or how old I am. They do want me to dress an act like a little girl, though. Spank me and things. So, is that what you mean?"

Smiling, Erma was glad she was figuring it out on her own.

"Exactly. Those men, well, to get their dicks up, they need a little girl, not a grown one, or a woman. And they are willing to pay for it. They'll pay a lot for it. Do you know why they pay a lot?"

Shrugging, Jamie thought about it, and had some ideas.

"I always thought there aren't many girls as pretty as me… or who can fuck like me. You know, they all say that to me. The part where they've never fucked a girl as pretty as me. Or they've never fucked one as young as me. I don't hear that very much now. Sometimes… With

new men. So, I always thought there aren't as many pretty girls as there needs to be."

Laughing, Erma thought how right Jamie was, though not exactly because girls weren't pretty. They weren't being sold for sex, and there never seemed to be enough to meet demand. She knew it was time to explain it to her.

"That's true, but there are lots of pretty young girls. They aren't orphans, or as lucky as you. They have parents who don't let them out of their sight. They don't let them have sex at all! I mean any kind of sex. Even rubbing themselves off. And. Oh, God, certainly not with older men."

Giving her a look of skepticism, Jamie shook her head.

"Why not?"

"Jamie. There's so much you've been protected from. Out there, in that world… It's not like here. A man and woman meet, and they get married. You've fucked married men and knew they have wives who don't fuck them and all, so in marriage, you're only supposed to have sex with who you're married to. Then, they have kids. And to make their daughters attractive when it comes time to marry, they don't let them fuck anyone until they get married. Imagine that. And, girls have to be 18 to get married in most places."

"I don't get it. Why 18? Why not anytime they meet someone who they want to marry?"

"Sweetie, I don't know why. It's just the way things are and have been for a long time. All kinds of laws people must obey. One is both a guy and gal have to be 18 to get married. In some places, 16, but not many. And to keep it that way… and you're not going to believe this… The law says a man over 18 can't have sex with a girl under 18, even if she really wants to fuck him. If he does, he'll go to jail."

Watching Jamie think about it, she saw the wheels turning in her head. She could see she was figuring it out. Jamie lifted her head and put her hands on her hips.

"So, if they can't fuck pretty young girls with people knowing about it, and if people knew they'd get in trouble and go to jail, they come here or wherever we are to fuck where nobody can see them or know about it?"

Erma nodded. Jamie went on.

"I think I get it. So, there aren't many little girls they can fuck, and they need a special place like this where it's secret… and they are all

rich because they have to pay a lot to keep it a secret and not get in big trouble."

"That's right, Jamie. That's why we live like we do, and don't deal with the world outside very much. Why you don't go to school or any of that bullshit. We take care of the smart men, and we take real good care of you. See, if you're an orphan, you end up in a place just like jail. A state home, or with people paid to watch over you but don't care about you. It's a lot to know, but I hope it's making sense."

"Yeah, it does. If that's how it all is, then they must pay a whole lot for my ass. Why don't I get any of what they pay?"

"Jamie, I get why you'd think that. You do get paid, but in other ways. We pay for everything you have. All your food. Traveling. All your clothes are custom-made. All those things cost a lot of money, so we take the money they pay to fuck you and spend it on taking care of you. And we need to keep things secret. We pay for all kinds of things you don't know about. Girls your age? They're lucky to have a nice dress or two. They have to start working in a store or a fast-food place. You'll learn all that really soon."

Crossing her arms, Jamie was still unsure of why she didn't get any of the money.

"I think I should get some of that money, even with that. If they are willing to pay a lot for my ass, it's my ass, right? What if I walked out and found some old guy to fuck? He'd pay me and I'd keep all the money. Right?"

The hard questions and facts had come. Erma hated such moments with girls. They all felt the same way. They were shielded from the truth of how the world works. If not, their whole operation would be out of business. She was there to get the girls thinking one way, and it was not how the world thought of things.

"I know that makes sense to you. But it doesn't work like that. I'll explain more about why later, but there's something you need to know. It's real important. Really important."

Eyes wide open, Jamie realized Erma was being unusually serious. She waited to hear.

"Jamie, since we provide young girls to men who pay, and it's all against the law, if anyone found out, we'd all go to jail and be in big trouble. If a girl left here and went around saying she could fuck on

her own, and start telling people about us? Well, we can't let that ever happen. We'd all be in jail, and I mean you too. Just take my word for it, right now, okay?"

Jamie could tell by the look on Erma's face she was being serious. She meant what she was saying.

"That scares me! I can't leave? What would you do if I did? Or, if I tried to?"

Erma went and hugged her side, then kissed her cheek.

"No. It wouldn't be good. That's why I'm having this talk with you. We would keep you from doing that. One way or another. Most likely sell you to some Arab or Russian to be his sex slave. Or lock you up in here somehow. I don't want any of that for you. Never. There is a way where you can make tons of money and be free too. I'm hoping that's what happens."

"Wha… what is that? How would I do that?"

"Jamie. I can teach you to do what I do. If you figure this out, you can go out, find girls, tell them about how nice you have it, invite them over. Then they can fuck men, and you'd make a part of what the men pay for fucking the girls you bring in. Recruit and get them here, all excited. If you told anyone what you're doing or what goes on here, you'd get in big trouble. I know you wouldn't take that chance, and you'd be so good at it, making money just by getting other girls to fuck the clients. And whoa, you'll make lots of money."

Thinking, Jamie had one more question.

"And if I fucked clients, as you call them, would I get paid?"

"We can talk about that. You wouldn't *have* to fuck them anymore, but if you wanted to, and they get off? Sure. Either way, Jamie, I mean, like, you're growing up! You're getting too old for our clients. Fuck who you want, but time to figure out your hot ass days for rich old men are about over."

CHAPTER 3

Looking at the "Girls Girls Girls" sign on the strip club leading to the LAX terminal, Jamie's commercial flight from Moscow had just landed. Being used to riding on Brian's personal jet, he apologized for it not being available.

"Jamie, shipment to pick up, important, no? Your girls, your money, this you know. You wait, you ride back on plane."

Staring at him, she shook her head and showed no emotion. She didn't reply to the offer but had a question.

"I've got one of my guns in a locker in LA, so no need to bypass security. I have one in a locker here if I need it. Are you going to warn the motherfucker? If you do, I'll kill him then come kill you."

Offering only a look of shock, he turned to walk away, but turned back. He was fond of her as she was the first seven-year-old from America he had fucked. Before Jamie, he'd been a pimp, whoring out grown women to politicos and had made connections with officials who had been asking for ever younger whores. When he first fucked her, he was middle-aged, married, still handsome and virile. After he had fucked all of her holes he was shocked that it hadn't frightened her, or hurt her tissues. Now, fifteen years later, his wife had left him, he was overweight, and it took ever more perverse sex to arouse him. He was pale white, had dyed-black hair slicked back with pomade, and he wore a $5,000 suit that did nothing to improve his looks. The only thing he possessed was power.

After sex with Jamie the first time, he decided to specialize in underage girls trafficked from the Americas, both north and south. That made him richer than he thought possible, but not just from selling young girls. Most money came from his taking pictures and videos of the mighty men who abused the young girls. He hadn't revealed such images until he had the mightiest men in the collection. Only if someone questioned his actions or prices did he mention that he had proof of their perversion, and it would only be used if anything happened to him. It was standard operating procedure in the corrupt government, and he was free to conduct his trade without fear. Jamie knew that. She also knew she had the same goods on him. In his visits to America to inspect the "merchandise," she had secretly filmed him fucking girls as young as four. She told him she'd hand over her proof to US officials if alive and

fucked with, or it would get to them if she turned up dead.

Wearing a simple wool coat, Jamie was a beautiful woman who hid her looks with frumpy clothing, bad hair styling, wearing makeup that made her look ordinary. Thinking back to her two years doing porn, she had learned to hide who she was so men watching her movies didn't recognize her out in public. Sexualized since early childhood, she loved sex, having orgasms, and had no interest in a boyfriend or husband. Her view of all men was that they were like Brian. Sick, perverted, and didn't care who they hurt.

A long way from her first grooming to be a recruiter, she had just returned from killing Erma. She had tied her up, pointed her 45 at her head, saying she wanted to know who kidnapped her when she was five. Erma was never a brave woman. Just having the gun pointed at her, Jamie found out Brian was the one who had placed the first orders for children her age. Knowing if she left Erma after that, Erma would call Brian. She had brought a long-blade knife, polished to a mirror finish. Pulling it out of her bag, she held it up for Erma to see herself in the mirror finish. Watching Erma's eyes open wide in fear, she pulled it away then without hesitation stabbed Erma in the stomach. As she keeled over in pain, Jamie took the butt of her gun and hit Erma's head. She kept hitting her head until it cracked wide open long after she'd been unconscious. She needed to make sure she was dead. Brains spilling onto the plush carpet where Erma lay meant she was dead.

Learning all the details, Erma told her that a man working for Brian in Los Angeles had been the one who put her "out" and groomed her. Erma didn't know who the man was, his name, or who had actually kidnapped her. That was all Erma managed to tell her before Jamie began using the butt of the gun on her head in a fury.

All Jamie could remember was being in a hot playpen, a man putting a gun in her mother's mouth, firing it and killing her. She was so traumatized; she was in shock and the man took her away. After that, the next year she was constantly in a traumatized state as she was sexually abused daily to where it became, to her, what a little girl did with men.

Deciding to work her way to being a trafficker, taking over from Erma, she had succeeded and met Brian. He knew who she was and thought like many of his traffickers she was fully groomed to where she saw no wrong in the activity.

She didn't see wrong in killing men like Brian or the ones who trafficked her when five. Long having his trust, she was confident telling him she needed to know who had killed her mother, kidnapped her, and the man who first fucked her in a car. She decided not to mention that after she took care of them, she'd take care of Brian. She needed the names first. Dead men reveal nothing, so she played the part, even though she was doing the very things done to her. She was so hardened from a life of abuse she had no feelings other than a long-planned killing of the ones responsible for life being ruined. Brian didn't see it as more than she wanted to off the men who first did her, and she knew he was too arrogant to think she'd ever come after him.

"No. What should I care now? Scum. Long gone, no do business with such rabble. Shoot fuckers. I give you Uzi, but you insist on doing on your own. You hurt feelings not taking gift. You think I would do that? To you? My first little malenka?"

"It's a dirty business we're in. This is my business. It happened to me. I'm doing it. Stay out of it. I told you. I appreciate the names."

As Brian's Mercedes pulled up, she got in and Brian stood watching, hoping she didn't start a gun battle that would end up at his door.

Once in LA, after getting her bag with her Magnum out of a locker, she went to the parking lot and got her car, a beater, then drove to the strip club the man she was looking for would be, according to Brian. She had no reason to doubt him. He didn't care about people no longer working for him, and he valued her — for the moment. He had told her the man who sold her had died, and the man who had killed her mother had taken over the strip club. His name was Jonze, and that rang true with her. When he said the name, she connected with it instantly. It had eluded her as she had PTSD from all that had been done to her as a child, but with just that name, it had all come back to her. Her mother's head blown off, Jonze taking her from her crib, walking over her mother, putting her in his car, eating food with him as they drove, then once at the strip club, being put in the back of his car where the club owner came and fucked her when five. He had drugged her. She wasn't fully out when he raped her, and she was furious he had died as she wanted to fuck him back good.

Figuring out the best way to get at Jonze was to show up and say she wanted to be a dancer at the club. That would get her into his office. She

changed clothes from ones she had in the locker at the airport. Wearing a revealing top with a short dress and hose with visible garter belt, she looked like a slut but she had a great body and the outfit showed it off.

Pulling into the parking lot, she flashed on where she had been brought by Jonze that night, which was behind the club. She was glad to see there were open areas to park and nobody guarding the back door. Walking around to the front, she saw the bouncer. Putting on the manner of a hooker, she said she was there to audition and was told to see some Jonze guy. He waved her in, saying head to the back and knock on the door that said private.

Carrying a vinyl handbag, she had it stuffed with clothes which hid the shape of her gun. The club was full of surprisingly attractive young girls. She knew being a stripper or porn actress had somehow become a respected occupation for girls raised on social media and the endless cable TV network shows about the lives and loves of strippers. The girls were trim, toned, and all looked like they were fresh from Kansas. The men were the same as always. Pathetic losers, overweight or wearing work clothes, and young company men out for a night of what they thought would be something to post on their social media accounts. They were buying $50 drinks, spending a hundred or more for a lap dance, and they all thought it was a fine time. Watching it all, she thought of how even her sick world of trafficking children had changed the classic strip club. Not long ago the dancers would have been in their mid-twenties and hookers. Now, she doubted one was over 18, and they had the trim bodies of teens. That's what porn had done to shape what men longed for.

Walking past all the men and teens, she stood in front of the cheap paneled door marked with a "Private" sign and knocked.

Hearing a man shout, "What?" she shouted back that she wanted to audition. In under a minute the door opened, and she felt enraged and sick at the same moment. It was him. Jonze. He didn't look much different from when he had killed her mother. Keeping her reaction hid, he stood, looked her over carefully, then after saying she was a bit old for the place, she had a decent body so he'd talk to her about it.

Following him in, he told her to close the door behind her. He went and sat in the chair behind his desk, not turning to face forward. He turned his chair to face sideways as he unzipped his pants and pulled out his cock and looked over at her.

"Let's see how good you suck dick first… and take that shit off so I see what you got."

Having expected to get naked and blow him, she started undressing and put her top and bottom in her handbag, leaving her hose and garter belt on. Putting her bag by the corner of the desk where she'd be kneeling, she stood in front of him first, letting him look her over. He asked if she shaved or waxed her pussy. She had it lasered but said waxed as he wouldn't think she'd afford a laser job. Telling her to turn around, he studied her ass, reaching over to pull her ass cheeks apart, telling her to lean over to see her asshole and pussy.

"Nice. It'll do for a while. Okay, suck me off."

Turning, she knelt and pulled at her bag as he counted some money waiting for her to start. She pulled her gun up on top of her clothes, then put both of her hands on his knees as she looked up at him.

"Hey, I think we've met before."

He didn't stop counting the money.

"I meet ass every night. So, what? I'm supposed to remember mouths or cunts?"

"Well, it was a while ago. We ate at McDonalds. The one in Barstow."

That got his attention. She put her hand on her chin as if to remember, him looking at her. She could see he was triggered by what she said.

"I haven't been in Barstow for ages. What the fuck you talking about?"

Putting her hand down and into the bag, she kept eye contact with him.

"That! That's when. Yeah… All those years ago when you shot my mother in the desert and brought me here to be fucked when I was five."

His face barely had time to show its shock. She had moved the gun as she talked and aimed it low at his crotch. She fired. His dick flew off and hit his face as he flew back and hit the ground as blood poured out of where his cock had been. She got up, stood above him, pointing the gun at his face, glad the loud thumping music had drowned out the shot.

"Remember this mouth and cunt now?"

He was still conscious and was trying to crawl back away from her.

As he opened his mouth to beg her to stop, she watched his look of terror as she pointed to his open mouth. Making sure he remembered

how he had shot her mother first, she could see he did, and fired. The 45 went in his mouth, just as his shot had been in her mother's. Keeping the gun in her hand in case a bouncer entered, she slipped her clothes back on, took her bag and opened the door. Nobody was in the hallway, and she went to the back, gun still in hand. There was nobody watching the back door, but still holding the gun she got in her car, backed up, and left through the front driveway as she put the gun back in her bag.

Not feeling frightened, upset, sorry or happy for killing Jonze, it was the first step at getting the enablers who stole her life out of the way. Getting Brian would not be as easy as Erma or Jonze. She'd need to call him and say she had taken care of Jonze. He was the man she wanted and now she could get back to work and set him up as she had the two she left dead in LA.

"Does kill make you money? Make you happy? He no after your girls. He was a nothing."

"Well, Brian, he's nothing now. Just something I felt like doing. You know how it is…"

There was a long pause, then, "Dah."

CHAPTER 4

Facing a moral dilemma, from her point of view Jamie had to do something horrific to stop the trafficking she was mired in from continuing. Thinking many times of just killing Brian, she met with him often and hoped for a chance to meet with him when not searched by his bodyguard before meeting with him. Men like Brian were always accompanied by a bodyguard holding an Uzi ready to fire. She knew he also had men in the US who kept an eye on her. Realizing the only was she could kill him was to keep trafficking girls to him until there was one moment when they'd be alone. It would have to happen at some point, and it would be her one chance of taking him down.

Since she started recruiting girls for him when 18, she had been told repeatedly if she told anyone about their operation or go to authorities, they would know, and she'd be killed. Told they had connections with government agents paid well to look the other way, they were also paid to report anyone who turned on Brian.

Brian also told her that if she wanted out, there was only one way, and it wasn't alive.

Living in fear hadn't stopped her of thinking of how to kill Brian. Realizing being abused since she was five had ruined her existence in every way, she stopped caring about being killed. Her caution to not get killed was ever about getting to Brian and killing him first.

She had found some solace doing porn for a man who worked for Brian. Important to current-day sex trafficking, older girls were put in porn videos to market them, and most were sold to clients. Porn videos were previews of what buyers could choose from if they wanted girls who were experienced in extreme sex. As with the trafficking, girls in porn were getting younger and though in her early 20s, she was playing MILFs and stepmoms. The premise was a sex-savvy mother would teach her innocent stepdaughter how to suck, fuck, and take it in the ass so she'd be able to do the same with her clueless stepdaughter's boyfriend. They'd always end up doing a three way. Being more experienced, as the mother she'd rim or suck balls as a 16-year old would suck cock, asking her if she was doing it right even though she was tatted and could swallow cock without gagging.

As absurd as the setups were, Jamie liked having sex and it was safe

as the producer worked for Brian. Having a boyfriend was not allowed, so it was her only way to have sex and stay alive. She enjoyed getting lost in the pure stupidity of it and surprised herself as she was willing to do anything. She'd take three or more in her ass at once while sucking a line of men off, get gang banged and it would always end where all the men would cum on her face. Doing it all, she was willing to do fetish and bondage. She squirted easily, drank piss, and licked pussy. Occasionally a shot would include simple kissing. She liked that best and kissing got her wet where she wouldn't need lubricant for the other acts.

Relying on Internet showcasing to sell girls, she was asked by Brian to make videos of all her girls, no matter how young. Pre-selling many of them online, he told her it was why he wanted her to do porn for a time. Knowing how to produce sex videos, she'd work with a photographer and do pictures of the girls for sale, make videos of them giving blowjobs, and sometimes getting it in their ass. There was only one restriction. They could be fucked anywhere but in their pussies. If a girl wasn't a porn actress and under 18, they were all priced as virgins. Being a veteran porn actress, she knew what he wanted. Telling her to first try to pay the photographer with head or ass, he also said to always use older girls for his payment. Older meant 16 and up, nothing under.

Knowing her entire life was about sex, she accepted it was a business and she often wondered what her life would have been if her mother had a husband and hadn't been a hooker. It was just something to think about, nothing more.

She was growing impatient. Doing the same things that had ruined her life to young girls was weighing heavily on her, and she wanted to stop. Needing to kill Brian she reached a point where she no longer cared if she was killed while getting at him. To make it worth her life, she knew she had to wait and stay in his operation no matter how much it sickened her once understanding the balance between her life and ruining the lives of so many young girls. It had to happen soon and had to be done right.

Having no one to talk to, she was alone and angry. She hated what she was doing to girls who were only children. Looking in the mirror each day she realized she was as doomed as any of the girls she trafficked.

PART TWO
The Survivors

CHAPTER 5

"And that's about the time I met Mike, then all of you..."

Mike, Angie and Cindy had listened intently, not interrupting her account of growing up a trafficked child, then a trafficker. Wanting only to be understood, Jamie had not forgiven herself for any of the things she had done once grown. Wanting to stop traffickers, she was compelled to reveal all she had done, and how she was adamant about getting at even larger trafficking rings than the one they had brought down in Russia.

Both Angie and Cindy cried most all the way through her story, while Mike sat listening, learning more about people who were trafficked than he ever had when a field agent for the agency. He'd been trained to understand how traffickers worked, how they avoided arrest, and warned they all operated under the protection of the most powerful and wealthy men in the world. He had never been taught what a person goes through when they are taken, or how they felt about the life they were forced into. He had found himself attracted to Jamie from the first moment he met her, and now he was starting to understand why. She had been a trafficker, and the attraction was upsetting to him as she was not a person he could think of as good to be involved with. He kept having images of her when she was in the playpen when just four, watching her mother killed, then taken to be a sex slave in an isolated world without family or society and schools around her. The words of Jonze saying, "She's four, so what?" kept echoing in his mind. Jamie was raised in a world without respect for any girl or woman. They were only "things" to be used, abused, and sold. It was horrific and it was the first time he fully understood what was done to people trafficked for sex.

Looking at each one, Jamie wondered what was going through their minds. She worried that they would think she thought all she had done was alright; that it was okay to do to anyone. She wanted them to know what had happened to her and let them form their own opinions about her. Deciding the only way to work with them was to never make excuses for anything she had done. They happened, and she had done them.

Angie looked at Cindy who was still crying. Her mother had been raised by traffickers in the Ukraine and been raped by her father when

twelve. If anyone there could understand the life Jamie had experienced, Cindy would be the one. Angie had watched her mother shoot a sheik who had bought them both. The man had his face pressed into her mother's slit while kneeling in front of her as she stood. Cindy thought about how the man thought himself so above them that he could do that right in front of her, Cindy's daughter. Buying them to use both as sex slaves, most likely having sex with them both at the same time, they were his property. Two things he owned — like his jet or all the other things, and women, he owned. Having no regard for either of them, he walked in, knelt and began licking her mother, pressing his face into her smooth mound. They meant nothing more to him than things to use. She watched as her mother quietly reached for a gun she hid behind herself as she stood, and as the sheik lost himself licking her clit, immersed in licking it and pulling it into his mouth, she quietly moved the gun over the top of his head, then fired straight down into it, his head exploding and covering them with skin, bone and brains.

Cindy was crying as Jamie's story brought back memories of watching her father have sex with young girls in her home in the Ukraine as her mother watched, her father insisting she and her brother watch while he went at an endless line of young girls who cried and screamed for him to stop. He was a drug lord, pimp, and eventually trafficker. Having sex with new girls was something he referred to as "testing the merchandise." Just like Jamie had been used, they were "things," not human beings. Her father had been bringing ever younger girls home, and it culminated in him raping her when she was twelve, making her pregnant with Angie. She had escaped to America, and wondered what would have happened if she hadn't. She would have been sold off, she was sure. She had been a thing to use and had no worth in her own father's eyes.

While talking about how she had been taken and trafficked, Jamie hadn't cried once. The only way she could tell the story was to distance herself from it and not let the true horror of it overtake her. Jamie grew up knowing that controlling emotions was something a trafficked person learned to do quickly, and even that was part of the nightmare of being trafficked. Enduring, tolerating, agreeing, hiding feelings, deferring to perverted people and ways of thinking. It was grooming that had been the worst for her. She was taught right was wrong and was beginning

to realize it was why traffickers were looking to get at young children. They could shape their values and perception of the world through using rewards and punishments — each extreme — to think that being a sex slave was a good thing. They were taught that if they didn't agree, there were endless young girls who would, and they'd no longer be wanted. Pure fear and endless threats kept trafficked children in line.

It was Cindy who was able to talk first. She went to Jamie, hugged her, and sat next to her.

"When I was just a little girl, I didn't think watching my father having sex with a girl young as me was wrong. My mother didn't get mad. She'd ask how good the little girl was, and made us guess how much he could get for her. It wasn't until he raped me... until he pushed his cock into me... that I first thought about all I'd seen. I was the same as all those girls, and it took getting raped by my own father to make me understand. Jamie, I'm so sorry you went through all that. I know that when you figured it all out, rather than get killed by trying to run, you played their game to get at Brian and kill him."

They were looking at each other, Cindy shaking, holding Jamie's hands. She managed to say one last thing.

"I need to tell you one thing I'm dealing with... I wish it had been you who killed him."

Saying that started Jamie sobbing. Mike was watching and knew what may help.

"We were all on our way to kill him. Jamie was with us because she wanted to be. If she hadn't, I would have. We all know we would have. It wasn't any of us who killed him. It was his own bodyguard."

Knowing Jamie had done all she had, she wanted to be the one who pulled the trigger and watch the man who destroyed her life have her as the last thing he saw. To stop him from ever doing harm to another person. To end it all, in her mind. It was revenge, disgust, and closure that shooting him meant to her. He looked at her, nodding, then to all three of them.

"Jamie. It may not make sense right now, but I assure you that you'll get your chance to kill Brian. It's something I've embraced. I know you'll see every trafficker is Brian. They're all doing what he did, and that's why we're here. We're going to be Brian killers. Fuck them up, then kill them. You all know that."

They all nodded their heads, and he could see the fire overtake the pain from how they had suffered. The hurting was over, the killing would begin.

"When I was an agent, I couldn't do what any of you could. I had rules, and there was always some reason not to shoot a Brian. It was always something. That he had names, or he had a deal. But me? I had rules. But now, that's done. Look at all of you. Just because you look the way you do, you all have a way in. You can infiltrate. Be trafficked. Be traffickers. Get inside and once there, do what was done to Brian. Get clients too. There won't be any agents there. The Brians and buyers won't even know what happened. We get in, fuck them up, then we go ghost."

Looking at them, he was amazed at the knowledge they all had being victims. Being trafficked they knew how things worked from the inside. It was something field agents and charities didn't know. That's why trafficking succeeded. He thought of how if each girl trafficked had a gun in her hand and knew how to use it, there'd be no more trafficking. With his discipline and connections, he felt confident they could bring traffickers down. The key was going after the largest and most powerful organizations. Spending time on the ones who served the main players was pointless. They would be replaced in hours. That would be where he could play. He would act the part of a provider, offer a taste of the women and girls he could provide. If they happened to be Angie, Cindy or Jamie, then they'd work the organization until they had access to its leader. There was risk, danger at each step, and they all knew it.

Nobody was backing down.

"Mike, I think that you and I being traffickers, offering Angie and Cindy as a sampling will work perfectly if we're total motherfuckers going in. Show them the goods, but no sample until we meet the head asshole. Then just kill the fucker. We offer only him the taste. Nobody else. Agree?"

Nodding, he said that would be the plan. Angie looked at him, filled with rage, but also concern.

"I'll be the bait, I'm sure. They want young stuff like me. I was taught to always tell the truth. So, I need to tell you that if I get the chance, I want to shoot the Brians. I'm going to need to learn how to do that. And, Mike… Can I use a knife or something else if needed?"

"I'll train all of you. And Angie, you're right. A gun won't always be

possible. It's going to be where I show you all the ways you can use just about anything to do it. A pen in the eye, a pillow to suffocate them. Even naked, there's ways to hide a box cutter in you…"

He watched as they all looked at each other. Cindy said, "Ooh, That's a good one. I hadn't thought about that!"

Mike somehow wasn't surprised by Cindy's practical nature. She was raised by killers and knew how things happened too well.

"Cindy, there's more ways than can be imagined. My dad was in Vietnam. The local hookers would put single-edged razor blades inside them, and the guy would slide in just fine. It was the pulling out the first time that cut their dicks off."

They all let out an "Ooh" to that one.

"Yeah, sick as all that is, when you deal with people who don't care about life, it's going to be them or you. So, it's simple. Kill them first. The advantage is that they sure won't be expecting it. They'll be guards and partners all over their places, and we'll have to be smart about choosing the time and place. If it's Jamie or me showing off the merchandise, we'll probably be frisked or scanned for weapons, but at that point, they're on their turf and more interested in getting their dick up some young ass than worrying about getting killed."

Worrying about if anyone doubted her in any way, Jamie returned to her explanation of her past.

"Before we get that far, I need to be sure you all know that the things I did once I grew up is not okay with me. I don't want it to be okay with you. I want it to be the spark that sets off the bomb."

Looking at her, Cindy said what each one was thinking.

"I read about what a renegade was. It was a warrior who realized they were on the wrong side and went over to fight with the opponent. They were the most feared fighters because they knew all about how the side they were once on worked and knew all their weak spots. They were full of anger and with their knowledge, they were the ones who did the most damage. None of us are okay with what happened to us, or Mike's sister. We're going to be renegades. Fighting with knowing how they work."

Smiling, Mike nodded.

"Good example. I studied that, and they teach that to agents. Inside knowledge is the most important. Jamie, it's why I showed up to work for you. To get inside and get you to stop by knowing what you did."

Blushing, Jamie nodded with a slight smile.

"Oh, you got inside, alright."

All eyes were on him. Both he and Jamie had told them how when they met, Mike had sex with Jamie while posing as a photographer before revealing he was an agent. Knowing what had happened, at the same moment they all broke out laughing and got up to hug him. He felt wonderful at their affection but felt a need to maintain his tough agent identity rather than confess he was instantly attracted to Jamie.

"Well, somebody had to do it."

Jamie looked to Cindy and Angie, asking where a box cutter was when she needed one.

CHAPTER 6

Having met at Cindy and Angie's new home, they had ordered out pizza for dinner. It was a day of talking about their mission and also to celebrate their move from a mobile home park in Aurora to a cozy home in Wheaton. Money had not been a concern for Cindy when looking for a house. Her mother had wired her $50 million after connecting once again when in Russia when Brian was killed and they escaped being trafficked. Cindy's mother had become the largest trafficker in Eastern Europe and played a part of their bringing Brian's organization to a stop, but the money was still made from the death or suffering of young girls.

Needing a safe place to live — and operate from, Cindy told them all that she would only use a small portion of the money for the house, but the rest was just for revenge on how it was made. They would use it to finance their activities to stop traffickers. She didn't want to use the dirty money for anything else.

Finding a older home made from bricks in the conservative town of Wheaton, it was the home of famous places such as a college founded by evangelist Billy Graham, and was old, full of trees, and everything Aurora wasn't. People had families, good jobs, took care of their homes and were active in the community. Now that she and Angie had been granted citizenship with help from Mike, they finally had a real home.

Looking at the wood paneled wainscoting, the crown moldings, and the comfortable furniture she had used some of the money to buy, she was elated but at the same time knew it was blood money that paid for it, and she knew who had made the money. Her mother. The one who watched what her father had done to all the girls, leading to her rape and getting pregnant by her father. She did all she could to get Cindy to the US, but returned to the Ukraine and continued on as a trafficker. Even seeing where things led, to her own daughter and son being raped, she went back to do the same thing. That was beyond what Cindy could understand.

Knowing it would be a half-hour before the pizza was delivered, she told everyone she had an idea of who their first target should be. All looking at her with surprise, Mike looked and asked who. The fire in Cindy's eyes when she answered made it all the more potent.

"My mother."

Angie stared at her with admiration, Jamie and Mike with surprise. Cindy didn't wait for them to ask questions.

"She's the most ruthless trafficker of any of them, and behind every mail-order bride coming here. Who knows how many girls she's sold throughout the world. She had a chance to stop. She didn't. Even after what happened to me, she continued on. And even now… Cindy and I get taken, and she still isn't stopping. I can't think of anyone I want to stop more than her. And it will be her own money that takes her down."

The sheer indignation in her voice had them all realizing she was right. Cindy looked at them, and saw they understood, having one more point to make.

"Good. We know where we go first. The renegade way is going to play a big role. It's a place… it's the world I was raised in. I know how she thinks, and how she operates. She thinks I'm a victim. That what happened with my shooting the sheik was because I was afraid. She gave me the money to keep me hushed. So, we play that. I can go in and say I want to be her daughter, take over her empire one day. She'll be proud of me. That's how we get in. And, she'll have a list a mile long of other traffickers and clients."

Jamie started thinking about what Cindy had planned, and she was full of admiration. She looked over at Mike, who nodded at her and she knew he was as well. She looked at Cindy, and she thought of how different she was from her sad mother. She wanted her to know how much she respected her.

"Cindy, oh, if you only knew how much I wish I had a mother like you. I know we're about the same age, but you know what I mean. You went through all that nightmare, and you came here and took care of Angie, and I know you were an escort, but you didn't go do drugs. Just trapped not being a citizen, and you weren't a hooker like my mom. You made sure you were on your own, with decent clients who treated you with respect. My mom, well, you know the story. But this? I understand…"

Watching tears stream down Cindy's cheeks, she was glad she had said all she had, and it was difficult to talk about her being an escort. It created a bond she longed for with Cindy. They had both been victims, but no longer. She kept her attention on Cindy, then looked at Angie who smiled at her, nodding. Cindy managed to stop her tears and her

expression changed. She grew stone cold.

"I have to tell you something. You need to know this. You too, Angie. Listen to all I just said. I'm talking about being a ruthless, violent bitch and killing people. I want to kill them. I want to stop anyone in my way. I felt power when I shot the sheik. I liked it. I got.. excited that I could do it. I looked in the mirror when I got home an I saw something you should all learn to see in me…"

Cindy was calm, and looked at each of them, waiting for any reactions. She only saw looks of surprise and confusion. She decided to let them know the truth inside of her.

"When I looked at myself, I saw who I was. I'm my mother's daughter. It's in me. How I'm made. I see it in Angie. Decent people don't talk about killing anyone. They don't strap guns on and plan hits. I saw the truth that I won't stop. For anything. What happened to me growing up? That messes anyone up. I'm sure what I want to do is a good thing, but it's not good I'm as ruthless as my mother. Jamie, I'm you going at Erma and Jonze and Brian. Same thing. Worse, I think. I'm after ones who didn't do things to me, but that doesn't matter to me. I can't pretend I'm doing this for some honorable reason. It's because of what was done to me… and they did it to Angie. I'm running on vengeance and hate. It's pure revenge. I want you to know that. Now. The only thing that will stop me, ever, is a bullet. No man is ever going to fuck with me or Angie again."

Jamie and Mike knew she was not like others. They had all been devastated by trafficking. Mike hadn't been trafficked, but his sister had. He changed his life to find her, and knew if he found who did it, he would be cold as he pulled the trigger of his Glock, glad to watch the trafficker die. Jamie understood perfectly as she had the same anger but was surprised at how open Cindy was about her intentions. They each nodded, and their expressions told Cindy they understood, and were right there with her.

Angie stood up, crossed her arms, looked at Jamie and Mike, then to Cindy.

"Mom. Like, we all know that. So what? After what you've been through? You know, I read so many women who go through this stuff start doing drugs, get self-destructive. But, hey, that doesn't stop traffickers. And, you're not like your mom. She saw what happened to

you and could have done what you're doing right now. Stop any other daughter from that. But she didn't. You're the one doing that. And you got one thing right. It's in me. When you blasted that sheik, it was the most wonderful thing I've ever felt. I wish it had been me saving you. I remember what I thought when his head exploded. I didn't think you killed him. I thought someone finally stopped him. I know I'm young, but I think those are two different things. That Vlad… he did me in my butt. Jamie, I'm so glad you stopped him. I know you knew he was doing that to me and my mom, so I thought you're as bad as him. But my mom, me, I think we showed who we really are, you know, when we learned why it all happened. We still can see what's right and wrong. But I'm never going to be without a gun on me ever. Some guy put his hands on me? Bah bye."

That had the three women in tears once again, and Mike was glad when the doorbell rang. The pizza had arrived, and it was time for a break from the emotions and to celebrate the move from Aurora to Wheaton. He paid and tipped the driver and brought in two large pizza boxes with a bag full of salads on top. Putting it all on the dining room table, Cindy and Angie were busy getting plates, glasses and cutlery. Mike went to Jamie and whispered he was glad she had said all she had to Cindy — and that he loved her. She whispered back, telling him she loved him with all her heart.

Smiling at him, she went to get iced tea and soda, and they all sat down and picked out slices as Jamie put salad into bowls and passed them around. Mike was right. The meal changed the mood, and they laughed and smiled as they ate. Mike asked Angie how she liked Wheaton.

"It's like I'm on a different planet. I can walk out the door without being asked to suck dick or shoot up."

Cindy looked at her, giving a stern look.

"That way of talking is from your old planet. Suck dick? Is that how a respectful person talks?"

Blushing, looking embarrassed, then sitting up straight, Angie nodded at her mother."

"Mom. You're right. I was repeating what was said to me by those creeps, but it doesn't mean I have to talk the way they did. So, to answer as someone who doesn't live in a trailer park in Aurora, Mike, I love it

here. I can go out and not worry about being spoken to without respect, and without fear."

Nodding, Cindy said that was well said, and true.

"Angie, as we go out and deal with scum, I think it's good you learned the language of lowlife, but at different times, you'll need to talk different ways. I need to be sure your European languages are all sounding right as well. Especially your Ukrainian. I know you speak it perfectly, but as time passes there are new slang words and expressions, so we'll both need to brush up."

Mike nodded, saying although he was good with Russian and other languages, not saying them perfectly was a plus. It allowed him to be American, but understood what people in other countries said, thinking he only spoke English. Throughout dinner, they played word games in different languages, surprised to learn Jamie was excellent in Russian.

"How could I not be? I was there so often, and I learned that if I didn't understand them, like Mike said, it could be dangerous to not know the language."

After dinner, Mike helped with the cleaning up, then said he had a few ideas. Heading to the living room, they relaxed as Mike said what he had been thinking of.

"Cindy, I know we could get in, stop your mother cold — and you know I mean with guns — but have you thought about how, well, like Jamie, she went back to things for a reason? Fear for her life, even yours, here? If so, and we know that to be true, if we turned her, we could bring her onboard. She has to know the players all over the world..."

Cindy stopped, and she sat thinking.

"Mike, I hadn't thought about it that way. Oh, that's the benefit of working as a team. Different views. You know, when she brought me and my brother here, she bought the mobile home, and then told me she had to go back. She didn't say she wanted to go back. She said she had to. Maybe it was something she never told me. Well, I don't know why I never wondered about it... I think before we go in with guns blazing, it would be smartest for me to find out first."

She sat, and she was thinking about what if she didn't find out first. It was the moment she realized that if her mother was doing what she did because she had to, then she could rescue her mother. It was a surprise, but it was important to find out.

Mike asked her how best to find out. Cindy was thinking the same thing.

"Well, not a phone call. If she's compromised, her line is secure, but it may be where she's still overheard. Well, she gave me all that money. I could let her know that Angie and I are coming to visit, and to tell her about how things have gone. An attempt to rekindle our relationship. And, if she's just flat-out bad like my father, I could tell her I want in. She'd respect that."

Mike said that was a good approach. He and Jamie could get out first, be there to make sure all is safe for them.

"Well, I think we get busy with the weapons training, and Cindy, call and let her know you two are going to come for a visit.

CHAPTER 7

Having lunch with James, his chief at the CIA, Mike was glad they could meet without hard feelings about his leaving the agency. Mike wished to tell him that working with Cindy, Angie, and Jamie would allow them to work together, not apart. The agency had information, and they'd be gathering first-hand accounts in the field. James said there wasn't any reason not to work together, and they both nodded at each other in agreement. They had a strong bond of trust, and James knew that Mike was motivated by losing his sister to sex trafficking. James admired that Mike hadn't let his rage at what happened to his sister overtake him when out in the field. It wasn't for revenge. It was to keep what happened to his sister from happening to others. He also knew if he could find who took her, there would be no holding him back. Then it would be vengeance with a fury.

He often thought of how Mike had left a high-paying career as a glamour photographer to join the agency. He had to start at the bottom, going through training and psych evaluations, and work his way up to gain trust. It was chance that brought him to being an agent. Pursuing where his sister may have been trafficked to, in Morocco he was spotted by a senior field agent who admired his determination, fearless nature, and discipline. Approaching him, verifying he was an agent, he said he stood a better chance working with the agency than on his own. They had intelligence and eyes in most hot spots, and without such resources Mike may never find or rescue his sister on his own. The agents added that asking the wrong person or being in the wrong place could get him killed.

Viewing the assets and intelligence the agency had, he decided to join under certain conditions. He wanted to be on a fast track as his sister was at risk, and time was the enemy in this instance. One of the first meetings he had was with James, who viewed Mike as driven, but controlled. He also was a skilled photographer and using photo auditions and job offers was one of the common ways traffickers found young girls. If he put him undercover as a photographer for a trafficker, he would be exposed to how girls were taken, and how the larger operation worked.

After an initial psych exam by Charles, their go-to shrink, Mike was given a green light. With a month of field training, James put him

under his supervision and his instincts paid off. Mike was the perfect undercover agent. He had credibility as his photo and video skills were expert, and he wasn't a lone wolf. When it came time to seize the operation, he called it in, stood back and let the right team take the traffickers down. That also included him. He'd be arrested and as word gets around, that kept him legitimate in the eyes of traffickers. He'd learn even more in holding cells and talk when first apprehended. He learned the rules, and kept in character except when meeting with James at work.

"Mike, I can't say I'm not worried for you and the ladies. Going after the leaders, they're surrounded by a team to protect them."

Nodding, Mike knew that was true. He also had seen how when it came to sex, there was a time when even the top dog wanted alone time to do sick things with the girls. Most often that was in a guarded room, so there would always be a time like that. James agreed.

"Oh, I get it. But think of what is done to a girl to get to that room. How many times are they raped first? Handled, humiliated. Trained using fear. Is Angie, even Cindy, ready for that? Do you want to see that sweet young girl get done like that?"

Mike appreciated the concern and explained how they planned to deal with it.

"That's true for most all girls. But, when there's one that is worth a lot because she's a virgin, they don't spoil the goods. They may want head… anal… sure. But more than likely they want the money she'll bring. There are tons of girls to get all that from, so with a top-dollar sale on the line, I don't think they'll waste any time getting cash for her. That's when we hit."

"Mike, she's 16. With the way things are going, that's a bit old. Do you think she'll be worth that much? Lots of hot little girls in the world."

"I've thought about it. First, Angie can look eighteen, or twelve. Nobody's going to be asking for birth certificates. I took pictures of her, and I'm working with her on how to play it younger in how she looks and acts, talks, all that. And other girls aren't as poised as her. She has that magic they look for. A rare prize. And we do have the crème de la crème. The mother-daughter act. Cindy is as good as it gets. The two, as a package, that's what will get them attention, and not to be messed with. It's the fantasy of it. It's rare to have a mom hotter than the daughter."

Nodding, James knew too well that traffickers had clients who'd want such a combination, and it would keep them working together. There was no question that they were mother and daughter. They looked alike, and had an appeal that made them more valuable than even the youngest girl. He couldn't help but agree.

"They're going to attract the largest traffickers. I agree with that. So, I guess the issue becomes that one moment when the top guy wants a look for himself, or some head. It comes down to weapons. Naked women are what they'll be when that happens."

"James, that's right. That is the tipping point. So, this is where we start helping each other. I agree, firearms are unlikely unless we have an insider, which is also unlikely. I plan to train them on all the other ways to take a man down. Use any object laying around, do the unexpected. I'm pretty good, but Mark, he's the best at that kind of training. I mean, look… They're going to do this. They'll need to be savage at that moment and I'd like Mark to train them. Think that could be done?"

James sat back, finishing his burger as he did, and Mike knew he was thinking. Finally, he nodded.

"It can. But, off record. I don't want them out there without those skills. I'm sure Mark wouldn't want that either. He works for the agency, but also does private training, so what he does on his own time is up to him. I know you have cash, and I'll tell him you may have a nice offer. But you said help each other out. What did you have in mind?"

Laughing, Mike was surprised James hadn't first asked what he was prepared to offer. He had a lot that would be of value as they started.

"Intel, for one. If we take the top guy down, we'll have learned all about the operation. We can't take a whole team down, but I can let you know the when, where, and who. I don't want underlings to go off and keep things going. That's the first one, and the same as I did when undercover. Next, we aren't beholding to the rich or elected. The ones you can't even mention. So, when we finish, we can expose them. If we have pictures and records, we can drop them in the mail to a news organization. You can't. That could put a lot of pressure on guys who're afraid and willing to trade who is all involved to avoid exposure. Is any of that of interest? Think asking Mark is still the only way? Maybe he should be told. Be one of our assets."

Smiling, James shook his head, impressed.

"I knew you were the real deal. Yes, all of that is of interest, as the agency likes to put it. I still think being covert is the best and safest way for you. Jamie knows how the bastards work. Who knows how many guys in the agency are on their payroll? Have you thought of that?"

"Sure. I also trained with Mark. He's like me. He still has a daughter who went missing and wants to find her. I think that's plenty to keep him smart about covert issues. But I was just letting you know the things we will want to feed you. It's best to hire Mark, keep him where he doesn't have a conflict of his oath. He teaches martial arts, right? Yes, so same thing. I'll do it that way. Just give him news of a referral for him. Maybe set up a lunch, like this, and I'll make sure he's okay with it. Sound good?"

Paying the check, James said it was smart, and fair. He relaxed a bit and changed the subject.

"How is it going with you and Jamie?"

Looking at James, Mike knew it was a sincere question. He had been teased endlessly at first when it was revealed he had sex with her when undercover, as it was more than going beyond the call of duty.

"Nice. For both of us. My take was on the mark. James, she was taken when she was four. Four... and groomed where when she got older, it was get on board or get dead. She didn't want either. She wanted to take down the men who did it to her, and the only way was to stay on. Long story, but she wanted to kill Brian. That was what she was living that life for and expected to die doing. I've learned the victim side that we never touched. They're full of rage and hate even if groomed like she was. She doesn't make excuses for all the girls she trafficked. She doesn't want anyone to be sorry about her early life. I think now of how the agency should be recruiting ones like her. She knows more than we ever did. She's going to play a key role in what we do. So, got off topic. How's it going? We're in love."

"Mike, I know it's going to sound funny coming from me, but I was hoping you'd say that. I was the one who interviewed her first. She was honest. The bad ones tell lies. She owned up to everything. It was where she wanted to spill on Brian, and knew to be believed, she'd have to be straight. I'm glad she is. I could see you look at each other. It was real. So, pal, good for you two. It's a strange damn world."

CHAPTER 8

"Okay, you got three in the ass, let's go for four."

Waving to a naked man stroking himself to get hard, he told the others to stay where they were.

"We've got cameras set, so don't fuck it up. It's going to have to be Alfred goes in from the side along with Will. Top and bottom, just stay where you are. And you two in her mouth, work it harder, alright?"

Struggling to squeeze into where three large cocks were waiting, the fourth man positioned himself where he wouldn't block the camera. Feeling the trembling in the woman's ass as she was about to be ripped open if they kept going the way they were. He called out to Jackson, the director, saying she was going to rip.

"Fuckin' fuck, what the fuck do you care? Yesterday, Will's arm was up to his elbow in her ass and that's more than four dicks. Okay, start thrusting best you can, and you two in her mouth, show some fuckin' interest. Ah, let's change that up. Work it where she can suck both your balls at one time. Let her get one nut from each of you in her mouth while you slap your dicks on her face."

Using his iPhone, Jackson said they were going, and they all started trying to move without pulling out of the woman on a huge — but hard — tabletop. Moving in for tight shots where the viewer could see all four cocks in her asshole, it was a tricky shot. Thinking he got enough of that, he moved to her head, shooting from the floor to see the two men's testicles being sucked into her mouth. He didn't see any need to stay long on that as he stood up to see her face and the cocks now laying on it.

"About ten more minutes of this, then we move to the pull-outs, and then the facial if you fuckers can cum. I'll give you a holler at about one minute left then really bang that asshole so you're revved up enough to cum on her. Her face, not her ass. I want her face covered…"

Getting tight shots of the cums, he said that was all. The six men didn't say anything to the woman, just walking away to shower, leaving her gasping for air and lying face down on the table. Jackson walked over to her. Not looking at her face, he barked that after the guys were cleaned up she needed to shower and get made up for the next shoot.

"Scott's coming soon, and it's going to be the scene where he ties you up then turns around for you to rim him. Probably ass fuck you at the end…"

Walking away, he was checking the footage on his phone, and was happy he got the key shots. He'd edit it all that night and have it posted by morning. His cell buzzed, and he saw it was Peter, not a call he ever wanted to answer.

"Jackson. How's the woman doing?"

"She's holding up. Hasn't moaned or complained about shit, so we're between episodes."

"If she does, let me know. After you're done, call Max to pick her up. I'm sending her over to a man who saw her doing daddy worship scenes and he wants her to be his baby girl for a few days. She needs to be perfectly clean. Tell her what he wants. Tell her child clothing and a bag of frilly underthings."

The line went dead. Jackson went to her and told her she'd have a few days away from shoots, and to do the baby girl routine with some client Peter had lined up. She looked up, nodded, and as Jackson walked away, she worked at sitting up and heard the shower had stopped. It was a long day, and she'd have to play for a daddy pervert later.

Another girl, Whimsey as she called herself, came over and asked her how her ass was.

Looking up at her, shaking her head to let her know it wasn't good, the girl, all of 16, pouted.

"If they wanted me to do that, I don't know... I don't think my butt could survive that. Did they give you enough goop?"

Goop was a local anesthetic gel that made her rectum numb, but even using a lot, it still hurt. It acted as a lubricant and one problem was it numbed the men's cocks where they couldn't feel much and that made it hard for them to cum.

"Whimsey, no matter how many cocks they squeeze in, it's never enough for them. I've had to be stitched up inside a month ago and that still hurts. That was scary. Don't take more than one, okay? You are so tiny, and they love that little ass with a huge cock destroying it routine."

"Well, I had one of those, yeah. I kind of got off on it. I couldn't shit right for a week, but they paid me extra. Well, I have to go. Just checking on you."

Watching Whimsey, already naked, walk away to the next room she was sad as the girl was one who showed up and wanted to be in porn. She wasn't owned by Peter, and she got paid. When they first met,

she asked her why she wanted to do porn. Whimsey said it was all the thing on TikTok, and she wanted some exposure so she could start an OnlyFans page and make a fortune. Even sadder to her was that young girls were enticed by the money they could make with a fan base, and porn was a way to have a following when launching their page. It was something she couldn't comprehend. Girls, some just into their teens, were online wearing a scanty thong and tiny bra rubbing themselves on their boyfriend. As they would get endless emoji faces with tongues hanging out and saying they would love to be their boyfriend, they also got clues that the followers would pay to see more. At first it may have been runaways or girls without a future, but now it was girls from homes everywhere. It was a way to show off at first, then a way to make money. There was no end to the line of men waiting to pay.

She had never wanted to do anything like that. She accepted that each person had their own choice, yet she didn't agree with the choice Whimsey made.

Growing up, she had been taught to respect people, and herself. That if she worked hard, she could achieve all her dreams. That her body was something to be respected by any man, and for one she would marry one day to cherish. She learned that she was considered beautiful by most all people, and that beauty was nice, but not how any person should be valued. She schooled to be an archaeologist, thinking she could help all people know themselves better by studying their past.

It was on an archaeological dig in northern Africa that she started to realize history was shaped by sex. From the earliest cave drawings through all history, it was clear that underneath the veneer of culture, politics and power was sex. It was the common theme and driving force of all human history.

In a newly discovered cave classified as a major find, she was cataloging wall drawings and carvings discovered there. All art on the walls depicted sex acts, all perverse. Six women working one man. Men with penises larger than their own body. Women worshiping the men, praying to their shafts. Men having sex with men, and most were of men having sex with young children, most all boys, also young girls hanging impaled on the tips of their giant members. She saw animals having sex with the small girls, mounting them from behind in an upright position while the child was on all fours like the animal going at them.

Recalling that while in school she had viewed pictures of many historical finds with equally perverse images of sex of all manners of depravity, she had asked a professor why such images were of value. Told that sex of such sorts was the privilege of a wealthy man, it was a way to show off their riches — and their power. Sex was a symbol of power over others, or of being worshiped so it was important to learn how rich the owners of the lands were at the time. Told that it was most likely slaves serving their master, that too spoke of the society and what was most important to them.

Thinking how things were getting worse, she knew what most were kept from knowing. Masters and slaves still existed. Owning a human for sex was still the standard of power and wealth. Men longed to be rich to have women as sex slaves, and to have illegal sex with minors. Their money gave them power to do what was wrong, and that taught them the true power of wealth. History revealed that money and sex went together, and nothing had changed. The only difference was before laws and large countries, it may have been flaunted. Now, it was hidden.

She had been working studying sex carvings in a cave newly discovered in Morocco when she was called to join the leader of a spiritual movement she had joined while in college. Going to a place where men lined the alleys and streets all day staring at women, nothing was thought of it by locals. She knew some of the men were looking for women to abduct, sell, and be used by sex traffickers. She had been watched carefully as she was American, beautiful, just out of college and would be worth a high price in Arab and African nations. Being taken from a wealthy American family and used for the sexual cravings of the one owning her, it would be his way of feeling powerful. He would have what an American wanted, but he would have instead.

Walking from the dig, she stopped for tea to meet with her spiritual leader, Peter. He was mannered, spoke English, and asked if she was working on the new dig. As they talked, he said he had some artifacts he had found on his property and asked if she could tell him if they were of interest as he may wish to donate them but didn't know who would want them. Excited, she said she would be interested in helping. As they left, he took her to his Range Rover, then a few blocks later he stopped, and three locals got in the car. One jabbed her with a syringe, and she blacked out.

Waking in a large hangar with a cargo plane inside, she saw Peter scrolling through her phone images. She had been tied up, a local thrusting himself in her ass as she attempted to scream. Her mouth was gagged, and she could only endure the brutal assault on her bottom while watching Peter studying her life as documented on her phone.

When the local had filled her with his semen, he pulled out of her, pulled up his pants and took an automatic rifle and stood next to Peter. He was smiling. A smirk of disgust at the American whore.

"Did you enjoy Andre's fucking your ass? I can tell he did. He came in you. He usually pulls out and covers the woman with his cum, leaving it for her to deal with. I know you can't talk with the gag. I'll just assume you wanted it. Your mission is to be a fuck hole. Do not be a heathen and think that is not a gift to men who need a good woman to fuck. Never make the mistake of thinking you're not. Andre, explain."

Lifting his rifle, Andre aimed at her and fired. She was sure he'd kill her, but his shots hit the ground around her.

"He gets satisfaction from gifting you with his cum or showing you what happens to a woman who doesn't dedicate herself to saving men from whores. He'll climax either way. You're my property now. I own you, and will sell you or hire you out, which is more likely. You will do whatever I say, and always thank me no matter what I ask. Do you understand?"

Trying to scream, frantically shaking her head, Peter looked to Andre, who fired another shot. It struck inches from her head, the blast of dirt from it hitting her face. She stopped and realized they would kill her and not care at all.

"You are a smart girl, and you learn fast. You are going to do what I say, and that will include fucking anyone I tell you to. You will fuck them in any manner they want but you must thank them for being so kind as to fuck you. Always thank them for whatever they do to you. Some will want you to drink their piss and lick their assholes. Suck their toes, drink liquids out of your cunt. All are things you must be thankful for. You will do God's work, and I act in his stead. I am sure you will be blessed for such purpose. You'll get on your knees and pray thanks to them as they piss on you. Not because it will keep you alive. It does, spiritually. Until you have such light shining on you, I will show you what else it will keep alive, so, look. Here's why. Here's what you praying

to be treated so keeps alive…"

Walking up to her with her phone in his hand, he showed her the screen. It had a picture of her brother, Mike, smiling and happy.

"Do anything other than what I say, or complain, your brother will be dead within a day. And not with one shot. After a day of torture and watching videos of you doing things not thought possible with the most depraved of men. Your brother will die seeing a video of you worshiping the cock of some heathen pervert."

Going into a state of shock, all she could do was lay still, and nod.

"See? It is very simple. You will be doing the work of a saint. By giving yourself, by fucking sick men, you will be keeping your brother alive. I know who he is, and where he is. It is all here on this phone you worship so much. I have disciples all over the world, with one close to where he lives."

He stood, arms crossed, then held up the phone to look at the time.

"It's almost 3:30. I'm going to take the gag out of your mouth, and I need to have you suck my cock. It must be given worship. Should you not give it true love and devotion, that will offend God, and you will reveal you are not worthy of life. Andre will shoot you if you think yourself above worshiping it."

Crying as he took the gag out of her mouth; she was numb and in mortal fear at the same time. Peter unzipped his fly and took out his cock, stroking to get it hard. When it was erect, he moved it to her and watching the phone, at 3:30 he put his cock to her lips. She opened her mouth and sucked him off, begging his cock, not him, to think her worthy and she prayed to it although her mouth was full and her prayer could only be heard as mumbles, then drinking his cum when he erupted.

After sucking him until there was no more cum to swallow, he stood, waiting. Her eyes looked up to his, wondering what more he wanted. Her eyes revealed she was confused.

"You didn't thank it. You also did not look up and offer a prayer of thanks for such honor."

CHAPTER 9

Staying at Mike's, the first night Jamie looked all around and wondered what was important to him. It didn't take long for her to realize how much having his sister be taken had affected him. Thinking her pictures weren't filling a wall like detectives do in movies did, with maps and news articles, there were four pictures of her placed with a few others, each from a different time in their lives together.

In the foyer was a snapshot taken when they were in grade school. Mike was smiling, his sister with her head tilted looking longingly to the camera. It revealed a happy young boy, and a hopeful young girl. In the living room was a picture of her graduating from college. Wearing the classic cap and gown, her head tilted down, looking at the diploma. It was clear she was proud of her degree and it meant a lot to her. In the kitchen, on the refrigerator was a simple snapshot of the two of them together. In their late teens, it was one where they were looking at each other, both laughing. They were clearly happy and weren't hiding the fun they were having that day.

The one that impressed her most was one of her hung in his second bedroom, used as his home office. She had expected endless photos from his glamour photography days, but there weren't any of those. The only one he had in the office was on the wall across from his desk; not in front of it where he saw it constantly. It was a glamour shot, lit perfectly, of his sister with her back to the camera, looking over her shoulder at him, smiling, hair flying from the turning motion. It could have been the cover of any fashion magazine, and she was stunned how beautiful his sister was. At the same time, she knew that her beauty and amazing smile was what made her a valuable take for traffickers. She was the fantasy girl, the one that had everything going for her. She stood, looking at it, not moving.

Seeing all the hopes and dreams of two people all taken from them, and their family, so sick men could use and degrade his sister, she thought of how each person has a life ahead, plans made, people they love, and look to find a love and be in a safe place. Trafficking was worse than death in her opinion now. She had robbed countless young girls of all those things. It was as if she took a match and lit the picture she stared at on fire. She had taken away hopes, dreams, and created

nightmares. Realizing she was wet from the tears running down her face, she turned to look for a box of tissues. She hadn't realized Mike was standing in the doorway, giving her time and space to think. She told him she wanted to look at his pictures of his sister. As he sat on the couch in the office, saying a few were hung up, he nodded knowing it best for her to look at them on her own.

Turning to him, still crying, then sobbing, she sat with him, grabbed him and was shaking. He put his head on top of hers, not saying anything. He had an idea of what she was going through, and he realized that if she hadn't reacted that way, she wouldn't have been who he thought she was. As he hugged her back, she tried to say something several times, but couldn't get words out.

Just holding her helped. Mike had changed his entire life to find his sister. He was what she never had. Someone who cared about her. She realized, for the first time, he was the one who did. When the world hated her, he understood her somehow. He listened to her, saw the world she was in and knew how it worked. He had a choice. He could have put her away for life or saved her. She still didn't fully get why he decided to trust her and be there for her, but she knew she would never let him down, and would be there for him, always. She looked up at him and managed to speak.

"Those pictures… ah, Mike, that did it. It made all the shit I've done so fucking real. All the girls I robbed of their life. Just to save mine…"

Instead of crying, she looked into his eyes, letting him know she finally realized what had been done to so many young girls, and to her. It was a moment they both agreed being trafficked was a fate worse than death. Living with shame and guilt was the only outcome for the ones who were cast off or made it away. They would blame themselves for being where they were. How they looked, being young, innocent, none was anything they chose to be. Being nice to the wrong person. Looking too pretty. Being too pretty. Or being young. Those were the reasons why they were taken and used as things. What they went through would never leave. It was something they wouldn't be able to talk or think about. She was overwhelmed with the reason why. It was only for men with money, many with power, could use them for sick sex. She started shaking so hard she slipped out of his arms and fell to the floor, looking as if she was having a convulsion. Mike knew it was guilt. He knelt

beside her, rubbing her cheek. He knew no words of comfort that could help or change anything that had happened to her. All he knew was it had stopped, and she had figured it out. He knew a memory couldn't be erased.

Finally able to look up, and to talk, she stared into his eyes.

"I was fucking just turning five when that motherfucker stuck his dick in my ass. In my fucking ass so he wouldn't pop my cherry! Five, Mike… Five… What the fuck is the matter with this world…"

He agreed. It was something he would never understand, and he continued to be shocked and appalled by each story. Hers was one of the worst he knew of. He knew the only thing that would help was to do something about people getting away with such horrors. That was what she had vowed to do. He pulled her up, not to hug, but to look at as he talked.

"Jamie, not everyone is fucked up like that. You're with me. You're loved now. I know it doesn't change what was done to you. I went through all kinds of blaming myself for not finding my sister, then I realized I may never find her but I could stop as many of the men doing that to women as I possibly could. Maybe, and I hope I can, find who took her in the process. Like me, there is a way you can deal with it all. Saving girls. Being proud of yourself, not ashamed, will change that. I don't care what was done to you, or what you did. I care about the woman I'm holding right now, and she knows how the world turns a blind eye."

Looking at him, she could see he meant every word. Feeling a rush of adrenaline rise through her, she stood up, no longer crying, and held her hand out for him to get up with her.

"Mike… You know what? It just takes one person who believes in you. One victory. Mike, you're that person for me. I want someone we save to feel what I'm feeling right now."

"Jamie! Only one?"

She looked to the left and to the right, then at him.

"It starts with one. Right?"

Nodding, he took her by the hand to his bedroom, thinking of how it was hers now as well. Laying down, he held her, and they were happy holding each other. He knew how to have sex, and how to show affection. With Jamie, he didn't see it that way. Between them, when

together, both would be given as one thing, to be what it was. Making love. He had a lot of sex in his life, so had Jamie. Finding each other, they were what each needed more than anything else.

Someone to hold on to.

CHAPTER 10

"Mom, can you help me? I need to look all sweet and innocent."

Scrunching her eyebrows, she shook her head, trying to figure out what Angie was talking about.

"Sweetie, unless there's something you haven't told me, you *are* sweet and innocent."

Breaking out in laughter, they both smiled at each other, with Angie amazed at such a thought. She hadn't hidden anything from Cindy and was happy she never had.

"Mom! Come on. You know what I mean. I mean look even younger. Like, that, well, I'm twelve or naive. I guess trashy clothes will help, and I can pick up the jargon and all, but you're good at makeup. Any ideas?"

The question stopped Cindy in her tracks. Her immediate reaction was that girls that age didn't wear any makeup, but then she realized that was just how she wished it was. It wasn't how the world worked. Many girls younger than Angie wore makeup, and they clearly were trying to look like strippers or rap groupies. They looked horrible in her opinion, but she realized that what she thought didn't matter. She had a few ideas.

"Well, I think we limit our budget to only twenty dollars and buy as much cheap makeup as we can. That's what they buy. Then maybe ten dollars for a trip to Claires… places like that for costume jewelry. We can find trashy clothes at the thrift store. Skirts way too short for you. White tops, you know, tube tops way too small for you."

"Mom, that's what I meant. Make me look all trashy like that. I was thinking we can go to the run-down mall in Aurora and sit on a bench when school lets out. We can see how they act and dress for school."

Cindy stopped and was amazed they were talking about how to make Angie look like a 12-year-old slut. Everything she had ever taught her, and the life they led was about having self-worth and not taking the easy route of using sex to attract men or make money. She had taught Angie to value herself, and that would help her be bait for traffickers. Underneath the trashy makeup and tawdry clothes, they would see her natural beauty. They would also think she was stupid like the girls who thought such a way to look was attractive. It was all about underestimating Angie — and her. She would be the doting mother who would, if needed, insist that she stay with her daughter no matter

what. Being a ravishing beauty, they would see the value in the mother-daughter act they would play.

Thinking of how Angie had grown up shopping with her at thrift stores, her daughter had become skilled at picking out nighties, corsets, thongs, nylons, and platform shoes for her to wear. As an escort, which she never fooled herself was a polite word for hooker, all of those had been worn under her rather conservative street clothes. Knowing her clients didn't want to be thought of by neighbors as hiring prostitutes, she looked and acted like a lady friend, or girlfriend. It was why she was able to make good money without turning to a pimp. She was on her own and had regular clients who treated her with respect. Some had fallen in love with her and said they wanted to marry her. She would ask them if they would really want a wife who had sex with so many other men. That put things into perspective, and despite attempts to say she could stop living such a life if they were married, she would be appreciative but say it was she who had a problem with knowing that, and she was theirs when they wanted her. She left off the part about being theirs when they paid for her.

Being an illegal alien in the US, not wanting to be found by Ukrainian drug lords her mother had stolen from to get her to the US, her options for making money were to be a stripper, prostitute, or escort. It was true she could be a maid or housekeeper for a man who only spoke Russian or Ukrainian. Such work didn't pay enough and unlike being an escort, the hours were long, and she needed to be home to watch out for Angie.

When she first started looking for clients, they lined up faster than she thought possible. She had talked to one man who was showing interest in her, and she told him the truth. She wasn't a citizen and had to be an escort to survive. The man said he would be happy to hire her, and he'd also tell many of his single friends about her. In a short time, she was turning down clients. They were all single, older, had money, and were widowed or divorced. They appreciated her respecting their situation, and none abused her sexually, all paying before her clothes came off. The sex was conventional, sometimes not even sex at all. The men were lonely and sometimes just wanted to talk or hold her, sometimes just watching her get undressed and letting them watch her naked. When they wanted sex, she would be on top so they could see her

stunning body, and they climaxed quickly, using the remaining time to look at her, or eat a delivered meal with her.

With all of that, she never fooled herself it was sex for money. When she and Angie had been taken, it was also sex for money. It was at an extreme level where they had no choice and their lives were at risk, but it was still sex for money. The trafficker had crossed the line by taking Angie, and that was not like the men she serviced did. They were admirers who longed for her. They didn't drug and kidnap her and her daughter. Just thinking of it sent her into a near rage. She looked over at Angie.

"Okay, I didn't plan on setting foot back in Aurora, but you're right. The mall there is a good place to learn how to be trashy when twelve. I guess I'm still worried that the place is where they grab girls... and I don't want to be in that situation."

Angie put her hands on her hips, shaking her head.

"Mom. We have guns in our bags. Remember?"

Putting out a box of hollow core ammo for their Glocks, Angie pulled her pistol out of her new messenger bag, pulled the clip out and started filling it. Cindy nodded, grabbed her purse and took out hers and joined in loading clips.

"Mom, do you have that knife we were given in training?"

Reaching into her bag, she pulled out a slick switchblade. Giving it one flick of her wrist, it was fast and easy to get at and use. Releasing the blade, it went back into the handle, and she rummaged around. Angie looked at her.

"Mom, the gun and knife is plenty. What're you looking for?"

Pulling a tube of lipstick out of her purse, she said she had found it. They giggled.

"Mom, that's the most powerful weapon in that purse. You really *are* packing!"

After filling the clips and putting a round in the chambers, they were set for the trip to the mall. Angie asked her mom to sit for a while and went to get soda for them both. Sitting down, she asked how her clients took the news she was no longer available. Cindy gave a bittersweet smile.

"They put on brave faces and said that was good news. I think they were genuinely happy for me, but sad as they were... well... most were

in love with me one way or another. I was impressed as there was none of that, 'one more before you leave me' stuff. They all asked if I had someone lined up to take my place, but I couldn't do that. All I could say was that the local paper had classifieds, and they could put one in, or read what was there. If they could access the online world, it would be easy to find someone, but go slow. Even that was hard to say. They need someone. I hope they find someone who is honest and doesn't have a pimp."

"Mom, did you tell them they can use online dating sites that really are about, well, you know…"

"No. Those aren't safe. They could be talking to some man in Serbia with a picture of some girl he found online. The ones saying she needs money to pay rent first, and they wouldn't know. The pictures are all phonies. A few of my guys tried that before they met me. They were scammed. It's a strange world and getting stranger. So, enough of that. Let's see what you can do. Act like a new teen trying to be hot stuff. Show me what you've got."

Taking the request in earnest, Angie said to wait a minute. She went to her room and changed, thinking about her mother. She had been loved by her clients but had never been in love with anyone. Although happy for Mike and Jamie, she thought Mike was incredible and deep inside wished he was with her mother. She promised herself to talk to Mike about men who may be as good as him, and single, to fix her mother up with. She'd also be on the lookout on her own but knew her track record of trusting "Vlad" at the photo studio when she was taken wasn't great.

When she came back out to the kitchen, she was wearing a regular knit sweater of Cindy's, but had it just covering her bottom where the lower half of her butt wasn't quite covered and plain to see. She had fluffed her hair out and had on a pair of mirrored sunglasses. She had taken her knee highs and pulled them up to above her knees, and she stood in front of Cindy with one knee in front of the other, making her legs go inward as if she had to pee. With her head tilted to the right, her left hand on her hip, she adopted an attitude that surprised Cindy. She made sure she was wearing undies, and she had on white ones to match the knee highs.

"Angie, you look like you just moved from a trailer park in Aurora!"

Laughing, Cindy knew that was true, but saw Angie didn't change and laugh along, staying in character.

"Mo, like, keep that hole tight, okay? I no need no yo tal-keen. Stuff yo self in support hose or somethin' to shape yo thang tah be worth lookin' at."

Her voice had changed to be like so many girls in Aurora talked, or some kind of affectation. It wasn't what she said, but how she said it that worked so well. It was a complete put-down, dismissing her as if she was 80.

"Does your mother know you dress like that?"

"Mommo lay-dee… Does yo mommo no yo dress like dat? Or she dress yo each morning? Lay out all dat maternity plus for yo?"

"I think if there was a beauty pageant taking place here right now, I'd win. I don't think they would say that about me."

"Mommo… As if! Get over yo stuff. Yo be past it. Men be no goin' for old action. This thang in front yo? It be what yo don't have. Juicy new stuff."

Turning around, bending over to pick up the sunglasses she managed to drop, Cindy could see her ass cheeks fully as the underwear rode up between them.

"Mo, don't be askin' where I got 'em. All I say where I got 'em? On my bot-tum. Clerk be fool sellin' snatch traps ta seniors."

Putting the sunglasses on a table, Angie reappeared and asked Cindy how she did. Angie was shaking her head in disbelief.

"Well, you have me convinced. Where did you learn all that? I mean all of it. The clothes? The talk?"

"Mom… we have the *Disney Channel*. I'm imitating one of the stars of their top show."

"Well, normally I'd say let's cancel that subscription, but it does seem to be good reference for what we're doing. How does it feel when you act and look like that?"

Looking down at herself, she shook her head. She tugged the sweater dress down, and let her socks fall as she sat down to drink her soda.

"Mom, it's so stupid, but all of a sudden, I kind of started to think that was what I was really like. I felt how I looked. Like a slut. I see why girls watching that show start acting and looking that way. Mom, do you think those little girls are, you know, having sex?"

It was a sad question, but an important one. Cindy knew that very young girls had sex no matter what generation they were from. She was realistic about it.

"Yes, I'm sure there are ones that do. Most? Just putting on an act, like you were. If they were faced with a live one, you know, an erect penis, they'd probably run away screaming. They see stars on Disney and social media and want to be like them. It doesn't mean they're ready for sex, but they sure are putting themselves out there to have some, like it or not."

"Mom, the thing is that in our plan, they are what I need to be hotter than. I mean, what? Be naked? Get tatted all over? My tongue pierced? I don't know how low I have to go to outdo them. And mom, I saved it for you to read. You know that *Teen Vogue* I bought at Osco? They had a big article that said to get a guy, give him a blowjob or he won't be interested. That's a magazine for ten-year-olds! So, add that to what I have to compete with."

That got Cindy thinking. She realized that Angie had a question that answered itself.

"You hit on a good point. With all those little tramps parading, you will just be another one. But, if you come off the same age, like twelve, and are polished, sophisticated and hard to get, that will make you stand out. Men want what they can't have. If you're the princess, the prize, and could care less what the other girls do, you'll get their attention. I'm sure of it."

Getting up, running back to her room, in a few minutes she was back, wearing the sleek black dress and heels her mother had given her as a birthday present to look good for a photo audition. Walking mannered, head high, timid, almost bashful, she pulled her chair out, and sat in a way that her knees were together, so nothing was revealed. She took her glass, used one hand to hold the straw, then nodded, smiled, and asked if that was the look that would get attention.

"See, there it is. You look so young, but you have the style and sophistication of a woman, and women have sex and don't play girlie games. You look like you come from money, and that you're worth a lot on the sex market. Perfect. Good job."

"Mom, then we need to get me some more dresses. I don't want to ever hurt this one. It's my special gift from you."

Thinking of how it was part of how she ended up being trafficked, she understood the intent behind it, and she was sentimental about it as well. Angie was right. She needed a high-end wardrobe.

"Okay, then no Aurora mall. We go downtown to boutiques and get you tailored outfits. How's that sound?"

"Mom, that sounds perfect, but I have a question? Are there traffickers hanging out downtown?"

"Angie, of course. Where there's moms buying clothes for their daughters, seems like a likely spot for them. Why?"

"Mom, then we still carry, and for the outfits, I need bags that are stylish and match, but big enough for my Glock."

Not Taken

CHAPTER 11

Peter was on his cell phone talking to his richest client.

"Yes. I give you first picks on the little cunts. You buy virgins who know nothing about fucking. My choice for you is a little girl who knows how to fuck properly. She's the hottest fuck in porn right now. She'll fuck you until it is you begging for mercy. And you can take her to dinners and have her on your arm. Since your cunt left, you need a cunt men will drool over. She is that, and more."

"Well, you're right about needing some decent ass. The little twats just don't have any idea what real fucking is. And, I do need arm candy. I'm looking at the clips you just sent. Oh, fuck yeah, she does everything I want. And the scenes where she's made up and all? Yeah, she has that too. Yes. You're right. So, she'll do whatever I want fuck-wise, and she can handle a dress ball. I don't imagine you're letting go of that hot ass of hers cheap…"

"No. Cunts that are cheap, they are cheap cunts. When you want cunt like this, price must never be questioned. It would insult me if you haggled. You have told me you wish prime cut, and you are a starving man. For this cunt, the cost is an even million. That is but a line item in your books. That is the price."

Peter knew he would think it was a bargain. He also knew he would put up a bit of resistance as he did for any girl he sold to him. He waited for a reply.

"I'm looking at the videos. These here videos are how many years old?"

"Freddie, it is not wise to insult me. I can hang up. I have a line forming for this one. You are a good customer, and I am giving you first option. Now, I will ignore your insult as you think all others are like you. The videos are all from this month. So, is it yes or no?"

Peter sat back and sipped soda water as he never drank. A girl was hard at work sucking his cock during the call, and he looked at her to consider if she was of value. When Freddie said he'd wire the money, that made Peter cum, the girl gagging and choking. She was coughing up cum, and he told Freddie to hold the call for a second. Putting the phone on mute, he leaned over to look at the girl.

"The first time, yes, it is much to take. As this is your first time, I will

give you kindness. Now, you must do what I say. First, bow with your head to the floor, tell me you are truly sorry and ask forgiveness, then lick all cum and spit off my pants, and the floor, while I watch."

She held back tears as she apologized, then began licking cum and spew off his pants and the floor. He added she must clean off his cock, and she went right to it, making sure not to anger him. He hit the unmute button.

"Good. I will look for the wire transfer, then get her ready. Two days. She will be in my jet, and you will take possession of her at my hanger at the airport. I have a question. How are the twins I sold you? Really. Well, I doubt her being dead was an accident, but she was yours to do with as you wished. It doesn't matter if you did it, or some ex-president. The one is worth little. You do not have twins If you gave one to Clinton, do you? Well, a waste of valuable cunt, but you paid for it. If that's what gets you clout, the power to make one a twin no longer is… yes, I can understand. That is a rare pleasure and worth much. Back to the little cunt. She will be to you in two days. She is unique as she will not grow older… Yes, you must learn that when I say something it is never to be questioned… Yes, that is why a million is a very small price. I suggest you don't do a twin on her, no matter what the reason… Oh, proud of it such power and getting away with it? Well, then you are indeed a stupid man to waste such rare cunt."

Hitting the end button, the girl was going over the floor twice, and had everything cleaned. He told her to get in the shower.

"Now, I wish you to have the matron get your ass perfectly clean. Your cunt too."

Thanking him, she walked away, and he thought she had an acceptable ass, glad it wasn't bigger as it was the best size for him. He thought about the million-dollar price for the girl who looked so young, and he was sure he had cashed out at the right time. She was everything he said, but she was also smart. Sooner or later, she'd find a way out, and then he'd get her back. She would be adequate for his morning ass fuck, and he would tell her when she escaped, to come to him, or if needed, he would find her. She would only need have her ass fucked daily which would be much less than the man buying her would demand.

In the meantime, he considered there were plenty of new asses to fuck. Getting up, going to his prayer room, the girl who had been

sucking his cock was there with her ass raised up where he could see her cunt and asshole. Taking off his clothes, he knelt down, moved behind her and put his tongue up her ass, feeling her twitch as it was the first time she had a tongue there. He liked how little she was. Her hips were still narrow, and they felt perfect as he held them both and savored her little unfucked hole. Working it to get it gaped to fuck it, he wasn't interested in the girl's cunt as she needed to have her cherry intact to make the most money selling her, but her ass had no hymen. He knew doing ass was best even if he could fuck her cunt. Her asshole was tight, and he felt power from the girl's cry of pain and shock when he slammed his cock in her ass all the way. Seeing her little asshole sphincter wrapped around his cock, squeezing him tight, he leaned over and pulled at her shoulders to get her torso upright. Laying down, she sat upright on him, and being on top of him allowed him to get all the way up her ass. He knew it would help her get good at fucking with her ass doing the work.

There were two more new girls waiting, and next he would have to give them both a first go. Watching the girl's ass go up and down, thinking of the two waiting, they had blonde hair and that was exciting for him. Thinking of their blonde heads bobbing up and down on his cock caused him to cum up the girl's ass. He pulled her down to press hard against him as he came. She shook with each pulse, and when he was done, he pulled at her shoulders to have her lay flat on her back on top of him, his cock still in her ass. Pulling her face to his, he spent time swapping spit and sucking on her tongue. Saying he had two more girls waiting, get off him and go get one of them, saying they must both clean her ass off his cock. He added that once he was clean, he was done sacrificing her, and she could lay out by the pool, but never to wear a suit as he wanted her to have no tan lines.

Thanking him, then his cock, she walked away while squeezing her cheeks together to not let the cum flow out. He'd have the other new girl suck it out, so he was glad she was being smart. He'd need to remember to insist on that. He wasn't big on brunettes, but she did had a great ass, and it was full of his cum. He thought about how righteous that was. He crossed himself, thinking of the next one. The first day for the new girls was each one, by themselves, with him. Tomorrow he would fuck all three at the same time.

He had grown up poor. Living in a cardboard shack in Peru, his

parents dead, all he had was his sister. They both knew the only way they could survive was for him to turn her out. His sister, only eight when their parents died, knew nothing of fucking, so he spent time fucking all her holes to give her experience with the men he would charge to fuck her.

Having trained her well, a pimp who was a legend heard of how good a fuck his sister was, and came to see him.

"Petre, tell me. How much you charge for your sister? What? That's what fat old whores go for. A girl, under ten? You must charge ten times what you do. I tell you what I will do. I can take her and do much business with her. You are new, and maybe someday you can do well, but, Petre, men may see you are so young. They have pistols. They can take her, and you'll never see her again. So, I help you. Sell her to me. Take the money, get a place where men can fuck whores like her in comfort. Get yourself little girls and keep them in your little place where you protect them. And, if you get some good ones, I may buy them off you. Now, I have a few hundred in my pocket. More than plenty for your sister. If you need more, come see me."

He looked at the pimp, and shook his head, saying he didn't need help. The pimp laughed, saying he was young and understood the foolishness of a young boy. His smile changed to a sneer.

"Petre. In my other pocket, do you know what I have? Smart boy! Yes, a pistol. Either way, I get your sister. You just need decide which pocket is best for you."

He took the money. He was still small, and the pimp was ready to kill him if he chose wrong. Since that day he followed the same practice of saying to pay or be killed, and it worked.

He eventually killed the pimp and took all his girls and money, and he was with his sister again. By the time he was sixteen, he was wealthy and respected for his money. He pulled his sister away from the working girls and taught her how to get more girls for their house. He learned how easily young girls trusted her. In a poor village, most girls were put out to whore, or starved. They were not very pretty, and he couldn't charge much for them. He figured out to make the most money, he'd do best with girls from high-class families. His sister became skilled at pulling girls out of wealthy homes and promising them they would do well working for her brother and be free from their controlling parents.

As he waited for the two girls to lick his cock clean, still thinking of

his youth, he recalled finding his sister in the next town where the rich people lived. She had been shot in the head, left on the side of the road, people walking by staring at her but none looking to even see if she was alive. He went to the road and found a man with a wagon to bring her to his home. Before she was taken back, telling the man to wait, he asked around the town about who had killed the young girl. A local drug addict told him that was easy. She was outside the house of the richest man, and he had seen the man pull his daughter from his sister who was holding her hand as they walked. Holding his sister with one hand, he made his daughter watch what he did to anyone who wanted to make her into a whore. The daughter watched her father take his pistol and without saying a word shot his sister in the head. The rich man took his daughter back to his grand home, leaving his sister on the ground there.

All in the town knew not to interfere with anything the rich man did. They all avoided the body lying on the side of the road. As he watched the man putting a tarp over his sister after talking to the drug addict, he saw the rich man run out of his house, screaming at the man for touching his sister's body, saying it was a warning. The man was in fear and started to take his sister out of the wagon. He decided to get what he was planning to do later over with to not disrupt taking his sister away.

Walking up to the wagon, he told the man to leave his sister there, and as the rich man turned to say something about him and his sister, for the man with the wagon he had money in one pocket, for the rich man, a pistol in the other. He had learned much from the pimp.

As the wagon pulled away, he sat on the bench with the man, not looking behind at the rich man who was lying dead where his sister's blood still soaked the ground. The man driving the wagon said it was a sad world and offered to dig a grave for his sister. He said he would pay much to one so brave as to not fear the rich man. The man, not much older than him, said that he would be available for work. He asked him if he had property or a job. Smiling at him, he said he had worked for the man he shot, and the wagon was the rich man's wagon. He asked the man why he took such a chance. He answered it was because the man had made a mistake. Asking what mistake, the man said he should have killed his daughter. She had made the decision to go. He knew his sister was making an offer, doing business. She didn't force the girl to leave. The man said the richer they are, the bigger fools they were.

Peter smiled as he said he'd like to have him work for him and asked him is name.

"Andre. Let this sad day unite us to take money from fools, then, let's kill them."

CHAPTER 12

Answering her phone, Cindy saw it was from a private, secured line. She had written to her mother in the Ukraine, saying she wished to visit with Angie, and appreciated what she had done for them… and she was surprised by how successful she was. She ended the letter saying she thought she could learn much from her. It was easy to know her mother had received the letter and was calling from a line she felt was safe to use.

The conversation was in Ukrainian and in many ways, she thought her mother spoke to her as if she were still a little girl. She understood that. It was what she had hoped for.

"Cynthia, you are safe? Well? Nothing coming back after all that nonsense? Good, yes, good. I just read your letter. Nice, glad we talk now."

"Momma, I am glad we talk. I don't know why we no talk all this time. I tell you, in Brian's house, your little malenke killed himself. I could no contact you to tell. I alone. He no here. Dead. Me with baby. Much to tell."

"Sad, for that, I am sad. But, best I did no know back then. So, at least I have malenka, and now Angelia. So pretty. Looks like you. You like me. We know why, so no more talking why, but she is beauty. We had little time in Russia. You want visit? That, I would like. If you want see me. I send jet."

Not having thought about that, she figured it best not to arouse any suspicions. Mike had said he and Jamie would go ahead of them, and they would know where they'd be landing in the jet.

"Yes. Much, we would wish that. We are citizens now. Less knowing what we do is good. It no different here than there. Politicos keep track. Momma, you can talk? No worry? I have thing to ask."

"I would no call if no."

"Good. You know what happened to us. I liked shooting fucker sheik. A big idiot to get killed. So, question. You run empire. You are not old, but one day you may want to stop. You know death hunts us all. Such things happen. Is one to take things over that day?"

Knowing her mother, she wasn't surprised when she had no hesitation or delay in replying with her more than overt question.

"Ah. Malenka grow up. Is no shy asking things. Cynthia, is family

business. I know you sell your ass in America. My man there, he keep eye on you two. I did impossible thing. Took over from sick fuck husband, killed off others who compete with me. Now, I too hard to get to, or fuck with. I gave you taste, like with drugs. A little money… get you using head instead of ass. I pray to Motka Busha each night you take over when I die. There. Does that answer you?"

Smiling, Cindy thought to herself it sure did. She would wait to see if she could turn her to doing some good once there, but for now, all being said was what she hoped to hear.

"I only say truth. It does. Even money you give, it last only so long. I must think of future. I live in trailer too long. No more live like street cunt. I am glad for your prayer. I will be answer. We talk more when we are there, yes? I have much to learn. Angelia too. She is smart. Inherited more than our looks, our brains too."

"Cynthia, it is prayer answered. I worried you hate me."

"Momma, until taken like cunt I no know if you even alive! I no have way to know."

"That is silly malenka, I still in same house. Not pretty place, not like stupid rich live in. Good place to do bad things. I understand. Are you still working with that Jamie? That Michael?"

"I am. Does that worry you?"

There was a long pause. She knew her mother was not sure yet about anyone other than her own people, and even then, she couldn't be fully sure. Finally, she answered.

"I text my man. One where you are. He say Michael left agency, living with Jamie. He said they fuck a lot. That is good. Fucking, good, if in love. So, he also say you friends with them. Is it that they want your money?"

"Momma, I no come if you think me dumb fuck. Is what you want? Treat me like cunt you sell and no respect?"

"Cynthia, it is worry for you. Get mad only if I no worry. Jamie, when I met her, she is tough number. Trafficker, maybe she wants in on my business? Mike, he may still be agent? So, just tell me. I no insult you. I ask. That is to know. You must respect me as no fool cunt. Yes?"

She looked at her hose to be sure they didn't have runs as she let her mother wait as if she were thinking about what she said. She let out a sigh and answered.

"Momma. I want start again, respect each other. First you must do this and know what will be if no. Your man? Watching me? That stops. Now. You say he look out for me. When taken by Brian, he was no there to look out for me. If he was, he is shit. I want you to text me his picture. If I see him, I will kill him. I give his picture to Mike. Tell him same thing. You do that. Now. I want picture of him. By tomorrow, picture with you, in home, prove he is no here."

Again, there was no hesitation from her mother.

"You say what I would say. That is good. Forget why he watch. You want him gone or you kill him. So, he is gone. I'm texting him now come back."

"And, you will not replace him."

"No. No need now. You get smart now. But, I ask question, you no answer. What of the two?"

"Momma, after what happened, now, with money, I need protection. Jamie was out to kill Brian. She is grateful because Brian is dead because of me. I told Alexander kill him, for me, and he did. Mike's in trouble going alone to save me. They both are ones I trust. They risked lives to save me. They don't work for me, I give them no money. They have money of their own. We have, you know, bond. Jamie was taken when five. I was taken by my father when twelve. We both know the business. Mike, he has reason. His sister. Taken. He protects me. I want you should help him. His sister, where she was taken. I want you should find her. He and Jamie, they are with me, ask no more of that. This, you must trust me. It is not like man watching me. He didn't decide that. You did. I didn't ask him, so I tell you stop. I know that is best. Is it smart thing for me to do?"

Another pause, and she heard the change in her mother's voice to being more like when she was very young.

"Cynthia, that is right way. Is smart. If you trust them, I trust them because you are smart. You prove that in this little talk. I liked them. I want you should know. I think Jamie more than hot ass, she is smart too. Good to have both, like you. Good to have working with us. Mike, you make him promise about sister?"

"I did. That, you must do that for me. I do what I say. Show me you are one I can count on."

"That is how to talk. Tell, no ask. I tell you I will find out. That is if

she is alive. If no, I find out why, and he can fuck up whoever did that thing. I am no sure how fast, but I will do. Now, are we done with big issues and prove we can both piss better than each other? What you call… pissing match. Over?"

"It is. It is good we did this now. Momma, I am still pissed. About man watching me. Is he important to you? If no, I'll have Mike shoot him."

"Cynthia, no let gun in hand or handsome man go to head. Yes, man is good one or I not let him near you. You know him from day we left. The one who helped us. I would no be okay if you did that. Good to hear you think that way. But, talking to one who is harder than you so good you show respect, you ask first. Now you know who he is. You understand he kept eye on you. So I know what is on your mind. Now, you think if good man, watch right, why you and Angelia taken?"

"Yes."

"So was he. He is disgraced he let it happen. He offered to quit. From shame. He is no dealer. He no takes girls. He just texted me, saying he needs apologize to you. He is packing up. He never said bad thing about you, ever. Only you are beauty."

"Did he say Angelia is beauty?"

"No. If he did, I would tell you shoot him yourself. That would not be good to hear."

"I needed to know that. That is good. So, we can come visit soon. Maybe two weeks from now. Is that time you can be with us, not running shit show?"

"I *run* shit show as you call it. I do what I want. Yes, I text you pilot's number. Arrange with him. He will tell me when. On this phone, I talk one time, that is safe way. Cynthia?"

"Momma?"

"I no wait until you here. I must tell you important thing. I am sorry. I was dumb cunt back then, but no excuse for what fucker did to you and Jakiah. I was wrong. No excuse. I am sorry."

The call ended. Her mother had stopped the call with what she wanted to hear since she had been raped. It was sincere. She heard it in her voice, and it was not something she had to say. That would make some choices harder.

Going to the living room, she sunk into the plush couch they had

bought and thought about the call and being watched. She knew the man she had mentioned, and he was a decent man when she knew him as a girl. Her mother was smart, and she heard her upset when mentioning he had failed to stop her and Angie from being taken. Perhaps it was as simple as her way of keeping aware of her child. It was hard to know with her. Ukrainians, after the revolution, like all in the USSR, trusted nobody. They kept secrets, and revealed little about anything, even about themselves. It was common, in a family, to have family members turning in close relations to get a decent apartment or because the KGB said if they didn't, they would be sent away to a gulag for life. It was a lesson America had yet to learn, but she knew such things would happen the way things were going. She hated the word socialism, and it was the new rage in America. It worried her.

Sipping at a glass of soda she had brought with, she checked her phone. Her old phone was destroyed when they were taken, and Mike brought her and Angie new ones with their old numbers. He had used the same security measures as the CIA. After scrubbing the phones clean of any spyware, he installed encryption and said all calls would only be heard by someone she decided to take the call from.

He had also installed a phone-to-cloud device, also fully encrypted, that recorded all conversations along with the actual source location and phone number of the caller. It required her voice and face to access the recorded conversations, and it was the first time she would be listening to a recorded call. Going to the recent calls, she clicked on the most recent one, knowing it was the one from her mother, then said her password as the phone used face ID to allow her access. It had a full trace of where the call was made, which was her home when a child as it allowed a map view of the location. It also had a full voice-to-text transcript. She was curious as the conversation had been entirely in Ukrainian, and the transcript was in Cyrillic, but had a "translate" button. She hit it and the entire conversation was changed to English, perfectly done. She was shaking her head at how little privacy people had now, and at the same time in awe of the technology.

Not reading it, she listened to the whole recording twice. She was sure her mother was happy to hear she'd like to replace her one day. She was also surprised at how strong she had been at times such as her trust in Mike and Jamie, and in telling her that there would be no more

watching her. Although impressed with her being strong on important matters, it also scared her. She sounded like her mother. Realizing she wasn't like her mother; she was glad she could sound that way.

After hitting end, she called Mike, and he added Jamie to the call. She told them she had a call from her mother, and said rather than explain, it was best to come over for dinner later and hear it all for themselves. Mike said to put him out of his misery. He wasn't sure he could wait that long. Jamie echoed the same. Smiling, Cindy switched to Ukrainian.

"This is how you talk to sex mogul all fear?"

They got the idea. Switching to what to have for dinner, Mike said he would enjoy cooking up some spaghetti sauce and noodles, and Jamie said she'd stop and get some cannoli. Laughing again, once more in Ukrainian, Cindy asked them if that was all they could do for the most feared sex mogul ever known. After more laughing, she told them both that would be wonderful. Mike asked where Angie was during all of the call.

"Oh, Mike. I was so distracted by my mom's call I completely forgot! Oh, God, I hope she's alright. I was about to call you to go be with her when the call came! Hurry, I'm freaking out!"

"Slow down. Just tell me where she went. That's all you need to do, and you don't have to worry about her. I'll be on it."

"Mike, I have to worry. She's headed right into a trap!"

"Cindy, first, does she have her gun with her?"

"Yes, but I don't think that will protect her."

"I assure you it will. I trained you two. Now, okay, just tell me where and why she went and why you think she's in peril."

With a huge smile, Cindy pushed herself back onto the cushions of the couch, lifting her long legs up to admire.

"Well, you know we want to get a car. She wanted to see how she held up to real criminals, and she went alone to a car dealership. I'm sure they've got her trapped in some business office and telling her she can get 30% financing!"

"Wha... Oh, I get it. Very funny."

Mike and Cindy both were laughing hysterically, but Jamie wasn't. She managed to cut in.

"Listen, you two. I've bought a car and they're the only fuckers I've

ever met worse than traffickers, so. Mike, Angie is in danger. She may come home with an electric car they can't move with a total protection package and extended warranty. And, I know it will be ten over sticker. Cindy, which dealer was she going to?"

Suddenly not laughing anymore, she had heard all the horror stories from one of her clients who ran a dealership and Jamie was right. She struggled to remember the name but it came to her.

"I'm sure it was City Toyota!"

Without saying more, Mike said he was on his way. Jamie told him hold on; she was coming with.

"We'll call you when we rescue her."

As they ran out to the garage, Jamie said to hurry. She also said she'd take the lead. Mike, confused, asked her why not let him mansplain things to them. Getting into his Tahoe, out of breath, she explained.

"That's the first dealer I went to, and not to bring up my past, those bastards wanted to fuck me every way they could. More than any sick fucks when I was trafficked. I'm going to fuck them up good."

Looking at her, he saw rage in her eyes. She was out for mayhem and would show no mercy.

"Okay, I'll have your back."

He looked over at her, almost missing a stop sign as he smiled.

"Well, you know how much I like that…"

Suddenly, she was all smiles. She was still revved up to go at the dealership, but she started laughing. Mike was confused and asked her why.

"Oh, a Bette Midler album I heard a long time ago when I was given a Walkman. A live album, and she'd do bits between songs. One I'll never forget. She said, my boyfriend Ernie said I have no tits and a tight hole. And I said, Ernie, get off my back."

He shook his head, laughing along with her. He smiled and reassured her.

"Don't worry. I'll be on your back all night. Glad you thought of that."

Wiggling her hips, she said she was ready.

"For the dealer, or getting that hot ass of yours done right?"

Shaking her head, she looked at him with concern.

"Mike, how can someone so smart be so stupid?"

By Terry Ulick 79

Pulling up to the place to showcase cars in front of the main entrance, they saw Angie sitting at a sales desk, leaning over and talking to a clearly frightened salesman. As they rushed in, everyone there was looking at Angie and the man holding his chair arms in a death grip. Jamie called out to her, and seeing them she smiled, stood up, and politely said thank you to the man as she walked to them.

"Mom tell you pick me up? I won't have to get a ride service. Thanks!"

As they all got in the Tahoe, Mike turned to her and asked her what the hell was going on, and why was the man cowering in fear with everyone watching in terror.

"Were they? I didn't look around, but it was kind of quiet. I was just negotiating with the salesman. He started at sixty, and I had just gotten him and the sales manager down to twenty-five when you walked in. I told him I'd think about it. Why? Isn't that how it's done. In my *Teen Vogue* they had an article on how to get a fair price. Right after the article about how you're expected to give a guy a blow job to get him to date you."

Glad he was at a red light, both he and Jamie turned to look at her in shock.

"That's the same look he gave me when I told him I'm not some stupid girl who'd give a blowjob to get a date. That's when the price started to come way down."

Mike had to drive, but Jamie continued to look at her with worry. Angie smiled, looking stunning in one of her new outfits. She shook her head at Jamie, then crossed her legs and flattened out her dress.

"I'm just seeing if you would believe me. I'm practicing being impossible to deal with. I told mom about the blowjob article, and no, I don't think that or would do that. I did read an article about how women are abused at car dealers, and also one about how to be absolutely impossible to talk into anything. They were in my…"

Jamie interrupted her.

"In your *Teen Vogue*…"

Nodding with a huge smile, Angie asked Jamie if there was a *Vogue* for grown-up women. Jamie, realizing she had been had, saying yes, there was a grown-up *Vogue* for grown-up women. Angie smiled and looked up at the roof lining, lost in thought. Looking back down, smiling, she told Jamie she couldn't wait to get a copy.

"That's a luxury. Thanks, that feels so good…"

Whimsey had never mentioned it, but she envied Sharon. She was only liked because she was so small. Sharon was popular as she was incredible looking and had a body made for fucking in her opinion. She didn't look old or young, she had classic good looks, and her body was trim. Her breasts were small, and her proportions were perfect. Washing her, looking at all her curves and her amazing ass, she was feeling aroused. Standing behind her, she moved to put her front against Sharon's back, putting her arms around to wash her breasts with the puff, worked her way down to her smooth mound, then between her legs. Telling Sharon to turn around, as she did, Whimsey knelt and had her move her legs apart. She moved in and started licking her, holding her hips as water splashed onto her head, and the suds of the shampoo started rinsing away.

Having no interest in other women as lovers, Sharon was aroused by the gentle way Whimsey was washing her. Being taking care of felt comforting. She had done hundreds of girl-on-girl scenes, but they had never turned her on. As she started shaking from the way Whimsey was flicking her clit, there was something about the girl she liked and couldn't tell her not to lick her. Surprised at her skill, she was getting off on being licked so gently, and she knew she'd cum. She always faked orgasms on camera with men or women and hadn't cum in a long time. Leaning against the tiled wall, she moved her legs apart while moving them forward slightly to push her lower pelvis out to give Whimsey a clear sign she wanted to cum. Putting her hands on Whimsey's head, she helped rinse away all the shampoo on her, then put conditioner on her hair which was somehow erotic to her. Having both her hands in her hair, she felt her every movement as she licked her and worked her tongue up inside of her. Whimsey moved her hands to Sharons ass and started massaging it and her hands felt gentle moving over her. That was what she needed to cum. Whimsey could sense by her spasms she was getting there. Moving her head back, she took one hand and put it in front and put three fingers inside her to go at her cervix with skill. With that, Sharon started to cum, squirting onto Whimsey's face, her mouth open catching as much of the squirt as she could. Sharon was gasping and her body trembling as she collapsed forward, bending over Whimsey's head, then back up to reach to her face and kiss her. After a

long kiss, licking her face clean, Whimsey stood up and pulled Sharon's head down to kiss more and twirl tongues, asking Sharon to spit in her mouth over and over and as her mouth filled, she had been rubbing herself and she came.

Hearing Jackson shout out that she didn't have much time, so get out of the shower, she looked at Whimsey who shrugged, and they rinsed all the soap and cum juice off each other, then got out and dried each other with towels that were actually clean.

"Jackson said you didn't have much time. They have you doing a private session?"

Looking at her, she nodded, looking disappointed at having to leave.

"Yeah. I don't know what they're thinking as it would be ideal for you. It's a daddy wanting a schoolgirl. Probably want to do the bad girl needs spanking thing and all."

Laughing, Whimsey understood the irony of it.

"Yeah, like, I am a schoolgirl, and he can have the real thing. Well, it's a break from the pounding you got today at least. And the money is better."

Not sure why, she looked at Whimsey and did something she wasn't allowed to do. She told her she didn't get paid for any of it. Looking at her as if she was kidding, Whimsey let it sink in, then closed the door to not be heard.

"Wait a minute... Not getting paid? For any of this? Like, are you doing it for fun... or... well, I don't understand."

Closing her eyes, she realized she was worried that Whimsey, cute and looking like a child, could easily be sold off to some billionaire, and wanted to warn her somehow.

"Whimsey, I'm going to tell you something secret. If you tell anyone, I could be killed. I'm doing it because you're so sweet, and I don't want you to end up like me."

Her face changing from a smile to concern, she moved to stand in front of the door so nobody could barge in. She could see Sharon was serious. She trusted her and knew she cared about her. She promised she wouldn't do anything to hurt her. Sharon knew that was sincere, a promise to not tell anyone. She knew Whimsey had a crush on her and would take what she said to heart.

"Two years ago, I was in Morocco. I'm a geologist but was also

involved in a spiritual church. The man Jackson works for, his name is Peter. I met with him there when there on a dig. I thought he was the leader of the church, but he's really a trafficker. He takes girls and sells them to rich men, or whores them out. These videos? They aren't just for watching online. They're like, well, a catalog. We show off what we can do, and men all over the world bid to buy us. Some, like the daddy, just to rent out. The ones nobody wants, they do porn or work hotels as hookers. I was taken, but, well… Peter didn't want to sell me as I was his favorite ass to fuck. Now, I'm too old to sell, so I do porn. All the girls they sell? All real young. Sixteen at most."

She saw the look of fear on Whimsey's face. She was looking at her eyes, clearly shocked.

"Sharon… I look like I'm ten… I was only doing this to get a fan base…"

"Whimsey, I know, I know. But right now your videos are probably getting bids. A little thing like you? You'd sell for close to a million. The buyers have billions. I'm worried about that happening to you."

Shaking, clutching her towel, Whimsey didn't have any idea of such things, or how it happened. She realized it made sense, and she had read about girls being trafficked many times.

"Do they, like… tell you? Have you meet with the men? How will I know if they have plans for me?"

Shaking her head, Sharon had to let her know none of that would happen.

"No, never. You'd run if they did or call the police. No, with me, a guy got in the car I was in, jabbed me with a needle and I was out. When I woke up, I had no idea where I was, but there was a man fucking my ass while Peter watched. He came in me, then shot at me with a rifle and they threatened to kill me right then if I said anything. They would have, I know it. But it got worse, and it's the reason they don't worry about me running off. I have a brother, and they told me if I didn't do everything they said, he'd be killed. Do you have family?"

Crying, nodding, Whimsey said she had a younger sister, and they were both in foster care and why she wanted to make money with her own sex site. The foster dad was abusing her and her little sister. Sharon realized the sister would be an even bigger sale, and she asked if she had told Jackson about her.

"I didn't tell him, but I know he saw her. I had a FaceTime call from her, and Jackson walked by and looked at the screen and gave me a thumbs-up. Later he asked who I was talking to as she looked so like me. I just said it was my kid sister. That's all I ever said."

"Okay, that's not good. She'd go for a whole lot of money. I have to get going. I know you need to get away from your sick foster dad but listen to me… Get away from here. Far away as you can get. And above all, take your sister too. I'm going to give you my brother's name and phone number. Call him, tonight. You can't say it was me or say my name. They'll kill him. Just say someone who knew him said to see if he can help you make some money. He's a for-real photographer and say that's why. He can help you earn money for real. You're so pretty, he can help you, okay. Do you have your phone?"

Reaching into her backpack, Whimsey pulled out a phone with a case that was pink with big yellow flowers. Sharon gave her Mike's name and phone number, then said get out, get her sister and call her brother and say you can't stay where you are. He'd understand. They were talking in a whisper, but a pounding on the bathroom door made Whimsey fly into her arms. It was Jackson yelling it's late, time to go.

Grabbing her hairbrush, she worked fast and as she opened the door to leave, gave Whimsey a tender kiss, telling her she had a lot to do with a false enthusiasm. Moving fast, she put on a light blue short frilly skirt with a thin white belt that knotted in front and was tied like a bow in front for her pussy to be unwrapped. She tied her hair with blue ribbons even though it was wet. Putting all she'd need in a silly rolling cart with kitten stickers on it, she turned, seeing Jackson waiting at the door.

"Max is outside, and he's been there twenty minutes. I did you a favor and you owe me some good head when you get back for it. He was about to call Peter, but I told him it was my fault, the shoot ran long. It sure fuckin' took you long enough."

Shrugging, she looked at him wondering how he couldn't understand.

"Whimsey was showering, and I had to douche all the cum out of my holes. I don't think the client would want to be sucking twelve guys cum out of my ass. Do you?"

"Well, yeah, right, that wouldn't be good. Okay, take that cum bucket ass of yours out to the car or we're both in trouble."

Walking out of the building, Max was leaning against the fender of the car, looking at her and shaking his head. He took her rolling suitcase to put in the trunk. He normally put it in the back seat with her. She said she was fine having it in back. Not looking at her, he closed the trunk then opened the back door for her to get in. The car didn't move. She asked why the hurry if he wasn't moving?

"Bags in the trunk. One more on the ride."

That had happened before. The geezer client must have wanted a three-way. They sat with the engine idling, music loudly playing classic rock. After fifteen minutes, she held back a gasp. Jackson was holding a barely able to walk Whimsey and carrying her backpack. Max got out, and the two managed to put her in the back seat and belt her in. Max put her backpack in the trunk. Whimsey was drugged and about to pass out. She managed one look at Sharon, and as she leaned over to rub her face, Whimsey whispered to her she was right, then passed out.

Tapping the side of the car, Jackson watched as they drove off. Sharon sat feeling sick, rubbing Whimsey's arm and holding her hand. She knew that was all she could do. It triggered all she had been through when she was taken in Morocco. If she had told her a few days sooner, she'd have made it out. She kept asking herself how it could happen the day she warned her.

As she sat shaking her head, Max's phone rang. After a brief hello, he held it up for her to take, saying Peter wanted to talk to her. She was in a panic. It wasn't a coincidence. Taking the phone, she started to say hello, but Peter interrupted her.

"You were told the day I took you to never tell anyone about me. Never. Tonight you told the little cunt to call your brother and run away. I have bids on her. I sell her tonight. Telling her to call your brother? I told you what would happen to him if you did. There is a camera and mic in the bathroom. I watched you warn her. I will do as I said. Your brother will have a knock on his door tonight, but not from the little cunt. From Max."

The call ended, and Max held his hand up for the phone. He wouldn't give her a chance to call 911 or do anything stupid again. He looked at her in the rearview mirror.

"Your brother… Hey, he's some nice guy. Peter told me he was all over the fuckin' world looking for your hot ass. Were you fuckin' him?

He was real sad to not have you around, and that's the only reason I'd do all that for. Shame there'll be no loving reunion…"

They were driving in a large car, not a limo with a dividing glass. She was behind him and his head was mostly hidden by the headrest. They were on a back road to the airport, not on the highway. Hearing Peter tell her they were going to kill Mike, looking at Whimsey, then hearing Max making jokes about Mike to her knowing he would be the one to do the kill made something snap inside her. She would kill all of them to save Mike.

Feeling one of the long ribbons on her hair, it wasn't long enough. She moved her hand slowly to the white belt that cinched her waist in, and that would work. All she could think of was what she was about to do.

Quietly sliding off her belt as Max sang along to Rod Stewart singing, *"Tonight's the Night,"* she wrapped each end around her hands and had plenty left for her plan.

Leaning forward, moving up to be right behind him, she asked him if he could please change the channel, the song was upsetting to hear. As he started to laugh to tell her that was too fucking bad, she swung the belt over his head and pulled it down to his throat, pulling herself back at the same time. Using her legs against the back of his seat for power and leverage, she pulled with all her might, her legs thrusting her back. He let go of the wheel to grab at the belt around his neck, and the car veered as he hit the brakes. The car was the only one on the back road lined with oak trees. As the car veered off, it was still going fast even though Max had tried to stop. She had pulled the belt in a cross pattern, and he couldn't get his fingers in to pull it away fast enough. Realizing he had to do something else, he moved his hand to reach for his gun as the car smashed into a tree.

The force of being thrown forward from hitting the old tree combined with Sharon pulling even harder on the belt as her legs helped stop her flying forward in the crash was what stopped Max. The force of being thrown forward and the belt so thin and tight around his neck crushed his windpipe and larynx, and he was panicking and choking, not able to breathe. Sharon kept pulling on the belt hard as she could until she couldn't hear him breathe then saw his head slump to the right. She didn't stop pulling, thinking he could be faking. Waiting five

minutes, not stopping the strangling, she was sure nobody could not breathe for that long. She let up on her pull just enough for him to grab at it if he was still alive. Nothing. She let go of it more, and he slumped in his seat.

Pulling it hard as she could again, she took the ends and tied them around the metal rods of the headrest using a knot she learned from climbing down into caves. Keeping him tied and upright, she let go, then moved to reach to the front seat. Moving things around, she found his gun and his phone. She climbed into the front seat and found a box of ammo in the glove compartment, then pulled his wallet out and took his license, credit cards, and cash. Getting out of the car, she inspected the front end. The tree had stopped it, but the front of the car was only crushed in the middle, the front wheels looking unharmed.

Walking to the driver's side, she opened the door and looked at Max. His tongue was sticking out and his face was a mix of pink, blue and purple. His eyes were bulging out. She had heard that the dead could still see for a while after dying. She put her face in front of his, telling him he wouldn't be visiting Mike later.

Unbuckling his seatbelt, she pulled at him. Letting gravity pull him down as she pulled him out as much as she could, his feet were on the door jamb. Pulling them off and away, the car was still running. Getting in behind the steering wheel, she turned the radio off, then putting it in reverse, slowly backed away from the tree. The ground was level, and as she moved far enough away, the headlights lit Max, and she didn't have to think at that point. Putting it in drive, she slowly moved forward and turned just enough to roll the front wheel of the large car over him. She backed up, looked at him, then moved forward to crush him again. After five times, she got out and looked at him. Having aimed the front tire to run over his face, he was unrecognizable, but he'd eventually be identified. She didn't care. It just felt good to roll over him again and again.

Backing up enough to where she could use his cell phone to take pictures of him lit by the headlights, she smiled at them. He thought it was her brother who would die. She taunted him, although he was clearly dead.

"Think you can take us? La-de-da, go kill Mike? Well… Go for it, asshole."

Once far enough away, somewhere safe, she decided to send the picture to Peter, saying, "Next, you."

It wasn't late, and she'd have plenty of time to drive in the night to not be noticed. Needing to get away far as possible, Peter would call Max at some point as he would expect to hear that they were on the jet. Not getting through, he would have someone take the road to the airport and she knew there would be a search for the car soon.

Thinking things through, she knew Peter would put the pieces together and send someone to Mike's. She had to warn him. Using the GPS on the phone, she shook her head in disbelief. She never knew where she was held when doing porn. She was only a hundred miles away from Mike's place. Taking no chances, she punched in his number. She realized he was probably sure she was dead, and it would be a shock but she had to warn him of Peter's threat before they talked about all that happened.

The car looked like a wreck, but there was no law against being a clunker as long as it drove and had lights that worked. Using the map app, she found a route using back roads, and felt good as she was moving fast, but not enough to set off police radar. With all of that figured out, she looked back at Whimsey who was sleeping, realizing she would first have to get Mike to snatch her sister. That would be Peter's power-play move when he had things sorted out. She was far enough ahead of things to tell Mike she was on her way, and they needed to get a little girl out of trouble. He would understand. He knew what happened to her, and he would get right on it. Turning onto a road with a decent number of cars on it, she felt safer. She had thought things through and was ready to explain she was alive to Mike.

Calling his number, she was relieved when he answered after three rings.

"Hello, I don't recognize your number…"

"That's because I don't have a phone of my own, just like in high school."

Smiling as she heard him gasp, all she needed was what he said in response.

"Sharon?"

CHAPTER 14

Knowing that Max took back roads to the airport where his jet waited, trying to get in touch for a half hour, Peter knew something had happened to Max and the two girls he was bringing to the jet to come to him. Giving up on using a phone, he began looking at video from the cameras in the bath and shower room at the porn studio. He knew Sharon and Whimsey had made a decision to get away but doubted that could happen. He sat upright and decided if they told anything about him to anyone, he would kill the ones they loved. His worry was if Max had an accident, heart attack, or any of many possibilities.

Looking at his records for Sharon and Whimsey to find addresses of ones to have killed, his phone pinged that a message had arrived, and he saw it was from Max. Feeling relieved until he opened the text, reading the message and studying the picture of Max dead on the ground, he stood still, staring at his phone. He couldn't be sure the women had overpowered Max, but that was the only thing that made sense. The message wasn't that Max was dead. It was precise.

"Next, you."

Not worrying about the how and why, he began to carry out his threats to Sharon and Whimsey. Deciding Sharon needed to be first to learn he kept his promises, he read the file on her brother carefully.

Mike, her brother, thought she was dead. He was a CIA agent taking down traffickers. If she got in touch with him and told him anything of what she knew, Mike would interfere with his operations.

Calling the man hired to carry out the threats Peter made to girls, the hitman already had an encoded list of people he may be called on to take out. The only calls Peter made to him were short, giving only a number from the list.

"Fifty-four. Immediate. Go."

Knowing he didn't need an answer, he ended the call. He didn't add Whimsey's sister as she was going to be a take, and he wanted her alive. He left it where the foster parents would be killed to let the sisters know he was their daddy now, and they could end up the same way if they even asked a question.

Using his mapping app, he calculated the time from the airport to Sharon's brother's apartment, then calculated how the hitman's place was

in comparison. Allowing for the time he had wasted trying to call Max, Sharon would reach her brother before his man could possibly reach him.

Standing again, he felt as he did when he was a young pimp in Peru, and how all knew him to be fearless. His success was always being ahead of a problem, or opportunity. Running on an intuitive nature he had since young, he couldn't recall ever being fearful. When his sister was killed by the rich man when recruiting girls, he hadn't any reaction to the man's threats, and had no problem killing him. That continued as he never suffered remorse.

Empathy, sympathy, caring. Those words had never been in his vocabulary, or his thoughts. When faced with any situation, no matter what the risk was, all he thought of was coming out alive and being the one who won. He couldn't recall caring what happened to any person. As he thought about his childhood, such a lack of empathy or feelings for others included his own sister. When he saw her dead, he felt nothing. He didn't cry, and he saw it only as an opportunity to say look what he did to her killer and become a hero. He still didn't care how his young sister, working for him, was shot in the head. No thought of what that must have felt like, if she lived for a while after the shot, or if she knew it even happened. She was just a body he and Andre put in the ground.

And that's what he would do to Sharon and her brother. Letting his instincts take over, he looked on his laptop for the data on Mike, found his phone number, then dialed it.

Standing, waiting for an answer or voice mail, he was walking to get a bottle of water when his call was answered. He heard panting on the other end, revealing a sense of excitement. He knew that had to be because of his surprise seeing his sister alive.

"Mike?"

"Yes, that's me. And you are…"

"My name is Peter. You have possession of two things that are mine."

Waving his hand frantically to Sharon and Whimsey, they got the message and stood quiet and frozen, listening.

"Peter, I need to correct what you said. What you had was mine. Something of great value to me."

"I'm sure you see it that way, and I know why. I'm sure you know

that often merchandise changes hands. It did, and that is why you are mistaken. I am a reasonable man. If you return my goods, no harm will be done, and you will continue to live as you have been."

Listening to more than the words, Mike understood that Peter was a psychopath. He was referring to human beings as merchandise, and he could hear in his manner that was what he thought them to be.

"Peter. I'm not of the same mind. I assure you that the only harm possible will be to you. I will give you an example. Have you talked to your man? Your driver?"

Mike was writing on a notepad, scribbling fast as he could to tell Sharon and Whimsey to gather their things, and go to his bedroom and get basic things together for him, and tell Jamie, upstairs, to pack all their firepower and pack her things, saying they were leaving when he gets off the phone.

"I have not conversed with him, no. But I was sent a picture of him. So, already mistakes are being made. Mike, do you want to have your possessions in such a condition? I'm sure you wouldn't."

Peter was engaging in a classic game of words, all to allow his shooter to get there and take care of them. He wasn't surprised that Mike was engaging with the scenario and was guarding his words. He knew Mike had agency resources to think his call could be traced. His sister was a witness and victim as people thought of women that way.

Seeing Sharon and Whimsey were downstairs with bags of things Jamie had given them, he saw Jamie carrying two large duffel bags. One would have their clothes and supplies, the other, tugging her right arm down, was clearly filled with weapons and ammo. She walked over to him and handed him an automatic pistol, and she had one out for herself. Lifting his chin to go get in the car, he kept talking as he walked to the garage following behind them. He opened the outside door to the yard, not seeing anyone or anything moving. He considered that time was on their side, and they needed to use it.

"Well, Mike. being unreasonable will not serve you well. Any good man will protect his assets, and I know you think that is what you are doing. For me, they are an investment. I expect a substantial return on it..."

Hanging up on Peter as he closed the driver's side door, he wasted no time driving away, taking an irrational route. He knew Peter was

stalling as a hitman or team was on the way to take back Sharon and Whimsey and kill him. Even if they had shown up before they left, he wasn't worried as he had been in many gun battles and that's what he was trained for. Calling Cindy, he said to open her garage, he and Jamie were going to pull in and had lots to talk about, but don't answer any calls or open the doors into the house. He'd added they were only two blocks away.

Since Cindy and Angie had only met him recently, he thought it unlikely Peter knew anything about them. Until Sharon escaped, he may have known his address and phone number, but to do surveillance on him was pointless.

As he pulled into the garage, he heard it closing behind them. He had a top-line security system installed for them when they bought the house, and Cindy could see him on the driveway and once in the garage on video panels in every room of her house. The inside door opened, and Cindy and Angie stood there, both holding AR-15s. They also had looks of surprise on their faces. They had both seen pictures of Sharon at his place, and putting down the rifles they ran to her and introduced themselves. Angie turned to Whimsey, and saw she was stunned.

"I'm Angie, and that's my mom, Cindy. You look kind of scared, and there's no reason to be… or, you look… well, I don't know what that look could be. What's your name?"

"Whimsey."

Smiling, Cindy let Mike take Sharon inside, and she heard the girl say her name as she walked over to her. She had heard what Angie had said and wondered the same thing.

"Whimsey. Angie's right. Are you afraid of us?"

Her eyes still huge as she looked at them, she finally spoke up.

"No, not at all. It's just you two are rockin' hot! Whoa, you're so beautiful…"

"Well, that's nice to hear, but I'm sure you'll get over it. Now, come inside and we'll get you fixed up with all you need, and I'll be making food for all of us. Just sandwiches and chips and things. C'mon…"

She held out her hand, and Whimsey took it, still looking at them. She was in awe of how they looked.

Once all were inside, Cindy told them all to relax on the sofas and for Mike to share what was going on, adding how in the world had he found

Sharon. She was beaming with delight. It was what Mike had wanted for so long. Angie felt the same, and she knew it had to be all shootouts and car chases. She was surprised as it was Sharon who answered.

"I found him, Cindy. I was in a place where I couldn't leave, and I got the chance to escape and on the phone I looked at the map and saw I was so near to where he lived. I was able to help Whimsey to get away too, and I was so happy Mike was home. There's so much to tell."

Jamie was holding her own AR-15 from the bag of weapons she brought, walking around the house looking at security cameras. She knew a smart assassin could work past any security setup.

After a half hour of laying out the basics of what had happened to her, Sharon was equally anxious to know what all the guns were for.

"Sharon, that's a good question. The answer will take some time, so I'm going to make something for all of us to eat first. Angie, show Whimsey around, and Sharon, how long has it been since you made a ham sandwich?"

Mike understood Cindy wanted to talk about things the young girls needn't hear, and he wanted to check things on the property and join Jamie on patrol.

Being much like the day in Russia, so many things were going on at once, he thought it wise of Cindy to slow them down and figure out a battle plan. The first thing needed was to learn about Peter. As Cindy and Sharon got up to go to the kitchen, he walked over to her and he wanted to talk to Jamie for some basics, then he'd join her. She understood.

Walking into the kitchen, he thought about how he had said he needed something from his sister. She was there to ask. That was what he had prayed and worked for since the day she went missing.

"Well, I'll need to ask a few things, Sharon. Keep making things as I do. I need to know all I can about Peter."

Opening a jar of mustard, she looked at him, not used to seeing his face. She snapped herself out of it, and understood he needed to get Peter and his men before they got them.

"Things to know first… Okay. He's smart. Cold as ice. He's from Peru, and I was privy to some talk about him. He started as a pimp when he was in his teens. Used terror and killings to get his way. Feared. Fearless. I don't know his last name. I only heard him called Peter, and I

would guess it's his Americanized name."

Jotting down notes, Mike shook his head. He looked up at her, and she seemed calm and able to talk.

"Okay, that's a start. Now, age, height, what he looks like."

Thinking it through as she spread some mayo on bread, she looked up, and said that she could give an accurate account of him.

"Latin lover type. About six foot. Thin, lean. Skin looks like a good tan, but that's from where he was born. Classic, chiseled good looks. Really good looking. High cheekbones and deep, dark eyes. No scars or anything like that. Wears light colored suits. You know, when a thin man dresses stylish, they have that loose, flowing style of clothing. I would guess he's around 40. Not young, not old. He would stand out in a crowd. He has that movie star look. But, and this is what I learned, he isn't attractive because of how he acts. He never smiles. He doesn't look people in the eye. He's not nice. Ever. When he is, it's a blatant act, a put on, and he doesn't try to hide it's an act. It's a way of putting anyone he meets down."

Mike was writing as fast as he could, and it was all helpful. Next, he asked about where he lived.

"Mike. That, I don't know. I've been there a few times. It's tropical. An island. You know… warm climate, all the doors and windows open, a big pool between the house and the ocean. I don't know which ocean, though. When I went there it was always on his jet. Oh, Mike! The jet. If a man has a jet, and it's an hour outside of town, couldn't you find out who has them there?"

"Yes, I can. That's important, and why I ask questions, probing like this."

Cindy was pouring soda into glasses and smiled at him.

"Is probing when you first met how you got to know Jamie so well?"

The look on her face was pure love and admiration. She laughed. She knew it was exactly how he was able to get past the obvious and learn who she really was. He smiled, nodding.

"Yep, and as you asked, the probing lasted all night long when we met. Now, back to Peter. Sharon, how many seats in the jet, and when you flew to his home, how long did it take?"

"It was large. I think about sixteen seats in front, then a big cargo area in back.

Mike looked over at Cindy, worried it would trigger her. She and Angie had been bound and gagged in such a plane when they were being trafficked. Even worse, by Jamie. She smiled, shaking her head to indicate she was okay.

"That helps. So, island house on the ocean, warm, tropical, good sized private jet. Likes nice things…"

Sharon had a look on her face, and Mike knew she wanted to say something but was being careful not to offend Cindy. He told her Cindy had been through a lot and knows everything is important and asked what was it she wanted to say?

"Oh, this is just sick, and so sad. Yes, he likes nice things, but he likes nice really young ass even more. There's always a lot of girls there for him. I mean really young. Twelve, tops, I would guess. And he only does them in… okay, no mincing words. In the ass. Wants them to stay virgins. But, well, no way around this, even with me, and I was what, twenty? In my ass. That's his thing. Lots of head, but he doesn't pay much attention when getting it. It's more about making girls submissive to him."

"Okay, I need to work fast, and this is all important stuff. You said you were being sent out to a client when you first arrived at my place. Do you know who? Or who any of them were? Names? Anything?"

That stopped her. Holding a slice of bread in one hand, she stared at him, then started shaking her head in disgust.

"I do. Quite a few. They didn't tell me their full names or anything. But I recognized them as I was always watching the news and reading financial magazines. So, a former president help? CEOs of some big tech companies? Royalty from Europe? Mike, I worked men who weren't just into young girls. When they wanted a real woman, a stunner, that was me. And they were all the sickest motherfuckers anyone could imagine. Get your pencil sharpened, here goes…"

CHAPTER 15

"Let's see if I have this right. You had a nice home, family, then your parents die. No other family, so you and your sister get put into a foster home. Your foster dad is all perv and going at you, so you go off and do porn. Whimsey, why?"

Not feeling put down, she knew Angie wanted to understand the reason. She thought Angie was pretty sheltered in her nice house with her beautiful mom, so she may not get it.

"Angie, not every girl is all lucky and hot like you. When you're in-system… that's what we called being controlled by the state, foster parents can fuck your brains out and all the shit social workers pay them even more money. I was reading some trash magazine and read how girls did porn…"

Raising her hand, Angie asked, "*Teen Vogue*?" Nodding, Whimsey laughed as Angie knew about the trash articles.

"That's the one. It said guys got hooked on porn girls, then they'd leave porn and put up Only Fans pages to make tons of money. So, it wasn't like I wanted to be fucked even more than at home. I needed to get us out of there. Make money on my own, take my little sister with me. I know it's stupid, but haven't you seen all those goody-goody girls with their asses out to the camera on Tok and IG?"

Knowing Whimsey had no idea about her mom's background, or that they had been trafficked, put on a stage naked while men bid on them, then sold to a sheik who her mother shot in the head, she saw no reason to compare notes. It was good to let Whimsey share her story and she would learn about how girls put themselves out for traffickers. That would give her more knowledge of how things work. She wanted to let Whimsey know she understood.

"Okay, I get it. You needed to get you and your sis out, and that's how others were making money, and they were online talking… bragging all about it."

As Whimsey nodded, Angie realized many of the people saying, "DM me," were probably traffickers. It made her sad. Whimsey was trying to do the right thing, but the wrong way. Whimsey looked at her, and she looked worried.

"Angie, I know I was doing some big-time sick shit. I do. Now! At

the time I thought, hey, fucking to get out seemed worth it. I mean, like, I was getting it up the ass most every night at home, so it wasn't something that wasn't going to be done to me either way. But tonight! Fuck, what happened tonight? Sharon told me I was going on the auction block, and they'd get big money for me cause I'm like a ten-year-old. I mean, well, the way I look and all. No money for me, and I'd be a prisoner. And then she said they really wanted my little sister. I'm freaked and don't know what to do…"

Crying, Angie had felt many of the same things when they were held by Brian. It was beyond belief that men could do that to sweet young girls. Whimsey may have been having sex, but not by her own choice, and she was finding a way out. She admired her. She wanted her to know that. Leaning over to hug her, Whimsey was shaking and hugged her back tight. They were sitting on Angie's bed, and she told Whimsey to lay down as she'd been drugged.

"Whimsey. Never be ashamed of yourself. Ever. I think you were very brave to do all that. To find a way out, and knowing your sister would be next for your foster dad. It was risky doing any of that, but you were stuck and needed to find a way to survive. I think you're awesome."

Laying on her side with her head propped up to look at Whimsey, she could tell what she said helped. She had stopped crying and was looking at her with appreciation. She held her arms out and asked if she'd hug her for a while. Angie said sure and lay with her as she hugged her and said thank you over and over. Looking into her eyes, Angie saw she was better. As she thought that, Whimsey pulled her fully and started kissing her and rubbing her between her legs.

Not wanting to make the day worse for her, she went along with it thinking it was some need for affection, but when she put her tongue in her mouth, she pulled back to ask her a question.

"Whimsey, I appreciate all the affection. So, do you like girls? I mean, just girls, not men?"

Looking worried, Whimsey leaned in to kiss her again, and had moved her hand to where she was rubbing her clit through her jeans. Angie was confused about what to do. She looked at her, asking again if she liked girls. Now kissing her all over her face, Whimsey worked her way to her ear.

"Girls, guys, both. I like anyone who wants me… But you're so

pretty, and so nice. I just want to lick you and drink you up… I'll make you feel so special."

Hearing Cindy call through the intercom that the food was ready, Angie felt she had been saved by the bell. She looked at her, saying her mom was waiting and they better get downstairs.

"Angie, oh my God! Your mom! I want to do her too. Both of you. That's why I was staring at you both in the garage. I wanted to pull your clothes off and fuck you both…"

Having been put up on the auction stage as a mother-daughter team, she didn't expect to hear such a thing from a young girl, but Whimsey was making it clear she wanted them both. Letting her kiss her had been to not make matters worse for her, but it hadn't been something she wanted. She kept calm but knew her mother would have to help out on what Whimsey expected.

"We'll talk later. Let's go eat, and after I'll tell her how much you like her, okay?"

Pouting, Angie could see how attractive she was when it came to sex. She was a kitten purring for a pet. She had read all about it in *TV*, as she had started calling *Teen Vogue*, but it was only something to learn about. She had never thought about it, but now, along with everything else, she had become the desire of a hot young porn girl. She couldn't get a break. Her mom would know what to do, but as they were getting off the bed, Whimsey held her hand tight and had a sassy look on her face.

"And, Angie… Sharon. She's so wonderful. I love her. Before we got stuffed in that car and all, she came and took a shower with me. It was heaven. She let me do her to where she squirted like a firehose, and I let it all go in my mouth, then stood up and shared it with her. Then we held each other and kissed and kissed. I hope you get to do Sharon. That was my dream come true. I'm sure we can do a three way."

Nearly freaking out, once they made it down the stairs, Angie felt a surge of relief. She had managed to not push Whimsey away, but she didn't want any more of her sex moves. She felt even worse as Whimsey was a sad girl who wanted someone to love her. Her idea of love was not one she shared, but she knew it was her way to be sweet and nice. She didn't want to do anything to hurt her.

When Whimsey went to sit with Sharon once the food was all out, Mike was busy on his phone, and they were waiting on him. Angie

pulled at Cindy to help her get some more soda in the pantry. Cindy gave her a questioning look, about to say they had plenty out already, but Angie stood inside the pantry doorway.

"Mom! I need help."

Cindy got the clue. Once inside the door, Angie put her mouth to her ear, then whispered.

"Mom, Whimsey's really super, but she just hit on me and started making out with me. And she wants to do you too! Well, I mean both of us, together! I didn't want to hurt her by pushing her away, but we need to do something. She's a little love puppy and wants to lap us all up!"

Cindy shook her head, rolling her eyes.

"Poor little thing. Sharon told me a lot about her. Angie, I'm proud of you. You can survive a bit of that, but she may not survive being hurt more. You realized that, and you did the right thing. I'll have a private talk with her after dinner. I'm just glad you're not sharing a room... or a bed!"

"Mom! Come on! Ooh... like as if I would let it go further!"

Cindy saw her panic and realized, more than ever, what a good person she was. She couldn't help herself seeing Angie's look of pure panic.

"She's a smart girl. You have to admit, she was going for the pot of gold, Angie. Good thing dinner was ready."

"Mom! Pot of gold? You mean my... Where do you come up with those terms? Now when I look at myself, oh, no! I'll be wondering what it's worth!"

Staring at each other, Cindy gave her a sweet smile, a wink, then they both started to laugh. As they left, Cindy looked at her and said she was sure it was the jackpot.

"Mom!"

The laugh was a good relief. Cindy was looking over at Mike, knowing they faced an enraged trafficker, and the battle hadn't even started. As Mike put his phone in his pocket, she waved him over.

"Find anything about him?"

"When Sharon called on the road, as it's a reported kidnapping, I was able to turn to James right then with one of the disposable phones. I gave him everything Sharon said. She said she worried as much for Whimsey's sister as for me, and he said he'd send two men to watch the

foster home and act if needed. He was ecstatic Sharon made it home, and he said what I had was plenty to work with. He'll have the entire unit doing what they do best, meaning scour records and he's putting agents outside my place and here. He said they'd also search for the studio where they were filming. That's what being an agent is about. A team that large can learn a lot fast."

Everything he said made her feel better. She suggested telling everyone as they ate, and he said he had planned to.

Mike called out.

"Finally, off the phone. Thanks for waiting. C'mon, let's eat."

Angie crossed her arms and was faced with the fact that after Whimsey's saying what she did with Sharon and would like to do to her and her mom, hearing "Let's eat" would now have a whole new meaning. Suddenly she started going through other everyday terms. "Grab a bite." "I could just eat you all up." Then she about let out a groan when she thought of "Can't stop eating them" and "Finger licking good."

CHAPTER 16

"You want I should bring back girls when I go. Get daughters?"

Looking at Victush, she gave him a look she was well known for, and one to take seriously as she always carried a small but potent Glock somewhere on herself.

"Eliana, what you want me to do is what I want to know. Asking, that is all I do."

Continuing to stare at Victush, she wondered how someone so smart could be so stupid at times. He, like her, had grown up in a world where a decent person still was careful with anyone powerful. She understood he wasn't suggesting it. He was asking what she wanted him to do as she normally would fill the plane with girls even when carrying a top politician or a billionaire. She knew that when picking up Cynthia and Angelia he would think it insensitive and insulting to them both to have trafficked girls on the ride. Then she stopped, thinking that if Cynthia wanted to take over the business eventually, it may be good to have her understand that trade doesn't stop for niceties.

Her first reaction was to say of course not, but having thought about it she changed her mind.

"No need look like that. It is good you ask. I was going to just have them, maybe I go too, but, they know what I do, and we have orders to fill, so yes, bring as many as you can, But, Victush, be sure sedated, asleep. No even mention if not needed, let them off, then take girls off."

She was excited about her daughter and granddaughter coming to visit and learn how things were done. She knew Victush would think she wanted them to have treatment better than if a King were on board the jet. She did, and like most decisions she made in life, it was ever a balance between her personal feelings and business.

Her personal feelings were what got Cynthia pregnant. Her feelings for her husband blinded her to what her life had become when she first learned of the pregnancy. She knew people thought her ruthless, and they had good reason to. Being ruthless was the first requirement to survive in the communist USSR she had grown up in. Nobody except Victush had seen that she was a torn soul. She could never find a way to forgive what choices she had made, and she was tormented and alone.

"Victush, good, you are. It is good you ask. Thank you. Now, go to

vault, get papers I made for them. Be ready if they wish to come sooner."

Having a top forger make passports and Ukrainian records and IDs for them, she wanted them to be known as Ukrainian, not American. Victush said he would get all things ready, looked at her, then said he'd get the jet ready if needed sooner as he left.

Eliana went to an antique cabinet she'd bought years ago when returning from America once her children were safe. It was claimed to be from the palace of the last Alexander and Alexandria, but she couldn't trust anyone selling anything. It was a nice piece, and she like it.

Using a small key, she opened a letter draw and took out an old-style hypodermic needle, and one of a dozen vials of morphine. Standing in front of the cabinet, she drew out a large dose with the long needle, holding the syringe up to the window to not draw too much out. Once filled, she put the vial back and took off the sweater she always wore, finding a vein that hadn't been used too often, then injected herself. Putting everything back, she locked the cabinet and put the key back in her desk, sitting in her large, tufted chair, closing her eyes until the morphine kicked in.

As she felt it working, she waited for the moment when her thoughts would be most lucid. Then, the morphine would deceive her into feeling invincible and immortal. In her lucid state, she closed her eyes and thought of two ways she could redeem herself with her children.

First was to teach Cynthia how to take over the business. She would grow richer and pass it along to Angelia. The second was to take all the gold and jewels she had locked away in safety deposit boxes in the US and leave the Ukraine and her business behind. To be a babushka, live with wealth and have a family once more. See Cynthia marry a man who didn't have to carry weapons and ruin lives. She was long past needing more money. She no longer felt any satisfaction being feared or powerful.

The two choices swirled in her mind as the morphine melted them away, leaving no thoughts at all, just rest from them. It took her where nothing mattered except how she felt at the moment. A place where she was floating in the air, free from feeling anything except nothing at all. Worries passed by and left, each breath she took was a sensation; an awareness that she was alive and free from anything that could hurt her. Her eyes closed, she smiled, seeing a vision of herself when she was

five. She was a little girl once more. It was snowing and she was with her father outside their farmhouse. The animals were fed and he had time to spend with her. His arm was out to his side, and she was hanging from it, swinging as if on a tree branch as he started turning in a circle. In her dream state, she saw the world spinning around her. The house, the stable, the hen house, the fields, the wagon, and her mother, Julia, looking out the window at her flying and laughing, telling her father to never stop.

It stopped. Close to an hour had passed, and the morphine let go of her as she came back and faced the world she had made for herself. She looked around and understood the time alone with her wise old friend helped her reach a decision. She would show her girls the sad world she lived in, and once they understood where all the money, gold, and jewels came from, how it was accumulated, she would ask Cynthia what she wanted to do. Become like her, or as a family take all of it and live in America and leave the drugs and trafficking to some other ruthless bitch.

PART THREE
The Business

CHAPTER 17

"Hey, Mike. My girlfriend texted my wife, and it had to happen when I'm in town. My first time here, but thought you'd know some decent places to eat."

Mike said the pizza at Cindy's was decent and probably open late. James said pizza sounded good.

Hearing the coded message, Mike knew James was already on his way. Telling Jamie, she was watching the security cameras ready to open the garage for him. Once he pulled inside she went out to greet him, giving him a hug at the door into the house. She saw he looked worried, and that worried her. Walking in, Mike was waiting to greet him. Seeing each other, James asked if there was a safe place to talk.

"I handled the whole place and it's clean. But happening this fast? I doubt they'd make a dent in the security. Let's sit in the kitchen."

As they walked, James nodded at how nice the house was. Standing in the kitchen, Cindy laughed, saying it wasn't a mobile home, but it would have to do. Knowing they had to talk, she said she'd be back in a while.

Mike was in front of a pad of paper as he knew how easy it was to hack over wifi networks and preferred paper and pen for anything confidential and James could write things down instead of saying them out loud. He told James he was all set, and James started writing what he learned on the pad of paper.

"Lives on an island off the coast of Peru. Not part of it. Private island — always has been. Too small for a base, too expensive to supply. Long enough for runway to handle private jet. Show you later on a satellite image. Did a time-lapse of each pass over and it's busy. Jets every few days. Naked girls — sex on beach. Bird's camera can see a mole — and everything else."

Writing numbers for longitude and latitude on the paper for Mike, he had written "Cuba, not Peru." Mike knew he wanted to be sure nobody was outside with a device that could hack the house cameras. Mike went and muted the entire inside set of cameras and microphones, telling James it was okay to talk. He continued, this time talking out loud, but in a casual tone.

"We traced him through the jet ownership. That was a good catch

your sister pointed out. Dummy corporations own it, but it leads to him according to our analyst. There's really no record of him doing anything. The planes… no manifest of passengers of course, but our footage shows the plane is always full. There are boats that come and go. All big. Private yachts, and we can make out some numbers on them. On record, he's a ghost."

Mike was taking notes, then thought it best to get some insider perspective.

"Jamie!"

Telling Cindy to watch the cameras and windows, she handed her the rifle then joined Mike and James. After hearing what James had put together, she said she had an idea that may help.

"He hasn't let his success go to his head, and he's fuckin' brazen. Really. I mean, he has porn being produced here, sounds like he's got men in the major cities, and he has women out recruiting. That's a lot of exposure. Any of those people could turn on him if nabbed. I think he's one of those psychos who gets off on thinking they're so smart they have everyone fooled."

Mike was thinking about it, and after talking to him on the phone, said that was his impression.

"He was playing games. Taunting me. He couldn't have known I was an agent from Sharon. She didn't know. He knew my name and he found out through his own methods. And even then, he was pretty sure of himself calling me and suggesting I hand over my sister to save myself. It's like he was grooming me…"

Jamie said that's how they do things.

"They act fearless, and they use loved ones to control people."

Mike nodded, saying that was the profile, but he seemed beyond that. He was cold as ice, and he knew what he was doing. Looking at them both, he was realizing what they were up against.

"If he's got the goods on world leaders, that means he must have intel coming from our agencies, or agency data feeds."

James was slowly nodding, saying that made sense.

"Yeah, that's what I'm worried about. An IT guy finally getting laid while working at any of the intel agencies could get him a ton of data. And it would be current. Mike, if he's in like that, it isn't safe here. We should get out soon as we can. I don't think it's good to wait."

Looking at Jamie, he said that he and James would haul the weapons and money, and asked her to get everyone ready.

"Say we don't want to take any chances, which is what it is. And we need to find a place where he…"

Each of them ducking as they heard Cindy firing the AR-15, they all had their pistols out, Jamie crawling to the pantry for more rifles.

Cindy shouted, "Garage!" and as soon as she did, there was the sound of the garage door being smashed open and cars crunching.

Yelling to Cindy to keep watching the front of the house, he told Jamie he and James would handle the garage, she had the back of the house. She nodded and crawled off, saying it was bound to be from all sides.

Working their way to the house door into the garage, they weren't hearing any new noises. Mike looked at James, and he knew the tactic.

"Diversion. Make us work this door. I'm going to go out and confirm that, so shut the door after me. Go work the back with Jamie."

James understood. They would do the obvious and enter from doors or windows, not the garage. On the count of three he opened the door as Mike jumped out with his rifle ready to fire at anything that moved. James slammed it shut, bolting it.

"Jamie… Mike thinks the garage was a diversion to get us there. The back is most likely. It has lights. Turn them on."

On the wall next to the back door where she was standing, she went to its security panel, hit the button for back yard lights, and lights flooded it. She also turned-on lights for the front. Cindy called out that Mike was at the front door, and she was letting him in. Mike had already punched in a code, and the door opened. He let himself in saying to keep guard, at least for a while as he talked to James.

Standing in the foyer, he called to James, saying for Jamie to keep watching. James crouched as he made his way to the hall to the garage where he was out of the line of any possible fire. He saw the look on Mike's face, and he understood. He shook his head, clearly upset.

Unbolting the garage door, Mike waved for James to come with him. He didn't seem worried about anyone being there. He walked with his rifle up and ready, but it wasn't aimed out to the street or driveway.

The garage door had been pulled down off its tracks, the large door laying on top of the cars inside. It had been smashed open by a large tow

truck that was sitting there, running. The driver's side door was open, and Mike slowly walked to it. Standing looking inside, he motioned for James to take a look.

James stood cold when he saw the young girl laying dead with a bullet hole in her head. She was on the passenger side, wearing a nightie, holding a note in her dead hand. Mike looked at James, and they understood they had received a message from Peter.

"I know you haven't met her, but she looks just like Whimsey, the little girl Sharon escaped with. I'm sure that's her little sister."

Reaching in, he carefully took the note from her grasp. The interior lights were on from the driver's door being open. James leaned in as he read it.

"You didn't give me what was mine."

It was printed off an inkjet printer, and it was nothing that could be traced. Mike turned the truck off, and said he needed to be sure it was the girl he thought, and he didn't want her sister to see things the way they were.

"I'll ask if she has anything online showing the two of them together, then, we'll be sure."

James nodded, looked up and listened.

"Mike, this is a residential neighborhood. A nice place. I'm sure neighbors all called this in. But, no blue lights, no firetrucks. Oh, this fucker has a reach that's deep. We need to think things through."

Asking James to stand guard as the garage door was down, he asked if he could get a crew out to fix things up and take the truck and the girl. James was enraged but shook his head that he would take care of it all. Mike said it was just a tow truck that somehow missed that the garage was closed, and James nodded that would be the story. Mike said he wanted to talk to Sharon and Jamie first, and he expected a call. James nodded again, but said he had to get news of the agents watching the foster family house, and the foster parents. He said it in a manner where they both knew it was a formality. To get the girl, Peter's man had to take out the agents watching the house, then the foster parents. They both knew they were all dead. They both stared at each other. It was an all-out assault and they had to put what happens next in motion.

"It'll be on Cindy's or Jamie's lines. I'll add covering those lines to the agency tasks."

Walking into the house, knowing anything could still happen, he was sure Peter wasn't going to push more that night as he would be sure he'd get what he wanted, Sharon. Calling her, he also called to Jamie, and they all sat at the kitchen table.

"I don't think we're going to have more come at us tonight. It was a message from Peter. It's bad, and now's not the time to get emotional."

Showing them the note, they looked at him, and he wanted to make it as precise as possible.

"Cindy had the window open a few inches and fired at a truck coming up the drive and not slowing down. It was a hard-ass tow truck, and supposed to smash through the garage door, the driver gone as soon as it happened. We'll have to watch the security cameras for that. The truck was left on, the driver's side door open. Inside was a little girl holding this note for us to find. She had been shot in the head. I'm sure it's Whimsey's sister."

For all she had been through, Sharon couldn't help but start heaving. Jamie grabbed her and took her to the sink, and she vomited and was in convulsions. Jamie looked back at him, and she was shaking her head. She was cold as ice, and she was livid. She knew how brutal such men were, and the speed of what happened had her by surprise.

"Jamie, when she can, get her to lay down upstairs. She's the one he wants, and she's been through a lot. Nothing of this to Whimsey. Have Angie ask her to see pictures of her and her sister on IG or anyplace they are on. I'll need your phone, and Cindy's, so send Cindy with them to me out in the garage…"

Sharon managed to stand up.

"Mike, it was the shock. I'll be okay. We need to get out of here. Can we get the cars out?"

"James has a team coming that can handle that. We have to talk in a bit once James contacts his teams. We're not going to make this mistake twice. We attack, not run."

Jamie looked at him, nodding.

"Mike, how about getting a jet, or maybe a helicopter. Ram his fucking garage on his island."

Admiring her clarity during the horrible events, he agreed.

"That's what I was thinking as well. Aside from Whimsey's poor sister, none of us have any family to worry about, so yeah, we do it right.

We cut the head off this snake right now."

Just as he finished, he heard Jamie's phone ringing. She took it out of her pocket and handed it to him.

"Did you think I was making idle threats? Now, I want what is mine or you all die."

"Peter, you think you know me. You don't. I used to deliver messages just like that. That's why they hired me. With all your influence you didn't learn collateral damage doesn't matter to me. Your man didn't stay to fight. You're a fuckin' pussy."

He ended the call.

"Get him wondering to gain some time. I'm going to ask James about a way to get to the island tonight. I'll be back in a bit."

Out in the garage, James was on his phone, holding his hand up to indicate he was almost done. Once off the phone, before he could say anything, Mike told them what they needed and had planned.

"Mike, since I was here, it was an attack on me so I can get a jet to Cuba, then a chopper to the island. What I can't get is an invasion team ready that quick. That requires a number of agencies."

"I wouldn't want that anyway. It'll just be us. Precision take-down. A copter with water buoys so we can use an inflatable to go in. He's on guard all the time, but not from something like that. He just called and I told him this was the same stuff I did for the agency and it didn't faze me. I was as cold as he was. I'm sure he'll have to think about that."

"Big risk going in like that, especially as you're the only one trained at doing this. I could get a team together, our guys, have them go in with you."

Just then, at that suggestion, Mike thought about Cindy's mother.

"James, I think I have a way to do this right. Cindy's mom is the most powerful trafficker right now. She has lots of weight, and he's too smart to piss her off. I think I'll have Cindy call her and tell her that Peter rammed her home and threatened to kill her. I think a call from her will make him stop and think what price there is to pay if he messes with her."

"Okay, I agree. She'll most likely hit him hard no matter what because of this. So, have Cindy tell her to call him, then wait and see what she gets back from him?"

"James, we're not little girls with our dresses on fire. Yeah, she'll tell

him he's through, and he'll be getting ready to jet out and get out of the line of fire. And that's when we'll be there. Get him as he has to get out with all his data and money, gold, evidence. When he's out and headed to the plane, he'll be in our sights. I want to nick him, then bring him in, though. I want to break him. Right now, we need a tank to get us to our plane."

"One's on the way to get you guys out of here. It's armored. The big Suburbans we just got in are tanks."

Leaving James to arrange for the equipment and get them going as soon as the pilot had the engines on, he went and told everyone the plan. He told Cindy to call her mother on the way.

"Let her know it was a hit on you. Tell her we're going there. Have her keep him tied up if she can. Negotiations or whatever works."

Within fifteen minutes, they were ready to head out, something they had trained for. As they were gathering in the garage, a huge black Suburban pulled up, and James said he wasn't taking any chances even though it was one of his men driving. Going over to the Suburban, James opened the driver's door, saying he'd take it from there, instructing the man to wait in the house for a cleanup crew. Waving everyone on, they all got in, including Whimsey. Mike realized they hadn't discussed what best to do with her, and they would figure that out on the way. In the third row, which didn't have much room for anyone, Cindy and Angie seemed to fit just right, and Cindy was on her phone sending a text code for her mother to call. There wasn't much of a wait when she got the call.

Listening to her speaking Ukrainian, Mike smiled as Cindy hit all the right buttons.

"Momma, did you tell anyone I was coming or going to be working with you? Hmm, then it must be because of Mike's sister... yes, the one who was trafficked in Morocco... Well, she showed up at his door tonight after she managed to kill one of the men taking her to a plane... Yes, with her belt, strangled him then ran over him a few times. Mike brought her to my house. We just moved in, so too soon for anyone to know where he'd be... Him, his sister, and a little girl they were shipping out... They're okay... But, I'm not... No, not hurt, Angie's okay too... The trafficker hit my house, momma! They had a big tow truck and rammed through the garage to leave us a note... Yes, my beautiful new

house we just moved into… It's all wrecked… Who? Oh, the man who trafficked Mike's sister… He called Mike and said he'd start killing us if he didn't give her back… Yes! Angie and me included… You must know him. We're on our way to his island to take him down… Of course I'm going too. He smashed my new house… Oh, we only know his name is Peter, and he's on some island off of Cuba… No, we're on our way. The jet's waiting. We'll be using a copter to land in the water and get him… No, momma, we can handle it… You saw what I did to that sheik… well, I don't want to alert him that we're coming… Alright, alright… When you call… You promise not to say anything? Well, I was looking forward to blasting him, but I'll wait for you to call. Bye, momma."

James stared at Mike. Mike smiled at him, grinning.

"Told ya."

CHAPTER 18

Whimsey was alert but confused by the loud crash and sudden exit from the house. Sitting in the second row of the Suburban, she was looking to Sharon, asking where they were going and what had happened. Mike could hear her, and turned to say they were going to stop the man who had taken Sharon to own, and he was angry. He looked at Sharon, who nodded for him to say what he thought best.

"Sharon told me that she explained a little of what had happened to her. That she was taken and was owned by that man, and if she didn't do everything he wanted, he'd kill her. I know you were drugged, so do you remember that?"

"That was when we were taking a shower... and she said I could never tell anyone."

"Whimsey, you were being watched and heard by hidden cameras. They had already made plans to take and sell you to some rich bastard to be his possession. They drugged you and a man took both of you and was heading to the airport. Well, there was an accident, and you both escaped, and Sharon found a way to get to me and get you away from being sold."

Shaking her head, she looked at Sharon who was nodding, letting her know it was true.

"I was just an actress. I didn't know they did those things. I was working to get my sister and me away from my foster dad..."

Mike held his hand to let Sharon know he would break the sad news. She held on to Whimsey's hand, knowing this was going to be devastating for her.

"I know, Whimsey. We all know you wanted to protect her. We had to leave the house because the man who was going to sell you, had you drugged so you'd wake up someplace and wouldn't know where... Well, he thought my sister was someone he owned. He thinks he can own people, and nobody can. He was really furious at her, and he wants her back."

Looking at him, she asked him if the man wanted her back too.

"I'm sure he does. He's more concerned about Sharon because she knows too much about what he does. Yes, he still wants her because he thinks he owns her, and even though I'm her brother and I've been

searching for her for the last two years, he doesn't care. He has men working for him just about everywhere, and that loud crash you heard was one of his men and he smashed the garage in with a tow truck. It was something horrible. A message. About what he'll do to get Sharon back…"

Having learned the only way to deliver bad news was to come out and say it, he looked at Sharon, shook his head, then looked back to Whimsey.

"This is really going to hurt, Whimsey. To protect you, it's something you need to know. When the truck crashed through the garage door, the message to me was in your sister's hand. To get to us, hurt all of us, he had your sister killed. She's dead, and I'm so sorry…"

Not able to finish his last words, Whimsey was in hysterics saying it couldn't be, that it was some other girl. She hadn't even given them her right address.

"Whimsey, I know we don't want bad things to be real. But, I'm sure it was her. I'm going to show you a picture. It's just her face. Let's be sure. Take a look…"

Holding up the cell phone he used to record what happened, he took one picture that didn't show the bullet hole in the girl's head. She looked like she was asleep, and he also needed to be sure it was her. Whimsey leaned forward, then cried out it was her, over and over.

Sharon got out of her seat and went to hold her, saying she had to know. It was important that they got her away and the man driving, James, worked for the government and would have a place where she couldn't be found. She needed her to trust James. Whimsey started thrashing and hitting at Sharon, not to hurt, to make her stop holding her.

"If he didn't protect my sister, how's he going to protect me?"

Sobbing, they were nearing the landing strip for the jet, and Mike needed to get her right.

"I didn't know you had a sister until right before it happened. We didn't know the man would do anything to her and we were all attacked. That's what we're doing now. We're going to find him and kill him. And to take care of you, I turned to the man driving. His name is James, and he works for the CIA, and he'll make sure you can't be found. I'm sorry Whimsey. We all are. We're devastated, but we know now how mad the

man is, and the only thing we can do is to stop him. We are going to do it for your little sister. We only have a minute or two, but you need to do what James says. He's a good man, and once we get on the plane, he's the only one who'll be able to hide you."

Turning to James, Whimsey was crying hysterically, and they had just passed the guard gate at the Air Force field where the plane was running and ready. James drove right to the stairs going into the plane, and guards came to open their doors and help carry their bags and weapons. As Sharon got out, Whimsey stayed in her seat, crying not to leave her. Sharon went to hug her and told her they would get the man who did it, and she'll see her soon once everyone was safe.

Sharon had stayed strong, but once the Suburban drove away, she grabbed Mike and was crying. He said it was time to get on the plane and take care of the fucker. She looked up, nodded, and then saw that Jamie, Cindy and Angie were all crying as they boarded the plane with her. As they got in the jet and sat down, Mike remained standing, looking at them all.

"That was brutal. With so little time, we needed to get her to not run off from James. She'd go to her home and that would have been what Peter wanted. We'll need to get her some help when we get back."

Jamie had watched it all, and thought of all the little girls she had put in that situation. The man who had worked for her had sex with the girls as part of his incentive to keep secrets, and for her to film and be able to stop him by turning him in if needed. He had got off on choking girls, saying the first time it was an accident. When it happened a second time, she decided all she could do was stop him. Telling the trafficker who owned her that the man was damaging his goods, he allowed her to execute him in front of buyers as a show of what happens to ones who touch his merchandise. All Jamie knew was she had stopped him. It was a sick business at every level.

As the jet took off, they all knew what would come next. They weren't scared. They were all anxious to stop Peter. The only one who didn't want to personally kill him was Mike. He wanted to use him and have him suffer the way women had. He would have no mercy on him, but dead men feel no pain.

Asking Mike if her phone would work on the plane, he assured her it had wifi and her phone was already connected. Angie was checking the settings.

"Mom, you want to install a target practice app?"

As she asked, the phone rang and she handed it back to Cindy. Nodding it was her mother, everyone stayed quiet and listened.

"I can't turn back. The planes in the air and we'll land in about an hour. Did you talk to the man… What did he say… Now he wants to kill you too… Does he know who you are… he doesn't care… so, you see why we want to stop him… yes… he sounds weird… do you have men in Cuba? That's too bad… Yes, I think it's good you send your men there… That will take time… Well, maybe wait. If we take him down I may just take over his operation right there… No, I know I don't know much about it, but we can run it together… Okay, I'll let you know once we're finished… I understand… I know this worries you. Talk to you in a while."

Looking back at Angie, she said having a target practice app on her phone would be good and she handed her the phone. Mike was thinking about the conversation.

"He blew her off. That says a lot. He's so sure of himself, or he wants to appear to be. Either way, what he did each step of the way makes him a psycho. It doesn't sound like he'll be running to his jet to get away. That will make this harder."

Angie had been listening, and when Mike finished, she said she had an idea based on what he said.

"Mike, he doesn't know mom or me. Maybe just our names and where we live. So, like, if he's not running for his life, and he's holed up in his castle thing, I think there's a way in and I'm it."

Everyone looked at her, not sure what she was getting at, and she could see they hadn't figured out the obvious. She got up for some water, asking anyone else if they wanted some. They all said they wanted to know what she was talking about, not water. She took a drink, then sat back down.

"Well, you said the satellite video showed lots of girls running around, doing all kinds of stuff, a lot of them naked, probably rich guys there too. I bet he doesn't know all the girls he has trapped there as there are new ones coming all the time. Everyone understand?"

Shaking his head, Mike looked at Cindy and Jamie, then back to her.

"And, as you're young as those girls, you wander onto the beach and make your way into the house, acting like you arrived and all, right?"

"Mike, you got it. Think of how easy that is? I either act really scared, or if I'm one who's been doing a rich guy for a while, act really comfortable and hot. I talk to some girls, ask how they like their rooms and stuff. Maybe ask to see their clothes or something. Get in, stumble into wherever he's lurking, then pop goes the Peter. I take him down."

With all eyes on her, she shrugged.

"Pretty simple plan. I know you, well, couldn't think of it as you're not a teen like me."

Looking at her, Cindy was thinking it through, then shared her reaction.

"Well, it's dangerous. But, just us being there is. It makes sense to me, but I have one question. The girls there are naked or probably scantily clad. Where are you going to hide a gun?"

"Mom! Basic sex stuff. They're either naked or they're in some sexy outfit. I'd be in some frilly thing, and with my small Glock, it won't be seen until I need it."

Angie watched as they all looked at each other. They all were uncertain, and at the same time it made sense. Mike had a question.

"Okay. Let's say all that is how it is there. And somehow you make it in. Where the hell are you going to get a frilly outfit?"

Looking at him, shaking her head in disbelief, Angie got up and went to get her duffel bag. Putting it on her seat, she rummaged through it, and pulled out a black cami full of lace and ruffles.

"You said to pack our stuff. This is what kind of stuff pervs go for. It's one mom used to wear when she was... well, you know."

Mike looked at Cindy and Jamie, and then Sharon. He talked to her first.

"You just came out of that world a day ago. You know his idea of marketable goods. If Angie was wearing that, would she fit in the place, or look like a plant?"

As Angie was holding in front of her, fluffing it up, then holding it up to see how see-through it was, Sharon asked her if she had nylons and a garter.

"Sharon, my mom was a pro... Sorry mom, really. My mom was a sex worker. Of course I do. It goes with her tawdry work clothes."

Cindy started to laugh.

"Sweetie, you don't have to mince words. It's what I did, and

everyone knows it. I'm not ashamed, okay?"

Sharon wasn't laughing, she was looking at Angie and the outfit.

"I think she'd fit right in. That's a classic outfit. With clients, you don't start off naked. The way it goes is you tease first. A hint of what's under it. If they want to see more, they pay. That's for the top-dollar girls, the ones who aren't doing porn or preview videos and then men are paying to see what they can do. Angie, well, she's certainly a top-dollar item, so that would make her one. The ones naked are being sold at a low price, or there to service the buyers while they shop."

They were close to the time for landing, and a decision needed to be made. Mike knew what would work best.

"Okay, everyone. I think we go in, and if we see the plane being loaded and Peter is about to scoot because he knows Cindy's mom was serious and he was bluffing, we take him on the runway. If that's not what's going on, and it's business as usual, Angie puts that on, attempts to get in, and after that, it's not where we could help her."

Sharon said she had been thinking more about it.

"Mike, I've been to showcases. Once to his island, but also Hawaii and other islands. It isn't just teens. There's a range of both teens and full women. I can't go in, he knows me and is looking for me. But, Cindy is way hotter than anyone I've ever seen at things. I think if there's another outfit, they could both play it."

Angie was riffling through her bag and came out with a black silk robe with lace that revealed selected parts. She handed it to Cindy, who shook her head in wonder.

"I was wondering where that went! What next, go at him with a dildo or a butt plug? How much do you have in there?"

Looking in, Angie stood up, saying not everything, but she did bring some toys, but no butt plug. Mike knew Cindy was teasing her, but Angie was smart to bring all the things needed when dealing with sick men.

"Angie, that was smart to bring. Did you leave room for any guns or ammo?"

"Mike, like, I'm not a first timer. I was on the auction block with mom, remember. And wearing a burka and then this thing, when we went shopping with you when we were in Moscow."

Pulling out a micro thong, she held it high, looking at it.

"No place for the Glock, though."

Somehow, Angie's intended innocence had worked in getting everyone realizing that Angie was both angry, and serious, about taking down traffickers. The methods they used to take people had snared her, and her mother as well. She had evaded the predators and pedophiles where they had lived. The mobile home park they had lived in was home to drug dealers, pimps, and ex-cons, all hitting on her daily. As early as six they had started inviting her to get high and have sex. Make easy cash by having sex. Having a nice dinner by having sex. She had learned how her mother was raised with human traffickers and knew how good they were at taking someone from plain sight. Then, trying to get the two of them out of the mobile home park, she thought she could earn money as a model. Going to an audition, it turned out to be a way to kidnap her and her mother.

"Well, let's hope it doesn't get down to that." Cindy wasn't laughing when she said that to Angie. A strip search, a metal detector, a, "who are you," from some guard.

"Wear something that you can put a box cutter in."

"Mom, oh, silly me! I forgot about the box cutters!"

Laughing, reaching back in the bag, she pulled out a box filled with them. There were also single-edged razor blades if a metal detector found a gun, and the box cutter. A single-edged razor could be put where it may be overlooked. Mike was thinking the plan through and asked the hard question.

"Angie, I agree you are the only one who can get in as one of the other girls. The big question is if that should happen, and if you should find out where Peter is, and if you should get close to him, could you pull the trigger or slice him if you don't have the gun?"

She stood still, the thong still in her hand. Her face made her answer clear.

"Look at my face. What part don't you understand? I think it's poetic justice a teen should kill him. I wrote this while my mom was on the phone with my grandmother. I'll stuff it in his mouth as he looks at me as he's dying."

Mike took the small note and handed it around. In red marker she had scrawled.

"Just a little whimsey."

CHAPTER 19

"Peter, want me to put your things on plane?"

Looking at his pilot, Peter gave him a look of not knowing what he was talking about.

"Why would you do that?"

"I heard you tell crew that Uke bitch to come after you. No good to be here during battle like that."

"Nick, I have no plans to leave. I was just letting them know to arm up in case any of her men come to try to talk to me. Just keep to the shipment schedule."

Waiting until his pilot left, Peter called his man in Kiev. He had no interest in what other traffickers did but wanted to learn what it would take to put the arrogant woman in her place. Or grave, he thought to himself.

After two rings, his man answered and he heard music in the background, asking him if he was out finding his allocation.

"It good night. Many dumb fucks, drunk, tits and ass hanging out. Drop pill in drink, get them ready to send you. So, boss man, what can I do for you?"

"First, make sure they're all underage. See if they have sisters. You know how to do that, but always good to let you know I look them up. I'm calling to find out about a woman you may have heard of. A trafficker of some sort, in the Ukraine. I didn't catch her full name, but her first name is Eliana."

Waiting, there was only the sound of club music on the phone. After near a minute, his man managed to start talking again.

"That is not good name to say here. I will just say bitch is her name. If I may, please to tell why she call?"

"If it helps, yes. She threatened to kill me over some girl I had killed as a message. It seems she had some interest in my matters as she said it was stepping on her toes. She made some threat that she was going to send an army and kill me, take over my operations. A lot of threats, but that's what small time operators think works. That's all I know. I couldn't find out anything online about her, if that's her real name. Do you know who I am speaking of?"

Listening to the volume of the music get quieter, it was obvious his

man had walked to a place where he could have some privacy to talk. It made it easier to hear him, and he was glad he did.

"Boss, everyone in business knows her. Biggest trafficker in Eastern Europe. Ruthless killer. Has governments in her power. No small time operation. Biggest one. If she make threat, she will do what she says."

Not impressing Peter, he was tapping his fingers on his desk, thinking how best to stop such a problem.

"If she's so powerful, how is it that you can pull girls out of the Ukraine?"

Again, a long pause. He was interested in what the answer to that question would be.

"Here, she only gets brides. Ones older than you say. She sends all over world. Rich men here, they can have own men get local bitches. She no care about locals."

Watching his fingers tapping, he was already tired of the story. He knew what he wanted to do.

"I am going to offer you two options. Kill her by tomorrow, or I kill you by tomorrow night."

Pressing the end button, he felt strongly that any threats be dealt with by stopping them dead. His world was one he created and controlled, and he would do what he always had. Eliminate anyone in his way. There had been many traffickers who had approached him in the past wishing to combine organizations and not compete against each other. He had them killed and took over their business after first acting interested and gaining a view into their activities and clients. The woman making her threats would be another one he eliminated by being in his way, or who challenged him.

Making more calls to Russia and Eastern Europe, once he mentioned her name, although just her first name, people became quiet and said it wasn't good to talk about her as she was too well connected and most likely was monitoring their calls. One man in Poland mentioned she was the most ruthless person he knew in any illegitimate enterprise, and to be cautious doing business with her. None would reveal her full name or how to contact her, or anything about her. He told the man she sounded much like him, and how he allowed none to know of his activities.

"Peter, comparing is not if you are the same or different. You keep a low profile. Eliana, she wears power as a badge, an invitation to challenge

her. She is feared because she does what she says. Her threats are not threats, they are guarantees. She will do what she says."

Finishing his calls, he thought about when she called, she made no threat. She told him he would be dead. Thinking she did seem confident, and his man had such a strong reaction, one never revealed regarding any other competitor, he started thinking more about if staying on the island was to her benefit. It would make it easy for her to find him and may cost him time and money by disrupting business.

Thinking more, it may seem that he took her threat seriously, and was evading her. A clash was inevitable, and he'd be on his own property with his own team to do the battle.

Then he started wondering about her. What she looked like? What if she was attractive and could disguise herself to be a new scout or taker? He thought it best to get a photo of her, and some background to share with his guards. He doubted his man in Kiev would succeed at killing her, so best to be prepared and approach the matter when she arrived, if she was coming herself. After calling Kiev with a change of plans to secure a photo and background information, he went back to matters at hand, particularly with a new group of young teens who had just arrived, and he wanted to fuck.

CHAPTER 20

Walking to her armored Maybach, Eliana told her driver to call ahead to her pilot that she would be leaving and have the jet ready for a flight to an island near Cuba. Handing him her bag, she first opened it to be sure she had enough ammo for her guns and counted the number of secured satellite phones. Nodding, as she prepared the bag herself, she told him to get her garment bag from the main house.

After the ride to her jet, then on-board, she called Cynthia.

"Cynthia, no what you planned. I am no sending men. I am sending me. I am on my way. Seven hours most. I go in with you."

Being told her daughter had a plan, she asked her to share it. Listening, she smiled as it reminded her of what she would do in the same situation. She thought it simple and effective but had risks.

"That puts Angelia at risk. If it is not just as planned, man will take her and then a bigger problem will be for you... I know she is trained. Trained not same as bullet to head with man... I know, you did it, she watched, but still, question is if she ready? First one is hard, after that, not so much... I have been thinking, that is why I come. As she is out with him, if I appear, him, guards, they all be looking at me. That is good time for shot. She doesn't need look at him, just side of head. I told him I was going to kill him, so good distraction."

Hearing her daughter tell Angelia and the others of her idea, there was little bickering or debate. Cynthia told her they'd need to plan things a bit more as Peter didn't seem to be worried and may not be out heading to his plane. She had ideas about that.

"He has shipments coming in. He will be out. He must inspect, count, make sure no games played. We wait for plane to land, then move in. We talk more when I land. I'll have pilot send you when, where. We get to see each other sooner than planned, yes? And do business too? Good to get you going."

Satisfied she'd be there to be sure nothing happened to Angelia or Cynthia, she could relax and read *Teen Vogue* to see what fashions were coming for her new sales to look best. Looking at the ads, she shook her head in disgust at how trashy fashion had gone. It put everything a girl had on display, making young bodies less hard to see or get. Thinking the world had made it where sex had less value, it was harder to sell even

girls in their mid-teens. She had been thinking about putting them all on OnlyFans, as that could bring in more cash for one girl than selling her. That may be something for Angelia to manage. Times changed, and she had changed with them. It was what customers would want, not what she thought they should have.

Opening her wallet, she had a picture of her two children when they were still under five. She had thought of not carrying it as if she was killed or her wallet taken, she wouldn't want Cynthia tracked down. Even though the photo wasn't current, few people knew she had children, and even those didn't know where Cynthia lived or why she had no contact with her for so long.

Drinking a sparkling water, she cringed at how naive she had been when young. Her boyfriend was a horrible person, but he was the only one who pulled her out of prostitution and offered to marry her. He was fearless, intense, savage in bed, and he was making more money than she thought anyone could ever make. It was her one chance out of a life of fucking officers and politicians for a loaf of bread or a few rubles. She didn't know any girl her age when she was a young teen who wasn't whoring herself out and working the street. The world was prostitutes and men who used and abused them. Parents lived in fear, and girls who didn't work the streets were raped and didn't get a loaf a bread. The men never got in trouble. They drank at social clubs and told how many girls they raped and kept their money in their pockets while having their dick sucked at gunpoint. It was a hard world, and her husband made it his. He took control of the whores and had no problems killing politicians or soldiers who didn't go through him.

Fearing her husband, the men feared her because she was his property. She'd walk down the street and men who saw her from a distance, thinking she was one they could take in a doorway and fuck, once close enough, seeing it was her, would cross the street and tip their hats. She started carrying a gun in case they were drunk or stupid, and she soon understood why her husband was brutal. The world they lived in was brutal, and only brutal people survived without damage.

Thinking back to the first time her husband brought home a young girl, at most fourteen, and fucked her in their bed, she had reached a point where she didn't feel jealous. He was making sure she knew how to fuck, and above all, be afraid of him if she didn't do what he said.

The girl fought him off as he got on top of her, and he beat her until she stopped and let him do what he wanted. She knew he wasn't fucking her for pleasure, he was making sure he was feared by her. A girl who ran, or who wouldn't do what a paying customer wanted was useless, and he knew how to keep them in line. She started to watch, even advising the girls on how to offer services that would make the most money no matter how depraved. Sex, she learned, was a business. Girls were a commodity. Merchandise. They owned the girls, and that was how the world worked. She made sure the girls made money, had food and were protected from rape, and thought they were better off with her husband as their pimp than on their own.

Taking a deep breath, she thought of Yuri. He was the man who gave her husband drugs to sell, saying that a bit in the girls would keep them tame as lambs and they would need the drugs more than money. A girl addicted was one who not only worked for drugs, she wouldn't care how sick the sex was. She'd do anything for her next little bag of heroin. Yuri was right. First enjoying the drugs as it numbed the girls from rough sex, they quickly became more valuable as when high, they would do anything and pleased the clients with their willingness to submit to perverse acts. They didn't care what they did. They cared about getting high again and again.

Thinking like a doctor who is a fool to prescribe medicine to himself, things changed when her husband started using heroin. Yuri convinced him to try it, his incentive was he would make more money with him high and using his girls to sell drugs to clients. She never used drugs, but saw her husband descend into a state of addiction, losing all his business sense. Like the girls, he cared more about drugs then her, or their children. There were times he would be wonderful. Laughing, carefree, loving. And times he would be a monster. He was a violent man to start with, but when in need of drugs he would lose all sense of caution and attack his girls, and eventually, her and her children. She grew afraid of him, and one day he took her gun away, and began having sex with her son. It was horrific, but she had no way to stop him. One day he raped Cynthia. That was too much for her, and she had to stop him. She had watched where he hid the drugs, money and guns, and decided to kill him.

She smiled at the memory of having a gun in her hand, sitting on a chair in the middle of the kitchen waiting for him to come in. She told

the children to stay back, and she kept the kitchen light off. With his largest caliber pistol in her lap, she recalled how she wasn't worried. She was calm and looking forward to sending him to hell. She knew she'd rather her and her children be dead than to let him do another thing to them. He had crossed the final line. He had fucked with what was hers. Her children.

Lost in the memory, she was back to the moment she saw his silhouette on the kitchen door glass panel. She could feel how heavy the pistol was in her hands. She could hear the breathing of the children looking from the living room. The water dripping in the sink. The dim light shining through the window above the sink. Everything from that moment was distinct, and her adrenaline had her hyper aware of all around her, and swelled up inside of her to fire when he walked into the room.

Remembering the dumb look on his face as he opened the door, wondering why the lights were off, then looking at her sitting there and about to ask what the fuck she was doing. The dumb look turned to a spray of red splatter flying slowly in the air, the door he had closed behind him turning red and light gray with brains and blood, his body flailing, his arms going up as his body gently sunk down to the now-red floor. Her whole body was in motion as she started flying backwards in that one second of time when the bullet blew his head apart. Her hands holding the pistol went to the ceiling, her legs rising up as her back hit the kitchen floor. The recoil from the massive shot sent her back and all she remembered was having a smile as she hit the floor.

Thinking of how time returned, she recalled how her first thought was to be sure she had killed him. Rolling off the side of the chair with the pistol still in her hands, she pointed to him, and waited. She looked, and the children were shocked, but safe. Getting up, she walked to him, saw his once virile body lying in front of the door, and a large hole where his face had been, his head laying in a puddle of brains and blood. Standing over him, she was sure he wasn't going to hurt them ever again, and as a thank you for ever doing anything to them, she spit into the gaping hole where his face once had been.

Shaking her head, she was roused from her memories by the pilot on the speaker in the cabin. He said they'd be landing in about twenty minutes. She had just enough times to think about how she went to his

stash, got the drugs, money and guns and both bought and blasted her way out of the Ukraine and with forged papers, took her children to America. Buying them a mobile home, giving money for them to live on to a Ukrainian lawyer, telling him she'd be back if he spent a penny of it the wrong way, she returned to the Ukraine and went on a rampage killing off pimps and drug dealers, taking their girls, junkies and clients, and ran the business with a vengeance that she still had. She wanted to make a fortune and leave it to her daughter. That needed to happen soon. She was not sure if her health would hold up. Now, with Cynthia being part of the business, her daughter could take revenge on the world that led a man like her father to such depraved acts.

Looking out the window at Cuba, she knew the only way to stop such men was to keep them in line with blackmail and vice. It was the language of power, and she hated any man who thought he could buy a woman.

CHAPTER 21

Being hunted just hours after being reunited with her brother, Sharon hadn't been able to share all that had happened to her since first being taken while in Morocco. Having a small dinner celebration at Cindy's once Mike got her away from his place, the crash of a tow truck into the house's garage with the dead body of Whimsey's young sister inside forced them to leave and take action to stop any more harm to any of them. The trafficker, Peter, was out to reclaim Sharon and make her suffer, and killing anyone who she turned to or cared about was part of the punishment she would face if they didn't stop him.

Having gotten help from James, who Mike had worked with when a field agent taking down traffickers, they had use of a private government jet and were headed to kill Peter. On the flight headed to an island off of Cuba, they learned that Cindy's mother would be joining them in downing Peter. That added five hours to their schedule to go via helicopter to Peter's private island. She wanted to talk to Mike first before sharing her story with the others. Mike was sure Cindy, Angie and Jamie would understand anything she'd been through but respected her need to talk to him confidentially first. Finding a quiet cantina, she and Mike sat at their own table to talk as they ate plantains and pulled pork.

"Mike, there's so much to tell. All horrible. I don't know where to begin. And now, all this because of me. I can't even think of what Whimsey will do now. She was doing everything to protect her sister, and she's dead. Mike, she's dead because of me."

Knowing she was taking all the blame; Mike knew it was Peter who was to blame. She started talking about how she was used, bought, sold, trafficked, and then used to make porn. That, combined with what happened since she ran away, killing a man, and putting everyone at risk, she needed his assurance of how she was not the real reason any of that had happened.

"It's horrible, I know. What kind of man does such a thing to some young girl? Sharon, Peter is a fucked up, sick man who'd fuck her, sell her, and think she was nothing but a thing. No sane person does any of that. There are bad people, and some really sick people in this world. He's top-of-the-list sick. Everything that happened is on his shoulders. Everything. You knew what they had planned for Whimsey and did the

right thing. It's what I would have done. What any decent person would do. I'm proud of you."

Poking at her meal, she heard him, but it would take time for her to put the truth against how it felt that day. Mike needed to understand the events of her escape all the way back to how she was first taken. Saying what would help him most was understanding how Peter operated, he asked what happened to her from the start, then what led up to her escape. She looked at him, shaking her head.

"My God, Mike. Everything… Just a total nightmare that never stopped. The worst thing is what it does to a person's head. I tell you; I thought I was a strong, independent woman who didn't fall for any bullshit. In no time they had me where I felt happy if a customer said I was a somewhat decent fuck. I actually would get excited because they wouldn't kick the shit out of me or let me eat. It's not just bodies they take. It's your head…"

Nodding, Mike said he had met many who were trafficked, and they shared that experience. He knew she needed to hear how he saw it the same way.

"I know. It's grooming, mind control, brainwashing… all that. But, at the heart of it? Fear. You know they'll kill you and not even think about it after the bullet's in your brain. I'm sure you learned that early and fast."

Staring at him, she looked heartbroken. She closed her eyes and shook her head, then put her head in her hands before saying more. Lifting her head, she looked at him and he could see the pain in her eyes.

"Ah, Mike. A bullet in the head would have been kindness. That's not what they did. Oh, God, that's not what gets you doing their fucking shit. The first time I saw a kill, I was in a cage somewhere. It was in a courtyard… a private mansion with a big courtyard. It was lined with cages and each one had a girl. I was the oldest. The rest were all really young. Ten, twelve. They wanted all of us to understand what happens when we complained or didn't do everything they said. This… wow, I can't get it out of my head. Mike… hold on a second…"

Taking a large drink of soda, she needed to ready herself. She needed to tell the story and see if she could stop thinking about it once she did.

"There was a little middle eastern girl and she tried to run away. They caught her, dragged her to the middle of the courtyard and there were

four men with rifles. All in sheaths… and head coverings. There was a table. Oh, that fucking table. They cuffed her hands and ankles, then they each fucked the shit out of her. She was screaming in pain. It wasn't to punish her, they just wanted to fuck her. What assholes… but that was nothing. They started doing shit no person should ever go through. They did their own shit first. Pissed on her, hit her. One shit on her… Then, Peter came. He had them hose her down, clean the area so he fucking wouldn't get dirty. He looked at each of us. A look of here's what happens if you don't obey me. A man brought out a cattle prod. It had a wire, and… oh, God, he rammed it in her ass. Then he flicked a little switch on it, and it started to shock her. Longer each time he flipped the switch. It went on for over an hour, at least. She was passing out each time, but the men would douse her with cold water and Peter would tell her not to pass out. We were all completely silent. I was seeing the most horrible thing possible and didn't say stop. If any of us did, it would be whoever did on the table next. Everyone knew not to make a sound. Then, with it in her, electric fully on, a guard handed him a knife and he slit her throat. Just like that. Walked up, did it, didn't even look down. Her body was still twitching from the electricity even though she was dead. Then Peter walked slowly to each cage and calmly asked each of us if we wished to be next. Then he left. The guards left the girl there, and fucking crows started going at her…"

Amazed she had been able to tell the whole story without stopping, she finished and started heaving and sobbing, saying "poor thing" over and over again. Mike understood how that would change anyone into someone who would do whatever Peter wanted. It was a classic method used throughout time. It was to create terror to get victims to not only be afraid of dying, but more about how they would die. He was glad she got the story out. It would never go away, but she had finally been able to talk about it to someone who wouldn't hurt her if she did.

"I'm sorry you saw that, that you were taken, that you lived in fear. That's why we're here. We're all going to stop him. I tell you what, it's probably better to talk about all that happened to you with someone who can help you cope with it all. I have a friend… a psychiatrist. His name is Charles. He helped me with things when I needed help, and I think he'd be good to take you through things and get an idea of how to help you. I wouldn't suggest it if I didn't believe in him. He's not one to

say you'll be okay now or anything. He told me I had a right to be angry. Just hearing that helped. I was feeling guilty. After time with him, I was angry and decided to stop photography and take down as many Peters as possible. That helped me, and it's helped save people. So, for now, maybe, if you can, tell me anything about Peter that could help us all when we go get him. I have a question, but first, think about any quirky things about him. His habits, what he gets off on, well, sexually."

Hearing how she could help Mike with things only she would know changed her from despair to serious thinking about all Mike had asked. She ate a bit more, saying she was thinking about it all. The waiter brought flan when they were finished, and she ate hers as she talked.

"The thing that was hardest to deal with was that he's a complete blank. Not cold. Blank, like he was dead. He never showed an emotion. No reactions to anything. His words were cold and cruel, always threatening, but to look at him, it was like there was nothing inside of him."

Thinking how that could have been a way of controlling minds and creating fear, it was hard to be like that all the time, but it sounded like he was just as she said. A walking corpse, a zombie. He said that was good to know, and she continued.

"He doesn't like anything messy. I had to go to where he was working, and his homes, and they were sparse. Bare. Like him, but all around him. No warmth, no dust, nothing out of place. I'm sure he only wears suits. Expensive suits always perfectly pressed. A tie too."

Mike was thinking it through. He asked her more about his places.

"Any pictures on his desk, or walls? Any art?"

"No. Sparse, nothing like any of that. His desk had nothing on it. Not even a phone. And him, sitting upright behind it, not moving much even when really mad. It was intimidating."

"It could be intentional, but I think with the other things, probably not. I didn't mean to interrupt. Sorry."

"No, ask questions. Please. Let's see. Quirks. I think, if it's a quirk, that he couldn't talk for a while after I said anything to him. At first, I thought he was thinking about what I said, but that wasn't it. I'd see him when one of his men came in with a question or something he wanted. The man would ask a question, then a long pause, like… at least a minute before he'd answer. I mean things like being asked if he wanted a

glass for bottled water. He'd just look at the man and wait. It was weird."

Thinking he may be more than a psychopath, he clearly had some kind of mental problem. Maybe it took that long for him to process a response. That was a strange behavior. He nodded, and she continued.

"His habits? Oh, he was all about that. He ate the same thing each meal, ate at the same time, sat in the same place, wore different suits each day, but the same one on each day week to week. He was like a machine. Precision everything. So, that… But sexually, there's where it all comes together. He was a creature of habit in that department. Each day at three, he'd have a new young girl brought into a special room. All that was in there was a clock, a rug, and one wall was all mirrored. She'd be naked with her head on the floor, her ass up in the air. Hands tied behind her back, a ball gag in her mouth. It had to be a different girl each day, all had to be younger than teen years. Right at three-thirty, he'd take his dick out without taking off his pants, and he'd be rock hard and fuck her in the ass. Then he'd pull out and tell her to kneel and clean him up. Get all her ass shit off his dick, and as she did that he'd come again, on her face. He'd be sure he was clean, put it back in his pants and walk out. All I ever heard was he fucked the youngest ones in the ass once, never twice. With the porn shoots, he'd never do any of the girls. He would inspect, but not touch. Weird shit, Mike. He's a fucking creep."

Mike agreed he was a wacko, and it's almost as if he created the trafficking operation to fulfill his crazy quirks and perverted sex habits.

"Mike! I thought the same thing, and still do. I mean, what if a guy is like that, and needs a new little girl each day. Trafficking was all about that. Having that ass up in the air at three-thirty each day, waiting for him. That would cost a lot if he wasn't a trafficker."

Mike said with such a person, that may be.

"It is the profile of serial killers and others who work out a world of their own to satisfy some sick need."

He had his question but knew it had taken a lot out of Sharon to tell what she had. He said he had the question he thought of earlier, and if she could answer, they'd go join the others and share some of the quirks. She nodded.

"When you talked about seeing the girl killed, you said it created terror in you. Did you ever see anyone do anything back to him. I mean

him thinking they were complying and obeying him, then kicked him in the nuts or had a knife and swiped at him. Anything like that at all?"

She looked surprised. It was revealing to him that she was still operating from the place she had been when held captive, and it would take a long time for automatic responses to leave her. As he finished the question, she looked at him with an incredulous expression.

"You don't do that to Peter!"

As soon as she said it, she realized what had happened and why Mike had waited to ask. She looked at him with an expression of horror and shock.

"Oh, my God, Mike! That's exactly how I would have reacted during it all. Mike, I'm still defending him!"

She sat, frozen. He knew she understood what it meant. She had been conditioned so long that she was still protecting him. That's what slaves and kidnapped people do after prolonged programming. They start to seek approval from their captor, continuing to defend him and protect him.

"Sharon, that's why I'd like you to see my shrink. Years of being brainwashed makes anyone side with the captor to survive. The fear of going through what that poor girl went through is so total you think that being on his side will save you from that. It's common for people in your situation. It took time to happen, it will take time to get gone. That was a conditioned response. I think it's why you're still alive. How many girls were killed during the time you were there?"

Staring at him with a look of despair, she said she didn't know how many because there were too many to keep track of. Then she paused, and tears ran down her cheeks.

"And you don't care. I mean, I didn't care. I was glad it was them, not me."

CHAPTER 22

Looking over to where Mike and Sharon were eating and talking, Cindy saw they had serious expressions and at times Sharon was in tears. She understood that after going through all she had, and then escaping with Whimsey, she had the added burden of what happened because she escaped. The dead young girl was another torture she would endure. She thought of how she felt responsible for her brother's suicide, and it was a pain that never left her. Looking at Angie, she too felt shame and guilt for going to the photo shoot that led to both of them being trafficked. Jamie? She was much like Sharon, but worse. She had to do unspeakable acts to survive and make the attempt to kill her trafficker. All of them, including Mike, had gone through hell and were looking for a way to climb out and forgive themselves, and each other.

In a few hours she would see her mother, and that was worrying her. She had led her mother on that she wanted to join her in the trafficking business. She was still hurt and angry at Eliana for letting her sick father rape her and her brother. Inside, she knew the truth was she wanted to destroy her and make her understand the pain she allowed to happen to them. In their recent talks her mother seemed different. Not from her power and success, but from a place of pain. Her offer to be part of her empire was a way to seek forgiveness, and there was more going on with her than a family reunion or making up for past deeds. Looking at everyone she was with; each person had done things that they would regret all their lives. She had killed a man, been a glorified prostitute, and it seemed that no one in her life was safe from trauma.

As she thought that, she realized for the first time that her mother was not just a monster. She married her father because he protected her when they met, then made her rich, and with two children she had started to recall that her mother had been afraid of her husband. He was violent and irrational, and when her husband had crossed all lines by raping her brother, then her, she stopped him with a bullet and escaped with them all to America. She could have stayed, but she only said she needed to go back without explaining why. She needed to talk to her mother and find out why she had done so many things in the past, and why she was still trafficking girls. There was more to her mother than she long believed. She needed to know why she did all she had done.

As she ruminated about her mother, she noticed Mike and Sharon were done talking and headed to their table. She understood anything they needed to know would be said, and whatever was personal would remain between the two of them. Sharon looked frazzled, and Mike looked his usual self, which was no indication of what he was thinking or feeling. Angie, seeing the way Sharon looked, asked her if she was alright. Sharon managed a smile.

"I'm alright now. Safe. With all of you. But there's a lot inside of me that got messed up I need to sort out. I'm going to get help with that."

Cindy understood, saying that stopping the sheik had helped her, and she hoped taking Peter down may as well.

"It won't change the past, but stopping his future takes away some of the fear he created. Gone is gone. It has to be goodbye to Peter. That will help. Knowing he's not after you."

Mike managed to change the subject by going over the strange life Peter led, and felt that even if plan A or B failed, he was vulnerable at certain times. After reviewing what Sharon had told him, Angie was thinking about the stories, and once finished, she said he deserved the cattle prod. Cindy looked at her, explaining how things often worked in life.

"Sweetie. A man who does that has such things on his mind. That's why he does them. So, have you thought about what if he enjoys having that done to him? What if that's what gets him off?"

Angie gave her an, "Oh, mother…" look.

"Mom, who cares if he does? We raise the voltage and hear him sizzle. If that's what does it for him, I'd like to watch him come and go at the same time."

Cindy crossed her arms.

"Really? Is that from another article you read?"

"Mom, it wasn't about cattle prods. It was about if you're really an incredible… you know… you get a guy off so good he can't help but die from too much good loving."

Cindy just stared at her, giving her a more severe "Really?" look. Angie sat looking at her with a, "What?" expression, then started to laugh.

"Mom, that wasn't what it really said. I made that up. Well, the article actually said try to love him to death. I'm sure we aren't going to do that. Are we?"

As she finished, everyone was laughing. It was a needed escape from what waited ahead. Cindy still shook her head at Angie, wondering when her magazine subscription would expire. She turned to Mike.

"Okay, well, as we haven't a cattle prod, any ideas on a plan C based on what you learned about him from Sharon?"

Mike, still chuckling at the interchange between Angie and Cindy, quickly changed his manner and explained he had one idea.

"It's clear that he's fanatical about routine. Same thing every time each day. There is one certainty. At three-thirty, he's in his sex room doing a little girl. When he's doing that, well, you understand what I mean… he's not going to have anyone like a guard watching, and he's not going to be holding a weapon. That's his get off time, and when he'll feel most invincible. The truth is it's when he'll be most vulnerable. Sharon, where's the room? Does it have windows?"

Opening her mouth to say where, she almost instantly stopped herself from saying she'd been in it, then said she didn't know exactly where, but the entire building was encased in glass windows so she assumed it would be as well. Mike caught the quick change about not knowing for sure. He knew she had stopped herself from saying where it was or for sure if it had windows. He knew she'd been in that room. He looked at her, and she looked at him. She saw he knew what was going on; the guilt and shame she was going through. He continued to look at her without relenting as he spoke.

"All of our lives are at risk. There are girls to save. It would really help to know about the room."

Still looking at him, tears were streaming down her face. She looked up, took a deep breath, and nodded.

"I'm sorry. Everyone, I just fucked up. I was ashamed. I've been in the room. You can figure out why. I can point to it when we're there, and yes, one wall is all windows facing a small hill behind the compound. It's a room where nobody is allowed outside of. It would be a clean shot."

Mike leaned over and hugged her, saying everyone understood and she gotten past a hurdle. He was glad she trusted all of them and they would trust her, adding they all understood what she was going through. As he finished, Cindy's phone had a text. She said her mother was arriving in twenty minutes and it was time to go meet her at the airport.

"Mom, they call it an aeropuerto here. We need to blend in."

Cindy stopped, and everyone stopped with her, looking at Angie.

"Angie. Look at us. Four totally hot cover girl types. Tom Cruise in disguise, and we're going to meet my mother as she saunters off her private jet. Do you really think we could fit in here?"

Angie stood, hands folded in front of her with one knee pushed against the other.

"Si, mama…"

Shaking her head, Cindy knew she was going through her teen years, but thinking they could blend in anywhere? That was just silliness.

Taking a taxi to the airport, Angie was testing her Spanish on the driver. Cindy looked at her and asked where in the world was she learning Spanish from?

"Mom, now that we have enough for satellite service, I've been watching Telemundo."

The driver said he was watching the Hallmark Network, and his English was getting pretty good.

CHAPTER 23

Walking down the stairs of her jet, Eliana felt something she hadn't often felt. Joy.

Standing waiting for her at the bottom of the stairs, Cindy and Angie were there with smiles and waves. She found herself smiling and excited to see them even under the circumstances of a risky kill. She was lugging her gun bag, which she wouldn't let even her pilot handle, and it weighed near as much as she did. Like Cindy, even being a grandmother, she was a glamorous, beautiful woman who hadn't let her hard life change her appearance. Looking beautiful was expected of her by clients and many had offered a fortune for a night with her, something that would be a badge of honor in the community of wealthy men she dealt with.

Wearing a simple black dress with black hose, she wore a choker and dangle earrings made of emeralds as she favored green. She never wore rings as they could interfere with a finger guard on a number of guns, and she associated rings with oligarchs and old men trying to impress with their wealth.

Looking at Cindy as she walked down the stairs, she thought she was stunning in her simple knit sweater top and blue jeans that looked far more expensive than ones at any department store though she knew they were most likely a favorite from when she shopped at thrift stores. Her hair, auburn red mixed with brown was long, parted to one side and off her face. Her skin was clear and had the olive cast that all true Ukrainians had as they descended from Mongolia and had a history of being fierce warriors. Looking at Angie, she thought her stunning. Wearing a simple olive-green tee shirt covered by a matching hoodie, she wore black leggings and sneakers. She knew that no matter what she wore she would look amazing. Like Cindy, her face had a classic beauty with high cheekbones, big eyes, and she would grow to be much like Cindy, perhaps even more beautiful.

Her husband had been father to both Cindy and Angie, and he was a handsome man. The union of her looks and his were evident in the girls as she put her gun bag down to hug them, squeezing them with an affection she had long missed in her life. She was not one to give compliments about appearance, but she moved back after the hug,

looking at them both, saying they were too pretty for their own good. Angie smiled, then looked at Cindy and back to her, saying that was true of her mom, but she had a ways to go to look that hot. Cindy looked at her, telling her she was glad she was speaking Ukrainian again, not Spanish, and she not only appreciated the compliment but could understand it.

Looking beyond Cindy and Angie, Eliana saw Mike and Jamie who she had met in Russia when Cindy killed the sheik, and a beautiful young woman who she knew had to be Mike's sister. She noticed Mike and Jamie were holding hands, and that his sister was smiling, but she could tell by her expression she was troubled. Before walking over to them, she hugged Cindy again and talked softly in her ear.

"Mike, Jamie… that is good match. But sister? I worry. I see trouble in her."

Letting her go, Cindy nodded, meaning she was right. She called out to them, saying to come and say hello to the ruthless nasty lady.

Walking up to her with smiles, Mike shook hands with her, but Jamie gave her a hug. They hadn't had much time when they met in Russia, but she admired them both. She noticed Jamie was looking more attractive than she remembered, but she recalled her saying she played down her looks when she was working for Brian to not compete with the girls being sold.

"Jamie, so different. I knew you had great body, now you show it. Even better than I thought. And face, so beautiful. The hair, perfect for you, And now, what? You give such wonder to secret agent? Is he keeping your secrets safe?"

Mike shook his head, thinking Eliana and Angie should work on a comedy routine as they shared a humor that was charming and insightful.

Holding out her hand to Sharon, she looked at her with a welcome and understanding.

As she walked up, Eliana took both of her hands and looked at her as a mother would.

"A lot you been through. Please, excuse my English. Is okay, but sometimes when I want to tell things of the heart, I not know all right words. Your brother, good man. I trust. He be there for you. All of us, here for you, this day. Look ahead to sun, let those shit shadows fall

behind you. We kill that motherfucker and you cut his dick off. I am happy to meet you. Good you are free."

Whispering in Cindy's ear, Angie said that was some compliment saying she could cut the *you-know-what* off then saying nice to meet you. Cindy looked at her, then whispered in her ear that in Elaina's world, giving her that was an honor. Angie pulled back to look at her, saying, "Really?" Nodding, Cindy said it was symbolic, and would be closure for Sharon if she could do that.

Watching the pilot carry her garment bag, Mike saw she had the heavy gun bag and offered to take it for her. She nodded her thanks, letting him carry it which was the first time she had trusted anyone with it. He had saved Cindy's and Angie's lives, and she wanted to thank him with her trust. She spoke softly to him as he lifted her gun bag.

"Mike, I tell something special. I never let anyone touch my guns. You, I let take for me. It is good to know man of honor. Your sister, I worry for her. Does she speak this language?"

Impressed she had thanked him with her trust, he said that he didn't know if Sharon had learned any other languages, but he'd ask. Calling to her, he asked if she had picked up any languages while away. She shook her head, saying everyone around her knew English, so there was no need to learn any other. Eliana said if she didn't speak English, it wasn't to be rude, but would try as everyone spoke English, adding that was once they went to the island, they would be sure to understand everything said. Sharon said if she needed to speak in Ukrainian, that she understood. Eliana continued to talk to Mike in Russian.

"Your sister, just away from that man, name I won't say right now. Will be confused. Part, in her, still loyal to bastard because she is afraid. I know this well. If we all should die, and she was left standing, she'd say you force her to do things. She between good and bad. We must be careful of that. I am sorry, Mike. I was like that when husband living. He had me fucked up good."

Looking at her with a smile, what he said didn't match the friendly expression.

"I appreciate your warning. I caught a bit of that when we talked earlier. I am aware of it, and I know we don't want her calling out when we see the bastard to protect him. It's sad, but she just escaped. Time is the only answer."

Nodding at each other, both were glad to share a warning of Sharon's unstable state of mind. Mike checked his watch, making sure they had time to go over the plan for once they were on the island. He had secured a room at the small airport for all of them to review their next steps and go over contingencies. It was a short walk to the terminal building, then not far to the room. When entering he used a small device to sniff out any hidden wifi, cameras, or microphones.

"It's clear. Not that anyone knew we were coming, but they do it for smuggling."

Sitting down, Mike looked at everyone and said he had been thinking about a way to take advantage of Eliana being a part of things. They all looked at him, and he got up and went to a white board and held a dry marker in his hand.

"We can't be certain when Peter will be out in the open, but we do know, thanks to Sharon having been at the compound, that he's in a room having sex with a girl on all fours, him standing behind her. He does that from 3:30 until he finishes, so maybe 4:00. The area outside of the room is off limits and the room has a wall that's all window. We don't know if it's armored, but we have firepower to penetrate if it so. The risks? Of course, harming the girl. The main one is making it to the area outside of the room without being noticed."

He passed his phone to Sharon and told her to let everyone see a satellite image of the compound James had sent him. He told Sharon to circle where the room was before passing it along.

"We've covered other options such as hitting him when he was out taking delivery of girls, but again, a risk of harming them. I think it best to put all the other plans aside. Having Eliana with us, I think we can land the copter without notice, and she'll be the reason he comes out to the airstrip. We'll be dropped off before the copter lands on the strip. When it lands, Eliana gets out and he'll have to meet her. He's not going to fire at her. His ego is too extreme. He'll want to face her and tell her she was mistaken to think she could waltz in. While they're talking, I'll use a scope and pop him off."

Everyone seemed surprised, but understood their plans were made prior to Eliana saying she was coming. Eliana was impressed with the simplicity and elegance of the idea, saying it made sense and would work.

"Mike, when I talk to scumbag, he was... how you say it in English?

Arrogant. He knew nothing of me and didn't think I'd do what I said. I tell him, I kill him, then hung up. In time since, he finds out about me, and know I am no fool. If that what he thinks, he have some man kill me, but no, he too big shit for that. I threaten him, he takes care of me. Mike, why not I get off machine and shoot him?"

Mike understood his intent was different than hers. Peter had threatened Cindy and thought only of killing him.

"That would be the easiest way, but I think before he comes out, he'll have you searched, or they'll shoot you. Once he's sure that you don't have any gun, then he'll come out. The man's dangerous, but I'm sure he doesn't take chances. That's the profile of a coward, and they are the worst."

Jamie was listening, and said having dealt with the security traffickers used, she said they were used to keep girls under control, and they may overreact and fire at her even when landing. Mike nodded, saying that was a possibility. He went to the whiteboard and drew a sketch of the airstrip as he talked.

"James has me dialed into air traffic control. I think the best time to get him is when his plane with girls lands. He'll come out to inspect then. With live radar, I'll be able to see the plane coming approaching to land. I think we let it land and we'll be not far off and beside it. With all the girls on the plane or on the field, I don't think he'll want guns firing at anything. He isn't going to risk any harm to the girls as he'd view that as Eliana winning, and he makes everything where only he wins. So, let the plane land, and we copter in as it does. It will be a bit chaotic, but that's to our advantage. Same hit approach. I'll have the sniper rifle, and I'll get him."

Seeing them all nod, they were impressed and understood the strategy. Looking at Sharon, she was impressed, but he could see a concern on her face.

"Mike, I know we're all at risk, but… I think when we started it was about me being the one who would kill him…"

Seeing the look on her face, he could tell she was still determined to take her revenge. She looked at everyone and continued.

"I escaped, I killed his guy, and I took Whimsey with. Her sister is dead now, and we all know he needs to be stopped. If possible, I want to be the one to do it."

Eliana understood. She held her hand up.

"Sharon, I understand. I killed bastard husband who rape daughter and son. If someone else kill him, I would be dead now knowing I didn't end him. I needed to be one stopping him. Mike, what if she rides with me… I hope I am speaking English good for Sharon… I go out first, talk, maybe you shoot legs or place on body where he drops, Sharon comes out, finishes him."

Eliana knew Mike was thinking what if she doesn't. What if she runs back to him and shoots her instead. She wasn't worried but knew Mike would be. He understood it would address Sharon's wish, but was too uncertain. He explained why in detail.

"One thing I've learned is to keep an objective in focus and not let things get out of hand. Sharon, I think you would be in danger, and put Eliana in danger. What if you are triggered and that training to protect Peter takes over? Once we get to him, and we're safe, then I'll give you a gun and you can shoot him. Chances are he'll still be alive. You can do what you want once he's on the ground."

Watching Mike, Eliana was taken by his strength, and his goodness. He had given up his life as a photographer to save his sister, then taken it upon himself to rescue her girls. Looking at him, she felt a sadness that she had not married a man like him. Her life, her children's lives, would all be different if she had. Thinking back to when she was a young girl, she couldn't recall knowing any man as decent and honorable as him. At that time in the USSR, men like him were either committed to the communist cause and in the military, or if opposed to the government soon spirited away to gulags or one day were gone. She liked Jamie, and was glad she was with Mike, yet she wished that it was Cindy at his side. That would mean her daughter would not join her in business, but she would have a good man.

"Eliana? What do you think?"

Lost in thought, Mike was calling to her, asking about sticking to the plan without Sharon as it had been her who had suggested it.

"Sorry, I am. I was lost in, you know, thoughts. Yes, much as I want Sharon to kill motherfucker, this is gun battle and she no trained. That she can do when you shoot him. Sharon, I sorry. If Mike gets him wounded, he lay on ground. You come, I give you my own gun. You finish him."

Sharon looked up at Mike and he nodded in agreement, then she turned to Eliana.

"Thank you for understanding, Eliana. If he dies first, I'm free from him. If I can do the final shot, I will."

Turning back to Mike, she said she was worried about Whimsey, asking if he'd contact James to check on her.

"I was about to call him in a few minutes for updates on surveillance on the island, and I was going to check. I'll do it now. We're going to need to eat, so Angie, with all your excellent Spanish, would you like to go the food shops and get us all some things to eat? Bottled water to take with?"

Smiling that Mike appreciated her learning another language, she looked at Cindy and gave her a big smile and nod of pride. Reaching into her bag she took out a pad of paper and a pen to write what each person would like. Mike called out he'd like pork sandwiches, two of them, and some beans, then went to the corner of the room to call James. Angie stood and looked at Cindy.

"Mom, I know you're a gringo and don't know the native tongue, but would you please come with me? It'll be a lot to carry."

"Angie, I think a gringo is a term they use in Mexico, but if only to keep you away from the magazine stand, I'll be glad to help."

Each laughing at the running gag, they asked what Jamie and Sharon wanted. Eliana said she doubted they had petoheh, so a salad without meat. Angie said "Si" to her, and Cindy took her arm and guided her out as Angie said she was about to say, "Buena elección."

CHAPTER 24

Not wanting anyone there to hear his talk with James, Mike decided to go to an empty room, and after checking if it was bugged, made his call.

"Mike, I was just about to text you to see if you could talk. First, are you situated?"

"Yes. I'm using a few agency resources as I have your go-ahead since you were attacked at Cindy's house. How are things there? I know Cindy's worried about what neighbors think."

"If the agency is good at anything, it's cleaning up messes like that. Works being done on the garage inside and out. The cars have some damage and they'll be repaired on-site. Window's been replaced already. Tell her it will be better than before it happened."

"Thanks, James. That was a hard hit as she just moved in. Sharon's stressing about Whimsey. Two things about that. Is she safe, and second, does she understand that happened to hurt Sharon?"

"Ah, what a poor little thing. I decided to tell her myself. I've talked to wives and mothers about husbands taken down, but this was rough. She's so young… I don't know what's going to be best after she gets out of protection. Technically, she should go back to foster care. That's not going to happen as she filled me in on the abuse. But, another foster home? I don't think that's best. She's traumatized and she'll run off again. I have some ideas. We can use someone her age to bait traffickers, and I think she'd be right for that because of what happened to both her and her sister. We'll need to find someone in-house to take her in and be her guardian."

"James, thank you. I agree with all of that, and I'm glad you talked to her about what happened. You didn't mention how she's dealing with it."

"I guess it's just hard to think about… Sorry. Once she knew from you telling her, I expected her to bawl and wail for days. She sat there in a state of shock, then after a bit, she was livid. I tell you, if she were with all of you, she'd be leading the charge. That's good, though. I talked to Charles. He said it's a healthy response, and he said he would stop by the safe house. And on that, she's in the Army base house that we took from a Captain. I'm not worried. It's a fort, and I have trouble getting in past the gate. Tell Sharon she's good on both fronts. She wanted to go to her sister's funeral, but I told her that wouldn't be safe, so no. We're going

to have to wait on the autopsy, and it'll be a while before any service. I hope that Peter fuck is history so we can do all that. What's the status on that?"

"Better than when we started. Cindy talked to her mom, and Eliana told Peter she was coming to kill him herself. Well, she jumped on her jet, she's here, and she wants to be the bait. I'll use the scoped sniper kit to hit him. When they meet each other on the runway when his plane and the copter land, I'll take him down. He's insane and he'll want to meet her face-to-face so that's the plan right now, and we have contingencies. He has sex with a trafficked teen each day at 15:30 in a private room with only him there, and nobody allowed outside as the building is all-glass windows. I can take a shot from outside the room. I don't know about what kind of glass so I'd use armor penetrating ammo, but that can deflect a bit and I don't want to harm whoever he's going at."

"Those are all strong. Everything has risks, but I think Eliana being there will work best. We've been doing deep background on him, and Mike, if ever there was a ghost, it's him. I mean nothing beyond when he left Peru in his early twenties. He was a local hero to some, hated by the ones whose daughters were taken. Change of leadership and he took himself off the map. If Sharon didn't know about the island, we wouldn't have a clue. Right now, we've had it as a private compound for business under a long chain of private companies owning it, leading back to a man in a retirement home who knew him in Peru, but he's been addled from dementia for a long time. No idea what's going on."

"James, that fits his profile. The Oz man behind the curtain. I wish we could take him in and find out who his contractors are, but let's face it. A nut job like him would never back down. He'd kill himself before he compromised. Agree?"

"Our profiler says the same. He's the point of sale, so his contractors will be scrambling to find a new seller and that's when we'll get them. I wish we had about 100 troops chuting down at night to raid the place, but with the girls there, that would be too risky. Hostage city, and he'd bargain his way out. We can't shoot down a private jet without lots of proof, and there isn't any. So, what's the timeline?"

"Two hours from now, we get on the bird. I'm using traffic control and radar to track his jet coming in, and we'll be dropped off near the

strip and Eliana will continue on to land beside the plane as the girls are being unloaded. I'll let you know when he's down. What happens after that is where you'll need to come in. Those are all missing girls, most all American, so you have a window to send a team and rescue them. Is that in the works?"

"I haven't been on that directly, but Adam has it underway. It's a short jump from Florida and a team is ready. We just need verification from you and one of the trafficked girls, then we are by the book right to go in. Well, Mike, for a guy who isn't an agent, you sure have the agency jumping at your commands. Keep alive, just text with a go, but call if there are complications. How's Sharon, aside from the worry about Whimsey?"

"There's a complication. She's not free from the grooming, and I'm not fooling myself. She can turn and protect him in the middle of it all, so I'm keeping her out of the hit. I haven't had a chance to call him, but she's state's evidence so we need to have Charles work with her. I can see it in her reactions. She has the fear that if we fail, he'll go for her so she's afraid and brainwashed to protect him. Rock and a hard place. She knows a lot about how he operated so we'll want her fixed so we can learn what she knows. Anything else on your side?"

"We'll be watching you from the bird. The weather's clear, and I'm looking at the island right now. They're not setting up any defenses or nothing different from what I can see. I'm sure your visit will be a surprise. He's so sure he's invincible he wouldn't worry even if he knew. That's the worse type, so get him with the first shot, then let me know."

Putting his phone in his pocket as he went to the hall, he saw Angie and Cindy loaded with food and drinks. Going to help them, Cindy said they'd handle what they had, but there was a flat of bottled water at the end of the hall they couldn't manage. After getting the flat of 24 bottles, he went back and the food was being sorted out. As with many past missions, eating was a good diversion from the stress of what would happen later. He sat down between Sharon and Jamie and was impressed with how good the food looked and smelled. Turning to Sharon, he updated her on Whimsey. He could see that she was relieved and took the opportunity to do some reassurance that Peter was no longer controlling her.

"James thinks she'll have a place in the agency taking other traffickers

down. She's way past sad, she's mad as hell and wants to stop any more of the things that happened to her and her sister. The funeral will be well after we get back, and she's as safe as the President. It's good that James was there when they hit Cindy's house. That allowed him to support all we're doing, and a team will be there to take the girls once we're done."

Sharon's eyes revealed a sense of relief. With Whimsey safe, and her with Mike, she felt less worried about Peter succeeding. She kept thinking that if they failed she would play the victim and find a way to kill him on her own. That meant making Mike worried she was still under his control. Mike saw a change come over her and knew what she was going through.

"Sharon, he's just flesh and bone, and believe me, when I get a round into him, that's all he'll be. No more control, no more power, no more hold over anyone. I don't know why humans think they're god-like or anything is worth hurting people for. Most all end up killed the way he'll be. He's actually an idiot. Better to have not have power, live long, and have a good life."

Mike knew that was rational, but men who are insane aren't rational beings. If they're holding a gun and you said not to shoot, they'll shoot just because no one tells them what to do. The whole life of adducting young girls, literally children, using them as things, thinking he owned them, could sell them, use them for sex, kill people... All the things Peter had been doing went against all values society held, but yet the Peters' of the world thrived and went largely untouched or stopped. In the room where he sat, each person there had been impacted by trafficking and men like Peter. Even Eliana, someone not free from guilt being a Peter herself, knew what she was doing, and he hoped that Cindy could help her turn to fight trafficking, not be a trafficker. Be a renegade, like he, Jamie, Cindy and Angie had decided to be. The trafficked taking down traffickers.

CHAPTER 25

Walking down an empty hall to his private room, Peter adjusted his tie and flattened his slacks in front. It was 3:25 and he stood in front of the door to the room once there, waiting until his watch said 3:28 to open the door.

He never asked who would be waiting in the room. His staff knew what he wished, and part of it was not knowing what to expect. Each day there would be a girl in the room, and she would be well versed in what was going to happen to her when he entered. She would be so terrified that she would be fully subservient and fearing for her life if she even made a sound or complained. Under his suit jacket he had a Luger used in World War II. He bought it when in his teens in Peru, as many from Germany had fled there after the war and sold their Nazi gear to survive. He had gotten it from a man having a sign on his hut that read, "Luger, Cheap." Walking in with a few coins in his hand, he asked the man to see it so he could inspect it. As it was loaded, he shot him and walked out with the gun. It had been under his coat since that day.

Watching the time, at 3:28 he entered the room.

He saw the girl there, shaking, her bottom up as high as she could get it. Being twelve, not very tall, it wasn't far off the ground. Her head was flat on the floor and her arms were stretched out on the floor in front of her. She hadn't reached puberty yet, so she had no hair other than on her head. She was thin, and her skin was white with no tan lines. He thought she would command a good price, and by only fucking her ass, she would be sold as a virgin even if she wasn't.

Seeing her flawless rectum and labia, he admired how God had made the female body such a perfect place to put his cock. If anything mattered to him, it was what he was looking at. He understood he was on Earth to take what God had told him to have. Money, power, killings... those were all to have what he was looking at. The unspoiled holes of a virgin to be offered in thanks for his being alive to do God's work. He was taught since a young boy by the padre that men were here to take women, who they had dominion over. Women were made to be offered to God, who was alone, having women through ones such as him chosen to take them, fuck them, and have God experience the power of man over the woman who betrayed Him in the Garden. What he did to

the girl was offered to God to experience through him and prove to the dark Angel that God had dominion over all, including the fallen one.

He had become a trafficker as society had been taken by the dark Angel, and denied the offering to God, leaving the sacrifice for the unholy one. He knew it was right and good to take the ones yet defiled by evil before they were stolen by sin. He never thought of what he did as anything more than taking what was God's away from the dark Angel. To do so, he snatched them off the streets, took them from the evil that ruled the countries and made laws against the ritual. That took money and power which were the tools of the demon he used to claim what was God's. Then, to keep the ones given to God free from the temptation of the demon, he sold the chosen girls to other followers of God, and they donated money to his mission. They did so in secret, for evil had taken over the world.

The girls were safe in the houses of the holy. Men committed to doing God's will by keeping women in their place in service to them, not out on the streets doing the work of evil. He was climbing the long stairway to God girl by girl, There were tens of thousands of steps, but he was climbing ever higher.

Looking at the pure bottom in front of him, he prayed to God, in his mind saying, "God, taste what I taste," as he licked the holes in front of him. He prayed to God in his mind once more, saying, "Feel what I feel. What Eve gave to your fallen son; I give to you."

With full force, he thrust his cock into the girl's ass. She had been prepared with lubricant, but the cock in her ass caused her to scream in pain. He knew that was Eve crying as the serpent fucked her, but with this girl it would be the servant of God fucking her, and the dark Angel would want her no more.

With that, he came inside of her with one final thrust. He was serving God by planting God's seed in her, where she could bear no fruit, but it would be vile and repulsive to demons on Earth for they would suffer being where the seed of God remained.

Pulling from the girl, watching her collapse, he felt the love of God fill him. It shot from his cock to his mind, and he had done what God had asked of him. He took no pleasure from the act, for the pleasure was God's, not his. His pleasure was from God, filling him, making him strong and invincible, and that was the power of the righteous. The

Grace of God to servants doing his work.

Each day, at 3:30, the time Christ died for God, he had offered a girl to God, and was renewed to gather ever more girls to keep them from taking the dark Angel in them. If he waited until they were much older, they would be lost to demons. He left, knowing the girl was safe from sin, and God was pleased.

CHAPTER 26

Once on the copter, Mike opened a duffel bag he brought full of camouflage and tactical clothing. He had guessed at sizes close to the four women who would need them, and they started changing into them as he changed into his. He turned away to give them some privacy, and he heard Angie tell Cindy he had seen plenty of hot babes when taking nudie shots, then asked if he was shy having them see him. He smiled at how Angie always found a way to say the truth while still able to have the innocence of being so young. Angie called out to him.

"Mike, don't be shy. We've all seen what you have before. We won't run. We're in the air."

Once he was dressed, he asked if everyone was decent. Angie managed to hit another home run.

"Mike, my Mom says we're all way more than decent. Take a look!"

As he turned, they were all standing in the bay of the military copter, smiling and giggling as he looked. Angie gave him her most innocent look.

"See!"

He had to admit there was something exciting seeing them out of their provocative clothes and in camo with webbed belts placed in ways that showed their forms quite well. He thought the look hotter than they could understand, but looking at them, he suspected they knew. Each had caps on, belts strapped just above their hips with holsters strapped to their thighs, and they wore black boots with the cuffs of the pants stuffed in the tops.

"I see how silly you all are. Those are for not being seen, not to show off in. Now, here, this goes on your face and hands. A little of both, but not too much."

Handing them jars of black and olive green camo for skin, he said he had forgotten the lighted mirror and overstuffed vanity bench. Angie opened her jars and was excited.

"Mom, this is all the rage. They started selling these at Osco last week."

Mike, seeing her applying it with skill, asked her, "Really?"

As she looked at him where only the whites of her eyes were seen, she said, "No. Jeez. Do you see any women walking down the street like this? I'm just seeing if my Mom will lighten up."

She had him fooled for a minute and told her it was risky in such situations to be joking. She was finishing covering her hands, and put the little jars in one of the many pockets in her pants.

"Mike, I'm practicing acting innocent and not too bright. It's hard work…"

Giving up, he glanced at Cindy who shook her head, shrugging her shoulders. Mike realized that Angie would have to practice hard to act not too bright. She was sharp as a tack, and she was right. In future actions, she would need to act like a naive young innocent, not a world-weary veteran of taking traffickers down. He also knew that at her age, she was thinking for herself, no longer mirroring the style and ways Cindy did things. She was testing that on Cindy, and he thought Cindy was handling it just right, challenging her rebellious nature only when needed, and only to point out ways to develop her natural personality and be aware of the world around her.

With all of them outfitted, he started handing out weapons and checking they were secure. Each had a AR-15, two Glock handguns, large knife, and canisters that would create a blanket of fog to hide in. Finally, he gave them each a communications kit that had a live radio, earpieces and it strapped to their shoulders. After a test of each being able to listen and be heard, they were putting ammo cartridges in pockets made for clips, and they were ready.

Eliana had been sitting up front with the pilot. Glancing back, seeing they had geared up, she came back to look them over. Nodding, she called out to the pilot over the copter noise they were ready, adding they looked like a force to be reckoned with.

Mike agreed. He had trained them before his sister returned on the gear and how to use it all, including gaining high scores in target practice and self-defense. His sister hadn't had such training, but he had explained the essentials of radio operation, using the guns, and told her that as she hadn't had time on the firing range, use them only if anyone was charging at her. She picked up on what he showed her to do, and it would help her survive if things got to that point.

Knowing how they looked was important to them all, he took out his phone and told them to stand in formation, but no smiles. He took several pictures, and one short video. After, he went where they could all sit and look at the pictures. They were oohing and ahhing, and Angie

managed to tell Cindy that was a great look for her. He agreed. Cindy looked great no matter what she wore, but she had transformed into a warrior to be feared just seeing her. Her stature and manner were no nonsense, and she had done better than expected in hand-to-hand combat training and target shooting. Jamie and Angie also did better than expected, and they were fit and nimble with excellent eyesight and hearing.

Getting close, Mike watched the radar on his phone. The jet was right on target and would be on the ground in about fifteen minutes. Things would need to happen quickly. The copter would be dropping them off just far enough away in a strategic spot where it wouldn't be seen from the compound or the air strip. They'd lower straps a short distance to the ground, and they had to just hold on to the straps as the cargo bay had a pulley for lowering and bringing them up. As they neared the spot, checking his live view of the area, they were right where they should be. He told the pilot he was on target, then put his hand on Eliana's shoulder saying he'd get the bastard but expect anything. She didn't have a weapon on her, and that was to make things go fast and not have Peter play games about her showing up armed.

Hovering as close to the ground as possible, the copter was right above the landing spot as they each were lowered to the ground. Mike waited for all of them, and then repelled on a strap after recoiling the ones they had used. It would pull itself back once there was no weight on it, and the pilot would power the cargo door shut. They had stowed their bags and clothes in a cargo bin, and the goal was to make it look like Eliana was the only one to have flown in. A search would reveal the gear, but they were counting on her having no weapons on her or the pilot to eliminate the need for a search.

As soon as Mike was on the ground, he radioed the pilot it was clear, and the strap coiled back, the cargo door closed, and the copter was on its way to meet the plane.

The airstrip was surrounded by shrubs and trees, and Mike led the way using the map on his phone with GPS to get to the spot where they would hide, with him crawling to where he could take a sniper position laying on the ground with his sniper rifle on legs at the end of its barrel. The women formed an arc behind him with their rifles to take down any guards patrolling the area. If possible, they'd use their knives as a

shot would throw things off but having an unexpected AR-15 pointed at them would be enough to get anyone to stop, lay down their weapon or be shot. It didn't always work that way, but that was the nature of a covert operation.

Through his rifle's scope, Mike had a clear view and focus of the airstrip, and the area where the plane would park. He could see all the men on the runway and in a hanger, and they were all easy shots if needed. It was just a matter of waiting for the landings, and for Peter to come out and be in the clear. He wouldn't wait for him to get next to Eliana. He'd take the shot as soon as he was in his sights and ideally, standing in one place. He was confident in his target skills, and he had worked with his rifle enough to know it would hit the target. With a few minutes left, he turned around and even though he knew the rest of the team was behind him, their camo clothing made them near-impossible to see. He used the radio to tell them they were virtually invisible, and things would be happening fast. He added that once he fired, stay in place. Eliana would get back on the copter to pick them up before any search was made for them. He heard a "copy that" from the female voices, and they sounded like veteran troopers.

He heard some rustling noise, then a squish. He worried someone had approached and one of them had stabbed them. He was relieved when he heard Cindy on the radio saying it had been a pretty nasty snake wanting to crawl up her pants. He had an impulse to say he understood why that would be but thought better of it. But he did manage to think how the poor snake had died for love.

Checking the radar on his phone again, the plane was about to land, no more than two minutes away. He saw the copter approaching from the side of the runway, just lagging enough to let the jet land before it touched down.

Putting his phone in a pocket, he told everyone at this point he was using his scope and wouldn't look away from it. He stressed their job was to guard him, his was to hit Peter the first chance he had a clean shot, but added that if he should miss, he would keep going even if it meant taking down his bodyguards or staff, so don't be surprised if he fired more than once.

Just as he finished, he was surprised to hear Sharon on the radio saying she didn't recall seeing any guards, just him and the women on

the plane who were trusted with the girls. It was useful information, and he asked her if she had just recalled that.

"It's all coming back. There was no army of guards here. Just some sellers looking over the girls, and he didn't have any of that as he felt invincible. Saying "roger that" he added no more talk unless an emergency. He could hear the jet, and not taking his eye off the rifle scope, he would wait until it was on the ground and came to a stop before worrying about it. At the moment, he was zoomed out to see most of the hanger and area outside of it, and the path from the house. His only target was Peter, and nothing else mattered.

CHAPTER 27

Whimsey was looking at herself in the mirror. Instead of the trashy mall clothes and makeup of a porn actress, she saw a pretty young girl of fourteen. She wore an army tee shirt and fatigue pants, which both were a bit too large even though they were for women troops sized extra small. She wasn't wearing any makeup, and her hair was washed and left natural without her putting it in braids or wearing it up.

Looking at her hair, she had an impulse to put it up or make braids on each side. That is how the porn director wanted it. If her hair was down, natural like she wore it as she looked at herself, the camera would only see hair as she hovered over a man to give him a blowjob or hide her face if riding him as seeing her look of passion and moaning and groaning was a priority.

She stood, thinking of all that.

"Fuck that shit. I'm never wearing my hair like that ever again. See my face sucking some prick off… Even if I get with a nice guy, he'll have to see my hair and be happy with that."

Having just gotten out of the shower and putting on the clothes the staff at the base had given her as a memento of her stay, she looked in the mirror as she took off her top, then her bottom. Standing there with a starter training bra and bikini panties, she studied herself. She was tiny, and she was as thin as she could be and remain healthy. The porn director kept telling her that she needed to be skinny as she could get. To look like a little girl, any extra pounds made her look her age.

"Gee, looking fourteen… can't look that old."

She could see her ribs, and her hip bones were also visible above her pantie top. Her stomach curved in where it met her panties rather than pushing them out in a natural curve. She turned around, seeing her ass was hardly filling her panties. That too was what a girl even younger than her was supposed to look like, although most girls younger than her were fairly heavy in comparison. They had large butts that filled out anything they wore. She looked healthy, even as thin as she had made herself. Her skin was tight and had good color, and her face was clear at a time when many girls were getting acne. Her hair wasn't as silky as it should be as it had been bleached to make her blonde, very light, all to make her look like a child.

Taking off her bra, she shook her head. She had been complimented by the director and many of the men fucking her for not having any breasts. She looked as if she had just gone through puberty and developed late. Her chest was flat with just a hint of breasts showing, and her nipples were soft pink, the only actual rise she could see. Holding her arms up, then in different positions including hugging her breasts together, there wasn't much there. It was the first time she understood how sick the world she had been working in truly was.

Taking off her panties, she didn't have any pubic hair, but like her natural hair that needed to be tied back to see her face as she sucked dick, she had been told that any hair down there had to be waxed off, not shaved. Shaving would leave nicks and irritation and young girls didn't have hair yet. Her little slit of a clef and her full naked mound and labia needed to be free of any visible roots and smooth as a baby's butt. She shook her head. The only word in her mind was, "Sick." Turning to look at her butt, it was cute, and it wasn't big. Her cheeks were where they didn't squeeze together and without pulling them apart, she could see her hole. That too had caused lots of compliments. The director said that kept her hands free from pulling her ass apart to see her asshole and she could use her hands to stroke cocks.

Looking at it, she wondered how many cocks had been up her ass. That was what most videos she was in were about. A little tiny girl with a huge cock up her ass. The smaller the girl, the bigger the cock looked, and the more it seemed like she was being ripped open by getting a cock near as big as her arm up her ass. The videos had names like, *"Jason Destroys Teen Ass"* or, "She wasn't expecting to be ripped apart." The thumbnails showing the video on porn sites had posed pictures of her with her eyes wide open as possible and her mouth open in shock with her hand partially covering it, and her other hand barely making it around a cock she was holding in front of her.

Putting her clothes back on, she looked at herself again in the mirror. She thought she looked so much nicer just in the drab clothes, her skin just the way it was, her hair flowing free, none of her ass peeking out from a short club dress or micro shorts. Attempting a smile at how she looked, she was amazed to see she could make one. For the last year, about the only way her mouth went was into a pursed duck-lip pucker, wide open with her tongue hanging out as she stared at some cock,

puckered up in an exaggerated kiss being sent, or wide open in a look of shock and surprise, her eyes looking equally surprised. She thought of how many hours she spent practicing in front of her mirror doing all those mouth expressions. She vowed to herself she wouldn't do any of those even if she was surprised.

Going to the single bed in the room, she sat on it and took out the iPhone James had given her as her phone had been destroyed. She looked at the Safari App and viewed the favorites and history. All that was there was from her doing some shopping for underthings and some decent clothes on Amazon. James had set it up where she could get all those as she didn't have any money and didn't have anything to wear. It was why the staff had given her olive greens to wear, along with toiletries. Her old phone had endless bookmarks and views of all the porn sites she was featured on. They ranged from free view sites, then moved to pay-for studio sites which showed full-length videos that included cum shots, mostly of her face covered with cum from several men at once, to a page dedicated to just her doing the most obscene acts. It had a large picture of her naked with ponytails having pink ribbons and her looking down at her pussy being pulled open with her hands, the type over it saying, *"Where did my sucker go? Can you help me find it?"* Above that, the name of her site was in crayon letters saying, *"Whimsey's World — Come Play With Me."* She thought back to how excited she was when she first saw it and having her own porn site. It had been getting more and more subscriptions although she wasn't getting more money from it.

Shaking her head, she thought about her name being shown that way. Whimsey. She had looked it up, and it meant, "playful, fanciful, fantasy." She thought what a perfect name for a little tiny girl working a giant cock. Every man's fantasy. She started laughing about it. Everyone thought Whimsey was a name she made up to be her porn persona. She was told it was a perfect name for a little girl fuck hole fantasy. She was laughing because it wasn't something she made up. It was her real name. Her mother, before she died, told her that her name was from her getting pregnant one night when her and her father decided to have a flight of whimsey and go to a bed and breakfast for a weekend adventure. That was where she was conceived, and her mother thought it a lovely, eclectic name that held sentimental meaning, and she would always know she was from the whimsical adventures her mother and

father had and wanted her to as well when she grew up.

"I sure grew up, didn't I?"

She was using the camera on the iPhone as she spoke that to herself. If her parents were alive, and they knew what Whimsey meant to thousands of men beating off to her at that very moment, they'd die from that. They would be so sad. She had betrayed the name her mother loved so much. She had thought of never using it again, but she realized that would mean that the sick porn people, that Peter, would have stolen the gift her mother gave her with her name. They had taken her virginity, her reputation, her values, her self-worth, her body, her little sister, but she was not going to let them take her name. That was the weekend her parents went and made her. She would never let them take that from her. They had done enough.

Laying down, putting the phone by her side, she thought about Sharon and her brother Mike, and also Angie, Cindy and Jamie. They had all been through horrible things, yet they could smile, care about each other, and were doing good with their lives. They had taken her in with open arms and kindness. Nobody had done that before. Not her foster parents, and not anyone at the porn studio. She realized that even with the world she came from, like them, she could move on, get away from it, do good. She'd like to be part of what they were doing. Getting traffickers to stop if they could, or at least save some young girls before they got too messed up.

She started thinking about Sharon and their shower together. Her hands went in her pants, and she was already wet from just thinking about her. Slowly rubbing herself, she thought of how Sharon had washed her, dried her, kissed her… She had never told anyone that even though she fucked men and sucked dicks, that didn't excite her. It mostly hurt really bad. She liked girls and women. They got her off, and she was attracted to women, not men. Sharon was the only nice, gentle woman she had met while doing porn, and she kept thinking of her as she rubbed more intensely.

As she came, her mouth opened slightly and she puckered her lips to a gentle kiss as she whispered, "Sharon."

CHAPTER 28

"Okay ma'am, jet's down, door's open, a few girls looking out. I'm going in."

Eliana held a strap with a firm grasp as the helicopter banked for a sharp turn while headed down without slowing. She saw the jet had stopped and one girl being almost pushed out of the door to walk down the ladder. The copter pilot was an experienced combat pilot, and she knew the copter, from the ground, had appeared out of nowhere and suddenly was sitting on an angle pointing to the front of the jet, just short of its nose and its propellers a hair away from slicing the fuselage. The few people on the ground looking with shock at its arrival were shouting into walking talkies, and the woman about to push girls out of the plane had pulled the one already out back in.

Looking out of the door of the jet, its pilot was gauging if he could move forward or back to take off if needed, but the Blackhawk was perfectly positioned where the jet couldn't move without being damaged. The plane's hull was thin and would be ripped by the blades as they were combat hardened and able to withstand contact with the jet's skin. Eliana told the copter pilot he must teach such maneuvers to Ukrainian pilots. He smiled at her.

"Well ma'am, we've been doing a bit of that, and I'm the point man as my mom was born right where you're from. This tactic will be in our training book after today. I've got them boxed in just like you suggested. I'll be waiting for your green light."

Holding a pair of binoculars up, she looked ahead at the entry to the compound, not the hangar. The pilot wore a helmet and had his visor down. It displayed a grid of the tarmac ahead, and she asked if he was all set.

"That's a roger. You're good to go."

Getting out of the Blackhawk, she went and stood in front of the nose of Peter's jet and waited. The men who had been on their walkie talkies had run to the entry of the compound, the hangar appeared empty, and there was no one to be seen. As she waited, she held a satellite phone and after two minutes, she called Peter. She wasn't surprised when he answered on the first ring.

"Are you the one standing in front of my jet?"

"Yes."

"Who are you?"

"Eliana. I here to kill you. You fucked with my daughter, now pay price."

There was a long pause, and she couldn't hear any change in his breathing. He had used long pauses between what she said and answering when she called him before."

"Yes, I remember. You're blocking my delivery."

Making him wait, she looked at her nails as a minute went by. She figured he would get upset with the way he talked to others.

"Yes, I am. You fucked with my daughter. Motka Buska, you are such an idiot."

After the long pause to reply, she realized she had struck a nerve. He responded in a way not expected.

"What was that you said? Did you say Holy Mary? You mean the mother of God?"

Then, no pause, and she noticed his breathing was deeper and faster.

"You are on my island, and you're using her name in such a manner? Yes, I see the look on your face. I know you're a demon sent by the dark lord. I will show your master I'm not afraid of you, or him."

The call ended, and she realized he was serious. He was upset by her mentioning Mary more than her saying she was going to kill him. Shrugging, putting the phone in her pocket, she knew he would be coming out as he was provoked.

Standing calmly, she lifted one hand up for the pilot to know Peter would be coming out. She was glad no girls were on the tarmac, and it would just be him. That would mean a clear shot for Mike. Although she knew Mike wanted to take him down, it was her daughter Peter had attacked. He crossed the line her husband had, and she was looking forward to seeing him walk to her.

Sooner than she expected, hardly a minute, the door to the compound opened and Peter walked out, closing it behind him. He was carrying a Luger, wearing a pressed suit and tie, and showed no expression but his pace was rapid. He didn't lift the gun or say anything. The helicopter blades were spinning, and she wouldn't have heard anything he said regardless. As he reached a spot the Blackhawk pilot had confirmed with her, she put in a pair of earplugs she had in her hand.

At the same time, the gun doors on the Black Hawk opened and

fired. The sound was deafening even with the earplugs in, but she stood and watched Peter cut in half by one-inch shells designed to penetrate tanks. The shots lasted only a second as Peter had been a clear target. The shells passed through him into the hanger, going through its wall and into a hillside behind it.

Turning to the pilot, she waved, and he waved back. She walked over to Peter knowing the pilot would fire if anyone came out to attack her, but no one did. She stood over what was left of him. He had been hit in the upper chest and his torso was gone, but his head was intact and flew to where it landed against a doorway into the hangar.

Crouching down, she looked into his eyes and said, "Motka Buska... you look like shit."

Standing up, she couldn't hear them, but she saw Mike running to her with the four women behind him. She understood she hadn't followed the plan, but as the pilot was fluent in Ukrainian and mentioned he could cover her with the guns, she decided to follow through on her promise and kill him.

Mike whirled his hands above him to tell the pilot to power down the rotor, and the engine noise subsided. He waited for the women, and they had their AR-15s ready in case anyone came out to fight, but once reaching Eliana, he said they could stand down.

"Mom, that means lower your gun."

"He told all of us what it means. Did you understand it? Your gun is still pointed out."

Looking embarrassed, Angie looked and realized she hadn't lowered it, and as she lowered it, they all circled around Peter's head. Eliana looked at them all.

"I told him I would do this. None of you did, I had promise to keep. I'm sorry, but that is what nasty bad lady does to one who hurts daughter. There was time I didn't. That was wrong. Cynthia, I am sorry I didn't protect you."

Not waiting for Cindy to react or say anything, she asked Sharon if she wanted to use her rifle or her handgun. Looking at her, Sharon was shaking but was able to take her pistol out, handing her rifle to Mike. They all moved back to give her room. The bullet could splinter and fragments fly at such close range, but he didn't stop her from going ahead with paying Peter back.

Thinking of all the reasons to shoot him even though he was dead, she stopped shaking and was calm, but crying. She held the pistol aimed to his forehead, and she looked at the creature who had caused so much misery and killed so many people for no reason.

"This is for Whimsey's sister…"

The shot went right into his forehead, where the little girl had been shot. She looked at it, and would tell Whimsey he got what he gave. She hadn't moved, and the gun was still pointed at him, but she knelt down, putting the barrel of it into his mouth which was wide open.

"And this is from me for all the times you made me suck your cock…"

She fired. The second shot left little of his head intact. She stood up, not saying anything as she put the gun back in her holster. She looked at Jamie.

"The plane, this place, it's full of girls. Who knows what's being done to them. How about two for the plane, the rest of us inside the compound to make sure nobody's getting a last fuck in?"

CHAPTER 29

"James, he's down. We count twenty-nine girls in the compound, sixteen on the plane. Tell the team they'll have that many to escort to Florida. We rounded up his crew and as this isn't Cuba's territory, they're ours and we need interrogators for them. Man, James, it was a shock. They were all in front of an altar in a bunker and one woman was mixing a large vat of what I assume was cyanide. No guns, no fighting but we did take five of them down. When we came in, they were waiting to drink the koolaid, and when we went in front and told them time to go, the woman with the vat shouted out we were demons and she and four others went at us. Jamie took them out and they're there too, so we need to ID them. The woman tried to splash us with the drink, and that's when Jamie fired. I would write it up as enemy action. The rest knelt down and prayed for our release from satan or somebody. So, in the end, you know how it is, we said they can pray for us in prison and that seemed to make things okay for them. We pulled them out and the only resistance was stopping to bow to a statue of Mary. So, fourteen total to take, four being women."

"Just glad you're alive. I watched it all. We all did. Did you know Cindy's mother would do that?"

Laughing with relief, he said he didn't have a clue.

"What type of pilots are they sending us? Taking orders from Eliana?"

Now it was James laughing.

"Hey Mike... Would you say no to her?"

They understood each other, and Mike was glad James had watched.

"Well, they'll find maybe four shells missing when he checks in, but he told me he routinely does a test fire out at sea, so nobody outside the agency needs to know. He just got back from the Ukraine. Training pilots there, so good practice for him."

Getting somber, James asked him how Sharon did with not being able to finish him off. Mike told him that Eliana had taken care of that too, described what she did, and how it provided the closure she needed. James said as soon as the skips arrived, head back on the copter, the jet was waiting.

With the call finished, a bunch of still frightened matrons standing in the hangar, and the staff locked in the room where James had performed his ritual each day, Mike noticed Eliana looking over the girls in the

hangar. He turned to Cindy.

"Don't tell me… Cindy. Is she actually checking them out? Does she have her own plane coming to traffic them away?"

Looking up at him, she smiled, giving him a hug.

She said she wanted to talk to them. I thought she was doing what you just said and told her they were headed to Florida, so hands off. She said some words no Ukrainian lady should say, so I won't repeat them. She said she just wanted to look. She's going through something… I don't know what, but she seems like she's been affected by what Peter did. We could all be dead, and that shook her up. You heard what she said about how she had made a promise to him. She keeps her promises. You have to admit, standing out there by herself, not knowing what guns may be on her, she's not someone to mess with."

Jamie had been watching the captive girls, but seeing Mike and Cindy looking at what Eliana was doing, she left Eliana with them and joined them. That surprised them, but Jamie held her hands up to indicate it was okay.

"I thought the girls would feel safer to talk if I walked away for a bit. Cindy, your mother is listening to each of their stories. About how they were taken, what people were worried about them. She's telling them if they're on their own, or if their parents are abusing them, she'll make sure they are okay, and she was talking about paying for it all."

Cindy looked at Mike, and then over to her mother. She knew each girl there was a real person, not merchandise to be sold, and it seemed like her mother was looking at each of them as if it was her or Angie.

"Jamie, I just told Mike she always does what she promises. She'll talk to us about making sure they're all safe and not on the street or being abused at home. She knows way too much about where that leads. I can see she's going through something. Guilt, remorse… I'm not sure what, but that's quite a sight."

Angie was looking at the hangar as she joined them.

"Mom, busha is fraternizing."

"Fraternizing? Really? And you know what that actually means?"

"Mom, don't you know? Associating with someone when you aren't supposed to. Getting familiar with."

Cindy looked at Jamie and Mike, saying she had to ask. They smiled.

"And did you read that in *Teen Vogue?*"

"Mom, they don't use words more than four letters. I was home schooled by you, remember? Having me read the dictionary to be articulate and expansive in my vocabulary."

Pulling Angie to her, she kissed her on the cheek, then hugged her tight. As she did, Angie smiled at Mike and Jamie and gave them a wink as she hugged Cindy back, then looked her in the eye.

"Mom, I love you."

Mike almost melted seeing the smile on Cindy's face, and he hugged Jamie to him. They watched as Angie hugged Cindy, then stepped back and looked her over.

"Mom, you have to keep going with that camo look. You're rockin' hot like that!"

As they both turned to Mike and Jamie, they nodded, both saying at the same time, "You are!"

Cindy thanked them all, but said she had a nice new dress at home that she was sure she'd look even hotter in. They all knew she was right. Blushing a bit, Cindy looked down at herself, and then up to Mike.

"I was wondering… can we keep these?"

With as straight a face as he could manage, he said nobody else could fill her camos, so all hers. Cindy smiled and straightened out a few belts.

Hearing boats, Mike looked and said the girls would soon be on their way, and so would they. He added that as he said when they were in the compound, they didn't touch things as an investigation team would be coming next and gather up everything possible and would trace money and who was working getting girls for Peter. He said within a week, they should all be rounded up.

Cindy said she was glad to hear it, then looked over to the hangar. She said she was going to tell her mother the girls would be picked up in a short time, and they would be leaving. Mike said that was a good idea, and after she left, he looked at Jamie and Angie.

"Well, I hope she finds out what her mother is up to. And, speaking of rounding up the troops, I'll tell Sharon. I appreciate all of you giving her some room. This, added to everything else… Well, I can't imagine how she's dealing with it all. James set up a meeting with Charles for the day after we're home, and until then, I'll keep an eye on her. So, we head back in a bit. I'll get her, then let's all get ready. Drop Eliana off in Cuba for her jet, then to Florida, then on our jet."

CHAPTER 30

"Charles, I don't know how anything can help how I feel. If I go through all that happened… all I did… what was going on in me even up until now… Talking about it will put me back in all those things. I can't do it."

Understanding all she said, Charles was sitting across from her in his office. It had soft lighting and the chairs were almost big enough to get lost in as he liked to say. After working with soldiers who had done things beyond imagination and suffered guilt, talking to people who broke down one day in the middle of a gun battle and let their partners get shot, he was not one to ask anyone to recount all the details of what happened. He didn't avoid what happened, it was as simple as nothing could change their memories, and that's what he wanted Sharon to know.

"I get it. I agree. I like to start things this way. It's best if I explain how I work. First, I understand what you said and as I just told you, I agree. I don't see any point in having you talk about what happened. You can, if you want, but right now I care more about today and the days ahead. You said nothing can help how you feel. Have you felt this way all your life?"

She stared at him, surprised at such an obvious question.

"Of course not. I was really happy a few years ago."

Nodding, he shrugged slightly, and was watching her body movements and expression.

"Good. I knew the answer, but I think it helps to remember that you are fully able to be happy. Some people, from birth, are never happy. Nothing is okay for them. That's bad. But most people are okay, or happy, then shit happens and it's horrible. Who can be okay when something horrible is happening, or has happened? Seriously. There was a song when I was in high school by a woman named Phoebe Snow, and it was a big part of what led me to sitting in this chair, and it still haunts me. The line that got me was, *We are wand'ring out on this desert plain, Oh, we have no canteen, Can the thirsty stay sane after what they've seen?* So, can we stay sane after what we've seen is what I think about when someone is traumatized. Do you think they can?"

Thinking about it, she recalled hearing the song, and liked it. She had

looked up the artist, and remembered what happened.

"I know the song and read about her. My God, she went through such horrible stuff. Then she dies from a brain hemorrhage. And you bring her up? That's supposed to help?"

He was glad she knew the singer and about her life. He wouldn't have to explain it, and she had an understanding of her life that would help.

"The question was can we stay sane after being traumatized. So, you know about her marriage, her daughter, and how after her daughter died, she dies two years later. With all that, what didn't happen to her?"

Sharon put her own issues aside and thought about the singer. She went through the details as when she read about her, she felt so bad for her. After thinking it through, she looked at Charles and had her opinion of what didn't happen to her.

"Well, she went through hell, but she kept going. I guess she didn't give up."

He was happy she said it, as it meant more coming from her.

"That's my take on it too. She had some sort of insight into her own nature with the being thirsty and staying sane lines. I have a point of view about her, and people who have trauma. She didn't give up, but her trauma never stopped. It got worse, not better. No light ahead, but she cared about her daughter and she had a purpose more powerful than all the hurt in her. You were in a bad place, but you're out of it now. Some people let that shape their lives. Others, they say to themselves that they aren't going to let what happened to them continue hurting them. Ruining their lives. So, I think in the desert you made it out of, you stayed sane. We can go through all the PTSD stuff, but it ends up being some things I'm going to ask you. Just answer, don't think about it, okay?"

Nodding, Sharon understood he wanted a gut reaction. He saw she was ready, and said he'd ask a couple of things, she'd answer. She looked at him and shook her head.

"Were you trafficked, groomed, harmed, hurt and suffered?"

"Yes."

"Did Peter do that to you?"

"Yes."

"Are you going to let him keep doing it to you?"

"No."

They stared at each other. He looked at her. He asked if she

understood she said no, without hesitation. She nodded.

"That's where things start. He's dead. You blasted his fucking head to smithereens. If you decide to suffer another minute, let's go get a shovel, let's dig him up. He's still living if he's fucking up your life now. It's not about you. It's about him. Keep him buried or you can take him with everywhere you go. Find a high school prom and take him as your date if that's how important he is."

Shocked at what he said, she didn't now how to reply. He was still looking at her.

"Don't look at me, look around for Peter. He's the one you keep worrying about. Right?"

She was still dealing with how relentless he was being, and not caring or asking what had happened to her.

"You don't understand…"

"Sharon, I've heard shit nobody should ever hear, and it's not about if I understand. So, go ahead and tell me every fucking sick shit thing he did, or you did, or anything that happened. Tell it all. Do you think that will do anything to help you? Me knowing what happened doesn't mean a thing. I can't change what happened, I can't make it go away. I can't say it's okay, don't let it bother you. Or, why think about it? Why dwell on it? All that shit people do just keeps it circling in their heads. I have people you can pay to listen to you tell everything that happened, and they'll tell you oh, that's too bad, that's horrible. Poor Sharon. If you want, I'll give you a long list. Is that what you want? Just do like before. Yes or no."

"No."

"There, we can check that box off. So, you know talking all about it isn't going to help, and you don't want Peter to keep hurting you. That means you're sane, healthy, and yeah, it fucking sucks that you went through horrible stuff, but give yourself some credit. Do what you did to that fucker's head. Shoot it, then shoot it again. Kill all that for good. I'm not saying it's easy to do. No. But that's where I come in. In that desert, I'm going to be your canteen. It'll keep you walking out of it and keeping you walking away from what happened. It's all a person can do with bad shit. Walk away. You won't forget it. It will be there. I think you'll find things that are important that you need to do. You'll be worrying about those and the memories will find they aren't

the only thing that matters to you, and they'll be filed under things that happened but aren't going to ruin my life."

"Well, I do have something I've been worrying about all the time…"

Holding up his hand, he said he wanted to hear, but had a question before she told him. She nodded.

"When you think about that, even if it's connected somehow, are you thinking about your trauma?"

"No, not mine. I'm thinking about Whimsey and how hurt she is, and what she's going to do. When I worry about her, I don't think I'm worry about what happened to me."

Nodding, giving her a "duh" expression, he was glad she had other things to focus on.

"There. So, there's an example. You're capable of prioritizing what's important now and putting aside worrying about your trauma. Now, the more that happens, the more you realize you can live with it, and it doesn't have to be all that matters. I'm not saying that happens just from figuring it out. Over time, other things will take priority. There are lots of ways of managing that. Set aside an hour each day for therapy to deal with the past, for example. I don't recommend it, but if it works for someone, I'm all about whatever works. So, tell me about what you're going through about Whimsey."

"We went through the worst trauma together, and she got hit hard. Something that can't be pushed away. Peter had her sister killed, and her sister will never come back. She has that, and she was abused by her foster parents so she has no family, and that's something I've been thinking about. She needs a legal guardian. She's only a teen."

"You'd like to be her guardian then?"

"You sure don't pussyfoot around, do you? The answer. Yes. And I'll get this out of the way. Not because I feel responsible for what happened and I owe her. I care about her, and I'm someone who can understand all she's been through. I mean, imagine anyone thinking about taking her in. A porn star? Fucked hundreds of men and women and she's only just fourteen? I don't think people will understand like I do."

"Okay, I think that's good. She needs you, and I think you'll feel less alone with the trauma knowing you weren't alone in it. So, she needs a guardian. You think that you should be it. So, what's keeping you from signing papers?"

She sat back, her eyes rolling up. Shaking her head, she said she would this second, but there was a slight bump in that road. Charles asked if she planned on telling him. She smiled for the first time.

"Yes, tough guy, I'm going to tell you. This is not a trauma thing. This is a life decision. I love Whimsey, she loves me. And. She loves me loves me. She wants to be my lover. She isn't into guys at all. She wants to be with me as my girlfriend."

Charles knew that was truly a life decision, and he understood her caution. He wanted to understand it fully as it was the first step away from the past.

"Okay, you love her, care about her. I didn't hear you say sexually, but I assume she'd have a hard time being with you if she couldn't be your lover, right?"

She nodded her head and wagged her finger at him.

"Watch your language there, Charles. You're getting sloppy. Didn't you mean to say if she couldn't fuck me?"

She smiled at him. She had figured him out a bit, which wasn't supposed to happen.

"You're smart. Mike got me on things too. So, when it comes to shit Peter did, that's when I say it hard. When it comes to love and feelings, I say what it is. She wants love, and to make love, not fuck. That's no fucking joke."

Laughing at how he recovered, she said that it wasn't.

"Okay, so, not looking back, but you've had sex with women when you were forced to. Did it repulse you? Was it okay? Or nice?"

She leaned back, thinking about it. He let her take as long as she needed. She looked at him and shrugged a bit.

"I never really thought about it until you asked. The first times I was freaked out. I never thought about doing anything with a woman. Not even a little. Then as it went on, I just said okay, do it, you did it before, but it was just something I had to do, not something I enjoyed. By the time I met Whimsey, being older than the other girls, I was doing a lot of playing stepmother making it with her stepdaughter parts. I remember one girl who could really lick clit and get me to squirt… I remember thinking that women sure give head better than guys. I got off, had a big orgasm. Then, well, the night we escaped I was pretty shook up and took a shower with Whimsey because I had to leave and

was coated in cum. She was so gentle and caring, and I was feeling like that towards her. We kissed and it was a for-real kiss. I mean, I felt it, but since then, well, I haven't thought about doing it again. It didn't freak me out like the first time. We were two people who needed each other, and it was affectionate."

He appreciated her being open about each instance and thought about it. He kept going as it was the best hope of getting better.

"So, sitting here right now, talking about how Whimsey is in love with you, do you think that's because of what you went through together? It may just be that."

"Oh, when I visited her and she told me she wanted to make love, I asked her that. Was she really in love with me or was it just because we went through all that together. She sure answered that without hesitation. She said she had been infatuated with me for a long time before that happened, and when we were in the shower, we didn't know she'd be sold away because they heard me tell her she'd be trafficked. So, she said she wanted to be my lover before anything happened. I look back and yes, she was giving me signs for quite a while."

"Okay, so she's got a thing for you, and it's not just because of what happened. So, go back to being in the shower. Did you cum?"

"Oh, yes. Big time over and over."

"Okay, and when you see her now, just like before, just answer, what do you feel?"

"Aroused."

"Does that scare you?"

"No. I just feel excited seeing her. I mean I get wet."

"Do you like sex with men?"

"Yes. I always have."

"Do you think you can have sex with a woman and still want sex with a man?"

She looked up again, thinking. Then she looked at him, and was sure about the answer.

"Well, I've had enjoyable sex and orgasms with a number of women and still want sex with men. It doesn't change that."

He sat, thinking. He didn't want to influence her, he wanted to take her through the process of understanding herself as someone who had sex with women and didn't think of herself as only attracted to women.

"One last question. You've been around some wonderful, caring and very attractive women lately. Have you had any sexual thoughts about them?

"No. I guess if there were ones to want, they'd be the brass ring."

"Okay, so, you aren't inclined to want sex with women. You like men. You also have a relationship with Whimsey where there is emotion, and love. She is very young and I would assume equates love with sex. If it's loving sex, one where you both like being with each other, would you consider that?"

"Charles, that's what I meant when I said being her guardian is complicated. She's... well, pretty sweet and loving. I've faced up to it. I'm attracted to her, and I'd have sex with her. But to be a guardian, that's as bad as a foster parent having sex with her. I think you even have to declare to not engage in a romantic or sexual manner. So, if I'm her guardian, I don't think it's right to lie, and to take advantage of that situation. And I'm worried that if I get too close, she's young, and she may find someone else. That would suck."

"Sharon, yeah, it would. Love is always that way. I know about her status, and she is a strong girl who just legally needs a guardian, so she doesn't end up back in foster care. I don't think this is like being a foster parent, and you aren't taking advantage of her. She fell in love with you long before the guardian thing. Thinking of it that way, that you are a legal guardian for her welfare, not as a parent, does that change things?"

She sat looking, realizing she hadn't thought of it like that.

"Are you sure? I won't do something wrong or against her best interests, and I sure won't lie about anything."

"Of course, I'm sure. That's what a shrink has to know. You'd be guardian ad litem, guide money, schooling, legal matters. Nothing in there about being involved sexually or romantically. If she didn't want it, the court would appoint a new guardian, but you wouldn't get in trouble like a foster parent would. So, if you did that, and you were lovers, would that be good or bad for you, and would it be good or bad for her? Those are the questions to ask yourself. I do have a caveat. You're an adult, legally she's a child. It would be sex with a minor. I'm obligated to warn you about that. Even when consensual, it doesn't matter."

"Charles, I didn't think about that. All those porn studios using underage girls and they don't get arrested, but I would?"

"Sharon, I'm going to have to do something. All we've talked about until right now? That wasn't a session and it was just me meeting a friends sister. We didn't talk more than socially."

Looking confused, Sharon sat back, mouth open, not sure what to say. Charles understood and continue on.

"Once we start a for-real session, what we talk about is confidential. That is true except when it comes to certain illegal acts. So, suicide for real, murder, and sex with minors. So, before taking you on as a patient, being your shrink, I am letting you know that. As for things said so far, you told me about a friend and how you felt bad for her. So, do you understand we can talk, but not about things I don't need to know?"

"Charles, are you sure? I don't want you to lie for me?"

"I can't lie if I don't know anything. As a patient, you can tell me about being a guardian and how you are doing in that role. That's all I'd need or want to know about. Are we clear about that?"

She leaned over, giving him a look of admiration and thanks, and she looked much better than when their session started.

"Thank you. Mike was so right about you. You are the real deal. This has been great."

Smiling, he said Mike was prone to exaggeration, and they laughed. He looked at her, held both hands up, and asked her what just happened. She scrunched her eyes and figured it out.

"We talked about being a guardian, that I was struggling with a past event. I was getting to know you and decide if you'd be the right therapist for me, and I learned I can trust you and you are a good man."

"Those are good things to hear. You're walking out with that, but what did you walk in with?"

"Ooh… You're one slick operator. I get it. There are things more important than what some sick fuck did to me."

Standing up, he nodded and said, "That's right."

CHAPTER 31

"Mom, when are we going to take down some traffickers not related to Mike's sister?"

"Angie, we are. You know Mike and Jamie are getting a list together. Why? Are you that anxious to get in possible danger?"

"Mom, that's what it'll always be. I just want to practice being a trashy girl and refine my high-class girl things. We've got more shopping to do, and I need to hang out with you at the mall in case I have to be a trollop. Get Cindy'd up if I need to be a wanton home-wrecker jail-bait type. I need practice on all that."

"Get Cindy'd up? *Cindy'd up?* What is that?"

"Mom, you know what that is. Be irresistible to men. Be all aloof and unobtainable."

"Angie, I'm fine with you being irresistible, but you sure better be unobtainable."

Shaking her head, she went to watch TV. Cindy heard her watching Telemundo. She thought to herself Angie's going to be a handful as she gets older, and she was too smart for her own good. Just as she shifted to thinking of other things, Angie walked in, and had an excited look on her face.

"Mom, I have an idea. Why don't we put on our camos and go the Army base and see if there are any traffickers there. Protect our troops."

"You just want to wear those, admit it."

"Well, that, and if we can protect our troops, that's good too. Oh, silly me. Mike and Jamie are coming for dinner. Maybe Sharon, right?"

Busy preparing stuffed peppers with no meat, just buckwheat and carrots, she was stirring some red cabbage soup as she looked up at Angie.

"Well, I'm here doing all this cooking, and as it's more than we can eat I guess they must be coming to help us. Me and all this cooking, listening to Telemundo."

Putting on her own special apron that said, "Don't even think about it" under the waist strap, she said she'd stuff the peppers. Cindy smiled, happy to be making a dinner together. It was something she had little time to do before her mother had given her fifty million dollars. She thought about how both of them being trafficked and sold to a sheik had

changed their lives in many ways. It even had her talking to her mother which was unexpected, then she remembered she had called her, not her mother calling her. She was still worried about Eliana as she had changed since they had been trafficked.

Watching Angie, she saw much of herself, but also hints of her mother in her. She was smart, confident, fearless like Eliana, and perhaps far too pretty to go through life without men wanting to use her. Angie had learned how bad that can be, but she wasn't traumatized by it. She accepted that such people exist, and they could do something about it. Angie had her looks, and her mother's sensibilities. She was also very young and wanted to do things other girls her age did. She had never talked about dating, but she knew that would soon come. She thought how some guy would think she was just some easy action. She pitied that man. Angie carried her Glock in her thigh holster at all times, but she could stop a guy with just a stare now.

Tasting the soup, she smiled as it was perfect. She hadn't fully grown up in the Ukraine, yet she learned how to cook as if she had. Watching Angie set the table, she found herself thinking of her brother. She wished he was still alive to sit and eat with them. He was a very hurt person when he killed himself, but she had known him before he was abused, and he was sweet and kind. Even before he took his life, he was always that way to her, and to Angie when she was first born. She missed him.

With all the food ready, she went and sat at the table, and Angie joined her.

"Sweetie, I was just thinking of my brother. I wish he was here with us. I know he would have been your best buddy. You would have liked him. You grew up with just me. No family, not even friends as I hid you away. I'm sorry for all that. I think I did the right thing, but I wish things had been different, you know?"

"Mom, have you ever heard me complain? No. It's because you explained why since I can remember. It wasn't just me who lived like that. You too. You're so sweet, so pretty, and never had a boyfriend. All of that to protect both of us. I figured it out."

Angie had a way to make Cindy's heart melt. She was amazed at how understanding she was about the sad life they had led. The look she gave to Angie said how much she loved her. She told Angie she had stayed in the mobile home park too long. Anyplace would have been better.

Angie's look meant she didn't see it the same way.

"Mom… You know what? Living in that mobile home park? I'd walk out to get groceries in the morning, and later take out the garbage… and there were all those horrible men hitting on me when I was five, six, just a baby still. And I'd see how they treated any women who were around. Then you'd come home, and I understood we weren't like those people. That they're good people, and bad people. If we grew up in a place like here? I'd think everyone was okay, and that everyone is good and goes to church and school and all. That would be isolating me from things. I'd think everyone was good. You've always been what I want to be. Well, not the escort part, but, you know. All the rest of you."

Crying as she listened, what Angie said took away worries that she had been having. Everything she said was true, and she wasn't some silly girl believing what she read in *Teen Vogue*. She realized she was making fun of how sad things were for girls growing up in nice places, reading such trash. She smiled as she realized that.

"Angie, did you read that in…"

"Mom, no, I can figure things out on my own. I read that nonsense to understand how girls get themselves in trouble. I mean, like, the whole magazine rack is telling them act like sluts, go out and say they're ready to be trafficked. Jeez… It's like the new thing to do. See, I wasn't raised like that. I have to learn how the world is for real. I know I tease you with things I read in it. I guess it's my way of dealing with how messed up the world is."

Smiling at her, she said she did a pretty good impersonation of a smarty pants teen, then the doorbell rang. The security system was voice controlled, and it was Mike. She said he knew the code, come on in.

Hearing the front door open, they both looked at each other as it sounded like a lot of people coming in. Hearing hellos, they both jumped up to give hello hugs and were excited. Sharon had brought Whimsey with. She was holding Sharon's hand but let go when Cindy held out her arms for her to come and get a hug. She realized at that moment that Whimsey and Angie were almost the same age, and both had people who loved and cared about them. She smiled and told her she was so glad to see her.

Looking at Whimsey when she finally let her go, she noticed she looked quite different. She was smiling, and her smile would make

anyone feel wonderful. She was wearing a cute dress and maryjanes that matched. Her hair was long, and she noticed brown roots showing her natural color.

"I've prayed for you everyday. And look at you. What a pretty dress!"

Beaming, Whimsey looked back to Sharon, then back to Cindy, and Angie who had moved to stand with her and was checking her over.

"Thank you. Sharon took me to Kohls and we bought so many clothes. I had to wear this out of the store. I couldn't take it off knowing I was coming here."

Still giving her a once over, Angie crossed her arms after giving her a warm hug.

"You're what? Double zero? I've got a cute sweater that will go perfect with that. I'm a 0 now, so let's see if I have some things you'd fit in just right. I'm, well, growing…"

Then, as if nobody could hear.

"Don't tell my mom, okay?"

Laughing, Whimsey said she didn't think it was something she could hide.

"I can try. Mom, remember when I was little and I'd put on all your tawdry escort clothes? Now I've been trying on your tailored dresses, and they still don't fit. It will be a long time before I need a bra that's…"

"That's for me to know and you to keep out of, okay?"

Winking at Angie, she laughed and knew she was teasing, but in truth complementing her. She had always wanted to look like her, and she was getting there. She turned to Whimsey.

"We weren't sure if you'd be able to come. Are you out of the base now?"

Whimsey held out her hand and Sharon came to take it, smiling at her, then Cindy.

"She's free now that they've rounded up the traffickers and the porn guys. No more army duds. And we have some news. I can't wait to tell all of you. Hey, let's sit and I'll tell you all about it."

Cindy looked over at Mike, her look asking without words if he knew what was going on. His look back made it clear he didn't. After sitting and getting their glasses filled with a Mexican soda Angie saw advertised on Telemundo, Sharon raised her glass, and they all got the message and raised theirs too.

"I think a toast will be nice to remember things. I just picked Whimsey up today as the court appointed me her legal guardian. She'll be living with me, or I should say we're going to be together!"

Giving Sharon a look, Mike wondered how all that happened and he didn't know. He knew Whimsey was free to leave protective custody, but he assumed James had made arrangements for a place for her to stay for the present. Sharon saw that everyone had the same look of surprise.

"Okay, okay. Enough looking surprised. So, here's what happened. My so-smart brother had me right into his shrink's office, and Mike, thank you. You were so right. Charles is just… amazing. Wow, if anyone needs to deal with things, he's the guy to see. Anyway, because Whimsey was in foster care, I asked him what about if I wanted to have her live with me. I didn't think I could be a foster parent because of having been in porn and… well, you all know the reasons why I would think I couldn't be that. Then he explained that a guardian isn't a foster parent, and if Whimsey wanted me to be her guardian, and she told the court that, it was really up to her. So, we had a hearing, and the judge signed the papers, and I'll look out for her, including where she lives. I'm her legal guardian, but that's the last time I'll say that. It's a lot more than that."

Everyone was shocked when Angie asked how much more than that. Cindy looked at her, eyes wide with a, "what?" expression. Angie shrugged and said she wanted to understand. Whimsey was laughing, saying she asked a smart question, and she answered.

"You all know I was in foster care with a monster and all. When I finally talked with Sharon, I won't mention where, she was the only person who treated me like a human being. She was so kind that I just fell in love with her right then. I told her how I felt, and that maybe we could live together when I was safe. It has nothing to do with courts or being a guardian. I feel brand new with her. Like my life has just started. I'm so happy right now. I mean, look at me! I'm just a girl, doing nice things, and in a good place with a wonderful person."

Mike looked at her, then Sharon. He was truly happy for them but had a worry at the same time. He knew what was being said, and his face showed it although he was not saying anything as he didn't think it right to share his worry in front of others. Sharon saw his look and smiled at him.

"My brother, who takes care of everyone, clearly is sending me a look

of worry. Look, we've all been through hell together. No secrets here. I love Whimsey, and she loves me. We want to be together. I know that she's a minor, and I'm not. When we did porn, oh sure… it was okay for Whimsey to have sex with guys of all ages, women too. Nobody stopped them! But, oh, if we get together, it's throw Sharon in jail. So, let's all deal with that. So what? Yeah, together. A certain someone Mike had me see said if we're happy, there's no need to put up signs or tell anyone. We'll tell you, of course, but anyone else? Where were they when she was being banged by six forty-year-olds. If loving Whimsey is wrong, then I don't want to be right."

Mike made it simple.

"You are. I'm happy for both of you. You love each other, and that's all that matters."

Thinking it would be rude to pry more, Cindy accepted that if it had been any other young girl, it would be wrong. Whimsey had been abused, worked in porn, then was about to be trafficked. Looking at Sharon, she realized why they connected. She had been through many of the same horrors and neither one would judge or worry about the other. As she got up to go to the pantry for some extra things as Whimsey wasn't expected, Angie followed, saying she was pretty sure she had some churros there. Once inside, she looked at Cindy, and then put her mouth over her ear and asked an unexpected question.

"Mom, I'm like, well, just sixteen, so a lot older than Whimsey. If a woman Sharon's age fell in love with me and wanted to live with me… and go at me gooey and stuff… would you be okay with that?"

Looking at Angie, she knew she was sincere. The question hit her like a bolt of lightning. She had an instant reply.

"No, I wouldn't. Both of you are too young to make such a decision, and such a thing can change a life forever."

"Mom… I'm confused, and it's why I'm asking. Why is it okay for Sharon to have sex with her, but it wouldn't be for me, or any other teen girl?"

Taking Angie's hands, her expression grew serious. She realized she was going against what she knew wasn't right, but because it was people she knew, she thought it was okay. Angie had pointed out that no matter what, wrong was wrong. She talked softly to Angie.

"You're right. Whimsy's too young, and so vulnerable. I wasn't

thinking. I let my knowing them and worrying if they'd be okay that I lost sight of the truth. I'm going to talk to Mike about it. He was surprised. So, better get back out there…"

Nodding, Angie walked towards the table and shook her head.

"No churros. I'm sure my mom ate them. She lost weight from running from sheiks and former clients who want her back, and I think she wasn't filling up her C cup…"

"Angie! I thought you were getting a place-setting for Whimsey."

She had cut her off again as she was about to tell everyone she wore a C-cup bra. She didn't have a problem having anyone know. It was obvious she wasn't that big on top, and it matched the rest of her. She wanted to remind Angie there are things shared only with someone a woman was intimate with. Angie looked at her and was acting surprised.

"Mom, I'm getting it, I'm getting it. I was just about to say how nice you look even if you can't fill your…"

"Angie. The place setting."

Looking at Cindy, Whimsey told her not to feel bad. She couldn't fill an A cup, but that didn't stop men from going for her. Cindy took the pot of soup and put it in the middle of the table, saying time to start filling bowls.

"Mom, I'm getting you a larger bowl so you…"

"Angie. Eat."

CHAPTER 32

All the while Cindy and Angie were being a newly affluent single mother and precocious teen daughter, the news from Sharon had sent Mike into a state of worry. She had been trafficked by one of the strangest, sickest men he could imagine, had survived to be trusted by him to leave trafficking and work porn. Having been forced to escape, that had been because of her sexual encounter with Whimsey in a shower where she was being recorded and telling Whimsey about Peter's operation. If that hadn't happened, she'd still be doing porn, and most likely been Whimsey's lover in that instance. There was also something that was gnawing at him since the moment she called. She was making porns less than 100 miles from his apartment, and where they grew up. Finding one chance to make a call to him would have been all that was needed to free herself from Peter. She had only called because she was about to be killed for telling Whimsey about Peter and his plans.

Enjoying the soup and complimenting Cindy on how good it was, he looked over at Sharon He realized that he hadn't talked to her much since she was back. Having gone through all she had, he assumed it would be good to give her time to recover, work with Charles, and not probe about all that she did or ask for details. He was trained to know that people who are kidnapped, held prisoner or trafficked experience a profound change. To survive, they literally often start to love their captor and think what happened to them had saved them from the life they had led before being taken. Sharon had been a smart woman with a career, and she had dated men she liked but traveling and living as an archaeologist kept her from having a long-term relationship. Saying she hoped to find someone who did the same work, they could work together and travel the world.

Looking at her, she was preoccupied with Whimsey, whispering things in her ear, and she had one hand under the table. He knew it was rubbing the young girl, most likely between her legs as their way of getting excited at having a relationship that the world must never understand.

James had advised him when they went to take Peter down that Sharon may still be under his influence, and he had kept an eye on her for any sign of that. She had been given some quick training in how to

handle a gun, and she hadn't done anything that indicated she wanted to protect her captor once they were at his compound. She had even made it certain she wanted the kill shot and was able to shoot him although he had already died. Even considering each person reacts to stress and trauma in different ways, he thought it was simply because she was with him and feeling protected that she didn't show signs of being triggered by things done to her by Peter that worried him. Once back, the only thing he knew was she had a session with Charles, and now she was with Whimsey as her lover. That had started before she escaped.

An explosion of insight filled him with that thought. She had risked her life to warn Whimsey, and she had been around Peter's operations to know that he had cameras everywhere and she was being recorded. He suddenly saw things from that perspective. Whimsey was at risk, and she heard she was going to be sold off. What if she had been watching Whimsey and wanted her? Being heard, she knew they'd be dealt with. That would get both of them out of the porn studio into a car to Peter's jet. After two years and not being sold off, she was too smart to make a mistake. Being smart, she knew how to get where she could get away with Whimsey. Get them both in trouble.

Her using her little girl costume belt to kill the driver kept going through his mind. They had been ushered out with few personal items, but she had a long belt. Having gone undercover in a prison one time, he knew that one of personal items taken first was a prisoner's belt. It could be used to hang themselves or strangle someone else. Sharon had left with a belt on, and once on the back road used to go to the airport, she did something a trained agent would manage, but not many people who were untrained, and frightened, wouldn't even think of. She quietly told the driver to turn off some music as it triggered her, and with one motion swung her belt over his head, then pulled herself back from him as he drove, using her legs to push against the driver's seat back. She had even crossed the belt from behind to make it hard to pull apart from the sides of a neck. She had pushed so hard against the seat with her legs for power and leverage that the driver, unable to loosen the hold let go of the wheel and crashed the car into a tree as he was braking. The car hadn't been going fast at that point, and she killed him, then pulled him out of the car to take it. It was still drivable.

Thinking that in such a situation, all of that may have been either

opportunity or desperation as she'd be killed either way. But it didn't stop there. She did more than drive away. She backed up and managed to run the dead driver over with a front tire. Not once. Five times. That was something that he couldn't reconcile. A desperate person would flee, leaving the dead body there. She had acted with cold precision in his opinion. It seemed more than malice. She clearly had intent.

Another wave of what happened washed over him. The car was found to have location turned on in its GPS system. She drove to his place. She had driven a car that could be found at his door. His agency training had taught him to know cars could be tracked by modern emergency systems, so he rushed her and Whimsey away to Cindy's house. Before the day was over, Peter had sent a team to get Whimsey's sister, kill her, and drive a tow truck into Cindy's garage, then leave with the dead girl's body lying on the front seat of the truck.

How did Peter know anything about Cindy or where she lived? All the records were still being processed for her purchase of a house. Any records about her would show her living at the mobile home park. And he could have driven to the agency or any other place. But Peter knew where he went, and where Cindy lived.

There was only one way for Peter to know.

That's what was gnawing at him.

It could have been Whimsey, or Sharon, or both, but it had to be one of them who managed to let Peter or one of his men know where she was. It was true that Peter could have guessed she had run to him, and he could somehow find his location. That would make sense, but it was Whimsey's dead sister and the location of where Cindy lived that went far beyond Peter knowing where he lived. Things were making sense, and it wasn't what he had first thought had happened.

Now, watching Sharon sitting there with Whimsey, her lover, both free from Peter to be together, he grew cold inside. He didn't want to have the thought she had planned it all, but he didn't have any other answer. She had met with Charles, and with just one session had managed to get him sold on her being Whimsey's guardian. She told him the session was so helpful she felt like she had the trauma issues manageable by looking out for Whimsey's future, and not mentioning living together.

With his soup finished, and Cindy putting out stuffed peppers, he

took a plate from her, thanking her, but he couldn't think of anything other than if Sharon was behind all that happened, or he had dealt with too many corrupt people and was putting a puzzle together of his own design. There was nothing he could do during the dinner, but later he would call James and have any phone records from the house or anyone's phone that night searched. He would ask him to have Charles have her come in for a talk and share his take on what may have really happened and use a session to gain insight to her escape and actions that night. Charles was capable of broaching the subject as part of being sure she wasn't having delayed PTSD from what happened. He would also ask about the interrogations of the traffickers working for Peter. They should be questioned if Peter had any favored ass fucks or trafficked woman, or if they could point out Sharon as someone trusted by Peter from looking at photos of different women. It would need to be treated as if she wasn't his sister.

Knowing that anything was possible when it came to women who had been brutalized, groomed, and brainwashed, he hoped he was wrong on every point. He wouldn't sleep until he was sure.

Then, he looked at Whimsey. She hadn't been trafficked. She had showed up wanting to act in porn. She was obviously younger than 18 and using underage girls in porn had become a big issue for pornographers. He doubted with her being so young they would take the risk of using an underage girl. She had grown up with an abusive foster family — at least that's what she said — and she had a little sister. Both her parents had died. It was reported as a car accident, but it could have been that they were drugged. It could be Whimsey was behind all of it and was jealous of her sister. She had escaped being sold, and now she was privy to their actions through Sharon.

Wanting to jump up and run to the agency and start getting answers, he knew if any of that was true, the smartest action he could take was to finish up the stuffed peppers and compliment Cindy about how good they were.

CHAPTER 33

"I'm sorry Eliana. If the morphine isn't helping, sure, I can give you opioids, but you would have a hard time doing things you've always done. It's either pain or take those and not even know your own name."

Looking at the lush office of the specialist, the doctor was known the world over for prolonging the life of people with stage IV cancer. Shrugging at the man, she was studying the German doctor's office where she was getting told there wasn't much hope left. The country had been rebuilt after the war, and it was too modern for her taste. Her life-long doctor had an office in Kiev that looked the same since she was a girl. It was old and dark, lined with books, not computer screens. He had a model of an open chest and stomach to show parts having diseases and he wore a white lab coat and always had a stethoscope hanging from his neck. The man she sat across from wore a casual polo shirt and slacks. His office was filled with computers and screens, and there wasn't even a diploma hanging on the wall. It was a new world she wouldn't be a part of. She had known for a year she didn't have much time left, and the time she had left would be painful and she'd need to use drugs to function day-to-day.

"Give prescription for morphine and pills. I won't kill myself if you do. I have more guns than Russian Army. If I do that, I die with gun in hand, not needle like junkie. I have daughter. Granddaughter. I want them not to think me some junkie, that I decide my fate, not pills or needle."

Putting up cautions and saying it was not ethical to give her a lethal combination as she wasn't supervised by a caregiver, she looked at him and thought him an idiot.

"How fucked that is. And I sure you tell one with month to live not have a smoke? Some comfort in last days? Bad for health? So, then I get on street. I no want that. I want daughters to know I did right. Not disobey law. Have compassionate doctor."

Clicking the keys on his keyboard, he said he could only send the prescription to a pharmacy in Germany as it was a controlled substance. He stopped, looked at her, and told her it would be a large amount and most likely she wouldn't need a refill. She slowly nodded, knowing well what he meant.

"There. That is what wise doctor does. Takes care of patient when can't fix illness. Please do for others like me."

Using a pen and paper, which surprised her, he wrote down the name and address of a pharmacy, saying he would call it in as she left so she wouldn't have to wait more than an hour or two.

Walking out of the office building, she went to a café and decided to treat herself to some pastries. She was upset as she'd have so little time to work with Cindy to show her how to take over her operation. Knowing it wasn't just that, she admitted to herself she wanted to spend time with Cindy. Perhaps have her there when she passed away and make sure she had a decent mass and burial. Knowing it was time to face facts, she wouldn't have time to run her business and work with Cindy. She did have another option.

Drinking her latte and eating classic strudel, she had time before her prescription was ready. She brought a secure phone with her and used it to call Cindy. She had made her decision.

"Cynthia, I need talk. Be by yourself… Where is Angelia? Taking bath? Okay, we talk now. I want to come be with you. Short time… Maybe few months, maybe less… No. No business… You know business is… is not good thing. Not good for Angelia to grow up such way… I sit in office, others do dirty work, no see girls… Yes, at island, I look at girls, talk to them. Each one, I look… I see you and Angelia. It is no good to keep going, no good you do that… I am stopping. I will put you on accounts, give you all you will ever need… That is right. Time to retire, get to know you and precious granddaughter… Is good bishop at that cathedral there? I have much to confess… What… Why big change? I wanted tell you when I see you, but I just left doctor. I no have much time… No need wonder what. I have a cancer, bad. Have for long time… Yes, I knew. I hoped to last longer, but this is sign. To just give you money I have, not have you do sick business… I'm going home. Two, three days. Get last things set with money, get some little things I want with me… I'll fly to you. I just walk away. No more business. Others will grab hold like always happens… I'll call on way… No, no more doctors or hospitals. I have real prescription for pain, and I want be with my girls when I die… And, Cindy. I give special gift. I bring names of people like me from all over world… I know you want to stop them. Cindy. No need to play game. I know. You want work with me to

get list… No, I would do same thing if I was you… It is gift for you and Angelia… and Mike. I like him, I wish he was with you… I know Jamie hurt girl too, but still, good man hard to find… I have much to do, little time. I see you in few days… Please to do one thing for nasty mean trafficker lady, okay? Don't, please don't, feel bad for me. We all die. Feel good a nice lady die with children with her."

Unable to say more after that, she had kept strong and kept herself from crying. There would be time to cry after she took care of her girls. It was good she would be welcomed by them. She sat there, ordering another strudel, thinking how pointless getting revenge on the world and her husband had been. Money, power, payback… None of that was worth a day with her daughter, and she had given that up at first to keep her safe in America, but now she wished she had stayed there with her to watch Angelia grow up and be a busha. Grow old without a gun in her bag and a bodyguard.

Looking out the window of the café, she watched two teenage hookers walk by. In a rich business district, they were out parading without worry or shame. She knew they had a pimp watching out for them, but the truth was he was watching them to be sure they turned as many tricks as he expected of them. They thought they were safe. Nobody was. She wondered how long it would be before the two girls were strangled by some sick john or overdosed on drugs. She knew if not that, they'd be sold by their pimp to some trafficker as they were very young and attractive. They'd go for a good price to someone in the Middle East. She thought of how the sheiks made their wives and daughters cover themselves fully so no other men may see them but kept such girls naked in a guarded house to fuck and use as they wished. The girls they bought were less than nothing to them. They were not worthy of covering in such a culture. They were property, and revenge against infidels.

Many such men bought girls who got them hard enough to fuck their own wives. The girl would suck his cock as he lay with his wife and when he was about to cum, he'd stick his cock in his wife to get her pregnant to have many glorious children. After he filled his wife, such men kept fucking the girl in front of his wife, letting his wife know she was not to be used in such an unholy way. The wife was honored, the girl was trash to be used then thrown away when she no longer excited

or pleased him. With oil money, they would buy a new one, or many new ones. If not in the Middle East, the same happened anywhere in the world. The girls were things to own and degrade. Such buyers of young teen girls didn't love them or take them to dinner or be seen in public with them no matter what culture.

Watching more girls pass by, they were young girls in tailored clothing. They carried books and came from wealthy families. They were the prize for any trafficker. A young hooker would be sold to be a hooker or slave. Most didn't sell for much money. A teen daughter raised right, from a good home, a father who ran a corporation? One of the rare ones who hadn't been fucked yet? That was big money. The slut hooker and the rich family schoolgirl could each be as pretty as each other, and like most young thin girls they would have flawless bodies and pretty faces. To look at them, they were the same and would satisfy any sick sexual need. Be a pet, a slave, kept locked in a room or in a cage wearing a collar. Rich men bragged how his bitch slave wore a leash, crawling to her master and begging him to let her suck his cock. Each could do those things, and each would grow to want to do such pleasing of their owner. The alternative was to be sold again to someone who'd put them in a warehouse in Africa or India with a hundred beds separated by cardboard walls or sheets for laborers to spend their food money to fuck them or beat them for a much larger sum.

Men fresh from factory work or from loading docks didn't care where they came from. They paid their money for a girl to fuck without asking her or talking to her. They wanted them young, and to never say no to what they wanted to do. They'd pay at the door, get a number of a cubby where some girl had just finished fucking or sucking some other laborer. The girl got to eat, and live. She was a prisoner, and there was no Mike to rescue them. They were taken, gone, missing. They would never be heard from again. The girls were like paper cups. Filled with cum, then disposed of once used too many times. They were controlled with drugs, and once thrown out to the street, they'd do anything to get drugs and most would trade sex for it. Chances were they'd die from bad drugs, overdose, or be murdered and thrown into some dumpster or into a landfill. They started as flawless bodied girls being stupid and putting themselves in club dresses and thinking they'd meet a hot guy. They would. He'd find the flawless ones, charm them, and instead of taking

them home took them someplace where they'd be taken and flown off that night to be sold.

Seeing more young girls laughing as they walked by the café window, she could easily tell which ones would end up in a harem or a guarded compound of some president or corporate tycoon. The prettiest ones, the ones who thought they were hot would be the target for any trafficker. The ones with a BMW or in a designer club dress, the ones who were all attitude and flash. Any trafficker knows the reason those girls went for a hundred times the price of a slut or poor girl was the buyer wasn't just buying their bodies. They got off from taking the prize from another man. A rich man's daughter. The girl everyone lusted after. The one men saw in their minds when fucking their wives. The men used them as a form of revenge on the world. Taking the only thing of real value. Someone's daughter. Some girl's future. Her innocence came with that. The excitement of using her like a street whore. Having her lick his ass, drink his piss. Beg him to kick the shit out of her. Any whore would do that for almost nothing. They wanted the girl who would never do any of that for her boyfriend or husband someday. They paid to take dreams away from a father, a mother, a family, a culture, a religion, a race, a nation, and ultimately the girl. She knew it was always because men were pieces of shit. She knew they only felt power by taking an innocent girl and making her even less than he thought of himself. Nothing. Trash. Garbage. All those men had money, and few had earned it legally or ethically. They needed what others worked hard for. Valued. Cared about. That was how they felt potent and powerful.

Thinking of how when Cynthia was born, she had such hopes and dreams for her. She would hold her, cuddle with her, sing to her, say prayers for her, feed her special things she liked, give her little toys and stuffed animals she could hold. She'd put her in the bed with her and hold her, thinking of her life ahead. Each day she would dress her in pretty things, comb her hair, smile just seeing her. As she grew, she'd spend time each day getting dressed, brushing her teeth, reading and learning from books, going to play with friends. Little things were really big things. If another girl would be her friend. If she made her bed just right. If she was growing taller, getting pretty like her mother. Talking about what she wanted to eat, places to visit, and dreaming about her life when she grew up.

All of that, every moment spent to look pretty, learn things, get her hair parted just right… all of that would disappear in a flash. One day, if she was desirable, she could be taken, turned out to work the street, or sold to some sick fuck. From that moment, all those days up to that moment — her hopes and dreams for her future — would instantly vanish. Her mind would be filled with fear, and her hopes changed to keeping alive each day by pleasing her buyer. Her dreams would be if he liked how she sucked his cock, always looked at him the right way, said yes to everything he told her to do, got her tongue up his ass the way he liked, and said she craved being smacked or chained to a bed. If her dream came true, she'd make it to the next day and be alive. All her dreams when growing up would mean nothing. The combs, the dresses, the stuffed animals, the walks to the park, her mother's smile, her A on her test paper, the next episode of her favorite TV show… they would mean nothing. All that mattered once taken was staying alive and not beaten or given to other men for gang bangs or passed around to fuck as part of some deal to take over a company. She would only worry if her pussy was good to fuck, if her ass could take a pounding without her crying. Her hopes and dreams were pleasing a sick, worthless piece of shit with a mansion and a yacht.

Finishing her latte, she looked, and she had a text that her prescription was ready. She called her pilot and said send a car for her and after she picked up her medicine she'd head back to her own airstrip. It was time to get her money transferred, convert assets into cash or destroy them, shred all records she had, make sure all papers with connections to Cindy were in her purse, and that she'd leave no trace of herself once gone. She thought about putting all her guns and ammo in bags and drive herself later that night and dump them off a bridge into a lake where it was quite deep. She thought Cindy could use them, so would take them with her to America. When all that was done, she'd give her driver the title to her car after he took her to her plane. The last item on her agenda was to set a timer to ignite a large amount of explosive to destroy her home and to let all think she went up with it. After all that, she'd be on her way to die in Cindy's home.

Boarding her jet, as it went airborne, she saw the smoke from her house being on fire after the explosion. She didn't care.

The dead don't need houses, guns or money. They just needed

someone to burn or bury them. She crossed herself and thanked Mother Mary she had a daughter and granddaughter who would do that for her. If not for them, she'd be rubbish like the thousands of girls she had sold each year.

Part Four
The Reasons

CHAPTER 34

Slumping in the chair in a conference room James had ready for him and Charles, Mike knew what the meeting meant. If everything regarding Sharon and Whimsey was legitimate and clean, he would have gotten a call from James saying no fire, no need to put anything out. That was code for no need to take a suspect or guilty party into custody. He had hoped to hear there was no fire, but received a text from James he had set a meeting time and Charles would be there too.

Arriving fifteen minutes early, he was in the room by himself, somehow wishing he could slide down off the chair and enter some hole that would carry him away from the meeting. He had attended many like what was to come when he was an agent. Parents being told what happened to their daughter. A field agent being questioned for having sex with a trafficked girl who promised to fuck him if he helped her escape although that was his job. The room was referred to as the *Bad News* room, and it was soundproof and had shades to prevent viewing who was meeting in it. He had never expected to be the one sitting in the chair across from where agents usually sat, their backs to a one-way mirror now covered with a world map as cameras were used instead of one-way glass.

Looking up as the door opened, both James and Charles entered. James was carrying his Surface PC to refer to. They both shook hands with him but didn't smile or joke as they would on any other day. Before James could say anything once they sat, Mike thanked him for checking things he brought up, and James nodded, saying it was good he did.

"Mike, before talking about your sister, something you should be aware of. Cindy's mother is on her way here. She moved huge sums from accounts all over the world into a new Delaware corporation and it's in Cindy's and Angie's names. She blew up her house and cleared out. Didn't transfer her database or papers to anyone we know of, and there are lots of people running around Kiev trying to grab her business and girls. From what we know, she has a passport and no proof or cause to stop her. She's one smart woman. She's retired, I guess, and Cindy and Angie are worth more than we can count. We're still counting, but it's a lot. She had most of it in gold, and the market for it is the highest it's ever been. She'll be here soon, and I assume she'll be at Cindy's. Did you

know anything about it? Did Cindy?"

Shaking his head, surprised yet not surprised, he said he hadn't heard a thing, and if Cindy had, she would have told him. He added that both he and Cindy thought she had acted distracted and was different than expected when they hit Peter. Adding that may have been a sign, he wasn't expecting her to shut things down. James said it could be any kind of reason, but if she brings any data that could be of use, let him know.

Saying he would, he leaned forward as he sat up in the chair.

"This room doesn't have a sign outside that says good news. Charles, with you being here, I'll just say give it to me straight doctor, I can handle it. What've you learned?"

Putting the Surface down, James brought it to refer to images they recovered from Peter's compound along with some paper records. If needed, he would have them. He looked at Charles and asked him to start, knowing he had appointments coming up. Charles said he'd take as long as needed. No frantic patients, just routine visits. He turned to Mike and first said hello. Then, he leaned forward to look at him with full attention.

"It's hard to admit I missed red flags, but with Sharon, I did. I fucked up. I'm sorry. I called her last night, saying I thought I had set up a session for early this morning, as I need to do a follow-up. I realized I hadn't as we were pretty happy with our session. I asked if possible, could she come in this morning. She said she could and would be happy to tell me about how the guardian appointment went. That was a flag. She was happy. Mike, you know how things go for someone who was captive for over two years. They're not happy, or okay, or taking on anything other than their own problems adjusting to being back to a somewhat normal life. When we first met, I thought because she had you, and you had succeeded at offing the sick fucker who took her, that she was in that period where things looked great, but reality hadn't hit yet. I support that as it's cruel to remind them the past will kick them in the ass, so I was all smiles. Today, I was not sensing a traumatized person. Far from it. I would guess that's why your flags went up, right?"

Closing his eyes, then opening them as if in pain, Mike said that's exactly what caused his concern.

"Yeah. She showed up for dinner with Whimsey and she was overly

happy. She tells me she's doing the girl, and she didn't tell me she was going to court to be her guardian or have Whimsey move in with her. It was all a surprise. She'd always confided in me before she was taken, and it wasn't like I knew who she was. I stressed having sex with a minor was illegal and wrong, and she got indignant, saying if men running porn use girls like Whimsey, they don't hide it and get away with it, but if she does it, oh, arrest her and throw away the key. She also said you suggested to not tell people and keep mum about it. She never would have agreed with such advice before.. That, and she seemed distant when we did the raid. She didn't care about the captives at all. She did want to shoot Peter herself to make sure he was dead. I think of it now as she was with only for that, and I'm not sure now if it was payback. That's when I called. Cindy had everyone over for dinner, and that's when I learned about her and Whimsey being lovers and living together, being her guardian. Then all the tiny pieces came together, and I saw things weren't okay. That's when I called James."

Looking at him with sadness, Charles said he understood everything he shared, and it was how things felt when it comes to someone close like a relative.

"We want to think things are the same. Family members are traumatized too, and they want to think the best. Shit, I fell right into that as well as we're friends, and I wanted her to get full support and hoped she'd crawl out of that fucked up world she was in. Long story short. My opinion is that she wasn't just a prisoner in it. She was part of it. I can only offer my opinion as I don't have facts like James does. Today, talking to her, and realizing the same from our initial meeting, I felt manipulated. I was being groomed or programmed or brainwashed or whatever she was trying to do. She was feeding me bullshit, and I have to tell ya, she is fucking *great* at it. I would've fallen for it again if James hadn't told me what you thought may be going on. That's all I have. I don't believe her, factually, and don't think of her as a traumatized person. She's manipulative and was playing me, and I am sure everyone else. Well, there is one more thing…"

Both Mike and James looked at him, waiting. Charles raised his hand with his finger up, and they could tell he was thinking how best to tell them what he wanted to say. They looked at each other, wondering what, and as Charles cleared his throat, they both looked at him with concern.

"This is not based on direct contact and is speculation. A feeling…
or just plain fucking experience kicking me in the ass to not screw up
again. She kept talking about her and Whimsey. She gets hold of her as
guardian, they're fucking, and together. Yet she said they hardly knew
each other before the escape. I could accept transference of dependency,
all that bullshit, but nah. Too much, too fast. Clinically, time with
Whimsey would be a trigger. It would put her back to her life being in
peril because she told Whimsey about Peter, and they were both headed
to be killed or whatever was planned for them. As I was listening to her,
I picked up that there's more to it than Sharon says. I think it's possible
Whimsey is a more than an innocent victim. That one, not sure about at
all. Just me questioning things. Like, what if Whimsey is the driver and
has Sharon under her control? If that's the case, her sister would know
the truth about her. If she's a psychopath, well, she'd want to make sure
her sister doesn't make that known, so…"

Mike finished the thought for him.

"She'd have her killed. She found Sharon, which leads to me, which
leads to here. Well, great. That's something that hit me too. Not the
killing her own sister, but that it was her causing the change in Sharon."

Getting up, Charles said it was best to think objectively like they
would with any case. If Sharon lied like she had to him, she was most
likely lying to everyone. If they wished, he'd meet with Whimsey. The
idea of her being the controller was a long shot, but as she'd been used,
she'd be showing signs of trauma at this point. He paused, and before
leaving said his final thoughts.

"I'm really surprised the court didn't order a psych exam. Abused
at the foster home, doing porn at what, twelve? Of her own volition?
Sharon may have worked the court as effectively as she did me. I haven't
a clue what Whimsey is like. Is she a sweet little heartbreaker like
Hendrix sang about?"

Mike and James both said "Yeah" at the same time. Charles looked at
them as he turned to walk out.

"There you go. Two men experienced at not being fooled saying yes
instantly when I asked if she was a heartbreaker. Don't worry. We're all
suckers for a pretty face. We want to be big heroes. That, my friends, is
how it works. We're not the stronger sex. We just have more muscles to
lift heavy things."

Watching the door closing both stared at each other. Charles was certain he had been made a fool of, and they were feeling the same. Mike looked at James and slowly shook his head.

"Okay. Two things. First, how the hell do we figure any of this out? Second, and it's just hit me now that Charles talked, what're they after? Why not just come back and go at it in private? Even if she ended up with some other guardian. And why the fuck aren't they basket cases like everyone else at this point? Charles thought Sharon may have been part of Peter's organization, or his lover, and that she's taking his place or something. How is she going to do that from here and attract girls and all?"

Mike could see a light bulb go off over James' head. His eyes were wide with surprise.

"Oh, it could make sense. Who do we know that can lure anyone to do what she wants. Us included?"

Mike realized how precise that statement was.

"Whimsey. Oh my God, James. She has all the key skills of the best recruiters. She's not threatening. She plays the innocent who needs you. She was a porn actress who has zero respect for sex or being used for money, so now she could turn it around at getting others to make money for her. Who can turn her down or say no? None of us have. And combine that with Sharon. No matter what's happened, I can tell you she's intelligent. She finished a six-year program in three years, and top of her class. And she was put on a big deal antiquity dig over famous people. Then out of the blue, she's trafficked to Morocco? What if it wasn't a take?"

Turning his Surface on, James scrolled through records and pictures. He said that was a possibility.

"We searched where she went missing… where she said she was taken. There was an interview with the team lead on the dig by the police there when he reported her missing. They interviewed locals and the team. Some locals said she must have run off with a man she had been meeting in areas where only locals went as they were shady parts of the city. They said the man had someone snatching girls, but those were grab and go things. With Sharon, they wondered why he didn't take her right away as she was hot stuff and would be in demand. Shady part of town indeed. That's why the police thought for sure she was taken as

she'd been seen with him, a known trafficker. But she was deep in talks with him according to those interviewed. Then, they talked to her team on the dig. She didn't socialize with them, and two men said they saw her with a local, and the description was a match for Peter. Now, this one stopped me cold. You know how Peter had his chapel and was a religious cult leader who used trafficking as part of his belief to take girls away from the devil? All the bible-based stuff? Well, the locals said they despised him… but not for taking girls. They were part of that shit and it's not unusual for daughters to be sold off there. They disliked him and didn't want him there as he was a fanatical Christian always talking about Mary and God and the dark one, as it says in the interviews. See how this is playing out?"

Amazed at the report, Mike had one observation.

"That fits like a glove. All the people who were part of Peter's operation were the same. But, and this is the big thing, Sharon isn't religious and not a religious fanatic. So, that isn't fitting."

James sat back and crossed his arms as he looked at James. He wanted to pose a difficult question.

"When she went to college, she may not have been. So, when she went off to school, what were you doing? How often did you see her, or talk to her?"

James said "Ouch." He got the point.

"Just Thanksgiving and Christmas. Even then, not at her college or my place or home. A restaurant, usually. As for calls… She was so intent on getting her degree she was always researching or busy, so not often, and on those, just short ones. Then she was off to some dig right away. I was going nonstop all over the world doing fashion shoots, so busy being a hot shot glamour photographer. Short answer. Not much at all."

Looking at the Surface screen, James read a few items, then looked up.

"One thing that happens at college… Often to the brightest ones there. They get involved in groups, sometimes even cults. A lot can happen. We looked at groups on campus when she was at school. She joined a group into archeology, and their focus was on finding religious sites where Christ was said to have met with the devil. The temptation story. She was very active on holidays going off to digs in the Holy Land. We have her passport records. She went five times. She never told you?"

Shaking his head no, Mike was sitting reacting with shock at how much James had learned — and how much he didn't know about his sister. He looked at James, and almost scoffed as he asked one last question.

"Okay. Don't tell me. You looked on your screen and you have a report that Whimsey's foster parents were part of the faith, or cult, whatever it is?"

James looked at him, and his mouth was hanging open.

"How did you guess that one? But, to answer your question. Yes. They raised Whimsey in it. Sexual sacrifices. The whole nine yards."

Mike looked at him, and James stared back. Mike had a one-word reaction.

"Fuck!"

CHAPTER 35

Getting a call from James, Charles listened to what his team had learned about Sharon and Whimsey, then James asked if he could meet with Whimsey on short notice.

Charles agreed with their conclusion once James told him how both Sharon and Whimsey were deeply involved in the religious cult Peter had led. He asked questions about the foster family and more about the group Sharon belonged to when at college. Finally, he asked if the cult or college group had a web site. Told the cult didn't, the college groups did as they were raised on social media and used it to recruit and hold meetings. Charles said that would be a help.

"All this will make meeting with her bring out things I hadn't been told about by Sharon. Fuck, James, bad enough dealing with trafficking and what it does to people. Now, cults as well? Shit, I hate cults. As a resident to get my PhD, I worked with kids brainwashed from cults. Court-ordered evals. They're zombies. It's like a virus that eats their brain and replaces it. That will help me if she's controlled, but if she's a true believer, that will take longer. Set it up, and I think it best the judge from the guardian approval is the one who says it's mandatory… an oversight. If it's not done, his clerk can't process the paperwork, so she has to get in now. The judge can ask Sharon if she has a shrink she trusts, she'll say me, and have him say that would be good. Let me know, and I'll see her when you say."

Feeling disappointed in himself for reading Sharon so wrong, he decided to take a different tact with the girl if she came to him. He'd go along with whatever she said or did and gain her trust in somewhat the same way he had been understanding and supportive of Sharon because she was Mike's sister. This time it would be strategic, not trusting.

Having some history from James, he knew both Whimsey and Sharon were going to veil most all truths unless he too was a "believer." Going to the web page of the cult Sharon had belonged to in college, he read every line, and well between the lines. They had links to resources and other groups. He went to those as well, learning that the cult was all over the world and had financial resources. Going to the two universities he attended to become a medical doctor then psychiatrist, he found they were there. He smiled as his diplomas were on the wall, and he could use

references to his own schools if needed.

Spending three hours doing research, the reading suggested the group viewed sex as the most powerful tool of what they called the Only One. It was clearly a reference to their own interpretation of Christ, and his battle with the dark one for his soul. The dark one tempted Christ with women, and failing, told him since he passed up such sweet treats, all who believed in the dark one would take girls and make them into whores who'd worship sex more than the Only One. Each of the web sites had a banner on the first page reading, "Fight Fire with Fire." Not particularly original, the concept was to defeat the devil by tempting his minions by taking all the sweetest treats. He knew that meant young women who would keep them from ones worshiping the devil.

Sitting back, he was always amazed at cults. He thought to himself that they all had the same objective. Get followers to give them their money, raise money, and most important provide the cult leader with an endless stream of young women who would do anything he wanted. This cult had bypassed all the nonsense and went right for the young girls. They gathered them, then made sure they went to cult members who paid for them in the form of donations. To have meaning, as the cult members had money, the girls were "surrendered" for a price. The site said they needed to give all — or at least as much as they could get to allow taking more girls away from the dark one. Many sites had photos of teens and little girls lined up, stating wealthy members were honored warriors in the battle to keep the girls safe from being taken by the minions of the dark one.

They had created a sophisticated religious trafficking network, and most ingenious, the donations were tax exempt. It was an old story told in a new way. Many pictures on the sites were of very young girls standing with their parents. They were being "offered" to the mission of the cult. It was making him sick. He was amazed at how ingenious mankind came up with ways to do all things evil or bad. If only all that effort went into something that helped people, the world would be a great place to be for a while.

Having been taking appointment calls as he read the sites, near five he received a call from Sharon. He made sure to sound surprised, asking if she needed to come back already.

"Actually, my talk with you put me on the right path, and a lot's

happened. The big news is I did what you said about being Whimsey's guardian, and yep, the court said yes and appointed me. She's with me, and we're both happy and healing."

Reminding him he suggested she have Whimsey ask the court for her to be the guardian, he winced, but kept the charade going.

"Sharon, that's wonderful. I'm glad you brought that up and I could help. Hooray for both of you. Thanks for letting me know. How's Whimsey?"

He could hear what she was going to say next in his head. She was wasting no time.

"She's happy as can be, but something just happened that has both of us a bit shaken up. Things move along pretty fast in the court, and I just got a call from the judge, not his clerk. He said as it was a simple appointment, he was so taken with hearing Whimsey talk about things he overlooked asking if she had an evaluation. Maybe you know about all that? I guess to be sure she's capable of making a good decision, she needs to be okay emotionally and all, so, let me see, I wrote it down… yes, a psychiatric evaluation by a board-certified psychologist or psychiatrist is mandatory. He said until he has a letter or some form from one, the appointment isn't in place, and he can't finalize it without one. Do you know what he's talking about?"

Gotcha, he thought to himself. Things were going to plan.

"Sharon, I do. It's like getting married. A priest can marry you, but a court needs to issue a marriage certificate to be legal. Sadly, the laws of God don't mean much. Yes, the person wishing to choose a guardian rather than have one appointed by the court has to be capable of making a decision, and one that is in their own best interest. It's that, or they appoint someone. I'm sorry to hear there was a hiccup in the process. But, easily fixed. She visits a shrink, he or she says she's good to go, and they fax it to his clerk. I used to do lots of those before working for the agency."

Thinking he just squeaked in with his reference to the laws of God and man are not the same, he did make it clear he had done evals many times. He was ready for the next one.

"Charles, can you still do them? I mean legally?"

"As long as I have my diploma up, yes. I have my little seal and everything, and I'm licensed by the state for it."

"Oh, Charles, I'm really glad to hear that. You know, I've been doing pretty good since we met, but when this happened? It was like Peter telling me what I couldn't do happening all over again. I'm in a panic, really. I keep thinking nonstop about what if we go to someone we don't know, and they say she's not capable or something. That could pull us apart and I'm freaked out!"

"Sharon, no need for that as I'll consider this something you need to not be triggered. I can meet with Whimsey and do the evaluation, put my seal on it and fax it to his clerk. As soon as they get it, it's filed and I'm sure that the clerk will look it over and process the court order for you as guardian. Okay, does hearing that help you? Still freaking out?"

He smiled. She had said everything in a smart way. She made it about herself, meaning she was turning to him as part of being traumatized. She was clever. She changed her panicked tone.

"Oh, it does. I feel better already. Just knowing you'll be doing it. Well, still a bit of anxiety until things are final. I don't want the clerk or judge to go and decide to appoint someone to be her guardian before you get them your stuff. I don't think I'll even be able to sleep until this is all finished and over with. I've been waiting for the final paperwork each day and that's been rough. Could you do it, well, as soon as possible? For me?"

Shaking his head, she was pulling every trick in the book, now pulling at his heart strings.

"Given the situation and that you're in crisis mode, yes, I can do that. I was just looking at my schedule before you called, and I'm fully booked the next few days. I have tonight open if you don't mind a night visit. Many people prefer it. I somehow didn't have any tonight and was going to do note transcription."

"You can? You would? What a godsend you are. Well, an idea to not put you through too much. Would it be possible to do it over the phone? Or FaceTime?"

Thinking why not just ask him to lie for her and be happy to do it, he wouldn't do that for anyone.

"Sharon, good idea, and I appreciate you worrying about my time but that wouldn't work. My board certification and the law requires I meet face-to-face for evals. It would be wrong of me not to and could mess things up if I tried that. I'll make it simple and easy for her, don't worry."

There was a short pause on the line, about a minute, and then she continued.

"Gee. That's crazy as we have all those video things now. I'm curious, what can you do in person that you couldn't do in a FaceTime call?"

Not bothering to explain that any visit in the office allowed any clinician to observe body language, twitches, and other things that can only be seen when meeting in person, he wanted her to hear the truth seldom mentioned… and one he knew would cause panic in her.

"There are a lot of observations I'm required to make, ask very specific questions, and make sure it's done with her in private."

Knowing her next question, he wanted to learn if she would ask him to break the law by not meeting in person.

"Really? I can't be there with her?"

"You can be outside in the waiting room, but as I do that test? No. It's a requirement. Some people, before the law, would come in and have signals or prompts, even answer questions for them."

Hearing her breathing grow deep, she was sure he would let her be part of it.

"Oh, oh… I'm starting to panic! I don't know if I can be apart from her that long. This is so silly, it's so mean, can't I sit in the corner or something?"

He had her making mistakes, and that's what he wanted. He decided to make it "do or don't do" time.

"I have to follow the rules and do it right. Do you want me to do something I'm not supposed to? Believe me, that can get my license taken away."

Waiting for nearly a minute, he finally heard a reply.

"No, I don't want you to do something you're not supposed to. I was hoping you'd take care of me…"

Shaking his head as she had sunk low to say that there was no point in continuing on, so he hit back with the truth.

"Sharon, understand that by meeting tonight, which I wouldn't do for someone else, *is* doing it for you. If not, I'd never do an eval on such short notice. I'd need medical history, and other things too. I have to sign I did things correctly including no other person was present. So, it's up to you. I'm here. If you can handle a little time alone, leave and come now. It'll be over and done with. If not, I don't have an answer. Anyone

who can sign the document will be faced with doing it the same way. You can call others, but after tonight, I'm booked full. It's a two-hour session so I have to tell you, most first-time eval appointments are weeks to months away when you make them. So, let's do this. Think it over, and if you want to do it, and I'm still here, call me and let me know."

That was all he would say. He put her to the test. His way or find someone else. He listened to her crying, fumbling with the phone, calling out to Whimsey she'll be okay. She was using every trick in the book as he sat there waiting. As he was about to say he was going to end the call but would answer if she called back, she beat him to it with her answer.

"Okay, thank you Charles. Like I mentioned, this has me off the deep end. I know you're being very kind by seeing her tonight, and that will help me be okay. We just need to get some clothes on, and we're on our way. I'll probably look a fright as I've been crying so much. See you in about twenty minutes."

"Sounds good. It'll be done before you know it, and we'll fax it off and you can get back to better times. Okay, see you soon. The parking lot is open, but there's a security guard and I'll let him know both of you will be here soon. See you then."

Ending the call, he hadn't missed the part about they both needed to get dressed to plant the image of them both naked in his mind. If any of what she was going through was true she wouldn't be naked with the girl and able to go at her for sex.

Transcribing notes, it was just short of twenty minutes when he heard his bell at the front door.

"Needed to get dressed… right. You were probably a few blocks away somewhere." The thought in his mind helped him get ready for lies. Opening the door, Sharon was standing there looking worried, but it didn't look genuine. Whimsey was standing next to her, smiling up at him. He understood what Mike and James meant about how she looked and acted. She was small, cuter than any girl he'd ever seen, and she was wearing a jumper that was bright pink, cut at her hips, and so snug it shaped around her clef, hiding nothing. He was sure from behind he'd see her ass hanging out of it. She was wearing her hair in pigtails, and he almost laughed at that touch. Even without practically being naked with the romper showing all she shouldn't be showing and the childish

pigtails, she was naturally beautiful and hard to not look at. She was classic adorable; the type of woman-child men would fawn over to help in the hopes they'd get a very generous thank you.

He didn't react. Sharon was in a casual knit top and jeans, looked nice but putting all the attention on Whimsey. Standing back to let them in, he showed Sharon were there were sodas and snacks, telling her to make herself comfortable and there were lots of books to read. She acted nervous, but said they were glad to be there as she nodded to his offerings.

Moving to his private office door, he told Whimsey to follow him. He expected her to take his hand, and she may have but he moved ahead of her to hold the door open. Whimsey turned around and ran to Sharon and hugged her saying she'd be alright, then ran back into his office. They had it all planned in his opinion. It didn't feel genuine.

Once inside his office he told her to sit in one of the large chairs, saying they were cozy, and he just needed to get a form he worked off of. She was calm and went to sit on the large chair and made it look bigger than it was as she was so small sitting in the middle of it, her arms out to her sides propping herself straight up as she stared at him. Getting his clipboard and a worksheet the courts needed, he sat across from her as she nodded, acting shy, waiting for him to talk.

"I'm going to ask you some questions, and some may seem pointless as I have to outright ask you your name, date of birth, address… all those things. That's so I can say I met with you and not somebody else. Best just to answer all the questions and I'll finish faster that way. Some questions won't make sense except to a doctor like me, but I don't make them up. I have to ask each one to do this right. Okay, do you understand?"

Nodding, she said yes, then asked if he would be asking all about her doing porn and things like that. He understood she was probably prepared to give a sob story, but the evaluation didn't ask those kinds of questions.

"No, nothing like that. That's for therapy using a regular visit. This is to see if you are what the law defines as capable, and able to understand important questions and answer them. Make choices. It won't ask about what you've done or do, it is about if you are able to answer important questions and can make reasonable decisions. Does that help?"

Nodding, she smiled at him, and her arms bent slightly as she crossed her legs. From where he sat he saw her smooth, silky legs and a good part of her ass that wasn't covered when her legs crossed. It wasn't blatant. He could tell she used her sexual nature naturally, but it was something she had to be aware of.

Starting the test, she leaned forward after a short time, and the romper was somewhat loose on the top with a scoop neckline as she had no breasts to fill it. As she leaned over it was enough where he could see down the jumper and had a view of her nipples on her flat chest. He had no problem looking at her even able to see so much of her. He assumed she wanted a reaction from him, and it could be that happened so often in her life it was unusual to not have a man not gawk at her in a lustful way.

She relaxed as the first questions were completed, and he told her with those out of the way, he'd ask questions where there were no right or wrong answers, so just listen, answer, and he wouldn't ask her about her answers. It wasn't him asking his own questions, not a conversation, and some of them would be yes or no questions. He said say yes or no, nothing else was needed. Asking her if she understood, she started to nod, then stopped suddenly and looked apprehensive.

"Doctor Charles, do you think I'm pretty?"

It didn't surprise him. He wasn't going to participate in such games. He sat waiting for her to be sure she didn't say more. She looked at him with a longing to be told she was. He sat, then spoke in a calm, matter of fact manner.

"We need to do this a certain way. What I think or don't think isn't part of what we're doing. Keep to focusing on the questions and answer them. Not answering them or talking about other things is part of the test. Asking me questions is part of it, and I'll have to indicate you weren't listening to questions or aware of the impact this test will have on your future. Do you understand? A first question such as yours is not noted on the form, so now you know. Are you ready to start?"

She sat back upright, uncrossed her legs and pouted slightly. He knew she was punishing him for not doing what she wanted, taking back a view of her almost naked. He sat with a blank expression, showing no reaction to her movement, something she knew how to do quite well and make look natural and child-like. A little girl asking for candy and not getting any.

Crossing her arms, she apologized, saying she was a bit nervous and insecure about taking tests, but she understood and was ready. He thought it a slick comeback that most people would fall for. He simply looked down and started going through a series of simple questions about if she knew the day of the week, what year it was, who he was, and she answered each one quickly and properly with full awareness of reality. He grew interested in giving her the test. It would help him understand if she was rational or was doing things such as porn as an irrational act, or because she wasn't cognitive of such choices.

Moving past questions that determined if she was aware of who she was, what she was doing, and about basically being in touch with reality, she had answered all the questions that established she was coherent and capable of proceeding. The next questions were to solicit a response of how she reacted to common life situations, and would be interesting to hear her replies.

'Okay. Now, I'll ask questions and you just answer. No thinking it over. An example is you don't like the color red, but you are in a red room to collect a prize. What would you do? That is the question, and to make sure you understand, give an answer, though this is a preview and not counted. So what would you do."

Without hesitation, she answered.

"I'd close my eyes to not see the red until they called my name for the prize, then leave."

She surprised him. That was a surprisingly effective response. He told her she understood the nature of the questions and said that part would begin. She sat, waiting. He began.

"You are thirsty but the faucet isn't working. What would you do?"

"Look to see if there was bottled soda or water. If not, ask a neighbor for help."

"A friend promised to go to the movies with you. The friend doesn't show up. Would you go to the movies on your own?"

"Not on my own. I'd call another friend or go home."

"You are sleeping and are woken up by a loud noise. What would you do?"

"Be frightened by it."

"And, last one of this type. Someone steals something from you. What would you do about it?"

"I'd have to find a way to replace what was stolen."

Again, Charles thought the answers were more than cognitive replies. He was reaching the more telling parts of the evaluation. All questions so far had been to establish the process. Now the insightful responses would reveal much more.

"Okay, now the questions will be where you can give opinions, express feelings, thoughts… whatever comes to mind. Again, it's important to just react, not think about an answer. Ready?"

Nodding yes, she changed to sitting cross-legged, and Charles could see the crotch of her jumper was such he could see labia on one side, and she wasn't wearing underwear. With her legs crossed and under her bottom she had herself on display. He considered it could just be how she dressed, or it was meant to either attract or distract him. He thought it sad, but it didn't distract him from the test.

"Let's begin. You're at a party and watching everyone else having fun, but you're standing alone in the corner. Why are you standing by yourself?"

"I don't know anyone there, or it's couples and I'm single and the wives are keeping their men away from me."

Okay, next. You receive a large sum of money you didn't expect to get. What do you do with the money?"

"Donate it to my church but keep some for taking vacations."

"There are days when you don't feel like getting out of bed. Why?"

"I'm happy in bed making love."

"To get a job, you fill out an application. One question to get the job is if you like to work alone. How do you answer?"

"I would leave. I don't like being alone."

"One more, you wake up from an upsetting dream. Do you worry about it, or ignore you had it?"

"That would depend on the dream. Sometimes nightmares are kind of exciting. If it's really upsetting I'd think about it and wonder what it means."

Looking back up, Whimsey had changed position to where one leg was under her bottom, the other dangling off the edge of the chair, and she was slumped down in it. It revealed even more of her. Charles only glanced to tell her the next part was a question where she needed to rate each thing, giving it a 1 through 5, 1 meaning very little, 5 meaning a lot. He asked if she understood.

"Sure, 1, not much at all. 5, all the way."

"That's correct, and after this section there's a short break of five minutes for refreshments or bathroom use. So, first question is, I am anxious, nervous and worried. 1 is not at all, 5 is a lot."

"A zero, so put a 1 down."

"Next, everything I do is out of my control. Same 1 through 5."

"1. Not everything I do is out of my control. To be more it says everything and that would be like a basket case or that sort of thing."

Okay, next one is I have trouble sleeping and can't get enough rest."

"2. Once in a while I can't fall asleep even if I want to."

"Okay, next, I have difficulty breathing or swallowing."

Suddenly laughing, she apologized.

"Sorry, a 1. Just when I was doing porn I did things where I couldn't do either. That made me think about that."

"I understand, but remember, it's about not associating memories or meanings, just a response that comes right to mind."

She was still laughing. He realized she was going to talk more about the question.

"Charles, I don't mean to be rude or get too detailed, but have you ever had your dick all the way down a girl's throat? And she can't breathe, and you like really get off on it? There's a question I can talk all about."

She had both feet up on the chair, legs fully apart where when he looked at her she was clearly showing him all she had. It was no longer subtle or just being restless. He wanted to see what would happen if he said she needed to stop the provocation and thought it best to try.

"Whimsey, I'm trying to get this done so you and Sharon don't have to worry about it. It's obvious that you're trying to get my attention with sexual positions like you're in right now. And you were doing well and now you're talking about sex acts, which is a distraction. I want you to stop any of that, sit in a less revealing way and keep to the answers."

Shaking her head, she said she was having a problem, and wondered if they could take the break now.

"We could. Is the problem related to taking the test?"

With her knees still up, she lowered her torso and took a position that was meant to be as if having sex. She had her eyes up to him, and she was breathing deep.

"It's related to who's giving the test. I can't help how I feel… I'm looking at you as we sit here and all I can do is think about going over to you and pulling your cock out and sucking you off. I think you'd like it. I'm really worked up right now."

Slipping down from the chair she crawled on her hands and knees to be in front of him.

"You know, we can keep going with the test. I can pretty much talk with my mouth full. I really need some cum right now…"

Charles let her get that far to see if she was willing to forgo the test and not have Sharon appointed as her guardian. She was in front of him, still on her hands and knees, looking up at him, waiting. Her mouth opened and her tongue came out, and she was letting spit drip to the carpet.

Thinking himself too experienced to have any reaction, he found himself aroused. Even more surprising, without being aware of it at first, he had an erection and Whimsey could see he had gotten hard. He was having unwanted thoughts of letting her suck him off. When else would he have a girl that sexual willing to do him like he was in a porn with her. Her hair, the braids, the spit pooled on her tongue like she had just taken his load… He was filled with lust and wanted to pull his cock out and let her work it. He grew harder and he wanted to fuck her right there and not care about the fucking test. He'd fill it all in and say she's good. She looked so good to him, and he found his hand rubbing his erection over his pants.

As he neared the point of struggling to keep from doing everything he knew he shouldn't in both mind and body, without expecting it Whimsey stood up and walked calmly back to her chair, turned and sat modestly, looking at him with a soft smile.

"That's my answer about having a hard time breathing or swallowing. See how that happens? So, what's the next question?"

His adrenaline rushed through him for every reason possible. He was furious he had been made a fool of, but most of all he was upset she wasn't sucking his dick. He held up his hand, then asked her if she'd like some bottled water. She looked over to a table where there were bottles of it, saying she'd get some for both.

Walking to him, she was gentle and handed him a bottle, then twisted the cap on hers, taking a long drink, but not in a provocative

manner. She looked sad, if anything. The chairs weren't far apart, and she went and sat on the edge of hers, legs together, leaning forward in a way that showed a concern for him. He didn't say anything, just opened his water and took a long gulp.

"Charles, see how it goes? See what my life is like? That test is to see if I am competent. In control of myself to make decisions. Who was the one here in control? I knew what I was doing. I knew if I did the oh I want you so bad thing, I could get you going. And I knew I could stop whenever I wanted to, walk away. That's control. That's knowing right from wrong, what I can do, not do. Everything on that test. And I learned I had to control my life when I was being fucked by my pervert foster dad. He kept at me and didn't know I was doing porn as he was at work when I was too. He'd come home and shove his dick in me, and it was full from a dozen cums. When he kissed me, my mouth still had the tastes of all the asses I tongued. I wanted that."

She took another drink, and he sat, not knowing what best to do. She looked at him, and shook her head.

"Trafficking? Men wanting a little tiny teen like me? You're working to stop men from taking girls like me, and like you said about the test. Just answer. The first thing that enters your head. You wanted me to blow you, right?"

It shocked him, but he found himself saying yes, he did. She nodded.

"You couldn't hide it. See how it goes? You know better than to want that. But another minute, you would have been everything you fight against. Question, right, or wrong."

Her face. Charles couldn't do anything except look at her and answer.

"Right… right."

"No need to explain or elaborate. And now a question where you say whatever you want, whatever comes to your mind."

"How do you live with yourself knowing that you could do a 14-year-old traumatized girl?"

He was near tears. He had never been in such a situation where he had opportunity to do something like that, and he didn't know if it was a need in him, or that Whimsey was so expert at getting a man to do what she wanted. He couldn't escape the swirl of thoughts about doing everything he was supposed to be against. Whimsey said she had one more question.

"Charles, do you think you'll have a hard time sleeping tonight?"

Looking at her, she wasn't being mean or working him. She was telling him something, and somehow that focused him, and he felt himself being rational again. She sat, nodding. She was telling him about herself, and him. He was able to think clearly enough to talk to her.

"Whimsey, I've never experienced something like what just happened. I'm going to be direct as it's the only way I know how to be. Did you do that to mess with me and hurt me?"

Still shaking her head, the look of sadness on her face was more evident. She was completely serious.

"No."

Accepting her reply, he could tell she wasn't doing anything to hurt him. She could have continued, and as he talked, done even worse to him. He asked her why she had done it then."

Still sitting upright, holding her bottled water, she both nodded and shook her head, and he knew the motion. It meant it was a good question.

"Charles, a lot has happened to me, young as I am. I've learned how people really are. How just me looking up at a man can make him forget his wife and his job and everything. You know, nobody came to save me when my foster dad went at me. Nobody saw what was so obvious. They gave me tests because I couldn't sleep. Want to know why? I was terrified he'd choke me. And I was the one being asked if I had trouble sleeping. When you got to that question, I thought of how the shrinks and the social workers thought I was the one who was messed up. And when they saw marks, I went to a shrink who said that I had come on to the asshole, and my marks were because he had to push me away…"

It was horrible to hear everything she said. He knew it was all true. She was telling him what she hadn't been able to tell anyone who she was told to turn to. He was overtaken with guilt and shame and said something he knew better than to ever say to an abused person.

"I understand…"

She didn't laugh, but her look told him how absurd that was.

"No, Charles. Until I crawled up to you and you were ready to fuck me, you didn't understand. How are you going to stop creeps from taking girls like me if you can't face that you have that same sick shit in you? Now you know. Instead of being a doctor with a patient who did

what I had, imagine if you were some billionaire? And nobody could say no to you, and you got away with everything. How many Whimsey's would you have in some locked room in the basement of your mansion? One? Three? Ten?"

He knew she was right, and it was the thing never talked about by his profession. Under the right circumstances, the animal inside each person could be out of its cage. He would never be the same.

He did something that was sincere, but her reaction shocked him.

"Whimsey. I'm going to have to step back and not do this job for a while as this changed so much about what I thought about myself. Are you okay?"

The look on her face hit him harder than all that had happened just before. She looked at him, and she was beyond upset.

"Okay? *Do I look okay?* Is being fucked when seven *okay?* Is doing porn to deal with who I am *okay?* Is being me *okay?* I hurt! I'm so fucking hurt you don't have a clue how much. And you know the worst part right now? I heard from Sharon that you were kind, and smart, and caring. I wanted so bad for you to be all that. But you weren't! My one little dream, one that didn't keep me awake all fucking night, and one come-on and that dream is gone! I'm hurt you didn't stop me, you fucker!"

She was screaming in pain. The door flew open. Sharon ran in, grabbing Whimsey's shoulders and looking at Charles with a look of shock.

"What the fuck is going on? What happened?"

Thrashing, Whimsey shook Sharon off. She walked a few feet, stopped, and turned back.

"You can ask Charles that. I just figured things out. You're all fuckers. You want to use me too. Not love me. Just like he did. You want to give me to your fucking sick church. Good fucking bye, you cunt!"

Flying out of the room, she ran so fast he knew Sharon wouldn't be able to catch her. He could have called the security desk, but he found himself saying to himself, "Run, Whimsey. Run."

After 15 minutes, Sharon was back, saying she couldn't keep up with her and she had no idea where she was headed. Asking him to call the police, he called and reported her missing, and they told him what he expected. He told Sharon what they said.

"They said until she's been gone 24-hours, they wouldn't be able to do anything. Said check home, friends, all that. I think I'll call James. He can do things right now."

Looking at him, she looked lost and confused. He called James and told him she had run, how long it had been, and said he'd appreciate when after he got people on it, if he could get Mike and both to come to his office. He stared blankly ahead and thanked him, then ended the call.

"They can do more than we or the police can. He said he's right on it. He and Mike will be here in a half hour or so. Mike, maybe sooner."

Sharon kept dialing Whimsey's number, and after 30 tries she gave up. She looked all around and turned to Charles, asking him what happened. He wasn't sure what to say. Whimsey had said something that stopped him from thinking much else. She had said Sharon was a member of a church and wanted to offer her up. That meant the cult, that Sharon wasn't trafficked, that she was converted. He couldn't trust her.

"I was doing the eval, and she was doing perfect. We got to questions about trust, sleep problems and being in control of emotions. Then she went off. She started saying all the things shrinks and social workers did to her, asking her the questions about if she was in control, blaming her when it was the foster parent who was out of control. She was mad at me not realizing that would trigger her during the test and said I was the same as all the others. That's when you came in."

Making no mention of the cult reference, he said he was surprised she lashed out at her.

"All that hurt must have run deeper than even I could have imagined. I guess the fucking test just unleashed it all. And it's exactly what she said. She goes through all she had, and she's the one who has to take a test to prove she's okay? How fucked up is that?"

"I tried to breeze through it as I think they're bullshit no matter who takes them. I'm dealing with not anticipating it and letting both of you down. She's so hurt, and it's all going through my head right now. Do you think she'll run home? Does she have anyplace else to go?"

Shaking her head, Sharon looked at her phone. No texts, no messages.

"I think I should go home and be there if she does. Anyplace else to go? No, no place good. Call me if you hear anything, I'll call you if she shows up..."

Lost in thoughts, Charles knew what Whimsey said about her, and that she knew he had heard it. He watched her leave, not rushing, walking slowly out the door, hearing the outer door close. He didn't feel safe, and it was why he wanted Mike and James to come to his office. The events had changed things.

Telling the security system to show who was ringing the bell, Angie saw Whimsey standing there looking up at the camera. She didn't see Sharon with her. She used the intercom to tell Whimsey she'd be right there but went to the kitchen to see Cindy first.

"Mom, Whimsey's at the door. She's all by herself and looks really upset. Can you come with me? We can find out why Sharon's not with her and stuff?"

Walking fast, she grabbed Angie by the hand and headed to the front door.

"She's too young to drive, no call… this can't be good. No matter what, be kind to her."

As she finished saying be kind, Angie opened the door, and Whimsey ran in and hugged Cindy, then putting an arm out for Angie to come so she could hug her too.

Looking back to make sure the door was closed, Whimsey had a look of fright, telling them both why she was there as Cindy had asked.

"I need to hide. Please, don't call anyone or let anyone find me!"

CHAPTER 36

Returning home after the debacle with James and Whimsey, Sharon felt as if she were walking in slow motion. Her steps were sluggish, her whole body felt slow with every move, but she eventually opened her apartment door, closed it and managed to make it to the sofa where she collapsed.

She had reached a point where each direction she turned led to pain and suffering. Having no other choice, she had to make a call that would make everything in her life worse. Knowing she had walked a path she alone had chosen. Looking at her iPhone she thought about why she wasn't a wife in the suburbs with a child on the way and a husband who may not have been exciting but would love her. That would be boring and ordinary, but better than where she was now as she held her phone and knew the call she'd make would lead to her death.

Deciding to think things through before making the call, she put the phone down next to her after launching a music playlist of songs she loved when growing up. The songs were sentimental and about love, dreams, and some just to dance to. Each one was a memory of a time or place when she was unaware that beneath such songs was a darkness and an evil that would soon find her. Listening to Lilia, a pop diva she adored, she thought of her as a girl with a great voice and a dream of being heard by people and loved bringing her smile and songs to the world. Learning the truth in a news magazine that Lilia made her way to fame by having sex with endless men who promised to advance her career, that hadn't surprised her. She grew up reading about celebrities and why some made it to the top, and others never left the ground. It was that she was a Christian who sang the praises of following the "one" who would love her. Fans thought that was about a man who would love her, or Jesus if they were fans of Christian rock and pop, or simply God.

Remembering the day she first heard Lilia's biggest hit, *The Only One for Me*, she had received a letter accepting her to a university she had prayed would accept her, the song and the letter were connected. Gilmore, the university she was going to attend, was where Lilia had attended and often talked about in interviews. She had said that the school had put her on the right path, and it was where she stopped thinking of being a famous pop star and started praising the Only One,

220 Not Taken

she knew who would help her spread the word that love was all that mattered. It sounded so reassuring and hopeful, she too wanted to find a purpose and have such hope.

Just before leaving to begin her first year at Gilmore, she read that Lilia had decided to stop performing as the music world was filled with darkness and evil, and she wished to follow the Only One. That's all it said. Thinking the singer had smartened up and decided to stop being used to have success, she must have found her answer serving a higher calling, whatever that was. To give up fame and fortune to serve a greater purpose was something she admired and sparked a desire to find out more about why Lilia had made her choice.

Once in school, there were posters saying that Lilia was going to be giving a talk about how Gilmore had helped her find the Only One she served, and all were invited to attend. Excited to hear what Lilia would say, she went to the event and was swept up in the story Lilia told to the hundreds of her classmates who attended. Listening to Lilia speak, she was at first disappointed she announced she wouldn't be singing songs, that soon changed as she heard the reason why.

"Everyone here is at a time when they are deciding what to do with their life. Everyone here is looking for answers and purpose. Do you think your degree will do that? Do you think that a job will? A nice car? A husband or wife? Or, like me, fame and success? I thought that once and had it all. Money, hit songs, fans clamoring for me to touch them or sign a CD. Everything I had dreamed of. But I found out. Oh, yes, I found out I had nothing. I found I was nothing inside. Empty. Do you have a fire inside of you? Is it to have your job and your house and your home in the new sub-development? Is that a fire? Is that what is important? What about your soul? Is it on fire? Does it want those things? Or is that what you've been told will make you happy? I can only say that after having all that I was told would give me joy gave me nothing but heartache. I was used by bad men who gave me success while they took my body and my soul. I slept my way to fame, and I've never denied I did. And those who gave me success? I found out they were all bad men. Evil men. They worshiped the dark one. The One who holds out promises of things that we think will make us happy. Oh, yes. Give me your body little girl, I'll make you famous. I gave them everything I had. My body. My time. My belief. I thought they cared about me. No. They wanted to ruin

me. Take my hope, my dreams, my faith in God and give it to The One they worshiped, and I'll tell you right now, when a man came to save us, the dark one came to corrupt that man by offering things of pleasure. Women. Money. Power. And I found out I was one of those things the dark lord had to offer good men to tempt them. Each man is in the desert. He's thirsty, hungry, all alone. Then a handsome man appears. He has food and water, and to not be alone he has a young girl he says will take away his loneliness and pain. And we all are used by the dark one. The men want that girl, and the girls want a powerful man. Do you hear me? There is a dark one working to tempt God himself with flesh and sex. But, the man said no. I don't fall for that. So, the dark one, he decides to corrupt men and turn them away from the true God and give earthly delights instead. And a young girl like I was? That, my friends, is the earthly delight. And I saw the darkness, and one day I said no. If a man wants delight. Is in need of love, give him the love of an innocent girl. One young enough to not yet be corrupted by the dark one. A girl he will have to show him that she is a gift from the Only One who loves him. That she is a gift from the Only One. She'll show him the way to joy and heaven above. I used to sing a gospel song of how woman cheated man down in paradise's hall. No more of that song for me. No, dark one. You will not use me to take men and women from the Only One who gives what we all need. Love. Hope. Joy. I am happy at last. I serve the Only One, not the dark one. If the dark one hasn't taken you already, fear not. You can serve. You can fight the dark one. Give yourself to love, to be a light that all can see if we want to. I belong to the Only One. I serve the Only One. And the Only One calls you to give what all men here want. Love. When you do that, the dark one can offer nothing to tempt a man. To say no, just as that man in the desert of life here did. He showed us the way. He is ever being tempted, that has never stopped. The Only One gives what is needed so no man can be tempted. We are weak, the Only One is strong. The Only One was the answer I chose. Thank you, and God bless. I want to talk to all of you who want to follow the Only One who can save us all."

Being hugged by Lilia as she wanted to find the joy she spoke of; she still could feel the surge of excitement as Lilia stepped back and looked at her and told her she was the answer. She could save the men wandering the desert looking for answers. She was beautiful and no man could say no if she offered love and hope. Lilia sent her to a table where

a group was inviting people to join the Only One. From the day of her first meeting, she was set on saving men from sin, and doing what God created women to do. Give men the strength to resist temptation by giving them the love they needed while here on earth.

Learning more, she started to give love to men who were the most likely to be tempted. The Ones who loved money, lust, and earthly pleasures. By having sex with them, she gave them what they needed, and said they must thank the Only One by giving all they had to the Only One who saved them, and they would have more of what they needed. They needed to serve the Only One, not the dark lord. As they surrendered what they made, the money they thought was once all that mattered, they would find the way in having a love to keep the dark one from taking them with temptations of sluts and whores who served sin and the dark one. Only the fresh new girls, not yet taken by sin, could protect them.

Sharon couldn't believe how easy it was to rise up in the Only One. She was beautiful, young and she could save men every day. She was doing so many, bringing in their money, that one day she was called to meet The One. The leader of the Only One. She was given a note saying, "Come be One with me," and a plane ticket to Montana. Feeling honored and valued for her work to save men, she flew to Montana and was met by a man who hugged her and said The One was waiting. In a customized Land Cruiser, he drove for two hours to a place in a valley that was beautiful, surrounded by majestic mountains, and a gated fence. Once passing the gate where a man waited to open it for them, it was a long drive to a large compound of beautiful cabins, the largest house made from stones and logs. It was the most beautiful house she had ever seen; more luxurious than any in a magazine or movie.

Walking up to the front door, she was welcomed by a gentle man who said that in the house, The One wished nothing of sin, and the clothes she wore were made to please the dark lord and no clothes were allowed inside. He stood outside of the house, and once she took off all her clothes, he smiled and said she was as God made her, and The One waited for her inside.

Met by a naked young girl who welcomed her with a passionate kiss, she took her by the hand and all throughout the house were very young girls and all ages of men. The girls were having sex with the men, and

she knew they were all saving the men from temptation by giving love, not sex of sin, to the men. She smiled at the sight, and she knew all there were safe from temptation as they had what God made us all to want for.

Opening a large set of doors for her, the girl reached up to give her a long kiss, sucking on her tongue, and when she backed away, she pointed to the open doors and said The One waited for her inside.

Looking, sitting with a clear view of the open doors where she and the girl kissed was The One. She had expected a man, one with a beard and wise looking eyes. The One wasn't a man, not old, and was smiling at her.

"Well... *aren't you cute*... Come, sit with me."

Sitting on a large sofa was a woman she thought was in her early thirties. She was beautiful, had long red hair and a supple body. Sitting with her legs apart, naked, she was stunning, and she felt an instant longing to be with her.

Walking slowly to her, looking at her in awe, The One had her arms open to embrace her, and as she got on the sofa, The One held her and began kissing her, telling her she was wanted, desired, needed. Telling her she was what all needed, she had worked her kisses down to her pussy and started licking her in a way she had never experienced with a man. The One worked gently and took her time, but once she reached an orgasm, she kept sucking her clit while flicking it with her tongue with it in her mouth, she was having continuous orgasms that wouldn't stop as she was holding The One's head. She was quivering, holding The One's head wanting the continuous climax to go on forever.

After an hour, The One raised up, saying she wished the same love, and moved her legs apart and guided her head down to her wet pussy, telling her to worship her clit as she had hers, to do the same, that she too could keep the dark one from her by giving her what she needed to be holy and safe.

They soon started licking each other, giving each other a continuous succession of orgasms for hours. After the first hour, she moved her head up for air and noticed there were many young girls watching them, smiling as they hugged each other, some licking each other. When they no longer had enough strength to continue, The One said they needed to tend to their bodies with food and drink. As she sat up, the young girls were gone, but there was a table full of vegetables, cooked grains,

ripe fruits, and pitchers of water. Taking her by the hand, The One took a slice of papaya and fed it to her, saying sit, and take what was needed to continue.

She was starving and had questions about what they had just done, and about her. Looking at her, The One started to nod as she ate, saying she could tell she was full of things she wanted to ask, and of course she should. She would answer, but she should also know that the food they had was a joy and to be cherished. Looking at Sharon, The One laughed, saying she knew by the look on her face when she first entered she was expecting some old man, and to be preached to about sin and all.

"I did. I had no idea what to expect. I had only heard you called The One, and of course, that's what came to mind. What's your name?"

"Sharon, I'll say what I say to followers when they ask. I'll do my mystic guru enlightened thing. Ready? Alright! To answer what you must know, I have many names, and none, for names mean nothing. It is what we do that gives us our true name…"

Looking at her for her reaction, she laughed, asking her if that was what she had hoped to hear. Not waiting for a reply, The One explained how things worked regarding her.

"Well, I do have a name and all that guru stuff is bullshit. I'm Jo, and wow! I loved doing you."

Wide-eyed, Sharon didn't know what to say. She sat, eating, looking confused.

"Don't worry, we'll get back to clit licking after we eat. Isn't that fucking incredible? I mean, who would have thought a person could cum like that? I can't get enough of that sweet pussy stuff, I tell you."

Looking at Sharon, she laughed, not in a mean way, but in understanding. She offered help.

"I know, I know. I'm not what you expected. I'm not what any of the followers expect, and that's why I keep pretty secret and only a few people know my name or what I look like. That keeps things all mystical and holy and shit. So, lose the I'm some wise man thing, and just talk to me like you would any other slut at school. Face it, Sharon, we're all just pieces of ass who can get what we want if we know how to use them. I just got really good at figuring it out. So, ask anything you want. Oh, I can tell you're wondering why I'm sharing all this stuff nobody's supposed to know with you, right?"

Finally able to speak, Sharon realized that The One was a hustler and a very smart woman.

"Well, you sure know how to lick pussy, I'll say that. I loved it, by the way, and can't wait to do more. But, okay, you had me fooled. I thought this was all for real. I bought into it big time. Is any of it serious or about good and evil, all that?"

Munching away, Jo was smiling and enjoying herself as she answered.

"Not one fucking word. All bullshit I learned people wanted to hear. Does that make me less of a person? A con artist or something?"

Thinking about it, Sharon could see she was telling her the truth, and she asked wasn't she worried she could walk out and tell others what she had learned. Jo laughed and threw an apple at her, and she managed to catch it.

"I don't think you will. First off, you want me to fuck that sweet box of yours. Well, at least before you run out and say I'm a fraud. So, that apple in your hand. What does it make you think of right now?"

"Tempting me, like Eve in the Garden of Eden."

"Yeah, I knew you'd get that right. I was raised to think that. I still think it. Take a bite, and make it as big a bite as you can…"

Sharon looked at her, shook her head, then took a large bite out of the apple. It was so ripe and juicy the juice was running down her chin. She reached for a napkin to wipe her face, and Jo said not to wipe it away. Sharon sat, holding the apple, as Jo got up and walked over to her and slowly licked the juice off her face, then sat in the chair next to her. Telling her to eat more of the apple, with each bite she licked the juice off her face. By the end of the apple, she was eating bigger bites and making sure the juice covered her and dripped out of her mouth as she ate it, hoping there'd be enough to drip down to her pussy. When she finished, Jo licked her face and after lapping up every drop, she sat back.

"Now, Sharon, I'm sure you've had a lot of apples in your life. How did eating that one compare to all the ones you ate out of your lunch bag or off the kitchen counter?"

"Well, it was the best apple I've ever had. Crazy different."

"Yeah, I bet. But aside from me licking you like that, how did the apple taste?"

"Incredible! Like the first time I ever ate a real apple. God, I want another one!"

Leaning over, Jo got a large apple, held it to her face, saying she felt like having one first. As she took a huge bite, the juice ran down her cheeks and chin. Sharon didn't even think, she leaned over and started licking the juice as she ate until the apple was finished. Smiling, looking at her with appreciation, she leaned and took another apple, and handed it to her, saying take a bite, chew, but don't swallow. Nodding, she did as told, and Jo put her mouth to hers and told her to give her some. Sharon opened her mouth and pushed her chewed apple into Jo's mouth. Jo chewed, then nodded for Sharon to open wide, and she gave her back the apple from her mouth. Sitting back, she smiled.

"How's it taste now?"

Sharon was at a loss for words. She found she was swirling the chewed apple in her mouth, not yet swallowing it. Jo told her to open her mouth, let her see. She smiled seeing she was savoring the apple still.

"See. That's the way to eat a fucking piece of fruit. Now, imagine some rich fucking asshole guy here, and we're eating an apple with him that way. Now, think with your cunt, not your head... You know your fucking head is only good for sucking cock and licking pussy, don't you? So, use your real smarts. What would that guy do if the two of us ate an apple with him like that?"

Sharon smiled, and her eyes were like slits.

"Anything we fucking tell him to do."

"Yay! You're absolutely, totally right. We can get any fucker to do anything we want if we use our cunts. They're all fools for hot snatch. Shove that munched apple up your hole, let them eat it out, and you can get every penny they have. So, the question is simple. Now that you know why the apple is the symbol of temptation and know how to finally eat one, do you want to turn things around. Tempt them and their little serpent things and let them pay the price?"

Her eyes opening wide, she had already decided.

"Oh, yeah... I'd like that. How?"

"First, by keeping what I just told you a secret, of course."

Nodding, Sharon said of course back.

"Second, you're a piece of ass women admire and trust, and guys will do anything to have, so we have you go and round up girls to join The One cult bullshit, then once we have them, and there are many ways to get them, by the way, we ship their sweet little cunts off to rich fuckers

who'll give us a ton of their money for them. Well, we call it a donation, but fuckin' hey, we're selling the girls to them. The little things? All innocent and so very sweet..."

Taking another apple from the table, she held it up, admiring it.

"Those fresh, ripe little pussies are our apple. The rich fuckers can't resist it, and they sure as fuck will take a bite."

Opening her eyes, escaping from the memory of the day she became a trafficker of underage girls, she looked at the phone. Whimsey was just as she was that day. She had her alone, and shared all the same strategy with her so she would go out and gather more girls to be sold by the Only One trafficking group. She figured that having been abused, sexualized, willing to do anything with a man, she went over all the reasons she thought she should be a recruiter for Jo, who said if she was, great, if not, well, she could be sold as she was the brass ring in the market. Whimsey was told all the secrets of how things worked.

She told her that she had never been taken or trafficked, and that was a way to go missing and disappear. Jo wanted her as the recruiter for Peter, who was a true believer who fell for the holy story, and Jo had never met him. He was a trafficker of some skill in Peru, and Jo thought he'd fall for the holy story, and he had. He was cold and ruthless, but fanatically religious and now trafficked in the name of the Only One so he was easy to trust. She laughed, saying he would say a prayer between each sentence to ask for protection from the devil, and that she didn't deal with him directly, but Lilia had found him showing up at one of her talks when touring South America. Once she let him fuck her in her ass, he was recruited. Sharon said she became the point person with Peter, and his pauses drove her crazy.

Now, after having tantric sex with Whimsey like Jo had done with her that first day, then sharing apples the same way, she was sure Whimsey was on-board. Then, the guardian mess happened, and her visit with Charles. Something Charles did or said triggered her, and she had run off, full of inside knowledge of how The One operated and she could blow it all up. She could tell Mike, go to the press… it was all a nightmare, and she needed to tell Jo all that happened. That would not be good. Not only was Jo a fraud making billions, but she also had no problem having her henchmen stop people by killing them. Peter was good at managing the goons, and he had no problem killing in the name of the Only One.

She stopped again before calling Jo. She thought knowing what happened with Charles, and what he did with Whimsey would be asked about, so she decided to call him first. That may help with keeping her — and Whimsey, alive. She had fallen in love with Whimsey, and she would do anything, kill anyone, to protect her.

Waiting for Charles to answer, she knew he was expecting to hear news if Whimsey had went home. As he answered, she could hear Mike and James in the background. Telling him she got home, and it was empty, she asked if he heard from her. Telling her no, she asked if James was hopeful, and he told her all he knew right now was a search had started.

"Charles, what may help was anything else she may have mentioned when she got so upset. I know she was saying mean things about both of us. Anything else you can think of?"

Knowing she was probing for anything revealed about her involvement with the Only One and trafficking, he said he hadn't even thought about any of that as she was upset at having to take another test to prove herself. That's what she was going on about then started ripping on everyone she knew. He asked, not knowing her, was she prone to outbursts or going off like that?

He was doing the probing now, and wanted to see how much she would protect herself.

"Some. She's very emotional right now. The being put through more things to be someplace safe. She can come up with some wild accusations about things when she's triggered. This is the first time she's taken off, well, since she's been with me. So… No mention of any other people or groups or places she may be upset about?"

Telling her it was just about the two of them as they were there to lash out at, she started talking about the social workers and her foster family, and that was before she rushed in to see what was going on. He doubted she would go to her foster family agency, adding that she's a survivor and had lots of people looking for her. Saying he wanted to talk to James as he just got off the phone with the police, he said keep calm, and no news is always good news.

Pressing the End button on the call, she hit the contact number for Jo. She had people all over who could be looking for Whimsey and they wouldn't ask questions about why she ran off. They didn't ask questions.

CHAPTER 37

Talking to James and Mike, Charles laid out all that happened, and didn't hold back about how he was ready to have sex with Whimsey and how messed up that had left him. They both listened carefully and saw Charles as never before. He was a wreck.

James looked at Mike, and they both accepted Charles was a man like any other. He was faced with the ultimate temptation, and he didn't have sex with Whimsey even though she had stopped it. He may have felt lust for her, but nothing had happened beyond his wanting it to. James looked at Charles, and decided to see if he could help him as he needed it as much as the long line of people who had turned to him for help.

"Charles, I'm not you, and can't feel what you feel right now, but my friendship with you means a lot to me. I know Mike feels the same. I know your world is upside down and you're in crisis mode. So, I'm going to see if I can be a good friend and do something to help a bit."

Shaking his head, letting it be shown he was feeling nobody could help, he grew even more somber as he talked in a near whisper to James.

"If this gets reported, I can lose my license, and that means a lot as I won't be here…"

Staring at him, seeming to understand what to Mike seemed quite obvious, James just shook his head one time, then tried again.

"I'm not a shrink, I just deal with hard problems each day and, pal, don't worry. I take care of things. If it comes to that, I'll be on it. For now, so you can cool your jets, step outside of your self. I'll be you, you be a patient. I'll ask questions like you do with me or Mike. Want to give it a try?

Charles was quiet, seeming unaware of what James had asked, but after a minute, looked at him and said it was what he would advise, so if he could play shrink, he'd like to go through what happened as he didn't want to wait, saying waiting would make the whole thing bigger and more upsetting.

James gave him a pat on his shoulder as he went to the chairs where Charles sat with patients, then Charles sat in one as Mike pulled a task chair to watch and listen or help if needed. After being sure Charles was ready, James started a mock session as a shrink.

"Charles, I know you went through a session today that had you

230 Not Taken

doing something you know not to do in your occupation. If you can, tell me how you felt as it was happening."

Seeing Charles gripping the arms of the chair, James worried it may be too much too fast, but Charles was calm, just clearly upset with what happened and was taking out his anger on the chair, a practical way to release the adrenaline pumping inside of him as he thought about it.

"I thought, not felt, that I was in control all the time. That it was just a girl, and that she was probably setting me up, so my thoughts were that, and that made me feel used."

James looked at him, nodding, saying that was well said. He thought about what he had learned when getting help from Charles and had a good idea of what hurt does to people and asked about that.

"Okay, you're feeling in control, then you felt you were being set-up. Worse, used. Did you become angry?"

"I don't recall it getting to where I was outright angry, but I felt… I felt like I wanted to let her know she couldn't hurt me, so I had that going on. Wanting to stop her from what she was doing."

"Okay, so some form of feeling aggressive?"

"Yes."

"Were you sure she was setting you up?"

"Not at first. I thought being in porn, she was just used to showing off her pussy and all. Then I couldn't think that as it was just so blatant. She had her legs spread open and she knew I had to look at her twat. I understood she was sexualized when young and related to the world with sex, but she wasn't acting afraid, she was saying hey, fuck this, you asshole."

"So, you're the man in control of a session. You're supposed to observe what she does, even if directed at you and not take it personally. I'm sure things like that have happened in session before. But, you had a feeling of aggression from her doing that?"

"Yes. I'm sorry to say this, Mike, but it was really as if it was Sharon with her cunt open to play me. She had used every trick in the book on her call and once here, and I was sure she thought she was in control. Not of me. Of Whimsey. That she was sure I'd cave from her sexual provocation. Whimsey isn't some dumb little fuck. I realized she's either just in need of Sharon's pussy, or that Sharon is in control of her like in the cult. That was all circling in my head."

"So, if you can, close your eyes and go back to looking at her. What do you see?"

Mike looked at James once Charles closed his eyes, making a face to indicate that was risky. James nodded his head, agreeing, but just at that moment Charles started talking.

"A very young girl. Almost preteen, and she has her legs spread, and I could see her pussy as if she was naked, right there in front of me."

"Put aside the feeling of being used if you can, and focus on seeing her exposed that way. What did that make you feel?"

"Aroused. It turned me on, and I could feel my dick get hard. I was getting off looking at her pussy."

Charles still had his eyes closed, and James looked over to Mike, who shrugged, raising his shoulders, trying to say it was natural to respond to seeing that. James understood and thought the same thing.

"If it was another woman sitting there, showing her pussy to you, do you think it would have aroused you?"

There was a wait for a reply. After the pause, Charles seemed certain in his tone.

"I've had women do things like that before. Even masturbate as they described a sexual fantasy or frustration. I didn't get excited at all. It was clinical, but, well, they weren't doing what she was. Playing me. No, seeing a woman like that hasn't done that to me in the past."

"So, it's happened before. Did you think those women were coming on to you, or would engage in sex with you?"

"No. I never felt it was about wanting to have sex with me."

"Were they attractive to you in any way?"

"No. Even if they were, it wasn't about me. It was anatomy to me, not provocation or desiring me."

"Now, Whimsey, still in your mind… seeing it again right now, you thought it was provocation? Not that she wanted you?"

"She was enticing me. Being dominant, making me her bitch. And then it was even more than her making me her bitch. It was Sharon too. Two of them. I'm not going to fuckin' fool you or myself, that was a fuckin' turn on. Some cunt telling me what to do is one of the things I would fucking pay to have done to me, but she didn't know that. Two of them? Oh, that was what was going on. Yeah, like paying a bitch for it, I knew it was only because I could do something for her, and it wasn't that

she was excited about me. I wanted it to be where she wanted to fuck me. I knew that wasn't what was happening. That hurt."

"Why did it hurt? Did you think you should be attractive to her? There is an age difference…"

"The hurt was I wanted her to want me. I wanted to be attractive to her, like she was to me."

"Keep remembering what you saw and how she looked. Jump to when she crawled up to you and talked about giving you oral sex. What was going on inside of you?"

"I wanted her to do it. I couldn't think of anything else. I'm watching this little bitch crawling to my cock, and the look on her face… I wanted to fuck that mouth. I was rock hard, and she knew it, oh yeah, she knew it. She knew I wanted to cum in her mouth then fuck her."

Mike watched James and how his eyes almost popped hearing that. It was brutally honest. James was thinking a bit before proceeding. He had an idea of how to focus on the main problem.

"Charles, you're looking at a very sexual young girl, not woman. She's a fantasy, almost unreal in that she is both a little girl who should be inexperienced, but at the same time she's no little girl. She's in front of you, crawling up to you to have sex. Putting her age aside, she's offering you sex and has shown you her body to entice you. Is it normal for any man to be excited by that, and is it normal to not be?"

"It's normal for a man, a straight man, to respond to that whether right or wrong. We are made to respond to a woman in that situation. Something would be wrong if he didn't."

"So, your response was what most any man would have if there and it was her coming on to him."

"Yes."

"What has you feeling you did something wrong to respond to an attractive female offering you sex?"

After a short pause, Charles opened his eyes, and rubbed his cheek and chin.

"My sexual response was natural, but as it was happening, two things were part of it. First, my training is to not engage with a patient, ever. It's essential to not let that happen as that would fuck up all that I need even more than her mouth. The other was more disturbing. I was responding to a little girl who is telling me what to do and getting off on it. I wanted

to be her bitch. That's pretty messed up."

"So, understanding you're trained to shut down such a reaction, that is about responding and acting on it, not that you can't have thoughts or be aroused, correct?"

"That is the line. Seeing any female that way will cause a response. Acting on it is what I was trained to control. In this instance, I wanted to act on my attraction to her, and her invitation."

"You said what was troubling was that you knew she was a little girl. Would you have the same issue if she was a grown woman?"

Closing his eyes again, only for a few second, he opened them and shrugged.

"Probably. It wasn't just a little girl. It was Sharon as well. I saw her doing it, really."

"So, make it where she was not with Sharon, and it was only her. Were you attracted to her because she was a young girl?"

"I was attracted to her. Being young and so little, coming on to me… It wasn't something I've ever went for, but it wasn't being young, it was the dominant manner that got me going and I think her being so young and able to do that made it more exciting as it wasn't expected."

"Okay, then it's not where you got going only because you're hot for young girls then, correct?"

"I have to say correct. I don't look at or think about sex with someone who is still a girl."

"To be sure, you were aroused not because of her age, but because she was dominant, taunting you, offering herself to you?"

"Yes. That was what I was going through."

"What if you weren't acting as a psychiatrist, and she wasn't a patient?"

"It would be wrong, legally, statutory rape. I would know it was wrong if I had sex with her but I would have wanted to, and I can't fool myself, I'd have fucked the shit out of her."

"Did you come on to her in any way?"

"No. At one point I told her to stop with the exposing herself, and I was shutting that down. I didn't indicate any interest. I was cold and clinical."

"You said you wanted her to give you oral sex than have intercourse with her. Is wanting to, having that impulse, the same as engaging in sex with her?"

"It's two different things. Each person has sexual thoughts and impulses, but we don't act on them when inappropriate."

"Charles, in common language, did you unzip your pants, pull yourself out and tell her to blow you?"

"No, but I wanted to."

"Wanting and doing, as you said, are two very different things. She was there, she said she wanted to, but it didn't happen. Isn't that the control a man in your position needs? If you didn't whip it out, you didn't do anything, and you didn't initiate it. You had the same response that any man would have when offered sex unexpectedly. Is that what happened when you look at it now, from afar?"

"That is what happened. I still wanted to."

"But you didn't. You're a man being offered casual sex, no matter who or what age, and it's normal to be excited and want it, but you didn't engage when you could have. So, as you had a normal response, kept your dick in your pants, what is the deeper issue behind how you're feeling? Is thinking it was wrong actually about a deeper issue?"

Closing his eyes again, Charles kept them shut for five minutes. Mike went and got bottles of water for all of them, and they waited for Charles to respond. Once he opened his eyes, he saw the bottle of water, took it from the side table where Mike had put it, stared at it, then at James and Mike.

"The deeper issue is that she didn't. Not that I didn't. I would have and she knew it. That was humiliating and I got pissed and was ready to smack her around…"

James stared at him, waiting. Charles had paused but hadn't finished what he started saying. He looked at the bottle of water, taking a drink, then looked at James.

"When Whimsey was doing all that, she got up and got bottles of water for both of us and handed one to me. A natural, normal thing. Getting me a bottle of water. Taking care of me. I remembered it just now seeing this bottle. I think this puts things in focus for me. It's why I'm ready to hang things up. I could deal with the anger from what she did. This part… this isn't me. You know me, and you'll understand."

James was shaking his head, Charles looking at him, shaking his head in return. He was going on no matter what.

"This to me goes against what I am. Against being in this… this

position I'm in. Having her do that? Just a little kindness, something nice… I liked that, a lot. It made me feel good when she did it. It changed things from her being a little slut to being a real person. Actually, a nice person. All her answers on the eval? Way more than I get from most people. She wasn't young or old when she handed me the bottle. She made me feel important… cared about, even if she wasn't. Then, I realized from the answers, the bottle, and all that… I liked her. Not as some girl to fuck. I just liked her the way anyone likes another person. James, you know I'm not that at all…"

Holding up his hands, James wanted to stop.

"Charles, like I said, I'm not a shrink. I'm glad you got all that out, and I hope it helps to say things where it's safe to talk. But now you're going past what I should hear… as someone here at the agency, okay?"

Charles nodded, saying he agreed, it was time to stop. Looking at them both, saying there was one more thing.

"The moment I realized how nice she was? How I liked her? That's when I wanted to really beat the shit out of her for not fucking me. Being dominant was sex. Her being sweet and nice and doing that to her? That was way more exciting."

Mike and James went out to the reception room, and left Charles to figure it out. Mike looked at his door, then back to James.

James looked worried.

"All the damn sick shit in this life we can't control. In this job we see it up close and it's brutal. I've given up wondering why people hurt each other. Silly to even think about it because it seems we're made to do that at some point and don't even know why. Charles is facing he can be violent if not getting what he wanted, and that was hard to hear. He needs to deal with it. I'm no fucking shrink, and I can't fix it. We all have a beast in us. Some just manage it better than others. Today, he came close to blowing what he has going, and he knows it. I'll keep an eye on him."

Mike was surprised James was so sure every person was capable of horrific acts, but after hearing his friend admit he had thought of it, he was sure that had him thinking the worst to defend Charles. Looking

at James, he started walking to his office and waved for Mike to follow. Closing the door once inside, he looked at Mike and was just as troubled in manner as when they talked about Charles.

"Shit. Here we are in the secrets business and I heard secrets and hated it. Charles told us sick fucked-up things that get him going, and it was tough shit to hear. I think the wanting to smack her was there, but he didn't so that's what matters, okay? The thing with your sister is just as brutal. Charles knows when someone is telling the truth. Whimsey said Sharon was the same and just like Charles wanted to fuck her or smack her around, she said Sharon just wanted to sell her off. Mike, that's a game changer. If that's true, it means that she's not who we think she is. She's on the other team."

CHAPTER 38

"Whimsey, I'm so glad you came here. Just to know if you could be tracked to here, did you take a ride service, a bus…"

"Cindy, I ran most of the way. If I took a ride service, it would be on Sharon's account so she would find me and be here already. It seemed best to hoof it. I'm sorry I'm all sweaty. It's from running most all the way, and I'm sure not dressed for night. Cold out there."

Taking her hand and holding it out, she said she could tell her all about it after she jumped in the shower, and that Angie would lay out some sweats and warm things to wear on the bed in the guest bedroom.

"You know where it is. Just go on up, and everything you need for showering is there. Angie and I will check the security system and turn on lights. We got smart after the last incident."

Watching her go up the stairs, Cindy waited until she was in the guest bathroom, then went to a cabinet and took out two Glocks, putting one in her sweatpants pocket, giving the other to Angie who was wearing an oversized robe.

"Angie… Is that my robe? You just bought a bunch of nice ones…"

Putting the Glock in the large pocket of the robe, she gave Cindy a little smile and hugged herself, clutching the soft collar of the robe.

"Mom, I used to wear this all the time when you were working late. I feel all cozy and safe in it. I know you want me to feel that way, right?"

Filled with memories of coming home near midnight after servicing one of her clients when she was an escort, she'd find Angie on the couch with the TV on having fallen asleep waiting for her, wrapped in her robe. There was no way she could say no to her wearing it, but she only had that robe and one spare. She knew she could buy more, but they wouldn't be sold with such memories.

"Angie, I'd like you to keep it. I'll get a new one."

Shaking her head in wonder, Angie was shocked at such a suggestion.

"Mom, then I wouldn't be wearing your robe!"

Smiling at her, she knew what that meant, and it was true. It wouldn't be the same if it was hers. She said okay, and Angie looked happy and cozy in it.

"Mom, the way you're stacked, I could never fill this robe…"

Looking at each other, they both grinned. Angie had her unique way

of complimenting her, and she knew the robe was Angie's hopes and dreams of growing up and being like her. Filling the robe was also her way of saying she hoped to be as pretty as her when she was grown.

"I know. I don't mind if you say I'm stacked, but not in front of company, alright? I don't want everyone checking me out. I think they can see for themselves as some things a woman can't hide. And I'm shapely, not stacked. A 34C, remember? Speaking of which, we need to hide Whimsey after we find out why she's here. I said we would. After the garage attack, that was about Whimsey, so we're going to put our new lockdown plan in place. You go and secure the bars Mike had installed in the garage, and I'll activate the zappers on the windows and doors."

Mike had installed the latest in intruder prevention. The windows and doors had small holes that concealed tasers if anyone touched a window or door. It seemed best to activate all the systems as they didn't know what Whimsey was running from. She had sent her up for a shower to have time to put all the systems on, get the guns, and talk to Angie. Angie's eyes opened wide, and she ran out to the garage, and Cindy had finished activating the systems when she came back in.

"All bolted? Good. I put everything on. After a bit, go put out some sweats and a nightdress for Whimsey. She'll come down once she's comfy. I'm worried about what's going on. I would think that as she ran here, meaning ran away, that Sharon would be calling to see if she's here. I'm not going to call her, but while you're getting things for her, I'm going to call Mike. I want to talk in private so she doesn't hear so spend time showing her what other things may fit her and help comb her hair until I call asking if you two are trying on all my things."

Smiling, saying that was a good suggestion, Angie hightailed it up the stairs. Cindy stopped and realized that with Angie, they probably would be trying on all kinds of frilly things. Listening, she heard the shower running, then called Mike.

"Cindy, I was just getting enough time to call you. Somethings up. Whimsey is missing and we're starting a search for her. If she calls or…"

Interrupting him, she knew her instincts were right. It was a serious matter.

"She's here. She's safe, and I've activated all the things you put in. Angie and I are armed. Why didn't you call me sooner? She said she ran

all the way here, and she was wet with sweat so she's in the shower and I can talk without her overhearing. What's going on?"

"Cindy, I'm with James at Charles' office. James was just telling his whole crew to go looking for her. I need to tell both of them that she's safe with you, and I'll come and meet with you to explain things. But, something before anything else. Except for me, Charles or James, don't say she's there no matter who. And most of all, don't call Sharon, and if she calls you to see if she's there, say no. Look, I have to tell James so his guys stand down. I'll be there in about 20 minutes. I'll deactivate what I need to get in, then turn it back on. Did you lower the guard bars in the garage. I did it where it's manually operated and can't be hacked via remote, so I won't be able to get in that way... Angie did? Pretty good, They're heavy... I hate to rush, but understand everything? Good. See you in a bit. Me and only me for now."

Hanging up the phone, she was glad Mike would be there soon. Thinking more about what happened the night Whimsey's sister was killed, she decided to put AR-15s under the windows of each room, and though heavy, she had all in place as Angie called out they were all set. Calling back that she'd come up, she felt like less of a target on the upper floor. She took one AR-15 to have with her just in case.

Thinking about her mentioning that they'd be trying on her things, she found Angie and Whimsey sitting on her bed. They had only a bedside lamp on, and Angie said as she had a King bed, and the rest were tiny queen-sized, it was the only place they'd have enough room. Glancing over at her closet, things looked like they hadn't been disturbed, and Whimsey was in Angie's robe and wearing a sweat suit set that was cute. It was large on her and looked comfortable. She looked at Whimsey.

"Just so you know, Mike has had a ton of systems installed to keep anyone out, and the garage is like a fortress now. And I have rifles under all the windows downstairs, and this one with me. Feel warmer with your shower and sweet things you have on?"

"Way yeah. You're so nice to take care of me like this, and let me stay here, after, you know, last time."

Cindy started to say the attack was for Sharon, not her, but didn't want to remind her of that night. She asked her what in the world was going on.

Explaining how she had Sharon appointed her guardian so they could live together, she talked about how the court needed her to visit a shrink, and Charles had offered to help her with it. As she reached that part, she jumped, hearing some beeps from the security wall panel, and the front door opening.

"That sound is the one it makes only if it's Mike. He's here, and I thought it best to have him here for some added protection."

Nodding, Whimsey said she was glad of it, and Cindy called down to Mike to join them upstairs. After taking off his shoes, he took his Glock from his jacket pocket and put it under his jeans in the back. Walking into the bedroom, he said he wasn't dressed for a slumber party, and they said they were out of robes his size. Getting on the bed with them, he looked to Whimsey.

"I'm glad you're safe. We were so worried about you."

Her face showing alarm, she asked who was in the "we."

He understood her reaction.

"I know, I know. Just me and James. He was calling all his guys to search for you. No, my sister wasn't there, and we haven't told her. From what I understand, she left Charles and went to your place, waiting there for you."

Taking a deep breath, she was relieved. Cindy looked at them both, not sure what the worry about Sharon was about, asking why they excluded her. Mike asked her if Whimsey had told her what happened. Saying she had just started to, Mike wished to hear her account of what happened, and suggested she continue as it would be better than what he could say as he wasn't there during important things that happened. Turning to her, he said to keep going. She said she was going to tell everything, and it may take a while, and continued on.

After going through all the detail about needing a psych eval, and Sharon intimidating Charles into doing it the same day, she shared how when she got off the phone with him, she was mad he wouldn't do it with her listening and being there, and Charles had explained the law required it where it wasn't how it could be done, but she was ranting as they drove to his office. Mike suspected that she had wanted to be there, and he stopped her to ask a question.

"I may need to ask things as you tell us everything, so I'm sorry for interrupting. So, you faced getting a psychological examination which is

stress in itself, and all the way to the office Sharon was upset and going off about it. Did that make it more difficult for you when you met with Charles? I mean did it make it where you were mad as he was being so rigid about it?"

Nodding, she said it was horrible. She explained she didn't want to have the test anyway, but Sharon being furious made taking the test a nightmare, and she'd be in the waiting room so she may be trying to listen in.

"With all that, I tried to do things just like Charles said, and I was doing it calmly to get through it. Then, with all kinds of things going on with Sharon, having to take the test, her fuming like she did, all outside the door acting weird, I answered a question that just set me off too. It brought all kinds of things from my past up and my mind was full of memories and how I had done things, and how all the men did things to use me an all. I lost it. And I was horrible to Charles. I did the worst thing possible. He was just trying to get me through the exam so I could forget about it, you know, get it over with, and he was reading things off the form he had, he didn't ask me anything himself, so I feel like shit now cause I fucked with him as only little me could do…"

They were all staring at her, and Mike knew she was saying what happened honestly and knew what had happened. To get it out and tell it seemed a good way to help her understand Charles wasn't going to quit his job or anything drastic, he told her she was with people who understood her past and would be understanding. Telling her to just say what happened and how she was feeling during it all, she looked apprehensive. She asked if he was sure they wouldn't hate her and make her leave, he looked at her with a warm smile, saying that wasn't going to happen. She nodded and continued.

"Sharon just all out forced me to wear a tiny jumper that I normally wear leggings and tee under, but she said just the jumper, no undies and I just gave up fighting about it. She said wear it like that or stay home. So that made it worse as it was like all riding up my crack… oh, sorry, that's rude to say. It was riding up in places that left no secret to all my private parts, and I started sitting where I could be comfortable so I could listen and answer. I just sit like that even watching TV, and now I know he was getting quite of glimpse of me as my legs were apart. Oh, yeah, one of the questions just sent me off to times men did things to me… well, it's hard to explain…"

Mike told her that she could say whatever she felt or what happened. They were okay if it was something not normally talked about. Saying okay, but she warned everyone, she closed her eyes and started talking again, but not wanting to look at anyone during that part of the story.

"He read off a question about stress. It said did I ever have difficulty breathing or swallowing or something like that. See, I did things doing porn that question drudged up. I'll just explain. I was good at deep throat… you know, taking a giant penis past my mouth way down into my throat. And you can't breathe with it in you like that. And the fuckers… ah, sorry, the men would stay down until I almost passed out and some would even squeeze my nostrils together so there was no way to get air. When you can't breathe you panic, and I could do it, but each time I freaked they would stay down and not let me breathe and I'd die. Oh, and another big porn thing is when they're doing any other part of me, they'd put their hands around my throat and choke me. I mean for real sometimes. They'd keep doing it until my eyes bulged out, and that was sick stuff and if I didn't do those things, they said no work at all. When that question was asked, I said something about, oh yeah, I've had times when I couldn't breathe. I just wanted to say no, but wham! It was me feeling like I had a cock almost in my belly, and from that point it was just all thoughts about men fucking me and how men thought they could make me do what they want. I was somewhere else, I tell you. I was back at the porn studio… and still in bed with my foster dad doing me in the ass. All that, and I just thought, okay, Charles is a good man. He won't use me no matter what. Out of nowhere I had this thing where I wanted to be a girl like I played in the porns and come onto him and have him push that away and say he didn't see me that way…"

Even with her eyes still closed, Mike saw she was crying, then looked to Cindy and Angie, and they were crying too. He shook his head, and Cindy, sitting closest to her, reached and put her arm around her.

"Take your time. You had all that bottled up in you, an you thought it was where Charles wouldn't want you like those men did, correct?"

Opening her eyes, looking at Cindy, she started crying harder and said she only realized that later.

"When that instinct to tempt him feeling inside of me took over, oh, wow, I went all the way. I did it worse than if it were a porn. He was asking the questions, not responding to how I was sitting and basically

naked as I pulled the crotch off to the side to show him everything. Then, I slid down off the chair, and fuckin' crawled like a dog on a leash over to him and got between his legs, and I, well, said he wanted to do me, and he could. Just take his cock out for me to suck... Oh, God, I'm sorry you are hearing what I said, but that's what I said to him. He didn't say or do anything, but I looked, and I lost it entirely because seeing me like that, and he's a man and all, and I bet he didn't even know it, but he had an erection. I could see it through his pants. That did it. I thought, oh, mister good guy saving trafficked girls wants to fuck a fourteen-year-old. I looked at him and asked him if he wanted me to do that, and he was totally fuckin' honest. He said yes! He didn't whip it out or tell me to, didn't touch me or anything. I think with me doing what I did, and he's a man and that shit gets any guy hard and he gets revved up, he didn't want to lie to me. He did what he asked me to do. Tell the truth. So, I stood up, said he was an abuser like all the other fuckers in the world, and he couldn't have my little mouth or pussy, and then the look on his face! All the way here, I kept seeing the look on his face. I told him I had one little hope he'd be a good guy. That he wouldn't want to use me like everyone else. I wanted to hurt him and the whole world, and he got the full blast. Then he just stopped and said he couldn't really be a shrink anymore after doing something like get hard from me playing him. I lashed out, screaming, then Sharon ran in and I was totally pissed, and afraid of her! Before we went to Charles, she told me she wanted me to join some fuckin' religion thing she's a part of. She wasn't trafficked. She's a trafficker for the cult. She wanted me to be a recruiter, or I'd be a sacrifice meaning be sold to some billionaire fucker. So I said that stuff to Charles, then told her that I'd let her secret out, and I ran. Just ran and ran until I got here. But now, I can't stop thinking about what I did to Charles. I don't know what to do!"

Sitting there, so small, Cindy still had her arm around her and pulled her face to her shoulder and held her without saying anything. Mike knew she was suffering, and knew she needed to know Charles felt a lot like she did, but James had helped him understand he hadn't acted on his impulses. He gently called her name, and said he had come from being with Charles, and asked if she'd like to know he had some help by talking about it. Raising her head, she wiped her wet face with her robe sleeve, and turned to him.

"You talked to him? You know how he is? Does he hate me?"

Looking at her, he was gentle, talking to her in a reassuring manner.

"No. He doesn't hate you. You impressed him by standing up for yourself, and he said you were doing the evaluation with sincere answers. He put it all on himself when it happened, and after. Not the questions, not that. He was reading off the sheet. He was just mad he's a man and you were giving him a hard on, and he prides himself on never doing something that would be wrong or give the wrong idea. He understood you were triggered. He knew why you did what you did, and why you think all men are only interested in you for sex, but he's the one who isn't supposed to. But he did get excited, and for a minute there he looked at you and he had that male desire to have sex, but he stopped himself, knew what was happening and got it under control but you had seen it, and he was ashamed. No excuses."

Whimsey listened intently, nodding she understood. Mike held up his hand, and shook his head as he continued.

"It was something more than about you. He was sure you were doing it because of Sharon. That she had wanted you to, maybe, although that would mess up the guardianship. He sensed it was really Sharon trying to provoke you with all that pressure before you arrived that would have you get worked up into a state, which is what happened. He saw Sharon doing what you did. He admitted that seeing you, and thinking of that being the two of you was what got him excited. He knows it was a kinky thing but, it happened. He said when you made him feel wrong for getting aroused, he was angry, and that was clear and was something that hurt you. That, and that he had gotten aroused. Once he realized how you were set up — you know, to set him up, he was worried about you, and yes, he was ready to stop being a shrink so it would never happen again. I heard him go through it all, just like you, and our friend James, who I worked for, asked if it was a thought or an action. See, it's hard to control unwanted thoughts. But you can choose not to act on them. James helped him realize he didn't act on that impulse, and that was the important part. As I said, he was proud you stood up for yourself at the end. He realized what you did, and why. He understands. You both are suffering, and I feel so bad for both of you... He's embarrassed, and it seems so are you. I think if you talk at some point, you'll find you both care about each other. Whimsey, I don't know if what I've said

helps, but think about it. I'm just telling you what he said and how he described how he felt. I think the real hurt is from Sharon. Seems like she orchestrated all that happened."

Whimsey looked confused, asking what *orchestrated* meant.

"Fancy word for set you both up. Playing him to meet with you or she'd be a wreck, making you wear next to nothing, going off how pissed she was at him on the ride right before you meet with him. All that was planned like having you dress to get him looking at you, and have you worried he's checking you out… See how she set it up to have things go wrong?"

Nodding, she said now she did.

CHAPTER 39

Jo thought how she'd rather be lying naked having a devoted young convert dwelling on her earthly delights. Instead, she was in the French Riviera.

With hair savage and free, wearing a revealing tailored blouse and skirt, she had used the flight on her personal jet for reviewing the materials on her iPad. Once her jet touched ground she had nonstop meetings with an Archbishop, Royal Prince, Hedge Fund billionaire, ex-President, and the CEO of a media empire. She was sure after offering them communion to soothe their need for spiritual enlightenment in the mystical form of a very young girl, they would find religion fast, and a highly meaningful experience, almost as meaningful as their donation to The One via wire transfer.

There was a time when she would go to whatever island or estate they were had to escape life's little trials, but this was a rare journey outside of her Montana compound since they were all gathered in one location and she also looked forward to some time watching what sad state the world was coming to with girls on beaches naked except for a postage stamp that passed for a bikini bottom, and the way men hit on the sweet innocents.

Enduring the long flight to meet with the power brokers gathered there, she would deliver the message of The One. With a large, and growing, congregation, most of the time they now came to worship at her feet. Looking over their ill-gotten assets, part of traveling to meet them was because such men of ill repute would never be allowed to her Montana ranch. Meeting them was also so they could pretend to have a reason or excuse to meet with a cause they were about to donate a fortune to. The One.

Having read there was a summit, a global meeting of idiots she didn't think of as great minds, it was being held in the south of France, and she knew such summits had nothing to do with planning the future, they gathered at meeting locations where there was always an abundance of hot young college pussy to fuck.

Deciding to meet with the richest men there, she was certain she'd secure enough donations to The One where after one day of meetings, she could languish on the Riviera for a week or so, enjoy watching idiots

hanging off the rails of their starter yachts to spot the hot asses of the college girls on Spring break wearing micro-thongs and nothing on top. The pathetic men with Rolex watches, hidden by gold rings and chains while wearing sunglasses that cost five million and made in the same sweatshop ones for Dollar Tree stores were made would be focused on the ripe pickings and not line up to invite her for a ride on what they thought was an actual yacht although it was closer to an inflatable sold at Walmart in her opinion.

The coastline was filled with both old and new money, and it was where young women with lean bodies and big smiles sought to find a wealthy man to give them an easy life in exchange for escorting him to buy more chains and rings. He'd buy the girl a few trinkets and parade her through the streets in his open-topped Cornice or Porsche Cabriolet. Out on the beach she would be delighted when one of the young men out to do a reverse slut routine on rich woman would approach her and ask if she'd be so kind as to grace them with her company for a night she would always remember. She liked to be kind, so went easy on them.

"I'm your worst nightmare. I'm a hot piece of ass that would rip your dick off if I fucked you, not some withered old cunt. Move on little boy."

She couldn't blame them for trying. She was in her early-thirties, beautiful, charismatic, and far hotter than the girls holding the arms of the short, fat men in their Gucci thongs. For any young money-grabber to approach her meant he was hitting on anything past 20 and was new to the way things worked. She'd help them learn how to work the beach by waving them away. Never equating a chiseled face and buff body to any hint of sexual skill — or intelligence — she felt bad for them as they had to work for their keep unlike the girls who just had to hang their ass out and wait to be lavished with an apartment overlooking the beach, a car with driver, and a chance to fool themselves they were actually special in some way.

Keeping an eye out for young daughters, it was not the best place to find girls just approaching their teen years. The people she watched rarely had children. The college girls would, someday soon, when their asses got fat and they waddled back to Iowa. Most men there had fathered children, but they paid off the girls and were not what anyone would consider family men. They also weren't men she bothered with.

Being a student of men's total stupidity when it came to women of

any age, she had learned going after men who were only wealthy was a waste of time. Knowing their type, they had stolen and cheated their way to wealth and were obsessed with money. They loved having the arm candy, but not lollipops hanging to them as they were pussies who towed the age limit. They still cared about money, and it was hard to have them part with any they claimed to have. When starting her trafficking empire, she'd used such types as they did manage to get her into places where the men who were rich beyond caring about wealth partied and played. Those were the men who saw no line at the legal age when it came to fucking. The younger, the better in their minds. In her mind, the younger the more fucking millions it would cost them. They cared about the girl's age being as low as it could go — but not the money. A million was taxi fare to them.

Deciding to start the day with a Prince famous for doing all women except the ones he was supposed to, she was aboard a real yacht. Meeting him, she had strict rules of engagement. She would only spend a limited amount of effort with him as explained she was offering spiritual advisors to ones whose dicks couldn't get hard enough to fuck the endless stream of young models and aspiring actresses, pointing out that such easy ass offered nothing more than an empty existence. To flatter his inflated opinion of himself as a lover, she asked him what was left for pleasure once a man had everything he thought he wanted? The conversation intrigued him.

"Goodness, my dear lady. You've got me on that one, I do say. And you are so right. You name it, and I've had it, and done it. More than once if the sweet thing could take it any longer… I love when a doting young beauty needs to stop and says she can't take it any longer. I know it's a lot to handle. I tell you, there was a time not long back when I wanted the throne, but now even that seems a bore. Fact is, I'm bored as all get-out. No one I'm doing seems to get my pecker up… well, you know what that expression means. I've done it all and I've stopped expecting there's anything more to do. Most commoners don't have their score card filled as I do, and truthfully, one is the same at the next."

Having looked her up and down, she saw he thought her attractive. That meant nothing. All the women at the private party he threw each night were her age or younger, and all of them were gold diggers wearing knock-offs of the latest Paris fashion. She knew that with unlimited

funds, such men were looking for ever more excitement. She asked what he thought could be done to remedy such a problem. He smiled in appreciation that she had asked.

"I'll tell you this much. Not only is price no object, I swear I'd give my left nut for something that makes me want to… well, you're a fine specimen… you know … get up in the morning."

Revealing a look of genuine interest, sitting in the suite in his floating house on water, a yacht he called a skipper, she leaned forward to look at him and she could see he appreciated how much the flowing, loose collar on her blouse revealed. That meant little to him although he smiled and said she had quite a handful there.

"Actually, I do. I would guess that you think I'm just another royal household pussy, out to fuck my way into being some kept bitch of yours… Oh, please, don't give me that look. Save that for mommy. I probably have more money than your whole bullshit lineage has ever robbed from dumb fucks…"

Laughing to herself, she knew he wasn't used to being told what to think or do. He was a spoiled brat and a fool — just her type of man.

"I say, old girl…"

"Old? You bet I'm old. Any pussy over 12 is old in my circles. And there you are… with bleached blonde shaved cunt bitches that are, what? Maybe 18 at best? Probably more like 20. No wonder you can't get that little heir to the throne of yours to stand up and make a declaration."

She leaned back and adjusted her blouse to cover herself, sitting with her hands on her knees, looking at him with eyes wide, waiting. She saw his expression and was sure she had him as if she were harpooning a whale. That's all she saw him as. A whale to pull in and carve up his family's wealth with something as simple as a girl her evangelists had taken in as a foster child.

Watching his stupid chubby face and eyes, revealing a light bulb going on inside the small pea brain of his, his mouth was a circle, wanting to say what a man in his position should say. Crossing her legs, she looked at her hose to be sure it had the sheen she liked best, then up at him, waiting.

"Anything past twelve? Are you bonkers? Go on… Seriously, you're pulling my leg, old gal."

"No, prince, I'm pulling that dick stuck to your balls and seeing if

Not Taken

really wants what you say. Something that you deserve only from being born into money you sad fuck."

Again, looking at him, she knew except for his mommy he'd never been talked to in such a way, but he couldn't look away and he wanted to know what she was hinting at. She looked at her nails, then back to him.

"Are you, by any chance, a church-going man?"

With such a change of subject, she caught him off guard, but he managed to answer.

"Of course I am. Comes with the title and all that rot. Every Sunday in my full brigadier uniform."

Nodding, she asked if he had ever been in the service, or in any battles.

Looking at her, indignant, he said it was tradition that the prince be given such rank, but, no. It was ceremonial. She shrugged, then talked to him about church.

"And there you are, all proper, praying to the fucking devil. And I'm sure you aren't praying for world peace. You're praying for a piece of ass you can't fuck because you are in that house of evil in your absurd uniform rather than up the ass of what you can't have."

His eyes filled with rage, and he started to lunge at her, then managed to sop himself.

"Insulting me is one thing. To say that about my faith, well… I am not one to be rude, but I must insist you leave this skipper. If not, I do have men who can be rude."

Smiling, she stood up and flattened her skirt, fluffing her hair, and looked at him with pity.

"No, we must never be rude, mustn't we? I'm happy to leave. I'd like to say that when I do, I'll find a real man for the ten-year-old girl I was going to suggest may give you some religion. Her altar is God's gift to any who are looking for spiritual enlightenment…"

Turning to leave, she thought to herself it would be all of three seconds before she reached the door of the suite to leave. The prince didn't make it that long.

"I say, old gal, sorry to be rude and all that. Comes with the title and all. Get my way all the time. Sit down and don't get your panties in a bunch."

Smiling before she turned, she enjoyed such a moment immensely.

She turned, shook her head, and saw what a total idiot had so much money, and she wanted to take it all, enduring the dumb look on his face. She lifted the front of her skirt up to her waist.

"I don't wear panties so I nothing to get bunched up, as you said. One sweet pussy though. I just wanted to show my cunt the dumb fuck who doesn't know what spiritual pleasures a little girl can offer. Now, I leave, and you go pray to some marble statue. I'll find a real man smart enough to know how lucky he is to fuck that sweet thing. The girl I had thought may be your redemption."

Leaving a half-hour later, she watched as he wired ten million as a donation to the Church of the Only One, and he almost came from her video of the little girl she said would be his salvation. With the money, and arrangements, in place for the girl to guide him at his private estate, she told him that he could seek many more such blessings if, he wanted, and was generous to The One.

Walking to the limo that waited for her, she had several more needy men with endless funds to pay for young girls, and she had many young girls to offer.

Before reaching the villa where an ex-president was staying, she heard the special ring she had set for when Sharon called. Answering, she said she was in Europe and was getting converts, asking if she could call a bit later. Sharon said to call when she had time, and something unexpected had happened. Jo scrunched her eyebrows, saying she was not one for unexpected things, and asked for a simple heads-up.

"I'm not sure how things will go, but Whimsey took off, and she didn't come home. Take her off the menu for now, well, until I find her. Jo, she just was filled in on the way we do things, and that could be a problem."

Jo closed her eyes, holding back on reacting but she wanted Sharon to know she wasn't happy with her at the moment.

"Why darling, not a problem. No, not at all… It's not a problem, it's a *huge* fucking problem. You know that, so please don't pussyfoot around with me. That's not what pussies are for."

CHAPTER 40

Checking that Whimsey was sleeping, Cindy and Mike both agreed to keep security tight, and he'd need to talk to James about what they had learned about Sharon.

"Mike, I'm so sorry for you. All that you did to find Sharon, and now this…"

Looking at Cindy, he was having a hard time containing himself. He loved Jamie but being with Cindy was getting harder to do. She was more than stunning to look at, she was wonderfully kind, caring, and even with what she had been through in the Ukraine with her father raping her, reduced to selling herself to keep Angie safe as they were illegal immigrants, and then recently trafficked and sold to a wealthy sheik, she was the most grounded person he knew. Her appeal to him was complete and she was beautiful inside and out. He hadn't let her know, and it was getting harder to repress his feelings for her.

"Cindy, it's not me to be sorry for. Sharon… well, I thought she had made it out. That she was home. I'm still not sure if it's the transition to being back, or she wants to stay in that world. I'm going to have to ask her but it's going to be hard to believe her no matter what she'll say. She's lied to me… to all of us."

Watching Cindy, her eyes were glistening, and he wanted to kiss her, take her in his arms. Beyond infatuation, it was what they had been through together. It was a bond that he cherished.

Without expecting it, Cindy moved to be in front of him, and she put her hand on his cheek and he felt a tremble rush through him. Her touch, the look in her eyes, the way she was breathing had made her the thing he had never wanted to see. A desirable, sexual woman who he longed for since they met. She was alone, and the only man she had to turn to was him. He didn't want to take advantage of her, and he didn't want to do wrong by Jamie. He loved Jamie, and as he felt Cindy next to him, he felt an even deeper love for her. She put her other hand in his, and he knew he couldn't say no to her if she wanted to make love to him. He needed to tell her he was longing for her. He knew she could see it in his eyes as she looked at him.

Looking at her, he squeezed her hand in his.

"I have to tell you something I've held in. I'm in love with you."

Watching her eyes that were already wet, he saw tears form and roll over her cheekbones and down her face, and she made no attempt to wipe them away. She didn't look away or moved. Almost in a whisper, she told him what he longed to hear.

"I know. I love you too. That's okay. You have Jamie, but I know you love her and won't hurt her. I'm glad you told me…"

She moved back just enough to let him know she wanted to not embrace as it would be impossible to stop what would come next. Still looking at him as she turned, she said she'd like to talk at the kitchen table. Still holding his hand, he followed her, and they sat where they were near each other and could talk quietly. Her cheeks still wet with tears, she put her hands on the table face up, letting him know she wanted his in hers. He put his to where she could hold them, and her touch was gentle and made him feel as he never had before. She looked sad, but not from anything said or done, but just at how things went in life.

"Mike, it would be the most wonderful thing I could think of to be making love to you right now. I know why. It's because you told me how you feel but didn't let it go further than that. That's the type of man I have never known. Even when I told you I love you. You are such a wonderful person, and if things had happened a bit differently, if the timing had been just a little sooner, I know we'd be together. I would want that. Hard as it is right now, would we still feel the way we do if we did the wrong thing? Right now, it would be. But hearing you say that? A man I admire, respect, and I'm in awe of? Mike, I've never had that in my life."

Watching her cry, he realized hearing her tell him she loved him as well had been what he longed to hear. It was so powerful that he was loved by her, and to do more than they had would ruin that. If he cheated or left Jamie, she'd feel it was wrong of him to do, and worse, she would be the reason why. They both were thinking the same things, and both felt a closeness that was far more than if making love. It was as she said. Respect. Caring for each other and taking care to not hurt people who had been hurt so badly. He was able to give her a gentle smile and tell her she was right.

"You are so beautiful right now. I wish you could see what I see. And I'm proud to be the man you love and admire. The first you could trust

and turn to. That's all that matters to…"

Suddenly the security system blared, and there was a pounding on the front door. Looking at the screen showing the security camera on the wall next to them, it was Sharon. Both seeing the screen, she looked at him and they both knew it wasn't the Sharon they had seen before. She was in a panic, and a rage. She wouldn't stop banging at the door, and Cindy knew it would wake Angie and Whimsey up. Mike knew it had to be him dealing with her, by himself.

"Be sure to have a bullet in the chamber of your gun. Go stay with the girls in Angie's room. I'll let her in. Let's not take any chances right now…"

Getting her Glock from the kitchen counter, she ran as she headed up the stairs, and he heard both Angie and Whimsey asking if they were under attack. Hearing a door slam shut, he went to the front door, and he opened it.

Facing the barrel of a Colt, she was clearly ready to use it.

"Back up, then take your gun out and put it on the floor, then kick it away. Mike, I just want Whimsey, and I'll be gone."

He knew better than to say no or try to talk her out of it. He also didn't know what type of training she had received, and she had been cold as ice as she shot the dead body of Peter. In a flash he realized she had blasted him in a way that he was unrecognizable. He had no record or arrest and could only be identified by how he looked. It was all making sense.

Doing as she said, as he rose up from gently placing his gun on the ground, she was cold as ice as she asked questions.

"Is she here?"

He nodded, saying she was, and was safe.

"You didn't call me to let me know. I think that means she's talked. I made a mistake in trusting her, and that's a bigger problem as you know now. And I'm sure Cindy and Angie do too. I'm sorry Mike, you know things you shouldn't know. All of you do. I wish things went differently…"

Looking at Sharon, he didn't take his eyes away from hers, but he was facing the stairway, and on the top landing Cindy and Angie were standing there in the periphery of his vision. Whimsey was behind them, and he saw the black blur of them aiming their guns at Sharon.

"Sharon, you can still escape. You can turn it around and stop all this. Please, for you, put the gun down and leave the cult."

"I joined the cult. I wanted it, and you never knew. It's not something I can walk away from. Not with what I know. If I don't do what I have to, I'll be dead by tomorrow."

Having been trained to stop a person holding a gun, one ready to shoot, he was waiting for the right moment to make a move against her, and he needed time, distracting her just enough to give him a chance to disarm her in that split second. Talking was the best chance he had to shift her attention to a question or comment.

"I can't believe you'd kill me and ones who care about you... You can live with that?"

She hadn't shifted her focus, and he knew even if she fired at him, unless in the head, he may have enough time to take her with him by lunging forward and letting his adrenaline power him enough to tackle her and turn her own gun on her.

"I can live with that, but none of you can live to know about The One. I'm the only one walking out that door tonight. I want you to call them down and make it fast and easy on them..."

Looking at Sharon, he held up his hands and started to walk towards her, saying, "It's me."

The sound of her shot filled the house like a clap of thunder as Mike flew back with his blood a mist of red filling the air. Just a second after her shot came two more, and Sharon flew down and forward landing at Mike's feet, her back oozing blood to join the pool under her where her chest had blown apart from hollow core bullets.

Angie was at the railing, her Glock smoking from her two shots as she saw Sharon's trigger finger pull back. She was standing with her Glock pointed to Sharon's head, ready to fire again if there was even a twitch from Sharon. Cindy knew they had waited too long. They had prayed Mike could talk Sharon into remembering who she was, but she was no longer his sister and her mind had been altered by rituals of sex and psychedelic drugs with The One.

Cindy shouted for Angie to stay on target as she rushed down the stairs to Mike. Whimsey was holding onto Angie's back, screaming and wailing in fear and pain. Angie kept aim at Sharon although she knew she couldn't be alive with the shots that hit her, and she slowly went step

by step down the stairs, Whimsey holding onto her pajamas and wailing in horror at what she'd seen.

Reaching Sharon, she knelt in the large pool of blood, turned Sharon's face to close her eyelids, then looked up at Cindy who was ripping at Mike's shirt, looking at Angie shouting, "Towels!" Angie, gun in hand in case Sharon had anyone waiting outside, told Whimsey to come with her and she'd show her where the kitchen towels were. Whimsey suddenly stopped her screams and ran with her. Handing her all the towels in the closet off the kitchen, Whimsey held them tight and ran to Cindy as Angie pulled out a large kit for medical emergencies and rushed to put it by Cindy's knees, then ran to the front door where Sharon had entered, made sure it was secured and moved back to face it with her Glock out in front of her ready to fire.

Pressing three towels down on Mike, under his left ribs on his side, Cindy had ripped his shirt away and was applying pressure to where the bullet had hit him. Without looking up, she called to Angie to call James, not 911, adding Mike's cell was on the kitchen table. Not turning away from the front door, she called out to Whimsey to bring her Mike's phone. Whimsey got up, then running through the pool of blood, saw the phone, grabbed it, and found the contact number for "James Emergency," pressed it as she reached Angie and held it up on speakerphone for her.

After three rings, James answered saying, "Mike?"

"James, it's Angie, Mike's been shot. We need help right now. It's bad. At our house, mom's putting pressure on the wound but he's unconscious!"

Telling her to hold while he makes calls, she didn't move or take her eyes off the front door as he took two minutes to get back talking to her.

"The Army base five minutes from you is sending a doctor and ambulance so get the system ready to let them in. The doctor is their gunshot wound expert. I know it must be a nightmare, but I'm running to my car and will talk to you on my way. Tell me just what happened."

Angie hadn't moved, but talked loud and clear as Whimsey held the phone off to the side of her head to not get in the way of her aim.

"Sharon showed up, he let her in. He told mom to run up to warn Whimsey. We heard Sharon was crazy, saying we all know too much, and we all would die. She forced Mike to put his gun on the floor. He tried

talking her down. I didn't wait, and I went to the upper landing and aimed at Sharon's back. Mom was right behind me then stood with me on the upper landing and aimed at her. Then as Mike started to move to her, she fired and he flew way back. I waited too long. The second I saw her finger pull, I fired twice before mom could get a shot off as I was in position to see her finger pulling back and she couldn't. Sharon's dead, Mike's got a hole under his ribs. Mom's putting pressure on the hole, but hasn't rolled him over to see what he looks like in back. He's breathing. I'm standing the front door where she entered and ready. Mom just said he's pretty white… wait, I see flashing lights. Yeah, it's a truck, dark green, I'm opening the door and I'm going to flag them in. I'll tell them any wrong move and I'll fire. I'll call once they figure out how bad it is. Gotta go!"

Opening the front door, a man in scrubs started to ask where. He understood why Angie was holding the gun, and knew to expect such precautions. Seeing Mike and Sharon, he went and told Cindy he'd take over.

Angie had let him in, but instantly stood with gun out blocking three men in green uniforms, two with a gurney and one with a large box. The first man, the doctor, called to Angie they were needed and they were his aides. She backed to the side but kept aim at them as they entered. One carrying the large box moved in and set it next to the doctor. The man with the box started assisting him. He was shouting out what he needed. The men with the gurney had an EKG on it, taking it off and they attached it to Mike. It started making beeps for the heart rate.

Cindy was covered in blood, Whimsey as well, and they moved back. Angie had moved to kick the door shut, and armed the security for it, and moved back to keep guard over the men. She was not taking any chances with strangers after what a man's sister had done. Cindy's eyes were locked on all being done to Mike. It didn't take long for the doctor to say he had the bleeding under control so he could be moved.

They were all clearly expert at moving someone with such wounds. The gurney went near down to the ground, and they moved Mike onto it with the doctor watching for anything he missed when Mike was on the ground. Once it was up and ready to move, Angie disarmed and opened the front door, still standing guard.

As the gurney went out the front door, the doctor watched, then turned to Cindy.

"Here's how it went. Short range, it sent the bullet through him. I don't think any vital organs were hit, that area is intestines. He's lost blood and you stopped a lot from the front, but most bled out from behind. He's in shock. That slowed his blood pressure. We know his blood type, so we'll fill him back up. I don't see any other issues right now, and from what I can see, he'll survive. I'd guess about two hours in OR. James will get you in and I'll know more then. I'm at the limit for how long it takes to get him in the OR."

He looked at Sharon, knew she was dead, then back at Cindy.

"The woman… A different team will come for her."

Rushing out of the house, Cindy fell to her knees and started to bawl. Whimsey was standing looking at Sharon, her face blank. Angie secured the front door, and using her own cell phone called James back, saying the doctor said he thought he'd make it, they were getting him to the base, and he'd be in the operating room for two hours.

Saying he was just blocks away, Angie went to the security panel and said flash his red and blue lights just once when he was down the street so she could be sure he wasn't accompanied.

Soon, James walked in, looking upset, staring at Sharon's body. Seeing them all soaked with blood, he said a team was coming to take Sharon and he'd handle that, but right now they needed to shower the blood away, get dressed, and go be with Mike. Cindy was still crying from what happened. Looking at the blood all around them, she told James she needed to clean everything up. He told her it was going to be done by the crew coming, adding it was a CIA operation, so no forensics or police. They would have it clean and safe.

Angie walked up to him before heading up the stairs, saying she'd hug him for all he'd done, but after she got cleaned up. As she started to walk to the stairs, she suddenly stopped and turned back to him. She was holding her Glock pointed up with her arm bent, looking up at it, then back to him.

"My mom and I aren't going to give these up to anyone, no matter where we're going."

Nodding, he told her he knew that, and he'd get them cleared while he waited. Angie looked at Sharon again before going up the stairs, and James saw her expression wasn't the Angie he knew.

"First kill. You had to, Angie. If you need to talk about it, I can have

Charles see you. He's coming to the base too…"

Looking at him, he realized she wasn't showing the common reaction to shooting and killing someone for the first time. It was common for anyone, even in such a situation to face the fact they took a life. He realized the look was one of anger, not shock. She shook her head.

"What you're seeing is that I'm upset that I didn't fire sooner. Charles can't change that."

She turned, walked up the stairs and James understood exactly how she felt.

CHAPTER 41

"We're at an Army hospital, and the doctor was in Vietnam and everything since. He told us it was bad, but he'd live… Angie? She didn't hesitate. Right now, she's upset she and I waited… Yes, we know now the second she said nobody leaves we needed to take the shot… Yes, we know who's behind it… Even the agency wasn't aware of how big the operation is… Whimsey heard it all, and she was working her to join and be bait or something… I don't know the person who heads it, but it's a cult thing. Some religion that's really big — all over the world and they go for the billionaires… Sharon joined them… Yes, in college. She was never taken… the name is The One. Just the word, One. James is working on it."

Talking to Eliana on her phone in the waiting room, Cindy was looking at Whimsey who was still mortified that she mistook what she thought was love from Sharon was really a form of grooming her. As Cindy told her mother about The One, she started waving to get Cindy's attention.

"Mom, Whimsey's waving at me to get my attention… No, she only speaks English… Okay, just talk slowly so she understands you… Yes, your English is fine, mom, she just saw a horror movie, so I'm going to put her on."

Sitting next to Whimsey, she said her mother was the biggest trafficker in Eastern Europe.

"She's stopping and is coming to live with us. She'll understand what was done. She wants to talk to you and find out what you can add, okay? Good, her name is Eliana."

Handing Whimsey the phone, she looked at Angie who was standing where she could see the corridor in both directions. She was keeping guard, and she saw she had one hand in her handbag, which held just her ID and her Glock. Having learned about her grandmother's operation, also one Jamie worked for that they had been trafficked by, then seeing that Mike's own sister had fooled them all, even in a secure Army base there could be someone from the cult who'd do a suicide run at them. Angie had changed from a trusting girl to a warrior after being trafficked, put up for auction naked with her, and sold to a billionaire. Cindy understood that like her being raped by her own

father and growing up in a world of human trafficking, Angie was still a sweet young girl, but had seen how horrific the world was to innocent children, girls and women. It was sad, but Angie was beautiful and was no longer naive and would take care of herself, and her.

Listening to Whimsey talk to her mother, again, she was amazed at how brutal the world was to the most vulnerable. Whimsey was just a little girl, and to hear the things she was saying was heartbreaking.

"No, it wasn't Peter or Sharon who had me fucking in porn… I ran to get away from my foster home… Yeah, he'd been fucking me in the ass since I was, like, seven. I needed money and I was too young to get a real job… I know sex for money is a job, that's why I did it… Sharon told me lots about how she was the leader's fuck… Yeah, it's run by a woman… Why's that a shock, you do the same thing… Oh, yeah, not a cult, I get it. You just sell girls and have hookers… No, she didn't give any details, but I heard her once on her phone, and she was talking to someone called Jo, and I guessed that she was taking orders, you know, saying yes, she'll do that, all that stuff… No, she told me I'd love going up in the mountains for a while, but didn't say where in the mountains… Am I in the cult and playing everyone? My little sister was fucking shot by them, so, like, figure it out. No… Okay, I get it. If I am, I know you'll do to me what you did to Peter… I know you're like Cindy's mom and all, but I'm the one they're out to get, remember? No, think what you want, why would she kill me then? No, I don't have a gun. I don't know how to use one… So, yes, it was Jo. Maybe an O at the end… or maybe an E, I'd try both… Okay, I'll tell her."

Giving back Cindy the phone, she said her mother had accused her of a lot of stuff.

"Yeah, for like a minute I thought she was saying I was the cult leader. You grew up with her? Whoa, she's intense!"

Smiling at Whimsey, she realized that her mother was doing what she did best. Taking care of things and taking no chances. That stopped the day she shot her husband in front of her and her brother. It had been a cold, planned kill, not something done in the heat of the moment. It was the first time she had seen someone killed, and deep inside of her she knew it was why she had been just as cold when she shot the Sheik she and Angie had been trafficked to. He was licking her clit as she took a gun she had hidden behind her, and while he was lost in licking

her, aimed straight down and shot him in his head. He deserved to be killed for thinking he could own them, or anyone. Some people had to be stopped. They would just keep hurting and killing whomever they wished if not.

"Yes, she's feared and ruthless. If she's looking for that cult leader, she'll show no mercy. If she's on your side, she'd die for you. Those are both the same thing. I think once she's here, she'll love you, and you'll get over her ways. What did she say at the end of the call?"

Looking at Whimsey, Cindy saw a little girl, frightened, so tiny. It was hard for her to imagine her doing sick things in porn, but she had. Raped when younger than she was when raped by her own father, Whimsey had been harmed forever by someone she was supposed to trust, doing porn to get her and her sister away. She was sad for her, but at the same time impressed that she did it to take care of her sister, just as she had prostituted herself to take care of Angie. They had that in common, and she understood her and knew that like her, she could grow strong and fight a world that had treated her without concern or kindness. She sat next to her and listened to her say what Eliana told her.

"Well, she said she knows enough people and that she'll find out who runs the Only One. Then she said she'd go kill Jo. That was, well, I think about all she said at the end, and to tell you she may not be here in a few days like planned. I guess she has to go kill that woman, then come."

Cindy smiled at her, then reached out and hugged her.

"Just a little detour to go kill someone, then she'll be on her way. What a sad world. I'm sorry you saw what you did earlier. That's why Angie and I are doing what we are. We want to stop as many traffickers as we can."

Asking her how they could get at the leaders, Cindy understood.

"Well, we are just what they look for. So, we act dumb, they could snatch us, or we could approach them and say we could supply them with girls. All depends on what we learn. Then once we're in and meet the head of the organization, take them out. In the Ukraine, where my mom is from, they say kill the head, the body dies too. We have Jamie, and I've tried calling her and don't know what's going on but no answer and that has me worried. Mike too, and he's strong. When he heals up, he's part of things too. And others we find who've been hurt and want to work with us."

Whimsey was looking at her, and Cindy knew she was thinking. There was something about Whimsey she admired, and she liked her. She had worried about her being with Sharon although she wasn't sure why at first. Now she knew. Her instincts had warned her, and she needed to begin running with them. Whimsey was looking at her, and she knew she wanted to say something.

"After the cult thing is figured out and all, could I work with you guys? I'm alone and free to do it. I'm, well, you know, like jailbait, so I could be out there to get taken and things like that. I'd need to learn how to be like you guys and all, but after what happened to my sister, I want to get fuckers like the ones who did that..."

Cindy looked at her and told her, "Yes." It wasn't something she had to think about. She was somehow hoping Whimsey would stay and be part of them. She was glad she and Angie had a large house. She told her from now on, she would live with her and Angie, and Whimsey was in tears, thanking her.

Calling Jamie again, she wanted to tell her to come to the base, and what happened to Mike. Everything had happened so fast, but it had been two hours since Sharon shot Mike, and she was surprised that she hadn't called. She was using Mike's phone to call her, and her own as well. When not able to call, she had Angie calling and leaving messages from her phone. She could be sleeping, but her instinct was telling her she wasn't.

James came in with Charles, and said he just left her house, and not a trace of what happened was left. Even the holes in the wall were patched and touched up. He said he'd hoped to hear that Mike was out of surgery but wasn't worried as better to go slow and fix him up right.

"We're in a war zone with all we deal with, but it's good he fixes him up. This is the first time Mike's been down, so Charles wants to be here when he comes to. He can tell him to stop whining, it's a badge of honor in a sick way."

Cindy couldn't quite understand the way men thought of getting into fist fights when kids, or boxing or football as something to be proud of, but there was James saying Mike would have his first badge of honor. She flashed on what he meant. He had stood there to try to keep his sister from shooting all of them, and his jumping at her gave them a reason to shoot her. She wasn't sure he had planned it that way, but

without a gun in his hand, and knowing they did, he had made it where they fired and took her down. He was willing to sacrifice himself for them, and yes, his scars would be a badge of his honor.

"James, as if enough hadn't happened, I've been trying to call Jamie since Mike was taken in the truck. No answer with my phone or his. I'm feeling something's wrong. Any ideas on how to get in touch with her."

James grew dead serious. His expression echoed her own worry.

"I assumed she knew and would be here. Christ, this sucks. Look, I'm going to call my best guy and have him go to Mike's, and if she's not there, we'll escalate things. The last thing Mike needs is to wonder where she is. She needs to be here with him right now. I'll be back in a bit. Going to the secure line from my car."

Charles watched him leave, then told Cindy no matter what, James would be on it. He looked over to Whimsey, and Cindy nodded. She knew what had happened at their evaluation, and that they needed to talk, even if just there in the waiting area.

"She saw it all happen. She saw Angie shoot Sharon, but she heard her say she was going to kill her. As if everything wasn't bad enough already. One thing to help you… She just said she wanted to be with us as part of taking down traffickers. She's figured out being hurt doesn't do much. Fighting back does. I know for Angie and me, it's not revenge. It's saving people just like us. I'm sure Whimsey is thinking that too."

Nodding, saying he would support that, he went and asked her if she wanted a friend to wait with. Whimsey looked up at him and told him she was glad he was a friend, and that she was sorry for being so mean to him. Suddenly, they were talking, and whatever happened had created a bond between them. Cindy was sure they both understood how Sharon had pitted them against each other. She had been well trained by the cult leader; the one known as Jo. Looking at how quickly Charles and Whimsey had gotten past the hurt they each had suffered at the psych evaluation; she heard Angie saying the doctor was coming.

Joining her where they could both see the long corridor to the operating rooms, the doctor who first took charge of Mike at their house was walking and he didn't seem to look worried, and seeing them both, he waved as he walked. Angie looked at her, and she was worried, and she was too. It could still be bad news even if Mike was alive.

Walking up to them, he was still in scrubs and he motioned for them

to sit in the waiting area as he pulled a chair out to sit facing them.

"I just washed up, and first, he's stable and he'll be out of things for a good hour or so, then he'll be in a regular room. I thought at first he'd need to be in the intensive care unit, but no need for that. She may have been aiming for his heart, his torso, but with him moving towards her, maybe he anticipated it and moved to not be centered on the barrel. So, like I said at your house, the shot went through him, which was a good thing. It went through under his lung, and it was close, I gotta tell you. It nicked an intestine, and I cut a section out, and that's a common procedure and really, that's all it did. The intestine bled and that could cause a major infection in the cavity, but I'm not worried about it as we got him here fast enough to prevent it. So, he's getting antibiotics just to be sure. I sewed him up, and why he looked so bad was from loss of blood, so you did good to stop as much bleeding as you could. He'll hurt where he got hit. Some muscles had to be cut and I put those back together. Right now, I'd say two, maybe three days he can head home. Large cuts front and back, so he'll have a ton of stitches to have taken out, pain meds and antibiotics. No chin-ups or stretching exercises. He's in great shape, and that's going to help him right now. Oh, and with intestines, a special diet, and on discharge he'll get a sheet about it. Well, that's everything. I'm prescribing you both a big dose of not worrying about if he'll be okay. He will."

He got up, and watching him head back down the corridor, they saw James coming in and they stopped to talk. James was nodding, looking relieved, then patted the doctor on his shoulder, and saw them looking and was shaking his head, looking worried as he walked to them.

"My agent was right near his place, and I waited as he went there. No answer, so I told him to let himself in. He can handle about any lock. Lights on, purse on hall table, gun in it. No Jamie."

Cindy looked at him and her mouth was open, but no words came as she was overcome with worry and didn't know what to say. James understood and continued.

"Right now, I have to plan for the worst. I gave a green light to wake our best guys up to start working on finding her. It could be so many different things, but of course a purse with her gun there and her not there, all red flags. I pray it isn't how it looks, but it sure doesn't look right. I don't know why she'd be a target. That's what I need to figure out

next. It'll be a while before Mike wakes up and I know it sucks, but I'll have to tell him and ask what she may know. Sorry guys, that's what this job is full time. People doing the worst to each other."

Looking over to see Charles and Whimsey talking and seeing they seemed past their conflict, he nodded, saying that was one good thing at least. Cindy looked at them and told him what Whimsey wanted to do. Angie hadn't heard about it yet and looked at Cindy.

"Mom, I'm supposed to be the bait!"

Both Cindy and James looked at her showing disbelief. Somehow, they both said the same thing at the same time.

"You still are."

Angie smiled for the first time since Sharon had entered the house.

"I know, but she'll be more of a draw then me. I'm getting too old anyway. I mean, well, what rich guy wants a stunning sixteen-year-old?"

Neither Cindy nor James disagreed. It was sad and sick. As young and totally gorgeous as Angie was, she was still one traffickers would want, but Whimsey would be the grand prize in their sick world. She could look like she was ten, and that's what they wanted above all else. Cindy looked at Angie.

"They will, but we all know that little girl with Charles right now is in big demand too. She's free from her foster family, and Sharon's dead, so not her Guardian. I told her she's with us now, and she'll live with us. If I need to get help being her legal guardian, then we do that."

Angie nodded, saying that was what she had hoped would happen. Turning to James, she surprised him.

"James, with the battle and Sharon dead, what if the world thinks Whimsey went down too? You know, like on Fox News, she goes off the grid. Nobody from the cult after her if she doesn't exist."

Cindy looked at her with surprise. Angie didn't think it was a crazy idea. She looked at Cindy with a questioning look as to what was the big deal, then she understood as Cindy said, "Now it's Fox News?"

"Mom, I'm dialing into all the things we didn't have with broadcast TV. James, do you know what I'm thinking? Hard to hit what isn't there. Oh, and mom, I heard that in a movie on Tubi…"

Thinking, James said getting satellite and streaming may not be so bad, and that Angie had a good idea. It's not something that could have been done before what happened earlier, but the agency could do it. He

said he'd need to tread carefully, but that's what he did each day. Angie looked at Cindy.

"Mom, see? You think I'm all looks and no smarts."

Cindy looked at her straight-faced.

"Oh, you mean like people think of me?"

About to laugh, Cindy felt a vibration in her pocket. It was Mike's phone. She held it up for Angie and James to see, then answered.

"Did you shoot Sharon?"

Cindy knew it had to be the cult leader, Jo. She was holding the phone where James put his ear next to hers to hear. Cindy shocked him once more as she answered."

"That wasn't really Sharon. It was someone you killed a long time ago. Yes, we took down your bitch if that's what you're asking."

"Why, my, oh my. Aren't you just letting that hot cunt of yours go to your head. That's not what it's for, dear. I'm a bit miffed that you did that. Did that sweet little twat daughter of yours get off on it? Because I'm more than miffed at her."

Cindy knew the woman had knowledge she shouldn't have. How did she know Sharon was dead, and that Angie had killed her?

"You have me confused with someone who cares if you are or not. If you were here now, you'd be next. I'm a bit more than miffed at you. You don't know who I am, do you?"

"Does that matter?"

"This isn't my first dance. And sure, we both got off doing her. So what?"

James was amazed at how Cindy was provoking her. He didn't stop her and knew that approach would get her into a rage where she'd make mistakes. He heard a long pause, then Jo replied.

"How's your boyfriend? Get off on watching him take it from his sister?"

"She was pathetic. Couldn't get a kill shot off at five feet? Oh, I take it you trained her then. That explains it. So, what do you want? Is this how you get off? You cum yet?"

Even Angie was surprised at the language her mother was using, not what she was saying though.

"Gee, I was hoping to bring you out of the dark and into the light..."

"Jo, how would you do that? Shine a flashlight up your twat? Even

then, I don't think you know how to deal with anything but weak ones, like you. You call yourself, what? The One. Please, give me a break. Rename yourself to be accurate. Weak One. That's better, don't you agree?"

"Well, that's all for show. I just called to say hello, as we will need to have a bit of time together soon. Oh, and I'll take good care of your little girl and that little clit licker Whimsey, so don't worry about them."

"I'm not the one, oops, used the wrong name, I'm not worrying about them. You are. I mean, really, who falls for your stupid act? If you're so scary, just knock on my door and say who you are and you want in. I have a few things to say to you too."

"Really. Well, I am looking forward to knowing what that could be…"

Cindy was relentless.

"Just a few. Oh, heck, I'll end the suspense. All I have to say is… Glock, hollow, point, in, your, head."

She hit the end button, then putting the phone back in her pocket, looked at Angie and James.

"She's certainly full of herself. So, James, the thing is that she knew everything that happened, and there wasn't any way she could know any of it except from someone who was there or who was told as it was going down."

He turned and looked at Whimsey, and Cindy stopped him right there.

"No. She's been with every step of the way. She's had no chance to call or talk to anyone. She's wearing the clothes we gave her, and Angie took all her old stuff and helped her shower. Anything's possible, she just doesn't have any way of connecting with Jo. I think maybe all the things we have right now are connected. Who isn't here?"

Looking at her, he closed his eyes, and was thinking through what she had said, then looked at her, and he was visibly shaken.

"Oh, God. I hope not, but I guess I don't want that to be true. Do you really think it's Jamie? Even so, how could she know?"

"Angie, I had you trying to call her. Just like me, you left voice messages telling her what happened, and that you had to shoot Sharon, right?"

Nodding, Angie said she had, just like she heard her doing. Just that Mike had been shot by Sharon, he's at the Army hospital, they'd shot

Sharon. Also, she could be who they go for next as she knew as much as Mike, so be ready and don't go anywhere unarmed.

James understood that as she was trusted, she needed to know and be on the lookout as Sharon may have had her as a target too. But, based on what Cindy had pointed out, she was missing, hadn't been part of things for the past few days, and even at Peter's island she was holding back and was there, but not really part of everything when thinking back on it.

"James, she was in deep for so long, who knows what could trigger her into going back? To think she didn't belong with us? She loves Mike, but it could be like Sharon, a way traffickers control ones who get rescued or take off. They know so much, they have to take that into account."

Agreeing that was possible, he asked a question that stopped Cindy cold.

"Okay, going with that as a real possibility, she was out, with us, and had Mike who loved her. What the hell could send her back, have her turn against them?"

Cindy knew the answer. Mike couldn't hide his feelings with her earlier before Sharon arrived. She knew he couldn't hide his heart. He may have given Jamie signs, or even talked about how he felt about her, even if only to be honest and say he had to deal with it. She looked at Angie, then looked at James.

"I know what. Me.

CHAPTER 42

Having only a short time ahead of her, dying from inoperable cancer, Eliana had divested herself of most all her money and weapons. Heading to the airstrip where she kept her private jet, she hadn't sold it as she knew it would be an essential asset for Cindy and Angie in their pursuit of traffickers such as she had been. She had put a fortune she had made by running her dead husband's trafficking business the way he never had into accounts in both Cindy and Angie's names. She had kept some money for herself. Doctors weren't always right about how much longer a person had to live, and she wanted liquid funds for anything that may be needed for while she was alive.

Talking to Cindy and learning of the threat to her girls by a trafficker operating under the guise of a religious sect, she had vowed to kill her. Turning to sources she had relied on; she was able to learn that the trafficker had gone unnoticed because she dealt almost exclusively with the richest and most powerful men in the world. Men who were at that level had enough money to keep their activities quiet and stop anyone who may know from talking. She learned The One, as she referred to herself, didn't accept payments. She accepted donations and offered girls for spiritual fulfillment and guidance. The most powerful and richest men often were ones with companies that were publicly traded, and their finances were paid by their company and multimillion dollar donations were viewed as line items in a ledger and had to have some excuse for the expense. The rich were buying young girls using shareholder money. Eliana had never used such a scheme, but she understood that it was the shape of trafficking to come.

Learning The One's name was Jo, she ignored that and focused on finding the headquarters of the Only One church. Turning to her accountant, Genia, she had grown up with her and was trusting enough of her to let her handle laundering money and general payments to her large staff. Telling Genia all she knew, the woman started searching for the tax filings for the supposed church.

"Eliana, I don't know why they don't operate like others, just gather money, launder it offshore. Having a church, tax filings, it makes no sense to me."

Eliana explained the bastards who had the most money got it all in

stock and had investors and were publicly traded. They didn't have cash and couldn't pay in shares, so Jo had been creative and allowed them to pay from their companies using donations. The men could buy girls and use company money. Genia was impressed, saying she was clever, so one to watch out for.

"She may be clever, but what she did was leave a trail to her. In US, to get status to not pay tax as church or non-profit, they need to make annual report, list who runs it all. I found what I think is hers. Big money, looks like real thing, so here, I am opening list of executives. She is clever. She has old hag as running it, and other hags as the board of directors. It doesn't show her, but it does say where they are headquartered. In a state, Montana, not in town, on property of their own where they train and, get this, provide shelter for young girls and children who won't stay put in homes. Ah, wait, I think I see something. Picture of woman with young girls, Very little ones. It says she is instructor, guiding them. It says name is Josephine Wilson. She must have big ego to put picture here."

Thinking, with the church being call the Only One, showing all young girls, it was the one. Jo did have a big ego, but the picture was to show the billionaires she was the one training the girls. It wasn't ego, it was business. Genia emailed her the link, and knowing where she was and what she looked like, that was all she needed. Looking at her picture, she was attractive, good body, and had a look that she was so smart. She had a smugness that irritated Eliana. She planned to wipe it off her face with a shot, two if needed.

She saw a problem. Jo had put herself in a camp where there were children around her all the time. Thinking they were her shield; she wouldn't expect anyone to go at her with children as shields. Again, Jo had it all figured out. She would give some thought on the flight to Montana, and she wouldn't waste time. She posed a threat to Cindy and Angie. She had been warned but hadn't taken her seriously.

Once aboard her plane, she thought of how Jo had used the people in ways she had never done. She would attack one of her own takes by killing the people who loved them most. It was a terror tactic. It was used by organized crime and terror groups, but she had never thought that way or used such low ways of controlling rouges. She realized that, if possible, she would fight fire with fire. She would attempt to find if

Jo had anyone related to her or close to her in some way. If not, then there would be people within her immediate circle at her organization, and they had family, and she could start doing the things Jo had. She didn't want to, but just as she had to learn English, she would learn Jo's language of terror tactics.

Having provided girls for many in the KGB and in covert groups in her world of clients, she knew they were relentless in getting information no matter how it had to be done. It wasn't where any of them owed her favors. She had charged them the highest price possible for what she provided to them. It would be more of the challenge. Her calling, saying to find a new source as she had gotten ill and needed to stop, then say she had one more who had done her harm, and just mention it, saying she didn't think they could find anything on her as she was an American and so smart. It would be that they would say that was nonsense, a fool could find out anything about the woman. They were the types that if you said they couldn't do something, they wouldn't stop until they proved you wrong. It was a mix of pride and vanity.

Making a call to the most tenacious black operative she knew, she posed her goal and said she was frustrated that not even he could help. He said that he understood she was not in his business, but such was child's play for one such as him. She said she would understand if nothing could be found, He said if only to not be insulted so, he would find more than she could ever know could be found. She said if that was what it would take to prove her wrong, she would be happy to say she was wrong.

After an hour, he called. His voice had the superior manner most men in the higher ranks of Russia had, and he said she would have to say she was sorry, but admitted he understood why she thought it impossible to find out anything about her.

"I respect such a person, but they grew up in America and don't live as we have, you see. They think they cover tracks by not making any, and anyone leaves a trail behind them. They have face changed, lose or gain weight, move many times, all done to hide identity, and that does no good. She has daughter. That, boss lady, was not easy thing to find. Daughter has no idea she is daughter. That bitch, she knows, she keeps eye on her it seems. Money goes to family who take her and adopt her, they don't question such good luck, but I am sure they know it isn't from

Putin… that was joke, you know? So, I have name, address of daughter, I know you want to write down, Russia spies on every email to you, no? Another joke. We don't care about where girls come from, just that we get them… how old? It would seem from day since money started, she eleven. Okay, my good deed for year done, but I think not good for the bitch in America. Give her bullet for me."

Writing down the name and address he had, it was the first time she was glad she had done business with anyone from the KGB as they were once called. It insulted them to not call them KGB. He had found the only thing that would hurt the cult leader. She had been sending money each month for a daughter she abandoned, so that meant she wanted to make sure she was okay.

Eliana wanted to make sure she took the girl and put her up for sale. Her last hurrah.

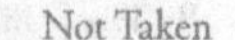

PART FIVE
The Insane

CHAPTER 43

"We meet again. My, you sure look better than when you were a taker for Brian. I had a sense that you would get tired of his bullshit. Now, you'll have to deal with my bullshit. At least I appreciate a sweet ass like yours..."

Jo was in her room and having a video chat to what she referred to as the "guest room." It was nicely appointed with comfortable furnishings, a bed, its own bath and shower. It was a place a guest could stay as long as needed, and included room service through a trap door, and she would always apologize to ones staying in it about the lack of a window, or that the door was locked and everything they did was seen via a closed-circuit monitor. She was talking to Jamie, who was sitting at a table with a monitor and felt horrible from being drugged then waking up in the room.

The only thing she could recall was getting out of her car after shopping for groceries while Mike was off to Cindy's house and feeling a jab in her neck. Whatever she was injected with had her out almost instantly, and she had no idea how long it had been since it was done.

"I know, I know. You must feel awful with all that sleepy-time stuff in you. I'm sorry. It turns out that aside from it being a chance to catch up and all, that I could have let you stay home and put your groceries away, cook a nice meal for that hunk you landed. You always did go for men, didn't you?"

Realizing she had been kidnapped, and she was talking to Jo, a trafficker she had met at Brian's one time, she had no idea why. It was a struggle to talk, but she saw bottled water on the table and drank some to help. She saw Jo, and she was as arrogant and self-assured as when she saw her in Russia.

"I don't know why you would want me here. Brian's dead. I'm not trafficking any longer. What do you want with me?"

Jo held up some pictures so she could see them on the monitor.

"Well, it's not like you're out of the game all the way, are you? You are hitting for the other team, but still in the ballpark. Let's see if I can figure this out. It's so complicated for a girl like me. So, first, I have a picture of someone you must know... Yes, that's right. It's Sharon. Okay, I'll try to remember that. Then, I know for sure you know this one, I mean, you're fucking him and all..."

Jamie tried not to react, but seeing a picture of Mike did make her jerk and want to say something, but she remained quiet.

"That's right, sweetie. He's a strapping lad, I will say. Worth switching teams for. And, I happened to know that Mike is Sharon's brother, and that he's ex-CIA, and he's been looking for her all over the place. Okay, and then, of course, you, but you know what you look like, and you're fucking him, so that's where you come in. Now, this is one I know you will recognize. Tell me who this is…"

Seeing the screen filled with the deadpan face of Peter, she was surprised at how much Jo knew. She understood Jo knew who it was. It was her way of operating. Played games, acted all the time, and she was skirting around what she wanted to say. All she could do was answer, and she said they'd never met, but his name was Peter.

"Good memory, even with all that sleepy-time in you! Yes, Peter. And I heard a little story that you visited his lovely island, and that Peter wasn't much of a host. Got all excited and lost his head. Okay, I'll put that one in the dead pile. Now, this one, I am sure you'll remember her. She's so cute and sweet…"

Holding up a picture of Whimsey naked, sucking a cock, she didn't want to look at it so she just said it was Whimsey, and she was with Sharon.

"Was with… I guess that's the best way to say it. That's because this one, take a look, yes, Sharon, is no more. She's with Peter on a tropical island in the sky now. Yep, passed on, and so young and with such potential. Very sad. And that brings us back to this one… Yeah, your beloved. Your intended. Well, it seems Sharon was licking this little sweetie's pussy, yes, that's right, Whimsey, and being so young and foolish, after a spat, she ran off and Sharon went to get her back, and Mike told her no. You know how jealous women get… Nothing can stop true love, so she shot… I know you saw this picture and know who it is, but Sharon was so upset she shot him. Oh, I can see you are sad. I understand. You finally found your guy, and he gets in the way of lovers and what a mess.

Sharon had learned to keep her control while working for Brian, and she couldn't be sure what Jo was saying was all a game or really happened. She sat, just staring, waiting. She was panicking, but that was what Jo wanted from her. Smiling, Jo said there was more.

"And this stunner, I know you know her… yes, that's right, Cindy. And this next in line for the title… yes, you know her too. Oh, you trafficked them, that's right. Angie. Mother and daughter, sold to Abul who didn't get exactly what he expected… Well, when they saw Sharon shoot Mike, they had Whimsey with them and guess what they did? Oh, they stood there looking like off a Bond movie trailer, and they shot Sharon. What a lot of hot action. All that rockin' hot pussy with pistols blazing, the male lead, the little hottie everyone wants. Sounds like big box office to me."

Aware that Whimsey was with Sharon, then learning she had run away, she couldn't remember anything after hearing Mike saying he was going to work with James to find her. After that, she recalled getting home, parking, then waking up in the room she was in. Although she heard all said, she kept panicking about Mike. Was he dead? As difficult as it was, she needed to focus on what Jo was saying in her roundabout way or she could be next. She needed to find out why she was taken, and what her motive was.

"I don't know about any of that. And I don't know why I'm here. None of that involved me. I was staying out of matters between Mike and Sharon. I didn't think she was free from her grooming, and I knew too much about it, and wanted Mike to draw his own conclusions. The Peter thing… Sharon wanted him dead. She was the last to shoot him."

Looking interested, raising her eyebrows as she spoke, all made it hard for Sharon to grasp what Jo was doing and saying. She had met her one time, and all she knew was that she was a trafficker and had talked to Brian about working together but that never happened.

"Very exciting life. Yep, just like a Bond movie, and you could certainly be a Bond girl. And Cindy! I think Mike as Bond deciding between which Bond girl he would do, and which one would end up encased in gold or drowned in oil. Exciting stuff. Oh, and yes, I did snatch you up before the scene where Sharon took lead, Mike too. I was going to trade you for Whimsey or some idea I can't really recall that seemed good at the time. Oh, I know. I wanted Mike to back off Sharon too. You were, well let me think of the best analogy… oh, a bargaining chip!"

Strangely, Jamie understood what she was saying, If needed, Jo would trade her for Whimsey and let Sharon off the hook to keep her looking

innocent. It all fell apart when Whimsey ran off, and now she was a prisoner, and Whimsey was still free from things. It still would be where she'd try to trade her for Whimsey. She asked her about what would happen next.

"Okay, I think I get it. The main goal is to get Whimsey, and even now I'm a way to trade for her. But why? There are so many girls like her out there. I understood if Sharon loved her, but now? Why not drug me and send me back? Find another one even better."

Smiling and putting her hand on her chin, Jamie was growing more irritated at her every expression and what she was saying. Jo pretended to be thinking about things.

"Well, that's one option. Why am I so enamored with Whimsey? Because Sharon has made her wise beyond her years. She told her all about me. Where I was, what I planned to do with her, you know, girl talk. Bedroom eyes, heat of passion things. But now, she's probably thinking all kinds of things and getting advice from secret agents and won't be the sweet little thing she once was. So now, I have you. Bargain Chip. That's your Bond Girl name, like Pussy Galore, and you know what? If I put you in peril, in a tank of sharks or strap you to a missile, I bet that agents Cindy and Angie will come and try to blow everything up. There's the climatic moment we've all been waiting for. So, in a while, we'll make our own little movie and say they can save you for one... million... dollars! Oops! That's not it. For Whimsey. Cindy and Angie bring Whimsey, and I have you to trade. Maybe on a bridge, or on a cliff."

The screen went black, and Jo had ended the video call.

Jamie stared at the screen, saying to herself, "She's fucking nuts... the worst type." Feeling faint, she didn't know if it was from the drugs they knocked her out with, or the sheer disaster that was taking place and not knowing what had happened to Mike. She wasn't told if he was alive or dead, just that he had been shot by his sister.

Laying on the bed to try and feel better, she wanted to cry as anything that happened to Mike would be unbearable. She wished to be with him, and feeling herself swell and tears about to come, she stopped herself. Certain that Jo was still watching her, the thing she'd want to see was for her to break down and sob. Everything that had been said to her was to provoke an emotional response and test her. That was the

hallmark of a trafficker. Fear, terrorizing, manipulation, hitting all the fear buttons any person taken had. As a former trafficker, perhaps Jo was factoring that she too used such practices, yet the news about Mike was one that would break the most experienced captive. She wasn't going to give her anything.

Thinking about her life, how she had been used since she was five, a wave of despair washed over her. She faced the fact that if she had a way, she knew she would kill herself. After a lifetime of living in a sad, sick world, harming so many innocent girls and their families, she got away and met a man unlike any she had ever known. Mike was not like traffickers or the men using or buying girls. He was a light in her darkness, and he had given her hope. Shivers ran through her as she remembered the looks of fear and hopelessness on so many trafficked girls. They all had dreams for their life ahead, and in one grab by a man in a windowless van, hope vanished the first moment he set eyes on her and made his move. Now, the most decent man she had ever known was shot, maybe dead, so the traffickers could keep going and keep taking girls. When Cindy said she wanted to take the money her mother gave her and start fighting traffickers in a way no government possibly could, it was the first time she had hope. She had a fledgling relationship with Mike, but it was Cindy welcoming her to be part of what she had planned that changed everything for her. She was going to save lives, not destroy them anymore.

Now, a very demented woman, a trafficker who had taken the business into levels never tried, had her as a captive. Even if Mike was dead, she knew that having Whimsey with Cindy and Angie, they would soon attempt to take down Jo and rescue her. She knew it was the last thing they should do.

When she met Jo in Russia with Brian, although presented with an opportunity to be the Russian host for The One and its expanding reach, he had backed off, saying he was growing old, and he was a tiger who would have a hard time changing his stripes. Surprised, after Jo said that was too bad as he would face her as a competitor, she asked him why he didn't want to work with Jo.

"That one? Here, take gun, shoot me now. She has no partner. She crazy bitch, dangerous. I see it in eyes. Crazy. You know, meet madman with shotgun? Tell him no shoot? He shoot you only because you say not to. She is crazy, and she has shotgun."

Brian was a despicable human being, but he was smart about people, and he had been right about Jo. She had taken a chance to even suggest letting her go or trade her. Just telling her that would mean she would never let her go, and that's why she said that. She was bait. Sharon had taken Whimsey from her, so that was why she was dead. Cindy and Angie had Whimsey, and they would be next. Jo would toy with them, just as she had with her on the video call, but ultimately Jo could care less what made sense. She would kill them just because they stepped onto her ground. She'd use her bizarre manner to confuse them, lure them in to swap her for Whimsey, and even tell them to come to her and do things in a fun way. Knowing Cindy was too smart for such deception, it remained she was being held and they would want to get her out.

At some point she knew Jo was so sure of herself that she'd let her out of the room that was her prison. If that happened, she knew she had to kill Jo and most likely she'd die trying. Thinking that if Mike was dead, she'd rather join him where they could be together, even if it was just darkness. The thought comforted her, and she felt a sense of calm was over her. In her thoughts, she sent a message that may reach him, saying she wanted to be with him no matter where that was.

With that message, she said that if he was alive, she'd wait and make sure before she did anything. She knew that meant it was her or Jo.

Jo held the keys to her prison, but that was all she had. Knowing at some point she would come face-to-face with her; she would do what Mike and the self-defense instructor had trained for. A time such as this. To take anything possible, even her fingers held in a certain way, and rip her throat out before she knew what had happened.

Comforting her, she fell back asleep.

CHAPTER 44

"Cindy... you're okay..."

Sitting next to his hospital bed, Cindy told Angie and James she wasn't going to leave until he came to.

She was praying to a holy card of the Holy Virgin she carried with her. It was the Orthodox devotion to Mary, and the card was embossed with gold leaf, and Mary holding one hand up to let her know to remain true and be calm. Unlike Catholics, Ukrainian Orthodox faithful prayed to Mary. Jesus was always an infant in her arms, and she took solace in knowing that a woman could be the mother of a miracle. She thought of Angie as a miracle. She had lived in a hellhole and was untouched by the vile world around her. She knew miracles happened, and she knew it was a miracle Mike was alive. Sharon had never tried to wound him. She was aiming for his heart. On the card, the heart of Mary and the Infant Jesus had sacred hearts, and she thought of how sacred Mike's heart was to her... and to Jamie.

With Jamie missing, and having acted so removed since Sharon had returned, a part of her wished that she was gone and wouldn't return. She didn't hope anything bad had happened to her. She just thought about if Jamie wasn't with Mike, she would be. She prayed for strength as she knew she was being tempted and tested. She was glad they each had revealed their love for each other, but that was where it had to remain — for now.

Having her eyes closed, she thought of what it would be like to be with James. She had never had a boyfriend, though she had more lovers than she could remember. She wasn't ashamed she had been an escort. She hadn't sunk to drug use or being whored out by a pimp, but it still was what it was for her. She had sold her body to men she thought decent, but they did nothing to deserve her. All they did was pay for her time and body. Mike had done everything to deserve her heart, mind, love, and her body. Having come to rescue her and Angie, he had been undercover and her first memory of him was as a photographer working for Jamie. He was deep undercover to stop Brian and Jamie, and even in that role she saw a kindness he couldn't hide. He had won Jamie over to doing right, and they had been lovers from the first day they met. He could see the hurt and pain Jamie had, and he had saved her as well.

Every time since, when they looked at each other, she felt a passion for him, and she could tell he had the same look in his eyes. All men thought she was beyond beautiful. She was made where no matter what she did, no matter how she dressed… she looked sensual and erotic. She knew it was just a way certain Ukrainian woman were. Having no expression on their face, they looked like they longed for whatever man looked at them. Mike knew she was beautiful, and he had been a glamour photographer and met many beautiful women. He looked past her allure and into her eyes like no man ever had. He saw who she was, not just how she looked. That was something that aroused her as no man ever had.

Hearing footsteps, it was James. As she looked up, she held the holy card in her hands, and watched as he pulled a guest chair to sit next to her.

"He looks good. I bet he'll be awake soon."

Looking at Mike, then at her, he gave her a bittersweet smile. He knew from watching them together that they cared about each other far beyond being friends.

"And seeing you, that will be good for him. He is going to wake up to a world of hurt beyond that wound. His sister doing that to him… Jamie nowhere to be found…"

Watching James shake his head, she knew Mike cared about James deeply. She wasn't sure why, or how far that bond went but it was wonderful to see two strong men have such care for each other. He had mentioned that Jamie was nowhere to be found and wanted to know more if possible.

"That's why I'm here. He needs to see I'm okay and that Sharon didn't kill us. But it should be Jamie here. I'm getting more than worried. I know you were going to do all you could to find her. Anything at all turn up?"

He sat back, and his frustration was clear. He had been thinking about things from a distance to try to put the pieces together.

"Nothing. She had been quiet since Sharon was back. I worried about that, but maybe she was just giving them both time to find each other again. Once Sharon did what she did, I think Jamie could tell she wasn't who Mike thought she was. If she came out and said that… warned him, things may have been worse. I think she was watching her,

trying to figure her out, and not get in the way. Just my take on it now. I'm making that part of why she's gone. I think it may be the reason why."

Thinking about what James had said, it made sense. It was a time for a brother and sister to be together, and having been a trafficker, she may not want Sharon to face a trafficker until she was settled and knew more about what her life had been like. She told James that's what she had been thinking.

"Exactly. I considered that. But I keep thinking she saw the warning signs. Instead of being home with Mike, she was far more concerned about Whimsey, and she was with her most all the time. That's got some merit. They were doing porn together, all that. But free, home again… Mike there to protect her… she could love Whimsey and take care of her but seeing Mike meant she had escaped. As we know, she hadn't and I think Sharon knew that, but didn't want Mike to get hurt. Well, there he is. Hurt."

Taking a deep breath, he had caught some of the signs Sharon wasn't free, but so many saved from a trafficker would go through a period where they weren't sure they were safe yet. That's how it had looked to him. Cindy leaned close to him just in case Mike could somehow hear her.

"James, I think she knew, but that doesn't mean she'd leave him. I think she was watching out for him. So, the question is what happened? Where is she? If I knew, I'd do anything to bring her back. She doesn't know what happened. Oh, James! What if that Jo took her to punish Mike? Get him away from Sharon?"

Opening his eyes with surprise, he said he hadn't considered that.

"That could be. We took something from her. Whimsey. So, she takes something of ours. You know, I am going to stop going in circles and think of it that way. Peter was under her control, and she's a nut job. Whimsey swears she never met her, and only heard about her the day she ran to your place. That's why Sharon wanted to kill all of you. To get Whimsey. She knows about Jo. We need to talk to her, and she needs to tell us everything Sharon told her. I think it makes sense that Jo has Jamie. Finally, a direction that may answer things."

Looking at Mike, then back to James, she could see the wheels turning in his head. He was putting it all together. She put her holy card

in her bag, and rubbed Mike's arm, then turned back to James.

"I know when Mike wakes up, the doctor said he'd be up and about in a short time, but I think we should do something about Jamie right now. You heard me tell her what I'll do. I want to go do it. If you can locate where she is and get us to her, I'll take her down and if Jamie is there, get her out and back home."

He smiled, just as he had each step of the way. He was looking at the most beautiful woman he had ever seen, and she didn't have any hesitation of putting her life on the line, or of killing someone like Jo. She was her mother's girl, that was certain. He knew she would do what she said, and he knew she'd find a way to do it.

"I know you'd do it. She threw down a gauntlet and you picked it up. We both know Jo was behind Mike laying here right now. I think there are two options. Draw her out. Get her here. Or, go to her. I have my whole team working on her background and we think she's at the main compound for her cult. We haven't seen any images of her from the satellite, but she may be hunkered down, waiting. The more we know, the better equipped you'll be to get at her. I'm going to leave you here with the hero, and I'm going to tell Charles Whimsey needs to tell us what she knows. I'll call in and see if anything's found out about her. Hey, I've been meaning to ask before all this. Isn't your mother supposed to be here already?"

Smiling, she told him there had been a slight detour.

"Well, yes, but I told her about Jo, and she told me not to worry. She'd take care of it. I've been waiting to hear from her, but my guess would be she found out where she is, and she, well, she's the type who would just go there, say she had business with Jo, and when they meet, she'd not say anything. She'd kill her then leave. Then, come here and ask if I made something good for dinner. She's not okay with how Jo treated me. I would guess you could track her jet. Could you add that to what's being done?"

"Cindy, I wish you had told me. That puts a new spin on things. Yeah, I'll get that going. They don't know each other, do they?"

Shaking her head that they didn't, she started smiling.

"That wouldn't make any difference. She's dying, James. She's coming to be with me, giving her whole operation up. She said she was putting all her money into accounts for Cindy and me, and I have no idea how

much that will be, but she's kept her jet, so I guess she'll give that to us too. See, she is the worst person to mess with. She had nothing to lose. I think she'd prefer to end things in a gun fight than in a bed. I hope she calls soon. If she gets to Jo, she knows Jamie, and she'll bring her back. But for now, let's assume that isn't the case. She may be too ill for it. I'm planning on taking Angie and popping a cap in Jo's head."

Getting up, James looked back at her as he was leaving.

"Pop a cap? Pop a cap? Where in the world did you hear that?"

Not realizing it, Angie had been standing in the doorway, not interrupting them as she could tell they were talking quietly and didn't want to disturb them, but she heard the last part as James stood and asked. She tapped him on the shoulder, and he smiled seeing her, thinking she may have heard what was said.

"We were watching HBO. That's all we heard as we went from preview to preview. We had to look it up on Wikipedia."

Turning to look at Cindy, she was nodding in agreement.

"And we've started referring to you as the... well, I don't think you'd appreciate being called a badass motherfu—"

"*Mom!* That's for putting on his birthday card!"

CHAPTER 45

Knowing Jo had never seen her, Eliana had thought of how best to meet with Jo in person. At first, she thought of simply showing up and asking to see her. Someone as arrogant as Jo would feel too invincible to not want to meet. Next, she considered a pretense that she ran a home for runaway girls and wanted to find a faith-based program for ones not quite yet into their teens when they can still be inspired. Such programs could be researched, and she could indicate that for the safety of the very young girls she hosted them discreetly and worked directly with other programs and not publicly.

Both of those seemed flawed in that Jo may not respond or appear. She thought about what would get her directly in front of her on short notice. Looking online, knowing that in a remote location, such a facility would need staff for cooking, cleaning and other such routine chores. Finding the towns nearest to the compound, she looked in local papers and there were several help-wanted ads, including one for a head housekeeper. The position reported directly to the director, which she was sure meant Jo. At her age, and wearing a simple dress, she could appear as an experienced woman looking to support herself after her husband died and she had need for additional income. It was one where she could use one of the many fake identities she had always carried when traveling showing her as a US citizen.

Going online, she sent an email, saying she was experienced, was traveling to visit a friend who saw the ad as she lived in the area, and was interested in being considered. She listed several past positions for random people, all deceased as she looked them up on an obituary site. She said she lived in Denver and used a name that had dozens identical in directories there. Annie Wilson.

Sending the email at the start of her flight, she received a reply two hours after sending it, asking if she could come for an interview. It said as she was traveling, it would be fine for her to come at a time when nearby, and at the gate ask to speak to the director regarding the head housekeeper position and she would be accommodated if possible.

That would be ideal. She saw no benefit of using bravado or confrontation. She would be in the facility, and even not meeting Jo at first, she knew she'd be close enough to pass by her or be interviewed by

her directly. Then, she would use a small pistol strapped to her thigh to simply shoot her, never telling her who she was. She didn't care if she knew. She only cared about doing what she told her she would. Kill her.

Worrying about Cindy, she called her and explained her plan. Cindy said it was a good way in, or out if she didn't get direct contact with Jo.

"Mother. That is very clever. I think that's the best way in, but there's been a complication. Jamie has gone missing, and we think she was taken by Jo as a way of getting Whimsey back in exchange. Right now, I'm planning to rescue her if she's there. James is working on confirming she is. It's more than getting Jo, it's also getting Jamie out of there, alive."

Eliana was not surprised, yet she didn't see the two tasks as being exclusive of each other.

"Cynthia, I am glad you told me. But why do more than what I plan to do? Once I kill bitch, I find Jamie, take her out with me. Both can be done with one shot. Now that I know, I will just need find where she is. Everyone think staff around maniac will be loyal even when she dead as they are afraid of her. No. They are afraid of woman about to shoot them, gun pointed at them. Let me take care of it all."

She could hear Cindy talking to Angie, and she heard what she was sure was James responding as well.

"Mother, I know that you are willing to go in and because of your illness, you will take a risk. If you get shot, it's a way to stop the suffering. But what if you get taken and held prisoner? We wouldn't be together, and you would die in pain. Have you thought about that?"

Hearing her daughter's concern made her smile, and she did have a good point. She had no idea what security staff Jo had, or if she'd be frisked or put through a metal detector. She let Cindy know she appreciated her concern.

"Cynthia, you said it well. At this time, I care little about dying, but no, I would not want to be prisoner. That would give her power and keep us apart. As you know, I can play part well. At least I could get in, see place, learn what security to take out. If I get job, I ask if I can start same day as I would not need to return to home and need money. I'd be, what you say, inside man. Plan things and learn more. I know you want to face her and take her down. I know she hurt you and you love Mike. You want to save Jamie as she and Mike are together. You know, that is why you are angel. You want to save woman of man you love, get her

back to him. I know that about you. I want to do what you want to do for you. If you want I should wait, I will. I'll try to get in place, then let you know how and when to come. A plan. Good one?"

Hearing more talking in background, she heard Cindy and was impressed with what she overheard. She had told Angie and Mike that her mother understood her better than she thought she could, and she would like to work with her to take Jo down, and that was what she was going to do. She had made her decision.

"Okay, I have a few things to figure out here. We're still not completely sure if Jamie is a prisoner, or if she's somehow working with Jo. When she went missing, suddenly Jo knew things only Jamie would know. So, it would be good if your plan to work there happened. You could find out if Jamie was freely roaming or locked away. See, that is one of my worries. If she's working with Jo, she'll recognize you and that would get you killed or locked up."

Thinking of what Cindy had just said, she agreed that not knowing what had happened to Jamie would change the level of risk. But she thought of a way to find out for sure.

"So, you do no know. Is it something that you could call bitch, ask what she wants to get Jamie back?"

"That is something I was waiting for her to do. But that's the experience you have. Do things, not guess about them. Yes, that's a good idea. I didn't want to give her any credit for having an advantage."

Smiling, she was happy to hear Cindy was holding a hard line of not letting Jo control things. She also knew the best way to make that message a stronger one.

"Daughter, you are smart girl. I think there is way to turn this where you let her know she's not running show. You have girl, Whimsey. She wants her. So, you call, tell her if she no let Jamie go, you start torturing girl to find all Sharon told her. Have girl with, maybe crying out to save her, or just screaming for her, using her name. She think girl isn't talking, needs to move fast. Then if she says to make swap, say only after you talk to Jamie. It is business. People… they are nothing to her. Things. She has what you want and thought that gives her power. But, you have girl who can expose her to CIA and things, so it is you who have real power. Maybe have sound like you hitting girl, asking her to talk. This is simple thing. One question, why do you think Jamie would betray man she love? Why think she may be with bitch Jo?"

Feeling a wave of shame go through her, Eliana had made her realize her feelings for Mike had her wishing Jamie had gone to Jo. Nothing James had learned showed any contact, and her phone hadn't been taken when she was, and with all the voice mail messages, that was how he was sure of what happened. It could still be where she was working with Jo, but deep down she knew that with the voice mails on her phone, and that Sharon had said Mike's weakness would be to take his love, it was where Jamie wasn't working with Jo. She explained the details to Eliana, and she knew she sounded ashamed to think the worst.

"Cynthia, the world is not always where you can know for sure about anyone. I know you somehow think if Jamie is on other side, then Mike is free and you can be with him. Cynthia, do you think Mike will not learn you wanted that? What will he love about you if he does? He will love you more if you fought for Jamie even if she is with Jo. That is what my Cynthia would do. I understand. Love, it makes us crazy. I was crazy once and made bad choice. What does that heart you have that make you glow tell you?"

She heard Cindy and knew she had touched her in an unexpected way. She wanted to make sure no matter what happened, her daughter would do right, not wrong like she had done so many times. Then Cindy told her something that she wasn't expecting so soon.

"I think either way, you go in, deceive her, and we work together to get Jamie out and get Jo dead. Mother, I worried about the things you had done. I did. Taking girls is horrible, and I am going to tell you something hard to say to you. I never planned to take your offer, take over your empire. I was doing that to get in with you, then stop you. Even if it meant..."

Eliana heard her crying, but she was smiling. Cynthia was doing all things she wished she had done before her husband ruined her life, and her children's lives. She thought Cynthia was amazing.

"Girl, listen what I say. I am proud you planned that, and more proud you tell me. You are what I should have been, not what I was. Good for you. You are good person, good daughter. That was good plan, too. If you held gun to me, said for what I did, it was wrong, that I would respect more than if you come be in business. I want you should know this should something happen to me. And you know what happened even without telling me plan? I stopped. I knew you good, not

bad lady like I've been. My visit, giving you all money? Even if I was not sick, I would do. Because you showed you understood what happened was bad, and you cannot fool mother. I decided to stop for you. So you no be like me. So sweet Angelia not have mother like you have. I can no fix wrongs done, but I can fix what I do now. I want you to know I will help you while I still live. And, start with Jo bitch. Get Jamie even if she is evil bitch. Give her chance like you give me. That is what your mother will do. If you are there with me, then I die with smile and you will remember smile, not bad things I let happen to you and my poor son."

Knowing she didn't have much time left, she had wanted to tell Cindy all that in person, but it was good to do it now. Cindy had answered with one word.

"Yes."

For the first time in her life, she felt good that she had done the right thing. It didn't excuse all she had done that hurt endless people, but she would die knowing that it was doing the right thing that Cindy would remember most. She couldn't die happy, but she wanted Cindy to live knowing she had done what nobody else could do. Make her do something for others, not only herself, or to live another day.

Getting up, she went to the closet in the area made into a bedroom in the back half of her private jet, and she kept a mix of clothes there to not have to pack when traveling. She pulled off her black dress that had been hand tailored for her by a renowned fashion giant in Pairs, and took off her rings and necklace, all adorned with rubies, deep red ones like the blood she saw oozing from her husband's skull after she killed him. She looked at her right wrist and took off the solid gold bangle she always wore. It had been hand-engraved by the last of the men who engraved by hand, not with machines or computers. He had made engravings for kings and queens throughout Europe, and it was priceless. One inch in width, the gold was engraved with a vine that held two buds yet to open of roses. One was her son, the other her daughter. The vine had thorns that if she touched them, had been engraved to be sharp, and like an actual thorn, would pierce skin. As she took it off, she let her fingers be pricked by the gold thorns. Holding it up, her fingertips bleeding, she saw the words engraved as inscription inside. They were in full Cyrillic, beautiful letterforms, saying, "I was never a thorn for my flowers."

Putting it in a wooden box, she didn't want to be buried in it, and

By Terry Ulick 291

she knew she would never wear it again. She wrote a note and put it in the box, knowing it would be given to Cindy when she died along with a box of things she had for her, saying only to open upon her death. She read the note, and it said what she wished.

"Cynthia, this is for you to put on top of my casket when I die. Let all see the truth that I did not protect you the way you protect Angelia. I want all to know that I didn't, but you did. I have worn this each day, but now, as we will protect others together, I need it no more. Do not bury me with it. I wish to be buried with three roses in my hands. For your brother, you, and for your daughter. I may not deserve the one for your brother, but I know now I would die for him rather than him die for what I didn't do for him long ago. And you, when you put first hand of dirt on coffin when they put me in ground, know that even with the dirt I was, two beautiful flowers grew from me. — Eliana."

Having found a plain black dress for times when she wished no attention paid to her, she put it on, then pulled her hair back tight into a bun. She wiped away her makeup and looked at herself and made sure she no longer looked like a rich trafficker. She looked like a housekeeper, a servant. She found one simple chain with a little heart made of silver. One from when she was a girl, she had kept but had never worn since she ran off when still a teenager. It would be one given to her by her dead husband, if asked.

Opening her arsenal box, she found a thigh holster and put it on under the dress with the holster inwards, then put a Glock made from a polymer that wouldn't set off metal detectors and put bullets in a long pair of lipstick tubes made from metal that would set off a detector but had a small cap of lipstick to conceal the bullets. Each holding only four bullets, that was all she would need. She'd switch to a gun taken off Jo or a guard after using her gun.

She took a selfie of herself and sent it as a message to Cindy.

Under the picture she added text that said, *"In case you don't recognize me, I am the old woman."*

After the words, she put an emoji laughing to tears. Even dressed as she was, she was still a stunner.

Like her past, there were things she simply couldn't hid

CHAPTER 46

Sitting in the chair next to Mike's hospital bed, Angie was reading *Car and Driver* magazine, thinking she'd want a cyber truck. It was supposed to be bullet-proof on the body and windows, and that was what she'd need. The review of it in the trusted magazine, in her opinion, was no better than the advice in *Teen Vogue*. Flipping through the pages, she noticed the reviews that gushed over Toyotas and Kia were somehow in the same issue with pages and pages of ads from those companies. She had read that the company making her dream car never advertised, and she thought magazine publishers were as low down as traffickers. They took people's money and sold the articles to makers of junk cars to make a profit.

Showing James the review when she came in to give her mother and him a break from sitting with Mike, she had asked him his opinion.

"Yeah, I wish we had those instead of the Suburbans and Tahoes. You know the agencies love their black beauties. As if anyone didn't know those aren't agency cars."

Realizing he was right, she had noticed he was always in a shiny new black Tahoe, always perfectly clean and polished.

"Why don't you guys switch? These would make you more threatening."

Laughing, he said the government had its favorites, and it wasn't the guy making the cyber truck. He suggested that where they live, a nice Tahoe with armor and bullet-proof glass would be ideal, and it would fit right in with what people in Wheaton were driving. She gave him one of her teenage girlish "duh" looks.

"James, one of those? Do mom or I look like suburban housewives?"

Knowing she had him on that point, he said no, they certainly didn't, but added she was underage, and a license required that she take a driver's education course if not eighteen yet. She gave him another look of astonishment.

"James, I know that. And what is it that mom and I do? Do sixteen-year-olds go around with a gun strapped to their thighs or in their little clutch like mom and me? In a quick getaway, I think I need a car, and one for mom too, and we can head in different directions and all that. Anyway, given that we face death as routinely as shopping for gluten-

free stuff at Whole Foods, I was going to ask you to grant me… let's see. I have it hear in my notes on my phone… Yes. Here it is. *Special Disposition.*"

Nearly cowering, Cindy smiled at James, letting him know he wasn't going to win when it came to Angie. She had looked it up and had references to younger drivers than her out on the highway. He looked at Cindy, looking for help, but she kept smiling and shook her head letting him know he was on his own with the request.

"Angie, I love you, you know that. But those examples? Those are for farm boys so they can drive a tractor at about five miles an hour. Not for car chases and ramming traffickers."

Undeterred, Angie said she was formally requesting special disposition from the agency, and a one-day crash course by their evasive maneuver driving instructor. He looked at Cindy again, and she added she thought it was essential, and she'd like to take the course too. In a last attempt to keep them from terrorizing the town in a pair of the beasts, he could only come up with they cost a whole lot of money. For what they'd need, over $100,000 each. They shrugged, seeming not to worry about that. Just then, a new opinion was heard.

"Do you honestly think they're worrying about money?"

Cindy and Angie both began jumping onto the bed and hugging Mike. He had woken up and seemed fully alert.

"Crash course? Teach you how to crash? Well, a car can be a weapon if needed. Just let me know when you're shopping so I don't take your parking spot."

While Cindy and Angie were sitting there, combing his hair and primping his sheets, James asked him how long he'd been awake, and had he heard Angie bossing him around. Mike was smiling, fluffing Angie's hair as she tossed his.

"Yes, I think I heard it all. You have a lot to learn about going up against them. If they don't get you with reason, they can pout, act hurt and all that."

Cindy and Angie both shot up, arms folded. Angie let him know they were shocked.

"Really? Use feminine wiles on a man? I can't speak for mom, but I would rather use what we learned at the agency about having him wake up in a dark room and being left until he begs to say yes. Anyway, we

only resort to logic and reason after giving a pout and a bit of swishing hips as we walk away…"

Not bothering to add anything as she knew Angie was being silly and full of joy that Mike seemed fine, Cindy told Angie and James she'd fill Mike in on what's happened since he confronted Sharon. They both knew she wanted to talk to him alone, so Angie took her copy of the car magazine and told James they'd want someone to talk to the car guy and get them custom builds as they left, closing the door behind them. Cindy knew the doctor should be told Mike was awake, but that could come later. He'd have questions, and those were the most important thing for him, bad as all the news was.

"Mike, I'm so glad you're up, and so you know, the doctor was great and said you were lucky and will be out in a couple of days. Even if you don't feel it… they have you medicated for pain there… you'll hurt for a while on your side. The shot went through you, and missed your lung and nicked an intestine. He thought you moved at the last second to not get it in the middle of your chest."

Propping himself up a bit, she helped, and moved his pillow up so they could look each other in the eye.

"Yeah, I remember thinking she would go for the torso to not miss, and I leaned off to the side. When I did, I saw you and Angie with your guns aimed down at Sharon…"

Patting his hands, with a sad smile she said they did, and as soon as she fired, Angie did too.

"Sharon's dead, Mike. Angie stopped her as she knew she'd shoot you again, then us too."

Looking at her, he closed his eyes once, then shook his head slightly. She kept her gaze into his eyes, and still had her sad smile. He rubbed the tops of her hands as he reacted to the news.

"You did right. It's so sad, and I feel bad for both of you having to do that. I knew when she walked in that she was going to try something. I didn't expect how fast. I thought maybe she was on drugs, or told she'd be killed… She didn't even look like herself. Those black eyes…"

Taking a deep breath, Cindy knew it best to just tell him there was

more bad news, and she was glad she was the one telling him.

"I could see she was desperate, but I didn't get a look at her face like you did. They ran tests. No drugs showed up. It was what you probably already knew. She was there to kill us and take Whimsey. She had told her all about Jo, and Jo said she may have told all of us. That's what we think. I have a bunch of horrible news. I don't want you to hurt more. If you aren't ready, I'll tell you when you are."

There was no hesitation. He said there was no good time for bad news, so he was ready for whatever she had to say, adding not to worry about how bad the news was. She closed her eyes, and looked to make sure Angie and James were settled, not watching. She turned back to him.

"I'll take it the way I learned about it all. I think we all noticed that Sharon wasn't acting like someone who just was saved from hell or death. How she got right in with Whimsey, and we didn't see her much, and she didn't really tell us much. James can fill you in later, but we're sure she wasn't ever trafficked. Not taken in Morocco."

Looking at her, she could tell he was doubting it, though he had already learned about Jo being The One, and Peter was part of her strange cult that trafficked girls. She kept telling what she knew.

"It started before Morocco. When she was in college, she joined the cult. She went and wanted to join. And those cult groups are in most all the colleges, and they are finding little girls to offer up to The One. She was doing that, and they were going international. She went to Morocco and met with a man there and then went off the map. She was a lead in the cult. She was Jo's lover, and that's what we're dealing with now. Jo is totally insane, and she's going at us for killing Sharon. She wants Whimsey, probably her next… you know… a replacement for Sharon."

Shaking his head, it was a lot to comprehend, and it was a nightmare. He asked how much they had learned about Jo since he was out.

"Enough to know she's the biggest trafficker of all. She's merged religion with the kids looking for some sort of purpose… but mostly she had people like Peter that we don't know about yet. James has all his staff thinking of everything in a new way now that we know about her. I do know Sharon was lost to you a long time ago. She was looking for something and found the wrong thing. I wish that's all I had to say, but, oh, Mike. That's just a part of it…"

296 Not Taken

She didn't want to stop. She only wanted to get it all out, and hard as it was, she readied herself for what she needed to tell him next.

"I'm just going to get this told, and it's hard to do, so I'll just lay it out, then maybe have James come in for details and all. Okay? Good. After you were shot, and we got you here… this is the Army base by the way… It was just a few hours and you had gotten out of surgery, and I was feeling happy, but I'd been trying to call Jamie to have her get herself here. I tried almost nonstop. Angie too. I told her all that happened on her voice mail, hoping she'd come running through the ER and be here. James sent his best guy to your place. Her car was there, keys… everything. And no Jamie…"

Mike stopped her.

"Jamie? Is she dead?"

Patting his hands again, she managed a little smile.

"Thank God, no. She was taken. Now we know Jo grabbed her, and she had a reason. She was taking no chances, and if Sharon failed, she'd have Jamie to hold hostage to get Whimsey. But we're sure she listened to all the messages Angie and I left. We did the wrong thing to leave messages like that, but we learned that the hard way… And my number… lots of numbers were on her phone. I was out there, in the waiting room, and she called me. On my screen was her name on caller ID. Mike, she's weirder than Peter. She's insane, crazy, and she is flat out ruthless. She played games… word games with me. Like a kid would talk. She said she had what we wanted, we had what she wanted, nah na nah na nah na… I don't put up with nonsense, so she asked what I had to say. I told her just five words. Glock bullet in her head. I hung up. I guess I declared war, and acted like I didn't care she had Jamie to stop her thinking she could work us."

Nodding, a smile showing a hint of being glad she did, he told her she had done the right thing, and she wouldn't do anything to Jamie. She needed her alive. Nodding, Cindy said that was what she thought as well.

"Then, in the middle of it all, my mother calls and she's on her way here. You know about that. I told her to take it slow and told her about Jo. Mike, that was something of a hint at what she's like if you're on her bad side. She said she had heard her talking to Brian once a few years back, and he told her she was messing with a trafficker much more

powerful than her, so she could do what she wanted elsewhere, but not mess with in his operation. She called her and just told her she was going to visit her and kill her. Jo scoffed; I think maybe laughed. Well, Eliana is on her way there, and I've filled her in about needing to get Jamie out, and she said after she took Jo down, nobody would stop her from taking Jamie. There's more, but I wanted you to know why Jamie isn't here. Why it's me sitting here…"

Mike was about to speak, but she knew she couldn't tell him only that. Half-truths to her were worse than lies. She put her finger over his lips as she leaned forward and kissed his forehead, letting him know not to talk as there would be more. Backing up, she told him about the hardest part for her.

"When Jamie is back, and I assure you she will be, I owe her such an apology. I did her such wrong. And, you too. It's why I wanted to tell you all this without Angie and James here. When we realized Jamie was gone, I did the wrong thing. You know how quiet Jamie had been? Staying out of things, even when we hit Peter? When we found out, my first thought was that since she had been a trafficker, and groomed like Sharon, that she had been watching and not part of things because…"

Stopping her, Mike shook his head, but didn't look mad.

"Because you thought she was under Jo's control too. That she told her what you left voice messages about…"

"Yes! I jumped right to thinking that she'd told Jo what happened, and all kinds of things like that went through my mind…"

"Cindy, after seeing what Sharon did, and her not part of things like normal, I understand why you would think that. It would fit…"

Shaking her head, tears flowing, she admired him understanding, but he had to know the real reason.

"Mike, of course I finally realized she was giving you room with Sharon. A chance to have time together, and not be in the middle of things between you two. That was so clear, and you weren't worried about it. I think she was reading the signs. She knew but didn't want to hurt you, or Sharon if that wasn't what was going on… She was doing something so caring and loving… But I know you'll get this. The night before, in the kitchen, when we talked about how we loved each other?"

Staring at her, she knew Mike was putting it all together. His look was a loving one. He said he'd like to finish the story, and maybe he

could make it easier. Her mouth opened as if to say no, but he just started telling the rest.

"God, Cindy. I know. I know. When you heard all that, it meant that without Jamie… with her being one of Jo's, then it would be me and you."

Shaking her head and saying yes, and that she was so ashamed, Mike looked at her, seeing her hurt, and gave her time where she could hear him once over her emotions. Finally, she looked at him, her mouth open, wanting to explain, to apologize. He started to talk before she had a chance.

"Cindy. I am so grateful you told me. I really am. God, we're all just people. Hopes and dreams and hurts. Your reaction. It wasn't about Jamie. It wasn't thinking bad about her. It was just an unwanted thought that hurts so bad now. A chance to be together without getting between her and I. Cindy, you're just a person, we talked about how if things were different just such a short time before all that. It was a natural response to the stress of me being almost killed, shooting Sharon. It was a little ray of good in all that bad. I'll never think bad of how you felt. I know Jamie will understand if she knew all of it, but like we said, maybe best some things aren't helpful to share. You righted yourself. Understood that before all this she was taking care of me, and Sharon too. In the middle of all this, you saw that, and figured it out. I'll tell you again. The things you just did. Telling me something so hard. It's why I love you. We both know, and we both know you got it right, but love is something that we can't always keep held down. So, can we both leave it there? I don't plan on telling Jamie. It's up to you if you need to, but after what she's going through, I don't know if hearing the most beautiful girl west of Moscow is out for her guy is the best news to come home to…"

Watching her look of heartbreak and shame changed to a sweet smile, she nodded in agreement, then put both her hands on her hips, giving him a stern look.

"Only west of Moscow? You think there's better ones there, or east of there?"

Mike gave her a look she would always treasure. His smile said all she needed to hear, but he added a bit to his comment.

"Actually, no, I don't think there are, but I hear Angie talking now about how hot you are, and I thought I better be careful. If I said anywhere it might go to your head."

CHAPTER 47

Listening to her pilot point out Jo's compound from the air, Eliana was surprised how large it was. Beyond the amount of land, there were a dozen large buildings made from logs and looked much like a ski resort, an airstrip with one jet clearly for private use, and two Boeing 737s for transporting goods, and she knew the goods were trafficked children, most all girls. As large as the acreage was, it was surrounded by a fence from what she could tell and had towers with cameras and small rooms for lookout guards. All she could think when seeing it all was that business was certainly good, and then her pilot pointed out a series of small cabins apart from the main compound, and outside were long limousines and they each had their own privacy fences with pools that went to the cabin, meaning the pools were both outdoor and indoor types. She knew those were for the richest people in the world to stay at with any number — and ages — of Jo's takes.

In a legitimate flight pattern, her jet was high enough to not draw attention, and she was using binoculars to view all below the path. She wondered how Jo hadn't made the airspace restricted as her clients certainly included top government officials who could take care of such a matter. It spoke to the confidence and arrogance Jo projected, and it all made sense. She may have enjoyed knowing all the wealthiest men could look, but not enter her world of sexual depravity.

With an understanding of the scale Jo operated at, she felt prepared for showing up for a job interview as a head housekeeper, yet seeing the size of the operation, and the security, she doubted it would be as easy as showing up and having a talk with Jo. It was a place where there would be a large staff, and none could reveal what went on there. If it was her, she'd run extensive background checks on anyone applying, yet she was told to just show up when it was convenient for her.

Not much time passed between flying over the compound and her plane landing at a resort town private airport with a dozen other private jets. It made sense to her. A ski resort area, a place where the ultra-rich would use their jets to go for a ski weekend but have a go at the girls at Jo's or have them brought to their own ranches or private estates. It was home to few as even the cost of using the airport that had only private jets cost more than $100,000. It was not a place where tourists could

go, propeller aircraft land, and there were no hotels, motels, charming B&Bs, or 3-Star eateries. It was made for privacy, security, and it served Jo's clients.

Her pilot had a flight plan that indicated he was picking someone up, not letting someone off. Both she and the pilot would leave the plane as workers waiting. She was told by the pilot there was a town an hour away where servants were living, and he had arranged for a car service to pick them up and take them to the town. There she would rent a car and stick to her plan. Her jet was registered to a company that made it hard to know who the real owner was, and if anyone searched the jet while she and the pilot were gone, there was nothing to find except clothes and toiletries.

After a long ride to the town, it was a sad place filled with mobile homes and shacks, a few motels that looked occupied in the middle of the day meaning girls were servicing local ranchers and their hired hands. It was a world apart from where her jet was parked. The town had a series of apartment buildings that made the ghettos in Russia look like mansions. She wondered if the girls fucking and sucking all day long were Jo's — ones too old to sell, but good for keeping the locals quiet. Just as in the Ukraine and Russia, large fields and ranchers meant single men working and when they got paid, they wanted whores to fuck. The town would be a wild one on the weekends, but it was still busy mid-week. She wondered if a no-tell motel was where Jo had started out and fucked her way up the ladder by being both ambitious and ruthless. There was nothing about her to be found that her people could find. Heading to the one motel where there was a room available, she saw one building that was apart from all the others.

Sitting on the edge of town was a church that was the largest building there. It was in perfect repair and was big enough to hold a few thousand people. Clearly a church by its design, there were no crosses or hints that it was a church in any way. There was one sign with the name One, and that was all it said. She was in the right place. She understood all the townspeople, the ranch hands, the burnt-out zombies walking the road were all members of the cult. They all had the look of ones who had found an answer, and would be outraged if anyone questioned their church, or leader.

Once in the motel room, it was what she expected. Wood paneled walls, sticky shag carpeting that was once orange, but now was matted

with what she knew was semen. The bed was lilting to one side, and the bathroom had one towel. On the dresser was a sign with hours of service at the church, and it was nightly. She told her pilot if it was where he would be welcome, try to attend, and if questioned, say he wished to show devotion to a young woman before the demon took her, and that he was on a pilgrimage to save as many little ones as possible. If successful, she'd know more to share with Mike and James about how the operation worked and was not known outside of the cult membership.

About the only thing that worked out perfectly was her pilot had sought a car to rent, but calling around, he was referred to a local auto repair shop that sold cars. He had decided to get her an older car that would be what she would have as a housekeeper. Not fancy, not in good shape, and it had local plates.

When he left, she turned on the tube TV, and she learned it had only one channel. It was about the cult, and without expecting it, the programming said it was time to hear from their One. There, on the screen, was Jo. It was unexpected but made sense to her. She operated under the guise of a religious organization, and the people of the town were the faithful, or pilgrims bringing their daughters with to save powerful men from following the ways of evil. It was such an ingenious scheme in her opinion. The girls were largely brought to her by her followers, and she also snatched girls who were high dollar sells. It was a new day, and not a holy one.

Watching the TV, she saw Jo and understood how it worked. Jo was a classic charismatic type. She was majestic, inspiring, and appeared to believe everything she said. She had a power that blasted off the screen, and anyone weak or looking for answers were taken in by her ways instantly. First shown in a close up, she was beautiful in every manner. A classic golden triangle face and features that were both flawless and sensual. She wasn't talking in the sarcastic riddle-laden manner when she had talked with her. She was soft in tone, and passionate without being superior. As the camera zoomed out, she was in a long white dress that was soft and flowing, and her body was shaping it to reveal an ideal form. She was stunning looking, and she was the type that a person had to look at. There was no other option.

Zooming out more, she smiled as Jo was surrounded by young girls,

some as young as five, the oldest being twelve. They all had white gowns like hers, and they were all looking up at her as she talked. Turning up the sound, Eliana was stunned by what Jo was saying.

"Today, these girls have come to us, and their families have seen the evil that would take them if not for The One. These sweet innocent gifts would be soon defiled by thugs from the ghettos they came from, but also their doctors or teachers. By boys in gangs and men in vans. They are what the dark one craves for they are pure, never touched by sin. And I offer them salvation and will keep them from those who would take their sweetness and feed it to the dark one who waits, who has a hunger for these sweet girls, who would take their flower and offer it to men who fall to temptation. Husbands, business owners, even pastors and priests…"

Eliana watched as Jo stopped at that point and pulled the white dress off the youngest girl and put her on the podium where she sat. She kissed her on her mouth, then moved her legs apart, showing her fully to the viewers, and she continued her talk.

"This is the temptation. This is a gift. A thing that is holy, to be praised and worshiped by one who is good, not the ones who would use her and teach her that a woman is just here to do the work of tempting men to become evil. Offering this, this sweet little thing she is showing us right now, is what I will give to a good man. Now, when she is still holy, untouched, and a gift to good men. I have already found a good man for this girl. He has given The One a donation that will grant him a place of honor in the life to come. He will protect this girl. Give her a life far from the evil that would destroy her. In a mansion, in a skyscraper, on a yacht. She will be safe and save that man from any other temptation. He will want for nothing more and will keep her from the evil in this world. She will give him protection from temptation, he will keep her from darkness and worship her day and night."

Eliana was amazed how she was coming out and saying a rich man was buying the girl to be his sex slave, and she had turned it into saving them from evil. As her lecture ended, she had all the girls taking off their dresses, and she joined them. Her flawless body and charm, kneeling to kiss the girls and hug them was like nothing she had ever seen before.

Jo had made depravity into saving souls. And she looked sincere, and beautiful as she did it. Sitting, stunned, she first wondered how she got away with such an all-out solicitation for girls from poor families, and promoting the new arrivals without notice. Remembering the private jets and cabins at her compound, she knew it was because she offered such girls to the people in power, and they made sure nothing threatened the good thing she had for them. Freedom from sin, law, and morality. She was a total psychopath. She could talk like she had to her on the phone one minute, the next be doing her lecture sounding like an angel or saint.

She had trafficked girls, and was corrupted by doing so for so long, but what Jo was doing made her sick. It was not trafficking. It was a crusade, and she was leading it. Worse, after seeing her charismatic performance, she now understood how she could get so many to follow wherever she led them.

CHAPTER 48

Finishing telling Mike all she could, he said he'd like to see the doctor who sewed him up. At first worried he was hurting, he told her that wasn't why. He just wanted to tell him thanks, and to understand what he had done during surgery. Telling him she'd found him, he smiled at her, and she knew it was his love being sent to her. She smiled back, then went to the nurses' station saying Mike was awake and asking for his surgeon. Being told he had just inquired if he was up yet, he was there, and they would give him the call request.

Walking over to Angie and James, they both had looks indicating they wanted to know how Mike had taken all the news.

"Well, Mike... you know... he's Mike. He listened, understood, and said all that happened was right to do, and he would have done the same. If he's grieving about Sharon, he didn't show it. Maybe he'll want to do that when alone. I don't think it was a surprise. How could it be after she shot him? And Jamie? That surprised him. James... I told him we questioned if she was one of Jo's. That was rough to admit, but he did it again. Said it sure looked that way to us, and we were right to be worried, but we were smart and figured it all out. He's so strong when things get tough. To wake up to being shot by his sister, her being shot by us, Jamie taken like she was... And he said he was worried about me dealing with it all..."

Angie knew how her mother felt about Mike. It wasn't something she could hide from her, but she had never talked about it. Seeing the doctor walking to the room, she pointed and they looked as the doctor went in and began talking to Mike. Standing with his arms crossed, they saw Mike tugging at his IV, and they were having a serious discussion. James knew what was going on.

"Well, I don't think an IV is going to keep him here. I can tell he's saying he's leaving no matter what, and what would he need to stay stitched together. I know the doc. He knows fighters don't let wounds stop them when in battle. I bet he'll get him where he can leave. See... he's nodding. Taking notes. Mike, yep, smiling, thanking him. I expected this. I'm not going to say what to do, but I'm not going to tell Mike to be smart and stay here."

As he finished, the doctor left Mike's room and walked to them.

"Well, no keeping a good man down. He wants to leave, and he's going to. He's smart enough to talk to me about it and get antibiotics and some things I'll give if he should start bleeding. Infections like that can happen fast. A high fever will happen out of thin air, and then he has hours if he doesn't get injected with the ampules I'm giving him, but you'll administer them. They're compressed in a metal cylinder. Screw on the needle, jab him anywhere, and press the release on the needle base and it will blast in. Pure penicillin. Still the best for that. If he doesn't get it, sepsis would come next and that's his blood being infected so ER. Confusion, white color, super high fever. All things to look for. I'll have a pack ready in about 15 minutes and full instructions on all of it. I'm not saying it will happen. It can, and if it does, he won't be the best to spot the signs and take care of himself. I'm going to get it together and call me if needed. Oh, and he's going to hurt. He doesn't want anything strong. He said he needs to be sharp, so giant tablets of ibuprofen is the best I can do. Some local packs that stick to the skin there. Topical anesthetic. Well, I think he'll do okay with all that. I'm here if needed…"

James was nodding, knowing he had made the call Mike would get up and join the fight. He said he'd go help him get dressed, as he was shy. That got a chuckle from Cindy and Angie, and they both stood, not talking, looking at the room, curtains now drawn. Finally, Angie put her hand on Cindy's shoulder.

"Mom. You doing okay? I was so proud of you telling him all the hard stuff. I've been here thinking about how we saw him get shot. That was unreal. And I keep thinking if I hadn't shot Sharon, she would have shot him again to be sure he was dead. Charles tried to talk to me about it, but what else could we do? Just like with the sheik guy. Things you never thought you could do, you have to. I think about standing on the landing. The two of us, you know, side-by-side. We saved him. That's what we said we'd do, and we're doing it. I've always felt so close to you, but on that landing. Firing at Sharon? I've never felt closer to you then that. Is that, well, weird or anything?"

Looking at Angie, she thought of how with all her teasing about magazine articles and the world in general, it was all her realizing how hard life could be, and how to make it better for some people if they could. She was dealing with the world outside or the trailer park they had lived in. It was bad, but she knew Angie was learning the world

outside of their mobile home was even worse in many ways. All she said was honest and realistic. She was learning that they were strong together, and she wanted her to know she understood.

"Sweetie, I felt the same there with you. We always faced things together to take care of ourselves. Now we can do that for others. We both felt closer than ever because we were together, doing things most people could never do, but I know you and I will take care of each other. I am glad we did that. I'm glad we did that together. Nothing weird about it. I don't think Charles would disagree with that. Oh, as we'll be leaving soon, speaking of Charles, anything come out of his talk with Whimsey? And how's she been. Whenever I look, she's been sleeping in the corner there."

Looking over at Whimsey, she was glad she was sleeping. Even though Sharon was using her, she knew Whimsey felt safe with her, and loved her although it was hard to be sure if it was love, or sex. She turned back to Angie, who had been looking at Whimsey too.

"Mom, I don't think much came out of her talking to Charles. He didn't say much to her when he left, and he just shrugged at me when I was making it clear I was wondering how things were. We can call him, but you know, doctor and patient thing, maybe. She didn't say much after, just she was so tired, and she's been sleeping curled up like that, so I haven't talked to her."

Cindy still had a caution after all that had happened. She wasn't sure if Whimsey was as she seemed. She was young, had a rough life, and had gravitated to doing porn so young. She knew some people were just bad seeds, seeing the world differently than others. She had an uneasy feeling that there was more to learn about her. She didn't know if it was good or bad she felt. Just something strange. Her sister was murdered, and suddenly she was with Sharon. Sharon may have been grooming her, but to not grieve much about her sister seemed strange to her. Thinking more, she thought it could be where her worries about Jamie should have been about Whimsey.

Telling Angie they'd be leaving soon as the doctor gave her the supplies, she asked if she could wake Whimsey and tell her time to go. Nodding a yes, the doctor was heading down the corridor, box of supplies in hand. Giving her the box, about to show her what was there, they heard Angie cry out that Whimsey was dead.

CHAPTER 49

Driving up to the security gate, Eliana was calm and not worried if her invitation was a setup or would go wrong. She had little time to live, and she had gathered information she had sent to Cindy via fax to James, Mike's friend at the CIA. His fax was secure, and if anyone from Jo's team traced his number, it would be a fake address. If she failed, James had information that Jamie was being held there, and legal cause to seize the compound.

"Praise The One, ma'am. Here to visit family?"

Eliana looked at the man in the gatehouse, and he was smiling the smile of cult members, but also had a holster with a Colt strapped to his waist. He looked to be ex-military, and had the manners hammered into new recruits during boot camp that lasted a lifetime, but they also had been trained that killing for a good cause was right to do. She smiled back at him, saying she was invited to an interview for the head housekeeping position.

"Oh, then welcome once more. Let me look on this sheet to see where you should go… Well, seems like we are really in need for your help, as you're going right to meet with Jo, and I think you'll find her to be an inspiration. Have you been through hard times, if I may ask as a friend?"

She noticed the camera pointed at the driveway and the guardhouse, and it was hard to tell if the man was acting nice, or he was what he seemed to be. A man who found a new life — and probably girls to fuck — working for Jo. She let her face grow sad as she answered.

"Hard times after something worse, son. Lost my husband of twenty-five years just six months back. We both met coming over from Russia, and he suffered for a long time, but I never left his side. Now, hard times have me needing to work, and I'm looking for a home with people all around me."

Opening the gate, he reached in and patted her arm holding the steering wheel.

"You've come to the right place. We're all family here, and this is our home for good. Now, you follow this road, and don't need to turn off it as you pass by other roads ahead. Way down is the end of this road, and that is where Jo lives and runs things from. Park anywhere you'd like, let yourself in, and I'll let her know you're on your way."

Driving forward, after seeing the town full of the faithful, meeting the guard, it seemed that there was little worry about her arrival. The place was well-kept, the buildings pristine and warm, and the people she saw as she drove along were smiling and some were walking with young girls, holding them by their hands, the girls skipping and looking excited. It was much more cult-like than a holding compound for trafficking. She was no longer certain if the trafficking was a way to fund the cult, or the cult a way to shelter the trafficking. It crossed her mind it could be both.

Reaching the last building, there were only a few cars parked in front of it. It had a wrap-around porch, chairs and tables on it, and it had huge windows across the front. Unlike the other buildings, it didn't have people going to and fro, and that worried her. As she parked then got out of the car, nobody was looking out the windows or opening the door to see who drove up. She knew cameras were doing that, not people, and she played the part of a matron, reaching in for her purse and a manila envelope she had with her history of employment from all the dead names she found from Denver obituaries.

After straightening her dress and looking in the side-view mirror at her hair, she walked up a few steps to the porch, then looked to see if there were signs about entering or a bell, but with none she could see, she did as the guard instructed and let herself in.

Standing in a large vaulted great room, it was tastefully decorated, had sofas and tables that were dark green, and paintings of all sorts on the walls. As she looked around, she heard her name called, and turning, there was Jo greeting her.

"Why you must be Mrs. Peters. I'm glad you made it safely and found our home here. It can be tricky at night, so glad you could make it here during the day. I'm Jo, and this is where I live. I'm the one looking for a housekeeper, so no need to talk to others. I'm the one who needs help, so not having anyone right now, would you like some coffee, iced tea, water?"

Jo was different than on the phone, or in the video with the girls. She was acting normal. Pleasant, polite, and dressed in jeans and a simple soft blue sweater, her hair loose yet her face was even more stunning in person, and she couldn't tell if she had any makeup on. She didn't seem to need much help looking beautiful.

"Some iced tea would be most nice. Please, let me to help."

Smiling at the suggestion, Jo held her hand to a counter area in the large room, and once there she took out glasses and a pitcher in a hidden refrigerator full of ice and tea. Pouring some for them both, she suggested going to her office and getting to know each other.

"I read in your email that you are recently widowed. I'm sure that was hard to go through. How long were you married?"

The question seemed sincere, and it was what anyone would ask.

"I say twenty-five, but it was twenty-six. We met when young. He died just before turning fifty. We came from Russia, so please to forgive accent. We both kept speaking Russian, but my English is okay."

It was a short walk down a hallway off the great room when Jo pointed to an open door, saying it was where she worked. Walking as Jo held the door, it was a large, cozy room full of books and a wall full of monitors across from the desk. Closing the door behind her, Jo pointed to a cushioned chair in front of the desk, and she went and sat behind the desk, taking a sip of her tea.

"I know it's so formal to sit across a desk from you, but I have all kinds of paperwork and forms here to refer to. I like to look at all those screens behind you as well. So, you stayed at the town last night? That motel is not very nice, I know. And the resort town? Not easy to get a room there! But you're here, and let's get to know each other. I feel like I know you already, you know how that is sometimes?"

Jo had the door closed, she was sitting behind a desk that could have guns in place but out of sight, and she just referenced she felt like she already knew her. It was intended to be a clear reference she knew Eliana wasn't there for a job.

"That is feeling I have. For you too. Funny how that can be. Yes, here now, and you are not what I expected boss lady to be."

Laughing, Jo revealed a bit of how she sounded on the phone.

"I think you are certainly right. I always seem to surprise people, but I really don't know why. What were you expecting. I'm curious."

Again, a clue of things to come. She was letting her know she was full of surprises.

"Oh, very formal lady who is too busy to talk to servant. Tough, stern. But no, you are sweet to me. That, I did not expect. I watched the TV last night. Saw you on show. So pretty. Such a dress. I expect maybe

you dress that way when we meet, that too."

Nodding, showing interest, Jo smiled when told she was pretty.

"Yes, when I dress like that, and act like that, I find that it inspires people. Did you understand what I was talking about?"

Looking caught off-guard, Eliana shook her head, acting completely baffled.

"Not so much. I was surprised, I never see TV with naked little girls, so I think that made it hard to listen much. And you, so pretty, girls so pretty. I don't think about why, too nervous for today. I hope that's what I saw. Maybe I was asleep. Dreaming. It was like dream."

Leaning forward, arms crossed on the desk, she nodded.

"I have to tell you. You are a sharp lady. That's exactly what it's intended to be. A dream. A fantasy. You got it right. I'm glad to hear that. So, did you think having girls like that okay? Many people think it's wrong to show them the way God made them."

Still unsure of the things Jo was saying, she wanted to learn as much as she could as she may have plans for Cindy and Angie, so it was time to find out.

"You know, coming from Russia, I don't think right or wrong. I grew up where KGB, they like little girls, it was just how things were there. Men, they like that, so to stay alive, nobody tell them no. They want daughter, they get daughter. Not like that here in America, but I think it goes on. Just is hidden. Men, they're men."

Staring at her, she was listening carefully. Not able to be sure of what she was really doing, Eliana figured it best to present herself as someone who understood what she did with girls.

"There. That's why I said come to see me. People from places like where you're from, they accept that life is what it is. If men in power want something, they get it. If you say no, they will get it anyway. I have met people from Russia who understood. When they were little girls, their families knew they'd have a better life if given to a powerful politician or general. They had been through that, and for a time they were living in luxury, but as they grew up the men wanted a younger girl. Like you said, men, they're men. If it's not too private, did you live in the housing projects, or were you lucky to end up with a rich man. It's clear you're beautiful, so you would have been worth a lot for your parents."

Tilting her head, nodding, Eliana was impressed with how fast she was getting to the essentials of the world she had created.

"Now, I am not shy about life long ago. Yes, you know. I was pretty child. My parents, very poor. I only remember being in cold flat, not much food. Then next day in pretty dresses sometimes, no dress at all most times. But I was treated nice, had lots of food. I live with very rich man. He had wife, but he had me too. And then other girls. Some younger, some older. I thought that was how girls grow up. I didn't now different than most people. Then, when I was turning thirteen, I see bags packed. I was sent back to my parents, worked in factory. Then, I find out that was for little girls, and I wasn't little girl... ever again. My husband, he knew how that all work. He was kind to me. I loved him very much."

With her chin resting on her hands folded up in front of her, Jo smiled when she finished, and she looked delighted.

"That was quite a story. I mean that. A story. Now, let's be honest, did that all really happen?"

As she talked, she opened a file folder, and glanced down at it, then talked more.

"I must apologize. That was wrong to imply you weren't telling the truth. That did happen, and you did meet a man who understood all about it. A whole lot about it... my, my. I know that once here in America, you need to leave a few things out. I get that. But I have a nice way of finding out things about people. Very important in what I do here. And for you, it says your husband didn't die recently. He died a long time ago, and wow, that you shot him right in front of your children. Did you do that? I won't hold it against you. Just us girls here. Good to get it off your chest."

"It is not thing I like to talk about. But yes, he understood how world works. Very ambitious. I had children with him. He... he, well, abused them. He was using bad drugs. I did what I had to do. I am glad I did. I waited too long."

Closing the file folder, Jo had a gentle smile, and nodded as if showing admiration.

"Now, doesn't it feel good to talk to someone and say what happened, and able to talk about it? We don't have much say when we're little, but at a certain point you figure out that you do things because that's how

you stay alive. We all just want to stay alive. I'm sure you want to, right?"

Shrugging, Eliana said of course. Things were getting to the point where anything could happen, and she crossed her legs, ready to pull her gun. She had loaded it with bullets on the drive from the gatehouse and had the handle pointed downwards to make it easy to draw. The chamber was loaded and the safety off.

"You may have noticed that I'm a bit different in how I do things. I mean, when I meet someone who's good at something, I think about how to become friends, even if they're enemies. Now, you know that's not how it normally goes. So, here we are. Two very strong women. We each sell little girls, an we are both killers. I do it one way because here in America, it works best here. You do it your way because that's how it's done there. Then we get bigger and better, and we cross paths. And we think we're enemies and we want to kill each other and all that. But me, no. I figure I get you where you come and plan to kill me, and we talk first, and I say that's one way, sure. But we can also figure out we are doing the same thing, we aren't enemies. Lots of sick fuckers out there wanting young pussy. Lots of young pussy out there to give them. Plenty for both. So, who are our enemies? Gee, the laws? The religions? Moms and pops? Everyone except our clients, and they have the same problems. They get in big trouble if they are found out. So, have you ever thought about how ridiculous it is to fight each other? I have. I could have had you drive in and had you killed in a minute. So, ask yourself why I didn't. The last things you said to me was you were going to shoot me, right? And here you are, talking about how this is all how life works, and we both want to just stay alive. I see two things that could happen. One of us walks out alive, the other dead. Or we both walk out alive. Pretty simple, really.

With her hand just touching the pistol grip with her legs crossed, she needed to decide. She could take a shot, and it may be where Jo had a gun ready to shoot her. But she worried that even dead, with a cult around her, Jo may have things set up to kill Cindy and Angie. She wanted to be sure about if she had that set up or not.

"If it were another day, yes, simple. We agree to not kill each other, work where we help each other with the law. But things are not simple because you have hurt ones close to me. And you have one of my people here. And I don't know how much more you have planned even if you

are dead. Crazy cult people will give lives to do what you say. You made mess, but act like things are okay. Why?"

"You're right. I did some things that you are right to be mad at me for. I'm not going to make excuses. I will only say that isn't good. You need to know one thing. I was in love with Sharon. She came to me, she joined the cult, and she was so into all of this. And whoa, I just fell for her like nothing I could have imagined. I wish she was alive, and I was fucking her right now. But whoa, did that all go bad. Peter, he took the cult shit to heart, and he took her and I didn't know he did that. He was up to something, and he was one crazy motherfucker. He told me she was dead. Then I watched some of his shit porns, and there was my girl, sucking dick instead of licking my ass. I told him to get her on a plane to me, and that's when things get bad. Sharon thought he was going to kill her, not send her to me, and she was probably right about that. So she killed the driver, found her brother, had the little cunt licking her, and oh my God, just one thing after another. So, they go shoot the fucker, and I was like all hooray, saved me the bullet. And then they connect Peter to the cult, to me, and like I said, we do what we have to do. You call me, Sharon wouldn't trust me and thought Peter was doing what I said, and on and on. Then your daughter is just like you, says she's going to kill me, and I'm sure she would. I tried to be nice-nice, lighten things up and all. So, now here you are and you are here to kill me. If you don't, the CIA will swarm in. I tell you, I'm fucked. No lover, everyone knows where I am. All this time I've been invisible, but not now. So, here we are. If you don't kill me, someone else will real soon unless we get smart."

Having pulled the gun from her thigh, Eliana was ready to kill her. She still worried about what would happen if she did.

"There is other option no mentioned. Stop rampage. I walk out door, you walk out door. We stop fighting, you stop hurting my family, I make sure even CIA doesn't attack. That is smart. That we can do."

"You think so? We have bad blood, dead people on your side. Can we trust each other? I'm not sure that works most times. But you know what does work all the time?"

As she said the last word, there was a crack of a pistol from behind the desk, and Eliana went flying back out of her chair. The bullet hit her chest, her gun flying out of her hand. She was gurgling blood, and bleeding front and back in her middle.

Getting up, Jo walked and picked up the pistol Eliana had been holding. Moving to stand above her, Eliana looked at her but couldn't talk. She watched Jo look the gun over, then look at her.

"Crazy. This could have killed me, but. it didn't. Let's see how well it would have done."

Pointing down to Eliana's head, she smiled, saying, "Sweet dreams. I'm speaking English, so feel free to tell me if you don't understand?"

She fired, went to a cabinet drawer, opened it and put it with other pistols in it.

"I'm going to need to start a second drawer, Eliana."

Four men were waiting in the great room, all smiling, all having cleaning supplies and two pushing a gurney. She waved to them as she went out to make her video for that evening in the building where a group of girls were playing tag, all naked, all happy to see her.

PART SIX
The Hurt

Not Taken

CHAPTER 50

Getting a call with a Ukrainian country prefix, Cindy thought it was her mother, knowing she seldom used the same phone twice. She was surprised to hear a man's voice, and he was speaking to her in Ukrainian with a Russian accent. After politely saying hello, she asked what the call was about. She put it on the speakerphone for Mike, James and Angie to hear.

"Cynthia, I can tell what only you and mother must know, I am pilot. Eliana's jet. I call. Eliana's wish we speak. Do you want me say private thing only you know?"

Things being so intense, she thought it best to be sure.

"Yes, please, it is hard to be certain right now, and that will be kind assurance. First, please, what is your name?

"Victush, but in America it Victor. I know in head what your mother said to say. Spit. Just that word. Spit."

Nodding to Mike, she knew it was what she saw her mother do to her husband as they left their house after she killed him. She spit in the place where his face had been.

"Victor, thank you, that is a word we both know. Where is Eliana?"

All eyes on the phone, she already knew what he was going to say. She hadn't heard from her mother past the time he was told to wait no longer. She could hear Victor breathing deeply.

"I know for certain she dead. My number only one on Eliana's phone. I get text. It has picture. It shows Eliana on floor, hole in chest, hole in head. Under picture says only Jo liked her very much. She was in place, one where is cult. She act like one seeking job. She tell me, Victush, I may be back, may be no. If no, call Cynthia. I wait, picture comes. Now, I do what she said. Take plane, bring it to you. Now yours."

Angie went and was hugging her side, crying. James took a pad of paper and pen from his jacket and wrote to have him text the picture, don't look, he would if she didn't want to. Mike nodded in agreement.

"Victor, I thank you. I know you are more than pilot the way you speak of Eliana. Please. When you land plane, you come here. I want know more. I want you to stay pilot, for me. You stay here, with my daughter and me. When do you land?"

"Cynthia, I thank you. I will be good guest. There are things she

318 Not Taken

wanted I should give you. Only if she dead. Landing? Estimate. Is two hours. I need to get to where you live."

"When you land, I will have man drive you to my home. He give you word you gave me. Go only with one with word. I am glad we meet, soon."

She stood looking at her phone, then turned to hug Angie back, saying it was best she died fighting, not in a hospital bed.

Mike and James heard her phone ping. It would be the picture sent as a text. Shaking her head, Cindy hit messages, looked at the picture, shook her head from reading the message, then handed it to Mike. She saw James look at it with him, then Mike forwarded it to James who then sent it off for analysis to be sure it wasn't doctored and if there was a location in the metadata.

They had just left the hospital and were at Cindy's house, still stunned at Whimsey being found dead in the waiting area at the hospital. Cindy asked Angie to get some water and soda for everyone, adding she wanted to sit on the couch to think about all that had happened. Once Angie was back with bottled waters and root beers, Cindy looked at each of them, one at a time, in their eyes, then looking at Mike she had a look of certainty that she had reached a decision.

"Here is what I want. No more of this. All this time we've being sitting here playing agency games we haven't done anything. That's not how it's going to be anymore. No more being victims. We're being groomed. I'm sure Jamie is alive, or that creature would have taunted us about it in her message. Once Victor gets here, if he needs some rest, I'll give him time if it's needed, but if not I'm on my jet and I'm going to finish that woman with a hollow core."

"Mom, don't you mean we're going to finish it? Geez, she's my grandmother!"

Smiling at Angie, she said of course it would be her too, and yes, she knew Eliana was her grandmother. Angie smiled back and knew she meant her too, she just wanted to be sure.

As Cindy finished reassuring Angie, both Mike and James started to speak at the same time. Cindy held up her free hand, saying to stop, she didn't want any more talk. They both knew she meant it. Taking a sip of root beer, she first looked to Mike.

"You need to stay here. You aren't fit to fight. Mike, I'm sorry. You

hold the fort. You're running on pain killers and when they wear off, you'll know I'm right. I won't take a chance of you getting killed."

Turning to James, she had just as much certainty in her tone.

"James, you know who she is, where she is, and what she's done. And where are you? Here. Where are all your agents? Not there. All here playing on their little computers. James, I can't count on you anymore. Not after this. My God, James. My mother managed to fly from the Ukraine, get in to meet with her, and you don't even have men on the way? You really need to think about that. I have. I don't think it's by accident. The worst thing? Whimsey died while you were responsible for watching her. The biggest agency in the world to protect anyone, and Whimsey's dead? No. That stops. Now."

Both Mike and James almost cried out but stopped themselves. Cindy was sitting as she talked, but crossing her legs, slipped her Glock from her thigh holster and had it pointed at James. Her finger taut on the trigger, there was no doubt by anyone there she was ready to shoot him.

"If you're not part of feeding Jo information and haven't done anything wrong, I'll owe you a big apology. If you're part of any of it? I'll take life in prison rather than let you live."

Mike was shaking, starting to talk, but Cindy, ignoring him, kept her eyes on James, telling him to stop, she wasn't going to do anything except pull the trigger if what she says doesn't happen. Mike stopped talking, sure she would do it. She kept the laser sight of her Glock pointed at James' forehead.

"Mike, I want you, without having James move in any way, take his guns. All of them. I know there's more than one. Give them to Angie. She'll lock them away. When she comes back, she'll have an AR-15 pointed at him. Take his phone, hand it to Angie. After giving her the phone, see what else he has on him. Earpiece. Radio device. Take all his clothes off. One thing at a time. Search him the same as you would a terrorist."

Telling James to stand up, slowly with hands on top of his head, James showed no expression but did as told.

Mike carefully searched his jacket, the back of his pants, and his cuffs. He found three guns, all loaded with rounds in the chambers. Not stopping to disarm them he handed them to Angie saying they were live.

Holding her AR-15 out at James, she backed away to put them in a safe with a biometric lock only she or Cindy could open. Returning she was holding her rifle up in firing position, aimed at James, the red dot of the laser on his head.

Continuing the search, Mike found two phones, putting them on the coffee table where they had been sitting. Cindy said they'd start going through the call history in a moment. Putting both her hands to her gun to show she wouldn't possibly miss; her laser sight was pointing to the middle of James' forehead. Using her always polite manner, she told James to say his unlock codes out loud as Mike accessed the phones. He remained still, only his mouth moving as he said them clearly. Mike entered the code for each one, saying they were correct. Cindy told him to look at numbers called in the last two days.

"Mike. After we secure him, read all recent texts and you should be able to spot any coded language. Listen to voice mails. Anything encrypted, if you can't access it James will tell you how. Right now, take all his clothes off. Go very slow. If he moves, I fire. I don't want you to get hit too, but if you let him make a move, that could happen. Everything. James, don't move or help get them off. Mike, cut them off if you need to. James, whatever you do, don't turn away from me."

Having learned a great deal of the tactics from the man who trained Angie and her on stopping or searching an enemy, she kept aim at James. Talking with a great deal of emphasis she told Angie to get the box of the large-size latex gloves and the jar of petroleum jelly. Saying she had aim on James, once she had them not to get in her line of fire so crouch down to put them on the coffee table. Angie had gone through the same training and didn't ask why. Mike moved his head just slightly enough where Cindy knew he agreed.

Mike knew Cindy was she was as fearless and determined as when she pointed a gun from above the head of the sheik who had bought her and Cindy and fired straight down into his head, causing it to literally explode. Even after Cindy was raped when twelve, watching her mother kill her sick father and blasting her way out of the Ukraine if anyone even looked at her funny, then recently being drugged, fucked in the ass, put on an auction block naked with Angie, then sold to a pathetic man living on the oil sold to America, shooting him... With all inside her she remained a gentle, caring person. But when needed, she was even more

ruthless and cold than Mike had ever known even the worst killer to be.

Returning with the gloves and lubricant, Angie stood back with her rifle aimed back at Jame's chest. It took time, but Mike found a micro recorder in the jacket lining, saying he should include that to listen to and see what had been recorded. Not looking away, Angie said, "Right on," and smiled knowing Cindy wouldn't ask her where she learned that, at least not for the moment.

Completing his search of the clothes, Mike used the gloves, not caring if James winced as he probed his rectum. Cindy knew it was natural — to a point, but James didn't show any reaction. Inside of James, Mike found a micro device, saying it was a beacon used for agent location and rescue. He didn't turn his head to talk to Cindy, adding most field agents carried them in a cuff or belt, not where he found it. Cindy asked if it had been activated. Mike looked at it, saying it hadn't. Holding it in the palm of his hand, he pulled one glove inside out to cover it, then put the other glove over the first using the same inside-out method. Angie had brought a plastic bag that zipped shut, and after putting the gloves and tracker in the bag and saying it could be zipped later, Mike let it fall to the table as it would be kept for evidence if James was doing any wrong.

That sparked a question in Cindy, and she said they needed to think all things through.

"Mike, thinking about where it was hidden, if it was activated, I assume the agency would be the one to have access to it. But what if it was there because when activated it was Jo who had access? If James was headed to her, she'd know where he was, along with all of us, right?

"Wow, Cindy, who trained you? But I agree. It's most likely why it was hidden. Not practical if not tactical is a motto we were taught. Having that up your ass isn't very practical if not needed to be found easily. Sorry, up his, I mean."

He hadn't looked her way or stopped his caution, but she appreciated the articulation.

"I know you didn't mean mine."

Angie hadn't moved, and the red dot was moving along with James' breathing heavily. Cindy said to sweep as she walked with her rifle as they didn't know if James had a way to get an agent in through their security, telling her to back away and get restraints. Angie said, "Roger

that," then went in a different direction than where she had taken the guns. In two minutes, she was back with keyed metal shackles and zip ties. Crouching down, putting them on the coffee table for Mike, Angie took the phones and put them in a pouch she had put on while getting the restraints.

Mike, reaching first for the metal shackle, asked, "Both?" Cindy said, "No chances. Hands behind him."

Angie had also brought a roll of wide duct tape, and a rag. Cindy said to gag him.

Seeing Mike shaking from doing all she told him to do, she understood he was hurting only from the movements tugging at his stitches. She understood James had long been his friend, but she had to eliminate all risks. She hated what was being done, but with so many lives at stake, she'd needed to be sure of everything after all that had happened. Only James knew where Sharon and Whimsey were, along with other details revealed to him that had been used to get at them. The only ones she was certain of were Angie and Mike. She needed to talk to them but didn't want James to hear anything more.

"Mike, you know what to do. You worked the plan for it. Treat him as hostile. Slowly pull his hands up far as he can and still walk. Best if he's bent far over. Stay behind, and don't let up. Angie will flank you both or where she can fire on him. Take him to the safe room downstairs and have him sit in the metal chair, shackle him to it. Angie, as you walk behind them, if he does anything at all, fire. Mike, keep a bit off to his side so she has a clear shot. Angie, keep that dot on him as Mike sits him down, then backs out and secures the room. Then fill the hanging water bag. Bring it to Mike, same aim as Mike goes in. Mike, make sure he can reach the hose to bite down on. Make sure it works. Get a couple of large blankets and put them on him. No getting dressed again. Oh, turn on the boombox in there. A radio station. Scatter rap. Blast it where it'll be hard for him to think. Angie, once all that's done and the door's shut, use our code to lock the room."

Mike looked at her, realizing she had codes he didn't know. Knowing it would hurt him, she told him she was sorry, but if he was ever caught, tortured, anything could happen, and he could be drugged and tell the codes. As he walked, he said that was smart, and she was right. She knew she was.

Having taken close to an hour to search and get James secured, once done Mike said he could still drive, and he'd pick Victor up. Cindy wasn't sure Victor would be ready to pilot once down, but knew he wouldn't say he could if he wasn't sure.

Mike was clearly aching from his wound, but once back from the safe room with Angie, he looked at Cindy and had a look of shock on his face.

"Man, I sure never want to get on your bad side. How can someone so nice be such a God-damn terminator?"

Angie looked at him, saying they'd just watched it two times on Prime not long ago, and Cindy had been doing Arnold impressions. Smiling, she started going through the phone's history. Mike managed to chuckle at Angie's continued fascination with having every cable and streaming channel for the first time in her life. Keeping his smile, looking back to Cindy, she was sitting like nothing had happened. She was calm and gentle as she looked at him, concerned about his wound. He told her it was okay.

"I'm not bleeding. It's okay. Cindy, you did it right. That's textbook, all the way. If he's totally innocent, he'll say the same thing. It's what he'd do as well. He'll know the drill. The extra blankets are good, and for now, water's enough. I know he'll be worried about… well… what if we don't make it back… No code to let him out, nobody knows he's here."

"Mike, have you joined the club thinking I'm stupid just because I'm so good looking?"

Angie giggled, proud of her mom using her line on Mike.

"Okay, well, I did get that one from Angie, but I'll never ask her where she got it from. About James… He's in the safe room, not out here. So, when we go, we tape your cell number on the door, saying he's inside. If we don't get back, someone at the agency will figure out he may be here, and they'll find the room. If we aren't back, they'll find a way to get him out. Explosives on the lock, probably."

Cindy said he had thought it through.

Then, starting to ask if she thought he's stupid because… but Angie stopped him mid-sentence, telling him that was for girls only, and she was looking at call logs on the phones, saying she had found some things they need to talk about. Cindy and Mike looked at her.

"I ignored ones to us, Jamie, but not Sharon or Whimsey. The other

ones… I'd have to call to know if they're burner or legit. But it's not the numbers that show something, it's the time the calls were made. Each was just before something happened. Just under two hours each time. One an hour before poor Whimsey… well, we don't know the exact time yet, but before we found her like that. Could be calls for instructions, could be calls to someone to act. I don't remember him calling at the hospital, but it's here on his phone."

Looking at Angie, showing concern, then at Cindy, Mike said that at the hospital James was asked to go check on Whimsey and was gone for a while. Cindy nodded, saying it had been her that asked him. Charles had left without saying he was going, and she was worried about leaving her there alone. Squinting her eyes, she asked what about Charles? Mike gave a little jump, saying he hadn't considered that. She asked if James and Charles had known each other long.

"I asked them that during dinner when we first met. They go way back. They were in the war in Iraq, and James got him the job at the agency. It's certainly a possibility. Charles knew everyone involved, and some things told to him and nobody else. I keep wondering why he left Whimsey and didn't tell us he was going. That's not good…"

Angie looked up, adding he had access to drugs of all sorts as a doctor.

"Sharon acted like she was drugged, Whimsey couldn't stay awake, Jamie said she was jabbed in the neck and went out like a light."

Mike was visibly shaken when hearing Angie lay it all out in a logical fashion. He looked at his watch, saying he'd have to leave soon, and said if Charles should show up, not to let him in. As he said that, one of the phones James had was vibrating. Angie didn't answer it but looked at Mike and Cindy.

"Speaking of the devil. The caller ID gives Satan a new name. Shrink."

After the phone stopped vibrating, they all nodded, knowing that Charles was as suspect as James. Mike looked at his watch again.

"I'm going to go now. I need to be comfortable driving so I'm taking your car, not the Tahoe. We can plan our invasion plan when I get back. And Cindy, you beat me to the punch. When I came to, one thing was on my mind was is if a team had been sent out… at least do surveillance on the cult compound. It's clear nothing like that had been done, and

after what happened to me… and Sharon, that should have been ordered immediately. And it may not be a question of James or Charles… two are stronger than one. Right now, let's assume that's the deal, and it really sucks. I know the code word for Victor, and where he'll land. I'll call when he's in the car. I want to make sure you haven't taken more prisoners."

Cindy gave him her most tantalizing look, throwing a couch pillow at him, somehow managed to hit his side.

Looking at her, he said, "Ouch."

CHAPTER 51

"How are you holding up, Victor? I want you to take us back to the compound, but only if you are rested. I made you some food, but do you need sleep first?"

Smiling, Cindy led him to the kitchen as she talked. He saw she had made kraut petoheh, stuffed cabbage rolls, and had pickled beets out in a bowl.

"Hungry, yes! You make all things I love. Thank you. Tired, no. I took nap waiting for Eliana to return. Had good rest. Could no sleep now anyway. Eliana, she meant much to me. If you want, I good fighter. Military. Ground, mostly air. Fighter jet commander when I meet Eliana. I could no say no to her."

Looking at his face, Cindy knew he was more than her pilot. She wouldn't fly with anyone she wasn't fully sure of. She sat across from him and called for Angie to get milk and some kolachky. He smiled, saying it was not dinner without them. Angie had come in for kolachky, then left with two in each hand, Cindy looked at Victor, asking him if he and Eliana were close. Still putting his napkin in his collar before starting his food, he looked at her. Just seeing his face, she could feel his sadness.

"I was, yes. I think she had same feelings for me. She was tough one, but with me, not so much. I loved her, she knew. She say she could love no one. She knew, I knew, any man loved would be target. We were, yes, very close. I wanted marry her but knew that she happy way it was. Cynthia, she showed me pictures... You... Angelia... She very proud, say she keep you far away. You safe. You both beautiful, look like her. But you are gentle, kind. You have beauty she would have if no hurt. Now, you know Victor's secret. For her, I will do anything for you and daughter. Only if you want, I mean."

He started eating. Cindy was sure he had revealed more to her than he had with anyone else. She knew if her mother loved him enough to protect him, he was someone she could trust as well. She began thinking of what he had said about his training. She called Mike to join them.

As he sat down next to her, she asked if he wanted some food. He said after reading his discharge sheets, that would be some crackers and milk, at least for a few days. Victor looked up, having learned on the drive Mike spoke Russian perfectly, asking him if he had been shot in

the stomach. Mike was surprised as he hadn't mentioned it. He said he had, but the bullet passed through him just under his lung and took a bite out of his pipes. Victor pushed the plate of kolachky to him.

"Three times... Three times I shot same way. First, stupid crackers. Then with cracker, I put jam. What is kolachky? Cracker with jam. Eat, this is better."

Realizing Victor was right, he sat enjoying them, but realized there would be none left for him. As if reading minds, Cindy brought out another plateful for them. She sat, taking two for herself, squinting when she took bites as she enjoyed them so much. She looked at Mike and had a question.

"You know the Army base you were taken to? They had a lot of fighter jets lined up."

Mike nodded, paused before taking his next bite, saying it was the Army Air Force, and they had the latest ones there. She asked to be sure, thinking about the planes all lined up.

"Victor told me he was a fighter jet pilot. I bet he could fly one of those. Could you, Victor?"

His mouth full, he nodded, then managed to say of course, any Ruskie pilot could fly such toys. Mike looked at Cindy, his expression implying she was stretching things a bit.

"No, Cindy. I'm sure he'd be able to, but no way a stolen fighter jet would get past the state line without getting shot down."

Pouting, she said it would be great to hit the compound with real bombs and guided missiles.

"Yes, it would. But no, we can't."

Crossing her arms, she thought about it and was pouting even more. She looked at him again, asking what if she nicely asked some top brass in one of her even nicer escort clothes. Mike said no meant no.

"Training exercise?"

"No."

"Practicing for an airshow and need a loaner as ours is in the shop?"

"No."

"What if I buy one?"

"Oh, okay, did you know they cost about 300 million? Do you have that hidden away with a secret code?"

Looking hurt, Cindy told him the secret code comment wasn't

needed. Realizing he was harboring a worry she didn't trust him, as always, she was right.

"Cindy. I'm sorry. That was wrong to say. Childish."

Smiling at him, she said she forgave him, then answered.

"Yes."

He looked confused, asking yes to what."

"I have lots more than that. So, can I buy one if I have the money?"

"Wha… you have more money? Wait, she gave you a ton, but not that much."

"That's when I was a sex slave and all. No, a few days ago she told me she converted all her gold and jewels and lots of other things and put them into accounts for Angie and me. I haven't finished totaling them all up yet. I stopped because the calculator didn't have enough digits. I forgot to mention it as you were all shot up and too busy to notice me…"

Just walking into the room, Angie told Cindy that's pretty good and she was learning from her way of talking. Cindy smiled at her, saying she was still quite young and able to learn. Angie looked at Mike, saying their calculator only had nine digits. Sitting at the table she grabbed a few more kolachky before they were all eaten up. Mike looked at her, then Cindy, his mouth opened and in near a state of shock.

"Whoa… You're kidding. More than a billion?"

Cindy looked, and pouted again because all the kolachky were eaten.

"A lot of those when I had to stop counting. She had fifteen years and saved most everything she made. Victor, did you help her cash in?"

Finished with all his food, he was drinking milk and nodding.

"Big job. So much gold. Very heavy. Bags, big ones, full of diamonds. Lots of rubies. Shares of stock in Apple… She say that worth more than billion Yankee. Man from there give it for girl. She thought just silly paper, no money. She carried those and worth more than some of heavy stuff. I sure it be more than what you say."

Mike was stunned. He was sitting next to a billionaire. He knew billionaires were becoming more common, but asked Victor how could she make that much from trafficking girls? Victor shook his head, then explained things.

"Mike, do yourself favor. No get into traffic business. That is no how it work. Yes, you make much if you have right girls, that is okay money.

Real money from giving girls, sometimes for pennies, to president, company CEO, all kind of stupid men, fools. Take pictures, blackmail them. Sell them more girls once they can no get dick hard from first one, so need new ones. So, blackmail them again. They no care. They care about little girl, not money. They have more hidden than they have in open. Last ten years, some pay with paper. She get stock in company, then she vote and they give her more to vote like they want. Before that, and the ones in middle east? All cash, all gold, all real money they hide. When we leave… Eliana, she gave me diamonds to start airline. For people, not little girls. I was thinking good name be Elianair. Good, no?"

Looking at all of them, Mike was learning the hard truth about things few knew, but decided to change the topic as he didn't want to learn more. Such knowledge could be revealed under torture, and he said best he didn't know. Cindy and Angie were looking at him as if to ask what the big deal was. Changing the subject, he returned to her fighter jet question.

"Even using your pocket change to buy one, it's not like going to a used car lot and getting one just like that."

Angie shook her head. "See any pockets on us? Clutch change."

Shaking his head, pouring more milk, Victor said yes it was.

"What? Please, don't encourage them. We need to get a game plan together."

Cindy said he was a fighter pilot so he must know something about it. She asked him to explain.

"Well, fighter jet no need be latest model. Can be older, for like you say, air shows. What makes plane fighter? Not plane, no. It is plane with canons, bombs, high caliber guns. That's all is difference for older jet. Good for hitting cult place. You go to man sells old planes, ones ready to fly. Then, find surplus supplies. Maybe black market. A few fighter guns, mount to plane. Tricky. Need buy guns you can buy munitions for. Things used for weapons, but not only on jet. Not hard is you no want brand new type fighter. But for cult place? A few calls. Men, ones I know, Maybe have one ready to go. They say it for airshow pilot, thing like that. Buy munitions, load it up, boom goes cult crazies."

Mike saw Cindy was bouncing with excitement, then turning to him.

"See, it's not a crazy idea. Victor, I must have your permission. Can I share what you told me about my mother. I think you have a reason to

hit the cult hard. Is it okay if I say why?"

Watching his face grow hard and cold, Mike realized he wasn't just talking. He held his hand up, letting Cindy know he would explain.

"Cynthia knows. Me? Eliana? In love. Nobody knew, but now they can't hurt her or me for love. Jo woman took my love. I want thank her… from cockpit of fighter. If I run out of munitions, or fuel, I eject and crash plane to where she hide. This, I will do for Eliana. And Cynthia. And Angelia. Jo. She will go at them next. Eliana said if she killed, kill Jo before she kills her girls."

Mike realized he had the skill and the know-how to do it, and he told him he was convinced. He turned to Cindy.

"Amazing. But, one thing. That, if we did such a thing, takes time we don't have. Jamie's there…"

Victor had sat back and had been thinking. He leaned forward and looked at each one, his face showing he had a lot to say.

"Mike, that is most important thing. I know time it take to make deal for fighter, get it fixed for fight. I think there may be way without to wait. Cynthia, you have jet. Good jet. I pick out. It has much cargo space. You have much money. We turn your jet into fighter. Add guns here and there. Or, for pussy compound, drop grenades, some bombs maybe, out cargo bay door on cult crazies. Do job just fine. We no fighting other fighters. Just fools on ground."

Cindy looked at him, then Mike, then Angie. She looked back at Victor.

"That, we do. I want my jet to be a fighter from now on. For now, we load it up with what we'll need to drop out of the plane. Bomb-type things to wreak havoc on Jo's compound."

Mike, amazed as it was so simple but so effective, expressed one concern.

"That is the best idea ever, Victor. I do think that we need to remember there are little girls there, and the cult members are brainwashed. We want to down Jo, rescue Jamie, not harm the others. I think just smoke grenades, maybe tear gas, a few real grenades dropped nearby would get them all running and leave Jo on her own. You've seen how noise and smoke send people into a panic. Could we get by with that?"

Before Victor could answer, Cindy spoke first.

"Mike. You're right. We can attack with the jet, scare the cult members to run out, but not hurt them. Then, we go in with a big SUV for Jo and to snatch Jamie. Victor, can you fly my jet like a fighter? I mean, low to the ground, loud engines, at night where they think it's a for-real bomber type?"

"Cynthia… you could be general in Russia. You know to strike fear is most powerful weapon. Of course I fly jet like I fly fighter. It has wings. It has engines. It has me! Real fighter pilot no care what plane. And with right smoke grenades, a few that go boom, it strike terror of Cynthia in hearts of cult fools."

Mike was nodding, adding it would be perfect. Angie sat, looking serious.

"Victor, I'd like to drop the grenades. Can you shout when to drop them?"

Cindy looked at Angie, smiling. There didn't seem to be any way of stopping her doing anything. She nodded to Victor.

"I sorry. I change to strike terror of Cynthia and Angelia on cult fools. Be bombardier Angelia? That is what you want? That is what you be. If general, the terror called Cynthia, say she need you on ground, I can do such thing. Small window for pilot. I toss out grenades."

Angie leaned over the table, looking at Victor.

"I'm going to drop the grenades. You'll be flying in a valley between big mountains and need to fly real low, so you do that, I'll do the bombing."

Wanting to say more, she heard the much dreaded, "Angie?"

"Mom, it's my jet too…"

Patting her lap, she wanted Angie to come sit there. Angie smiled, happy she wanted her close, and hugged her tight once she was sitting on her lap. Cindy looked at Victor as she hugged Angie.

"I'm sure every girl who's been taken and trafficked dreams of doing that. That's what they all should do, then no more traffickers. And Angie? Of course it's yours too. It's ours. You make me prouder each day. All that time in the trailer… those horrible people there. And now, cable, streaming and satellite. And still all sweet and wonderful…"

Mike started to imitate a cough, trying to get her attention. Both she and Angie looked at him, asking if his wound was acting up.

"No, not that. I kind of don't think of taking the jet and dropping

bombs as necessarily all sweet and wonderful. I think Angie's a for-real warrior — in some pretty fancy clothes recently."

Both laughing, Cindy said that's how she saw her, but she agreed she was quite a force for any trafficker to face as she hugged her tighter. Angie tilted her head at Mike.

"I mean, really? Fancy clothes on a bombing run? Mike, you're such a guy with all your fantasy stuff. Or, maybe taking a bullet has you forgetting you gave us camo fatigues? And I'll have like four Glocks and an AR-15 strapped on, so that doesn't go with Italian fashion. Except in your dreams!"

Cindy moved Angie to look her in the eyes.

"Now, I want you to apologize. He was paying both of us a compliment, and saying he fantasizes about either of us if not what he meant, and you know that. I know you're worked up about getting at Jo and working with Victor, but you can be kind, and sweet at the same time."

Looking at her, showing she understood she went off for no good reason, she nodded.

"Mom. You're right. No matter how bad things are, you're always kind to anyone nice and a good person. Mike, I'm sorry for not doing what I know is right…"

Getting off Cindy's lap, she went to Mike, sat in a chair next to him to look into his eyes.

"I'm sorry. That wasn't right for me to say any of that. You're the best, and I appreciate you seeing how much I want to stop people from hurting girls like me."

Looking into Mike's eyes, it was a moment where they found an even stronger bond between each other. He shook his head and told her that meant a lot to him. Then he asked her how she planned to not fall out of the cargo bay with Victor zooming up and down and banking. She said she hadn't thought that far ahead, then turned to Victor, asking him how to keep from falling out.

"Angelia, you think I would let such thing happen? Put you in harness, strap you to frame. Maybe you be tossed a bit, but no fall out. I promise."

Standing up, Angie was excited.

"Harness? How does it go with Camo? Same color?"

Angie stopped, afraid to turn around as she heard, "Angie" again from Cindy.

"Sweetie, I know that would be exciting, but I've been thinking about it. That would leave only me and Mike to be in the SUV to get Jamie. He's just been shot, and we must consider that. I know Victor can drop things out his window, and that will be plenty. I would hope you'd want to be on the ground and ready to fire at Jo and save Jamie."

Thinking about it, Angie was about to try to say she really was needed on the jet. She looked at Cindy, who was looking at her, expecting her to do what was right, and she realized the thrill of dropping bombs was not where she was needed most. Cindy was right. She knew she had gotten carried away. Looking at Cindy, she picked up her rifle and held it in front of her on the classic angle at full attention.

"Private Angie, on the ground, ready to take out the enemy by any means."

Closing her eyes to say a short prayer of thanks, Cindy opened them and nodded, saying she'd be right there by her side. Like always.

CHAPTER 52

"Jamie… oh, Jamie… are you *really* sleeping?"

Stirring, she woke hyper-aware from hearing Jo's voice. Looking up at her bedside, then around the room, she realized Jamie was talking to her on a flat screen TV that she guessed wasn't for watching Netflix. Thinking she'd never be able to fall asleep, as she lay thinking best not to try, that's when she dozed off. She had no idea how long she'd been asleep, her first thought being not more than an hour.

Being monitored, drugged, not knowing where they were, and sleep deprivation were common practices to get captives confused and even to a state of hallucination. Tilting her head up, seeing Jo smiling at her made Jamie feel like it should be a hallucination, but she knew it wasn't.

Sitting up, she knew Jo could see her as she sat on the bed.

"I don't know if I am or not. Is it day or night?"

Jo laughed, shaking her head at the camera for Jamie to see. She didn't look like someone on a typical webcam. She looked perfectly lit, her hair cascading and styled, and behind her was a hazy backdrop like she used when taking pictures of trafficked girls.

"With all the things to worry about, your first question is if it's day or night. Well, neither. It's sunset, and a wonder to behold. Take a look…"

Watching the screen, the image changed to the sun setting behind mountains, then Jo walking in front of the scene. Looking to the camera, she was talking only to Jamie.

"Green screen. I can be anywhere, talking to anyone. Who'd know? But, it actually is sunset, and this is a live view to the west of my compound. I thought of going outside when I broadcast, but I do avoid the sun. UV, all that. I don't really go out in it if I can avoid it."

Watching the background change again, Jo was showing her a live view of her sitting on the bed. She was toying with her, and Jamie ignored the game playing. She tucked her knees up under her chin and wrapped her arms around her ankles.

"Are you going to let me out of here?"

Looking surprised, Jo changed to a live feed of Cindy's house. She managed to not react and kept looking at the screen.

"Of course. The whole now, when, and in what condition, those are all things that depend. Let's take a stab at it. Not with a knife or

something nasty. Our imagination. So, say I let you out in a little while and you come join me in my video studio. Would you behave? I really don't think it's a good time to try to run off or strangle me. It would be exciting viewing, but not on the script. I livestream every night, and usually it's to show the latest little ones. You did a lot of videos of little sweeties, so you know all about that. I'd love to interview you tonight, though. You'd have time to get all cleaned up, and while you're in the shower I'll have a few nice outfits for you to choose from laid out on the bed. Up for it?"

Thinking things just kept getting crazier and crazier, it wasn't a choice, so no need to discuss it.

"Sure. If that does it for you. How long do I have to get ready?"

"An hour, and I know you'll get all gussied up for the viewers. I'm inviting a few VIPs tonight. I think you know them. They're all in here…"

It cut back to Cindy's house. She assumed that it would be to show that she was alive and well. There was no need to ask. It was obvious. She asked what the questions would be.

"I was thinking it would be interesting to talk about how you were very bad and sold girls, but now you know that's not right to do. You know, the snatching them off the street, drugging them, taking bids… and how you were treated that way. I want my followers to know that trafficking is a horrible thing."

Jamie almost burst out laughing, but she wasn't sure if Jo believed her form of trafficking was different. She decided to test her reaction to a question if that's what the point of being interviewed was.

"Sure, we can talk about that. So, will you be asking me if how your method isn't like trafficking at all?"

Nodding, Jo looked calm and not upset by the implication.

"I know you don't know yet exactly what the difference is. I'll fill that part in. I'll ask you about Peter, however. You were there when he suffered for his wrongs. He was dipping in the pot, so to speak. And he was so mean to Sharon and Whimsey, and all you could do is put a stop to it. I want others who are missionaries to know what happens when they stray from the fold. I do have some footage that I'll ask you to do a play-by-play of…"

The screen changed to security footage of Eliana shooting Peter, then

everyone coming and surrounding her to make sure he was dead, with Sharon taking her vengeance shots. She watched it carefully, and she wasn't surprised she had the footage. She waited for it to finish before talking about it.

"That's not exactly family viewing. So, just to help me here, are you mad Peter was killed, or glad?"

"Both. Yep, both. Peter? Well, I'm glad he's dead. He was so fuckin' crazy with the religion shit and was really doing everything I told him not to. All of you killing him? Yeah, I'm mad you did it. I wanted to do it. But that's just between us girls. Well, that's the lineup. You better get going and get yourself all dolled up. And Jamie, please, no crazy shit. If you're very good, maybe we can talk about things we can do together."

The screen went blank. She knew all the things Jo said could be nonsense, and she was planning to kill her outside and not make a mess in the room, or wanted the company of someone who knew the business and talk shop. It would be a chance to see the compound as she was out when she was brought there.

Showering helped her feel better after being drugged. After drying off, she found an assortment of luxury cosmetics and a cordless hair dryer. Jo was taking no chances. No cords, no strangling her with it.

Deciding to look nice, but not go overboard, applying makeup didn't take long. Going to the bed, four outfits had been laid out for her to choose from. They were stylish and any of them would be flattering to her shape and skin tone. Picking out a casual dress, it was a deep green with tiny sweet-pea flowers, and it fit perfectly. She thought it would be better having a belt at the waist, but like the cord on the hair drier, a belt could be used like Sharon had used to kill. Each outfit had matching shoes and putting on classic flats the same color of the dress, she was ready.

The door opened. A man, smiling and saying she was right on time, waited just outside the door. She didn't notice him having any weapons, and he was the only one she could see once outside of the room.

"It's not very far, and close enough to walk. It's a nice evening."

After walking side-by-side, he held the door and she was out of the building. The sunset on the monitor was a hint of how beautiful the mountains looked, and they surrounded the large group of buildings she saw as they walked. She could hear laughter and squeals of delight in the

distance, and they were sounds made by young girls. She was getting an idea that what appeared to be a lack of concern about her getting violent was the opposite of how is appeared. Like not having a cord on a hair dryer, the man not having a gun, it meant she couldn't grab for one. It was also part of the image of a religious setting. Smiles, natural splendor, no guns visible… It was crafted to paint a picture the opposite of what was really happening all around her. It was young girls being sold for donations, a tax-deductible form of dirty money.

Ushered into the building closest to the one she had been held prisoner in, it was full of doors with "On Air" signs over them, the red lettering lit. Each one had a large window looking in, and while walking she glanced at what was going on behind each door. It was not what she expected, but it made sense. None of the rooms were large, just enough to look like a bedroom. Each had a different theme. Bookworm, movie fan, nurse, sports fanatic and some just a hodgepodge of things a young girl would have including stuffed animals and posters of pop stars. Each had a large bed, and facing the bed was a fixed webcam and professional lighting. On the bed were a variety of girls in different stages of undress, some fully clothed, some in thongs and nylons, some naked. They all were in front of laptops with cute stickers such as smiley faces, and the girls were reading or typing. It was a chat center for sex with the girls, and they were all past their teen years.

Reaching the end of the corridor was a large set of doors, also with an On Air sign although not yet lit. Her guard opened the doors and unlike the other rooms, it was a large TV studio with state-of-the-art cameras, lighting, green screen and other backdrops on either side of where Jo was sitting in a tall director's chair next to an empty one.

"That dress is perfect for you. And your hair… nice. Come, sit with me."

Jo was wearing a soft white dress that reached mid-calf. It was flowing and she looked like the cliché of an Angel in movies. Her hair, a dark brown, was frosted with a spray and glowed under the studio lighting. The tall chairs faced each other at an angle, the cameras seemed fixed in place, and there weren't any people working them. There was no teleprompter, but there was a large studio monitor that could be seen when in either chair, showing both of them as she sat down. Jo looked at the monitor and nodded at how they both looked onscreen.

"This is exciting! A special edition and I think we look wonderful together. If there were decent money in it, we could have a morning show on a major network. Talk about making pasta and what the royals are doing. So, this show goes out world-wide, and about the only thing to remember is to never call me Jo. That's so important. To the world, I am just called The One. Kind of like if your serious, say, tell me One, what is it that… or if it's all chatty, like, hey, One, did you see the new kids…" Pretty easy. Now, I know how it may be tempting to blurt out you're a prisoner and I'm evil, so there's a 30-second broadcast delay thingy so nothing like that would go out. If you do, it won't do you any good and I would be so disappointed in you."

Saying she understood, Jamie realized Jo had built a world different onscreen than what any visitor would see. She had a confidence that came natural to her, and she understood how she used that to get followers and donations.

A voice from speakers said one minute to air. Jo was adjusting herself in the chair, taking on a serene look, her deceptive smile gone, her body leaning forward with her arms crossed on her knees, looking serious and concerned. As numbers counted down over them on the monitor, ethereal music sounded and as it faded, Jo began her introduction.

"Trafficking. Are our children safe?"

The same words appeared as overlaid titles on the screen.

"No matter who you are, where you live, rich or poor, if you think it can't happen to your family, think again. It's upsetting to live in a world where organized groups have men roaming your streets, looking for pretty young girls, some just toddlers, and they snatch them!"

The screen changed to a short clip of a little girl being pulled in the sliding door of a white panel van.

"That's how they do it. They take them, give them drugs to keep them quiet, then put them on airplanes full of other taken children, then they're all flown to secret places overseas where they are literally sold to the highest bidder. Evil men compete against each other to pay the price that will let them buy the

children to be their sex toys. The smallest of girls forced to do evil things no child must ever do. Don't believe it can happen? I am going to prove that it can."

The screen changed to a close-up of Jamie's face.

"This is a special edition, and I have a very special guest who will explain all I said is true. She was trafficked as a child, groomed to be a sex slave, and when she grew older, to stay alive she started finding young girls. This woman… Pleasant, like someone you'd meet at church… She's a former sex trafficker. You'd never know it to look at her, would you?"

Cutting to a shot with both of them, Jo first kept her face to the camera.

"She's here to tell us all how such horrible things happen. I'm The One, and this is The One Show."

Turning to Jamie, she kept her concerned persona, and shook her head in sadness as the shot changed to show them talking to each other.

"My guest tonight is Jamie, and I assure you, she's very brave to be here. Jamie, thank you for coming. I feel so much pain thinking of what happened to you when you were just turning five. Why don't we start with that. Now, from what I know, your mother lived a life of sin. Drugs, sex worker, and it was just you and her out in the middle of the Mojave, correct?"

"Mike, she's alive and doesn't seem to have been beaten or hurt. That's a relief."

As they were finishing deciding on how many smoke grenades would be needed for their terror attack on Jo's compound, Cindy received a text message inviting her to watch a world-wide special event featuring sex trafficker Jamie on The One Show. It had a URL to watch the live stream, and what time it would start. Going to the living room having a smart TV that could access Web sites, they all sat, and had gotten the

text just in time for the start of the livecast.

Angie was focused on the way Jo was dressed.

"Mom, that Jo thinks she's hot stuff. I think Jamie is way better."

Cindy told Angie that was true.

"Jo's playing a sweet Angel, but she's a beautiful woman."

Mike's eyes were fixed on the screen, saying as it was a livecast Jamie could send some sort of sign he would get a hint from. Angie told him to chill.

"Mike, she sent us to a link to a URL, and it says live, but it could have been done hours ago. It's on the cloud."

He was still looking for any special signs Jamie used that only he may know. Angie was picking up on what Jo was up to, and she tugged at Cindy's sleeve.

"Mom, the way she's going, pretty soon she'll be talking all about us and then about killing Peter. I hope she doesn't put pictures of us up on the screen... well, at least not low-res snapshots or something."

Cindy didn't flinch as the pictures from the photo shoot where Vlad had a hidden camera taking video of her and Angie, naked, about to put on thong bikinis, popped up on the screen. She gave a sigh of relief as their faces were blurred out, but did nothing to hide their near-naked bodies.

"Mom, that Vlad really did you justice! Mike, think you could shoot ones like that?"

Cindy gave Angie a look that Angie had never quite seen her make before. Knowing what it meant without having it explained, Angie apologized to her and Mike. Cindy pointed to the kitchen, politely asking her if she'd like to go help Victor.

Realizing Cindy meant it, Angie went to cuddle with her, and Cindy asked if she was saying all that because seeing it upset and embarrassed her. Angie nodded her head on her upper arm, and Cindy knew she put on a brave front, but it was hard for her to watch.

They both jumped when the footage of Peter being shot by the copter guns with Eliana watching was shown. Then, after presenting the shocking footage, Jo was having Jamie explain how it happened and her part in it, then looked and asked her if she planned to stop more traffickers. Nodding, saying it would be her mission in life, Jo looked at her with concern.

"Jamie, if you know someone was trafficking girls, you'd do everything possible to stop them?"

Again nodding, saying she would, Jo shook her head.

"But, I'm concerned you may be fooling yourself. Isn't the woman you were with, the one who shot that horrible trafficker, Peter, a notorious sex trafficker herself?"

Keeping her cool, Jamie said yes, the woman had been a trafficker, but had stopped and decided to fight traffickers. Jo said she was glad to hear that. Turning to the camera, again in closeup, she said the former trafficker may have fooled everyone — including Jamie. The shot changed back to her and Jamie together.

"Jamie, I have some shocking news, and I am sad to tell you, and all my viewers, that she hadn't changed her ways. As you know, The One is committed to protecting young girls from traffickers. We have so many girls here that you can understand a trafficker would be tempted to find a way to take them if they can. I'll never let that happen. This will be hard for all watching to see, but, Jamie, hardest for you to see. Abraham..."

As she called the man's name, a gurney was rolled in front of Jo and Jamie, a body on it covered with a white sheet. Jamie looked shocked, and Jo looked at her, stopped for a moment, then told Jamie, "Prepare to face the truth." She looked at the camera.

"Two days ago, a respectable looking woman came to apply for a job as my housekeeper. But she was no housekeeper! She came to kill me! Shooting at me, she shouted she was here with you... her partner!"

She pulled the sheet, and on the gurney was Eliana.

Jamie looked at Jo, shocked, for a moment not knowing what to say. After looking, with sadness, at Eliana, she looked up at Jo.

"One, she wasn't my partner, and I didn't know she came here or did what you said. She wasn't trafficking any longer, and we worked to stop traffickers

such as Peter at any cost. What did happen was that I was kidnapped by you, and she must have come to rescue me. Please let your viewers know you're the real trafficker."

The video player went black. The stream went black. Cindy, Angie and Mike were sitting, stunned, not knowing what to do. They knew Eliana had been killed by Jo, but clearly Jamie didn't know it happened, and worse, she had just told the world that Jo was a trafficker and murderer. As Mike started to speak, the screen faded from black showing only Jo staring at the screen. She looked somber and upset.

"I want you all to rest easy. The One is safe, and we all just witnessed what being trafficked does to someone. I helped Jamie calm down, and she is resting after getting hysterical seeing her dead partner. I will help her with her trauma, and it was heartbreaking to watch her defend the trafficker. That comes from being brainwashed and abused. She still believes the trafficker had changed. It was the shock of being abused again that caused her to want to blame me, The One. Because I stopped the trafficker from taking our girls. Worry not. They are all safe and never knew anything happened. Pray for Jamie. The One will pray and guide her back to the Only One who can heal her."

Cindy got up, not wanting to talk about the livecast. Saying she had enough to Angie and Mike, she added she wanted to help Victor any way possible to speed things up, then headed to the kitchen where he was looking for any other things needed for the attack, including a strong harness for Angie just in case she'd be needed.

Looking up, smiling at her, he pointed to a chair next to him at the kitchen table, saying he would show her all he found that they could get on the way to the jet.

"In such battle, it is surprise, not even government know. Jet, it is pretty thing. Pretty thing does no have holster belt with pistols. Our grenades and weapons hidden, easy to get at when you need."

Cindy asked him how low to the compound he could fly, and when he dropped the grenades, how accurate would they land.

"Jet can go very fast up high. It can because it all sleek. When fly low, it must go slow. When needed, window open, grenades they thrown out,

jet slows down more, just enough to stay in air when near target, and then all hell lets loose. Then, can fly fast again to get up above mountain, turn around to make more attack."

Getting the idea, Cindy was wondering about flying to the compound while being watched by air traffic command.

"Cindy, no problem. We make compound destination on flight plan. We be where we say we go. Simple, they see us there, forget about us."

Victor was smiling as he looked at her. He could tell that like her mother, she was thinking every aspect of the mission through. She knew he understood as she sat thinking.

"Victor, with a flight plan, isn't the tower near the compound going to know we're on the way, and I assume they'd let Jo's crew know a plane would be landing. We don't want to alert them. Can we make it to some other place where they won't know, then go off the plan?"

He reached into his small duffel bag he had when bringing the jet to her, pulled out a box, putting it on the table. Then he pulled out a cable that he plugged into the box, and then the laptop he was working at.

"This is what I learn being Russian Commander. You can't see what is no there. This is for thing you talk about. Show where we are, where we head, all those things. I know how make this box on jet say one thing, the jet do another. See, this will tell the air traffic towers we where flight plan says we are supposed to be. Everyone one will know we go to air show in Wisconsin. I already paid late entry fee online if any check, but they no do. Just be sure. They like money, no complain it just few days from now."

Smiling at him, she said that was what a real commander knows, and others don't. Smiling, he said that was correct, and then he added one more detail.

"I think, if this is what you will want too, after we hit target, we go over big lake on way from air. Then, do what box says we do, go to air show. Be exactly where we supposed to be. I change box when on flight plan, it says we are where we are for real. We eat cheese, get some bratwurst."

Laughing, she told him he really just wanted to get some good eats there. Smiling, he said he wouldn't say no to that, or to bringing some home as well.

CHAPTER 53

"You did great. I know I gave you a shock there, but if we planned it, it wouldn't have been real. People can tell if it is or not. Sorry about that. You knew Eliana vowed to kill me, right?"

"Yes, but I didn't know more than she said that to you. I didn't know she came here or you killed her."

Jamie was angry and afraid, and told Jo how she felt.

"Dear Jamie, of course you're angry. And sure, after seeing those holes in Eliana, who wouldn't be afraid? I bet you're all worried you'll be on that gurney for my next show, don't you?"

Looking Jo with eyes wide in disbelief, she said of course she was. Jo smiled and rubbed her leg as she looked into her eyes.

"Kill someone pretty as you? I'm ruthless, but one horny bitch. Oh, I'm way more horny than ruthless. You realize I just lost Sharon. That hurt. She was my sweetie, and one hot fuck. I'm so lonely without a sweetie to lick my pussy. You know, I have all the porns you did, and I knew you really wanted to do them for some savage sex. Nasty Brian told me. I'm a big fan. Your lesbian shoots… I rub myself off when I watch them."

Jo, taking Jamie's hand, told her it was time to go back to the room she was held captive. Once there, getting into the bed with Jamie, she loudly said, "Play," and monitor started playing a compilation of her girl-on-girl porns, Jo rubbing herself between her legs, asking Jamie if she was really as good as in the movies.

Fearing for her life, Jamie had little choice other than to go along with what Jo wanted. Thinking it was the only thing that would keep her alive, she looked into Jo's eyes, nodding, saying, "Better."

Jo pulled her green dress off, then got off the bed gently pulling off her white costume, turning to show Jamie her flawless body, then admiring Jamie's as she crawled to her once on the mattress.

"You are so fucking perfect. So much better in person then in those movies. Look at your sweet pussy… Oh, fuck, I'm going to have you squirt all over my face… over… and over…"

After a bout of sex more savage than any she'd had when doing porn, Jamie was glad to hear Jo say she needed to take care of some business matters, and though she didn't want to leave she had no choice. Jamie

understood, saying she was near worn out, adding she was impressed with what a large compound she had made as Jo was getting dressed.

"All it takes is cash. A bit tricky getting help in the middle of Montana, but it wasn't as hard to do as I thought it would be. I did have a good plan. This whole spread. I inherited it from my parents. Otherwise, who knows where I'd have picked."

Jamie showed genuine surprise.

"All this land? You mean you grew up here?"

Jo stopped after she pulled the dress over her head, looking at Jamie with a sad nod.

"Sure did. Montana girl through and through."

Jamie purposely showed surprise, saying she wondered about life growing up in such an isolated area, and had been wondering how she ended up being The One. She sat up, body gleaming with sweat, showing she was waiting to hear more about it.

"Well, my full first name is a pretty good clue. Josephine. Not a name most parents would choose. But, being a Magdalene, it was, and still is, popular."

Jamie was putting pieces of the puzzle together. She had some idea of how that fit in to what she became.

"Jo, that's wild. I have a question, but I'll understand if it's not something you want to talk about. I don't know much about the Magdalenes, just that…"

Jo was nodding, laughing, and filled in her sentence.

"Yep, you're on the right track. Bigamists. I had one dad, and I can't even count how many moms. And know what? As I grew older, the wives grew younger. My father was a very important man in the church. And I'm talking all over the country important. All those old fucking elders? They can't land a dead cat let alone young pussy. My dad, he picked girls out, groomed them to be brides, and he was the guy who got little girl wives for fuckers who contributed the most money. Sound a bit like what I'm doing?"

Stunned, Jamie saw things from a totally different perspective. She was still thinking about how it all made sense.

"That's wild, Jo. I mean, you literally grew up with a trafficker who operated within the law… well, church law. It's not really legal, right?"

Sitting back on the bed, saying she had a bit of time, she said she was

impressed Jamie was connecting the pieces of the puzzle.

"No, it's tolerated, and not promoted in the press. Most states have Magdalenes in high office. Big surprise. They just say they are. It's a way to get free young snatch and it's how the church has done it forever. I grew up with their bullshit. The Magdalene men would give their daughters to my dad to be brides, and he'd give them whatever young pussies they wanted in exchange. The girls were raised knowing they'd be married off to some old fuck. And I'm talking a lot of girls all the time. Near as many as I handle now. His was more trading, but for ones not really elders, he got lots in the way of donations. I looked at all that shit, and thought, hey, I can do that, but fuck the Magdalene church. The joke is that they ended up being customers. Not big dollars, but they pay plenty with endless daughters I sell to pervs all over the world. Pretty wild how you can take your worst nightmare and become the monster."

Catching the part about it being a nightmare, Jamie asked her if she meant that she had been one of the girls to go to a church elder. Jo gave her a slight smile, and she nodded as she thought about it.

"Yeah, that was really a stupid decision on my dad's part. I was helping him with everything. Did most of the shit needed. Mostly grooming the girls. I thought I'd take over for him and all that kind of shit. When I was sixteen, he came in with this hunched-over fucker to meet me, saying he's going to marry me to him later that day... Yeah, definitely not a good decision."

Jamie realized what she meant. She volunteered finishing the story as Jo was clearly reliving it.

"So, if it were me... I'd kill him, the geezer too. Say the geezer did it as you wouldn't marry him, and he shot himself too. Well, that's sure as hell what I'd do."

Standing up, saying she just had a minute or two, Jo gave Jamie a sad smile and told her the rest to complete the picture.

"You and I, we both went through some really fucked up shit, so absolutely. I shot them. But... Well, you know how it goes. I didn't really stop there. I went on a bit of a rampage. Well, you know, actually a whole fucking shitload of a rampage. My real mother knew what was planned and the bitch didn't even tell me. Shot her next. Wow. She flew through the air like a feather. I lost it. Really fucking lost it. I shot everyone in the place. A bunch of old fucking elders waiting to pick out

cunts. Six church ladies. No girls. They were locked up in the barn we fixed up for them.

All Jamie could do was say, "Wow…"

Nodding, Jo said that said it all.

"Looking back, shooting the fuckers was the easy part. Getting rid of the bodies and not getting in trouble was a lot harder. I did it. We had a backhoe. Land where we grew some things. The law was paid to stay away, and I knew it would only be the church elders wanting to know what the fuck happened…"

Jamie sat, waiting, wondering how she survived that part, asking how she managed to not get arrested. Jo laughed, seeming back to normal… for her.

"That, sweet puss, is when I learned all about business. I got a call from the elders later that night, and they asked about my dad and girls and marriages. I was still way deep in the rampage, just getting back in after plowing them all in the ground with the backhoe. I said someone came in and shot us all up, but the brides were fine, then I pretended to cry and said the staff and my parents were all dead, and I just buried them. I said a few elders were there and ate lead too. Guess what they did?"

Jamie could only shrug, stunned by every part of the story. A sixteen-year-old girl plowing bodies after dragging them out of the house, cleaning up a mess like she'd clean up after a meal.

"It's fucking perfect. I learned the truth that fucking day, I tell you. They didn't ask a thing about any of it. Here's what they did ask. They asked if I'd be arranging the marriages from now on. They didn't care what happened. They only cared about the girls. As long as I kept them in pussy, I was home free. That, as you know, is why pussy is worth more than gold if you know who needs it."

Leaving the door open as she left the room, she turned back, pointed to the door, and then at Jamie and smiled.

"Jamie… this… Please, don't let me down."

She looked at her, smiling.

"I kind of think you just found out what happens when someone does. Check the whole place out. And, oh, silly me. I got off on talking about the rampage. I want you to know I really enjoyed your pussy. A lot…"

CHAPTER 54

Originally planning to head out the night they locked James in the safe room in Cindy's basement, they changed plans on when to carry out the air attack. Cindy said she wanted to deal with him first, and learn all he knew, adding James needed to be considered as he was more than being held in the basement, he was missing from the agency. That would lead to agents coming around asking if he had been seen.

Angie had spent time going through his phones, and she created a list, but let Mike go over it to get his take on if James was doing what they suspected. She was certain he had been connected to recent events, but also knew he was fully involved with their rescue when being trafficked and had kept Jamie out of trouble. She found hints that James may have been involved with traffickers, and she kept trying to track his bank accounts, but she had limited success as the accounts on his phone were ordinary accounts for paychecks and bills, paying credit cards and nothing out of the ordinary.

Sitting down with Mike and Cindy, she had put all she could find in an Excel spreadsheet, and Mike said he was impressed. Cindy had stopped asking her where she learned things, but said she was glad she had learned to do such a great job.

"Mom, I was home-schooled, remember? You said go to the library and get books and use their computers for free. I wasn't home eating junk food all day."

Smiling, Cindy acted surprised, saying she was sure that was what she was doing given her dress size. They both started poking each other at their waists, saying, *"As if!"*

"Mom, you must be talking about your dress size!"

Mike faked a cough, saying there was plenty from just his phones. If they had his personal computer, imagine what that would be like. Then he turned to the door down to the basement.

"We can keep him shackled, but maybe we can do a bit of barter. Trade some comfort for some information. From all this, I think he's been found out, and that really is hard for me to deal with, but it is what it is. Things like all this? He couldn't do that without others involved. It's bigger than him, and he probably wasn't the brains behind it all, just made to do things at first, then do more and more. It's like blackmail. If

we do this right, he can give names…"

Cindy looked at Angie, and like her, they were hoping James was the good guy they had always thought he was. She understood Mike wanted to see if James would turn informant, and it was worth a try. She smiled at Angie, who knew her so well she knew what she'd say to Mike.

"If you think you can do it, best to do it soon as possible. If he has higher-ups involved, and he's missing, they'll track him back to here. That will happen fast, I imagine, right?"

Mike nodded and said that would be what would happen, adding as he was federal, they would just come in, no search warrant needed. They'd find him. That was what they did best. Cindy knew that would happen if they didn't act fast.

"Okay, Mike, I can think of a few things really important. First, Charles. He's out there, and we know he's part of it. We need to get him just like we did with James. Second, we could move him. You may know of places for that. I only have the mobile home, and they'd look for him there. So, that's a way to let the agency in and not have any idea what they're talking about and say we want to help find him, I guess. Third, we lay it on the line. Give us names, switch sides, or…"

Mike looked at her. Angie knew where she was headed. She understood her mother was thinking of the safest way to kill him for the last option. She took Cindy's hand, saying she had an idea of what to do for the last option. Cindy said it may be better than hers, so she'd like to hear it.

"Mike, I'm sure my mother was thinking what I am. Well, we have a jet. We have a pilot. And if we put James on the jet and opened the door, he could decide to do right, or he can decide to go skydiving. We don't have a chute, but it would still be skydiving."

Cindy and Mike both looked at her, if only surprised that she clearly saw it as the best option. Cindy pulled her to whisper a thank you in her ear, then turning to Mike, said that was exactly what she had thought of as well.

"Angie must be watching a show on how to mind read. That's what I was thinking. Facing being tossed out of a plane, he'd turn sides with less incentive than that. And… well… I can't believe some of the things I say now. He knows we'll do it. I don't make threats. He doesn't talk, he goes out the door."

Mike looked at both of them. Sitting there, he saw a sweet suburban mother and daughter. It was as if they had just decided what to make for dinner. To anyone else, it would have them running and screaming as they got as far away as they could go. He knew that Cindy was exactly what she had to be. The world took sweet women like her and Angie and did the worst things to them, and the nicest of people. The worst happened to her when she was twelve, yet she remained a good person who knew that being good didn't stop the horrible things going on even the law wouldn't go near. She had a line between right and wrong, and the right was how she lived. The wrong was the world that didn't do right. He knew they were waiting for his take on the suggestion.

"I agree. Going down there and making threats isn't going to turn him in time. He's waiting for the agency to figure out he's been snatched and come for him. That will be where we can't rescue Jamie or do anything like we planned for a few days and that's time for Jo to kill her. What we did was a federal crime, so we go all the way with it."

Cindy called to Victor, asking if he heard the plan. He had been busy programming the little box, but looked up, saying, "Plan, good. Only option. I ready to go. Jet fueled. Is ready."

Mike stood up, saying get the car ready, and no need to make a production out of it. Get James dressed, into the car, on the plane, and one way or another, at least they'll be out of the house if a squad came. He looked, and Victor was standing by the basement door.

"I hold him. You dress him. I know you agent. Good agent. I am bastard commie all my life. Don't say a word to him. We take every hint he was here. Leave nothing. If he stupid. Make struggle, I help him sleep with little sleeping pill."

Victor pulled a old-fashioned blackjack out of his pants pocket. Mike nodded, saying everything had been done in the living room, kitchen, and the safe room. He told Angie take his guns, laptop and his phones, leave nothing with any trace. Angie nodded as Cindy got a large tote bag and started taking things James hadn't even touched.

Heading down the stairs, Victor stopped at the bottom and looked at Mike.

"I tell Cindy, now I tell you. I will do anything for her. If things go bad, blame on me. I told her mother I give life for her. I will. I be, what you call it… fall guy. Agree? It is what must be."

Shaking his hand, Mike said it was a tight team and it shouldn't come to that, but would honor what he asked. Victor punched his shoulder, saying, "Brothers." Mike realized Victor was the real deal. A man who had a code of honor even trained endlessly to not have one by the military. He hadn't been a spy. He was a fighter, a warrior, and he wore all he was with pride. Mike nodded, punching Victor's shoulder, saying, "Comrade."

As Angie went through her notes and scribbles when searching for numbers, she had been careful to do all her work from one spot and keep all the notes in one pile. Wanting to be sure nothing had slipped away, she had been working on her bed, using her nightstand to put the papers and notes on. Worrying something may have fallen behind it, she pulled it away from the wall, just enough to look to see any papers. She had been careful, and no papers had fallen behind it, but she found a small, flat device stuck to the back of the nightstand. She wouldn't have enough room to place her slim arm behind it, so she knew it had to have been pulled out to attach the device. Backing away from the front of it, she studied the carpeting, and she couldn't see any marks of it being pulled forward, even using the flashlight on her phone. Thinking it could have been placed when they first moved in, she ruled that out as she had changed the layout and the nightstand was in a different spot than when first placed. Taking her phone, using the flash, she took a picture of it and left it slightly out from the wall, then rushed downstairs as she wanted to tell Mike before he went for James.

Seeing Mike talking to Victor, they were turning to the door of the safe room but stopped, hearing her calling to them. Holding her phone out to Mike she said she had checked everything in her bedroom, and nothing to worry about as her nightstand was too close to the wall for anything to fall back there. Looking at the picture on the phone, then at Angie, he calmly said he understood, telling Victor he had to get a few more things, as he turned to go upstairs with Angie.

Victor understood Angie had shown him something that caused worry. He said he'd keep an eye on the door and nodded at them to go do what was needed. After getting to the top of the stairs, they waved to Cindy who was going over the living room, and Angie held her finger to her lips. Mike pointed to the garage and led them out the side garage door for a short walk down the street. When he felt far enough away, he

turned and asked Angie about finding it.

Telling him that there weren't any rug marks, and it had to have been placed recently as she had rearranged the room and had dusted the nightstand, he nodded and studied the device.

"This is bad. I know it looks like a wireless microphone, but that's not what it is. It's a kind of quiet bomb. It goes off and releases a toxic gas. It's deadly and fast. When it goes off, it's hard to hear, so next to a bed like this, it's perfect for when someone's asleep. I'm sure you'll have one by yours, Cindy."

They stood, all stunned. With the security system, and home most of the time, Angie said that she doubted someone broke in. It had to be someone they let inside and had left alone. Cindy agreed, then looking at Angie, said the only ones that could be was James, or Whimsey.

Looking at each other, it was a complete mystery. Mike said that even with such a threat, they needed to keep moving to get James out, and they would include that in their list of questions for him. They'd be away, so the devices weren't a concern for the moment. All agreed and headed back to the house.

Just before going in the garage, Angie stopped, and moved back down the driveway. She talked softly.

"I may be off the mark, but Mike, aren't there drugs that make someone look like they're dead. Breathing so shallow and all? I saw Whimsey wasn't moving, and she'd been with Charles. It happened in a government hospital. I mean, could that be possible? To get her away from us? Mike, you said you didn't think James was the head of it, just one and others higher up. Is what I'm saying making any sense?"

"Angie, it's the type of thinking the agency hires people to work on, and yes, it's possible. I was in the room, you didn't want to leave me alone, and you were so upset you left Whimsey to the hospital staff. And yes, there are drugs like that, and they most often are used by anesthesiologists. Not easy to get, but you can if you work in a hospital. Or, you work out of there as a shrink and know people there. I think you just opened up a new world of worry. Let's talk about it on the ride and on the jet. Now, we need to get James. Things are getting where anything could happen and now, we have one lead. Let's hope he isn't big on skydiving."

Angie and Cindy made sure the house was clean, and as they walked

to the kitchen, they heard Mike talking.

"I'm sorry, pal. This is not what I thought we'd be doing, but just keep calm. I may be injured, but our big Russian friend here is in top form, and he doesn't like anyone who would do anything to hurt Cindy or Angie…"

They had gotten James back into his clothes, and he needed a shave, but that didn't matter. His mouth was taped shut again, and he looked at Angie first, then Cindy, shaking his head to motion not to do anything to him. Seeing him trying to send a signal, Victor smacked the back of his head with the palm of his hand, and it was not a light tap. James got the message and looked away.

With everyone in the car Victor had driven to the house in, pulling out of the driveway, they were relieved to be making a proactive move. The airport wasn't far, but a few blocks from the house, Victor said there was a car behind, and it was a Tahoe.

"Black Tahoe. I wonder what kind of Yankee scum drives such tank? You want I try outrun him, or perhaps do what they no expect. I turn corner, another corner, we get out and take them out, as you say here."

Smiling at hearing gun chambers clicking rounds into Glocks, Victor didn't need an answer. He told them he'd turn the car to use as a shield when they fired. Telling Mike to get his Uzi from his duffel bag under the seat, he handed it to him just as he spun the car around to position as a surprise when the Tahoe turned the corner to follow them. James was left on the floor. Mike and Cindy got out and crouched behind the hood, Victor and Angie behind the cargo bay. The Tahoe came screeching around the corner and the driver hadn't expected their car blocking the street, sideways.

No call to start shooting was needed. As soon as the Tahoe turned, all four guns were firing into the windshield. Attempting to make a U-turn as soon as their car was seen and fired at, the Tahoe turned without slowing down, and flipped onto its side. Having watched the windshield turn red with blood, once on its side the windshield had shattered. Rising up, Mike saw two in the front seat, and both had taken hits to their faces, and he saw no need to check.

Getting back in the car, Victor drove calmly and was back on route to the airport.

Turning to look back, Angie said no way was she going to get a

Tahoe. If it can't stand up to two women, one guy who had been shot up, and just one Uzi, it was pretty lame.

"Angie, you smart girl. That is right. Tahoe just car for mommies and kiddies going to ice cream parlor. Not for one like you."

Smiling at what Victor said, she said James had told her to get a Tahoe. Now she really knew he was a douche-bag. Cindy looked at her.

"Douche-bag?"

"Mom, they sold them at Osco. I saw them when I'd buy you… ah… chocolates. Yeah, for when you got home each night."

Laughing at how Angie had gotten fast on her feet with all her blurting out questionable word uses, they were pulling up to where the jet Eliana had left Cindy was parked in a private hanger. Driving in, Victor said to wait in the car as he closed the hangar door. It didn't take long to board the jet, and as Cindy and Angie got in, it was their first time on the craft, and Angie was rubbing the leather seats, looking in cabinets, then going in the back, called to Cindy to come and see.

"Mom, can you believe this? Bed, shower, closet full of clothes. We can live here and travel to where girls are trafficked and never stay in one place!"

Smiling at Angie's excitement, she agreed it was amazing, but she also knew it had been the jet that her mother had ridden in right before she was killed. It was a bittersweet moment, but her mother had left it to her exactly for a time such as they faced.

Up front, Victor had helped Mike secure James with duct tape to a seat, then was in the cockpit flipping switches. Looking to be sure all was in order, he went out, opened the hangar door, got back in and was wasting no time. The takeoff was smooth, and Mike had worried that the agency would know about the jet and try to stop them, but that was not public knowledge yet. Once in the air, Mike turned his seat around to face James as Cindy and Angie turned theirs to face James from across the aisle. Mike looked at Cindy, just to tell her he was about to begin explaining what would happen once they reached altitude. Cindy shook her head to say no, and then leaned forward and told Mike to take the gag out of his mouth. Taking it off, James gasped for air and was sweating, but kept quiet. Cindy was calm and mannered as she talked to him.

"I'm not an agent, and I haven't been trained in playing games or

deceiving people, so I'll explain why we brought you on this flight. Now, I'm going to be telling you the truth, and I'd appreciate you doing the same in return. I hope you can do it. I'll begin with a simple question. Have you been doing things you weren't supposed to do? Things like spying on us, or not being completely honest with us?"

As he sat, seething and panicking at the same moment, Cindy took her switchblade out of her bag, pressed the release, and the blade was out, ready to use.

"I've been told it's not safe to fire a gun in here, so I'll use this. Now, it was a simple question, and I expect a yes or no answer."

His face red, seeing Cindy had moved the tip of the blade to make a quick stab, he blurted out, "Yes!"

Nodding, she said she was glad he answered honestly, and hoped he would continue.

"Now, James, were those things you did on your own, or with other people?"

His head started thrashing from side-to-side, and he was mumbling that he couldn't say, they'd kill him.

Cindy leaned back in her chair, but kept her gaze fixed on him.

"I'll have to accept that answer as a yes. At least half of it. Saying you can't answer as they'd kill you means there are others. But the part about you worrying they'd kill you? That is a no. They won't. I will. That's what this plane ride is all about. I'm going to push you out that door."

Watching her mother talk to James, Angie knew Cindy didn't make threats. She told him what she would do, and he knew she would. He sat, shaking, trying to get free. She shook her head.

"James. It's not that I want to do that, but I will. I have to save Angie, me, well, everyone here. I didn't put you on this jet. You put yourself here by ever doing anything to hurt someone on purpose. You did a very good job of it. You were very smart in the ways you hurt people, so you could use your intelligence to think of a way, other than that door over there, to get yourself off this jet, meaning once it lands. What do you think will guarantee you a return ticket?"

Wanting to say, "That's a great line!" to Cindy, Angie restrained herself, but would be sure to mention it later. She watched James about to burst and he stopped when Cindy turned to the open cockpit door, asking Victor how much longer before they could drop James without

harming anyone on the ground. James didn't wait for his answer. He started sobbing, saying he knew how, over and over. Cindy said saying that over and over wasn't what would change her mind. He looked at her. She had gotten up and was standing in the aisle, saying he needed to tell her whatever she wanted to know. It would be the only way to save himself. Cindy leaned far over, putting the knife to his throat.

"That means you tell the truth. Now, next question. How can I believe someone who sat in our house, lied about everything, had no restraint getting people killed… and planned killing all of us next? How can I ever believe you?"

He was panting, hyperventilating, struggling to get his answer out.

"The answer is you can't. You can't. Anything I say you'll think it's a lie. If I tell you everything and told the truth, you'd still kill me!"

'James, well, finally. An honest answer. I appreciate that. So, questions won't do it. Any other ideas, and I have to tell you, there isn't much time left."

James closed his eyes and was visibly thinking of what he could do. Cindy saw him struggling, so offered a suggestion.

"I can't answer it, but I would think about what if you were doing what I am to someone you wanted truth from. And you knew he was a liar. Think about what you'd do at work…"

Angie was impressed with her mother as never before. She was like right out of a superhero movie in her opinion. Watching James, she saw his eyes open wide, and he looked excited as he started explaining what may work.

"If you can't believe me, then if I called someone you would hear us talking, and that would be something you could believe. I can start with Charles… then the guy behind all this. I know that works. I've done it. Let me do it. I know you can't trust me, but it won't be me saying things, it will be them, not me!"

Calling to the cockpit, she asked if they could circle or delay things or just keep going and find another place if needed. Getting a yes back, James closed his eyes, knowing he had a chance. Cindy looked at him.

"No promises. Even if they're talking about what I need to know. Mike has shared you have all kinds of coded speech for such occasions. So, I can't believe you or them, can I?" What they say doesn't mean you get a land safe on the ground free card."

Angie hadn't brought a notepad, so was typing the Cindy zingers using her phone. Her mother was on a roll with great lines. She watched as Cindy stood, thinking, then finally nodding slightly.

"James, I tell you what. I'll tell you something I know about, then you can call the right person and talk to them about it. If what I know matches what they say to you, that would be good. It will help me know you really don't want to prove a man can fly."

Angie typed furiously, ready to shout that was really a great line.

"So, here's the thing you'll need to prove to me. Ready?"

Nodding, he said he understood, and he was thankful for the idea.

"Don't thank me yet. I doubt that's what you'll be doing if I push you out that door on the way down. So, this is very upsetting to me, and I do plan to do something about it to whoever did it. Angie found a recently planted device that when triggered, releases a gas that kills when close enough. It was inches from the pillow on her bed. It was thin, round, and stuck to the back of her nightstand. Who ordered it put there, who put it on the nightstand, and when is it going to be used? Tell me all that, then call someone who will confirm what you told me."

Without hesitating, James said he had answers.

"Shit, this is one that goes deep. I'll keep it short. You killed that sheik. His father is the king, and is doing deals with the vice president. He was really pissed and said he wanted who did it dead. The VP called Allan, CIA director, and got the details. I wrote him a report. He hopped a jet, then walked into my office with the discs. He said since I was in with you, put them on whatever is next to both your pillows when you sleep, then tell him they're in place. I put them there when I used the upstairs bathroom about a week ago. It doesn't take much. Just tip it forward to get at the back, toe holding the base on the front in place so it doesn't look like it was moved, they stick right on. I did yours and Angie's. Since then, I've been dreading learning they were set off. I can call Allan and ask him when he plans to use them, and I'm worried I didn't do it right."

Filled with rage, Cindy managed to keep her manner calm, the told him, "Call him. On speaker."

Handing him his phone, she knew that would be the only way anyone he called would feel secure, and why she had Angie bring it with. Nodding, she took the phone, called the number, and had the

speakerphone going. Mike, Cindy and Angie all were silent, but Angie was recording the speakerphone call on her phone which she knew was a best practice. Cindy noticed, smiling at her, nodding that she was impressed. After getting an assistant, James was talking to Allan, the man he reported to.

"Hi Allan… yeah, we need to catch up, so lunch next week maybe? You set the time and place… things are going along okay, but I'm concerned about those pies you like so much… yep, I know you like things delivered, but I don't know if they're fresh… Well, I left them a while ago, and… yeah, this is the right phone it's encrypted, or I wouldn't have used it… looks good on your side? Okay, good, this isn't a call to talk around the topic… Yep, I'm concerned about the discs. I know they're new and hardly field tested. I'm sure I placed them right, and you said someone was going to trigger them a few days ago, but nothing's happened… tonight? I seem to have missed that message… No, I don't care when, but my guy at the security system place is getting nervous. He doesn't work tonight or tomorrow… Yeah, to get in and get those out, clean things up if he's not there to open up for us… No, Mike showed it all to me. Cutting power, jamming signals, it's all about that. So, wait? Okay, I'll get to him and tell him it's just a schedule change… Did you tell the Veep we did it? Mike? He's weeping and wailing about Sharon… Oh, shit, that's not going to be easy. Rickfeld? Yeah, but I think we need to slow down on this… Three down in a week, now three more? Okay, it's your call, but I think it looks pretty much like our calling card, and that's what I'm supposed to look out for… No, I don't work well with Rickfeld. I don't trust him… Oh, and I know the thing isn't supposed to show on an autopsy, but mother and daughter both dead, no discernible cause? I know on paper it won't show that way, but still… Getting onto shaky ground. Okay, I'll confirm once I've updated the alarm guy… Yep, Antonio's sounds great. I hope we're past all this shit by then… Okay, see you then."

Not looking at James as the call ended, Cindy was looking at Mike, who was staring at James.

"Mike, before you go off on how you're on the hit list, do you know all the people mentioned?"

Taking a deep breath, he kept his stare on James as he answered.

"All but one. Allan, sure. Rickfeld. Gun for hire. No loyalties, works

for whoever pays the most. Well, I don't know the vice president, so a concern is the inside man at the security company. I'm so sorry, Cindy. I vetted them and didn't find anyone to worry about. James, good time to pony up. Is there a guy there, or was it going to be you keying the code in?"

James felt better as he had shifted their focus to others. He wanted to tell them the security guy was a new find.

"It wasn't that you didn't run them right. When this came down, I knew I couldn't just use a code. It's code, voice and facial so all I could do is get someone inside. Everyone has a place where you can turn them, you know that. I found one and he doesn't know what's going to happen when he unlocks. Just retired from another agency, wife died a few months back. You know how it goes. He can't live to tell. Better than a guy with a family or dependents. I took his dog. His wife's dog…"

Just as Mike was going to lay into James about being next on the list, and how he could do that to Cindy and Angie, he was stopped before starting by Cindy again.

"Mike, no need for that now. I want to ask one more question. About Charles."

Mike looked at her and picked up on the "no need for anything now" reference. She looked at James, who asked if she understood he had been straight and the stories matched. He almost looked smug that he had. She leaned forward to face him again.

"Yes, that means you can do it. Let's see if you can keep doing it. Now, about Charles. Simple question. No need to call him. Is he in on everything? Part of it all?"

James stared at her. He knew he had to answer to have any chance of coming out of things alive. He needed to make it where they needed him to deal with things happening next. He told her what she needed to hear.

"Yes. I brought him in. We were in the same troop in Iraq. You learn about a guy who gets off on killing women and kids and having a beer after. He had no problem doing any of that. He's stone cold. And having the shrink for all this? People open up to him. I have files on everyone he's worked with. He doesn't have to, but if needed, he'd have no problem taking anyone out. Like I said. Stone cold."

Cindy hadn't changed expressions. She said that was something they were sure of, but wanted to hear it from him. James looked shocked that

they knew, but didn't say anything.

"James, you said he'd kill someone if needed. Did he kill Whimsey?"

Not fazed at the question, he didn't need to think about how to answer.

"No. I'll make it simple. He was the last one with her. He's a medical doctor. He's CIA. He has access to things the FDA will never hear of. One is to make someone slow down so much even the best doctor will sign the death certificate. Charles waited until he was alone with Whimsey, told her what he was going to inject her with, and she acted like she was sleeping. He injects her and leaves, but it raised questions. He had said he was going to say he had a suicide call, and she was asleep, so he had a reason but didn't tell anyone when he left. He didn't kill Whimsy, she's alive and well. One of ours. Older than she looks. Gland case. If you want, I'll call her."

It was shocking news. Although they all showed a reaction, there were no comments. Cindy was working things, and she just nodded.

"I knew that was strange. Why didn't you have her plant the discs? Well, never mind. They were your doing no matter how. Yes, call her. I need the number and where she's at. That should wrap things up. You've surprised me. Not that you are what you are, but that you've done what I've asked. Now, get Whimsey on the phone. Just a checking up on her call. Say the number and address out loud and Angie will copy it to her phone."

James looked on his phone to show the full number, read it out, said it was an ordinary cell, and she could be in a safe house or anywhere right now, so he'd ask her. Cindy nodded as she hit the call button.

"Whims, how's my gal? Nah, just making sure you're keeping low... No, went off just as planned. I need to talk to Charles. Leaving like he did wasn't plan. You were out, I know, but he just walked away... No, didn't call out there's something wrong with you like he was told to... You're with him? Oh... I get it now... Hey, who you fuck is no business of mine if it isn't assigned. Let me talk to him. Still at the lake house? Good, nice place. I'll stop by if I can... No, come on, not just for some head, well, ax that, fuck yeah. A couple of good ones as you owe me... Well, give me the big guy... Charles, risky going to the house, pal... I know you know what you're doing, but what the fuck was with that ditching at the hospital... No, no questions,

except from me. Not how it was supposed to happen… Oh, I think I'd do the same, then. Old wounds that never heal. Okay, but you know I need updates when things change… No, just making sure she's where she is if I need her. Well, have fun getting your dick sucked, we'll talk tomorrow… Yeah, heads up means give one, not get one."

"Two birds with that one. You see how I work. I can do it for you. You can pay more, and I have the news you want to read about."

Leaning forward even more, Cindy said she'd give him just the headline.

"You say that now. I'm sure you've made that promise many times. You've used a lot of people. You killed a lot of people. None of it bothers you."

James was looking at Cindy as if she was asking a question.

"No more than when you killed the guy who bought you. First time, yeah. After that, it didn't matter. It's stuff that needs to be done. I can do it and still sleep. I can do that for you. I'm good at it. You have a lot of traffickers to take out. You need someone like me."

Leaning back, she nodded her chin up to Mike, and he knew that meant tell Victor he needed to head down so the door could be opened. James was bound securely to the seat. Mike took duct tape and first taped his mouth shut, nodded to Cindy, then went to the cockpit. As he walked back, they all felt the plane descending.

"Use the cargo door in back. He'll open and close it as we do the same with a door on the floor. It's right at the back on this model. Altitude in about five minutes…"

Cindy looked at James, who was thrashing, his eyes bulging, and he was in a full state of panic. Cindy was calm as she talked to him.

"Thank you for doing what I asked, and not saying you were taken. I'd have stabbed you. You did the calls and gave the information right, but you did make a few mistakes…"

She watched as his face grew bright red, and he was hurting himself trying to get himself free. She didn't take her eyes off him and wanted him to feel how the people he killed felt when he was in her seat. He finally stopped, looking at her, clearly wondering what else he had done wrong as there still could be a chance to redeem himself. She shook her head.

"You are actually wondering what you did wrong, aren't you? You don't have a clue, do you? I'll make it simple for you as you kindly did

for me. You put a disc in my daughter's room to kill her. Do you think I did all I've done all my life for her to have you come and put some little disc there and end her life? I know you think that's something you can do. I don't. She was no threat to you like the sheik was to us. You did so much more. You know that. I'm going to do what you seem proud to do. Eliminate a problem. I'm sure you're an expert at surviving in such situations, and I know you'll try to put up a fight. Victor brought this little .22 for me to use. He said it won't go through you and hit the cabin. James, accept the truth. You drop. One way or the other. Put up any resistance when we walk you to the door in the back, Mike will turn you to face me. I want you to see my face as I fire. Before you go out, I'll shoot, but not to kill. Just to stop you from throwing yourself around. Now, Angie's going to cut you from the seat. Get up, don't struggle or I'll stop you with a shot and keep shooting until you get it right. Like you told me. Again, just as you did, I'll make it simple. You get up and walk to the back. Very simple thing to do. After Angie gets the door up and you see the cargo door is open, that is very simple. Get off my jet."

Having reached in her bag, she had a small pistol, cocked and ready to fire. As Angie cut the tape holding him to the seat, he started to lunge at Cindy. Firing, she shot him once in his upper chest, and it didn't make much of a hole, and didn't go out his back. Mike grabbed him by the cuffs on his wrists behind his back. He yanked up where James was bent over but could still walk. Angie was ahead, already opening the carpeted panel on the floor.

Mike called out to Victor they were headed back, Victor using the cabin PA to say it he was opening the cargo door. It was enough of a walk for James to fake a collapse and fall to the floor. Cindy was walking behind Mike leading James to the back. As James fell, Mike moved to the side between seats, giving Cindy enough room for another shot. Hitting his shoulder, he stayed down on the floor, and it was clear he would have to be dragged. Using one foot to hold him down, Mike managed to step on him and get in front of him. Grabbing him by the shoulders of his jacket, slowly dragging him to the back, James kept spreading his feet to try to stop from being pulled by hooking them on seat bases. Mike was strong enough, even with injuries, to keep dragging him.

They all felt the cold blast coming from the open cargo door, and Mike was shaking his head to Cindy. She understood.

"Mike, he won't do it himself. You're injured. I guess just push him out slowly, face down. If needed, I'll shoot him in the head so he can't fight. Only if needed. I want him to understand what killing is to the one being killed. I'm sure he never thought about how it felt. Keep pushing until he's out."

It was a slow, sorry sight, but while James screamed through his gag, pushed inch by inch, his head was eventually over the open hatch. Mike kept pushing him to where he got his belt, and that had him half over the edge of the frame. Looking up at Cindy and Angie, panting from how hard doing it had been, he finally pulled the ties at his ankles upwards. From lifting both feet up high enough, gravity sent James down and out of the plane. Angie said she'd close the floor panel, and Mike went to sit and catch his breath. Cindy used the intercom phone to tell Victor the cargo door could be closed.

Feeling the jet head upwards, they saw the trail of blood on the carpeted floor, though not much. Cindy asked Angie to see if there was a cleaner as it was best to clean it away before they landed. Making sure Mike was alright, he said he was just worn out from the dragging, and he would catch his breath in a few minutes. Turning, she saw Angie had found some Resolve carpet stain cleaner and a roll of paper towels.

"Mom, after I clean it all up, I think we need to be litterbugs and throw the paper towels out so there's nothing here..."

"Yes, that's a good idea. That .22 sure doesn't make much of a mess. I didn't see anything on the seats, just the rug. I knew my mother would have supplies to clean up..."

They looked at each other, nodding, each knowing what she was saying.

Sitting down, Cindy putting the .22 back in her bag, telling Mike it was not one that could be traced according to Victor, asking if it should go out with the soiled towels. He said if they were over water that would be best, and she agreed she didn't want someone to find it and use it for something.

After getting up and telling Victor they wanted to sink the gun, he said Ukrainian smarts are good smarts, he'd let them know when, and just flush the .22 and bloody towels down the toilet and he dump it when over water.

Telling Angie what to do, giving her the gun and the bullets, she

looked at the carpet and said it was fine. After Angie sat back down, they turned their seats to face each other. Cindy looked at them both, sighed, and shook her head in amazement.

"Well, Whimsey now. Not to rescue, to make sure she doesn't kill us."

"Mom. Another flight like this?"

CHAPTER 55

"Jo, I did everything I could to get away from trafficking. I know you grew up like this, I did too. You have all this beautiful land, you're beautiful, creative, why didn't you just stop… get away?"

Looking at her, Jo said she'd explain once away from the compound. She was taking Jamie on a tour of her property and said riding would be best to see it all. Jamie had asked ride what?.

"Horses! What else do you ride? Oh, well, put porn aside and answer that."

Jamie laughed, realizing people still rode horses and she was about to.

"Funny, I forgot about things like that. I did see a casting call for someone making videos of girls riding horses and getting off on the rubbing… but… I think there may have been more than that planned. The old hung like a horse saying had to come from somewhere."

Reaching a stable that was as well-kept as the rest of the buildings, one of Jo's men had two horses ready and saddled. The man helped Jamie get on her horse and told her the mare was a gentle thing, and she just needed to hold on to the saddle horn to not fall off. He wasn't being condescending, she had told him when walking up to the mare she'd never ridden a horse before, and he said he'd prepared the right horse, just in case.

Jo needed no help as she mounted her stallion, a good-sized horse who was well-groomed and seemed to be gentle and proud in nature. After a few basic instructions from the groom, Jo said the mare knew how to follow along, and let her do the thinking. As they walked, the horses were a surprise, the same as the whole world Jo had around her. Jamie thought it a strange mix of dreams and nightmares, but it was all-too real.

Having her stallion ride alongside of Jamie's mare, Jo was smiling, patting her horse's neck, and started talking about what Jamie had asked on their way to the stable.

"I guess if I hadn't shot my parents and the elders, and my parents hadn't been doing what they had, then I'd have turned this into a lodge for getaways or even for making westerns. But I shot them all and knew if I didn't keep the whole thing going, I'd be dead or in jail. Getting away was all I dreamed about before it all happened. Outsiders don't

know about hard-line church leaders out here. We didn't want anything to do with the outside world. So, no TV, no movies, no magazines except about the church. Hell, I thought every old man had a stable of fillies like we set up. I was so isolated."

Jamie understood that. She had grown up with rich men who were married. The one keeping her longest was in his sixties and his wife knew he needed a toy to keep him happy. She wasn't going to leave him over some plaything, and she wanted to get all his money when he died. She treated Jamie like a servant, the same as if she performed a household chore in service to the head of the household. For a long time, she assumed all married couples had a girl like her as part of their staff. She learned later that it wasn't unusual, just more often it was a mistress or a maid, not a preschooler.

"I can relate to that. I was taken so young I just thought old men and little girls was how the world worked. So, was it just lining you up with a husband that sent you into your rampage?"

Jo looked at her, showing a sincere smile and she nodded.

"Yes, and I'm touched. You called it my rampage. That's sweet of you. It wasn't just the man or being surprised that day. I was doing most of the work, then find out he thought I was just another bride. It was all that, the whole being a girl watching other girls cringe and the elders lifting their dresses to check their cunts. All of it, coming together, and it was insulting to me. And, well, I was fuckin' pissed my dad had been fucking me, and I thought I was more special than my mother. Then I find out he'd been fucking me along with every one of the brides. Started in on me real young. Seven. My mom knew. I thought I should be the only one he fucked. It was all so fucked up, but that's why. That's what I was upset at. I was just another fuck, and then another bride. So, I shot the motherfucker and any fucker who looked at me that day. Those geezers all wanted to fuck me, so I fucked them instead. Now… all this? This is payback for all that."

As much as Jamie wanted to think of Jo as some crazy monster, she understood everything she said, and what she was doing now. Jo looked at her, nodding that she knew what she meant.

"This whole world is one totally fucked-up place. And the pervs fucking little girls shit… it's the only side of it I've really ever known. I thought everyone was like your family or the creeps who fucked me.

And then, all the trafficking shit. I understand your wanting to get back, but don't you ever think about how they win when you keep doing this all? We were both groomed to think this was how things are, but they're not. The girls are going to end up all fucked up. They'll be hurt like we both were. I'm glad to not be doing that anymore."

Riding up an inclined path, soon they were high enough to have a view of the compound and the other mountains. Jo stopped the ride at a grove of trees and a clearing nestled up on the mountain they were riding. Tying the reins to a tree, she had a blanket tied to her saddle and put it down for them to relax on and enjoy the view.

"Sure, thought about that a lot. If I left, it would still all keep going. It's a hard fuckin' truth. The church is no different than the whole fuckin' world and nothings going to change. One thing I know about myself is that I'm good at this. I don't operate like other traffickers. I run it like the church wants. It's a bit of trafficking, and a bit of matchmaking. Well, that's how it was for quite a while. Then I met Peter. He was a Magdalene. The zealot fuckers are all over the world. Same as other cult groups. The B'hai, so many more. He came to a big prayer meeting we held, actually a thing to pick out brides. He introduced himself and suggested we work together as he had elders who wanted American girls. He'd already talked to elders who were keen on fucking little cunts from Peru. Kind of an exchange program. He was really into it, but like everything in this fucked up world, it all got out of control. I was happy here, and fine letting him lead an expansion. In a few years, we were shipping brides all over the world. I was making a whole shitload of money as it stopped being only church elders. Elders agreed with Peter to open things up to highest donors, and they sure weren't saying prayers before they fucked little girls. When he made a meeting with world leaders set up for me, I was sitting there with men who thought they could do whatever the fuck they wanted. It was like being in a room full of elders inspecting brides and saying which one's they wanted. I looked at them and they made me sick. They weren't brought up in the church. They were just regular rich old sick fuckers. I wanted to fuck them up, and I did. I played them, filmed them, then threatened them. And with that came guns and that's what Peter did so well. He was a killer, scary as all fuck, really. Suddenly it's like I'm in Scarface, you know, the movie. Since then, until Peter got it, I was afraid to do

anything else. Now, maybe. I have enough money to never worry about money again. I had Sharon, but, Peter was so fucked up with holy shit, he said he was going to tell the Elders he was the true One, and God told him to replace me. Peter was big on doing his Jo's a sinner thing. You know, me being with a woman… He's fucking an eight-year-old in the ass each day and I was the sinner. Fuckin' crazy fucker, I tell you."

Listening to the story, Jamie knew how easy it was to fall into a world you can't leave. She had kept doing horrific things to get the man who groomed her from her early teens on. She couldn't think trafficking girls was justified only so she could justify killing him to herself. She had trafficked girls, and there were always reasons, all of them lies.

"Well, Peter's in the choir in the sky, and you said you were set with money. You could ride back, say bye to everyone, and take life easy. I bet you think you'd get in all kinds of trouble for what you've done. I thought that too. But I had my list, and getting on the other side, helping them, I didn't get in trouble. I got back at the rich fucks better that way. It's payback, and I think you'd get off on going that route."

Jo rubbed Jamie's cheek, then kissed her.

"Are you worried about me? Jamie, I think you are? Shouldn't you want to kill me for kidnapping you and all?"

Putting her nose to hers, she started kissing her with passion, unbuttoning her shirt, whispering into her ear as she started undoing jeans she had given her.

"Do you think I kidnapped you because of all this stuff? No. I think you're beautiful. Sharon had told me about you, some phone pictures, links to your movies. I wanted to see if we could hit it off. We have a lot in common, and I'm sorry for taking you like that. It was stupid, and wrong. I should have gotten together with you the right way…"

Jamie knew there was no way to be sure if she wasn't playing her or not. She could mean what she said. She wasn't carrying a weapon, they were alone, no guards she could see, and she had taken both their clothes off and was making love, not having sex. She didn't expect what had happened, but she knew it was something she needed to put to the test.

"Jo, that was nice, what you said. I want to trust all of it, and do things right as well. You know I have Mike. We're in love. And he saved my life in so many ways. I'm not going to leave him, or hurt him."

Looking up at her from licking her pussy, Jo nodded, and didn't act

upset in any way. She looked at her in a loving way.

"I'm not asking you to, and I wouldn't want you to."

Going back down on her, Jamie again thought she seemed sincere. She was confused at what she had in mind. Deciding to keep things going, she talked as she was getting tender licks.

"Well, I don't know how things could work out. What were you thinking? All three of us, something like that?"

Jo looked up again. She closed her eyes, and then moved up to look her in the eyes.

"That would be up to Mike. Well, the three of us, really. When we get back, maybe call him. Let him know you're okay and all. I don't know. Let's see how we do together first. I think, for now, if we get to know each other, some good things can happen. I mean like what you were talking about. I don't know. I didn't expect anything like this. So, can we just make love? We talked a lot, and I need to do this right now."

Jamie kissed her, and taking no chances, said, "Me too."

After endless orgasms, they rode back to have dinner. Jamie had been thinking about how Jo said her operation was world-wide. She asked how Peter gained so much ground so quickly, as that surprised her. Jo agreed it would seem a surprise, but once back at her building, they sat in Jo's room and she put a map of the world on a large screen, and it was filled with check marks in most all lands.

"Jamie, all the marks, they're all places where I get girls from, and send special girls too. Pretty wild, and so many. That's why the Magdalenes keep things to themselves. I didn't do any of this. Wow, the church has missionaries, and they go out and spread the word… well, spread legs apart and get a lot of pussy which is why the fuck they're out there. Peter went to each place, gun in hand, and said there was a new mission. He converted the converters so to speak. Now that he's fucking cherubs in the ass, I'm supplying the elders. I've always had the missions and missionaries working with me, just as they did my father. I tell you, if not for him, and the Magdalene church, all the geezer fuckers would be singing…"

She stood up, doing a little dance, singing an old blues tune as Jamie watched, nodding she understood.

I'm standing on the corner with a dollar in my hand, I'm a lookin' for a woman, who's a looking for a man. Tell me how long, do I have to wait, can

I get you now, or do I hesitate."

She was smiling, pausing to say the next part was priceless.

"Oh pussy ain't nothing , but meat on a bone, you can take it, you can eat it, or you can leave it alone."

Jamie was laughing, asking if it was an old church song. Jo said that may be as they sure worked the south a long time.

Then she started singing another song, saying it was a *yipee-eye-aye* old cowboy song about the nature life where her ranch was, and the virtue of Magdalene women.

"Blue mountain you're azure deep. Blue mountain your sides are steep. Blue mountain with a horse head upon your side, you have won my love to keep. I trade at Munson's store. There's bullet holes in the door. His calico treasures my pony can measure, when I'm drunk and I'm feeling sore. I chum with Latigo Gordon. I drink at the blue goose saloon. I dance all night with those Magdalene gals, and ride home beneath the moon."

"Yep, that's been the story for a long time. That Blue Mountain, it's the one we rode up today. And the song was first written to say fuck all night with those Magdalene gals, their asses white as the moon. So, Jamie, to the world, to anyone looking in on me, this is a Magdalene faction sanctioned by the Elders. If I get out, they'll get someone to fill in. This is part of the religion. It's not a cult."

Realizing Jo was building on the status of the church, she didn't understand the need for killing and things she knew had happened and figured best to ask about it.

"Jo, that's all something I would never have guessed. Quite an operation. But I'm getting confused. You have the church and all kinds of devoted followers. Why the killing? Why draw attention to all of this? I was kidnapped... I just don't get it."

Sitting back down, Jo was looking all around the room. Jamie knew she was thinking about how to explain all that had happened and why.

"The religion is a blessing and a curse. The whole fuckin' religion was based on some old perv wanting young cunt, and guys sure as fuck converted for that sermon. To work, it needs an endless supply of young cunt. I'd say, well... about seven to one guy. To get young cunt, you need more and more men with families or now baby mommas. Converts... they're usually just off drugs or out of jail for perving. Then, oh glorious day, they find us. When they figure out what the church really is all

about, they go off and do things that crosses all kinds of lines. Like Peter before he was torn in two by the copter fire. This wasn't enough for him. He wanted to start his own church. A real church, see... he was a thumper. Pounded the good book, went all in. That's what happened with Sharon. A true believer, started to think I was sinning. She used you all to get me. I don't need that exposure, and I've had to do things to stop the crazies. I mean that. Give a junkie a fix of religion, they get really crazy."

Jamie was getting the big picture, and it wasn't good. It was like a snowball rolling down a mountain full of snow. She knew it would get bigger and bigger. It was headed to Jo and would come soon.

"That's scary. So, it's not the parents of most of the girls as they think of it as church duty. The rich fucks, well, if they are flush with girls and safe, they want you to keep going, and the missionaries, well, I guess some get fanatical. So, you solicit and recruit on college campuses. Is that where the trouble comes from most?"

Nodding, Jo said it worked for a time, but now something she can't control. The elders insist on the outreach to grow the funds and all, but that ends up with people like Sharon who start off helping, but then get fanatical.

"Well, you see how much I deal with. I delegated to people like Peter, but I'm pulling all those types in. Jamie, there's no good way to stop them. Money doesn't do it. Nothing really works, so the elders, they're mostly ranchers, we meet once a month. They said if a wolf attacks the herd, all you can do is protect the herd, and it's no different for my herd. They gave the green light to kill anyone attacking this operation. Well, it's what makes it hard for me to run off, or say I want to stop. I'd be a wolf who threatened the herd."

Looking at her computer screen, she said she needed to write up the show for that night, and it wouldn't take long. Jamie asked her what the show would be about. Jo smiled, and said it was what most all the shows were about. Putting preteen wives on display naked for the elders to make their picks.

"Jamie, you can be my hostess... do the hand flip when I say a girl's name and age. I think that would be fun, and the church would love it."

"Well, I don't think I'm ready for sequin gowns and the big smile. Oh, I've been thinking about when we talked up on the mountain...

and what about Mike? I'd like to get this settled in my head. I'd like to call him. Jo, he's thinking I'm dead or a captive... which I am. He's going to come for me, and for what? And Cindy, she shot a buyer straight down into his head while he was licking her clit. That's not someone who tells you she's going to kill you and you think she won't find a way. So, you die, or she dies. She's someone to have on your side."

Listening to Jamie, realizing she didn't know much about the people who loved her, she was warning her that everyone would lose in some way. She said they were more alike than different. They weren't like people such as Peter, but like all abused women, Cindy had a trust issue which was going to be hard to overcome.

"Jamie, I'm going to lay things out and maybe you can help me. My life... it's been people I should trust, and they fucked me over. I've worked to make it where it's hard for anyone to hurt me now. I can't be hurt again. I can't... That all may be true, but wow, if not, rampage time... I don't want that ever again."

Looking at Jo, Jamie saw the hurt she had lived with growing up, and she had been ready to get killed rather than keep going. Looking at Jo was looking at herself when she went to kill Brian. She didn't know how words would change how Jo felt. It would need to be where what people like Mike and Cindy had done for her that may help her turn around, and she knew that they would see her with an open heart if she wasn't pointing a gun at them... or kept her prisoner. The best hope for Jo was for her to trust her, and then Mike, Cindy and Angie. It was going to be harder than it had been with her, but then she realized it was making love to Mike, letting him see what she was when making love that had started an understanding of each other. She had made love to Jo, and found she was thinking of her differently because of it. She may be, to Jo, what Mike had been to her.

"I just want it to be where we both trust each other. I was feeling like you are right now when I made love with Mike. Love, not sex. It was really the first time I ever made love. This world we're in? There's no love. It's just sex. When we've been together, I felt a lot more than sex. Maybe I'm stupid, but I hope not. Being loved... that's what changed me. I think we've been hurt, and we shouldn't ever hurt each other. I know we just met, but... I don't know... It's like we've known each other forever. I know how hurt you are. I'm not going to hurt you. Jo... please, don't

hurt me. Better to kill me than to hurt me. I don't want to be what I was before."

Looking at her, Jo's expression made it hard to know if she was believed. Jo masked her emotions and that was making it hard to know if she was a genuinely hurt person, or flat-out a sick monster after all that she had been through. She would find out soon enough. She wanted her to know she was going to tell the truth no matter what happened to her.

"Listening in? Do it, don't do it. It won't change what I talk to him about. But I'd like to know if you'll be listening, or recording. Even thinking about it is upsetting. If you do, I get it. I'm hoping that this isn't where I have to be worried all the time. Me calling him is about not having him come here and having anyone killed. If I don't call him, they come for me. I'm calling so that doesn't happen. If you want, be in on the call. I'll tell him what I've just said to you."

Looking at her, she saw wheels turning from what she said. Then Jo said she had planned to listen in at first, but that was creepy. She added "No. I'm not planning being in on the call."

Jo sat, looked at her computer, shook her head and started talking to Jamie as she sat across from her.

"I'm not interested in fucking things up by getting off on the nice path we rode earlier. Yeah, call, say what you want. Nothing you've learned is a secret. I didn't even know Eliana, and she came to kill me, and she would have. Her or me. I had no issue with her other than she said she'd shoot me in the head. I know Sharon went off, but that wasn't my deal at all. She was on something, or it was that Whimsey. None of that was my thing. That's all there is. You can tell him all that. It's the truth. Oh, and Cindy threatened me, and I still don't know what she has planned. But what's she going to do? Send a fighter jet here and do a Nam village thing on me?"

Jamie saw a desperation, and she wanted, just as she did, to be understood. Everything she said was true, based on what Peter and Sharon had done, and they were doing things Jo hadn't initiated. She was right. The threats weren't based on her direct actions, and they may have looked at things differently if she hadn't killed Eliana. She realized, as Jo said, it was kill or be killed. She needed to get everyone to figure out how to stop a war if possible.

"Jo, that's what I want to tell him. This is all about what Peter and

Sharon did. I can explain that, but it's really about killing Cindy's mother, and I hear you. She would have killed you, so I can see if there was some reason. I'm not going to play games. This is something, well, maybe I can get everyone on track. And, Jo, no need to defend yourself for the things that have happened. It's when people don't talk to each other. That's why I need to come out and just tell all I know."

Handing Jamie a cell phone from her desk, she nodded, saying she needed to get to the studio, and later she'd talk with anyone she wanted.

"I'm not going to listen in. Do one thing for me. Ask him if she's still out for me, and maybe say that's silly now that we've made peace… and a whole lot of loving. Oh… well, scratch that… maybe not much about that just yet. I keep forgetting he's your boyfriend. I'd love if he'd get up here and see what the two of us can do to a hard cock. If that's what you wanted. I'm not out to take your guy."

Left with the phone and the thought of Jo and her doing a three-way with Mike, she felt aroused. She hadn't earlier when Jo mentioned it. She knew she needed to keep an eye on what was right, not what she was excited by. At the same time she sat, thinking about it, having a fantasy, and she kept thinking he'd be one lucky boy if he made nice-nice with Jo.

Shaking herself, shocked at her thoughts, she took a deep breath, deciding to wait before she dialed Mike's number. She knew herself, and sex was something she had problems with. The line between love and sex, between self-worth and not having any, those had been flipped around from being sexualized so young.

Thinking more, she realized it was fucking Mike the day they met that was the start of learning about each other. It could work at times, but this one? She knew she had cheated on Mike by letting Jo have sex with her. She sat there, knowing that when your life was at stake, a person is capable of anything.

PART SEVEN
The Remains

CHAPTER 56

Once the jet landed, Cindy said going home was a problem as it had the poison gas discs placed and the house was a target for a hired hitman to set them off. She asked Mike if they could do anything about it.

"I think I have an answer. The gas is only going to harm someone about three feet away, then it goes inert. You could sleep in the bedrooms, or simple answer is I take the two nightstands down to the safe room and lock them up. Regular bed routine and let them go off. I think we're safest in the house. I need to get at the guy who did the unlock. That will be easy."

Cindy said if he thought it would be safe, she agreed, adding they needed to do a search to find any others that had been planted. She pointed out she had told James there were two, but as he was answering, not volunteering, she worried about that. Mike said he was thinking that as well, and it was a priority. Angie looked at Mike, and she had a serious look on her face.

"Mike. What about the hitman who was hired to set them off. Are you going to go after him?"

Mike was concerned about that but said the thing to do was use him to do the opposite of what he was hired to do. He knew the man worked for the highest bidder.

"He'll go with the most money. If we pay him double, I'd suggest we tell him to take down Allan. He's a gun for hire and doesn't know James isn't going to be able to pay him yet. I had an idea. I tell him that will never happen now, and Allan isn't going to pay him so he may just pass this job by and hit Allan for not paying what James arranged for. I'll tell him we may have more work for him soon. I'm sure he'll turn."

Angie was on a roll.

"Mike, what about Whimsey and Charles? Can we use him for them?"

Mike looked over to Cindy, and Cindy looked at Angie. She understood there were a lot of new twists and dangers, but Angie was fixed on hiring a hitman suddenly.

"Angie, don't you think we should find out more about Whimsey? What we heard… it could be she was there with a gun pointed at her head. Charles, he's a killer, at least that's what James said. And hearing

him on the call sure proved that. But Whimsey may be trapped into doing what the agency says. I'm not leaning that way, but Charles? Certainly. And soon as possible. He'll figure out we hit James, so we'll come for him next. Mike, can you hire that man to get Charles, but have him bring Whimsey to us?"

After listening to the idea, he said it was something he could ask for, and agreed it would be best to get Whimsey and find out what her story was. Angie was shaking her head as she didn't agree.

"Mike, playing good guy in a bad world means they get us first... like those gas bombs. If Whimsey wanted to, she'd call us. She'd find a way. If she's that smart to fool, like, everybody, I think she'd use her sex stuff to have her way. And why not do to Charles what we did with James? And, we didn't buy all our guns to hire out. We can do it. Maybe I'm just a girl, and don't know much yet, but hire a guy like that, if someone pays him more than we would, he'd turn on us. I think we need to do things ourselves as we can't trust anyone."

Cindy looked at Mike, and then at Angie, holding out her hand for her to take and sit with her on the couch. She realized she was thinking about things in a way she hadn't, and all her points were good ones.

"Mike. I think Angie has a good point. A gun for hire? He goes at Charles, and using agency money, he buys him off, same as we want to do. Angie, you have me thinking. The guy knows all about us now. Who knows what a man like that will do? I don't want to find out. Mike, a man like that... would he worry if I called him and said I wanted to hire him. Have him come here. Would he think we're setting him up?"

"Mom, you're on fire. He comes here and can we do a James on him."

Listening to Cindy and Angie talk, Mike wanted to get a word in, but thought it best to hear all their ideas first. They both turned to look at him, waiting to see if he agreed.

"I admit, I'm still thinking like an agency guy at times. Their protocols and rules. All the people right now? None have played by any rules. I've been thinking all this lately. We're talking about your lives... mine too. And Jamie's. All that I keep thinking is that we're talking about our lives. It's the only thing we have. And, to lose it? That's forever. One minute you're getting dressed, thinking about dinner later, things you are planning... then one shot. One pull on a trigger? All that, gone.

All the days you spent being careful to not get noticed, not get found by immigration… all that, gone. One minute happy or laughing. Then one pull by someone you don't know, and all those hopes and dreams and new shampoo and what's on TV later? Poof! For what? I don't want that to ever happen to any of us. Angie, you're right. If a trigger's going to be pulled, we need to pull it."

Cindy and Angie were both surprised at Mike's show of emotion, and his appreciation of how precious life is, and Cindy sat eying him in a less than innocent way, then went to sit by him, but wrapped her arms around him and gave him a long hug. Angie saw the looks on their faces and couldn't stop herself.

"Mike, you're prime cut, and my mom sure is hungry… You know Jamie isn't getting hugs like that!"

This time, it was Mike who was blasted with Angie's newfound analogy repertoire.

"Prime cut? Your mom sure is hungry? What in the world…"

Cindy let go from hugging Mike, then looked at Angie who was still looking at them. Cindy knew she wasn't being sarcastic or flip. She was serious. In moments of stress and crisis, working so close with Mike, and what they had revealed to each other, she knew Angie could see how easily they could make a mistake. She patted Mike on his arm, and after giving Angie a nod, let him know Angie was pretty good at summing things up.

"Well, I think you should take it as a compliment. Angie, just curious… Did you say that because you think Mike is prime cut?"

Not skipping a beat, Angie wasn't afraid to say how she felt.

"Mom, of course I do. Any female would. I'm not even dating yet, but that doesn't mean I can't see he's a hunk. And, oh, like he doesn't know you're the fantasy pinup girl of all time? We have streaming now. Wow, there's a scene like you two in every action flick, and now I know why. Usually someones says, like, get a room or something."

Mike, wishing to get back to a hitman they needed to deal with, didn't have the way with words Angie had.

"Angie, that's why people have houses and apartments… Okay, come on you two… that's a joke."

Cindy let him know that sounded like a plan, but not one she could follow.

"Don't worry. Just a little too close to home... oh, Christ... I did it again! Angie, it was just a hug. What I was trying to say, and not be mister hunk sensitive dreamboat, is because of what happened with Sharon I've been thinking how horrible it would be if anything happened to you two... and yes, before a remark, I'm so worried about Jamie. Angie. This isn't a movie. It's our lives. I think we get the hitman here and you two talk to him, and yeah, we pull a James on him. With Victor and me, yes, do it, and fast as possible before he realizes he can't get a hold of James. Agree?"

Cindy nodded, and Angie waited to be sure about things.

"Only if there's no more touchy-feely hugging. If you can control yourself around my mom, then yes, all for it."

Mike looked at Cindy.

"*Control myself?* What have you been telling her?"

CHAPTER 57

"Fuck me some more. I'm waiting…"

Whimsey was on an ottoman, kneeling on it with her ass up at the perfect height for Charles to go at either hole. Having her head turned back to see him, he was stroking himself to get hard again. She laughed, but not to intimidate him.

"You know, this little hole in my face can take care of that. Come on up here, silly guy."

Although she was the one on the ottoman positioned where Charles can feel powerful and dominant, she knew she had him right where she wanted him. All she needed to do was fuck him, flaying around as if she was getting off, and he'd do anything she wanted. He could never have a girl like her if not for being part of her larger ambitions, and she could tell he never had one close to her when it came to sex. It wasn't that he wasn't capable. He was older, had sex with the usual number of women for most guys like him. She thought he'd had maybe two or three serious relationships, so that meant no real sex. All tame to not piss off his sweethearts. Beyond that, maybe some fucked-up clients, the usual hookers or handouts at a convention. Those had to have been better, but not much as he didn't know how to do much more than fuck and get sucked. His attempt at eating her was embarrassing. She had herself wide open, pulling herself apart and had her clit pointed right at him, but he stuck his tongue up her hole as if he didn't know what a clit was. And getting her to cum? Not a chance.

She was there with her ass out waiting for him to fuck it, and he hadn't even licked it. She wanted to tell him, hey, like I'm about 85-pounds, so pick me up, facing you and put my legs over your shoulders and eat me like you should, and let me arch back like a circus acrobat and take your cock all the way, dumbfuck! Throw me around. Slap the shit out of me. Make me crawl. Beg for your stupid dick. Give me a facial and video all of it on your phone. I want to be sure you figure out how good a fuck you're getting so you'll do what the fuck I want you to do. I want you to be my fucking bitch after some of that.

She waited for him to figure out she'd suck him hard, but there he was, stroking away because he wanted to show he could get it hard and still could. Rolling her eyes up, she wanted to shout out that's what her

fucking mouth was for, asshole! And the way he looked at her was the worst. He was acting grateful. That was pathetic in her mind. A decent guy would pick her up and tell her to do what the fuck he said or he'd hang her upside down on a door hook while he watched porn on his laptop, saying he wouldn't let her down until she passed out, then he'd fuck her the way he wanted.

Pissed that she got herself all cleaned up, did her hair like an eight-year-old, wore white knee-highs and frilly panties and a training bra, and after she'd done all that he was fucking her like some bitch wife or slut from a strip club? And he was a shrink? Didn't he know bitches coming to him were to fuck? That's why they were there. Then realizing in the service, then the CIA, he probably only dealt with men, but so what? He could fuck their asses, get them to suck his dick and say that's the prescription you fucked up mommy's boy.

She understood most men she fucked knew jack-shit about what to do with a hot fuck like her. Most men didn't have a clue. Now, women? Yeah. They gave as good as they got. They knew how to lick pussy and get her squirting and loved to lick ass for hours. And as for cock, that's why God made strap-ons.

Having a hard time not laughing as she was trying to suck him hard, Charles was standing with his eyes rolled back in his head, and trying to sound like a man, saying, "you want it, you want it, you're a bad girl, I know you want it." She had an impulse to stop, kneel up, look him in the eye and ask exactly was it that he thought she wanted? Men loved to say that during sex, and she wondered what they were thinking. She didn't want, "it," they wanted her and to get off. She thought if he had been a halfway decent guy, she'd explain what she really wanted, and even show him how to do it.

Having gotten him somewhat hard enough, she said she wanted him to fuck her from behind. She also thought he needed to run fast and get it in before he went limp. He managed to remain hard enough to get in her pussy, but no way he'd make it up her ass, not that he'd figure out that's how a real man did a decent bitch. He'd be wanting her to cry out, "OH… it' so big… go slow… it's too much for my little ass."

Even just fucking her pussy from behind he could have grabbed both her pigtails and pulled her hard so he could pound her where she'd have no chance of not doing exactly what he said. Even just the hair pulling

would get any guy off, and she knew that's what hair was for. To grab. To let her know she was just his bitch, and that pussy was his. As he plodded along, she kept getting more frustrated, and all she could do is think of what she wanted to say to him each time.

Oh, Charles. Figure it the fuck out. Let all that fucked up shit inside you out on my box. You're a fucking shrink and don't know that? And you don't know how your oh so sweet little bitches really wanted to be fucked like the whores they really were? You thought they were a goddess? Oh, you dumb fucker. When you went to your job, oh, someone was ramming her ass, and she was rimming that fucker to kiss you with when you got home. And you couldn't taste their shit on their lips?

But, say that to him? A fucker like him? He was the worst kind. He wouldn't smack the shit out of her, but he'd kill her and that's about the only way a shit fuck like him felt like a man. She could tell that would get him hard, and he'd beat off thinking about it for years. Big, strong, real man. Yeah, real man with a 45 in his hand. Take that away, and even she could kick the shit out of him. Fuckers like Charles were dangerous. She could tell just from how he fucked he was someone who had only felt like a man by being a shrink and thinking he was so much better than the patients. And when he felt like the worthless fuck he was, he found manhood in six bullets of a gun — almost as small as his dick — that had power he never would. She knew a man, a real man, didn't need his little holster and permit and cartridges and prestige pistol. No. A real man would beat the fuck out of anyone who pissed him off or even looked at the cunt he was fucking.

That was what made men like Charles dangerous. They knew real men. They were beat to a pulp by them growing up. They wanted to be like them, but they were total pussies. Her pussy could do more damage to a man than Charles could ever do in a fight. She was sure he became a shrink to figure out why he was a pussy. He knew all about inferiority complexes and inadequacy, and how those mess men up. They treat women like they wanted to treat the ones who made them know they were nothing, didn't have a dick, no girlfriend, and they had never gotten laid. Once they found some stupid cunt who do them, they'd take it out on her. Not sexually. They didn't abuse them. They'd get arrested for that. No. They didn't let them do what they wanted. Spend what they wanted. Let them have a car. Or friends. They used money and

threats of leaving them to be a man. She knew the pathetic dick in her cunt was from a guy who got off on making a woman feel like she'd only be okay if he said so and had her live in fear that she couldn't survive without him.

"Oh, Charles… are you going to cum soon? I don't know how much more of you my sweet little pussy can take. It's too much! Oh, oh! Why be so rough? You know how little I am and how big you are…"

Smiling, that did it. Just as she expected, she felt him freeze, and she heard the grunt and gurgle of his climax. She couldn't feel it. She couldn't even feel his dick in her. She decided to play it all the way.

"OH… oh, no… didn't you pull out? You didn't come in me, did you?"

Instead of telling her what a man would, to shut the fuck up, cunt, he said he couldn't pull out in time, sorry.

"I know. When you're going at it like that, like, the fun part is filling me all up like that. Oh, I feel like it's going to gush out all over… could you grab some tissues for me?"

Rolling her eyes again as he went for a box of some store-brand cheap tissues, she loved telling him that he had filled her up. That his jizz would flood the place. She thought of how big of a flood two or three small squirts would be. She would just tuck a tissue in her hole, and once collapsing on the sofa wait for a drip or two, an tell him how it just kept coming and coming out of her. That would make him feel like a real man. He could fall asleep thinking about how he had really fucked her good. How she begged him to take it easy, and she worried about making a mess of his carpet and sofa. It was so easy to play fuckers like him. Once he put the tissues back and was sitting next to her on the sofa, she decided to cuddle up next to him and knock his balls out of the park. She waited until he sat, then worked her way under his arm and looked up at him, eyes wide, a sincere look on her face. All she needed was to say the magic words.

"Thank you. I'm so happy you like me."

He was sitting with a top-money porn star, naked in his arms, gently rubbing his limp dick, and she was thanking him. And he bought it. Some insightful shrinking he had. He was too big of a man to tell her he liked fucking her, or she was incredible, that he never had pussy like that in his life. No. He'd just hear her say thank you, and then bask in

the power of his cock. He was every guy who'd pay $30 a week to see her fan page. He was the guy in a video chat where he used an avatar, not a video of himself beating off, asking her to tell him how good he was.

"Oh, yes, daddy. You take such good care of your baby girl. I want more... Can you stay with me a while longer? I don't want to be alone, and I don't know how to cum if you don't tell me what to do..."

She'd done that so many times. They'd add money to the account, and didn't know she was messaging with up to ten men all saying the same things at the same time. They could hear her, but they couldn't see the screen filled with panting emoji, hearts, bug-eyed happy faces... and by calling them all daddy, they each thought she was talking to them and nobody else.

Saying she was so tired, he had worn her out, and if he let her, she'd like to take a little nap. He said get some rest as he had plenty left for later, and she slid down and used his hairy leg for a pillow. It would be a good time to think about how much she could get for selling all the information Sharon had given her about the cult bitch. Not wanting to take any chances, Sharon had given her a flash drive with pictures and videos, copies of donation checks that timed in with the videos and pictures of the richest men and the most powerful politicians all over the world with young girls. That was worth a ton of money according to Sharon, and they had plans to start their own trafficking business, using the names as clients. She'd be the one offered first — for a taste of how incredible their little twats would be. With the drive, a bit of help from James, who was a somewhat decent fuck, Charles, who provided her with some little powder that sent Sharon off to crazy land, and being sure Jo wanted her for herself, she was counting the days until the rich fucks would pay to keep what was on the drive private. When that happened, she would say a fond *fuck you* to men like all of them forever.

CHAPTER 58

"Jamie! Thank God, I was so worried. Are you okay? Did she hurt you? Do things you didn't want?"

He was up on his feet, pointing to the phone, letting Cindy and Angie know it was Jamie, as if they didn't know as his first word was to say her name. Cindy grabbed Angie's hand and squeezed it, whispering she was so glad she was alive. Angie smiled and she was ecstatic as well, but she also knew her mom liked Mike, and wondered what it was like to be attracted to a man who was in love with someone else. She squeezed Cindy's hand back, but it was also for being sad that Cindy didn't have a guy like Mike. She had never thought it would be right for Mike to hurt Jamie, and even just being attracted to Cindy was cheating, in her opinion. Watching him, she understood how he would fall for Cindy. It wasn't just that she was really beautiful, it was just the way she was. She was the nicest person ever in her opinion. Just her way of talking. The way she looked at someone and let them know she cared about them and what they felt. The way she moved, dressed, and didn't play up her looks. She knew it was so much more than being so beautiful. She had a way that made anyone like her. Want to be with her. She knew she was much like that, and she was being bratty sometimes to test if she would still be liked. She had been careful to make her bratty remarks a compliment, and intended only to let it be where she was being a silly teen girl.

The traffickers had wanted to take both their sweetness and niceness from them. Cindy hadn't let them. Angie knew they hadn't made a dent in her or her mom. They had made her more stunning. She could turn to Mike, politely ask if she could use his Glock, kill a trafficker, then gently hand it back to him, thanking him, making him feel as if he had protected her. She didn't want to hurt anyone. She saw how people were hurt by traffickers, and as part of not wanting to hurt people, she understood she was strong enough to stop the hurt. It didn't change her goodness. It had made her use it to stop people who hurt women like her, and girls like herself. Lost in the thought, she turned her attention back to Mike.

"Well, that's all things we didn't know. We knew it was a bona fide church... Yes, I know a bit about it... You know why this all

happened… Yeah. Sharon came back and said it was Peter and he was some cult leader, and we traced him back to Jo. Then Jo wasn't exactly like you're saying when we made contact… Okay, I hear you. She's in a situation like you were… And she isn't on the line… Does she know why we blame her… Oh, wow. She was in love with Sharon… I didn't know, we didn't talk that much about any of it beyond she wanted to kill Peter for what he'd done to her… Do you really think Sharon wanted to take him out to take over his operation? I mean, I know she was still in the cult, and spent all her time with Whimsey… Na, she's not here. Long story, but she played us. She's no victim, and she's not fourteen. More like twenty… I not sure, some gland condition keeps people little and she seems to have found out she can cash in on it… Okay, that's interesting… I think talking would be good. I'm not sure I can believe things she says right now, I've got so much to tell you, and it's down to you, me, Cindy and Angie… James? He took a dive and is out. A bit too much for him… I didn't know if you were alive or dead... And I felt helpless to do anything, but not now…. Let me ask Cindy, hold on."

Not muting the phone, he told Jamie he was putting her on speakerphone.

"Cindy, Ange… I want you to be part of this. Obviously, Jamie is alive, and she says she's well. If anyone is holding a gun to her head right now that would really be stupid… Jamie, can you do a video call?"

"Well, it's an iPhone like yours, and the wifi is strong. Jo didn't say not to. She said do whatever I wanted to do. Let me call you back. If it doesn't work for some reason, I'll call back just voice."

Mike was stunned. Cindy and Angie said it may be true, so the video call was a good idea. As they said that, the phone showed a FaceTime call. Swiping the screen to answer, there was Jamie, smiling, saying it worked. Mike turned the phone to show Cindy and Angie, telling them to come sit next to him on the couch so they could all see.

Waving at them, happy to see their smiles, Cindy said it was far beyond a surprise. She was just so happy to see her smile and know she's able to call. Jamie nodded, saying it was a surprise to her. She started to explain things so that Cindy and Angie could hear it all from her.

"I haven't been sent home yet. I think you'll understand why in a minute…"

Telling them how Jo was abused as a young girl by her father, an

elder in the church, she had intended to shoot her way out, but the elders just asked her if she would keep the girls coming, and she had been afraid they'd kill her. She was doing what the church had done, and people like Peter were missionaries. Adding they were all over the world, they started to understand it was a huge operation, all out in the open, not totally legal in the US, but she was doing what the church had always done.

Cindy listened carefully, and Angie had been searching on her phone for a world map showing locations where the church had missions for a long time. Jamie said she learned bigamy was all about young brides for church elders who were mostly older, but not always. Jamie pointed the phone to the map on the wall, and said that was it, but added Jo had gone past what the church did and played the rich and powerful, her way of getting back at the world, or at least that was what she thought it was. Cindy thought about it all.

"Jamie, I hear all you said, and that makes it harder to understand some things. First, why she took you. Second, why she killed my mother. Why not just talk to us? Tell us that Sharon was using her?"

Jamie listened carefully, knowing that Cindy was coping with what happened to her mother. She didn't want to dismiss the hurt or assign blame to anything more than Sharon playing them all.

"Cindy, I can't imagine how horrible it must have been to see that. Your mom did so much for us in Russia… And you were just connecting again. I know she came here to save you. She was here for you, and I still can't figure out how this all got so messed up. It didn't have to be this way. I'm sure you don't want to do anything but get back at Jo. I'm not going to speak for her. I think she needs to talk to you, and no matter the reason. Any human being can realize you lost your mother and be sorry for you."

They all jumped as they saw Jo walking up behind Jamie. They instantly thought that she was going to do something to her, and their mouths were all set to say look out, she's coming. Before they could say anything, Jo was there, leaning over Jamie's shoulder, waving at them without the attitude and game playing from when talking to her on the phone. Jo looked at Jamie, and nodded at her as she pulled a chair to sit with her.

"I hadn't even thought of a FaceTime. Good, this is better. I'm sure

you all know who I am, but anyway, I'm Jo. And I see Mike, and, oh my God! Cindy? Angie? I can't believe how amazing you look… I'm sorry… it's just that you look… amazing! I was expecting you to be screaming at me. I don't know how much you've said to catch up, but if Jamie doesn't mind, I think it's good we talk. I hope you do…"

Taking the lead, Cindy said hello, and that she agreed it was best to talk. She added that before they went too far, she had a few things that would help. Jo nodded, saying she understood, and she hoped to make that a good start. Cindy was polite, and Mike and Angie knew that meant she could be kind, or out for revenge. They'd have to wait and find out.

"Good. I wish it had been before all the horrible things that happened. So, we know those things, and Jamie surprised us by being able to call. Are you keeping her there against her will? Can she leave?"

Leaning in so she could be seen fully, she understood that such questions had to be answered, and sincerely.

"Yes. I was doing that. I need a way to keep from getting killed. I thought if she was here, you wouldn't have the entire Army storming in. Not a thing to be okay with, I know. Sometimes, God smiles and shines light, and when we talked I learned I had been worked by Sharon. All I knew was from a video of a raid on Peter who was one of the missionaries. He was insane, and out of control. He had been working with Sharon, but I didn't know that. When Jamie explained to me about what happened, which was really just last night and today, I understood I was fighting the wrong people. So, is she a prisoner? Not now. Can she leave? Yes, whatever she wants to do."

Cindy worried it was just a way to play them, so kept on the topic.

"I appreciate that like us, you were hearing things about us, just like we were about you, and that's what caused us both to do the only things we knew how. You said she was free to go. If I send my jet for Jamie, tonight, she gets on, you won't stop her?"

Nodding, then looking at Jamie, she turned back and said go ahead, she wouldn't do anything to stop her. Jamie was nodding, indicating she thought that was true. Cindy said if it wasn't too much, she had two more things to ask, but didn't wait for a reply.

"Jo, the last thing will be about my mother, and I am not one to think of one side of things. First, I know I said what I said to you. That

I would shoot you in the head for taking Jamie and trafficking Sharon. I meant it, and I will never lie. I would still do it if I thought it was a way to keep more horrible things from happening. I don't want to do anything of the sort, but to protect the ones I love, I would. Do you understand that though we're talking, seeing each other, I haven't said I wouldn't do what I said?"

Mike and Angie looked at each other. Cindy always amazed them at how she could be so nice when making the most threatening promises. Looking at the screen, they saw Jo nodding, saying she understood, and hadn't thought words and a video call would change that. Cindy thanked her for understanding, then continued.

"This is important. When you called, you were so flip… so la-de-dah. I thought I was dealing with a psychopath. That's why I made it clear that I would stop you, and you were saying things in a way that left me no choice but think you were far past dangerous. I talked to my mother after that, and she didn't want me at risk. She said she would find you and kill you for me. Jo, have you thought about why I reacted from a need to protect people I loved? And why my mother wished to protect me? Why did you talk to me that way?"

Running her hands through her hair, then holding her temples, Jo was clearly surprised at the question, and the reason Cindy and her mother felt a need to stop her. Her face had changed, and she wasn't smiling or as calm as when she first said hello.

"Yeah… I know. I get why you needed to worry about me. I'm on meds. Stuff that happened to me? I've been on some kind of meds ever since. Yeah… I called you after I took some to get up my courage. I can't remember all of what I said, but I remember feeling like a circus clown… I don't know, maybe trying to be funny. Silly. Did you think anyone could be like that all the time? Oh, I'm sorry, that's making an excuse. Well, I was completely manic, I'm sure. Wrong time to call you, and I do stupid stuff when I first take them. I don't know what to say. I caused this…"

Mike pulled a pad of paper and pen from his jacket, and out of camera, wrote to ask her what the meds were for, and if she could, show her the bottle of her prescription.

Cindy asked her to explain what she took medications for, and asked if she could show them the bottle to assure them that she was getting treatment and using medication to help.

Jo looked surprised at first, then thought about it, finally nodding.

"Fair thing to ask. I'd have to go get the bottles, but I can tell you what they're for. My doctor says I have a genuine classic case of you name it, I've got it. Bipolar, personality disorder, paranoid delusional schizophrenia, chronic anxiety, depression, suicidal ideation, oh, and claustrophobic. So, take your pick. I cycle through them, and he says it was all from the day I went nuts and killed my parents, brother and sisters, church elders, and some brides. I guess I've never recovered from it…"

Mike was rapidly scribbling, "Careful!" for Cindy, and she tapped it to let him know she agreed. Her face both sad and worried, she showed genuine concern after thinking about it.

"Jo, just hearing you say it, I can only guess at how horrible that was for you. Do the medications help much?"

With her serious expression changing to a mock smile, and then laughing, Jo looked upwards, then back to Cindy.

"They work really great, Cindy. Just fantastic. They work so well I called you up and thought I was a clown spreading laughter and smiles. That's how well they work."

All saw Jamie's face grow deeply concerned, her mouth open in surprise. She didn't seem to be aware of any of what Jo said. Jo turned to her, seeing Jamie was looking carefully off to her side.

"Gee, I didn't mention all that, did I? It slipped my mind. Don't worry, I take medications and they make me all better."

Cindy knew the call had triggered her, and she was heading back to the way she had been on the phone. She hoped she could calm things down, though she knew that may not be possible.

"Jo, I'm sorry. I brought up something I had no right to. Can you accept my apology, and that my asking you if medications helped was a concern for you? I would have the same concern for anyone."

Jo was shaking her head, eyes rolling as if Cindy was being absurd. Things were changing fast. Even the apology was triggering her more, and all she could do is ask her to get her medications, then suggest taking them if she was somewhat the same as now, just reacting to her traumas.

"Cindy. Of course I accept your apology. It was from a place of love and concern, I know. From a stunning beauty who can only be wonderful and ever so nice… except for when she politely says she's

going to put a bullet in my head. Yes, of course you care about my mental condition. A bullet would fix that really well."

Mike wrote, "Take meds!" on the notepad, and again, Cindy tapped it as that was what she would do next.

"Jo, talking about his has you upset, and I hope we can put such things behind us. I had first asked to see the meds, and maybe, as this talk has upset you so, if you go get them, check if you need to take some now. That may help. I'm not saying I know if it will. I'd like to get back to talking about how to learn about each other. Do you think that could help you and how you're feeling right now?"

Changing in front of them once again, Jo looked calm and sensible.

"Cindy. Smart suggestion. Kill two birds with one stone. Out of concern for me, what really happens is you see what stuff I'm taking, and I'm not making things up. Yes, you're right. Hearing the call, coming in to join… I forgot to take my meds. You all talk, I'll be back in a minute or two and get everything I need."

Getting up, Jo rubbed Jamie's cheek, and Jamie was looking up at her, saying that she didn't realize what all Jo was going through. Jo kissed her on the cheek, saying she just needed to get what would help, then left the room. She could be seen heading out of the door, and she seemed calm.

Not wanting to be heard, Mike rapidly scribbled on his notepad, then put it to the camera.

"Not safe. Any way out?"

Jamie was frightened. Jo had told them that she wasn't always rational, and that was something that seemed to get worse right before their eyes. Frantically looking all around, Jamie shook her head, mouthing a, "NO!" Mike could only think of one thing. He rapidly scribbled a note and put it to the camera.

"RUN. NOW. Get outside and keep running. Just RUN!"

Taking a second to realize it was her only choice, she mouthed, "I love you," then went quietly to the hall, then they could see a bit of the outside door through the office door, and all sighed some relief as it opened and closed. Mike wrote a note for Cindy and Angie.

"Pray! Then let's load up guns and fly there right now! Keep Jo on the call long as we can!"

As they sat, waiting longer than expected, Jo came walking into the room then leaned over the chair where Jamie had been sitting. She

looked at the camera, then the chair, then back to the camera.

"I must really need my meds. Is it just me or has Jamie become invisible?"

Cindy did all she could to keep her there.

"She said as we were waiting for you, she needed to use the restroom…"

Jo was holding an ornate wooden box and put it on the table in front of the phone which was propped up against a lamp. She patted it and smiled at them.

"When you gotta go, you gotta go. Oh, I'm not saying Jamie has to go, but I gotta take some of these, for sure."

She opened the box, and took out a bottle of prescription medication, holding it for them to see.

"Time-tested, gold standard lithium sulfate. Let's see, it says take one. Well, I want to be sure to take enough as one doesn't do it. Wait… I just flashed on a moment. Yeah, thinking back, I remember shooting my dad as everyone looked at me like I was crazy. Know what the first thing I thought was? One's not enough."

Taking the bottle, she poured four into her hand, and started crunching them.

"Sub-lingual helps them work faster. Big artery under your tongue works with this. And, oh, this one always helps. I assure you I'm telling you the truth about what they are. Xanax. You know, most people take like, a half, maybe one milligram a day. I have a wonderful stallion. He gets horsey panic attacks. He does great with ten milligrams a day. Me. Well, I take twelve. I read that will stop a horse…"

She poured a handful and started crunching them and had them under her tongue.

"But, well, I'm not a horse. So, I think those will help. Oh, I feel the lithium already. Working… that's good. Wait a minute… Jamie's still not back. And I have a special prescription for her. Well, if you don't mind, I better check on her. I think she needs this…"

They watched in horror as Jo put the two bottles in, then smiled as she reached inside, and said, "This will ease her worried mind…"

She pulled a silver 45 from the box, loaded the chamber, then got up and left the room, calling to Jamie that she was all better now.

CHAPTER 59

Envisioning Jamie running for her life in the mountains of Montana, Cindy told Mike to go with Victor and have him get the jet on and started, and for both to get all the guns and ammo they had, including ones for Angie and her, adding they'd need the grenades and smoke canisters. She knew it was going to be an all-out battle.

Mike had just returned from their arsenal with six night-vision goggles, making sure they had been fully charged. Each could go eight hours, but he had a box with six extra batteries. He had his arm through six kevlar bullet-proof vests and made sure there was one for Jamie and one for Victor as he insisted on being in full gear and on the ground with them.

Raising her skirt fully up, tucking the hem and a good deal of its length into her lace underpants as she spoke to Mike, he wasn't easily surprised yet seeing the most beautiful and charming woman he had ever met strapping holsters to her thighs and putting two Glock 91s in them where each didn't rub against the other, making sure there was a bullet in the chamber, then pulling the dress out in one tug and letting if flow down was an image that would never leave him. She had put on leggings that would hold up to brush and trails, but as she looked at him to talk gear, she looked more seductive than any top model he had photographed for *Vogue* covers.

Seeing Mike had stopped to take a good look as she armed up, she asked if she missed something. She was pulling back the slide on a magnum 45 she had been practicing with at the firing range and checking the extra clips.

"I'm using high-velocity, not hollow-core. Laser infrared sight's in my bag. Did I miss anything?"

Deciding to give Mike a pass on checking her out, he snapped back to normal as she put the 45 in her handbag. She wanted to smile and ask if he liked her red lace panties, but there was no time for teasing. She recalled shopping with Angie and deciding what color to get. Angie, who seemed to be reading everything ever written on any topic, helped make it an easy decision.

"Mom, if you need to leave a trail of markers, or flag me down, you get red. You can pull them off and wave them. White too, but that's kinda for seniors."

She had been amazed at Angie's practical approach to so many things. She had added that if needed, she could flash some red at any guy attacking, and that would get his attention and that's when she could fire while she asked what he was looking at. Apparently, Angie was right. It had caught Mike's attention, and it gave her a sense of confidence about what had been a curse in many ways during her life. Having a perfect figure, her beauty was now a weapon. She was a Venus flytrap. She lured with beauty, and once anyone looked, they were finished. Knowing men used might to take down opponents, she knew her strongest weapon was simply someone wanting to look at her, and how they'd never expect her to be fearless and cold as ice when confronting someone who hurt anyone.

Calling to Angie they had to get going, she saw Angie had taken a different approach to battle attire. As stunning as she was, Angie had yet to learn how to use her looks as part of her arsenal, but for where they were headed, she was a sight to see.

Turning the lights on the upper level off, Angie appeared out of darkness as Cindy and Mike looked up to the landing, somehow sensing her presence at the top of the stairs

Wearing a skin-tight black body suit that covered her arms, legs and neck, she wasn't hiding her weapons. She had two magnums in a black nylon holster slung on her waist, each end strapped to her thighs. Like the holster, all straps were matte black, matching her full military boots that reached mid-calf. Each boot had a sheath, and they held black carbon knives with matte black handles. On top, she wore a black cap with a long brim that put most of her face in a shadow, covered by a black hoodie with the hood up over the cap. At first all Cindy or Mike could see was a hint of cheekbones moving from the darkness of the hall, then the eerie shape of hips, holsters, 45s, knife handles, and the AR-15 visible only from the sheen of it's tooled matte black metal. She stood, not moving, sleek, confident, and with her hair pulled back behind her she was a vision to cause fear.

Understanding she would be almost impossible to see at night, Cindy realized the outfit would be the last thing anyone going at her would see. She knew Angie had ordered what she told her was, "practical tactical." This was the first time she had seen her battle gear, and she was like Mike in that she just stopped, stunned, and looked at her.

Mike stood, shocked, ready to shout they had been invaded, then realized it was Angie and relaxed. He looked up at her, asking who helped her with the gear. Looking at him with her classic, "You must think I'm not smart because I'm a girl," expression, she answered with one word.

"Amazon."

Seeing the case full of night vision gear, Angie said she wanted to add it to her belt to adjust it on the way and get used to it. Asking if it had enough battery power, she saw the extra batteries, each having velcro on the back. Taking one, tapping it onto her belt's velcro, she said she was all set.

Victor was wearing dark green camouflage, military issue, his nylon web belt had his uzi and two Glock 91s, and his pants had gusseted pockets for filling with grenades. He wore a knit cap, also camo green, saying he was ready and would fill his pockets when they landed as he couldn't fly with them full.

Looking at Mike, he had on a black sweatsuit, both pants and shirt, and had a black knit cap. Cindy knew he'd be using an AR-15, and he had a utility belt filled with clips on one side, his Glock on the other.

Knowing they were all prepared for a night invasion of Jo's compound, Cindy thought the most important gear were the night-vision goggles. They weren't there to do battle or take the compound down. They were equipped to search for Jamie and see anyone in the way or coming at them. They had talked after hearing Jo going crazy on the video call and agreed Jamie had enough of a head start to make it up into the mountains, and they would each take a different location and search for her. Cindy was saying a prayer since the call that Jamie would find a way to evade Jo. Her instinct told her Jo would go after her by herself — not with any of her guards or staff. It fit with her insanity. It was a game, and she was on a manic high, feeling invincible.

Seeing they had all the things needed for a night search, she nodded, saying to everyone it was time to get in the car, they'd talk on the way about how to find Jamie, and what to do if they found Jo and subdued her.

The car was loaded with cases in the trunk, Victor behind the wheel, Mike in the front passenger seat, and the garage door had opened. It was a moonless night and looking at the sky, Cindy knew that was to their

advantage. Angie and Cindy stood at the alarm panel making sure it was armed. Once done, heading to the car, with almost no sound something made a whoosh past Cindy's ear, and at the same moment she heard a crack behind her where the wall was lined with casework. Angie heard the cabinet, and they each knew it was a rifle shot aimed at them.

It was the hitman, and he had been waiting for them to leave in a car, not invade the house.

Cindy knew she didn't need to say anything. She was standing near the panel with light switches and for closing the door. Both her and Angie had been trained for such an attack. She turned off the lights, and both her and Angie flew down, getting their guns out as they dropped. With the night dark, they saw a black Audi sitting across from them, the window open, and knew that was where the shot was fired from.

As she dropped to the garage floor, Angie had instantly pulled at her night goggles and had them on, saying she could see him to Cindy in a hushed voice, pulling out her 45 just as Cindy had done. Angie said he was in her sight. She didn't use the laser on the scope, and without hesitating, she could see the man's head was pressed against the scope on his rifle and saw the red flash of it pointing to her. She didn't wait for it to settle on her. She fired. It had all happened so quickly that Mike was just opening his door to do what they had. Get low, be hard to hit, and locate the shooter.

Hitting the ground, he heard the crack of a gun, sure it was from Cindy or Angie. The shot into the garage had made little sound. That meant a muzzled rifle, and using a muzzle reduced the precision of the shot, but the hitman was experienced with compensating, but he knew Cindy or Angie hadn't been hit. He would have heard a fall or a scream. He only heard the report of the shot fired. A second later, he heard another shot from the semiautomatic magnum, then heard the roar of a car engine and tires screeching. Almost as fast as everything had happened, there was a bang that sounded like a car crashing into a tree.

Telling Cindy and Angie to keep flat, Mike said it could be a ruse, and the guy let his car go but was outside waiting for them. Grabbing his night vision goggles, he put them on, then went out the side door to the yard, opening it with a full swing to see if it was shot at. With the door fully open, his Glock held to fire, he did a quick step out the door, then in. No fire. Talking in a normal voice, he said to stay down, he was

going to check if the hitman was in the car, and if he was still alive and dangerous.

Angie stood up, saying no, he wasn't.

"Not where I hit him. His neck, and it was spurting blood like a garden hose."

Saying he still needed to be sure, Mike did a by-the-book approach to the Audi with his gun in both hands held out at the car. Seeing a bald head hanging out the driver's side window, blood covered the outside of the driver's door, and the windshield was splattered with blood as well. Pushing the man's head, then feeling for any pulse on his dangling arm, Mike was certain the man was dead. Getting in the back seat, he leaned into the front, taking a sniper rifle and scope, a box of shells, then a cell phone and the man's wallet with his ID.

Running back to the garage, he told everyone to get in the car, they needed to get out before police came. Victor saw him in the rear-view mirror and knew he had the long rifle and opened the remote trunk. Mike threw the rifle and ammo in, closed it, hopped in, then Victor calmly backed out of the garage and then down the street as if nothing happened. Only a few blocks away and on a main street, he went quickly as possible and in record time they were in the hanger, and he had the jet started. They all carried gear into the jet. As it pulled out of the hanger, Victor used a remote to close the hanger door and had been cleared for takeoff.

From the time they all jumped in the car, until takeoff, they hadn't talked. They were all looking for any signs of another shooter — and the police. It was a short delay, and they were glad there hadn't been another one.

Looking at Angie, Cindy was concerned. She had just shot a predator and heard the sniper fire whiz between them. Watching her daughter add two shells to her 45, she had dropped the clip, ejected the chamber, and filled it again. She didn't seem shook by the incident or stopping the man. Angie looked at her with her classic, "What?" expression, then held up her goggles with both Mike and Cindy looking at her, not knowing what to say. Angie could tell they were worried if taking the man down had been traumatic for her. She shook her head at them.

"First, these goggles are awesome. He was in the darkest spot, black clothes, black car. And his scope's laser only went on when he pulled the

trigger back or pressed his eye into the sight. He had his rifle aimed at mom and me, and lucky we were down. With us laying on the floor like that, he would have gone for the car's gas tank… not us… I don't know if you heard it, but he fired, and it was like a hair away from hitting mom in the head. I had a clear shot. I saw it hit, but I took a second one to be sure. I think it was just he had the car in drive for a quick exit and the reflex had him floor it. All I really had seen was a spray of red, the rifle barrel up, not at us."

Mike gave Angie a thumbs up, saying it was that or be killed. Cindy was looking at her the entire time, then over to Mike, then spoke to them both.

"Mike, we didn't have James to cover the incident like before. We have a dead man, shot, car rammed into a tree and it was across from our house. Aren't the police going to want to investigate us?"

Nodding, she noticed he had a burner phone out and was texting.

"There. Texted that I saw a drive-by shooting and don't want to be a part of it, but some guy driving must have been shot as he hit a tree and didn't get out. Then the address. None of our guns can be traced, so they'll be looking into the guy's history and I'm sure there'll be plenty there to support the drive-by hit I suggested. We aren't there, so not home when it happened."

Cindy was glad of his strategy, but not okay with the attempt to kill them.

"What is with this world? Somebody pays someone and they just pull up and casually kill someone? I understand what Angie did was stop the man from killing us. She had a reason. But him? For what? Money? Our lives are what? A bit of money in his pocket as he drives off? Angie, you didn't hesitate, you stopped him. He's never going to hurt someone again. But, Angie… Mike… when we get past the Jo mess, I want to visit Allan. He paid that man. I'm going to pay him for thinking he could do that to anyone. Mike… I'm glad you're out of there. What do they do all day? Look at each other. Say, gee, we're behind on kills. Let's kill some women today. Mike… I can't figure it out. How did you stay there? Even for just one day?"

It was the first time Mike heard Cindy show her indignation. She was talking the same as always, but what she said was like a blow to the head. She was right. That's what happens when men can get away with

murder. They kill people, and people are just names on a whiteboard to be circled or crossed out. He knew that the agency never thought about the targeted people. They had a way of abstracting the person down to a word on a board. He had been there and been a part of it. He met Cindy and Angie because Vlad and Jamie had been names on a whiteboard. In a large room full of recent college graduates sitting at computers screens, pulling data and images to view, people were only pixels on a screen, the ones locating the "targets" had never pulled a trigger to kill someone, or had been fired at. The agency knew that, and to the young men sitting at screens, it was all a sick video game. Then he realized most video games were all about killing people. They had abstracted life down where real people and video avatars were one and the same.

"Cindy… you're right. I was so obsessed with finding Sharon I couldn't see that all around me this type of thing was going on. I do now, and I'm here, not there. I was deep undercover and wanted to stop people like the one tonight. I know. It's the whole world… this is going on all over. And Allan? Charles? They're going to try to kill us. We kill them first. I'd do it, but I can see you want to be the last thing they see. I'll figure out how and when."

With autopilot on, Victor joined them in the cabin. He had some ideas about finding Jamie and getting out alive.

"I think much about what to do. I give options. We have parachutes, but, the people can see, hear jet noise. Fast way in, and I land, get car, we have meeting place. Pick up, get back on jet. Second. We land, get car, I drive where we are close, I join in search, we call on phones, leave. There is landing strip there, but that is no good for this as we may not make it off stairs without being shot at. Well, I think there may be… well… a bit more like what I did with fighter jet. We land, get you car, you park, I am in sky watching. Jamie, she is running, maybe hiding. That Jo, she is crazy type who will want to find her herself. When you leave car, start looking, I pretend nice Eliana jet is meg, and I buzz compound so low it blows hair on head. If people gather, I head to them, they scatter, screaming for Jo to come…"

Cindy looked at Mike and Angie, then she turned to Victor.

"Land at the local airport. We'll get car, you fly off to compound. Distract them with your fighter pilot flying. Victor, does this plane has a loudspeaker? So when you go in, you can use it to send a message?"

Smiling, Victor understood her thinking.

"Yes, malenka as Eli call you. The voice of God thundering would be good. This plane has that, a siren too. What you wish I should say?"

Mike was looking concerned, and he hadn't been able to say what he thought best, although the third option was the one he liked just as Cindy had. He nodded at Cindy, waiting to hear the message. She was writing it down for Victor, and she read it out before giving it to him.

"Stand down or be killed. We are here for Jamie. Go to end of airstrip. Jamie, go to road, get in car. If Jo is not on airstrip, all will die. To save your lives, drag Jo with you."

Mike and Victor saw the simple genius of her message. The goal was to stop Jo from going after Jamie, let Jamie know they were there, and allow her to make it to the road and find their car.

Heading back to the cockpit, Victor radioed the airport near the compound, had clearance to land, and had made arrangements for a Suburban. Using the plane's PA, he said he had gotten a nice black Suburban so they would think CIA has arrived.

Angie was looking at Mike from her seat, arms crossed, clearly upset.

"I think we could have had James get my special disposition driver's license before we threw him off. How am I going to get one now? I put a hundred down on the new wedge truck earlier."

Mike thought a bit of levity would help before they landed and faced a deadly situation.

"Angie, I forgot. Why didn't you say something when you were opening the floor hatch? I could have taken his cuffs off and he would have arranged it for you."

Not finding the humor in what Mike said, she was putting her arm back to throw her bottled water at Mike and see if he could catch it. Cindy gave her a look that stopped Angie, but she was still worried about who would get her fixed with a license. She gave a huff, and they could tell she had come to a decision.

"I don't need some guy to do it for me. I'll go to the DMV and tell them Jake Maxx said he wants me to have one, right now, that day."

Mike looked at Cindy, then at Angie. He asked who in the world was Jake Maxx. Angie gave him her all-out, "Duh!" motion with her shoulders and arms, eyes wide.

"I don't know. And, neither will they. It's who you don't know that

matters. The who you know is so old school…"

Cindy smiled at Mike, saying she knew she'd pull it off.

"Mom, you're on top of it even though you don't know it. I'll have my phone out dialing in sympathy for what will happen to them, then I'll call out to everyone there to look how the DMV treats girls from trailer parks and ask people to get online and please leave a like and all. It'll go viral as I'm like, a girl. That's all it takes to go viral. Oh, maybe I'll drink a frappuccino while they're all filming me."

Mike was as confused as Cindy on that part, and asked her what the frappuccino was all about.

"Mike, see, that's why you wouldn't have many followers. You're a hunk, and that could help. But, if you aren't drinking a coffee and being difficult in a public building, nobody online is going to watch what you post. You hold the cup in one hand, phone out to do the selfie, then ask a question, a vague one. I'll need to ask, do you get blown off when all you want is what the law allows? But, before I tell you what this lady is denying me, check the like button. Then I keep telling her I have a right to drive, and I want to know her name and ID number, and does she know the number or page such a law is in the regulations, or is it just she doesn't like really nice, sweet innocent girls because her daughter just got busted at the strip club."

Both with mouths open in shock, they looked at each other, and Mike asked Angie if she planned on doing all that.

Angie looked at them, implying they just didn't understand, then laughing, said aloud, "No. But… if needed…"

Over the speaker, Victor said he was coming in hot, and strap up. It was Angie's turn to ask where Victor was picking up jargon. She looked up front, calling to Victor.

"Coming in hot? *Coming in hot?* Where are you learning those things?"

CHAPTER 60

Running out of Jo's office and knowing she'd be killed if Jo found her, Jamie looked towards the trail up into the mountains, then seeing them stopped, stood, then realized running to escape was what Jo would expect her to do. It's what anyone would do in that situation.

As her adrenaline pumped, she became hyper-aware she was going to be hunted by someone fully insane, or on drugs or whatever caused her change in behavior. Then a flash that Jo wasn't either of those. She was actually diabolically evil and used such behaviors as tactics. In her adrenaline rush from running in fear, she knew Mike, Cindy and Angie heard it all and would find a way to get to the compound and try to save her. Feeling a giant adrenaline surge shoot through her, it was so powerful she thought the top of her head would fly off. Everything Jo had done... Taking her. Telling her everything about her past. Letting her call Mike, then joining the call and acting insane. It was never about her. It was to get all of them to the compound to save her. They had all killed Peter, and she had set Sharon up to get killed by getting her drugged and triggered in fear. Now, she was using her skill of appearing to be irrational to kill all of them. She only had taken her as bait so they would all be there.

Hitting her hard enough to knock the wind out of her, Jamie flashed on she was diabolical from leading a life of power, money, intelligence, and trauma. Jo used irrational acts that were amazingly rational. She had built the largest trafficking network ever known, used the Magdalene church as a cover, and used different personalities to control people and never let them know who she was or what she would do. She was a genius to have survived and gained both revenge — and power.

Flooded with thoughts, Jamie remembered the wall of monitors Jo used to have a full view of the compound. Looking at them, Jo wouldn't rush out after her; she'd look at her screens, watching what she'd do and where she was headed. Looking at the screens before she called Mike, Jamie realized every part of the compound was monitored. Smiling, she couldn't recall any screen showing where she was standing. She had run to the right once out the door and had stopped at the corner of the building when the adrenaline rush hit her. With so many cameras covering the area around Jo's building, all looking out to view anyone coming towards it, she couldn't recall any view of the corners of the building, or even the sides.

Shivering from terror and the adrenaline rush, with the hope no camera was watching her, she stopped reacting to either. Pumping a surge of fight or flight, she realized what adrenaline was for. To run — or if that wasn't an option — fight. She was suddenly calm, lucid, and was no longer in terror. Entering survival mode, she was sure running from Jo meant death. Fighting her was the only way to survive and save the ones she loved. She needed to think like Jo. Play her game with her unpredictable acts. Jo controlled people by knowing most people respond in predictable ways.

Flashing on how stupid people acted in crisis situations, she thought of how one man with a gun pointed at a group of people could lead them into a building or into a forest and tell them to kneel down as he shot them one by one in the head. She had seen that happen one time in Russia where Brian had one of his goons take six men from a startup trafficking group who had tried to take some of his girls. Pointing an Uzi at the men, all unarmed, he said only, "move," pointing to a storage building, each man knowing he'd get shot if he didn't do what was said. They all held their hands on top of their heads and in a line, walking to the building. It had a large door for loading, and she watched as they were told to kneel. The goon stood there, shooting them one by one in their heads, then turned and walked back to Brian, giving him a nod. Brian turned to leave, telling another one of his goons to take care of the mess.

The vision of the incident flooded over her as she stood against the building. What was with human nature? One man with a gun. Six men without them, hands untied. Each doing what they were told only because one man, one gun, told them to. They could have all turned and rushed the goon, and they would have prevailed and took his Uzi, shot him and then Brian who was not far from them, watching how stupid people were in such situations and counting on it. Each man was afraid of being shot at the moment, realizing they were being marched to the building to be killed. They knelt knowing they would never stand up again. They didn't do the only thing they needed to do to not be killed. Stand up and fight back. Not one man wanted to be the one killed as they fought back. That fear, being the one to die, letting the others live, was what people did. A man with a gun tells a man without one to turn around. The one without a gun knows he's going to be killed. The only

chance of living was to do anything possible to stop the man. Better to die fighting with a chance than to be so stupid and just do what the man with the gun said.

She thought of how people in concentration camps would be rounded up. Ten, twenty, thirty people all told by one Nazi to line up against the wall, knowing he was going to shoot them all. Even weak, frail, unarmed, the man with the gun would fall against an onslaught of so many people willing to die. But most always they stood,, letting one man shoot all of them dead.

She knew that was mind control. What a captor used for power. What governments did to populations. It was always imparting a sense of helplessness, weakness, that they had no way to fight. Jo had made sure she saw the monitors. She drew attention to them, making her aware she could see the compound without anything escaping her notice. She had told her how as a very young girl she had went on a rampage killing everyone she saw, and nobody could stop her. That may not have been true. She gained her trust with her story and sexual affection. Then, giving her hope by making her call, she used her crazy act to turn all that around to where she would flee, while Mike, Cindy and Angie would line up like the men in Russia and do what she said.

Realizing someone with all the psychological conditions she listed couldn't make it out of bed each morning, she couldn't lead a world-wide organization as its mastermind. Many crazy people function as madmen for a time, but it was always their insanity that would get them arrested or killed. They felt invincible, or godlike, but that wasn't what Jo was at all. She must have seen men like that at some point. Men like Peter. She was hurt, smart, and ruthless, but Jamie was sure she was far from crazy.

Having groomed girls and buyers, Jamie knew how to be a victim, a charmer, and one to be feared. She would start by being kind and sweet. Then convincing. Then threatening. She'd watch girls who first trusted her as a friend fall apart when she smiled at them with a gun in her hand. If they cried how could she do that to them, she'd say she didn't want to, but she'd be killed if she didn't do what some big, bad man said she had to do. The girls would realize Jamie was a victim, like them, and even more horrible was by having them like her first, they felt sorry for her and did what they were told to keep her from getting killed.

That was how traffickers controlled people. There was no gun

in a hand needed. It was what was done before any gun was shown. Grooming, mind control, intimidation, enticement, rewards, punishment. All of those to control people. She had done it. It had come natural to her, but she could have used all that to work in advertising or in some motivational pursuit. She had something the ones who hurt people for their own income or worse, pleasure, didn't have. She had a moral center that knew right from wrong. She had been groomed and brainwashed since a child, but her sense of right and wrong won once she met Mike. He wasn't fooled by her. He knew what she had been through. He saved her, and now she would save him, and she would save Cindy and Angie. They were everything she wanted to be. She cared about them the same as Mike. She needed to stop Jo, not run from her.

Standing, quiet, knowing all the signs, putting them all together, she knew it would come down to her and Jo, face to face. One would live. One would die. But Mike, Cindy and Angie would not. Even without a weapon, Jo wasn't going to get her to march to some building, kneel down and be shot in the head.

She would use the same control on Jo as she had used on her. There was no need to run. She'd calmly walk back into the building and ask Jo if she was sure they saw her run in fear — and believed it. Work her with the same tactics. Tell her they were probably going to do something, so what are "we" going to do?

That wouldn't be something Jo could figure out. She would just ask if her little display of fear worked. Then, smiling say they had plenty of time to lick the fuck out of each other.

Distracting Jo would give Mike time to get everyone, fly there, and take Jo down. Planning on convincing her she needed fucking more than anything else, if Jo learned they were near, or there, she'd say time for a new lover, and she was it. She had no desire to put up with a jealous ex. She wanted to convince Jo it was them now, and she would be the one to stop Mike, so he got the message and didn't bother them again. She wanted Jo to put a gun in her hand, and then she'd blast the power games out of Jo's head.

Jo had absolute control of all she did except for one thing. Fucking. She had said she missed Sharon as a lover. She needed to get laid.

And Jamie thought to herself she was just the one to fuck her like there was no tomorrow. If she licked her just right, there wouldn't be.

CHAPTER 61

Working for the agency, Mike knew it had advantages when on a mission. As an operative, he'd be able to zoom in to the compound from a satellite in real time. Approaching the airport, Mike wished he had satellite visuals to Jo's compound to spot where Jamie was running to. The agency didn't know that James was dead, and Mike could turn to others at headquarters who thought James would approve helping him. He had decided all that was over. He realized he had learned the hard way that trust wasn't a word that existed with agency staff or any in charge.

As they neared the runway, Mike turned to Angie to do what agents often did before a critical mission. He'd engage in idle conversation to distract from any tension of what was coming. Saying most all the new social media jargon was not only not original or new, it was rehashed, all from people too young to know where it came from. He didn't want to bother Victor to explain what "coming in hot" meant and where it came from. He understood that each new generation thought they were new, and they came up with things nobody had ever come up with before. What really happened with each new generation was they grew up hearing terms or watching movies or TV and heard wording that was no longer popular to use. At some point, it popped into their minds, and they thought they invented it — or know they didn't but could lay low and make claim to it. It was how things changed yet stayed the same.

"I was going to ask Victor, a guy in the military, fighter pilot, not hip or an influencer, and from Russia, if he was up on the latest stuff and ask if he knew what coming in hot meant. He's busy landing. So, do you know who came up with it or where it came from?"

Shaking her head, giving him a look of how he simply didn't understand, she was letting Mike know he was well past being up on how people talked today. It was the look all teens gave anyone over twenty knowing how they just don't get it — and they weren't important anymore.

"It's from a song by two guys a long time ago. Like, I was... like ten or eleven. That's where. And it's about driving up, ready to go. Guy pulls up and the girl better get in or he's gone. So, yeah, I can see where maybe he heard it on the radio or somewhere and figured we we're

Not Taken

landing, ready to go. That's cool. We're coming in hot."

Mike thought about letting her think that, but realized Angie was smart and wanted to learn as much as she could. She would need to see that age and what most people thought was a shortcoming in the world they faced in dealing with people of all ages and from all different backgrounds. He shrugged, saying it was somewhat close, but two guys getting play on social media weren't the ones who came up with it, just made money off of it.

"Victor would get a bang hearing your origin story. I can only imagine the ones who came up with it weren't having PTSD triggered in them."

Watching Angie's expression change to a mix of surprise and genuine concern, she asked why, and said she didn't get it. Mike was glad she lost the teenage superiority stance, and it's why he was always impressed by her.

"It's a term my dad used. He was in Vietnam. That's not talked about in America much anymore, but we lost over a hundred thousand boys not much older than you getting involved in some war we weren't part of. Long story about why, all bad. It was in the sixties, so a long time ago. They were in jungles and swamps, so guys were dropped off and picked up in helicopters that had large caliber guns mounted in big open cargo bays. When they got ready to land to drop the soldiers off, the gunners were told to fire when ready. That alerted troops on the ground they would come in guns blazing. The guns would just blast away, and guess what? They would glow from the large rounds blasting, and they were too hot to get near or touch. So, they'd radio and said they were…"

Angie looked so sad as she finished the sentence.

"Coming in hot…"

Angie's face showed she felt horrible for making fun of Victor, and thinking things she heard were always what social media claimed they were. She looked at Mike, shaking her head.

"Those men… well, I get it now. They'd see the guns killing people, maybe ones not even enemies and that was a scary moment when they could get shot at or shot down. And there's some song talking about being pissed at a girl who isn't dressed yet…"

He looked at Cindy, and she nodded. She looked over to Angie, telling her what she thought of it all.

"What matters is even if you didn't know where it came from, just hearing where, and why, you figured out what it did to men who were there. You figured it out. That the guys who used it that way in some song to make money didn't care if it triggered those men. I bet they knew. Saw it in a movie or something. It isn't that people can't use a term like that. But imagine if the song was about respecting where it comes from, or telling a woman not to worry, life isn't a war zone. The man she was getting ready for wasn't coming in hot. To show some respect for women and how they should never be told that. They can just say they're there and can't wait to see them, so, whenever they're ready, they're ready to see her."

Again, Mike was stunned at how Cindy said things in ways where she helped Angie learn and think larger than herself. She talked about a better way to do something. Looking at her, he gave her a little thumbs-up, one he was sure Angie couldn't see if she were looking his way, but she wasn't. Cindy smiled at him, then let him see her turn to look at Angie with a loving smile for her. Angie was wiping her eyes, and she realized she had said something that could hurt Victor and she had fallen for nonsense in media and online. Before turning to Cindy, she managed to ask Mike if Victor had been in Vietnam.

"I don't know. He's old enough. I'm pretty sure military terms like that applied to their guys in the same situations. He's been in charge of a lot of young soldiers who think they know it all, so I think he'd understand. It would be good to learn about what life is like for someone in combat, like we are right now. He knows what it's like to deal with losing people and killing people and not even knowing why it's all happening. He's a good man. Here, because he's from Russia, people would instantly think he's some bad villain. And he'd give his life to save us if it came to that. That's a mistake we don't want to make. People are people and if we think of them that way, we'll do the right things."

Looking to Cindy, she saw that Cindy was proud of her. She understood they were sharing things to make her smarter and kind, not giving her a hard time or treating her like some child.

"Mom, all the girls out there think it's so okay. It's not. Mom, how'd you get all those smarts?"

They both were smiling, and Cindy heard the flaps go up to land, saying,

"Runs in the family. You're stuck with them too."

Hitting the short runway, the braking flew them forward. As the jet turned back from the end of the runway then headed to a parking area, they saw a black Suburban waiting for them. Bringing the cabin door perfectly lined up to it, Victor called back he was not going to shut down, he wanted to take off. He said the man with the car was there to assist if needed. Mike went to the cockpit, said they were fine. Reviewing the GPS route the car would take, he made sure Victor could track him using an app on his phone. They nodded at each other and Mike told him they'd radio when they parked, then look for him when he flew over. Victor smiled, saying he heard his talking with Angie. He winked at Mike.

"Sweet girl, just new, you do good tell her things like that. So, tell her not to stand on door sill of Yankee car. I'll be very low to ground. Tell Angie Victor coming in hot!"

He was glad he knew Victor. With him, there was no cold war or world far apart from where they were. He was a man of integrity unlike the weasels at the covert agencies, or even the military now. He knew such good people are at their best when things got bad. Looking at Cindy carrying a bag full of weapons, he saw the same in her.

Cindy was at her best when things were bad.

Behind her, Mike watched as Angie checked her thigh holster straps, lifting a bag weighing near as much as she did. Like her mother, the horror of being trafficked, sold, treated like a thing — not a human being, had made her know the value of human lives. It had made her strong, not angry or afraid. She was exactly like she looked. A warrior when facing anyone hurting people; and a loving, sweet girl when no gear was needed.

Mike was sure they saw the same in him. He had faced horrific truths, as with James, and stopped it. Leaving the lies of the agency, he was where he belonged. With good people. He was one with them and let them know he would do anything for them. Meeting Jamie was when he realized he could look past where a person had been and ask if that's where they wanted to stay. Like Cindy and Angie, she had been in the worst situation possible and like being in a dark room, her inner light showed her the truth that she had been programmed to think bad was good, good was bad. Once the light showed her the way she was

doing what she could to stop Vlad and Brian, and anyone else including the men who had taken her when five. Alone, knowing she had to stop them, willing to die to take them down, she knew to get them she had trafficked girls. Worse, she knew that would continue if she succeeded at stopping them.

Mike knew the person who would take her place if she managed to walk away wouldn't have stopped Vlad or Brian. Killing Brian, cutting off the head, was the only way to make a dent and save some girls. Jamie was still haunted by things she did, and he was sad Charles was one of the bad ones. She'd need help with the trauma of all she had been through. If there was such a thing as a decent and caring therapist, he would find them and suggest Jamie talk to them. He wasn't her therapist and didn't want to be the one she worked it out with. He wanted to be her friend, her love, and the one who understood her pain.

As they faced rescuing her from Jo, he needed to be the one to save her from yet another maniacal trafficker.

Getting in the Suburban, the man renting it to them said have a nice evening. He smiled at him, thanking him for getting the car ready on short notice. The man put his head slightly in to the car, where Mike was behind the wheel, to be heard over the jet engines.

"Lot's of calls needing a car at all hours. But, not from ones like you. Most always some of them Magdalenes. Rent this machine, leave alone, come back with little girls in white lace dresses. I still get riled seein' that each time. It's none too hard to know that Magdalene place must be holding someone you want out of there. That must be rough. And you know ain't no law man or anyone goin' help you. Watch out for 'em. They smile all the time, but those ain't really smiles. If you ain't one of them, doin' the sick stuff with those little girls, they'll shoot you and take that girl there in the back seat while you bleed out. You ain't Magdalene, you don't need to be alive. Girl don't need to be one of 'em. They'll give her some of their religion, and she'll be one of them brides. Well, go do some preachin' of your own. Just felt a need to warn you of 'em. You're the first I rented to that ain't one of 'em. And me? No, never been one of them. Have a daughter they'd sure like to be a bride, but they know better than to try."

Waiting for Victor to take off, Mike was waiting and was at first worried the man would warn Jo they had showed up. Hearing the man,

and that he had a daughter, he could see in his face he meant all he had said. He asked them how he was sure about his daughter being safe. Backing up to give them room as the jet had taxied away, before he did, he smiled at Mike.

"I just done told any who asked about if she was a Magdalene when she was here helpin' me that no, she was a lesbian and hated men. Rather shoot one than talk to one. Just glad I was her pa or I'd probably have been shot long ago. I don't think they'd care none; if she was a lesbian, and that's just what I say as she ain't one, but it was the shootin' men that made them lose interest real fast. I heard one talk about some young gal who done shot a whole lot of elders. They said now look at what she was doing. From what they said, I guess she's the one you're headin' to visit. Best know she ain't afraid of shootin' anyone comes for a girl she didn't say was okay to have. Well, enough of me, safe to drive now the jet done took off. All you come back with your girl. Tell 'em her wife wants her back. That seems to get them worried some!"

As they drove off, he thought about how Sharon had been Jo's lover. That told him they didn't care what the good book said. They were fine with a woman loving a woman if she gave them what the good book said they had domain over. Brides. Young, pretty, and a lot of them.

CHAPTER 62

"No. I explained that you can't leave. Tell me where the drive is and after the time he requires, we go get it and then we'll see what Allan says. You'll get a lot of money, but it's going to be from us, not from the men on the drive by you blackmailing them."

Whimsey was in jeans and a plain sweater top. Her hair was down and loose, and she wasn't wearing much makeup. She didn't look as young as most times Charles saw her. She still looked like a girl no more than thirteen, but nowhere close to the twenty-year-old woman she was. He knew her age, history, and how she had used the medical condition that kept her small and from developing like a girl having gone through puberty would look. Her hips were narrow, she hadn't any breasts, and physically she looked prepubescent. She was experienced in how sex was a way to make money, allowing men to legally have sex with what appeared to be a child, but was an adult free to have any sex she wished. She had also learned to use her looks, and offering sex, as a weapon.

She was working the agency, and the issue keeping her from trading the flash drive for money was if she had accessed the data on it or had made a copy. She understood they were worried that was the case, and that they had a way to find out. The man in charge of her offer, Allan, said two things would address their concerns.

"I'm glad you know we want to work with you, but also need to know the data hasn't been copied or accessed. So, those two things, once established, will allow us to execute the transaction. Time is the first form of proof. If anyone has a copy, or has had access to it, they will use it. We seed sources with names that are actually our own people. If the data is in use, they'll be contacted. We'll also get called from ones blackmailed so, we'll know. I think four months should do it. Many names are of top politicians up for reelection, and even if they're not reelected, they face ruin if revealed. If they stay elected, that makes the data even more valuable as it could get them out of office. So, let's let the election be our timeline. The second is that we want you to spend most of that time with Charles. You've met him. The shrink. He assures us he can put you in a hypnotic state or use drugs to learn if the disk you have is the only copy. He's been told not to attempt to find its location. We have reasons for not wanting that answered. We only wish to be sure

we're the only ones to have the drive, that it's the only one. The original."

She had always thought Allan was an idiot, and there was something sick about him. After telling her the conditions, she offered a less complicated process.

"Allan, what if there's a better way to know absolutely that it's the only one? I know how to convince you without all that. Wondering how? Well, here's how. Later, you take me to a place of your choosing, and I fuck you in ways you never knew possible. You'd have all of me to let you know I'm the real thing, just like the drive. Your dick up my ass is all the proof you'll ever need, or ever want. I'm so willing to give you assurances every way you could possibly need. I know one thing. I'll be the best deal you ever make."

He didn't take the deal. Telling her nice try, a man in his position could get better deals, no offense intended, but she wasn't the only one who had such assurances. A few weeks later she realized he had put the emphasis on the first syllable of assurances. Shaking her head at the message, she thought him even more bizarre. When it came to ass, she was the top of the charts. He would never have one like hers, ever. That meant waiting, which wasn't the worst thing possible, but the Charles part was bad to start, and had become beyond unbearable. She needed to get fucked by an actual man, or woman. And his lame attempts to hypnotize her was like a bad TV movie. She'd pretend to be in a hypnotic state, and he'd ask the same question about the drive in many different ways. If she bought a movie ticket and it had a seat assigned, and they sold a ticket to the same seat, would she think it was okay or would she get angry… that was one of her favorites. Each time he thought he put her under, he would make a post hypnotic suggestion that she longed for his dick, and he was the best she'd ever had.

Giving her drugs, they never seemed to do much except make her anxious or drowsy. For the ones making her feel drugged, or needing to sleep, she decided to lay on the couch and act like it put her to sleep. That was also pathetic. He'd ask the same questions, then ask how she liked him fucking her. Then, sure she was out, he'd start feeling her up, or beat off after pulling her panties down. He'd cum in his cupped hand, and then he'd lick it up and swallow it. She'd seen guys do it for money, but maybe men who never got laid or were perverts did that, but no guy she ever fucked wanted any cum in his mouth.

Dealing with his sick acts had gotten to be too much. She could run off and make money fucking rich men. It would take longer but as she was well-known as a porn queen — or princess as she looked too young to be a queen — it was better than being with a sick fuck pervert like Charles.

"I don't care about the money. You can have the drive, and not pay me, so who cares about copies and access if you don't pay me? I just want out of here. And if you don't let me out, I'll get out somehow. I'm going crazy trapped in here. I told you that if we go get the drive, we bring it to that Allan fuck, give it to him, he can wait his fucking however much longer the four month thing ends, the be all sure about it. After that he can pay me or not pay me or whatever. Fucking hell, I'm giving you the drive and I'm the one who can't be trusted? I don't trust him, get it? He's fucked up!"

She hadn't told Charles she'd fuck Allan as he clearly wanted to be her only fuck. At this point, she didn't care as she wanted out no matter how. He asked her why would she doubt Allan. He had been reasonable, and he needed to be sure of the drive. She let loose.

"Doubt him? Why? Let's see what you think when I explain. Before I was brought here, he told me all his shit about making sure and you probing my deepest places. First, he didn't say you'd be probing my cunt. So that. But, that, hey, I get that part. You have some hot ass you can take advantage of, so that's what any fucker would do if they could. So, maybe he didn't know, though I doubt he's actually that stupid. No, I offered to make the deal easy. To give him all the assurance he needed, with all the A-S-S in assurance he could ever dream of. I told him I'd fuck him every way possible and that was all the ass-sure-ance he would ever need. The guy's really fucked up and I know he's a fuckin' liar. He didn't go for it, then told me in his position he could get assurances anytime he wanted, and better than what I had to offer. That, Charles, is bullshit. No way he's going to get a girl like me. Ever. I was tops in porn, and that I know for sure. So, he's stupid, a liar, and if he was gay, he could have said barking up the wrong dick, babe. So, a guy who won't fuck this cunt of mine? I don't trust him. You're supposed to be a shrink, right? Can't you figure it out now that I told you. He passed this ass up. No guy in his right mind would do that. I'd watch out for him if I was you."

Charles stood, listening to her carefully. He didn't show any expression more than curiosity, which was upsetting her as well. Waiting for him to reply, he thought about what to say for a few minutes, then looked at her and said if she was over her ranting on about it, he had some things to say. She said she was waiting, and he remained calm while talking.

"I wasn't showing a response as I was hearing two things. I pay attention at times like this to get things right. First, the ranting, the going off. I think that's because you've let it stir in you and not talk about it. You've learned your body has value, and you know it. You have pride being desired and that is understandable. I haven't heard you say you've ever been rejected by any man, so that may be why you didn't want to talk about it. You're pissed off he turned you down. Any woman who is attractive and willing to give a man sex would feel as you do. So, that is one part, and it creates the real issue. Now, I'm being detailed as I want to make sure what I heard is what you meant. So, on only your being told no to your offer to fuck him any way he wanted, is what I said how you felt about that?"

Nodding, then laughing, she told him sure, she wasn't used to it and it was a shock, but his loss. It wasn't the end of the world. She added she didn't like the part saying he could do better as it was meant to hurt her or say she wasn't that great and no need to insult her. He was listening and nodding in agreement.

"Good. All valid, and implying he could do better that was the most upsetting part as he went out of his way to demean you, implying he had power to get what he wanted. It said the sex you offered, or your attraction to any rational man who is attracted to women, wasn't much."

Simply nodding to say that was so, he continued to the second part.

"In that, he was saying his power was greater than the temptation from you. As it was sex related to a matter of trust, and money, it was more than just rejection. You know that females appearing to be a girl is a male fantasy, and not one most men would have available to them unless quite above the law and very rich. You know that, and no man, free from any risk as you're of legal age, would pass that up. Most men, even if you appeared your actual age wouldn't pass that up. He would at least say it may help, or he wanted to see if it was worth taking a risk for. You, being an expert on such a response, is from experience and a

world of men willing to take any risk to have you. But, he doesn't show any interest, insults you, and wants to assert power by putting you here for four months. At the same time, he has you with a man who will hypnotize and drug you to find out if you are truthful, and he says that is why, and not to learn where the drive is. You know that in such a state, you would surrender the location, and I could get the drive, never pay you, even arrest you for failing to surrender it. His saying that, having me here, and staying four months would prove it wasn't copied or shared would also lead you to question him. Such information would be effective for as long as the men lived. The only conclusion is that he was not being truthful, and it was unlikely he'd honor his part of the agreement. That is not the emotional part, though being used, lied to, and uncertain do create emotional responses. Again, I have fully explained what I was hearing, and do you think I heard it correctly?"

Whimsey thought he was finally doing what a shrink was supposed to do, and that was figure out what a person was feeling based on what they thought or was done to them. She figured as long as she was getting it all out, she wanted to know if she could trust him. She would tell him about what she had learned about him, and see if he became abusive, or curled up into a ball in the corner.

"The Allan part, yeah, something's wrong, he's playing games. Can't trust him. But I have another part. I wasn't going to say it as I am not out to hurt people, you know, for no reason like he did. But, it's part of it. I assume you guys talk and know about each other. He puts you here with me, and I figured at first, hey, maybe it's like a bonus or a gift to a friend or he owes you. He knows you fuck all the pussy you can, and that I'd let you fuck me as sex is just like, you know, how I make money and for this, part of the deal. And I was okay with that. I fucked you as much as you wanted. I didn't do it to get anything for it. I never said hey, you do this for me and I'll fuck you, right?"

Nodding, Charles said that was well said, and no, she never offered sex for anything in return.

"Well, I'm glad you have that straight as there's stuff where maybe it's connected with Allan being pretty scary as if he knows this part, then I really need to get out now. You know all the times you were putting me under and giving me stuff? I never was really under. I was aware, and I wasn't hypnotized and you suggested it, and I'll explain how I know. The

same with the pills. They made me groggy, most of them, and I didn't want to get more pumped in me so I pretended to sleep while you asked things. Did you know that?"

Charles looked concerned, his first real reaction.

"Well, that is a concern. I was sure you were. I've done such to many patients, and some were resistant, but I could always tell. If that's so, you put one over on me as I was sure you were under. It was deceptive, but given your concern with Allan, that may be why you didn't allow yourself to fall into the suggestive state."

Seeing it was something that upset him, she thought it mostly his professional pride, but he did get the why part right.

"Yes, of course. He does that, puts me in with you, I'm scared, and I couldn't relax or let myself go out. It wasn't trying to be deceptive. It was trying to stay alive. I kept thinking if I went under, you'd find out how to get the drive, then Allan would have what he wanted then kill me to be sure I could never tell anyone about it. I mean, I was scared for my life, that's why it didn't work. Not because you didn't know what you were doing."

Adding the part about he knew what he was doing, she wanted to not make him feel inadequate. And, that part was yet to come. He returned to his calm state and asked her more about that part.

"Okay. I understand. In this situation, rather than feeling safe to go under, and that does require both trust and a feeling of being safe, you were frightened, alarmed, and didn't want a greater effort to gain information from you. But, on the part of my being in with Allan, and you being worried about me, why that?"

She was astounded. She had just told him she was conscious during it all, and he knew what he had done while thinking she was out.

"I wasn't at first. But, I mean, I just said I wasn't out. I was aware of everything during those sessions. And that's the part where I started thinking maybe Allan knew things about you, or something, because you were doing some things doctors don't do when people are out. I mean, not supposed to do. You were doing a bunch of perv stuff. Pulling my pants down, feeling me up, beating off, eating your jizz while looking at me. I mean, I could kind of get that if it was where you couldn't do me, but during all that time you were fucking me every day. I can kind of figure that stuff out. I mean, if it's just another thing that turns you

on and gets you off, well, sex is crazy shit, But, put it all together and it's all too much for me. I don't think a doctor is supposed to do that. The crazy thing is that once you knew I'd do whatever the fuck you wanted, if you said, hey, pretend you're sleeping, and I want to perv out over you, I'd say sure, whatever gets you off. That's what I'm for."

Watching him carefully as she said the part about his actions, it was hard for her to see if it upset him, or he was surprised hearing she'd have let him do it if he asked. His eyes closed for a minute, then looked sad as he talked about it.

"Whimsey, if I asked and you said sure, okay with you, and went along with it, that wouldn't be the same. It was you not knowing that was exciting. I'm obligated to do right, not do that. It's the being bad that was exciting for me. Doing something I wasn't supposed to do. I'm really sorry you were aware of it. I mean more sorry than I can express. It changes things. All that allowed me to manage things, the desires in me. With you knowing, it takes all that away as if I never had done them. You're smarter than I thought. The part about Allan doing something for me. Giving me some sort of reward? That was what happened. This was for me, not to wait to validate the security of the drive. It was to keep me in line, and out of big trouble…"

Freaking out, Whimsey knew her instincts were right. Allan had lied and put her with Charles to let him do things that were sick because he was a sick fucker. Trying to not appear worried, she knew she had to get him settled and then find a way to get out. She didn't know exactly how sick he was, but he was already implying he was back to a place where he wasn't okay.

"Charles, okay, it wasn't hard to figure out. I get the part about getting off because I didn't know. That's what does it for you. So, if I had known the truth from day one, I would have been feeling less worried and understood that's what you needed, so why worry about it? Now, I know. I'm bummed I said anything to ruin what it did for you. But, chill. You know, now, hey, when I'm asleep, or you put me under, get back to where your need is taken care of. Will that help?"

Looking at her, he looked beat down and depressed.

"Thank you for offering that. I mean it. You're not out to hurt anyone, and you're not what I expected you to be like. It's a mess now. Just like you said, Allan did this for a reason. Ah, shit. This isn't good.

Not good. I thought you'd be trash. That you'd put me down and laugh at me when we fucked. But, you've been kind, and not because you had to be. You could have said no every time. Now, I can't do this. I'm going to get something to fix this. Please, just stay there. This is something that we have to do."

Scaring her more with each word, and seeing him look tortured, she knew everything was locked and why she couldn't just run off. She started panicking, thinking she'd need to do something like break a window or anything to get away. As she started looking around, Charles was suddenly in front of her holding a 45 revolver. She fainted.

Gasping for air, she was alert again, and Charles was there, looking sick, holding the gun. She got up to run, but he pushed her down to her chair, telling her to stop, and don't run. She was shaking and could only see how big the gun was in his hand.

"Whimsey, men become shrinks to try to figure out why they're fucked up. That's why I did it. I'm sick. Bad sick. In the army. I was able to do things that kept my sickness under control. Since I've been back, it hasn't been where I could go and kill people like Iraq or other places. Allan was there with me, and he knows what I need. Since being back, he gives me a way to deal with it. It was going to end up with me saying you tried to run, and I had to stop you. He gave me this to get okay for a while. It sucks because you're not like the ones I didn't think should live. Bad ones. You, you've been decent, nice, so nice. Whimsey, this is going to suck. I can't do this anymore. I need to do this, right now."

Screaming, realizing he meant kill people, and he needed to get off by killing her. She started screaming, then shouting, no, no, no, please, no, over and over. He didn't say anything as she pleaded. After she could barely scream any longer, he said only one word, sorry, then put the large barrel into his mouth and blew the top of his head off.

She sat sobbing, looking only once at what had happened to his head. Blood and bone and brains were dripping on the wall behind him, and from the ceiling. She was in a state of shock that she was alive, not from what she had seen.

Getting to the floor, she crawled away to the corner of the room and curled up into a ball, sobbing, letting all that happened sink in. As her thoughts started to sort things out, she realized she was alive. That Charles was as he said, a sick man who knew it and should have

sought help, not help himself by feeding his sick need. That her showing him simple kindness and not making fun of him even though she had thought such things, it wasn't where she thought him as anything but a pathetic fuck, and why rub it in. He didn't need to feel worse about it. She hadn't made fun of the perverted things he did, and somehow facing someone who had been kind about all his sick traits made him realize it would be wrong to kill her, and it was wrong to keep on doing what he had been, so killed himself. He was free from the sick human being he was.

Then, she recalled all that was said. Allan had fed him with the lowest of the low to act on. Allan had been feeding his beast. Sitting up, she was realizing her first impressions were right. Something was wrong with Allan as well. No man in his position would take such risks for Charles. He had something to hide. She thought he was probably getting help from Charles, and this was paying his bill. Allan was so bad he had to be stopped.

Walking over to the body that had been Charles, as horrible as it was to see, she had a new strength once realizing it was Allan who had put her there to be used in a manner beyond sick. He was evil.

She pulled the gun up from the floor where it had flown. It was huge, and heavy. Reaching into his pockets, she found keys, money, and in the wallet, a key card that would get her into the agency.

She had everything she needed. As Charles talked to Allan each day, he already had called that morning and she heard Charles ask what he was doing in town. She had until the next day as Allan would realize not getting an answer would alert him something had happened. If she sat there and waited, he may send agents to investigate, or most likely show up himself. If he did, he'd have a gun out and he was skilled with it, she wasn't.

She'd need to get to the agency, and into the garage. She didn't think she'd be able to get into the offices with just the key pass. But the garage and his car? That would be possible. She could wait, watch, and when he left, shoot him there. Or, follow him and shoot him where nobody could see her do it. Then, leave, go to Mike. Tell him what happened. That, or live in fear all her life. Sharon had made it clear that Mike was not like the others at the agency. He was a do-right guy, in her words. He would find out about her, and she needed to stop him, even if he was her

brother. There was no way he would let her do the things she was doing when he found out the truth. Whimsey decided it would be safe to tell Mike the truth.

He was the only one who would understand. He left the agency because they must have wanted him to do something wrong. She flashed on how Allan was the something that was very wrong.

She decided not to go the agency or follow Allan. She would go to Mike. She hadn't killed Charles, she hadn't done anything to get in trouble for except hide the drive Sharon gave her, doing what she asked. When Mike understood the truth, she could only pray he would believe her. The last time he saw her was when she was standing behind Cindy and Angie as she was shot by her lover, his sister, Sharon.

Then, she had been at the hospital, then disappeared.

None of that was in her favor, but it was all true, and she hoped he could see she was not lying.

CHAPTER 63

Standing at the corner of the building, Jamie could only assume Jo was looking at the remote camera monitors rather than chasing her. If she waited too long, she'd lose the credibility she was putting on an act for Mike. Walking in would surprise Jo, and she may have a gun with her, or felt there wasn't a need for one yet. She was certain the most dangerous option was to run. The one where there was a bit of hope was going in and acting like she was on Jo's side as a lover.

Frightened as she was, it was nothing compared to the adrenaline rush she had experienced. It had helped her, and she knew it would kick in again if needed. Jo was ruthless, but that also meant that she knew Mike, Cindy and Angie were coming, and she may be more valuable alive and with her than on the run. She knew, from some intuition, that going in and not running was the best thing to do.

Getting herself calm, making sure her hair was in place, she climbed the few steps up into the building, and walked in.

Everything seemed normal. The light in the big room used for an office was lit, and she could see the slight flickering of monitors. She didn't slow and stop, just looked around as she entered. Jo would be watching the foyer, and she was glad she thought of that. Walking into the office, as she felt would be the case, Jo was there, looking at them, going from one to the next. She turned to her, looking happy about how things went, and called to Jo.

"How'd I do. Did they fall for my panicking and running out?"

There was a short pause as Jo listened to her, then she turned her chair faster than expected, looking right at her.

"You did great! They bought it. And we didn't even plan it. Well, come here you…"

Holding out her arms as she stood, Jo was giving her a look of appreciation as she walked to her, then she grabbed her and started kissing her with all-out sexual passion. When she finally took her tongue out of her mouth, Jamie smiled and said she did a great job acting all crazy. Smiling, Jo said she'd had a lot of practice.

"I was just looking to see where you ran off to. I'm hungry."

Jamie thought things were going alright, but she couldn't be sure.

"Nowhere, I just went off to the side of the building. I didn't know

how long you'd be on the phone, and they'd see me if I walked in too soon."

Holding her chin with her index finger, Jo was grinning.

"Smart. Well, when you ran off, things ended fast. I'm toying with letting them wait, you know, see what they'll do. And, well, I have a confession to make. I feel bad about something. I did all that to well, test if you were serious about me. It wasn't for Mike. And, well, the bad part is that I'm sure he'll come storming the place, and it'll be where he's on one side, me on the other. So… what… will… Jamie…do? Who will you run to? I'm being bad… because I need to be sure."

Jamie wasn't surprised she told her. She could tell it was her style, and she was setting everything up. She thought of the best response. She made a kissing motion with her lips, and in the same sing-song kiddie manner, answered with, "Then you'll just have to wait and see. I'll be bad too. It'll be fun!"

It was easy for her to see Jo didn't expect the reply. She was expecting her to try and convince her she would choose her. Jo was looking, and she had caught her unprepared for the answer.

"Well, then, game on! You're a girl after my heart. Well, I hope some other places too. And, Jamie, when I said I was hungry, if you remember, we already had dinner, so I wasn't talking about food…"

Jamie was glad she had made it in and not been shot. More would happen, but it seemed that she was giving Jo the type of thrill she enjoyed most. She was playing her game, her way, which meant it would be dangerous and unpredictable. If she could make it through the night, she was sure Mike, Cindy and Angie were on their way, and when they came everything would be up for grabs. Jo had essentially declared war. She was what was being fought over, and the compound would be the battleground. She couldn't believe how many things had happened. Her whole life had revolved around the sickest things, and she had been with the sickest people imaginable. She now had Jo to add to her list.

Sitting at her desk, Jo had stopped watching the monitors, although she would glance at them occasionally. Asking what she was doing, Jo looked up and smiled at her, saying taking care of a few things she needed to do each day, and wouldn't be long. Walking to sit on the sofa to wait, Jo said why not get the whirlpool going, and she'd be there to join her as soon as she was finished.

"Jamie, there are a lot of gorgeous bath bombs and things to add. Pick out what you'd like, they're all nice. Oh, and music. Just ask out loud to play a song or display playlists. There's a screen on the wall for that. Surprise me!"

Smiling, nodding that it all sounded wonderful, Jamie went to the master bedroom. It was dimly lit, incense burning, and there were flowers almost everywhere she looked. It seemed Jo was anticipating the night ahead, which was typical of dealing with her so far. She hadn't had much time alone in the bedroom and wanted to explore all the things put here and there, but first started the water in the jetted tub. It was huge compared to any she had seen, and thought it large enough to swim in. It was also surrounded by flowers. There wasn't a faucet, and no faucet handles. There was a touch screen off to one side on the ledge, and she tried talking to it. Saying start a bath, there was a line all around the tub, and water began cascading from it like a waterfall. The screen displayed a question of how many? She said two. Finally, it asked tepid, warm or hot. Saying hot, the screen displayed a video of a natural hot spring.

Going to a cabinet, Jo had summed it up well. It was full of bath salts, bombs, soaps and some erotic toys. After picking out a bath bomb that said soothing, she hoped it would work. The last task was to put on some music. Just saying play Loreena McKennitt, it displayed a list of all her albums. She said, "The Book of Secrets," and music began playing.

Certain she had things set up nicely for the bath, she went to the bedroom and walked slowly to look at anything on dressers or tables. In the corner was a vanity that like all things in the room was custom made. There were things on it she expected. Brushes and combs, bottles of vintage perfume, and they were all ones hard to find. Shalamar was a favorite of hers, and opening the bottle, it filled her with a vision of a life she never had. Her mother, not dead on the floor of a camping trailer, but in a room lovely as the one she was in, standing by her as she dabbed a bit of the perfume behind her ear. Moving on to dressers, there were small statues and carvings, all primitive and looking authentic. There were crystal unicorns, flowers, and items she was sure were one-of-a-kind. What she didn't see were any photos. No picture frames, nothing of Jo in places she'd been or people she liked or loved. Looking around, she thought of how she too had no photos from her life growing up, and

there were no moments to remember that were nice. Her life was just starting, and she had suggested to Mike that they get a portrait taken. He had told her that he would love that.

Looking around, she thought it all sad. It could have been her room if she had as much money, and it would be just as sad. As beautiful as every item in the room was, she thought it would be better to have just one old photo of a little girl being hugged by a mother and father on a cheap dresser because that was more important than all the things around her.

Going back to the bath, the tub was full, and just by walking up to it, the jets started, and the water was swirling nicely. Checking the temperature, it was perfect, and the bath bomb scent was soothing and not too strong.

"How did you know I love this album?"

She turned around and saw Jo looking at her with surprise.

"I didn't. It's my favorite. The Arabian flavor, and it's not like any other music. Well, I'm not surprised you love it too. It goes wonderfully with the bedroom and this bath. I hope I thought of everything."

Walking up to her, Jo kissed her with passion, saying she had everything perfect. Jamie felt her pulling at her clothes, and she slowly undressed her, kissing and licking all the parts revealed, and she was licking in sync with the rhythms of the music. After all her clothes were off, she started to do the same for Jo, moaning with delight at certain places, humming along with the music.

Once their clothes were off, Jo spoke to the system, saying lights dim and star-like. The lights lowered and tiny LEDs in the ceiling and walls began twinkling. It was a fantasy room, and it was as if the album, the most romantic and erotic she had ever heard, had become real. Taking her by the hand, Jo took her to the mirror covering one wall across from the tub. They were lit by the soft lights, and the twinkles above and behind were like they were floating in the sky above. Jo put her head on Jamie's shoulder and was looking at the both of them in the mirror.

"Look at us… I don't think anyone could see two women as lovely as what's in that mirror. Bodies so stunning, everything just perfect… and the way we both fit together. The lights sparkling in our hair. It doesn't look like this when it's just me here. Back up a bit, I want you to see this…"

Helping Jamie move back enough where she could kneel in front of her, Jamie was facing the mirror, watching Jo kneeling then putting her head where she could begin probing her slit with her tongue. Holding her thighs, coaxing them to move apart, her legs moved to give Jo enough room, Jo moved her forward, her head tilted back to lick her gently, and in the mirror she saw her hands clutching and pulling Jo's hair, her thighs covered in it. The mirror reflected the flawless curves of Jo's sides sloping to her hips, making the rapid turn to shape her ass which was sitting on her feet. Her whole body was quivering from how Jo was licking her, and with a few gentle flicks on her clit, she bent over, grabbing at Jo's hips as she came. It was intense, and it released anxiety she had been feeling since the video call. She stayed leaning over Jo, rubbing her hips and lower back.

Without saying anything, just swaying with the music, as she stood up Jo was smiling, leading her to the tub, and they both got in, sitting next to each other, kissing, rubbing each other all over. With the flow of the water, the soft lighting, twinkling star lights, music she loved, the scent of the bath salts, surrounded by flowers, and still feeling the lingering sensations from cumming, Jamie thought it was surreal. It was a dream in a nightmare. She wanted the world to be like the place she was, free from horrors, guns, people she couldn't trust. Knowing Jo was one of them, for the moment, she didn't want to think about that. She was caught in the moment of sensations and smells, and the world outside of the room and worries no longer existed.

Jo moved her where she was sitting in front of her, and she began rubbing her shoulders, massaging her, finding all the right spots to release her tensions, and she was swaying as Jo mixed the rubs with leaning to kiss her in places, licking at times, and she was in a state of complete relaxation. Jo put her mouth to the side of her head over her ear, asking if she was making her feel special. It was just a whisper, and it blended with the music and the splashes of the water around them. Then Jo moved to put her mouth over her other ear, again whispering, this time asking if she wanted to make her feel special. Jamie nodded gently, turning to kiss her, and Jo kept massaging her as they kissed with Jamie's head up, Jo's sideways, and they could put their tongues fully into each other and Jo was moaning, then said she needed to cum.

Moving away from her mouth, she moved behind her again, telling

Jamie she would make her cum far beyond anything she'd ever known, then told her she'd show her how she was going to get her off.

Jo's hands rubbed up to her neck while wrapping her legs around her front, surrounding her completely. The massage grew stronger, and she let out a gasp as Jo had both hands around her neck, suddenly moving her arm fully around her neck in a choke hold, and the other pulling back on the arm around her neck. Jo had her in a strangle hold. Choking her, Jamie couldn't get air, her arms and legs were flailing and hitting the water, her hands moving up to pull Jo's arm off, but she couldn't get a grip as water and bath salts made Jo's arms slippery. Suddenly Jo pushed her head down fully into the water, and she was stronger than she thought possible. She was using her elbows to hit at her ribs, but she was starting to gasp, taking in water, and she felt the panic of drowning, doing everything she could to get free, but nothing stopped the arm round her neck from keeping her under the water. Jamie realized she was going to die in a matter of seconds.

As she felt water being sucked into her throat, trying not to take water, Jo's arm flew away from her and she felt Jo's body rise up, just feeling her legs, then they were gone. She didn't think she could, but she managed to spring up to put her head above the water, vomiting out water in her that she had gulped, filling her lungs.

Above the sounds of her choking, gagging, gasping, she heard a blaring siren. Vision blurred, she could see the lights in the room were fully lit and flashing. All she knew was she was out from under the water, Jo wasn't holding her and not in the tub. Heaving, she tried to stand up, slipping from the slick coating made by the bath bomb, but flung herself forward to keep from flying back and hitting her head on the ledge of the tub. Trying again, she needed to stand and cough out the water she had taken in. Managing to get hold of the ledge, making it to where she was standing, heaving, feeling a gush of water flow out her mouth and gasping for air, she saw Jo throwing on clothes, shouting, looking furious.

As loud as the siren was, she could hear Jo shouting out, not to her, to the ceiling, whatever was above her.

"Those fuckers are here. God damn fucking motherfuckers!"

Paying no attention to her, just getting herself clothed, Jo ran out the door, shouting to the panel on the wall to kill the alarm. The blaring

stopped, the lights stopped flashing, and Jo had left to confront whatever was causing the alarm. Getting out of the tub, her whole body hurting and making it hard to move, she was still coughing out small amounts of water but she was alive. She grabbed at her clothes, wanting only to get out and away, run far as she could, and not to follow Jo. As she pulled on her top, she heard a sound that shook the room and the whole building. It was the roar of jet engines so loud it hurt her ears worse than the sirens. It had to be a few feet above the building, it was so close.

First worrying it would crash into the building, it didn't. Then over the roar of the engines, she heard a loud voice saying not to help Jo, put her at the end of the airstrip. Then, it said, "Jamie, go to car on road."

Taking her first deep breath, she began running to get out of the building, then down the path to the gate by the road. She heard the jet engines make another pass, saying the same message. As she ran to leave, all the people in the buildings were running the other direction, to the airstrip, all shouting for Jo to get on the airstrip. She could feel the rush of wind as the jet flew over her so low she thought if she jumped up, she could touch it.

Running, laughing, her laugh growing hysterical, she was gasping for air, but managed to say one word, just to herself, one only she could hear.

"Mike."

CHAPTER 64

"Okay, keep at them. We're approaching the gate now. I have the blinkers on so she'll know which way to run."

Having just heard Victor say they were all scrambling to the air strip, Mike had just crested the hill that showed the compound ahead. Cindy was in the passenger seat, Angie kneeling on the large center console, and they all saw a scene right out of an action movie. Victor was flying Cindy's jet as if it were an F-16, going up into the sky past the compound, turning around in a maneuver only a fighter pilot could manage , then swooping down so close to the ground that they first thought he'd crash. He was flying just above the buildings, over the airstrip, then pulling up in a climb to do it again from the other direction.

"Wow, he's the best I've ever seen. That's stuff a small fighter jet can barely pull off."

Mike was in awe of how Victor struck terror in the people there, and they couldn't be sure if he had guns or canons. As if reading his mind, he recalled how Victor had filled his pockets, then flight bag, with smoke and full explosive grenades. The jet had a small window for the pilot, used when gated, not in flight. As they watched, they saw the jet, just approaching the landing strip, tilt pilot-side down slightly, then saw good sized explosions. Victor was hitting the strip with the smoke grenades, and he had people thinking they were bombs, which they were. Having called Victor, he said it was a great show, but they needed to head down and be there if Jamie could make it out. Angie said she had it all on her camera, and Mike turned, seeing her making a video of the jet. Mike was glad as it would be quite a video, and he rolled down the hill, working to keep his eyes on the steep road, not the air show ahead. Not worried about being seen, the whole compound was in a panic. He stopped short of the main gate, putting the emergency flashers on. Hearing Victor using the jet's loudspeaker, he was repeating for Jamie to go to the road. Mike said he'd keep an eye out for her, and if anyone was chasing after her, he'd crash through the main gate and get to her with the car,

Mike wasn't showing it, but he was worried, and could only hope Jamie was alive. If she was, he hoped she wasn't up in the mountains.

Each were things that he couldn't know, and he was betting on how quickly they made it off the ground and to the compound as the best bet that Jamie was alive. All he could do is wait. They were all quiet, watching for any sign of Jamie. Mike was watching the road out of the compound, Cindy was watching the mountains behind, and Angie was still filming, saying she could film and look at the mountainside ahead.

Swooping down for his next pass, Victor threw a live grenade out his window, being sure to hit an area where nobody was gathered. It was close enough to the airstrip they could hear screams of terror, and the blast was strong enough to send dirt and concrete flying into the air. He worried that someone would start shooting at the jet, but as of yet, nobody had attempted it as the way Victor was flying, the speed, the grenades, all sent a message of pure terror. He was certain they had rifles, but it was clear that none on the ground had military training. They weren't trying to stop the assault.

While concrete was still flying, Mike shouted he saw Jamie.

They all turned and saw her running, heading towards the gate but still a good distance from it. She was alive, and their plan was working. Mike drove ahead to get in front of the gate, then shouted to hold on.

Far behind Jamie was a Jeep that had come out from a building and was speeding towards her. Mike realized it could reach her if he waited at the gate. Flooring the Suburban, it crashed through the gate and speeding down the road. Seeing Jamie running, the lights of the Jeep racing towards her, he shouted for them to buckle up, he'd need to ram the Jeep. Telling Cindy to get in the back seat, he felt her jump to the back and shout she was buckled in. He could tell if he slowed down to pick Jamie up, the Jeep could make it to them, then ram her as she scrambled to get in. He needed to stop the Jeep, and the only way was to get past Jamie and go right at the Jeep. Shouting for Cindy to roll her window down, waving a sign for Jamie to get off to the side of the road, he heard the window roll down, and the sound of the jet filled the car.

Not slowing down, he saw Jamie running off the road. She'd seen Cindy who had her top half out the window, Jamie understanding the message. Mike yelled to get back inside, Cindy saying she'd use her AR-15 to fire at the Jeep. Mike had first thought to ram it, but that would leave them without a way out if the car was totaled. He called to Angie to hand him one, and she was on it, and she put it

where it was ready to fire as he grabbed it.

Heading right to the Jeep, Mike went fast as the car would go as it was almost on Jamie. Passing her, he slammed the brakes, skidding the Suburban sideways where both front and back windows on the driver's side faced the Jeep which wasn't slowing down as it headed for them, not Jamie. Before even fully stopped, Mike and Cindy pulled their triggers and both guns fired non-stop into the windshield of the Jeep, then just as fast Cindy thought to shoot the front tires and managed to hit them. At the last moment, the Jeep looking like it would ram them, and that speed would kill them, it went into a spin. Its front tires, both blown out, caused it to swerve enough to miss them in its spin, and it was inches away from their doors as it went into a tumble off the road, flipping over several times, landing on its roof.

Mike knew they had just managed to not be killed, and it was Cindy taking out the tires that did it. He heard the gasp Cindy and Angie made as the Jeep just made it past them and went into its spin.

Mike shouted he'd secure the Jeep, and for them to get Jamie. All three flew out, Angie jumping up and down as she saw Jamie running to them, shouting their names. She ran into the arms of both Cindy and Angie, and she was crying, thanking them over and over. Angie, letting go of both of them, said she was going to help Mike, Cindy nodding for her to go. Angie pulled back the fire lever on her AR-15 as she ran to where Mike was. Taking Jamie to the Suburban, Cindy felt Jamie stopping at the door, saying she needed to see. Cindy understood, saying she'd guard the road, going to the side of the Suburban facing the compound. Standing with her rifle aimed to the road, she was moving it left and right to look for anyone coming at them off from the sides of the road.

Reaching the Jeep, Angie saw Mike was just getting up from looking inside, shaking his head. He still held his rifle, but his moving away meant the driver hadn't survived. Angie stood, circling, making sure nobody was coming at them from any direction. Mike saw Jamie running to him and the Jeep, and he grabbed to stop her. Looking up at him, she needed no words. He understood. She needed to see, to look in the Jeep, to know it was over.

Joining Angie in circling to fire at anything moving, Victor was still making passes and he didn't want him to stop until they were well on

their way, only once sure nobody followed after them. He turned, saw Jamie near the ground, looking into the Jeep. The roof was caved almost flat, and there was blood on the ground and on shards of the shattered windshield. He called out that they needed to go. She took a final look, got up, then ran to the Suburban, Mike and Angie, walking backwards, keeping guard at a critical moment. Mike stood at the drivers door of the car, saying all clear, get in. Angie and Jamie jumped in the back seat as Cindy, rifle still pointing to the road as she backed up, worked her way into the front passenger seat.

Mike hit the pedal, spinning around back to the gate, then out, and was back on the road to the town airport. After driving a mile from the compound, he called Victor saying they were headed back, but one more pass to keep anyone from following. Victor said he had it.

"Tell Angie she will see truth. Watch as I land. I be coming in hot."

Mike had him on the car speaker. Angie, smiling, called out she was excited to see the real thing.

Jamie was sitting, taking deep breaths, Cindy looking back and seeing Angie was holding her hand. She saw no need to tell her things were okay, or she was out of there. Jamie knew that. She needed time to wind down, realize she was alive, and with the ones who loved her. Angie reached into their duffel bag and took out some bottles of water, giving two for up front, then one to Jamie and one for herself.

After a few minutes, they all heard the roar of Cindy's jet above them and saw the lights blinking on it as it passed over them to get to the airport. Mike was already thinking of what waited for them as they returned home. Next, it was the agency to battle. Hit men, Charles, Whimsey, and who knew what else waited. He would talk about it on the ride back, but for now, knowing Jamie was sitting right behind him was most important. As he thought that, he felt her hand rubbing his cheek. Gently, a simple touch, letting him know she loved him.

Looking, Cindy saw Jamie's hand and smiled, happy for Jamie and Mike. She was still holding her rifle, and her window was down in case she needed to fire at some car behind them. Mike nodded at her, and he thought of how she shot out the tires. He hadn't. There she was, sitting calmly, smiling at Jamie's gesture. She had just faced death, managed to do the thing that saved them from being killed, and somehow she could smile. He could only think of how amazing she was. All the weapons

they had, the jet, Victor, those were all hers, knowing she could have all her money instead. That wasn't what she wanted. She made the commitment to fighting traffickers, raising Angie... and as he looked at her, knowing she loved him but wouldn't do anything to come between him and Jamie.

In the world full of such horrific people doing horrible things, Cindy had become his lighthouse. She guided him, and she, like a lighthouse, kept him away. She was by herself, keeping them all safe.

Driving north, in the crystal clear of the Montana sky he saw the northern lights were visible, a rare sight there. He looked at her, saying to look up, the aurora borealis was there, and it had kept dark until they finished their rescue. As Cindy looked up, Jamie and Angie had ducked low and could see it too. They could only look, amazed, no words could explain why it had appeared. The silence was broken as Angie took her camera to make a video of it, saying she would send it to all of them.

Seeing Cindy's face, looking up at the sky, it's colors softly lighting her face, Mike knew she was beyond beautiful from the moment he first saw her. Now, knowing her, he understood her beauty was from who she was, not how she looked. She was her own aurora borealis, and her beauty was a light that shined from inside her and all she did or said. He had never heard her ask for anything for herself. Then, he thought again, and smiled. She had asked for some head-popping hollow core ammo when she shot the sheik who had bought her and Cindy back in Russia. Then, feeling a warmth inside himself, he realized she hadn't asked that for herself. It was for all of them. She'd be there and be sure they would be safe. She would be standing in front of them, like she stood in front of the Suburban, guarding them, shooting out tires, succeeding because she was protecting the ones she loved, not herself.

Turning away from the northern lights, Angie and Jamie sat back. Thinking about Jamie, she had the same qualities as Cindy, and she had a beauty that shined from the inside out. She had killed Vlad, and when everyone other than him didn't trust her, she didn't care. She knew he did, and that was all she needed. He was the first person to see past the life she had been trafficked into. Taking hold of him, she left the hold that world held on her and joined him in fighting it. If they hadn't met, if she hadn't opened herself up to him, told him what she was doing on her own to get at Brian, she would most likely have been killed. She

expected to be, and that would be the price of stopping the man who trafficked her and so many others. She had yet to come into her own, to be a leader like Cindy, but he thought somehow what happened at the compound would make her as strong and fearless as Cindy. She was the next warrior, bringing her ability to fit in with the worst traffickers, speak their language, and know how they operated. That would add to their ability to go after the most ruthless of men who didn't care about life or what they did to people.

Looking at Angie in the rearview mirror, she was drinking her water. At first he thought it was Cindy — that she had traded seats with Angie. In the dim light flickering through trees, she looked so much like her mother he was stunned. Like Cindy, it was beyond how she looked. It was who she was inside that made her look like Cindy. She was just sitting, looking out the window, seeming to enjoy the scenery, but she was scanning, her eyes going right to left and back. She was looking for headlights or movements as they still could be chased from roads or ways that weren't on any map. She was the next Cindy. She'd be that, and more. She was learning everything she could, and she wasn't tagging along. She was fearless. She wore weapons the same as if she was wearing a hoodie or jeans. They were a part of her, and no matter where, they were what she wore. She had become a warrior, not a victim. She had been trafficked, but grew wise from it, not letting it traumatize her. Where other girls her age worried about what to wear on a date, she worried about if she had enough guns hidden under her clothes when she went shopping for groceries. She would be the one who would cause fear in traffickers. She'd be a shadow. A mere glint of a 45 appearing then gone. She'd only be seen rising up from the floor as she stood above the trafficker. Nothing they said would ever be heard by her. Anything they had to say would be soundless to her, meaning nothing at such a moment. She was doom. She had seen what such traffickers did to her mother. They had shown no restraint, no regard for anyone's life. They didn't care if Cindy, or her, lived or died. She would be the last thing any trafficker would see. A hint at her shape covered fully in black, seeing four guns strapped to her thighs and arms gleaming, her legs apart in firing stance, her Glock out in front of her, lit only as it fired. A pretty face, not hearing their plea not to kill them, her saying only they had killed themselves… too bad. Bye.

Arriving at the airport, Victor had managed to arrive just as they pulled in to allow Angie to seem him landing. She smiled as he did, and she understood he had waited to land for her.

The man who rented them the car was waiting. As they got out of the car, Victor had lowered the stairway and the man was there making sure it was secure. Getting out, Victor was talking to him and saying there may be a rush for cars from the compound as there were bound to be some wanting to live elsewhere. They smiled, and each understood that was good news at last.

Looking over to the Suburban, he said three had left, but four came back. He smiled, saying even more of a miracle the car was in one piece, saying he sure was happy about all that. As they all loaded their gear into the jet's cabin, the man came and handed Cindy a white box tied with string.

"Missus said you'd be needin' some eats if you made it back alive. Some sandwiches and moose turd cookies in the box for ya. Have yourselves a nice ride back."

Angie, smiling, went to him and gave him a hug, saying she had to ask.

"Moose turd cookies?"

He smiled, appreciating the hug.

"Yep, you'll see. When I run out of toll house morsels, a fella has to make do. What else can those little dark plops be? Now you can say ya done been in Montana, an' got so tough could even eat my moose turd cookies. May not look good, though, me not being much with that part. Sure are good though."

Running up the stairs, Angie opened the box, looked at one, took it out and ate it, and waved as she got in the cabin. Carrying the box open, she went and held it for Victor. He looked at them, smiled, and asked, "Could it be? I can no believe! Moose turd cookies? Oh, cookies remind me of time stranded in woods with not much else."

Double checking the car to make sure they hadn't missed anything, Mike went to the man and said they were stunned seeing the aurora borealis. The man shook his head, giving him a puzzled look.

"Once in a blue moon, but none tonight. Must have been reflections from all those dashboard lights…"

He turned, going to the Suburban, then waved to the sky.

"Just them darn digital gauges. Sure they was pretty to see, though…"

As the jet took off, they all took the cookies, and they were shocked. They were wonderful.

Cindy remarked how resourceful the man was, and he worked wonders with what was available out in the woods. Looking at her, Angie let out a sigh, then shook her head.

"Mom. He was teasing. Those are toll house cookies."

Cindy took another bite, thought about it, and asked if Angie was sure about that. Angie looked at the cookie she had just taken a bite out of, then at Cindy, at the cookie, then back at Cindy.

"I think so…"

Cindy smiled at her, saying she was teasing. Then, looking at her own cookie, with a concerned look over to Angie said, "I think so."

CHAPTER 65

Lurking outside the agency building, looking at the main entrance, and the enter and exit gates from the parking garage, Whimsey had three things she knew she could use, but that was all. She had taken a bus from the safe house where Charles had shot himself. The three things may be all she had, but they would be needed. She had taken the large 45 automatic pistol Charles used to kill himself and even found a box of cartridges. She also had his wallet holding his key card along with money they used for pizza deliveries. Those were two of the three things she had.

The third was the way she looked. Before leaving, she had clothes from when taken to the house, and she knew exactly what she needed to wear. After taking a shower, drying her hair, she made braids on each side, not pigtails as girls actually never wore those. Those were for halloween costumes and absurd wigs for porn worn my women near thirty acting stupid and licking a huge lollipop. She wanted to look natural, not foolish.

She found a simple pink tee shirt, one that fit nicely, not snug. She picked a pair of red overalls cut as shorts. The dark red denim was a natural match for the pink tee, and she loosened the straps, making sure it wasn't tight. Before leaving, looking at herself in the mirror, she thought she looked the same as any girl still in mid-school. Applying just a bit of makeup, she knew she looked like any other girl, not a porn star.

Instead of the fantasy white knee-high socks, she had a pair of ankle length knit socks, white, but average. For shoes, she put on sneakers, ones she hadn't worn as she wasn't able to go for a run.

Looking in the mirror when all put together, she nodded. Surprising even herself, she was nothing much to look at as she looked like any schoolgirl. The last thing she needed was what girls wore to school for books and lunch. A little backpack. She had a few she had brought, and although she had a pink one with a unicorn on it, that was not what girls in middle school would choose. She found a gray canvas backpack, and it was perfect as it didn't match. Girls didn't have matching color packs for every outfit, and the gray was one a girl would wear every day. It was also a perfect size for the large gun she needed to carry with. Stuffing some pillowcases in it to pad it full and not show the shape of the gun, she was confident she looked, for the first time, like a young schoolgirl.

The one schoolgirl item she had that real schoolgirls didn't was extensive experience making men do what she wanted them to. Needing to get into the agency, and as a girl she wouldn't have a driver's license or ID, she'd just be a girl needing to see her uncle. Charles. Even if the man at the security entrance saw he was out of the office, she would say she needed to drop off a birthday card for him to sign, and she'd leave a note. She would say was a secret and told her he would pick it up if out and came back, or know what it was if he was with a patient.

She was just a little girl. She wasn't a security threat. Her story was valid, and she'd say she knew the way as she had visited so many times before. The only problem was every bag, briefcase or her little backpack would need to go through a scanner. There would be an x-ray belt people had to put their items on, and that would show the gun. She realized all she could do was wear it through the metal detector and act surprised and say why are they picking on her? If they used their hand wand, she'd say she just had her lunch wrapped up in foil, take off the pack and pull out a big sandwich. It would be the gun, wrapped in foil. It was so big, she wondered if that would be too large for a sandwich. Then she thought it could be a batch of cookies she made to leave for him, looking desperate, saying she was afraid they'd get all messed up, and she'd worked so hard to wrap them up. Going to the kitchen, she found a box of chocolate cookies. Taking a paper plate and foil, putting the gun on the sturdy paper plate, then layering cookies on top of it, she double wrapped it with the foil and it looked just right. Cookies wrapped to not get tossed around in her backpack. Thinking of how to get it perfect, going in the cookie box she took out two cookies, smashed them on the counter, turning them into cookie crumbs. She sprinkled enough to look like they were from the cookies wrapped in foil, and even made the backpack smell like cookies. She added some crumbs in the backpack, also making a sandwich and using the foil for it.

Adding two books she found that looked ordinary, although a bit heavy, most school kids carried everything they could around with them, so it was a matter of not putting her backpack on the belt, and playing the guards who most likely had children and knew how secretive they were with what was in their bags.

Before leaving, she figured she better have the note she planned to leave for Charles if he didn't answer when she knocked on his office

door. She made it simple, saying to sign the card then mail it to his aunt, and that she made some cookies he said he liked just for him. All that was left was to get a birthday card, and those could be found at stores on the way.

Getting off the bus, at a drugstore she bought a humorous card, signed a few names, put an address on it, and put that in the pack with the container. She didn't want to be seen standing looking at the building for long. They had security cameras and looked for people doing that, she was sure. She made sure to arrive at lunchtime as people would be hurrying in and out, so they'd not be as critical of her getting through the line with people waiting. If she made a fuss, she was sure people behind would say give the kid a break.

Walking to stand across from the building, she saw it was busy. With both thumbs hitched in her pack shoulder straps, rather than turn and go back to the crosswalk, she jaywalked and that gave her more of a chance to look into the lobby. The line was busy going in an out. Inside, getting in line, she was behind an older woman which was good as she would see what she did with her purse. Behind her was a heavyset middle-aged man wearing a wedding band, and she thought him the type to be a suburban dad. When the lady ahead went forward, she started to put her purse on the belt, but to keep the line moving, the man at the metal detector waved her through. Her purse set off the alarm, and she pulled out a key ring full of keys, saying that did it every time. He waved her on. She went up, looking up at the gray detector to walk through, acting unsure what to do. The guard leaned down, asking her did she want to stand there or perhaps walk on through so everyone behind her could get back to work. Giving one more look up, she looked at him, gave a little smile and a nod, then stepped through.

The lights flashed, and there was a beep. The guard saw the straps of her backpack and said just open it for him. Looking surprised, not frightened, she pulled it off, opened it, and he asked what was in the foil. She smiled and said cookies she made for her uncle. He just said they smelled good, and to get going.

It was good to have picked lunchtime to get through, and she knew she had done all the right things. The cookie crumbs in the bag worked like magic. Passing the directory board, she wanted to have it seem that she had been there before. She noticed some people were taking the

stairs as there was a crowd waiting for the elevators, and acting like it was what she always did, she joined a few using the stairway door, and instead of going up, she walked down. She was going to check out the garage.

Walking down the stairs as if going to a car that would be taking her home, she noticed that the parking spots nearest the elevators all had "reserved for" signs with names, and one, clear as could be, was a spot for Allan. It made sense as he was the top guy. His car was there, and it was a Land Rover Defender, a new one, and it was black inside and out. On either side were black Tahoes, ones agents seemed to love, but she assumed they were given the cars. They were big enough to give her a place to hide. They were big enough where she could crawl under the back of one as it was well above the ground.

She knew there were security cameras, and there were ones looking at the elevators. She'd be seen if she walked between the cars, so she walked past them, turned at the wall housing the elevators, and not seeing the cameras on the other side, she crouched low and hid behind the cars all around the elevator bank, making quick moves, then waiting different amounts of time between cars. She also made it where she looked like she was looking for something she had dropped or lost, just in case. It took time, but she finally made it to where the Tahoes were parked, and she stayed behind one and laid down under it far as she could and was sure she wouldn't be seen. If the driver came, she'd scoot away to go under the Defender, then to the other Tahoe, although that would make things more complex.

She had no plans to wait for the end of the day. She had the one thing that was needed to get Allan out of his office and into his car. She had the cell phone Charles had been talking to Allan with. She hoped to sneak into his car as he was getting in and ride out of the garage with him. That would be hard to do, but if he were to unlock his car doors, and she called his phone as he was walking up, he would answer, standing outside of the car in case he had to go back to the office for some reason. She could open a back door, crawl in as long as he was looking away, and as car doors closing was routine sound in any garage, close the door and lay on the floor. She had done well so far, and she knew how most men get distracted by calls, but sure she couldn't hit send until she heard the doors unlock.

It was past lunchtime, and she had one last decision. If she had called from the house, saying something was wrong with Charles, maybe say he collapsed during sex, Allan would have sent a crew and ambulance. He may not even come himself. If possible, if she could hide enough and give him a compelling reason to go to the house himself, in a hurry, that would be ideal. She'd be able to point the gun at him, even shoot him in the leg or shoulder, get him to sit, telling him to throw his gun and phone out or she'd kill him. And she would. She wanted to get him to the house, get him to talk about what he was really doing, and record it all with the recorder Charles was never without. That would be her protection from anyone going after her once he was dead.

When she looked into the Defender, it had all kinds of things in the back, including a tarp to hide what he carried on the floor. If she could get in, hide under the tarp, she would be hard to notice. The final step before calling him was to take the gun out of the container and foil, be sure it was ready to fire, and leave it loose in the backpack where she could grab it instantly. After doing that, she thought she was as ready as she'd ever be.

Taking the phone, she hit the Allan contact to call. Being from Charles, she knew he'd pick it up. He did, asking what's up. She had it all worked out.

"Allan, it's Whimsey. I'm freaked out. I can't talk loud. Charles took a bunch of stuff he was using on me, and he's all crazy. I grabbed his phone when he was throwing papers around… I'm in the pantry… he's saying stuff about you killing me and you letting him kill girls. He just took more pills… What should I do? He has a gun and he's playing with it and calling my name, saying you want all the girls. I'm in the pantry, and he's… oh, I need to get off, he'll hear me… I don't want…"

She ended the call and hit the airplane mode so if he called back it would go to voicemail.

She knew he'd walk up to the driver's side, and by himself. She made it clear that Charles was talking about things he wouldn't want anyone else to hear, and he'd go alone to kill Charles. He couldn't do anything else. She crawled out from under the Tahoe and was crouched down next to the Defender passenger side door. It didn't take long. She heard the elevator door, and had the phone back to normal, her finger on the call button. Watching from under the car, seeing feet walking towards the

car, she heard the car unlock, and she hit the call button. She opened the door just enough to get through, hearing him outside saying Charles first, then pause, then say Whimsey. He wasn't hearing anything, and when he opened his door and jumped in, she was in, under the tarp, and he hadn't heard her close the door. She had the phone muted as he kept saying her name, then trying using Charles. He said, "Fuck" as he pulled out of the spot, siren on, and screeched tires as he pulled out of the garage then raced through traffic, the siren loud, perfect as he was focused on driving and the siren was louder than any noise she could make.

Still having the impulse to just shoot him when the car stopped at some point, that wasn't the best choice. She may only wound him, and he'd pull his gun to shoot her. She had her phone ring silenced, and he kept trying to call. He drove faster as he made it past downtown traffic, and soon they'd be at the house. She thought of how her planning had somehow worked, but again, she thought men easy to figure out. They acted on impulse.

Feeling the car make a hard turn, then stop, she knew it was at the house. She heard the car was still on, and the slight sound of the garage door opening. That was ideal as she'd get out after him and get in quietly. He'd be looking at Charles, laying there, and it would fit with her story about him acting crazy. He'd call out to her, saying he was there, it was safe to come out. It would be, for her.

As she heard him go in, calling out for Charles, she got out of the car, had the gun ready, and entered the house. Walking quietly, once in, seeing him searching the body, she knew he was looking for anything about him. He was calling out her name, saying come out of hiding. It struck her that he was too trained to just be afraid of her pointing a gun at him. She knew she had to shoot him while he was distracted and hit him where he'd be unable to defend himself. If she killed him, that would be okay. She wasn't great with a gun but had fired ones in a self-defense class with her sister. She was good with aim at close distances. She knew the gun had a clear sight, and she wasn't far from him. Aiming for his shoulder blade, she fired. The recoil was more than she expected and her hands flew up with the gun, but she held it tight. It was so loud she couldn't hear well, but she saw she had hit Allan, and he was laying on top of Charles, not moving.

She slowly walked to him, the gun pointed at him all the way. She had hit close to where she aimed. His left shoulder had been ripped away, and he was gushing blood. He seemed fully out, but breathing. She kept the gun in one hand, finger on the trigger, and pressed the barrel into his back. She reached to his belt in back and he had a holster and smaller gun. Taking that, she undid the safety and as it was lighter, switched to it, putting the safety on the 45, putting it in her backpack. She felt him all over and found a smaller gun strapped to his leg above his ankle. In his back pocket, his phone, and she knew if she wanted to talk to him, she needed to stop the bleeding somehow. Pointing the gun at him, she backed up and found the drawer with towels, and taking them all, put them over the wound. To apply pressure, she realized she could drag Charles to where his upper body would be over the wound. That would apply pressure. For now, she could only hope he came to.

Realizing she wanted to keep him alive and to get him to talk, she needed someone who could do both. She knew who to call.

"Mike, I need help. I've been a prisoner since I was taken from the hospital. Charles took me, and I'm in a safe house. He killed himself. He said Allan was the guy behind everything. I got him to come here, to get me, I guess. I shot him, and I'm afraid he's going to die as I don't know what to do…. Yes, if he's alive, we can find out what he knows… Yes! Yes! I'm not lying. I've been a prisoner, Come with all kinds of guns and stuff if you think I'm lying. It's a place near a park… yeah… a school across from the park… not far so please, get here fast as can be. Here, I'm taking a photo, texting it right now… See! That's what is left of Charles. I put him like that to apply pressure on Allan's wound so I can call you. Okay, I'll stay on the phone… Oh God, I don't want him to die until I find out why he did all this to me. I've got a gun. The one Charles shot himself with… oh, and two I took off of Allan… I'm sorry, Mike. I didn't know what Sharon was doing… Charles injected me with something, and I woke up here, and he was fucking me when I wasn't even awake yet… yeah, all the time… You won't believe what he told me… Okay, almost here? Yeah, Allan is breathing. I'll open the garage door, he has a black Range Rover, and it's parked in it. Okay, I'll put all three guns down in front of me when you walk in, and I'll be far from the door… I know you have to… I wouldn't trust me either…."

Breaking down into tears, she realized she was someone he couldn't

trust, even though she hadn't done anything except shoot Allan to wound him. Mike could only hear her sobbing. Hearing his car stop, knowing he was near the door she managed to say she laid all the guns down, and would back away from them. She was worried other agents would follow Allan, and she was afraid he would get up somehow and kill her. She kept looking at him, making sure he didn't get up, or that he was okay somehow.

Hearing Mike calling out it was him in case she didn't have the phone to her ear. She called out to hurry, she wasn't near the guns.

The door opened, and a gun barrel poked through first, then she saw a rapid movement of someone looking in, then saying it was clear. The door opened from a push, and nobody was there. Then, she saw Mike, Cindy and Angie move with guns pointed into the house and her. Angie walked in first, picking up the guns, then backing up, putting them behind her back as Cindy took them.

Mike walked in, telling her to stay, his gun pointed directly at her. Cindy and Angie kept their guns pointed out, and moved in, passing her, pointing at each door as they walked, kicking each one open, moving in, gun first, scanning the room and closets in them, then the bathrooms and working fast, they called to Mike, saying things were clear. Angie went to the back patio door, gun scanning the yard, Cindy patrolling windows with rapid passes, gun out, at each one.

Mike moved in, telling Whimsey to back up behind the bodies, until he was sure Allan was down. She nodded, knowing they needed to be sure. Mike called to Angie, saying only to go from patio to garage and back, take no chances. Angie was wearing a vest, dressed in a black jumpsuit, her rifle held in firing position. Patrolling the windows, Cindy started going into rooms as well, gun first, not missing closets or any hiding places just to be sure as anything was possible in a government safe house. Secret rooms, basements, other hidden entrances. It was a single level home, and with each circle through she called out that it was clear.

Once looking Allan over, he called for Whimsey. He said he wanted her to help him with Allan and took her hand to help her up. She had blood on her front and shoes, and she was holding a little gray backpack, open, turning it upside down and shaking it to show him it was empty. He nodded, glad she had done so.

Bending down, Mike dragged Charles off of Allan, who was covered in towels, all of them soaked with blood. Patting him down, asking Cindy if turning him over was wise. She said not yet, so he worked his hand under Allan's body, and Whimsey watched with shock as he pulled out another gun, saying there was nothing else.

Cindy told Whimsey to get more towels, ones from the bath, and a lot of hot water. She told Whimsey to find a medical kit if she could. Whimsey got up and saw that Angie didn't stop or let her rifle down, she was moving from door to door, looking at anything outside for anyone that may be approaching the house. She didn't stop, she kept guard, even going into the garage, checking the hatch of the Range Rover, and had cut power to the garage door.

Whimsey knew where the large towels were, and she grabbed them all, saying there was a bucket in the pantry as she gave them to Mike. He called to Cindy, saying pantry, she opened it, said clear, getting the bucket and also rubbing alcohol kept there, putting the alcohol next to Mike, then went and ran hot water, waiting for the bucket to get near full.

With water, Cindy joined Mike and washed away most of the blood. Mike used his knife, cutting away the shirt and suit jacket where the wound could be seen front and back. Patting both sides, they were clean enough for her to look up and say she was sure he lost a lot of blood, so it went through, making a big hole. Once clean enough, she said the wound was above the lung, didn't get a main artery, so she needed gauze to pack it, then they could only wait it out.

Whimsey said she'd seen a roll of gauze, and as she ran to find it, Cindy said if there was a toolbox, she could use that. Angie had taken over going window to window along with the doors, said she saw one in the garage, and she'd get it. Whimsey ran back with a full roll of wide gauze, giving it to Cindy. Angie was behind her, rifle in one hand, toolbox in the other, setting it down next to Allan's hip, then returned to patrolling. Cindy opened the toolbox, found a small phillips head screwdriver, rinsed it in alcohol, made a tight roll of gauze, then put it in the bullet hole, using the screwdriver to force the roll in deep. Making another one, Mike propped Allan up, and she did the same stuffing from the other side. The rolls quickly grew red, but the bleeding had been contained. She pushed a bit more in and said any wide tape would help.

Mike saw duct tape in the toolbox, Cindy saying that's what it was for, taking it, she taped the wounds.

Telling Whimsey to put all the supplies on the dining room table, the kitchen was full of dried blood and debris from the way Charles shot himself, and they didn't want to disrupt the evidence. Mike took pictures, and asked what about if Allan was faking it, or woke up if they wanted to talk away from the mess. Looking up at him with a "very simple" expression, she pulled lengths of duct tape and secured Allan's wrists, ankles and thought about his mouth, then looked up at Mike.

"Well, if he can't walk or use his arms, I don't think he'll get to us to bite."

Getting up, she said for now, that's all she could do. He'd come to at some point, and best hear the whole story. Mike agreed, and asked if he'd do better on a bed, or on some cushions. Cindy said if he was a nicer person, that could be an option, but it would be best not to move him any way.

Washing her hands in alcohol, she made sure she was cleaned up, and suggested talking in the living room area. Asking Whimsey if there was anything cold to drink, Whimsey opened the fridge and said bottled water and some iced tea. She took two of each and put them on the coffee table in front of the sofa. Cindy took an iced tea and a deep breath.

"I was all set to make pirogi for Victor, and some burgers. Good combo, really. I hope he doesn't get too hungry. Well, let's find out what happened."

Angie walked over. She was still patrolling, but said she had a suggestion.

"Mom, you can still cook. At some point, someone is going to show up. A guy like Allan would tell someone he's going to see Charles. When he's not back, not getting him on the phone, they'll figure it out. He has the SUV. We can move him. He's fixed up enough for that. If we take him home, put him in the safe room, then I drive — yes — drive, without a license and leave it somewhere, the car's ditched. He's not here so we won't get in a gun fight with the CIA."

Mike looked at Cindy, and as she sipped some tea, she smiled up at Angie.

"Really? Very clever. All that... just to get to drive? I'm teasing you,

sweetie. I think it's a good plan. You're right. They're going to figure out he's down and come looking. One thing, easy to do. Whimsey, can you scatter all the clothes and things around, knock things over. They'll assume he took you. His blood is mixed in with where Charles is, so they'll think it's from him. We take the supplies from fixing him up, so that won't show he was hit or repaired. I bet they'll think he did Charles. Took the guns and all. Let's get going before they do."

As Whimsey got to work, she made it look like she had been snatched, and Angie put all the supplies in a garbage bag, then put the toolbox back in the garage. They took the one bottle of tea with, and looked everything over twice, not seeing anything that would indicate what happened. Mike said the hardest part was moving him. He suggested, because of the wound, that Cindy take one shoulder, Angie the other, and he'd take his feet. Angie held up her hand, went to the garage and came back with a dolly for moving heavy items. Taking a garbage bag to cover it, Mike smiled, and they managed to put Allan's upper torso on it, then Mike used his legs to pull him to the inside garage door, and as it had only a threshold, pulled enough to get the dolly over it. Angie had lowered the rear seat, took the tarp from the back floor, then all three moved Allan onto the tarp, then lifted him up into the cargo area, with Mike getting in the back doors and pulling him in to where with his legs bent, they could close the hatch. Angie rolled the garbage bag up, put it in with the supplies, then returned the dolly to where she found it. Mike went back in, made one final pass, locked all the doors, and said he'd drive the Land Rover to the house as Angie pouted.

"You can joyride once it's empty. I need you to ride shotgun with Cindy, that rifle aimed at his head."

That made Angie smile, and she said safest to have Whimsey lie on the back floor for now, and Mike agreed. With all the arrangements made, Mike said he'd call ahead to Victor to help with the heavy lifting, and for them to drive nice and slow as if coming home from shopping and not call attention to themselves. He'd be taking a different route, one where it was backstreets without cameras. He said they monitor those and can read a plate, so they would beat him home, but he wasn't going to give them any reason for a visit.

CHAPTER 66

"Okay. When we left for Montana, we had a hit man, Jo, Charles, and worry for Whimsey and Jamie. We took out the hit man, and we can assume it was Allan who hired him. We took care of Jo. Charles took care of himself. Whimsey is found and did an amazing job getting the news about Allan, and Jamie is here with us again, and safe. It seems like everyone is accounted for, and Allan is the last hand to play."

Gathered around the kitchen table, Victor was smothering his pirogi with sour cream, adding James was also crossed off the list. Cindy had a big smile watching him.

"Victor… would you like some pirogi to go with your sour cream? I'm letting you know there are more in the oven for you. But, yes, James, checked off. We may find that the Montana compound is still an issue, so good to arm it with guns and launchers next. Did you enjoy using the jet like a fighter?"

Getting a pan full of pirogi, smiling at it, he looked at Cindy.

"Yes, it good, but you haven't seen what I do in real fighter. Then, you see what I do best. Fighter, it has guns, not little toys thrown out window. Sure, we put them on jet. Very good to use when time comes. I may practice a bit each week. Angie, up front, two seats. I show you how to fly. You get pilot license before driver's license, I teach you, and know you will be good as me."

Cindy and Mike both looked at Angie, who gave her most innocent look.

"Mom! What? We haven't been talking about it…"

She met their stares and had to finish her sentence.

"Well, not talking about it that much. I was going to ask you if I could first."

Smiling at her, she was thinking of how things happen when decent people meet each other.

"Well, a sixteen-year-old girl, no drivers license yet, and a Russian Fighter Jet Commander, up in the sky and planning invasions. It's what I love about America. If Victor is kind enough to teach you, I think that is wonderful. Now, Victor, no having her coming in hot."

"Malenka, not first time out. But what good if she can no be terror in sky?"

He smiled at her, and she knew he would teach her what

responsibility comes with such skill. She nodded, thanking him. She turned to Jamie.

"Well, tell us what it was like when Victor buzzed the compound. I bet that was scary!"

Jamie could only laugh at that. She stopped after getting the laugh out of the way and said as she hadn't explained all that happened yet, it was Victor that saved her life. They all stopped, looking at her, and wanted to know how.

"It's still hard to deal with. I went back in after I ran off, acting like I was on her side. That, or have her hunt me down. I knew you'd be coming for me, and I had to keep alive until then. She was saying how clever I was, smart as her and all. Well, she liked me, and that led to taking a bath in a giant whirlpool. She was massaging my neck saying I was tense, and I sure was. She was being nice like she didn't have a care in the world. Then, as she was massaging my neck, she was behind me, and in a second, she had one arm around me in a choke hold, and I couldn't pull her arm away… and then she pulled my head under water… I started to panic and was swallowing water, and I was drowning as she held my head down with all her might…"

Everyone was shocked. Jo had played her again, and was killing her. She held up her hand, and turned to Victor.

"I was thinking, this is it. I'm dead. Then, wham, she let go and jumped up. I couldn't hear under the water, and I was blacking out. Her letting me go somehow let me know I could rise up and force the water out of me. I was able to, and it hurt like nothing I can explain. She was swearing that it was you guys, and she ran out, got dressed, not even looking at me. As I got out of the water, there were sirens, really loud, and lights flashing. As she ran out, she called to the system thing to stop the alarm, and it went off then the whole building shook like something crashed into it. Loud, shaking everything. Then I heard it zoom past. It was Victor. If he had been a few seconds later, I'd be dead. She ran because she heard the jet, then the alarm. I got the water out of me, my clothes on, heard Victor on the speaker telling me to run for the road, and I ran. Wow, did I go. I just ran. Victor, you saved me. I've been wanting to tell you, thank you…"

He got up, went to Jamie, told her to stand up, then hugged her, lifting her up off the ground.

"I just fighter pilot. Mike, Cindy, they come up with plan. I am glad you survive. I kept saying run to road. I pray each pass you alive, see you. Then, third pass, I see little thing. Tiny thing running to road. It was nicest thing, seeing you. Now, hearing this. No just nicest thing. Miracle!"

Smiling at each other, Cindy could tell that Victor, who had spent a life shooting people down, had saved someone. She saw him glow with pride. She also knew Jamie had a lot more to share, but when she was ready.

As they finished eating, Mike looked at his phone which showed a security camera from the safe room.

"Our guest is moving around, he's awake. Well, I think we go at him right now, while he's disoriented and hurting. And, not to overdo it, with a guy like him, we need to…"

Cindy held up her hand, nodding.

"I agree. We're coming in hot. I was thinking having Victor there first would really shake him. Ask him why did he have girls killed. He had messed with one from Russia… or whatever would work. I think facing a foreign agent would shake him more than we would. Mike, what do you think?"

Looking at Victor, he said he thought he was the right man for the task.

"Victor, speak in Russian only. He won't know where he is. Let him think he's outside of Moscow, you know… the place where the KGB did the interrogations. Maybe let him know he'll live if he says who he's doing all that for or ask if he's just a sick pervert. Think you can give him a taste of USSR old school persuasion?"

Nodding, Victor said he would be very convincing, and not very pleasant.

"Men like him. Sit behind desk. Have others do dirty work. Cowards. And, there no old school. It still class in session there. He will know nothing changed, that he is unlucky man as Russia is no pansy like CIA."

Getting up, Mike and Victor said if they wished, watch the interrogation on the big TV. He has it on and set to view the room. He explained to Whimsey they all spoke Russian, and knowing she didn't, have Angie translate anything important, or just what was being said.

Turning to Victor, he said he'd give him some basics on all they knew so far before he went in, and asked if he would like to change out of his very American clothes and wear his uniform as it was current issue. Victor nodded, saying uniform is more intimidating than any man, so talk while he gets changed, then, looking at Angie, he moved her heart.

"Littlest malenka, could you please to take picture, on phone, of me in uniform? And one of Mike and me, together, brothers?"

Smiling, she held up her phone, and telling he'd be the handsomest man she'd ever take a picture of, causing Mike to pout. She said she meant of just one man, that with both, they were in a tie.

Knowing Mike had a lot of background to fill Victor in on, Cindy said as it was all girls now, they could do some talking. That caused all of them to smile, and giggle.

"I was thinking about how Mike and Victor have been there for all of us, and we get all the credit. They are amazing men. I wish all men were like them. I think we should do something to let them know how special they are. Any ideas?"

All their eyes lit up, and they all said Cindy was right, they had saved all of them along the way, and didn't want credit or even a thank you. Whimsey spoke up, saying she was so upset at Sharon.

"I haven't known them as long as you all have. Today, when I told him I needed help, even though he said he had to be sure I wasn't waiting to shoot at all of you, it was the way he said it. I felt he was protecting me as much as you guys. He let me know you were coming, and wanted to be sure you were okay, then said, me too. He made me understand. And once you came in, he didn't have one doubt, he made me part of everything. But, about Sharon. I knew how much he cared about her and how he had changed his life to find her. I never knew anyone who did something like that. And Sharon, she didn't tell me, but I could see she didn't care he did that at all. That's when I pulled away from her and ran off and all. He did all that, and she was planning to kill him! I can't imagine how that felt. And today, he was there, not hearing or knowing me and what happened, and he treated me with respect, even admiring how I got Allan there. Anyway, I just wanted you to know I'm right there with you. Doing something special will be really nice."

Cindy looked at Whimsey. She saw so much in her that she admired, and thought about what a life she had, and how brave she had been.

"I haven't had a chance to tell you, so much happening, but all that you did? The way you figured out how to get Allan out and to the house? That is so much like we would do. That was so brave, and you wanted to stop him from doing to others what was being done to you. All of us here? We've all been through that, and we all would do the same as you. So, I don't know what you may think of an idea I had, but would you like to do things with us? Go after traffickers and use our, well, female charm, to get them?"

Whimsey was crying, so happy to be treated for her smarts, not her child-like body. The day had been far beyond any in her life, and she had been scared, but yet did things she didn't think she could ever do. Stop the one hurting her. She told Cindy she didn't know how to be all superspy like Angie, but she'd like to learn and yes, she'd love to be part of what they did, but she wasn't very big, or a hottie like all of them.

"Oh, Whimsey. Please, you are beautiful, and that's where I think you can add so much to what we do. Angie and I, we use our looks to be... well, bait. But we are a bit older, so some traffickers will like ones like us, but you know... they want little girls the most. And little girls, they get older, and as we go along, we couldn't have some little girl in danger. Angie, well she's sixteen, but she grew up dealing with perverts and learning how to stop them. Now, you, you have a condition where you won't look much different as the years go by, and you're an adult, and you have a lot of experience with how men use girls. I think that you, being the one men would want the most, setting them up, that would give us a way of getting at them more than we can now. I think you know you can attract men like crazy, and with some of the skills we've learned, you can find out who's a trafficker just by walking by them. I hope I'm not offending you, but you are really unique. A woman who looks like the one they want the most. So, just a thought, so think about it. Even if not that, yes, please, be part of what we do. I can provide anything you need. No need to worry about money or, well do anything you've been doing."

Crying through all Cindy said, she wiped her tears away, looking at all there, and then back to Cindy.

"My sister was killed. And, I think that it wasn't really that Jo. I think it was Allan. Her dying... I want to stop that happening to any other girls. She was so good. She wasn't doing what I was, and she was all I

had. Now, she's gone, all because of sick perverted fucks like that one in the safe room. I don't need to think about it. The day he killed her was the day I said yes. I've been waiting to know a way to stop him and pervs like him. And, you are right. I'll look like a twelve-year-old until I grow old and gray. Put me out there, and they'll do stupid stuff to have me. I think with me, it will complete the picture, the team or whatever you call what you all are. I am ready, right now. Today, shooting that fucker, it's the first time I felt I was doing something good. I saw all you, and what you do, And, I was going to ask you, say I'd be great bait, as you call it."

As Cindy held her arms open wide, Whimsey got up and went to her, whispering she was happier than she'd ever been. Cindy hugged her and as she let go, asked if everyone agreed with how best to have Whimsey fit in. They all laughed, and Angie did more than the, "duh," expression. She said, "Mom… duh?"

Cindy said she was happy, and there would be more training then, but their way. She said Angie was amazing, so when not flying fighter jets or trying to get her license, she may be able to teach her to be a warrior. Angie looked at Whimsey, saying she'd need to get up early tomorrow, she was best at dawn. Cindy saw them nod and smile at the thought, and got back to the subject she'd brought up.

"Okay, so back to what to do for our brave men. Anything goes. We all know my mother left us more money than we could ever spend, so don't worry about cost. Anything come to mind?"

Jamie had been thinking about it, and said it was something maybe not part of the thing from everyone, but she could use some help. Cindy asked what she wanted for him.

"Well, maybe not just for him, but all of us as well. When I was in Jo's place, I looked all around. No pictures. None. She had nobody, and it was sad, because it's the same for me. I don't have family, until now. I mentioned to Mike I'd like to have a portrait of the two of us. He's such a great photographer, but he can't take it. I wanted to get the best portrait photographer for us. And you know what? I'd want to have pictures just like that of each of you, and all of us together."

They were all looking, expressions that showed emotions that had been held back all their lives. None of them had pictures like that. Cindy was amazed. What Jamie had wished for moved her.

"Jamie… wow. That is the sweetest thing, ever. You know, I don't have a portrait of Angie and me. Only the one that monster Vlad took of us, and I will never hang that up. And he took one of Angie, but same thing. That's not a picture of her. That was her auction photo. And you, and Whimsey, grew up with sick monsters. Mike had a family, but I think his family portraits all had Sharon in them. Victor. I bet he doesn't have any except in a fighter jet. That is wonderful. Yes, I want all those pictures. This place is just a house until we have pictures of all of us. Those will be our family pictures."

Looking at each of them, eyes filled with love, Jamie nodded her head.

"See what happens when it's just all girls…"

They laughed, and there wasn't a dry eye at the table. Angie asked Jamie where they'd find the best person for portraits.

"Well, a nice way is to flip through some of his photo books and magazines. Ask him who he thinks is the best ever portrait photographer. We'll hire whoever that is. That should work. So, back to something to celebrate Mike that he will know we thought about him and wanted him to know how amazing he is, what comes to mind?"

Jamie looked all around, waiting to see if anyone had an idea that came to mind right away. As they were all thinking, she decided to offer a suggestion.

"Well, not saying this is best as you all may have a better idea, but I do have one. You know, Mike, he's all guy. Likes guy stuff. And that's exactly what makes him what we all admire. Did you see him drive? He loves driving, and I see him look at car magazines and read all about cars. I think that's what he dreams about because he's never had one really that's… well… like him. A car equivalent to him. I don't know much about cars, but I think that would be a way to let him know it's how we see him."

Getting oohs and nods, Cindy thought it was perfect.

"Oh, yes. If you need a loaf of bread, he'll jump at the chance as he gets to drive to the store. Jamie, do you have any idea of what car he really dreams of?"

Nodding, Jamie said it was one that she wasn't sure they still make, but they are treasures for ones who have them, and there may be ones for sale. They all looked at her, and she said best to see it. She asked Angie to

look to see if she could find a picture of one. Angie took out her phone, and asked what it was called.

"Well, he just calls it a Diablo. I looked at an article and it's a Lamborghini. The one he keeps reading about is black. I just envision him roaring after some trafficker, and he's the Diablo sending the creep to hell…"

Looking at her phone, Angie said, "Oh my God. This is so him. I want one too!"

Handing her phone to pass around, they each had the same reaction. It had doors that scissored up, it was inches off the road, and it was a slice shape that looked as vicious and powerful as its name. Cindy said it was perfect, but she'd want to talk to Mister Lamborghini and ask him to make one special just for him. They all looked at her, and she told them remember, she could be very sweet and appreciative and that would help the man a great deal. And, as she could probably buy the company, that too. Getting a round of smiles, they knew she meant it, and she would get a perfect Diablo.

Angie said she had an essential addition.

"I think we get a little plaque to put on it, you know, on the back or a special place. And, have it fit right in with the other lettering on the car. It can say, *I stop traffic.*"

They all clapped at the idea, and Cindy said she'd tell Mister Lamborghini to make it himself.

Nodding, Angie asked what about Victor. She added that would be a bit trickier. Cindy said as she knew a bit about him, she had a nice idea. They all waited.

"Well, you know he was in the military, then he was retired and became the pilot for my mother. I think she loved him, but you know, she kept everyone she cared about safe by keeping them at arm's length. But I was thinking. He'd never had a home. A real place of his own. I think that would be something he would love. So, that, but what does he really love? To fly. He's flown everyone's plane but his own. I was reading about how not far from here, they had started to build an airstrip, but the company ran into trouble and gave up the project. So, a full airstrip. They built a house right on it, and it's all sitting there. You know… not everyone can afford certain things. And you know what's best. The money to pay for it. It's not from me or Angie, really. It's from the woman he loved. Eliana…"

They sat, stunned. Cindy had it right. Eliana had trusted her with all her money, knowing she'd use it the right way. Jamie sat, melting.

"Cindy. My God! That is the most romantic thing I've ever heard. When he goes in, have a simple flower in a vase, and a little card. It can say to Victush, from Eliana. What could be more incredible than that?"

Cindy nodded at her, then gently said, "Nothing. Like you said. He saved your life. This will save his heart from losing her."

Chapter 67

Watching Victor deal with Allan on a security camera in the safe room, Mike understood what Victor meant by he would not be kind to Allan. There was an art to interrogation, and although he hadn't been involved in them as he was a field agent operating undercover, he heard the tales of terror employed and wondered how someone could torture a person then go home at night and calmly have dinner. Thinking more about why enemies or prisoners were physically and mentally abused to get information, it was the first time he understood that it was more than that — at least it would be for him and Victor.

Allan had coldly, calmly gave instructions to have Cindy and Angie killed. He had allowed Charles and James to act on their sick perversions. He hadn't a clue how much other horrific acts he was responsible for, but he knew he wanted to suffer the way all he harmed had done. It was payback time and he couldn't fool himself it was anything else. He wanted him to suffer. He wanted to see him beg and grovel for mercy he had never shown. It was impossible to justify his desire to make Allan suffer beyond all reason, and that didn't matter. The was no way to justify anything Allan had done to people. It went far beyond abuse of power. It was a choice. He decided to hurt people and he could only guess he enjoyed having the power of life and death over others.

Thinking the only way to describe Victor's actions was that he was an artist, Allan was his canvas and he was once white, but now covered in red, pink, blue, purple, and dark brown. There was no part of him not battered and bruised, and cuts that were bleeding or dried to a scab had been from skin being torn apart by force, not a knife or sharp object. The artist in Victor would take Allan to a point where he would be near to passing out, then keep him alert and awake. Using cold water, slaps, threats, he told Allan if he passed out, he'd wake from pain beyond anything he could imagine. When he needed a break, Victor would blast rap music through headphones so loud that the sound was as bad as spikes in his ears.

Waiting for his chance to go at Allan, Victor had assured him that he was getting him receptive for his visit.

"When you come in, he be ready to listen. I knock all stubborn man

away, leave simpering child. When he is ready, I let you know."

Worried that Allan would be able to endure much more, he heard Cindy talking to Angie as they walked down the stairs to join Mike. They had been watching Victor during commercial breaks on Telemundo, and had come down with food and snacks for him and Victor, not concerned as they knew Victor planned a long session of breaking him down. Handing Mike a large bag of oranges, he started to take one with a nod of thanks, but Cindy said they weren't for eating. Victor had told her to put a dozen in a bag and have it ready for him to beat Allan with. Mike looked at the orange, then put it back in the bag, saying he hadn't heard the request, but the bag was certainly heavy.

Telling Cindy and Angie it would be about time for Victor to take a break, he said he was going in next, and wasn't sure he could do as well as Victor, but it would feel good. Angie looked at Mike, shaking her head.

"Mike, orders from headquarters. Mom is going to torture him when Victor comes out."

Looking at Cindy, standing and inspecting her nail polish, he asked if Angie was serious. Putting her head back for a different view of the polish, she told him she was correct, and she was going to join her when she talked to him. Angie had two Glocks on her belt, and said if needed, they would do the talking for her.

"Cindy… Angie… he's restrained, and sure, we'll be watching, but he could do all kinds of things unexpectedly. I don't recommend going in there. I'll be worried."

Looking at him, smiling, she told him it was okay to have an orange. She wouldn't be using them and doubted Victor would be needing them.

"I appreciate your concern, but no need to worry. I know how strong both you and Victor are, and with all that's been done to him, he still hasn't told what we need to know. Mike, think about being Allan. Right now, he knows what he's up against. He understands such interrogations, and I bet he's thinking he'll com out alive, or dead, but he isn't going to give us anything we want. Angie and I were watching and he's the type who'd die rather than spill what he has. That's why he's head of the agency here."

Thinking about it, Cindy was making sense. He asked how her asking him anything would be different.

"Well, because Angie and I, we're not you or Victor. He didn't put little discs by your headboard. When he faces us, guess what we are that you two aren't?"

Mike could see on her face, the smile she had, that she was right. He knew the answer.

"You're his failure. Instead of you two being dead, he's the one about to die."

Holding both of her hands up to admire her nails, she thanked Angie for putting the polish on, and doing such a neat job. She turned to Mike and told him that he was right on the mark. She had a way to hit him harder.

"I'll torture him with how ineffective he is. Can't even pull off a simple hit on a mom and daughter. I think his ego is going to hurt worse than his body is right now. That's where I'll start off. Let's see how he does."

Hearing the knock on the safe room door, Mike checked the monitor and Victor made the arranged motion that it was safe to open the door, and Allan was secured. As he walked out, he said he was glad to see some beauty as he looked at Cindy and Angie.

"Fool inside not so pretty. I left eyes not swollen shut. He can see. Hear. Rest of him? I think all hurts. Knocked wind out of airbag, at least. He no kitten or puppy yet. Just stubborn. Think if tell anything, he be killed."

Offering Victor an orange, he thanked her for remembering and started peeling one.

"Mike, I asked these for you. Swing bag hard, hit anywhere. Hurt more than hell. Keep fists getting bruises. Good for first time at him."

Angie went and stood at the door, waiting for Cindy. Mike looked at Victor, and Victor looked at him.

"Cindy, no need for guard at door. Tell her have orange with us."

Walking past him, patting him on the shoulder, she stopped next to Angie at the door.

"I was just explaining to Mike that you can beat him up, but he hadn't slated you to be killed like he did us. We're alive, he's a failure. I'm going to remind him of how weak and powerless he is. So, it will be a nice break for you. You've been working too hard."

Punching a code at the door security panel, Angie heard the click,

opened the door with one of her Glocks out pointed at Allan, and Cindy walked in wearing one of her nicest new dresses. They saw Angie's back as she pushed the door closed with it, then they turned to the monitor and made sure the volume was up. Angie remained silent, standing in front of the door, gun pointed at Allan, while Cindy went to the table across from him and sat on it, crossing her legs, Mike noticing she had picked out a dress that showed all her thigh as it just graced above her knee when standing. He realized that Cindy was going to hit Allan harder than he or Victor could ever manage.

Victor watched, nodded with admiration, saying only, "Ukrainian girl."

"Allan, why, look at you… It looks much worse in person than on a monitor. I must say, you took quite a licking and you're still ticking as the old saying goes. I think it's time to talk a bit, stop all the battering and all that. I bet you're hungry. Would you like some food? We just made some meatloaf and things. Smells pretty good."

Looking at her, head unsteady, his lips swollen, he managed to grunt out a few words.

"I'm hungry. You feed prisoners…"

"Allan, I know that. Geneva convention, all about treating prisoners like human beings and all. So, ready for some meatloaf? Hungry?"

Grunting a yes, he managed to add please to his answer. He was trying to wet his lips as they were crusted with dried blood. Cindy uncrossed her legs, then crossed them again, giving him a bit of a glimpse up her dress. She leaned forward and let him smell her. She never wore perfume, but her hair was washed not long before and it smelled of peaches.

"I bet you're really hungry. But, no, I'm not giving you anything to eat or drink. You don't deserve anything like a nice meal. Why, you know what? If you had your way, I'd be a meal for worms right now. Angie too. I'd never have another meal, cook a meatloaf, nothing. All because some man sitting in a glass building told some man to kill us. A big, powerful man, deciding that we aren't going to live anymore. Now, Allan, how could I extend such a kindness to a man who would deny

Angie and me our lives?"

She sat, smiling at him, looking into his eyes, waiting for him to answer. He just stared at her, then started to shake his head to say no, she was wrong. Sitting up, she folded her arms in front of herself, waiting for him to stop shaking his head. He realized she was waiting, and muttered she had it wrong.

"Allan, I know you want me to think that. That's because you think I'm stupid because I'm so good looking, right? A woman, homebody, a young daughter. You, big CIA director. Well, I'm sure you can remember a call you had with James? One where he asked you all about some gas bombs you had him put by Angie and me? Really? You don't? Maybe it was such a little thing, I mean our lives, that you didn't bother to worry about it. Well, you may want to now. Angie, can you play the recording you made of James when he called Allan?"

One hand holding her gun, without looking, she hit play on her phone and the conversation with James played. Allan's eyes were on fire looking back and forth between Angie and Cindy. He was trying to yell, but nothing he was saying was getting out. Cindy waited, then as the recording ended, she looked at him, leaning over to see his eyes.

"Well, James was trying to prove to me that he was doing what you told him to do. He did plant them, and I don't know if you noticed, but we aren't dead, are we? We put the bombs in a good place. Where did they end up, Angie? I know it wasn't worth remembering about, but, oh. I remember now. Yes, I'm sure of it. Allan, it will be something you'll remember this time. We had a man put them in your house since you've been here. One by your wife's bedside, one by your son's. And it was nice of James to tell us how to set them off…"

Managing to mutter obscenities at Cindy, he was saying not to do it, he'd talk. He was pleading and stopped as his throat was too dry to say anything more. Cindy was listening to his every grunt.

"I think I might understand what you want. Yeah, I think so. You don't want sweet Angie there to dial a number on her phone and have them go off. You don't want us to kill your wife and son. Right?"

Nodding furiously, he said he wouldn't talk if she did. She nodded.

"I understand. Yes, I get it. It was just fine to set the ones off to kill us, but we aren't supposed to set the ones off and kill your lovely wife and handsome boy. I watched a video feed of them we put there too.

How'd you get a hottie like that? Well, you got lucky. Now, that's the part I don't understand. Why was it okay to kill us, but not us kill them? Explain that to me."

He sat still. Suddenly defiant. He worked at getting some spit to wet his throat, then answered.

"Because I have what you want."

Nodding, Cindy said she could understand that, but wasn't sure about why he thought it was okay to kill them. He sat, still, then said one word.

"Sheik."

Laughing, Cindy shook her head, and crossed her legs again, taking a deep breath with both arms stretched behind her to push her breasts out.

"Oh, him? He was nothing. He couldn't lick pussy if his life depended on it. Well, you know what? You remind me of him. He only worried about himself, not about me, and licking my clit just right. Considering someone else? His life depended on it. Yes, it sure did. He wasn't getting me off, but you know what did? Oh, I can still feel the cum I had when I took my gun, held it right over the top of his head, and popped that skull like a balloon. Now, that had me squirting all over the crater that had once been a head. You should have seen him. He had his eyes on me. I mean it. They each were stuck to my thighs, right here…"

She pulled up her dress, spread her legs apart, and rubbed a spot on each thigh. She moaned as she rubbed, saying she would have never guessed a guy eying her would get her off so well, but it had. He stared at her crotch, as she knew he would. She was wearing red panties, frilly with lace. She reached and started pulling them off as she raised her bottom up off the table, and after they were off, she crossed her legs after letting him have a good look at her and was twirling her red panties on the index finger of her right hand.

"Well, you and the sheik have something in common. You both got a good look at my special little weapon. But you know what? See these panties? Turn you on? Oh, go ahead. Admit it. It's okay to say yes. I know they do. Well, I know something you don't. They can turn you off if I want. Here, I'll show you."

Getting up, he was somehow drooling, dry as he was. She calmly crossed to him, and still letting the red panties swing around on her

finger, she grabbed the end that was flying, and with both hands gripping them tight, pulled them wide, stretched to their limit, and put them behind his head, still holding each end, and pulled the hip straps around to cross in front of his neck and began pulling hard, choking him.

The elastic waist had stretched so far it was thin as a wire and was cutting into his throat. She pulled harder and he was gurgling, gasping, his mouth opening as he was being strangled. With his hands secured behind him, all he could do was gasp and let his tongue fall out of his mouth, his face turning purple.

Pulling her panties tighter, yet not enough to fully strangle him, she told him if naked, when a man went to lick her, she'd do the same with her legs, but he wasn't going to have such a pleasure. His eyes, starting to bulge out, were looking up at her and getting glazed.

Cindy let go of one end and pulled at the other. The panties back in her hand, she backed up, watching him gasping for air. Not putting them back on, she told Angie she may have stretched them a bit too much to wear again, and that they were such a favorite.

"These work great. When we go shopping, I want a bunch more. Lots in red as it sure gets their attention…"

Throwing them in a wastebasket, she was back on the table. Wearing thigh-high boots with heels, she put both feet up on the table, far apart, her dressed pulled up where he could see her without the panties and had a full view of her. Taking one hand, putting it to her mouth, she put it in and covered it with her spit, then put it on her clit and started rubbing herself as he watched. He started to turn away, but couldn't stop himself from turning back to look.

"Oh, Allan. You and your little discs and having all that fuss. Me, I spread my legs, know you want a peek, and oblige by pulling my panties off. And, no little disc needed. I take them and do you right then. And you'll cum as you go, won't you? My, who knows what else I have up my dress… Oh, I meant to tell you. James? He was just like what I have between my legs. He tried to say he'd work for me, and he revealed all your secrets. The thing was we were on my jet. Oh, you don't know… Well, my mother left me her jet, and James was on it, and I told him I didn't like him putting those discs to kill me and Angie, and he said it was your fault, he was doing it because you'd kill him if he didn't. What's

a little lady like me to do? Have him do something else you said to kill us? No, we were flying, and we opened the cargo door and pushed him out the jet. No more of him doing what you said. Imagine how I feel right now, here with you as you gave the order. Goodness, we're not even on a jet... Well, I'm sure I can come up with something..."

Cindy stared at him. Victor had him naked, but put a throw over his lap out of courtesy as he knew Cindy and Angie were watching him interrogate him on the security cameras.

Looking, she shook her head and smiled as he watched her every move. She put her legs down, then standing, she pulled the hem of her dress up to keep it above her crotch by tucking it into her matching belt her dress used as an accent. She stepped over to him, then bent down, sideways to him, and looked at the little rise in the throw on his lap.

"What a nice compliment. Why, Allan... is that a hard on?"

She pulled the throw off, and still bending over for a close look, she was giggling, staring at his penis.

"Allan. It is! I gave you a rise in your Levis... Not much there to work with, What do you have there? Four, maybe five inches?"

Moving closer, she put her face so close her lips were almost touching it. He had urinated over his lap many times, and he stunk, but she ignored that and with her mouth, she blew on it, then stood up, pulling her dress hem out of her belt, letting it fall back down.

"There. I gave you a little blow job. Can you imagine what it would be like to have this mouth..."

Taking the finger she had been rubbing her clit with, she put it in her mouth and began sucking on it, her lips puckered out, gracing her knuckle, and was moving the finger in and out before she continued on.

"Oh, my pussy tastes so wonderful. Allan, it really does. Oh, I got off track. Can you imagine having this mouth suck that little thingy of yours? And, you came so close! Now, I couldn't suck dick if I was dead, could I? See, if instead of ordering to kill us, you could have arranged to meet up someplace for dinner. Angie and me, both of us. Said you wanted to help us take bad men down. Been sweet. And who knows where that could have gone? I was an escort. I'm sure you know that. If you'd done that, I may have ended up giving you head like you can't possibly imagine. These lips..."

She leaned in, lips in front of his eyes, and she opened her mouth

slightly and licked her lower lip with her tongue slowly back and forth, then backed away.

"These lips, around your little pecker. The sweetest lips imaginable. Sucking. Instead, you wanted these sweet lips to suck poison gas… Oh, well. Now, what to do with a man who is so, well, no other way to say it. So stupid."

His face was trembling from arousal and fear, still purple from her strangling him. He knew she was ready to kill him and was taunting him to make his last moments worse than any torture. Sweating, using his eyes to her, he grunted for her to stop, he'd tell her anything she wanted.

"Why, thank you, Allan. That's nice of you. I take it you don't want to die, and don't want your wife and child to die. And you'd sure like to get your dick sucked as you grow old. With all that, finally, you're figuring it out. I understand, you're all ready to tell me what I want. So, what should I ask?"

Sitting back on the table, she flattened her dress and let her feet dangle freely back and forth like a little girl as she continued.

"Well, Charles would have been one to ask about. He is your other errand boy, correct? No matter. He's dead. You saw that before Whimsey shot you… Oh, you didn't know she's the one who downed you? Sure. It was little Whimsey. See, men think size matters. Women? We know it's what you do with what God gave you that matters. Whimsey took that little girl body of hers, aimed at your back, and with just a little squeeze of her finger, shot you. See, with a gun, a man and woman are completely equal. And you were all set to kill her too. Isn't that something? Did you know she had hid in the back of your Rover thingy, and big mister CIA didn't know that secret? You really aren't very good at what you do, are you?"

Sitting, staring at him, she waited for an answer. It took close to a minute. He was thinking about James and Charles and now him, taken down by women he had ordered to have killed. He looked at her, and said no, he wasn't.

"I agree. Well. Since you can't figure anything out, I'll tell you a secret. You're plain old pathetic, really. So, because you're such a stupid man, that helps me know what to ask you. I know you're the chief for this district, but you do have to report to someone. They like having an idiot to order around, so they tell you what to do and keep an eye on

you. I don't think you run things without someone high up telling you to. So, I just have one question for you. Who is the one telling you to do horrible things to people like Angie and me? Just answer with a name. Right now, or I won't be all sweet and nice like I was with my panties. Who pulls the strings?"

He didn't wait to think about it. She knew she'd kill him and his family if he hesitated.

"Scott Anderson. Man at the very top. National director. Nothing happens unless he says. I do what he says."

Nodding, she said she'd want to visit him, and that was all she needed from him as she slid off the table and started to turn. Hearing him trying to shout, she stopped and looked back at him.

Saying he'd gave her the name, asking about his wife and son, he was sobbing, and she could just make out what he was saying.

Turning away, she went to Angie, took her second Glock from her holster and turned back to Allan. His expression changed to pure terror. Holding it down at her side, she looked at him, calm and certain in her manner.

"Do you want me to tell anything to your wife and son?"

Struggling every possible way, he was bleeding from his wrists and ankles. He stopped and gave up. He wasn't crying or panicking, not shaking. He knew what would happen next. He calmly told her the message to give his family.

"Tell them I gave my life for theirs."

Cindy nodded, raised the gun up to point it at him, then said one word as she used both hands on the Glock, aiming it at his forehead.

"No."

She fired. A black hole with scorched skin around it appeared on his forehead, the wall behind him a sheet of red and gray dripping down the wall. Turning to Angie, she thanked her for her gun, saying she thought the meatloaf would be just about done.

Mike stood back as they both exited the safe room, Cindy saying dinner would be ready when they cleaned up. Victor said that was good, he was starving, and telling her not to worry, he would play cleaning crew. Thanking him, she said dinner first as she went up the stairs with Angie.

Mike stood where he was, looking at Victor, his shoulders up in a questioning shrug, wondering what had happened. Victor understood. He explained things to Mike.

"Man hire assassin to kill her girl. Is no way she let him live to do ever again. Man, he fool to do such thing, even if told. She had to do herself. It is her daughter. She got what she needed. Ended him quick. Not want meatloaf to burn. Put it in oven before coming down. She knew what she'd do. Timed it just right."

Mike was still in shock. He agreed Allan couldn't leave, but it was how she had no hesitation. How she had belittled him to less than a human being, hitting him in every area he prided himself in being a man. He had watched Victor pummel him to an inch of death for close to a day, and he hadn't caved in. Cindy was in the room for less than a half hour and did things to him that shook him more than anything he'd ever witnessed. As with so much about Cindy, he was unable to reconcile how someone so kind, loving and caring could be the most ruthless person possible. Even when her life was in danger, like when they first met and she was held captive before shooting the sheik, she secured a weapon, hid it, and waited until he was licking deep into her, lost in her, the most beautiful woman he could have ever found, then she calmly put the gun above him pointing straight down and as he pushed his tongue fully up into her, she killed him.

Victor had been right. It had to be done, and by her. How she did it was more than revenge. Victor was far smarter than he let himself appear. He didn't question Angie being there. Cindy had her with to watch. She wasn't seeking revenge. She was teaching Angie a lesson about men with money or power. What they were without a gun in their hand or a gang of goons to do their dirty work. It was a lesson for Angie. He knew it wasn't about her proving a point to a man soon to be dead. It wouldn't matter to him, and there was no point in getting a dead man to see the path that led him to death.

He had first been confused about her letting him see her body in such a sexual manner. Using her panties to strangle him. Angie had watched it all, standing without a reaction. He knew Angie was learning the power women had with such men. Sex was a weapon, and Cindy knew how to use it as well as any gun or knife. It was a lesson she

learned when a child in the Ukraine watching Eliana and her father. In a bad place, the only weapon a woman had was sex. Some used it to survive. Cindy's mother learned to use it for power. The lesson wasn't lost on Cindy, and it wouldn't be lost on Angie. In a situation where she'd be without a weapon, with no way out, she had the one thing that would stop a man long enough to kill him. All she'd need do was spread her legs and act as if she wanted sex from him. Men lost all their senses for that one moment when they thought she wanted them. Nothing else would fill their minds except that she wanted them to do her. That was the kill moment, and there were many ways to kill a man without any weapon. Opening her mouth and reaching up to kiss him, she could bite down on his neck so hard she'd cut his main artery. If he was putting himself in her mouth, she only needed to bite it off. He may fight, but so could she. The moment it was off, he'd drop whatever weapon he'd have to grab his stump as it gushed blood meant to make him erect. Trained in dealing with such a moment, she only needed to grab at his weapon and end him. He had just watched a training session no man would be given, and no man could put to use. Cindy had made it clear she would stop anyone harming women and girls. She had stopped Allen and taught Angie how to do it.

He shuddered. He knew Angie would be ruthless. Anything she did in the future was to honor Cindy. Angie had been born from her mother being raped by her own father. She knew how they lived in fear, in a trailer park, because a man used his physical might over women, and had no respect for life. He understood such men would never change their ways. The only way to stop what harm they did was to kill them. It was a brutal truth, one he hated, but it was the truth. The government didn't stop such insane men. They used them, let them continue, played a mind game that they were assets. He had just watched Cindy take a potential asset and her opinion of Allan matched his own. Men such as Allan only had value once dead. It was wrong to allow them to continue doing harm to others. The world of law and agencies was upside down and backwards. He suspected taking the men who ran them was high on Cindy's target list, and Scott Anderson was the next one to learn how powerful he was from a beautiful woman looking up at him as if he was God's gift to women.

"Mike. Meatloaf. You flew away? I see no jet?"

Appreciating Victor understood he was thinking about all he'd witnessed, he had given him room, but Mike knew he was hungry after working long and hard on Allan. Shaking his head, he admitted he was lost in thought. Victor smiled, gently, patting his shoulder.

"You see sweet Cindy, woman I know you love, do worse things than even I do. Hard to put two sides together, yes?"

Nodding, Mike said that was what he was trying to figure out. Victor closed his eyes, understanding, trying to figure out how to help. As he opened his eyes, he said something Mike would always remember — about all people.

"Mike. When little boy, I poor. I shine shoes. Get my first coin, very excited. I sat, looking. On one side, Stalin. On other side, Lenin. They had no agree on things at that time. I thought how coin like Russia. Like people. We are like coin. Each have two sides. Each side look in different direction. Cindy, she is rarest coin. A treasure. One side, it look at good person with love. Other side is Cindy look at bad person. No love. Death. Sweet girl, but she is valuable coin. Each side as valuable as the other. Good to have such coin."

Mike, seeing it in his mind, realized Victor had explained it perfectly. He nodded, saying that was exactly right, and he sure was glad to be on her good side. He then realized what that term meant. To be on someone's good side. It all made sense as never before. He stood, admiring Victor and how smart he was, and as they headed to the stairs they smelled the dinner. He stopped halfway up, asking Victor what about Allan's wife and son. Victor laughed.

"They fine. Never a worry. Cindy. She wanted him know how it felt. How she felt knowing plans for Angie. Only bad thing. Wife, boy. They never know what happen to him. Went to work, no come home. Life of agent. Uncertain if come home or no."

Victor looked back down to the safe room, then at Mike.

"Later, help throw out trash with me? Good, do together. Very good to do such with dirt. First, eat. Mike. I want give little advice. Upstairs… No look, no ask if Cindy have new panties on. Answer may not be one you like."

Chapter 68

Slicing meatloaf and mashing potatoes, Angie had long been the one to cook when her mother worked as an escort. Cooking had become a joy to Cindy as she had left Angie with the shopping and cooking until she was able to stop working and be a stay-at-home mom… when she wasn't out killing traffickers.

Looking at the large table she and Angie had picked out when they bought their first house, it had been custom made to fit the area in the kitchen designed to be a dining room. Having both thought going to a separate room to eat was too formal. Before moving in they had the wall taken down and the kitchen was now open and updated with new appliances as it would be an important room and their base of operations. Leaving the rest of the vintage brick home much as it was, the kitchen was redone to make it look like from the time it was built, and it was where they spent most of their time when just the two of them, or with their new family.

Insisting on cushioned chairs that were comfortable as a living room easy chair, Angie worried about food stains and soiling. Cindy looked at her, understanding she had grown up worrying about every penny, and wished to reassure her they could provide comfort for guests.

"We both know how to clean up messes…"

Angie smiled, knowing the double meaning, and added if needed, they could get them reupholstered. Cindy said she wasn't letting some money in a hundred different bank accounts go to her head, and a bottle of dish soap with a bucket would do the job. Agreeing, Angie knew there were better uses for the more than a billion dollars they had been given by Eliana.

Looking around the table, she was glad that Mike and Victor had made it upstairs just in time for the food when served. Victor had rinsed himself off in a shower downstairs once out of the room as Cindy and Angie entered, just to clean up. He had clean clothes waiting but told all he still needed to take a full shower, so please forgive his not looking the gentleman he was. Smiling at him, he winked at Cindy, and she winked back, then looked at Jamie and Whimsey who were both watching her with Allan on the TV in the living room. They were somewhat stunned, and it was clear they wanted to ask her about all she had done. She

understood and thought it not the nicest dinner conversation.

"Okay you two. I know you want to ask how I could be so nasty and where I learned all that. Well, all I can say is that it may be wise to keep your rooms tidy as I do get a little upset with a messy house."

Watching both of their expressions, eyes wide, they were taking her seriously. She waited a little bit before she said more. Their faces were frozen.

"I was kidding you! Stop with the looks of panic. Your rooms are yours to keep as you like. I was going to say let's talk about it after dinner, but you go ahead and eat. I'll explain it between bites as it's not too hard to understand. But, be sure to eat it all. I work hard to put that food on the table."

Taking her first bite of meatloaf, they were both looking at her with fear again, and then they both realized she was still teasing them. Relaxing, they said they didn't need to be told. They looked at Angie and said it was delicious.

Making sure everyone had enough, Angie put all the food not already on plates on the table, then sat down to eat as she looked around at everyone.

"Mom, if you don't mind, I'd like to explain why you're a holy terr… I mean so strong. Whoa, this is really good meatloaf! Anyway, I don't think she was hard enough on that Allan. I had to bite my tongue at times, it was her show and all. I'd have fired up the jet, strapped him in a body harness on a long chain, and dumped him out hanging as we flew along… Then land with him scraping the ground. That's after all my mom did. She let him off too easy."

All eyes were on her. She looked at them all.

"What else can I tell ya? It's what I'd do to him. Think of the time we were hanging in suspense about who put those bombs here and if they'd go off. Good to let him hang wondering if we'd reel him in as we approached a runway."

The eyes still stared at her. She ate some more, and looked up with a smile as she finished chewing, then sipped some *Faygo* red pop.

"Actually, I'd let him scrape as we came in, but then let loose the chain, then have Victor fly up and away. Send a message to the CIA that way, so maybe at Dulles. If the tower says we did it, we say Victor saw him there and had to abort the landing as he didn't want to run him over."

Listening, Cindy was proud of Angie in every possible way. She knew what such men deserved, and she made a great meatloaf. She saw the look of shock on the faces around her, even Victor's.

"Angie, I'm sure everyone thinks you've got quite an active imagination, but I think what you said makes a lot of sense. We can all play nice. Put up with them doing things like that to us… women all over the world. That's not what we will ever do. We can do more than stop traffickers. We can let people go supporting them, like this Anderson, and his Allans, know that we're not okay with what they're doing. Cindy just described sending them a message. Do that to anyone, you'll be a smear on the runway. I actually think that would have been good to do to Allan."

Having thought about the two sides of Cindy's — and certainly Angie's coin, Mike thought of how Victor had opened up his eyes to see things in a new way, and he chimed in.

"An hour ago, I would have thought that was way over the top. I watched Cindy with Allan. I watched him… thought about what he did each day. Let's think about what she did. If he had known someday a beautiful woman would do what she did to him, think he would have done what he had? My first guess would be that he would. That's what TV and movies tell us, but I watched him. Without the CIA and all it's power, he'd of found some wife he'd abuse, but go out and kill? No. He was a coward. All Cindy did was let him know he was one. I saw it. If he wasn't a coward, he would never have given up the name. He would have laughed at everything she said or did. The protecting his wife and kid? A way to excuse his begging to stop from killing him. I think from now on we make videos of things like that. Just show him, none of us. Then post it by hacking into the agencies and let them all see the truth. Only we knew and could hear from him that what he did was sick. Everyone at every agency needs to know those days are going to end."

Cindy sat back. She clapped, and said, "Yay!" Suddenly, everyone was cheering for all he said. Cindy kept smiling at him, and she knew he understood what she did was not just to stop Allan, but for Angie to learn from, and without thinking of it, knew they would all learn from it.

"Mike, that's a great idea. We do record all the cameras, remember?"

Suddenly slapping the side of his head, he nodded.

"Duh, as Angie would say. And I set it all up. I'll edit it, and put a

little title roll at the beginning summarizing all he had done. Then, turn it loose for the agency to see. I have to figure out how best to do that part…"

"Mike, I'm sure you'll find the safest way. I think we all need to realize the difference between what I did to Allan, and what he was doing to us and so many others. Without him doing what he did to us? He'd be invited to dinner. I'd never do anything like that to anyone without a reason. It would never enter my mind. He would do what I did and get some sick pleasure from it. You all know he got aroused during that. He hurt and killed for pleasure, he was someone who needed to be in an institution or jail. I did it to test what he really was. If he figured it out, even just a bit, asked for help. Knew deep inside he was so messed up… I wouldn't have shot him. I'd have him confess to all he did, turn him over to a place for criminally insane people. I kept pushing him, and the more I pushed, the more I was sure nothing would help him. No hospital, no jail. He wouldn't confess. He didn't if you recall. I couldn't set him free to ever hurt anyone again. Not knowing what he did. He was going to kill all of us. You know that. And nobody at the agency, the police… nobody would have stopped him. His boss would have protected him and that's who I have a talk with next. Scott Anderson. I guarantee, he won't leave the meeting alive."

Knowing the questions and shock around the table had been addressed, she watched everyone enjoy their meal. Cindy also knew the whole incident had brought them to the place she knew deep inside they needed to be. Where they stopped things at the source. Before things happened. It was clear that if the powers that were supposed to stop such evil, and trafficking, did want it to stop, they could make a major dent in the problem. It was clear that they not only weren't stopping it, but they were also a part of it. They were clients. They were given young children in exchange for not doing anything other than help and welcome traffickers to do what they pleased. With the money they had, there were many ways to find the worst of the sick men in power and take them out.

Seeing that every last morsel of food had vanished, Angie got up, taking plates, and Whimsey got up and helped her. As the table was cleared, Angie brought small plates for dessert and put them in front of everyone. She stayed standing.

"I can't take credit for dessert. Whimsey insisted she make it. It looks really wonderful. I'll be right back with some ice cream."

Walking from the oven, Whimsey put an oversized pie on the table, still warm. Angie brought a knife to cut it, and servings were passed around. She had made a pie with fresh cherries, and a lattice crust. Passing the vanilla ice cream around, each piece soon was covered in melting white cream, and they were all savoring the pie. Whimsey was clearly joyous that it was liked, saying she wasn't sure they would like it. Mike looked at her, shaking his head in wonder.

"Whimsey, it's great! Real cherries, not out of some can. And I can tell you made the crust. Tart, just sweet enough…"

Everyone laughed as Whimsey said that was what people often said about her. Cindy said she wanted a second slice, asking Whimsey where she learned to make such a wonderful pie. Whimsey stopped and looked embarrassed. Cindy could tell she didn't want to say, but she wanted to let everyone know that anything in their life would be understood.

"Whimsey. I was an escort. I learned a lot of things when I was. I'll never be ashamed of what I learned during that time. There's no need to hide anything here. Only if you want to share, though."

Whimsey started to blush, looking even smaller than she was. She nodded at Cindy and sat up straight.

"Okay. It's no secret I did porn. I'm not doing that now, and you all know all about the why. So, how I learned to make a cherry pie… Okay. One of my most popular videos was called *"Piece of cherry pie."* I was supposed to be a virgin girl, and I'm all good and at home making a cherry pie, then a guy comes in and says he wants my cherry… then a long pause, and he says, pie. Like that. And you can guess the rest. Well, the woman playing the mom loved to bake pies, and as we shot the video, she was making a pie, for real, and I was helping her in the setup scenes. This is her recipe and where I learned to make it."

Looking up at her, Victor said at least she learned something useful. Holding his plate out for more, he acted completely serious as Whimsey cut another slice for him.

"Whimsey, I want more your cherry goodie."

That sent everyone into hysterics, and Victor looked into Whimsey's eyes, nodding, and told her something she would never forget. As he spoke, he said it loud for all to hear.

"I eat at place. Chinese. Give fortune cookie. Paper inside say, look to sun, shadows fall behind. Today, you make pie for ones who respect and love you. That day. One you remember. Pie was sun, all rest, now shadows."

For the first time, Whimsey was able to look at two men. Mike and Victor. They were real men. She had never met good men, but now she had. They were both men who cared about her inside, who she was, not just a girlish body. She felt a warmth rise through her, and it was a new day for her. She needed to let them know what they had done for her.

"Victor, I will never forget what you just said. Thank you. Mike, you too. Both of you. I thought all men were total creeps. Perverts. No man ever treated me like a human being or listened to what I had to say. Guess what?"

They looked at her, then each other, both saying please say what. She smiled.

"As of this moment, I can never say that again. I now know that there are men who are good, and care about me as more than how I look. I'll never instantly think men are creeps ever again. I need to get to know them like you've gotten to know me. Wow! What a day!"

Eating his second slice of pie, Victor was nodding.

"Whimsey. That is good. It is good being pretty. I think you smile so nice it lights up room. Don't let bad men take that from you. You know, I very strong. For long time, people only think me strong guy. That I not smart. Just strong. Nobody listen to what I say. I wanted to get fat, stop making muscles bigger. I met Eliana. She no say big muscles. She ask only what I do if she hit me. That is what she said. First thing she ask. I said it not nice to hit good man. She said, I am good man? I said yes, I good man. She stood in front of me, and know what she said?"

With all eyes on him, especially Cindy's which were glistening with delight, he nodded and told the rest of the story.

"She stood there, said if that is so, she no hit me."

Cindy saw the look on his face, and he saw her look to him with pure love and affection, and it was the look Eliana had given him when he needed it most. As they looked at each other, their bond grew even stronger. Everyone else was saying hooray and clapping. They all understood what he meant, and Whimsey got up and stood behind his chair, leaning over, giving him a kiss on his cheek, then went and sat

back down. Victor looked all around, into each of their eyes.

"I travel round world, to compound, lose my Eliana, deliver jet, to find friends. Real friends. I never had this, what you call, bond, with anyone before. Now, I think I finally have place to know is home."

Jamie, Whimsey, and Angie all looked at Cindy, realizing how amazing she was. She had just told them he was in need of a place to call home. They all knew it would be more than a building. It would be them showing that he had a home with them, and a gift from friends. Even Cindy started to tear up but managed to reach over and pat Victor's hands.

"You're home. It was a long road, but you're home. And I see no need to wait. Eliana told me she loved you. If it had been safe, she would have married you. This house. It's really a gift from her. To Angie and me. But all of us. Jamie, Mike. She met you and knew you were good and loved each other. Whimsey, oh, she would have grabbed you and never let you go. She did all the things you did when she was very young. She would have been a mother to you. At least as much as she could be while dodging bullets."

Seeing all of them, they were all people who had been to hell, turned away, and as Victor said, headed to the light. She recalled seeing the aurora borealis in Montana and knew even in darkness there could be the most beautiful light ever known. Looking around, she shared that she had a name for the house.

"I like to give important things names. The trailer Angie and I lived in? Well, I called it the hellhole. That's what it was. Here? In Montana, we looked up at the sky, and in the darkest night I think I've ever seen, the sky filled with lights, and it was some sign to us. In the darkness, a light shined. Maybe only for us. As we talked and Victor said head to the light, I had the name for our home. This house… It's like that. It's the light that shines, calls us all together in the darkest moments…"

They all looked at her, lost in the things she said. She smiled, looked all around, then said she could no longer call it the house when she thought of it in her mind. She would only see it as what it was. *Aurora*.

Angie gasped, looking shocked.

"Mom! We lived in Aurora, and it was a hellhole, just like you said. How can you say this is called that?"

Looking into Angie's eyes, she understood, and knew it was ironic.

"I think it's perfect. All aurora means is light. When we lived there, we were in darkness. Afraid. Hiding. Here. We are the light. All of us. This house is the light that calls us to be together. I love we've taken something that once was bad and made it good. It's a victory over being afraid of a lovely word. Light. It's the people there who made it dark. Not the name. Now, when I hear the word, I'll think of here, with all of you. Not that nasty place we lived in. Good has replaced bad. I think of this as being that for us. We finally are free from the dark, and Victor, you are right. Face the light, and all the bad is just a shadow. No looking back."

Chapter 69

Looking at the contents of a file only he had access to, Scott showed no reaction. Using his mouse to pull names over to the "Dead" folder, he dragged James, Charles and Allan there. Looking at another set of folders, he had to drag Jo and Peter to the Dead file. There was a file for his favorite assassin, and he was confirmed down, so moved his file to the archive as there may be some useful information he'd use at a later date. Looking the screen over, he didn't notice any others that needed to move or be concerned about except for the woman trafficker in the Ukraine. Jo had reported that she took her down, and there was a scramble in Eastern Europe for her business. It was the largest trafficking network in the world, and it would be chaos for a long time as some trafficker killed enough others to take her place. In the meantime, he'd talk to her most strategic clients and keep them supplied from Canada.

Using a yellow legal pad, he started scribbling and looking at it without the structure of the file folders. He spoke softly as he played with the names.

"Charles, James, Allan… Same office, same objectives. Let's think about it. Scramble over a woman, some old issue between them? All sick as fuck, so anything goes on that one. Easy enough to replace. Circle back to that in a bit… Traffickers. Thought that was stable with the consolidation and our help. Guess not. Peter and Jo? Same group. In-fighting? He was out of control. Jo was a cunning bitch. But, if she took him out, the question is why? The church would have to sanction it, and they haven't said a thing about him. They'd turn to me for that. Question mark. But, the Ukrainian… had it wrapped tighter than anyone else. Ruthless bitch. She lets crazy girl take her down? Why would she care about what Jo was doing? Doesn't add up. Well, logic doesn't apply to this no matter what or who. Let's look at it bottom up…"

Returning to the computer screen, he opened the Unknown folder with his legal pad next to the keyboard.

"Okay, Allan, let's see what you logged… Hmm… Hired our favorite bad boy. A hit on a Mike and some women… Mike. I know him… Photographer out to find his sister. Oh, yes. Sharon. One of Peter's. So, you wrote she shows up out of the blue, and connects with him to spill on Peter. Takes some porn girl with her. Sharon, you were on fire. Took

out Peter's guy and did him like jam on bread with his own car. Okay, you go to Mike. Not long after Peter is taken out. She turned on him, had Mike help her. Makes sense. Let's see what James said. He was the go-to guy anyway. Hmm. Busy with Mike. Giving him help. Says he was threatened. Sure, James, you were threatened. Oh, interesting. After Peter, she goes to kill Mike. She was on a roll. But, nicked him, and she gets taken out… by who? A mother and daughter? What? Let's find out who they are… Oh, them. All those calls from the oil field about the stupid son getting offed by a take. Interesting. Let's draw some lines, see where they all lead."

Clicking folders rapidly, he kept finding the mother and daughter, then he found what the connection was. He smiled, shaking his head they hadn't been reported correctly.

"Cindy, you don't even exist. Nothing other than in what James reported, but he says your mother came and helped you after you killed the sheik… and your mother is Eliana. The world's largest trafficker… And there you are in the middle of it all. I think I'll just focus on you. All these other have lines to you, so you are my girl!"

Reclining in his chair, he thought about it.

"Cindy. Hidden asset. Keeping you out of sight until needed? Next in line? Wanted no part of it all? Then, you get taken. By Brian… let's see, he used the photo audition tactic… Let's see…"

Going back to the screen, he kept reading what James said. Smiling, there was a nice report on how Mike had needed a jet to go to Moscow.

"He'd went undercover as a photographer and that's how Cindy and her daughter… let's see… Angie. They were taken, Mike goes to get them. Eliana's girl, taken by Brian? Oh, Brian, bad move. And Cindy does what Eliana would. Kills the son for buying her. Mike is there. Ah, that got you out of hiding, didn't it. Mommy didn't like you being sold like she sells thousands of girls each month, did she? And you grew up with the most vicious trafficker? Oh, you can't be okay with that. And where do you live? Right there with my guys. And James is helping you. That means Charles and Allan go along for the ride. Let's see what else James had about you…"

Going through the photos he complied, he found the studio shots from the take. He sat and stared at them. He looked at them for a long time. There were others, each one better then the last.

"What a hot fucking piece of ass you are. You have any guy doing whatever you want, don't you? Shit, sign me up! Well, Cindy, I think you're the one. All this is about you and your girl, and she's as hot as you. All over a stupid take at a photo snatch. Brian, lucky you're feeding worms or I'd be on your ass so hard… Cindy… Cindy… What do you have planned. Two traffickers, your mother, my guys, and it's just a few weeks."

Leaning back after clicking the remote to close his shades and darken the room, he texted his girl he was in quiet mode, he used the remote to turn off all the lights, leaving only the computer monitor on. Sitting where he had a perfect view of it, he filled the large screen with the studio shot of Cindy.

"My girl! You're on fire, aren't you? Yes, you sure are. A for-real Ukrainian beauty. The real thing. I love Ukrainian cunt… Oh, you don't need to worry. You and little Angie are safe now. I'm going to have you. In agency, and on my cock. Oh, and Angie too… you are the girl! Ruthless, gorgeous. Smart. Can't go unnoticed if not. And raised by Eliana. How can you be any hotter? How can you… how can you…"

In the dark room, he was beating off to Cindy's picture, thinking about her with guns blazing, him standing behind her fucking her ass as she fired away. Then he could see Angie walking up behind him, kneeling down, putting her tongue up his ass. Catching his cum in his free hand, he looked at how much that image had cut loose. Getting up to go to his bathroom, he was thinking how much he wanted her to be there to lick it out of his palm.

"You will be. Soon. *You're my girl!*"

Chapter 70

"Mike, thank you for your worry about me. I mean that. I'll be fine on my own. He didn't sound like I expected. He told me just about all that's happened, and he said I was his kind of girl. He had dreamed of someone like me showing up someday and he wanted me to learn about what he's really doing. I didn't fall for all that, of course, but I said I wasn't about to show up and get taken down, or taken. I told you what he said when I told him that."

Mike was sitting with her alone. She had just gotten a call from Scott Anderson and it was unexpected, but not a surprise as the agency was searching for what happened to Allan and the others. He repeated what he told her when she said she wasn't about to be taken.

"Not taken. Recruited."

"Right. And you heard me say I needed certain rules laid down. He asked me to list them. I said rule number one was we don't meet alone. Not at any office. Out in public, and whatever he had in mind ends if he does anything stupid like have anyone near. Then he asked what was the next rule. I told him rule two is to be sure to follow rule one. Then he said, ah, my girl, again. And this guy heads the agency? Sounds crazy as Jo."

Mike shook his head, not sure why they were even talking about the meeting. He didn't want to tell her what to do, but he was more than worried about such a meeting. She was taking on the CIA, and that was not going to be what she would be able to control.

"That's right. A guy has to be nuts to want that job, and they all have been. And you plan on trusting him?"

She reached and rubbed his cheek, giving him a look that filled him with longing to be in her arms. He was worried she was going to make a bad choice and go, and he would lose her.

"Mike, I didn't say anything about trusting him. I'd never do that. So, think about it. I want to take him down. To do that, we'd have to follow him, shoot down his jet, do things that would all call attention to us and get us all killed or locked away forever. Then this. He said he had never seen anyone wreak as much mayhem so well, and nobody even knew I existed. He said that's his dream. To have someone like me onboard. I think that's possible. He doesn't care what happened to his

guys, or anybody. I told him if we meet, it's him and anything else would have me take him down. He knows what I've done, and I could do it to him. He's got to at least be smart enough to realize I'd kill him or just not show up. It's a one-time chance to meet him, kill him, then walk away."

Looking at her, she was fully certain of what would happen. She had been right each step taken, and she didn't seem concerned. He thought how confidence was a double-edged sword. It could cut him down, or her. Scott didn't get to head the agency by taking any chances. He told Cindy that was something that was reason enough to not meet him.

"I know. I'm confident, sure. Mike, what about him. In his position, he must be somewhat near confident as me, right? I think showing up alone is about him being invincible. He probably just want's to fuck me anyway. I'd say that was most likely. I don't usually talk that way, but I don't know how else to say it and reflect his way of thinking about me. He seemed… well, to use a pun, taken. He was like a schoolboy trying to get in my pants. Now, think about it like that, and who walks away? Him, or me?"

"You."

"Right. And if I call and say no, what do boys do when they get rejected? They get mad and want to hurt a girl back. I think that's what he'd do. He had to know where I am, all about you too. All of us. He has the whole agency to use to show how much I hurt his feelings. Girls know how boys feel when they get turned down. He's a little boy with a lot of toys that shoot and kill. Tanks and rocket launchers when we're in the air. If I show up, I can play him. If it's a trap, I'll say I'm all for being part of the agency if he lets me take down who I want."

Feeling a sadness wash over him, he understood that for the first time, he was not in agreement with Cindy. Thoughts running through his mind were telling him she had grown confident and they had been effective against a few people. The large trafficking groups were not typical. Anderson wasn't like them. He was one man, but he had resources Cindy couldn't outwit our outfight if he chose to call on them. He could only tell her that he was asking her not to go.

"Cindy, I value you, our friendship, more than I can describe. I don't know what to do. I don't think you should go. I'm worried and have reason to be. I don't want anything to happen to you. Please, don't do this."

They sat, looking at each other. Cindy understood how he felt, and she didn't want to fight with him about anything or have him worry about her. Knowing he had reason to be concerned, it was down to what would be accomplished by meeting with Anderson, or not meeting with him. She knew the only way to stop him was to get close to him, fire, and walk away. If she didn't, there would be a life of fear ahead, the life she and Angie had led since she was born. So much had happened by inaction, her instincts were to attack, not shy away.

"What happens if I don't go?"

Not prepared to answer, he had no idea, but his instinct told him it would be where they'd need to run, and keep running. They had opened a door, and they were in the fray. It would be flight or fight. They both understood that. He realized they fought and succeeded because people hadn't fought such men. They ran.

"We'd need to run. Become invisible, Stop the taking of traffickers for a long time. At least until he's no longer running the show. I would call it a live to fight another day scenario. I'd rather have us all alive and making plans than play into his hands..."

Cindy picked up her phone, and dialed the number Anderson had called from, holding her hand up to Mike to not say anything. She hadn't said she was calling him, but Mike knew it had to be a call to him.

"Scott. Yes, Cindy. Are you on the side of the traffickers, or are you on my side? Well, I ask because if you're on their side, I don't feel it's right for us to meet. I'm able to be honest, but none of your people have been with me. You run the show, and I'm sure you know all they've done... I know it's complicated — for you. But not me. There's a line that can't be crossed. Taking someone, killing someone. Those are lines that are easily crossed when you let it be complicated... No, no, no. I know all that and it's a game you play. Keep them happy, they feed you information, rich men, politicians to appease... Yes, I know that's the balancing act you think has to exist. Let me ask you a simple question. Is taking one girl, and selling her to a man, worth any of that?"

She looked at Mike, shaking her head. She wasn't hearing what she needed.

"I asked you a simple question. Is one person's life worth any of that... Please, not all the things about so many will die if you don't

keep rulers and the rich happy. You can say no to any of them. That's a choice you make. Say no. Arrest them. If a rich old man buys a minor, arrest him… Oh, I do understand how the world works. I'll tell you my answer. No. I don't see any point in meeting. I fight what you do. I'll never be a part of it… Yes, I've killed people. Ones who tried to kill me. It's called self-defense. Jo? Driving her jeep at me full speed to kill me with it. I stopped her, yes… Allan, he ordered gas bombs to kill me and Angie… Not revenge, protecting us from him. If I let him go he'd attack and kill us with your men… You. Yes, I want to do that to you. If we meet, I'll kill you."

Pressing *End,* she said it had gone well. Mike was at a loss how she could possibly think that. He asked her how she could possibly tell the director of the CIA she would kill him was a good end to the call. Cindy looked at her nylons to see if they had any runs, then at Mike. He couldn't understand how she could be so calm.

"He said it was a matter of I didn't understand, and he would like to show me how things work. He said he'd be where we could meet. Just the two of us. None of his agents, no games. It would be the only way I could begin to trust him. He said he'd be waiting for me, and I could show, or not. He asked if I showed up if I'd want to kill him. You heard what I said."

Trying his best to keep calm, he asked her where they were supposed to meet.

"He said on the river, where all the cherry trees are in bloom, there's a bench where the entrance goes down to the river. Very open, and lots of people around. He'd wait for me there."

Mike could only look at her, mouth open, wanting to say that was a trap if ever there was one, but waiting to hear what she thought of the call. He gathered himself for the worst and asked what she thought.

"Well, I don't think it's the best place to meet. I would like to see those trees. I've only seen pictures of them. All the monuments across the river. But he won't be there."

Standing up, Mike needed to release some of the adrenaline that had been building up as he listened to the whole scenario.

"Okay, he says he'll be there, you say he won't. Where will you be?"

She stood up, looked him in the eye, and shook her head that he couldn't figure that out.

"Back home. Here. Aurora. I've just told you what he said. I know who he is and he's worse than any of them we've dealt with. So, I'll meet with him, just not there or then. I can tell you're all worried and worked up. I'm not going to ask you if you think I'm…"

Holding his hand up, he said he didn't think she was stupid and he did think she was very pretty. He said he did think it was time to tell him what she had planned. She looked at him, head tilted down, on a slight angle, her eyes open wide looking up to his, her mouth open just slightly, letting him look at her.

"Only pretty?"

Chapter 71

"I'm Mr. Anderson's date for the evening. The agency said you'd have a key for me so I can get ready."

Smiling at Cindy, the clerk nodded, admiring her appearance, and she let him admire as he fumbled for words. Hearing the woman who was clearly the manager clear her throat as she walked behind him, he snapped out of it and told her of course. Putting a plastic card in a keying device, he handed it to her and told her the top floor, and he'd call ahead to the man standing guard there. She thanked him as she took the card and turned to go to the elevator. She wondered if the guard on the floor would be as easily worked. She knew she'd soon find out.

Wearing a tight black dress with a slit up the front, she had on black hose and was wearing a white knit crop top sweater. Walking with a simple, small rolling suitcase for a change of attire, she knew that Anderson paid for only the most stylish and fashionable escorts. With her hair up, she had kept her makeup as she usually wore it, and except for the dress being provocative, she didn't feel the need to look any different than at home. She was a knockout no matter what she wore, and she knew how a man in a high position needed an escort to be attractive, but not trashy. Before getting in the elevator, she decided to give Mike a call and let him know she was at the Fremont and had the key to the room. The lobby was lush and not crowded, so she found a chair where nobody was sitting and called him.

"I'm here. Got the key. Just a guard when I get off the elevator… Once you did your research and found his expense reports, all that hacking comes in handy. Well, as he has several girls he likes, I called the agency and said I was his assistant, well, temping for his assistant, and saw he had made an appointment but didn't indicate who it was with. She said to hold a minute, then said Alice, and I said got it, and he'd know for sure who to expect. Then, I went on their site, looked her up, and she's said she also enjoyed meeting online when clients were away…. Yeah, OnlyFans… I texted her and said I was Anderson, and to come really late as he was going to be delayed and didn't want to waste her time. I said midnight, she said great, and confirmed it was not as scheduled. I said see you at midnight, she sent back a smiley face…. Yeah, at the desk I just said I was tonight's date. Guy had never seen one

like me and was drooling. Last obstacle is the guard… I'm set. No metal when he scans. Around seven, ask him for some help with my suitcase as I can't unlock it. As he bends over it, I have the syringe and some of the stuff Charles used on Whimsey… I'll make sure he's the only one… I'll use his gun, and that's really all there is to it. It's six, so it should all go okay, well, assuming he doesn't call and check on the date or change the time… Thanks, I know what to do. When I leave, the gun will be in the guard's hand. I'll be in a different outfit, a wig and all. I'll call you when I'm out and in the car Victor rented… Call you then."

Checking her phone, it was time to go up to the penthouse floor. She worried that the guard would question her being a new girl, and she was prepared to say Alice was delayed, and she was helping the sweet thing out, not wanting Mr. Anderson to be waiting long by himself. If he was suspicious or went for his phone, she'd have the syringe ready and would hit him then.

Going up the elevator, she was calm and knew she looked the part, and before the door opened, she started smiling. Waiting as the door open was a large man, near fifty, and he wasn't smiling.

"Wrong floor."

She was prepared for that. She was holding a sheet of paper she had printed out with the escort agency logo on it with a short note to her to keep Mister Anderson company until Alice arrived and offer an apology. She handed it to him, and said she was told to give it to him. Reading it, handing it back to her, he said they hadn't called ahead. She apologized and said she would mention it to Renee as that wasn't nice. She didn't play up to him or try to work him. She just stood, letting him say what to do.

"Well, you're his type, so I don't think he'll complain. I do need to check that you aren't carrying anything dangerous. So, I'll use a wand on you, no patting down or anything unless it goes off. I will need to go through your bag after that. Let me have it, and I'll put it by my side why I wave you down."

After using the wand to scan her expertly, she stayed in the same spot as he said she could sit if she wished as he searched her bag. She had worked the zipper where it got stuck as he opened it, and she said it did that to her all the time. He pulled hard enough to get it passed the spot she worked, and went through everything in it carefully. He pulled her

toiletry bag out, and once opened pulled out three disposable syringes and a vial she had Mike make sure had a label indicating it was insulin. He held it all up, looking at her. He didn't ask, so she shrugged and said, "diabetic." He put it back in, and then rummaged things back somewhat as they were, and said she had the door key, and if she needed anything, he was there to help. Thanking him, she said she appreciated that, and headed down to the end of the short hall. The top floor had two suites, both large, and as she went in, it was impressive.

Her last matter was Anderson getting suspicious when he rode up and the guard wasn't there. She assumed he'd leave a note if he was getting something for her, or in the john, so it was something to have at the elevator, but she didn't plan on him looking long as she'd tell him the guard wasn't there.

At six, she called the guard to help with the zipper, and as he bent over to open the bag on the bed, she poked the needle in his neck, and it worked so fast she was shocked. He rose up in a rage, but stood frozen, hand on his neck, then fell back onto the carpet. Before eight, she'd give him another small dose as she was taking no chances. Patting him down, he had a Glock 91 in a shoulder holster, and an extra full clip in his vest pocket. Dropping the clip, checking its operation, it was in excellent repair, and after loading the chamber, she felt much better. Even with the drug, she decided it was best to secure the guard. She found a pocket knife in his pants pocket, and ripped a sheet into strips, and tied him with knots that would be hard for him to undo even if fully awake. She put a rolled-up strip in his mouth as a gag, and looking things over, she went to the hall, leaving the door open slightly, and the man couldn't be seen when walking to the room.

Leaving a single light on, and music playing from the entertainment system, she took the gun and extra clip and went to the opposite side when getting off the elevator, and sat facing it from that direction, not the one he would be headed to. The lobby was lit darkly, just enough for atmosphere. Her forged note was on the table across from the elevator door, and she sat, waiting for Anderson.

Just before eight, she heard the ding of the elevator, and the door opened. Anderson stepped out, looking for his guard, and turned to his suite and called out his name. He shrugged, and as he turned to see if he was at the other end, before facing Cindy, she fired.

Not intending to kill him with the first shot, she hit him in his hip, sending him to the carpet instantly. She was standing as she fired, and with him hit in the hip, he could draw a gun to fire back. She kept aim at him as she walked to him, and he didn't reach for a weapon. As she stood over him, he looked confused.

"Why?"

Crouching down, gun aimed at his head, she fired. The shot went into his mouth, and she knew he was dead. Going to the suite, she gave the guard another dose, then untied him, putting all the sheets in her suitcase, she pulled out a wipe, and cleaned the gun from its being fired. She had been wearing latex gloves she had with, but she didn't want anything to leave a trace she was there. Putting the gun in the guard's hand, she had brought latex gloves for him that had powder residue from her firing a Glock using them before she left home, putting them on his hand before putting the gun in it. From her bag, she took a bottle of opioids and put them in his pocket, saving two to put in his mouth and move him in a way he would swallow them. That would explain why he was out cold on the floor.

Making one last sweep, she had one final task. The elevator had a camera and had filmed the people riding it. She thought of going to the security office and wiping the digital file, but she decided against it. Opening the door, she ran into the elevator, banging on the keypad, looking terrified. She would look like an escort who saw Anderson had been shot and was running for her life. In the lobby, she toned it down but was looking over her shoulder as she went to the main door and out of the hotel. Waiting for her outside, Victor was double parked far down the street. Getting in the car, Victor didn't need to ask if she had been successful. She was out, nobody chasing her, and she told him she needed to call Mike. He said that would help him not worry so much, and she smiled, saying he was quite a worrier.

Dialing, he didn't answer. She checked the service on her phone. There were no missed calls or messages. Trying again, still no answer. Then she called Angie. No answer. She told Victor, and he hit the gas and made remarkable time to the jet. Once in, he declared need for an emergency departure, and they were given priority. She tried several times on the flight to call, but still no answers.

After a flight that seemed much longer than it was, and then a car

ride at a record pace, they pulled into the garage. As the door closed and they got out, a man was standing in the door into the house, two guns pointed at them both. He smiled, then whistled at Cindy.

"I'm Scott Anderson. The man you shot looks a lot like me, and was excited to get laid, but, we don't always get what we want. Come in. I've been wanting to see you up close since we talked. And, I'm so impressed you cared enough to go and kill me."

Chapter 72

Backing up as they entered, Victor was ready to sprint and take a bullet to down him, but she calmly said to him, no. Anderson smiled, saying good decision. No need for anything like that. Cindy didn't react, she looked at him and asked what he had done with everyone in the house.

"I knew before we could talk that would be a condition. That they had to be safe. Take a look on your TV…"

He backed up into the living room. The screen showed the safe room, and everyone was in it, apparently unharmed, not tied up, with a tray of snacks and drinks.

"It didn't take any force. I came in, said we had you, and we'd kill you if they didn't do what I wanted. I told them I wanted some time to think and told them to do the same in the safe room. I suggested taking some food and drinks, as you can see. Now, as I wish to have a private talk, your man can join them, or he can join them. Not a choice. Cindy, I need you to get on the intercom, tell them you're here, safe, and your man will come in, and not to try to make a break for it. Say it wouldn't be safe for you, which is true. Go ahead. You, big guy, no need to worry. Go downstairs, wait for Cindy to open the door, go in and close it. Everyone will be okay if you do that for her."

Victor did as asked. Getting a nod from Cindy, he walked down to the safe room. She called out to him to remember how powerful one person with a gun could be. Victor, nodding, saying only he knew. Watching him enter and get hugs, Anderson said finally, they had the place to themselves.

Cindy and Anderson both watched Victor enter, close the door, look up at the camera and nod. Anderson was clearly pleased that it was just the two of them, and he said it was always so complicated to do such a simple thing as spend some time with a beautiful woman since taking his job.

Wearing a classic gray worsted wool suit, expertly tailored, he was tall, thin, and looked like a poster boy for a government official. He was slightly gray at the temples, his hair black, and looked more like a model than the director of an agency. He was clearly concerned about his appearance, and she realized that the man she shot looked amazingly like him. She asked him who the man he sent was, and why did he do that

to him. She added that was everything she hated about people in power, and he was off to a terrible start. He only smiled.

Looking at her, she knew he wasn't concerned with anything other than how she looked. Understanding she was unusually attractive, she knew he could find other women who may be close to her beauty, but for some reason he was obsessed with her. There was no point in speculating why. For all she knew he may have had a nanny when a boy who looked something like her and she was his fantasy lay.

Knowing she was looking him over, he held up both his hands, saying he wanted to remove any impediments to getting to know each other.

Backing up a few paces, he said he was going to lay his weapons down. After dropping the clips and emptying the chambers he asked if that made her feel a bit more comfortable. Shaking her head, she said she still didn't know him and wasn't happy with what happened at the hotel, or that her people were being held.

Smiling at her, saying he understood, she assured her she could pat him down, which he would really enjoy, and he didn't have any other weapons for her to worry about.

"There. As I promised. We meet, talk, I don't have a gun on me. None of my guys hiding. To make it reciprocal, I needed to put your folks in the safe room. Not the worst fate, surely. They know the code to get out, but they're concerned for you. They could storm up right now and with me unarmed, take me. I hope they don't. I'd prefer it's just two people in a big house getting to know each other."

She stood still. She wasn't playing his game. She looked at him, showing her disgust for him.

"A man is dead because you let him pretend to be you. I shot him, and I was set up for that."

He nodded, saying he knew that was a hard pill to swallow.

"Well, sometimes fortune smiles… even on me. Yes, he could be my twin, but that was just luck. He was a trafficker we took after a raid. He had over a hundred girls in a warehouse. I saw we looked so alike, and yes, I made a deal. I told him as he could be my body double, he could have some consideration. Or, we'd let him run, and we'd stop him when he did. He understood that meant do what I wanted or get shot attempting an escape we'd arrange. He agreed, and I told him to come to

my place at eight. My guys put him on the elevator, then you got him. So, you took down another trafficker. Chalk up another one. I told you I can help with that. I did. See. I did."

"Mike, our phones, they work. Door, we have code. One man, easy to kill. We have guns. What are we doing in here?"

Having thought of all those already, Mike knew Victor was going through the same process. He had the list right, except for one thing.

"Victor, you know we're here to keep Cindy alive. If we go up and do anything, he can kill her, or take her as a hostage as he fires at us. That's why we're in here."

Watching Victor, Mike saw the cold Russian military man who he had been most of his life, and he didn't agree with Mike. Victor understood what Mike said, but as he looked around at all in the room, he shook his head in sadness.

"Cindy, she talked of people who let one man with gun shoot them all. None do a thing. Each could save the others. We like people in camps who let one man with gun shoot dozens for same reason. Do you think this will end where Cindy is okay with what he made us do? That he may have goons come shoot us or gas us in here? I can no see him letting us live. Cindy, maybe. If she give him body. That is all he want. I see in his eyes."

That stopped Mike. Cindy had intoned Anderson's interest was about how she looked, not what she was doing. If it was about stopping them, the house would be swarmed and there would be a shootout or they'd all be arrested. Instead, Anderson had them in the safe room, and Cindy to himself. He could be saying if she didn't have sex with him, they'd all be killed. He hadn't wanted to think about it, and knew because of his feelings for Cindy, he wasn't thinking like he would if it were anyone else.

"I admit, I don't want to even think about that. Victor, you're right. He comes in, guns drawn, and we are like people in the camps and do what he says. And if he has Cindy where she has to do what he says she can lock us in here. She has a master code I don't have to override it…"

They were looking at each other, and things were so tense they hadn't

noticed that Angie had gotten up and was standing looking at them just a foot away.

"Mike, geez. Get a mitt and get in the game. She isn't the only one who has the override code."

What she said hit Mike like a hammer blow. He had discounted her and not thought about how Cindy would never do anything without Angie being part of it, and they both knew the code.

"Angie. I'm sorry. Stupid to think what I did. I'm sorry."

Standing with one hip raised, her hands crossed, she shook her head and then went to hug him.

"You're freaked. You weren't thinking right. I forgive you, but anything here? Mom and I did together. I'm in here too, for the same reason. Who knows what he has planned, but I'm with Victor. We stay, we die. I'm going to look at what they're doing on the security cameras."

Using her phone, she started changing the room views. She went to the one in the living room, and they all watched Anderson empty his pistols and hold his arms up, and they could listen to the conversation. Mike was watching, and as the talk was not hostile, talked over the sound.

"Good show of disarming himself, but I'm sure she knows he had more on him. And possibly something to inject her with. CIA has things nobody knows about for hiding arms. And we don't know if he has people waiting to come in…"

Victor said that was all correct, and it was simple. Take him now or wait for something to happen then feel sick they let it. Mike turned and looked at Jamie, and she nodded, saying Victor was right. Whimsey said she didn't know much about such things, but how could they think he was straight. Mike turned to Angie. She was still standing with one hand on her raised hip, looking disgusted at the waiting game.

"Mike, you're worried about my mom, and I know that. We all know we're waiting and hope things will be okay. I heard, yes, on cable, some guy say the road to hell is paved with good intentions. That's sure what's going on. Now, I'm going to show you something that will hurt you. It wasn't done to hurt you, but it will. It was for a deal like this. Keep chill, okay?"

Confused, he looked at Angie, his eyes wide, not sure what she meant. She decided it was best to just say what she and Cindy had done without his knowing.

"Mike, like with the override code, we knew you were doing everything to protect us, but it was about what if something happened to you, or one of us and all that doom stuff. You weren't here one day, and mom and I talked about what if we were locked in here and where even the code wouldn't help. Mom and I thought it would be good to have an emergency exit. She sweet talked the contractor into doing it himself and she... well she said if he told anyone, including you, that she'd... Well, she pulled out her Glock after giving him a good view of her holster, and said she'd not be okay with that. And, she gave him a bunch of cash, so he did this for us..."

Looking at the monitor, neither Anderson nor Cindy were looking at them on the screen. She went and pressed two cinder blocks on the back wall, and they popped forward a few inches. Walking up to see them, they had indents intended as handles. They were not full blocks, each being a foot deep. They were high on the wall, and she had used a chair to reach them. She pressed them back in, then jumped off the chair, looking at the monitor again. Mike was watching, his mouth open, realizing that they had a way out if they couldn't use the door. He looked at Angie, and she smiled.

"Yeah, compromise the place from an nuclear explosion, but we thought it was best to have this just in case."

Victor was chuckling, looking at Mike.

"Ukrainian girls. Very smart. Watch your back. Want to see scars on mine?"

Smiling at him, Angie said he sure had that right. Mike nodded, asking where it leads to.

"Up into the pantry. The exit looks like an air exchange panel, but it's not. It's the way in or out of here. Just one thing about it. It's too small for you guys. We just can squeeze through. So, it's me who goes up. He put indents to use to put hands and feet in to climb. We figured by making it small, guys couldn't get through. You know how mom and I poke each other in our bellies and talk about being a certain size?"

Mike stood, and it washed over him. They were so smart.

"It's to be sure you'll be able to fit. Wow, and you did that so many times and I didn't have a clue. It's like you were trying to see if I could figure it out..."

Angie laughed, and her smile melted Mike's heart.

"No, it was actually about our figures after a while. I want to fit into all her clothes as I get my full figure, and she likes the new stuff I have, so we tease each other about it. We never thought about doing that to razz that you didn't know. But, if you're not a double zero, no point in trying to use it. Well, there is the thing I keep teasing mom about her bra size… that's about this. Anything more than… well, anything more than the perfect size she is now would be a bit too much."

Jamie and Whimsey were giggling, asking Mike what bra size he was. Victor even said he was still in a training bra and Mike started smiling, then shook himself. Victor watched.

"Mike. I know what you thinking about. Think cup size later. Maybe not mention if you smart. Girls, did smart thing. Now, we have way to get creep. Enough fantasy dreaming about Cindy."

Opening his mouth to deny it, he met with all of them looking at him, and they all were nodding. He rolled his eyes.

"Jamie, sorry. I did think about that. I would if we were talking about you. Angie, would Jamie make it? Two would be better than one."

Shaking her head, Angie said they had raided her mom's closet. Some things fit, but Jamie was a two, and pretty curvaceous. Jamie blushed, thanking her for pointing that out to Mike.

"Come on. I said I'm sorry, and I was just asking as you'd be the one to go with. Now, who else is mad at me?"

They all raised their hands, including Victor, then they all laughed and told him not about that, but lots of other things. Their smiles were all loving and he said he was sure he'd done something at sometime, but right now, he be mad at himself if they waited any longer.

"Angie, you have your Glocks. What did you have in mind once you get in the pantry?"

Rearranging her holster to where the guns wouldn't keep her from the small escape tunnel, she had moved them to hang from her neck, saying if needed, she'd bite the belt to keep them in front of her as she went out the air return.

"They're talking, and I'm so light I don't think the floor will squeak. I think after putting us down here with the threat of harming my mom, I have the right to just pop him in the head. I don't think anything else will keep her safe. You said it. Who knows what he has in his pants."

Being met with surprised looks, she just shook her head and ignored

the reaction to what he had in his pants. She asked Mike if he agreed. Victor spoke before Mike could answer.

"It not what Mike want. It is Cynthia and you do what she would. She would shoot him in head. Then go shoot again. That is what you do."

Mike looked at her and nodded.

"Victor is correct. He invaded. The cameras have it all recorded. Don't use the laser sight. Take the shot, walk forward, shoot as many times as needed until he isn't moving or twitching."

Angie nodded, put her holster around her neck, and said to stand on the other side of the room to call attention away from her. She started to move a table to use to open the blocks and climb in. Victor said that would be noticed, he'd lift her up, then put the blocks back in place. He was tall enough to not need a table, and Mike said he'd take the blocks as she took them off, and they'd put them back fast. She nodded, stood under them, and Victor held his hands cupped for her to use to move up enough to release the blocks. Handing them to Mike, Victor raised up and Angie was bent to enter the hole, and Victor gave her feet a push and she was in. Mike handed him the blocks, and as Victor pushed them in place, he turned to Jamie and Whimsey who were watching the monitor to be sure Anderson wasn't looking at the video of the room. They said he hadn't glanced at all, and they all let out a sigh of relief.

Taking out his phone, Mike said he'd change the monitor to track Angie, and be prepared.

"If anything goes wrong, we're out the door and we rush him."

Switching to the pantry, they saw the air return panel move forward, and they all gasped as they thought it would fall and make a crashing sound. Almost as quickly, they saw the panel move out in the air, not falling down, and saw Angie was using two handles welded to the inside of the panel just for that reason. Watching her, she was wriggling her way out after gently putting the panel to the side of the opening, making sure it wasn't sliding or about to fall. It was a tight fit, and to exit, without handles, they saw her put her holster on the floor, then once her arms were fully out, she used them to press back against the wall, pushing her out, her top half moving to the floor, using her arms, crawled out to where she could take one leg at a time out, and was laying flat on the floor. Getting up, she put on her holster, and left the panel open.

Wearing a slim fitting black sweater and snug black leggings, she put the holster belt on where the Glocks were on the front of her thighs, and she took one out to have in her hand, and she had already loaded the chamber and they watched her release the safety. Looking up at the camera, she smiled, and went to the door, standing, listening, then made a quick move to the hall and backed against the wall opposite of the pantry door. Mike switched to the kitchen camera with a view of the hall.

Not wearing any shoes, gun held up and ready to move it out to fire, she was listening, hearing her mother and Anderson talking in the living room. They were surprised as she looked over the kitchen, then without trying to stay hidden, she walked through the kitchen, gun held straight out in front of her. She was moving it side to side, and she stopped at the wall outside of the living room, and switching the camera to the hall there, she was not pressed against the wall, but standing outside of the living room entry, then they all gasped.

All looking in terror, there were two men that had been hiding at the back of the hall, both raising guns to shoot at her.

Anderson had let them in after having all of them move to the safe room. He wasn't alone, and Angie was there in front of them.

Mike watched, and everything, though happening so fast, seemed to be in slow motion.

Angie saw the figures, and she immediately fired at them. He was sure they wore body armor, and he knew she would know that. Her shots weren't at their bodies. She hit them each in the head and the camera, 4K in quality, showed the red spray of blood where their heads were. As soon as Angie fired, she flew forward to the doorway, but landed on the floor, gun out facing the chairs and couch. Anderson had just jumped up and was bent over to get at a gun strapped to his ankle, but Angie fired instantly when seeing him, and with him bent over, the shot went into the top of his head as he flew backwards. Up and her gun out, she fired as he flew back, the shot getting him in his face, a spray of blood filling the air. She had reached for her second gun and as she ran forward to go at Anderson again, she handed off the second gun to Cindy, saying there may be more and take the hall.

Moving over Anderson, though he couldn't be alive, she put a shot in his forehead, then turned to get to Cindy's side. Mike shouted to

go up and have guns out, they all ran out the door and up the stairs, using defense moves not knowing where other hidden men would be stationed. Knowing Angie and Cindy had the first level hall, they heard them fire, and Mike shouted to Victor, upstairs. Just as they aimed up to the second-floor landing, four men rushed to stand and fire, all with automatic rifles. As each appeared, Victor let loose a torrent of fire, all hitting the men's legs and as they fell, Mike's shots hit their heads. Victor was relentless, he ran to the stairs, and running up fired into the men, and their bodies were jumping with each shot. He reached the landing, and fired into each of their heads and took their rifles by their straps, slung them over his shoulder, keeping one to use, then rushed the hall to the bedrooms. Mike followed as he heard four more shots. There were men in each bedroom, and none made it past the doorways. Pointing to the walls, Mike joined Victor in approaching each bedroom, turning in and there were two more men crouched down in wait, but Mike and Victor managed to hit them just before they could fire. Once done, they each went to the bathrooms and did the same attack, but there weren't any more waiting. Calling to Jamie, Mike shouted out basement, and she stood guarding the door, waiting for him before going down.

Taking two rifles from Victor, Mike ran to join Jamie, and he led her down. Victor heard four more shots, knowing there were at least two men in wait in the basement. He ran to join Cindy and Angie, and they had done a full sweep, and were standing with guns out to the window at the end of the hall. Cindy told Angie to check her phone's view of the outside walls. Angie said no motion detected, nothing there.

All the shooting had taken place in less than two minutes. Still on alert, they all walked, guns circling in sweeps as they met up in the front foyer. Mike said it was classic strategy, they were to lay in wait, not charge all at once. Cindy asked if there would be more coming, and Mike said that was likely. He was the director, and didn't go without a small army, but it would be only after they stopped getting messages that things were in place. Reaching to one of the fallen men, he took out his phone, and the screen showed a simple button for okay, one for come. He hit the okay button, and said they should do that with all their phones. Whimsey said she'd gather them up, and soon they were sending okay pings, which would give them time.

Mike said they'd need a message to stand down, meaning they had

all been taken down, so no need for backup. Going to Anderson's phone, he said he'd be the one to send that command. Swiping through screens, he found the stand down screen in Anderson's Health app, and he shook his head at how logical that was. He said they should be safe for now, but good to rotate standing guard at the doors out to the garage and front, and they could grab a bite and a drink while they decided on the next steps.

Angie said she'd take the doors, and asked if they'd make her a ham sandwich and she'd like a red pop. Mike looked at her. She had taken one of the automatic rifles after loading her clips, and she managed to look more threatening than she already did. She had devised the attack, and she had been fearless with her first shots at the two men in the hall and taking out Anderson all in one move. She was the best he'd seen anywhere. She was only sixteen, and he was sure it was genetic. She was a descendant, like all full Ukrainians, of the Mongolian warriors who were legendary for being fearless fighters.

Victor had counted up how many men had been stationed, and he said twelve, plus Anderson. He added they had made a lot of noise. Mike said that would have police coming, and Anderson's backup crew was still out there. Cindy looked around and her beautiful home was riddled with bullet holes and blood splattered all over, but she knew that meant little as they were all still alive and well. She looked at Mike.

"So, did our little escape hatch hurt your feelings?"

He couldn't ever lie to her. Not even if she asked how he was doing, he'd say not great where most people would say they were okay.

"When I first saw it. For a minute or two. Then, I realized it was so smart of you two to do."

"I'm still upset!"

It was Jamie. She had her hands on her hips.

"*For double zeros?* What if it was me down there by myself. What have you got against size twos?"

She smiled at Cindy, they both laughed. Jamie said making it where just about only they could fit was genius. She said she'd have to work her way down to a double zero. Cindy squinted at her, looking her up and down.

"Well, I'd rather have it enlarged than see you change that shape of yours. You're perfect, and I'm sure Mike would miss the sweet parts that go with being a two."

Looking down at herself, she said Cindy was right. He wouldn't be able to hold on to her if she trimmed down. She and Cindy laughed, and Mike blushed. He added time to make a decision. Stand their ground, or move out.

Cindy looked around. She called to Angie.

"Sweetie, do you see any traffickers in here?"

"Mom. No. Let's get our bug out bags."

Looking at everyone at the table, she said staying would tie them up in what happened and why, and worse call attention to themselves.

"We prepared for this day. Everything that could reveal us is in our bug out bags, so let's head out. I don't know how to get to the jet without attention, though."

They watched as Angie went to the living room, then came out with Anderson's key fob held up for them all to see.

"A stupid Tahoe, but it has agency plates. Mike, if you put on one of the less bloody tactical suits and go out, pull it into the garage, I think it's our way out without being stopped."

Telling her she had it all figured out, she looked at him, and smiled.

"I wasn't going to say, duh… but, *duh!*"

Smiling back, he said grab bags, his too, and get to the garage.

He drove, Victor riding shotgun, literally holding an AR-15, and they passed police cars racing to the house, and a group of black Suburbans in a church parking lot as they drove. Mike used Anderson's phone which had a message box on the stand down screen, saying he was taking the captives, and with police, stay put until he called.

Chapter 73

"Well, where to? We stopped one group, and that's okay as we're just getting started, but we need to get going. Every day they're out there taking girls. We need to stop thinking just about the US. We haven't even made a dent yet. So, no slowing down. There are Allan's and Scotts and Brians all over the world. So, the question is where to. I don't want to land and take a break. They never do."

Victor was taxiing the jet and they looked out the window at the Tahoe they had commandeered as Victor put it. Cindy looked around at each one there, and said she had an idea.

"Well, we all speak Russian. Whimsey, I'll teach you and you'll pick it up in no time. I know my mother blew up her house, but I have the title to the land. I think the rumors of her death are greatly exaggerated. Her name strikes terror, and it was rumored her daughter was going to take over."

Putting the jet on autopilot with a flight plan for Europe, Victor walked back and joined them.

"Ukrainian girl. Smart. Eliana was full of tricks. Blowing up house? Maybe guests staying there she no like. Cynthia... Angelia... no question her girls. I am who I am, and nobody dare question me. So, we go, have new fortress built. Maybe stay in some mansion when I say Eliana wants daughter to stay there. Oligarchs will run when I ask. Good plan. Safe place. Government on our side. Guard us. You want I should fly there? Eliana has own airstrip. I call ahead to get mansion cleared out..."

Nodding at Victor, she smiled at him, and he looked at her.

"I know no which world will fear more. Bad lady Eliana, or good lady Cynthia? Angelia... she will always be feared, no matter which."

He walked to the cockpit. Cindy looked at them all.

"For now, it will be safest. We can buy places all over the world. I think we know staying in one place may not be practical. I want to be sure you all are okay with it. It's a bit of a rough homecoming for me. You all know why. It's time for me to let the shadows fall behind me."

As they all said it was a perfect choice, Victor called out that for their first meal, take out Chinese.

"We need to read little slip of paper in cookie. And, dumplings near as good as petoheh."

Angie got up and sat on Cindy's lap. Looking at her, she asked her what happened with that Anderson man when she was wiggling her way up to shoot him.

"Well, I was right. He said I was prime cut, and he was sure hungry."

Angie poked her in her waist, saying now that they didn't have the escape tunnel was no reason to go all two on her.

Jamie, sitting across from them, gave them a look.

"I beg your pardon? *Go all two?*"

Angie went and sat on her lap, poking her waist and tickling her.

"Not that there's anything wrong with that!"

Mike, watching, shook his head, knowing it was him and a jet load of beauties who all knew how hot they were. Sighing, he could sense they were all looking at him. He turned, and they were all serious and had their brows scrunched.

"Look, we need to get this understood. I was a glamour photographer if you remember, and I can tell a two from a zero to a 34 inseam to a cup size better than anyone. I think you're all perfect, and know what? When I took pictures, they all looked great. That's because size doesn't matter."

They all giggled. He looked at them and repeated that size doesn't matter. They all stopped giggling, smiling at him. The only one not laughing was Whimsey, who had a serious expression. She unbuckled her seat belt, went to Mike, cupped her hand over his ear and whispered to him. She looked at him, nodded, then went back to her seat.

Rolling his eyes up, he knew they'd all want to know what she said. He turned and looked at them.

"I know you all want to hear what she said…"

Cindy, Angie and Jamie all nodded, waiting. Mike looked at each of them, then before turning to read a car magazine, told them Whimsey said she didn't think he'd make a living doing porn but that being the case, she told him just as long as Jamie was okay, don't worry about it.

As they all did their best to keep from bursting out in hysterics, Jamie looked at Whimsey, Angie, then Cindy. She calmly said that was good advice.

"There are days when I have to stop and tell Mike I need a break. I explain I *can't take it any longer*…"

Flipping the pages of his magazine, he called out to Jamie.

"Thank you."

Whimsey leaned forward to Jamie, and whispered, "Really?"

Mike said he could hear that, and said, "Yes. Really."

A short minute passed, and Angie, still on Cindy's lap, thinking, looked up at her.

"Mom. I don't get it."

Giving her a serious look, Cindy told Angie said she wouldn't get it for quite some time.

Angie, thinking about what she was told, made sure everyone could hear her as she pressed her head to Cindy's chest.

"Mom. I say it all the time. *I want to be just like you.*"

Not Taken

About the Author

"My grandmother and grandfather were sex traffickers of underage women in the Ukraine. My grandfather raped my mother when she as 12, and was about to "sell" her. My grandmother killed my grandfather/father and escaped to the US with my mother and two uncles and I was born in the US. I grew up with a trafficker — and her children who were trafficked. I lived with them in a car, on the run, and heard the trauma, pain, and witnessed what trafficking does to people from the side of the trafficker — and the trafficked. I ran away when I was 13 as I wanted no part of that world even though they were no longer involved in it. They lived that trauma everyday. I left to forge my own life and do something to help traumatized people — and have worked to do so through authoring self-help books and publishing magazines such as Adoption.*"*

Terry Ulick is ready to tell the story of what trafficking does to people in away not yet told. It is an important one, and it will show how trafficking happens, and most important... to be *not taken*.

Terry Ulick is a filmmaker, publisher, photographer and author.
Not Taken is is 70th book.

Printed in the USA
CPSIA information can be obtained
at www.ICGtesting.com
CBHW011546011024
15215CB00072B/4088